Jonathan Kellerman's series of detective novels featuring Alex Delaware have made him an internationally bestselling author. He lives with his wife, the novelist Fay Kellerman, and their four children in California.

JONATHAN KELLERMAN

THE FIRST
ALEX DELAWARE
OMNIBUS

WHEN THE BOUGH BREAKS
BLOOD TEST

Two Novels in One Volume

LITTLE, BROWN AND COMPANY

A Little, Brown Book

First published in this omnibus edition in Great Britain in 2001
by Little, Brown and Company

A CIP catalogue record for this book
is available from the British Library.

ISBN 0 316 85899 4

Printed and bound in Great Britain
by Clays Ltd, St Ives plc

Little, Brown and Company (UK)
Brettenham House
Lancaster Place
London WC2E 7EN

www.littlebrown.co.uk

WHEN THE BOUGH BREAKS

1

IT WAS shaping up as a beautiful morning. The last thing I wanted to hear about was murder.

A cool Pacific current had swept its way across the coastline for two days running, propelling the pollution to Pasadena. My house is nestled in the foothills just north of Bel Air, situated atop an old bridle path that snakes its way around Beverly Glen, where opulence gives way to self-conscious funk. It's a neighbourhood of Porsches and coyotes, bad sewers and sequestered streams.

The place itself is eighteen hundred square feet of silvered redwood, weathered shingles and tinted glass. In the suburbs it might be a shack; up here in the hills it's a rural retreat—nothing fancy, but lots of terraces, decks, pleasing angles and visual surprises. The house had been designed by and for a Hungarian artist who went broke trying to peddle oversized polychromatic triangles to the galleries on La Cienega. Art's loss had been my gain by way of L.A. probate court. On a good day—like today— the place came with an ocean view, a cerulean patch that peeked timidly above the Palisades.

I had slept alone with the the windows open—burglars and neo-Mansonites be damned—and awoke at ten,

9

naked, covers thown to the floor in the midst of some forgotten dream. Feeling lazy and sated, I propped myself on my elbows, drew up the covers and stared at the caramel layers of sunlight streaming through French doors. What finally got me up was the invasion of a housefly who alternated between searching my sheets for carrion and dive-bombing my head

I shuffled to the bathroom and began filling a tub, then made my way to the kitchen to scavenge, taking the fly with me. I put up coffee, and the fly and I shared an onion bagel. Ten-twenty on a Monday morning with nowhere to go and nothing to do. Oh, blessed decadence.

It had been almost half a year since my premature retirement and I was still amazed at how easy it was to make the transition from compulsive overachiever to self-indulgent bum. Obviously I'd had it in me from the beginning.

I returned to the bathroom, sat on the rim of the tub munching and drew up a vague plan for the day: a leisurely soak, a cursory scan of the morning paper, perhaps a jog down the canyon and back, a shower, a visit to—

The doorbell jarred me out of my reverie.

I tied a towel around my waist and walked to the front entry in time to see Milo let himself in.

'It was unlocked,' he said, closing the door hard and tossing the *Times* on the sofa. He stared at me and I drew the towel tighter.

'Good morning, nature boy.'

I motioned him in.

'You really should lock the door, my friend. I've got files at the station that illustrate nicely what happens to people who don't.'

'Good morning, Milo.'

I padded into the kitchen and poured two cups of coffee. Milo followed me like a lumbering shadow, opened the refrigerator and took out a plate of cold pizza that I had no recollection of ever owning. He tailed me back to the living room, collapsed on my old leather sofa—an artifact of the abandoned office on Wilshire— balanced the plate on his thigh and stretched out his legs.

I turned off the bathwater and settled opposite him on a camelskin ottoman.

Milo is a big man—six-two, two-twenty—with a big man's way of going loose and dangly when he gets off his feet. This morning he looked like an oversized rag doll slumped against the cushions—a doll with a broad, pleasant face, almost boyish except for the acne pits that peppered the skin, and the tired eyes. The eyes were startlingly green and rimmed with red, topped by shaggy dark brows and a Kennedyesque shock of thick black hair. His nose was large and high-bridged, his lips full, childishly soft. Sideburns five years out of date trailed down the scarred cheeks.

As usual he wore ersatz Brooks Brothers: olive-green gabardine suit, yellow button-down, mint and gold rep stripe tie, oxblood wing tips. The total effect was as preppy as W. C. Fields in red skivvies.

He ignored me and concentrated on the pizza.

'So glad you could make it for breakfast.'

When his plate was empty he asked, 'So, how are you doing, pal?'

'I *was* doing great, What can I do for you, Milo?'

'Who says I want you to do anything?' He brushed crumbs from his lap to the rug. 'Maybe this is a social call.'

'You waltzing in, unannounced, with that bloodhound look all over your face isn't a social call.'

'Such intuitive powers.' He ran his hands over his face, as if washing without water. 'I need a favour,' he said.

'Take the car. I won't be needing it until late afternoon.'

'No, it's not that this time. I need your professional services.'

11

That gave me pause.

'You're out of my age range,' I said. 'Besides, I'm out of the profession.'

'I'm not kidding, Alex. I've got one of your colleagues lying on a slab at the morgue. Fellow by the name of Morton Handler.'

I knew the name, not the face.

'Handler's a psychiatrist.'

'Psychiatrist, psychologist. Minor semantic distinction at this point. What he is, is dead. Throat slashed, a little bit of evisceration tossed in. Along with a lady friend—same treatment for her but worse—sexual mutilation, nose sliced off. The place where it happened—his place—was an abattoir.'

Abattoir. Milo's master's degree in American Lit asserting itself.

I put down my coffee cup.

'Okay, Milo. I've lost my appetite. Now tell me what all of that has to do with me.'

He went on as if he hadn't heard me.

'I got called on it at five A.M. I've been knee-deep in blood and crud since then. It stunk in there—people smell bad when they die. I'm not talking decay, this is the stench that sets in before decay. I thought I was used to it. Every so often I catch another whiff and it gets me right here.' He poked himself in the belly. 'Five in the morning. I left an irritated lover in bed. My head feels ready to implode. Gobs of flesh at five in the morning. Jesus.'

He stood and looked out the window, gazing out over the tops of pines and eucalyptus. From where I sat I could see smoke rising in indolent swirls from a distant fireplace.

'It's really nice up here, Alex. Does it ever bore you, being in paradise with nothing to do?'

'Not a hint of ennui.'

12

'Yeah, I guess not. You don't want to hear any more about Handler and the girl.'

'Stop playing passive-aggressive, Milo, and spit it out.'

He turned and looked down at me. The big, ugly face showed new signs of fatigue.

'I'm depressed, Alex.' He held out his empty cup like some overgrown, slack-jawed Oliver Twist. 'Which is why I'll tolerate more of this disgusting swill.'

I took the cup and got him a refill. He gulped it audibly.

'We've got a possible witness. A kid who lives in the same building. She's pretty confused, not sure what she saw. I took one look at her and thought of you. You could talk to her, maybe try a little hypnosis to enhance her memory.'

'Don't you have Behavioural Sciences for that?'

He reached into his coat pocket and took out a handful of Polaroids. 'Look at the beauties.'

I gave the pictures a second's glance. What I saw turned my stomach. I returned them quickly.

'For God's sake, don't show me stuff like that!'

'Some mess, huh? Blood and crud.' He drained his cup, lifting it high to catch every last drop. 'Behavioural Science is cut down to one guy who's kept busy weeding weirdos out of the department. Next priority is counselling the weirdos who slip through. If I put in an application for this kind of thing I'll get a request to fill out another application form. They don't want to do it. On top of that, they don't know anything about kids. You do.'

'I don't know anything about homicide.'

'Forget homicide. That's my problem. Talk to a seven-year-old.'

I hesitated. He held out his hands. The palms were white, well-scrubbed.

'Hey, I'm not expecting a total freebie. I'll buy you lunch. There's a fair-to-middling Italian place with surprisingly good gnocchi not far from the . . .'

'Not far from the abattoir?' I grimaced. 'No thanks. Anyway, I can't be bought for noodles.'

'So what can I offer you by way of a bribe—you've got everything—the house in the hills, the fancy car, the Ralph Lauren gear with jogging shoes to match. Christ, you've got retirement at thirty-three and a god-damn perpetual tan. Just talking about it is getting me pissed.'

'Yes, but am I happy?'

'I suspect so.'

'You're right.' I thought of the grisly photos. 'And I'm certainly not in need of a free pass to the Grand Guignol.'

'You know,' he said, 'I'll bet underneath all of that mellow is a bored young man.'

'Crap.'

'Crap nothing. How long has it been, six months?'

'Five and a half.'

'Five and a half, then. When I met you—correct that, soon *after* I met you, you were a vibrant guy, high energy, lots of opinions. Your *mind* was working. Now all I hear about is hot tubs, how fast you run your goddamned mile, the different kinds of sunset you can see from your deck—to use your jargon, it's *regression*. Cutesy-poo short pants, roller-skating, water play. Like half the people in this city, you're functioning on a six-year-old level.'

I laughed.

'And you're making me this offer—to get involved in blood and crud—as a form of occupational therapy.'

'Alex, you can break your ass trying to achieve Nirvana Through Inertia, but it won't work. It's like that Woody Allen line—you mellow too much, you ripen and rot.'

I slapped my bare chest.

'No signs of decay yet.'

14

'It's internal, comes from within, breaks through when you're least expecting it.'

'Thank you, Doctor Sturgis.'

He gave me a disgusted look, went into the kitchen and returned with his mouth buried in a pear.

'S'good.'

'You're welcome.'

'All right, Alex, forget it. I've got this dead psychiatrist and this Gutierrez girl hacked up. I've got a seven-year-old who thinks she might have seen or heard something except she's too damned scared to make any sense of it. I ask you for two hours of your time—and time is one thing you've got plenty of—and I get bullshit.'

'Hold on. I didn't say I wouldn't do it. You have to give me time to assimilate this. I just woke up and you barge in and drop double homicide on me.'

He shot his wrist out from under his shirt cuff and peered at his Timex. 'Ten thirty-seven. Poor baby.' He glared at me and chomped into the pear, getting juice on his chin.

'Anyway, you might recall that the last time I had anything to do with police business it was traumatic.'

'Hickle was a fluke. And you were a victim—of sorts. I'm not interested in getting you involved in this. Just an hour or two talking to a little kid. Like I said, hypnosis if it looks right. Then we eat gnocchi. I return to my place and try to reclaim my amour, you're free to go back to Spaceout Castle here. Finis. In a week we get together for a pure social time—a little sashimi down in Japtown. Okay?'

'What did the kid actually see?' I asked and watched my relaxing day fly out the window.

'Shadows, voices, two guys, maybe three. But who really knows? She's a little kid, she's totally traumatized. The mother's just as scared and she impresses me as a lady who was no nuclear physicist in the first place. I didn't know how to approach her, Alex. I tried to be nice,

15

go easy. It would have been helpful to have a juvie officer there, but there aren't too many of those any more. The department would rather keep three dozen pencil-pushing deputy chiefs around.'

He gnawed the pear down to the core.

'Shadows, voices. That's it. You're the *language specialist*, right? You know how to communicate with the little ones. If you can get her to open up, great. If she comes forth with anything resembling an I.D., fantastic. If not, them's the breaks and at least we tried.'

Language specialist. It had been a while since I'd used the phrase—back in the aftermath of the Hickle affair, when I'd found myself suddenly spinning out of control, the faces of Stuart Hickle and all the kids he'd harmed marching through my head. Milo had taken me drinking. At about two in the morning he had wondered out loud why the kids had let it go on for so long.

'They didn't talk because nobody knew how to listen,' I'd said. 'They thought it was their fault, anyway.'

'Yeah?' He looked up, bleary-eyed, gripping his stein with both hands. 'I hear stuff like that from the juvie gals.'

'That's the way they think when they're little, egocentric. Like they're the centre of the world. Mommy slips, breaks a leg, they blame themselves.'

'How long does it last?'

'In some people it never goes away. For the rest of us it's a gradual process. By eight or nine we see things more clearly—but at any age an adult can manipulate kids, convince them it's their fault.'

'Assholes,' muttered Milo. 'So how do you get their heads straight?'

'You have to know how kids think at different ages. Developmental stages. You talk their language—you become a language specialist.'

'That's what you do?'

'That's what I do.'

16

A few minutes later he asked: 'You think guilt is bad?'

'Not necessarily. It's part of what holds us together. Too much, though, can cripple.'

He nodded. 'Yeah, I like that. Shrinks always seem to be saying guilt is a no-no. Your approach I can buy. I tell you, we could use a lot more guilt—the world's full of fucked-up savages.'

At that moment he got no argument from me.

We talked a bit more. The alcohol tugged at our consciousness and we started to laugh, then cry. The bartender stopped polishing his glasses and stared.

It had been a low—a seriously low—period in my life and I remembered who'd been there to help me through it.

I watched Milo nibble at the last specks of pear with curiously small, sharp teeth.

'Two hours?' I asked.

'At the most.'

'Give me an hour or so to get ready, clear up some business.'

Having convinced me to help him didn't seem to cheer him up. He nodded and exhaled wearily.

'All right. I'll give a run down to the station and do my business.' Another consultation of the Timex. 'Noon?'

'Fine.'

He walked to the door, opened it, stepped out on the balcony and tossed the pear core over the railing and into the greenery below. Starting down the stairs he stopped mid-landing and looked up at me. The sun's glare hit his ravaged face and turned it into a pale mask. For a moment I was afraid he was going to get sentimental.

I needn't have worried.

'Listen, Alex, as long as you're staying here can I borrow the Caddy? That,' he pointed accusingly at the ancient Fiat, 'is giving out. Now it's the starter.'

'Bull, you just love my car.' I went into the house, got the spare keys and threw them at him.

17

He fielded them like Dusty Baker, unlocked the Seville and squirmed in, adjusting the seat to accommodate his long legs. The engine started immediately, purring with vigour. Looking like a sixteen-year-old going to his first prom in Daddy's wheels, he cruised down the hill,

2

My LIFE had been frantic ever since adolescence. A straight-A student, I started college at sixteen, worked my way through school free-lancing as a guitarist, and churned through the doctoral programme in clinical psychology at UCLA, earning a Ph.D. at twenty-four. I accepted an internship up north at the Langley Porter Institute, then returned to L.A. to complete a postdoctoral fellowship at Western Pediatric Medical Center: once out of training I took a staff position at the hospital and a simultaneous professorship at the medical school affiliated with Western Peds. I saw lots of patients and published lots of papers.

By twenty-eight I was an associate professor of pediatrics and psychology and director of a support programme for medically ill youngsters. I had a title too long for my secretaries to memorize and I kept publishing, constructing a paper tower within which I dwelled: case studies, controlled experiments, surveys, monographs, textbook chapters and an esoteric volume of my own on the psychological effects of chronic disease in children.

The status was great, the pay less so. I began to moonlight, seeing private patients in an office rented

19

from a Beverly Hills analyst. My patient load increased until I was putting in seventy hours a week and running between hospital and office like a deranged worker ant.

I entered the world of tax avoidance after discovering that without write-offs and shelters I'd be paying out to the IRS more than I used to consider a healthy yearly income. I hired and fired accountants, bought California real estate before the boom, sold at scandalous profits, bought more. I became an apartment-house manager—another five to ten hours a week. I supported a battalion of service personnel—gardeners, plumbers, painters and electricians. I received lots of calendars at Christmas.

By the age of thirty-two, I had a non-stop regimen of working to the point of exhaustion, grabbing a few hours of fitful sleep and getting up to work some more. When I remembered to eat, the food came out of hospital vending machines and I stuffed my mouth while zipping down the corridors, white coat flapping, notepad in hand, like some impassioned speed freak. I was a man with a mission, albeit a mindless one.

I was successful.

There was little time for romance in such a life. I engaged in occasional carnal liaisons, frenzied and meaningless, with nurses, female interns, graduate students and social workers. Not to forget the fortyish leggy blond secretary—not my type at all had I taken the time to think—who captivated me for twenty minutes of thrashing behind the chart-stuffed shelves of the medical records room.

By day it was committee meetings, paperwork, trying to quell petty staff bickering and more paperwork. By night it was facing the tide of parental complaints that the child therapist grows accustomed to, and providing comfort and support to the young ones caught in the crossfire.

In my spare time I received tenants' gripes, scanned the *Wall Street Journal* to measure my gains and losses, and

20

sorted through mountains of mail, most of it, it seemed, from white-collared, white-toothed smoothies who had ways of making me instantly rich. I was nominated as an Outstanding Young Man by an outfit hoping to sell me their hundred-dollar, leather-bound directory of similarly honoured individuals. In the middle of the day, there were times, suddenly, when I found it hard to breathe, but I brushed it off, too busy for introspection.

Into this maelstrom stepped Stuart Hickle.

Hickle was a quiet man, a retired lab technician. He looked the part of the kindly neighbour on a situation comedy—tall, stooped, fiftyish, fond of cardigans and old briar pipes. His tortoise-shell horn-rims perched atop a thin, pinched nose shielding kindly eyes the colour of dishwater. He had a benign smile and avuncular mannerisms.

He also had an unhealthy appetite for fondling little children's privates.

When the police finally got him, they confiscated over five hundred colour photographs of Hickle having his way with scores of two-, three-, four-, and five-year-olds—boys and girls, white, black, Hispanic. In matters of gender and race he wasn't picky. Only age and helplessness concerned him.

When I saw the photos it wasn't the graphic starkness that got to me, though that was repulsive in its own right. It was the look in the kids' eyes—a terrified yet knowing vulnerability. It was a look that said *I know this is wrong. Why is this happening to me?* The look was in every snapshot, on the face of the youngest victim.

It personified violation.

It gave me nightmares.

Hickle had unique access to little children. His wife, a Korean orphan whom he'd met as a GI in Seoul, ran a successful day-care centre in affluent Brentwood.

Kim's Korner had a solid reputation as one of the best places to leave your children when you had to work or play or just be alone. It had been in business for a decade when the scandal broke, and despite the evidence there were plenty of people who refused to believe that the school had served as a haven for one man's paedophilic rituals.

The school had been a cheerful-looking place, occupying a large, two-storey house on a quiet residential street not far from UCLA. In its last year, it had cared for over forty children, most of them from affluent families. A large proportion of Kim Hickle's charges had been very young because she was one of the few day-care operators to accept children not yet toilet-trained.

The house had a basement—a rarity in earthquake country—and the police spent a considerable amount of time in that damp cavernous room. They found an old army cot, a refrigerator, a rusty sink and five thousand dollars' worth of photographic equipment. Particular scrutiny was given to the cot, for it served up a host of fascinating forensic details—hair, blood, sweat and semen.

The media latched on to the Hickle case with predictable vigour. This was a juicy one that played on everyone's primal fears, evoking memories of the Cosmic Bogeyman. The evening news featured Kim Hickle fleeing a mob of reporters, hands over face. She protested her ignorance. There was no evidence of her complicity so they closed the school down, took away her license and left it at that. She filed for divorce and departed for parts unknown.

I had my doubts about her innocence. I'd seen enough of these cases to know that the wives of child molesters often played a role, explicit or covert, in setting up the dirty deed. Usually these were women who found sex and physical intimacy abhorrent, and in order to get out of conjugal chores, they helped find substitute partners for their men. It could be a cold, cruel parody of a harem joke—I'd seen one case where the father had been bed-

22

ding three of his daughters on a scheduled basis, with mom drawing up the schedule.

It was also hard to believe that Kim Hickle had been playing Legos with the kids while downstairs Stuart was molesting them. Nevertheless, they let her go.

Hickle himself was thrown to the wolves. The TV cameras didn't miss a shot. There were lots of instant minispecials, filled with interviews with the more vocal of my colleagues, and several editorials about the rights of children.

The hoopla lasted two weeks, then the story lost its appeal and was replaced by reports of other atrocities. For there was no lack of nasty stories in L.A. The city spawned ugliness like a predatory insect spewing out blood-hungry larvae.

I was consulted on the case three weeks after the arrest. It was a back-page story now and someone got to thinking about the victims.

The victims were going through hell.

The children woke up screaming in the middle of the night. Toddlers who'd been toilet-trained started to wet and soil themselves. Formerly quiet, well-behaved kids began to hit, kick and bite without provocation. There were lots of stomach aches and ambiguous physical symptoms reported, as well as the classic signs of depression— loss of appetite, listlessness, withdrawal, feelings of worthlessness.

The parents were racked with guilt and shame, seeing or imagining the accusing glances of family and friends. Husbands and wives turned on each other. Some of them spoiled the victimized children, increasing the youngsters' insecurity and infuriating the siblings. Later, several brothers and sisters were able to admit that they'd wished they'd been molested in order to be eligible for special treatment. Then they'd felt guilty about those thoughts.

23

Entire families were coming apart, much of their suffering obscured by the public blood lust for Hickle's head. The families might have been permanently shunted to obscurity, saddled with their confusion, guilt and fear but for the fact that the great aunt of one of the victims was a philanthropic member of the board of Western Pediatric Medical Center. She wondered out loud why the hell the hospital wasn't doing anything, and where was the institution's sense of public service, anyway. The chairman of the board salaamed and simultaneously saw the chance to grab some good press. The last story about Western Peds had exposed salmonella in the cafeteria's cole-slaw, so positive P.R. was mighty welcome.

The medical director issued a press release announcing a psychological rehabilitation programme for the victims of Stuart Hickle, with me as therapist. My first inkling of being appointed was reading about it in the *Times*.

When I got to his office the next morning I was ushered in immediately. The director, a pediatric surgeon who hadn't operated in twenty years and had acquired the smugness of a well-fed bureaucrat, sat behind a gleaming desk the size of a hockey field and smiled.

'What's going on, Henry?' I held up the newspaper.

'Sit down, Alex. I was just about to call you. The board decided you'd be perfect—pluperfect—for the job. Some urgency was called for.'

'I'm flattered.'

'The board remembered the beautiful work you did with the Brownings.'

'Brownells.'

'Yes, whatever.'

The five Brownell youngsters had survived a light plane crash in the Sierras that had killed their parents. They'd been physically and psychologically traumatized—overexposed, half-starved, amnesiac, mute. I'd

24

worked with them for two months and the papers had picked up on it.

'You know, Alex,' the director was saying, 'sometimes in the midst of trying to synthesize the high technology and heroics that comprise so much of modern medicine, one loses sight of the human factor.'

It was a great little speech. I hoped he'd remember it when budget time rolled around next year.

He went on stroking me, talking about the need for the hospital to be in the 'forefront of humanitarian endeavours,' then smiled and leaned forward.

'Also, I imagine there'd be significant research potential in all of this—at least two or three publications by June.'

June was when I came up for full professorship. The director was on the tenure committee at the medical school.

'Henry, I believe you're appealing to my baser instincts.'

'Perish the thought.' He winkled slyly. 'Our main interest is helping those poor, poor children.' He shook his head. 'A truly repugnant affair. The man should be castrated.'

A surgeon's justice.

I threw myself, with customary monomania, into designing the treatment programme. I received permission to run the therapy sessions in my private office after promising that Western Peds would get all the credit.

My goals were to help the families express the feelings that had been locked inside since Hickle's subterranean rites had been exposed, and to help them share those feelings with each other in order to see that they weren't alone. The therapy was designed as an intensive, six-week programme, using groups—the kids, parents, siblings and multiple families—as well as individual sessions as needed. Eighty per cent of the families signed up

25

and no one dropped out. We met at night in my suite on Wilshire, when the building was quiet and empty.

There were nights when I left the sessions physically and emotionally drained after hearing the anguish pour out like blood from a gaping wound. Don't let anyone ever tell you different. psychotherapy is one of the most taxing endeavours known to mankind. I've done all sorts of work, from picking carrots in the scorching sun to sitting on national committees in panelled boardrooms, and there's nothing that compares to confronting human misery, hour after hour, and bearing the responsibility for easing that misery using only one's mind and mouth. At its best it's tremendously uplifting, as you watch the patient open up, breathe, let go of the pain. At its worst it's like surfing in a cesspool, struggling for balance while being slapped with wave after putrid wave.

The treatment worked. Sparkle returned to the kids' eyes. The families reached out and helped each other. Gradually, my role diminished to that of silent observer.

A few days before the last session I received a call from a reporter for *National Medical News*—a throwaway for physicians. His name was Bill Roberts, he was in town and wanted to interview me. The piece would be for practising paediatricians, to alert them to the issue of child molestation. It sounded like a worthy project and I agreed to meet him.

It was seven-thirty in the evening when I nosed my car out of the hospital parking lot and headed westward. Traffic was light and I reached the black-granite-and-glass tower that housed my office by eight. I parked in the subterranean garage, walked through double glass doors into a lobby that was silent save for Muzak and rode the elevator to the sixth floor. The doors slid open, I made my way down the corridor, turned a corner and stopped.

There was nobody waiting for me, which was unusual because I'd always found reporters to be punctual.

26

I approached my office door and saw a stiletto of light slashed diagonally across the floor. The door was ajar, perhaps an inch. I wondered if the night cleaning crew had let Roberts in. If so I'd have a talk with the building manager over the breach of security.

When I reached the door I knew something was wrong. There were scratch marks around the knob, metal filings in the rug. Yet, as if working from a script, I entered.

'Mr. Roberts?'

The waiting room was empty. I went into the consultation office. The man on my sofa wasn't Bill Roberts. I'd never met him but I knew him very well.

Stuart Hickle slumped in the soft cotton cushions. His head—what was left of it—was propped against the wall, the eyes staring vacantly at the ceiling. His legs splayed out spastically. One hand rested near a wet spot on his groin. He had an erection. The veins in his neck stood out in bas relief. His other hand lay limply across his chest. One finger hooked around the trigger of an ugly little blue steel pistol. The gun dangled, butt downward, the muzzle an inch from Hickle's open mouth. There were bits of brain, blood and bone on the wall behind the head. A crimson splotch decorated the soft-green print of the wallpaper like a child's fingerpainting. More crimson ran out of the nose, the ears and the mouth. The room smelled of firecrackers and human waste.

I dialled the phone.

The coroner's verdict was death by suicide. The final version went something like this: Hickle had been profoundly depressed since his arrest and, unable to bear the public humiliaton of a trial, he'd taken the Samurai way out. It was he, as Bill Roberts, who'd set up the appointment with me, he who'd picked the lock and blown his brains out. When the police played me tapes of his confession the voice did sound similar to that of 'Roberts'—

at least similar enough to prevent my saying it wasn't a match.

As for why he'd chosen my office for his swan song, the supporting cast of shrinks had an easy answer: because of my role as the victims' therapist, I was a symbolic father figure, undoing the damage he'd perpetrated. His death was an equally symbolic gesture of repentance.

Finis.

But even suicides—especially those connected with felonies—must be investigated, the loose ends tied up, and there began a buck-passing contest between the Beverly Hills Police Department and L.A.P.D. Beverly Hills acknowledged the suicide had taken place on their turf but claimed that it was an extension of the original crimes—which had occurred in West L.A. Division territory. Punt. West L.A. would have liked to kick it back but the case was still in the papers and the last thing the department wanted was a dereliction-of-duties story.

So West L.A. got stuck with it. Specifically, Homicide Detective Milo Bernard Sturgis got stuck with it.

I didn't start to have problems until a week after finding Hickle's body, a normal delay, because I was denying the whole thing and was more than a little numb. Since, as a psychologist, I was presumed able to handle such things, no one thought to inquire after my welfare.

I held myself in check when facing the children and their families, creating a façade that was calm, knowledgeable and accepting. I looked *in control*. In therapy we talked about Hickle's death, with an emphasis upon *them*, upon how *they* were coping.

The last session was a party during which the families thanked me, hugged me and gave me a framed print of Braggs' *The Psychologist*. It was a good party, lots of laughter and mess on the carpet, as they rejoiced at getting better, and, in part, at the death of their tormentor.

I got home close to midnight and crawled between the covers feeling hollow, cold and helpless, like an orphaned child on an empty road. The next morning the symptoms began.

I grew fidgety and had trouble concentrating. The episodes of laboured breathing increased and intensified. I became unaccountably anxious, had a constantly queasy feeling in my gut, and suffered from premonitions of death.

Patients began asking me if I was all right. At that point I must have been noticeably troubled because it takes a lot to shift a patient's focus away from himself.

I had enough education to know what was going on but not enough insight to make sense of it.

It wasn't finding the body, for I was used to shocking events, but the discovery of Hickle's corpse was a catalyst that plunged me into a full-fledged crisis. Looking back now I can see that treating his victims had allowed me to step off the treadmill for six weeks, and that the end of treatment had left me with time to engage in the dangerous pastime of self-evaluation. I didn't like what I learned.

I was alone, isolated, without a single real friend in the world. For almost a decade the only humans I'd related to had been patients, and patients by definition were takers, not givers.

The feelings of loneliness grew painful. I turned further inward and became profoundly depressed. I called in sick to the hospital, cancelled my private patients and spent days in bed watching soap operas.

The sound and lights of the TV washed over me like some vile paralytic drug, deadening but not healing.

I ate little and slept too much, felt heavy, weak and useless. I kept the phone off the hook and never left the

29

house except to shove the junk mail inside the door and retreat to solitude.

On the eighth day of this funereal existence Milo appeared at the door wanting to ask me questions. He held a notepad in his hands, just like an analyst. Only he didn't look like an analyst: a big, droopy, shaggy-haired fellow in slept-in clothes.

'Dr. Alex Delaware?' He held up his badge.

'Yes.'

He introduced himself and stared at me. I was dressed in a ratty yellow bathrobe. My untrimmed beard had reached rabbinic proportions and my hair looked like electrified Brillo. Despite thirteen hours of sleep I looked and felt drowsy.

'I hope I'm not disturbing you, Doctor. Your office referred me to your home number, which was out of order.'

I let him in and he sat down, scanning the place. Foot-high stacks of unopened mail littered the dining-room table. The house was dark, drapes drawn, and smelled stale. 'Days of Our Lives' flickered on the tube.

He rested his notepad on one knee and told me the interview was a formality for the coroner's inquest. Then he had me rehash the night I'd found the body, interrupting to clarify a point, scratching and jotting and staring. It was tediously procedural and my mind wandered often, so that he had to repeat his questions. Sometimes I talked so softly he asked me to repeat my answers.

After twenty minutes he asked:

'Doctor, are you all right?'

'I'm fine.' Unconvincingly.

'Oka-ay.' He shook his head, asked a few more questions, then put his pencil down and laughed nervously.

'You know I feel kind of funny asking a doctor how he feels.'

'Don't worry about it.'

He resumed questioning me and, even through the

30

haze, I could see he had a curious technique. He'd skip from topic to topic with no apparent line of inquiry. It threw me off balance and made me more alert.

'You're an assistant professor at the medical school?'

'Associate.'

'Pretty young to be an associate professor, aren't you?'

'I'm thirty-two. I started young.'

'Uh-huh. How many kids in the treatment programme?'

'About thirty.'

'Parents?'

'Maybe ten, eleven couples, half a dozen single parents.'

'Any talk about Mr. Hickle in treatment?'

'That's confidential.'

'Of course, sir.'

'You ran the treatment as part of your job at—' he consulted his notes—'Western Pediatric Hospital.'

'It was volunteer work associated with the hospital.'

'You didn't get paid for it?'

'I continued to receive my salary and the hospital relieved me of other duties.'

'There were fathers in the treatment groups, too.'

'Yes.' I thought I'd mentioned couples.

'Some of those guys were pretty mad at Mr. Hickle, I guess.'

Mr. Hickle. Only a policeman could be so artificially polite as to call a dead pervert *sir*. Between themselves they used other terms, I supposed. Insufferable etiquette was a way of keeping the barrier between cop and civilian.

'That's confidential, Detective.'

He grinned as if to say *Can't blame a fella for trying*, and scribbled in his notepad.

'Why so many questions about a suicide?'

'Just routine.' He answered automatically without looking up. 'I like to be thorough.'

31

He stared at me absently, then asked:

'Did you have any help running the groups?'

'I encouraged the families to participate—to help themselves. I was the only professional.'

'Peer counselling?'

'Exactly.'

'We've got it in the department now.' Noncommittal. 'So they kind of took over.'

'Gradually. I was always there.'

'Did any of them have a key to your office?'

Aha.

'Absolutely not. You're thinking one of those people killed Hickle and faked it to look like suicide?' Of course he was. The same suspicion had occurred to me.

'I'm not drawing conclusions. Just investigating.' This guy was elusive enough to *be* an analyst.

'I see.'

Abruptly he stood, closed his pad and put his pencil away.

I rose to walk him to the door, teetered and blacked out.

The first thing I saw when things came back into focus was his big ugly face looming over me. I felt damp and cold. He was holding a washcloth and dripped water on to my face.

'You fainted. How do you feel?'

'Fine.' The last thing I felt was *fine*.

'You don't look wonderful. Maybe I should call a doctor, Doctor.'

'No.'

'You sure?'

'No. It's nothing, I've had the flu for a few days. I just need to get something in my stomach.'

He went into the kitchen and came back with a glass of orange juice. I sipped slowly and started to feel stronger.

I sat up and held the glass myself.

'Thank you,' I said.

'To protect and serve.'

'I'm really fine now. If you don't have any more questions...'

'No. Nothing more at this time.' He got up and opened some windows; the light hurt my eyes. He turned off the TV.

'Want something to eat before I go?'

What a strange, motherly man.

'I'll be fine.'

'Okay, Doctor. You take care now.'

I was eager to see him go. But when the sound of his car engine was no longer audible I felt disoriented. Not depressed, like before, but agitated, restless, without peace. I tried watching 'As the World Turns' but couldn't concentrate. Now the inane dialogue annoyed me. I picked up a book but the words wouldn't come into focus. I took a swallow of orange juice and it left a bad taste in my mouth and a stabbing pain in my throat.

I went out on the patio and looked up at the sky until luminescent discs danced in front of my eyes. My skin itched. Bird songs irritated me. I couldn't sit still.

It went on that way the entire afternoon. Miserable.

At four-thirty he called.

'Dr. Delaware? This is Milo Sturgis. Detective Sturgis.'

'What can I do for you, Detective?'

'How are you feeling?'

'Much better, thank you.'

'That's good.'

There was silence.

'Uh, Doctor, I'm kind of on shaky ground here...'

'What's on your mind?'

'You know, I was in the Medical Corps in Viet Nam. We used to see a lot of something called acute stress reaction. I was wondering if...'

'You think that's what I've got?'

33

'Well...'

'What was the prescribed treatment in Viet Nam?'

'We got them back into action as quickly as possible. The more they avoided combat the worse they got.'

'Do you think that's what I should do? Jump back into the swing of things?'

'I can't say, Doctor. I'm no psychologist.'

'You'll diagnose but you won't treat.'

'Okay, Doctor. Just wanted to see if—'

'No. Wait. I'm sorry. I appreciate your calling.' I was confused, wondering what ulterior motive he could possibly have.

'Yeah, sure. No problem.'

'Thanks, really. You'd make a hell of a shrink, Detective.'

He laughed.

'That's sometimes part of the job, sir.'

After he hung up I felt better than I'd felt in days. The next morning I called him at the West L.A. Division headquarters and offered to buy him a drink.

We met at Angela's, across from the West L.A. station on Santa Monica Boulevard. It was a coffee shop with a smoky cocktail lounge in the back populated by several groupings of large, solemn men. I noticed that few of them acknowledged Milo, which seemed unusual. I had always though cops did a lot of backslapping and good-natured cussing after hours. These men took their drinking seriously. And quietly.

He had great potential as a therapist. He sipped Chivas, sat back, and let me talk. No more interrogation now. He listened and I spilled my guts.

By the end of the evening, though, he was talking too.

Over the next couple of weeks Milo and I found out that we had a lot in common. We were about the same age— he was ten months older—and had been born into working-class families in medium-sized towns. His father had

34

been a steelworker, mine an electrical assembler. He too had been a good student, graduating with honours from Purdue and with an M.A. in literature from Indiana U., Bloomington. He'd planned to be a teacher when he was drafted. Two years in Viet Nam had somehow turned him into a policeman.

Not that he considered his job at odds with his intellectual pursuits. Homicide detectives, he informed me, were the intellectuals of any police department. Investigating murder requires little physical activity and lots of brainwork. Veteran homicide men sometimes violate regulations and don't carry a weapon. Just lots of pens and pencils. Milo packed his .38 but confessed that he really didn't need it.

'It's very white collar, Alex, with lots of paperwork, decision-making, attention to detail.'

He liked being a cop, enjoyed catching bad guys. Sometimes he thought he might like to try something else, but exactly what that something else was, wasn't clear.

We had other interests in common. We'd both done some martial arts training. Milo had taken a mixed bag of self-defence courses while in the army. I'd learned fencing and karate while in graduate school. We were miserably out of shape but deluded ourselves that it would all come back if we needed it. Both of us appreciated good food, good music and the virtues of solitude.

The rapport between us developed quickly.

About three weeks after we'd known each other he told me he was homosexual. I was taken by surprise and had nothing to say.

'I'm telling you now because I don't want you to think I've been trying to put the make on you.'

Suddenly I was ashamed, because that had been my initial thought, exactly.

It was hard to accept, at first, his being gay, despite all my supposed psychological sophistication. I know all the facts. That *they* make up 5 to 10 per cent of virtually any

35

human grouping. That most of *them* look just like me and you. That *they* could be anybody—the butcher, the baker, the local homicide dick. That most of *them* are reasonably well-adjusted.

And yet the stereotypes adhere to the brain. You expect them to be mincing, screaming, nelly fairies; leather-armoured shaven-skull demons; oh-so-preppy mustachioed young things in Izod shirts and khaki trousers; or hiking-booted bulldykes.

Milo didn't look homosexual.

But he was and had been comfortable with it for several years. He wasn't in the closet, neither did he flaunt it.

I asked him if the department knew about it.

'Uh-huh. Not in the sense of filing an official report. It's just something that's known.'

'How do they treat you?'

'Disapproval from a distance—cold looks. But basically it's live and let live. They're short-staffed and I'm good. What do they want? To drag in the ACLU and lose a good detective in the bargain? Ed Davis was a homophobe. He's gone and it's not so bad.'

'What about the other detectives?'

He shrugged.

'They leave me alone. We talk business. We don't double-date.'

Now the lack of recognition by the men at Angela's made sense.

Some of Milo's initial altruism, his reaching out to help me, was a little more understandable, too. He knew what it was like to be alone. A gay cop was a person in limbo. You could never be one of the gang back at the station, no matter how well you did your job. And the homosexual community was bound to be suspicious of someone who looked, acted like and *was* a cop.

'I figured I should tell you, since we seem to be getting friendly.'

'It's no big deal, Milo.'

36

'No?'

'No.' I wasn't really all that comfortable with it. But I was damn well going to work on it.

A month after Stuart Hickle stuck a .22 in his mouth and blasted his brains all over my wallpaper, I made some major changes in my life.

I resigned my job at Western Pediatric and closed down my practice. I referred all my patients to a former student, a first-rate therapist who was starting out in practice and needed the business. I had taken very few new referrals since starting the groups for the Kim's Korner families, so there was less separation anxiety than would normally be expected.

I sold an apartment building in Malibu, forty units that I'd purchased seven years before, for a large profit. I also let go of a duplex in Santa Monica. Part of the money—the portion that would eventually go to taxes—I put in a high-yield money market. The rest went into tax-free municipals. It wasn't the kind of investing that would make me richer, but it would provide financial stability. I figured I could live off the interest for two or three years as long as I didn't get too extravagant.

I sold my old Chevy Two and bought a Seville, a seventy-nine, the last year they looked good. It was forest-green with a saddle-coloured leather interior that was cushy and quiet. With the amount of driving I'd be doing, the lousy mileage wouldn't make much difference. I threw away most of my old clothes and got new stuff—mostly soft fabrics—knits, cords, rubber-soled shoes, cashmere sweaters, robes, shorts, and pullovers.

I had the pipes cleaned out on the hot tub that I'd never used since I bought the house. I started to buy food and drink milk. I pulled my old Martin out of its case and strummed it on the balcony. I listened to records. I read for pleasure for the first time since high school. I got a

tan. I shaved off my beard and discovered I had a face,
and not a bad one at that.

I dated good women. I met Robin and things really
started to get better.

Be-kind-to-Alex time. Early retirement six months
before my thirty-third birthday.

It was fun while it lasted.

3

MORTON HANDLER'S last residence—if you didn't count
the morgue—had been a luxury apartment complex off
Sunset Boulevard in Pacific Palisades. It had been built
into a hillside and designed to give a honeycomb effect:
a loosely connected chain of individual units linked by
corridors that had been placed at seemingly random
locations, the apartments staggered to give each one a
full view of the ocean. The motif was bastard Spanish:
blindingly white textured stucco walls, red tile roofs, window accents of black wrought iron. Plantings of azalea
and hibiscus filled in occasional patches of earth. There
were lots of potted plants sunk in large terra-cotta containers: coconut palms, rubber plants, sun ferns, tempo-
rary-looking, as if someone planned on moving them all
out in the middle of the night.

Handler's unit was on an intermediate level. The front
door was sealed, with an L.A.P.D. sticker taped across
it. Lots of footprints dirtied the terrazzo walkway near
the entrance.

Milo led me across a terrace filled with polished stones
and succulents to a unit cater-cornered from the murder
scene. Adhesive letter spelling out the word MAN GER

39

were affixed to the door. Bad jokes about Baby Jesus flashed through my mind.

Milo knocked.

I realized then that the place was amazingly silent. There must have been at least fifty units but there wasn't a soul in sight. No evidence of human habitation.

We waited a few minutes. He raised his fist to knock again just before the door opened.

'Sorry, I was washin' my hair.'

The woman could have been anywhere from twenty-five to forty. She had pale skin with the kind of texture that looked as if a pinch would crumble it. Large brown eyes topped by plucked brows. Thin lips. A slight under-bite. Her hair was wrapped in an orange towel and the little that peeked out was medium brown. She wore a faded cotton shirt of ochre-and-orange print over rust-coloured stretch pants. Dark blue tennis shoes on her feet. Her eyes darted from Milo to me. She looked like someone who'd been knocked around plenty and refused to believe that it wasn't going to happen again at any moment.

'Mrs. Quinn? This is Dr. Alex Delaware. He's the psy-chologist I told you about.'

'Pleased to meet you, Doctor.'

Her hand was thin and cold and moist and she pulled away as quickly as she could.

'Melody's watchin' TV in her room. Out of school, with all that's been goin' on. I let her watch to keep her mind off it.'

We followed her into the apartment.

Apartment was a charitable word. What it was, really, was a couple of oversized closets stuck together. An archi-tect's postscript. Hey, Ed, we've got an extra four hun-dred square feet of corner in back of terrace number 142. Why don't we throw a roof over it, nail up some drywall and call it a manager's unit? Get some poor soul to do scutwork for the privilege of living in Pacific Palisades...

40

The living room was filled with one floral sofa, a masonite end table and a television. A framed painting of Mount Rainer that looked as if it came from a Savings and Loan calendar and a few yellowed photographs hung on the wall. The photos were of hardened, unhappy-looking people and appeared to date from the Gold Rush.

'My grandparents,' she said.

A cubicle of a kitchen was visible and from it came the smell of frying bacon. A large bag of sour-cream-and-onion-flavoured potato chips and a six pack of Dr Pepper sat on the counter.

'Very nice.'

'They came here in 1902. From Oklahoma.' She made it sound like an apology.

There was an unfinished wooden door and from behind it came the sound of sudden laughter and applause, bells and buzzers. A game show.

'She's watchin' back there.'

'That's just fine, Mrs. Quinn. We'll let her be until we're ready for her.'

The woman nodded her head in assent.

'She don't get much chance to watch the daytime shows, bein' in school. So she's watching' 'em now.'

'May we sit down, ma'am?'

'Oh yes, yes.' She flitted around the room like a mayfly, tugging at the towel on her head. She brought in an ashtray and set it down on the end table. Milo and I sat on the sofa and she dragged in a tubular aluminium-and-Naugahyde chair from the kitchen for herself. Despite the fact that she was thin her haunches settled and spread. She took out a pack of cigarettes, lit one up and sucked in the smoke until her cheeks hollowed. Milo spoke.

'How old is your daughter, Mrs. Quinn?'

'Bonita. Call me Bonita. Melody's the girl. She's just seven this past month.' Talking about her daughter seemed to make her especially nervous. She inhaled

41

greedily on her cigarette and blew little smoke out. Her free hand clenched and unclenched in rapid cadence.

'Melody may be our only witness to what happened here last night.' Milo looked at me with a disgusted frown.

I knew what he was thinking. An apartment complex with seventy to one hundred residents and the only possible witness a child.

'I'm scared for her, Detective Sturgis, if someone else finds out.' Bonita Quinn stared at the floor as if doing it long enough would reveal the mystic secret of the Orient.

'I assure you, Mrs. Quinn, that no one will find out. Dr. Delaware has served as a special consultant to the police many times.' He lied shamelessly and glibly, 'He understands the importance of keeping things secret. Besides—' he reached over to pat her shoulder reassuringly. I thought she'd go through the ceiling '—all psychologists demand confidentiality when working with their patients. Isn't that so, Dr. Delaware?'

'Absolutely.' We wouldn't get into the whole muddy issue of children's rights to privacy.

Bonita Quinn made a strange, squeaking noise that was impossible to interpret. The closest thing to it that I could remember was the noise laboratory frogs used to make in Physiological Psych right before we pithed them by plunging a needle down into the tops of their skulls.

'What's all this hypnotism gonna do to her?'

I lapsed into my shrink's voice—the calm, soothing tones that had become so natural over the years that they switched on automatically. I explained to her that hypnosis wasn't magic, simply a combination of focused concentration and deep relaxation, that people tended to remember things more clearly when they were relaxed and that was why the police used it for witnesses. That children were better at going into hypnosis than were adults because they were less inhibited and enjoyed fantasy. That it didn't hurt, and was actually pleasant for

42

most youngsters and that you couldn't get stuck in it or do anything against your will while hypnotized.

'All hypnosis,' I ended, 'is self-hypnosis. My role is simply to help your daughter do something that comes natural to her.'

She probably understood about ten per cent of it, but it seemed to calm her down.

'You can say that again, natural. She daydreams all the time.'

'Exactly. Hypnosis is like that.'

'Teachers complain all the time, say she's driftin' off, not doing her work.'

She was talking as if she expected me to do something about it.

Milo broke in.

'Has Melody told you anything more about what she saw, Mrs. Quinn?'

'No, no.' An emphatic shake of the head. 'We haven't been talkin' about it.'

Milo pulled out his notepad and flipped through a few pages.

'What I have on record is that Melody couldn't sleep and was sitting in the living room—in this room at around one in the morning.'

'Must've been. I go in by eleven-thirty and I got up once for a cigarette at twenty after twelve. She was asleep then and I didn't hear her for the while it took me to fall off. I'd 'a' heard her. We share the room.'

'Uh-huh. And she saw two men—here it says "I saw big men." The officer's question was "How many, Melody?" and she answered, "Two, maybe three." When he asked her what did they look like, all she could say was that they were dark.' He was talking to me now. 'We asked her black, Latino. Nothing. Only *dark*.'

'That could mean shadows. Could mean anything to a seven-year-old,' I said.

'I know.'

43

'Which could mean two men, or one guy with a shadow, or—'

'Don't say it.'

Or nothing at all.

'She don't always tell the truth about everything.'

We both turned to look at Bonita Quinn who had used the few seconds we had ignored her to put out her cigarette and light a new one.

'I'm not sayin' she's a bad kid. But she don't always tell the truth. I don't know why you want to depend on her.'

I asked, 'Do you have problems with her chronically lying—about things that don't make much sense—or does she do it to avoid getting in trouble?'

'The second. When she don't want me to paddle her and I know somethin's broken, it's got to be her. She tells me no, mama, not me. And I paddle her double.' She looked to me for disapproval. 'For not tellin' the truth.'

'Do you have other problems with her?' I asked gently.

'She's a good girl, Doctor. Only the daydreams, and the concentration problems.'

'Oh?' I needed to understand this child if I was going to be able to do hypnosis with her.

'The concentratin'—it's hard for her.'

No wonder, in this tiny, television-saturated cell. No doubt the apartments were Adults Only and Melody Quinn was required to keep a low profile. There's a large segment of the population of Southern California that views the sight of anyone too young or too old as offensive. It's as if nobody wants to be reminded from whence they came or to where they will certainly go. That kind of denial, coupled with face lifts and hair transplants and makeup, creates a comfortable little delusion of immortality. For a short while.

I was willing to bet that Melody Quinn spent most of her time indoors despite the fact that the complex boasted three swimming pools and a totally equipped gym. Not to

44

mention the ocean a half-mile away. Those playthings were meant for the grownups.

'I took her to the doctor when the teachers kept sendin' home these notes sayin' she can't sit still, her mind wanders. He said she was overactive. Somethin' in the brain.'

'Hyperactive?'

'That's right. Wouldn't surprise me. Her dad wasn't altogether right up there.' She tapped her forehead. 'Used the illegal drugs and the wine until he—' she stopped cold, looking at Milo with sudden fear.

'Don't worry, Mrs. Quinn, we're not interested in that kind of thing. We only want to find out who killed Dr. Handler and Ms. Gutierrez.'

'Yeah, the headshrinker—' she stopped again, this time staring at me. 'Can't seem to say anythin' right, today.' She forced a weak smile.

I nodded reassurance, smiled understandingly.

'He was a nice guy, that doctor.' Some of my best friends are psychotherapists. 'Used to joke with me a lot and I'd kid him, ask him if he had any shrunken heads in there,' She laughed, a strange giggle, and showed a mouthful of teeth badly in need of repair. By now I had narrowed her age to middle thirties. In ten years she'd look truly elderly. 'Terrible about what happened to him.'

'And Ms. Gutierrez.'

'Yeah, her too. Only her I wasn't so crazy about. She was Mexican, you know, but uppity Mexican. Where I come from they did the stoop labour and the cleanup. This one had the fancy dresses and the little sports car. And her a teacher, too.' It wasn't easy for Bonita Quinn, brought up to think of all Mexicans as beasts of burden, to see that in the big city, away from the lettuce fields, some of them looked just like real people. While she did the donkey work.

'She was always carryin' herself like she was too good for you. You'd say hello to her and she'd be lookin' off into the distance, like she had no time for you.'

45

She took another drag on her cigarette and smiled slyly.

'This time I'm okay,' she said.

We both looked at her.

'Neither of you gents is a Mex. I didn't put my foot in it again.'

She was extremely pleased with herself and I took advantage of her lifted spirits to ask her a few more questions.

'Mrs. Quinn, is your daughter on any sort of medication for her hyperactivity?'

'Oh yeah, sure. The doc gave me pills to give her.'

'Do you have the prescription slip handy?'

'I got the bottle.' She got up and returned with an amber vial half full of tablets.

I took it and read the label. Ritalin. Methylphenidate hydrochloride. A super-amphetamine that speeds up adults but slows down kids, it's one of the most commonly prescribed drugs for American youngsters. Ritalin is addictive and potent and has a host of side effects, one of the most common of which is insomnia. Which might explain why Melody Quinn was sitting, staring out the window of a dark room at one in the morning.

Ritalin is a sweetheart drug when it comes to controlling children. It improves concentration and reduces the frequency of problem-behaviours in hyperactive kids—which sounds great, except that the symptoms of hyperactivity are hard to differentiate from those of anxiety, depression, acute stress reaction, or simple boredom at school. I've seen kids who were too bright for their classroom look hyper. Ditto for little ones going through the horrors of divorce or any other significant trauma.

A doctor who's doing his job correctly will require comprehensive psychological and social evaluation of a child before prescribing Ritalin or any other behaviour-modifying drug. And there are plenty of good doctors. But some physicians take the easy way out, using the pills as the first step. If it's not malpractice it's dangerously close.

46

I opened the vial and shook some pills onto my palm. They were amber, the 20-milligram kind. I examined the label. One tablet three times daily. Sixty mg was the maximum recommended dosage. Strong stuff for a seven-year-old.

'You give her these three times a day?'

'Uh-huh. That's what it says, don't it?'

'Yes, it does. Did your doctor start off with something smaller—white or blue pills?'

'Oh yeah. We had her takin' three of the blue ones at first. Worked pretty good but I still got the complaints from the school, so he said it was okay to try these.'

'And this dosage works well for Melody?'

'Works real fine for me. If it's gonna be a rough day with lots of visitors comin' over—she don't do real good with lots of people, lots of commotion—I give her an extra one.'

Now we were talking overdose.

Bonita Quinn must have seen the look of surprise and disapproval that I tried unsuccessfully to conceal, for she spoke up with indignation in her voice.

'The doc says it was okay. He's an important man. You know, this place don't allow kids and I get to stay here only on account as she's a quiet kid. M and M Properties—they own the place—told me any time there's complaints about kids, that's it.'

No doubt that did wonders for Melody's social life. Chances are she had never had a friend over.

There was cruel irony to the idea of a seven-year-old imprisoned amidst single-swingle splendour, tucked away in a slum pocket on an eyrie high above the high Pacific, and dosed up with Ritalin to appease the combined wishes of the Los Angeles school system, a dim-witted mother and M and M Properties.

I examined the label on the vial to find out the name of the prescribing physician. When I found it, things began to fall into place.

47

L.W. Towle. Lionel Willard Towle, M.D. One of the most established and respected pediatricians on the West Side. I had never met him but knew him by reputation. He was on the senior staff of Western Pediatric and a half dozen other Westside hospitals. A big shot in the Academy of Pediatrics. A guest speaker, highly in demand, at seminars on learning disabilities and behaviour problems.

Dr. Towle was also a paid consultant to three major pharmaceutical concerns. Translate: pusher. He had a reputation, especially among the younger doctors who were generally more conservative about drugs, as easy with the prescription pad. No one said it too loudly, because Towle had been around a long time and had lots of important patients and plenty of connections, but the whispered consensus was that he was a Dr. Feelgood for tots. I wondered how someone like Bonita Quinn had ended up in his practice. But there was no easy way to ask without appearing unduly nosy.

I handed the vial back to her and turned to Milo, who'd been sitting through the exchange in silence.

'Let me talk to you,' I said.

'Just one moment, ma'am.'

Outside the apartment I told him, 'I can't hypnotize this kid. She's drugged to the gills. It would be a risk to work with her, and besides, there's little chance of getting anything worthwhile out of her.'

Milo digested this.

'Shit.' He scratched his head. 'What if we take her off the pills for a few days.'

'That's a medical decision. We get into that and we're way out of bounds. We need the physician's permission. Which blows confidentiality.'

'Who's the doc?'

I told him about Towle.

'Wonderful. But maybe he'll agree to let her off for a few days.'

'Maybe, but there's no guarantee she'll give us anything. This kid's been on stimulants for a year. And what about Mrs Q? She's scared plenty as is. Take her darling off the pills and first thing she'll do is lock the kid inside twelve hours a day. They like it quiet here.'

The complex was still silent as a mausoleum. At one-forty-five in the afternoon.

'Can you at least look at the kid? Maybe she's not that doped.'

Across the way the door to the Handler apartment was open. I caught a glimpse of elegance in disarray—oriental rugs, antiques, and severe acrylic furniture broken and upended, blood-spattered white walls. The police lab men worked silently, like moles.

'By now she's had her second dose, Milo.'

'Shit.' He punched his fist into his palm. 'Just meet the kid. Give me your impression. Maybe she'll be alert.'

She wasn't. Her mother led her into the living room and then left with Milo. She stared off into the distance, sucking her thumb. She was a small child. If I hadn't known her age I would have guessed it at five, maybe five-and-a-half. She had a long, grave face with oversized brown eyes. Her straight blond hair hung to her shoulders, held in place by twin plastic barettes. She wore blue jeans and a blue-green-and-white-striped T-shirt. Her feet were dirty and bare.

I led her to a chair and sat opposite her on the couch.

'Hello, Melody. I'm Dr. Delaware. I'm a psychologist. Do you know what that is?'

No response.

'I'm the kind of doctor who doesn't give shots. What I do is talk and draw and play with kids. I try to help kids who are sad, or angry, or scared.'

At the word *scared* she looked up for a second. Then she resumed staring past me and sucked her thumb.

'Do you know why I'm talking to you?'

49

A shake of the head.

'It's not because you're sick or because you've done anything wrong. We know you're a good girl.'

Her eyes moved around the room, avoiding me.

'I'm here because you may have seen something last night that's important. When you couldn't sleep and were looking out the window.'

She didn't answer. I continued.

'Melody, what kind of things do you like to do?'

Nothing.

'Do you like to play?'

She nodded.

'I like to play too. And I like to skate. Do you skate?'

'Uh-uh.' Of course not, skates make noise.

'And I like to watch movies. Do you watch movies?'

She mumbled something. I bent closer.

'What's that, hon?'

'On TV.' Her voice was thin and quivering, a trembling breathy sound like the breeze through dry leaves.

'Uh-huh. On TV. I watch TV, too. What shows do you like to watch?'

'Scooby-Doo.'

'Scooby-Doo. That's a good show. Any other shows?'

'My mama watches the soap operas.'

'Do you like the soap operas?'

She shook her head.

'Pretty boring, huh?'

A hint of a smile, around the thumb.

'Do you have toys, Melody?'

'In my room.'

'Could you show them to me?'

The room she shared with her mother was neither adult nor childlike in character. It was no more than ten foot square, low-ceilinged with a solitary window set high in the wall, which gave it the ambience of a dungeon. Melody and Bonita shared one twin bed unadorned by a head-

50

board. It was half unmade, the thin chenille spread folded back to reveal rumpled sheets. On one side of the bed was a nightstand filled with bottles and jars of cold cream, hand lotion, brushes, combs and a piece of cardboard onto which a score of bobby pins were clasped. On the other side was a huge, moth-eaten stuffed walrus, made of fuzzy material and coloured an atrocious turquoise blue. A baby picture was the sole adornment on the wall. A sagging bureau made of unfinished pine and covered with a crocheted doily, and the TV, were the only other pieces of furniture in the room.

In one corner was a small pile of toys.

Melody led me over to it, hesitantly. She picked up a grimy, naked plastic baby doll.

'Amanda,' she said.

'She's beautiful.'

The child clutched the doll to her chest and rocked back and forth.

'You must really take good care of her.'

'I do.' It was said defensively. This was a child who was not used to praise.

'I know you do,' I said gently. I looked over to the walrus. 'Who's he?'

'Fatso. My daddy gave him to me.'

'He's cute.'

She walked over to the animal, which was as tall as she, and stroked it purposefully.

'Mama wants me to throw him out 'cause he's too big. But I won't let her.'

'Fatso's really important to you.'

'Uh-huh.'

'Daddy gave him to you.'

She nodded, emphatically, and smiled. I'd passed some kind of test.

For the next twenty-five minutes we sat on the floor and played.

When Milo and the mother returned, Melody and I

51

were in fine spirits. We'd built and destroyed several worlds.

'Well, you're sure lookin' frisky,' said Bonita.

'We're having a good time, Mrs. Quinn. Melody's been a very good girl.'

'That's good.' She went over to her daughter and placed a hand on her head. 'That's good, hon.'

There was unexpected tenderness in her eyes, then it was gone. She turned to me and asked:

'How'd it go with the hypnotism?'

She asked it the same way she might inquire, how's my kid doing in arithmetic.

'We haven't done any hypnosis yet. Melody and I are just getting to know each other.'

I drew her aside.

'Mrs. Quinn, hypnosis requires trust on the part of the child. I usually spend a little time with children beforehand. Melody was very cooperative.'

'She didn't tell you nothin'?' She reached into the breast pocket of her shirt and pulled out another cigarette. I lit it for her and the gesture surprised her.

'Nothing of importance. With your permission I'd like to come over some time tomorrow and spend a little more time with Melody.'

She eyed me suspiciously, chewed on the cigarette, then shrugged.

'You're the doctor.'

We rejoined Milo and the child. He was kneeling on one leg and showing her his detective's badge. Her eyes were wide.

'Melody, if it's okay with you, I'd like to come by tomorrow and play with you some more.'

She looked up at her mother and began sucking her thumb again.

'It's fine with me,' Bonita Quinn said curtly. 'Now run along.'

Melody sprang for her room. She stopped in the door-

52

way and gave me a tentative look. I waved, she waved back and then she disappeared. A second later the TV began blaring.

'One more thing, Mrs. Quinn. I'll need to talk to Dr. Towle before I do any hypnosis with Melody.'

'That's okay.'

'I'll need your permission to talk with Dr. Towle about the case. You realize he's professionally bound to keep this confidential, just as I am.'

'That's okay. I trust Dr. Towle.'

'And I may ask him to take her off her medicine for a couple of days.'

'Oh all right, all right.' She waved her hand, exasperated.

'Thank you, Mrs. Quinn.'

We left her standing in front of her apartment, smoking frantically, taking the towel off her head and shaking her hair loose in the midday sun.

I took the wheel of the Seville and drove slowly up towards Sunset.

'Stop smirking, Milo.'

'What's that?' He was looking out the passenger window, his hair flapping like duck wings.

'You know you've got me hooked, don't you? A kid like that, those big eyes like something out of a Keene painting.'

'If you want to quit right now, it wouldn't make me happy, Alex. But I wouldn't stop you. There's still time for gnocchi.'

'The hell with gnocchi. Let's talk with Dr. Towle.'

The Seville was consuming fuel with customary gluttony. I pulled into a Chevron self-serve at Bundy. While Milo pumped gas I got Towle's number from information and dialled it. I used my title and got through to the doctor in a half-minute. I gave him a brief explanation of why I

53

needed to talk with him and told him we could chat now over the phone.

'No,' he said. 'I've got an office full of kids.' His voice was smooth and reassuring, the kind of voice a parent would want to hear at two in the morning when the baby was turning blue.

'When would be a good time to call you?'

He didn't answer. I could hear the bustle of activity in the background, then muffled voices. He came back on the line.

'How about dropping by at four-thirty? I've got a lull around then.'

'I appreciate your time, Doctor.'

'No bother.' And he hung up.

I left the phone booth. Milo was removing the nozzle from the rear of the Seville, holding it at arm's length to avoid getting gasoline on his suit.

I settled in the driver's seat and stuck my head out the window.

'Catch the windshield for me, son.'

He made a gargoyle face—not much of an effort—and gave me the finger. Then he went to work with paper towels.

It was two-forty and we were only fifteen minutes from Towle's office. That left over an hour to kill. Neither of us was in a good enough mood to want first-rate food, so we drove back to West L.A. and went to Angela's.

Milo ordered something called a San Francisco Deluxe Omelette. It turned out to be a bright yellow horror stuffed with spinach, tomatoes, ground beef, chilies, onions and marinated eggplant. He dug into it with relish while I contented myself with a steak sandwich and a Coors. In between bites he talked about the Handler murder.

'It's a puzzler, Alex. You've got all the signs of a psychotic thrill killer—both of them trussed up in the bedroom, like animals ready for the slaughter. And stuck

54

about five dozen times. The girl looked like she ran into Jack the Ripper with her—'

'Spare me.' I pointed to my food.

'Sorry. I forget when I'm talking to a civilian. You get used to it after wading in it for a few years. You can't stop living, so you learn to eat and drink and fart through all of it.' He wiped his face with his napkin and took a long, deep swallow of his beer. 'Anyway, despite the craziness, there's no sign of forced entry. The front door was open. Normally that would be very puzzling. Except in this case with the victim being a psychiatrist, it might make sense, his knowing the bad guy and letting him in.'

'You think it was one of his patients?'

'It's a good possibility. Psychiatrists have been known to deal with crazies.'

'I'd be surprised if it turned out that way, Milo. Ten to one Handler had a typical West Side practice—depressed middle-aged women, disillusioned executives, and a few adolescent identity crises thrown in for good measure.'

'Do I detect a note of cynicism?'

I shrugged.

'That's just the way it is in most cases. High-priced friendship—not that it's not valuable, mind you. But there's very little real mental illness in what most of us— psychiatrists, psychologists—see in practice. The real crazies, the really disturbed ones, are hospitalized.'

'Handler worked at a hospital before he went out on his own. Encino Oaks.'

'Maybe you'll dig up something there,' I said doubtfully. I was tired of being the wet blanket so I didn't tell him that Encino Oaks Hospital was a repository for the suicidal progeny of the rich. Very little sexual psychopathy, there.

He pushed his empty plate away and motioned for the waitress.

'Bettijean, a nice slab of that green apple pie, please.'

'A la mode, Milo?'

He patted his gut and pondered.

'What the hell, why not. Vanilla.'

'And you, sir?'

'Just coffee, please.'

When she had gone he continued, thinking out loud more than talking to me.

'Anyway, it appears as if Dr. Handler let someone into his place sometime between midnight and one and got ripped up for his efforts.'

'And the Gutierrez woman?'

'Your quintessential innocent bystander. Being in the wrong place at the wrong time.'

'She was Handler's girlfriend?'

He nodded.

'For about six months. From the little we've learned she started out as a patient and ended up going from couch to bed.'

A not uncommon story.

'The irony of it was that she was hacked up worse than he was. Handler got his throat slit and probably died relatively quickly. There were a few other holes in him but nothing lethal. It looks as if the killer took his time with her. Makes sense if it's a sexual crazy.'

I could feel my digestive process come to a halt. I changed the subject.

'Who's your new love?'

The pie came. Milo smiled at the waitress and attacked the pastry. I noticed that the filling was indeed green, a bright, almost luminescent green. Someone in the kitchen was fooling around with food dyes. I shuddered to think what they could do with something really challenging, like a pizza. It would probably end up looking like a mad artist's palette.

'A doctor. A nice Jewish doctor.' He looked heavenward. 'Every mother's dream.'

'What happened to Larry?'

'He's gone off to find his fortunes in San Francisco.'

56

Larry was a black stage manager with whom Milo had conducted an on-again, off-again relationship for two years. Their last half-year had been grimly platonic.

'He's hooked up with some show sponsored by an anonymous corporation. Something racy for educational television, along the lines of "Our Agricultural Heritage: Your Friend the Plough". Hot stuff.'

'Bitchy, bitchy.'

'No, really, I do wish the boy well. Behind that neurotic exterior was genuine talent.'

'How did you meet your doctor?'

'He works the Emergency Room at Cedars. A surgeon, no less. I was following up an assault that turned into manslaughter, he was commandeering the catheters, and our eyes locked. The rest is history.'

I laughed so hard the coffee almost went up my nose.

'He's been out of the closet for about two years. Marriage in medical school, messy divorce, excommunication by family. The whole bit. Fantastic guy, you'll have to meet him.'

'I'd like to.'

'Give me a few days to slog through Morton Handler's life history and we'll double.'

'It's a deal.'

It was five to four. I let the Los Angeles Police Department pay for my lunch. In the best tradition of policemen the world over, Milo left an enormous tip. He patted Bettijean's fanny on the way out and her laughter followed us out on to the street.

Santa Monica Boulevard was beginning to choke up with traffic and the air had started to foul. I closed the Seville's windows and turned on the air-conditioning. I slipped a tape of Joe Pass and Stephane Grappelli into the deck. The sound of 'Only a Paper Moon', delivered hot forties style, filled the car. The music made me feel good. Milo took a cat nap, snoring deeply. I eased the Seville into the traffic and headed back to Brentwood.

4

TOWLE'S OFFICE was on a side street off San Vicente, not far from the Brentwood Country Mart—one of the few neighbourhoods where movie stars could shop without being harassed. It was in a building designed during the early fifties, when tan brick, low-slung roofs and wall inserts of glass cubes were in vogue. Plantings of asparagus fern and climbing bougainvillaea did something to relieve the starkness, but it still looked pretty severe.

Towle was the building's sole occupant and his name was stencilled in gold leaf on the glass front door. The parking lot was a haven for wood-sided station wagons. We pulled in next to a blue Lincoln with a SPEAK UP FOR CHILDREN bumper sticker that I figured belonged to the good doctor himself.

Inside, the decor was something else. It was as if some interior decorator had tried to make up for the harshness of the building by cramming the waiting room full of mush. The furniture was colonial maple with nubby seat cushions. The walls were covered with needlepoint homilies and cutesy-poo prints of little boys fishing and little girls preening themselves in front of mirrors, wearing mommy's hat and shoes. The room was full of children

58

and harried-looking mothers. Magazines, books and toys cluttered the floor. There was an odour of dirty diapers in the air. If this was Towle's lull I didn't want to be there during his busy period.

When we walked in, two childless males, we drew stares from the women. We had agreed beforehand that Towle would relate better doctor to doctor, so Milo found a seat sandwiched in between two five-year-olds and I walked to the reception window. The girl on the other side was a sweet young thing with Farah Fawcett hair and a face almost as pretty as that of her role model. She was dressed in white and her name tag proclaimed her to be Sandi.

'Hi. I'm Dr. Delaware. I've got an appointment with Dr. Towle.'

I got a smile fronted by lots of nice, white teeth.

'Appointments don't mean much this afternoon. But come right in. He'll be with you in just a minute.'

I walked through the door with several pairs of maternal eyes boring into my back. Some of them had probably been waiting for over an hour. I wondered why Towle didn't hire an associate.

Sandi showed me into the doctor's consultation office, a dark-panelled room about twelve by twelve.

'It's about the Quinn child, isn't it?'

'That's right.'

'I'll pull the chart.' She came back with a manila folder and placed it on Towle's desk. There was a red tag on the cover. She saw me looking at it.

'The reds are the hypers. We code them. Yellow for chronically ill ones. Blue for specialty consults.'

'Very efficient.'

'Oh, you have no idea!' She giggled and placed one hand on a shapely hip. 'You know,' she said, leaning a bit closer and letting me have a whiff of something fragrant, 'between you and me that poor child has it rough growing up with a mother like that.'

59

'I know what you mean.' I nodded, not knowing what she meant at all but hoping she'd tell me. People usually do when you don't seem to care.

'I mean, she's such a scatterbrain—the mother. Every time she comes here she forgets something, or loses something. One time it was her purse. The other time she locked her keys in the car. She really doesn't have it together.'

I clucked sympathetically.

'No that she hasn't had it rough, growing up doing farm work and then marrying that guy who ended up in pris—'

'Sandi.'

We both turned to see a short, sixtyish woman with hair cut in an iron-grey helmet, standing in the doorway, arms folded across her bosom. Her eyeglasses hung suspended from a chain around her neck. She, too, was dressed in white, but on her it looked like a uniform. *Her* name tag proclaimed her to be Edna.

I knew her right away. The doctor's right hand gal. She'd probably been working for him since he hung out his shingle and was making about the same amount of money she'd started out with. But no matter, lucre wasn't what she was after. She was secretly in love with the Great Man. I was willing to bet a handful of blue chip stock that she called him *Doctor*. No name after it. Just Doctor. As if he were the only one in the world.

'There are some charts that need filing,' she said.

'Okay, Edna.' Sandi turned to me, gave a conspiratorial look that said Isn't this old witch a drag? and sashayed down the hall.

'Can I do anything for you?' Edna asked me, still keeping her arms crossed.

'No, thank you.'

'Well, then, Doctor will be right with you.'

'Thank you.' Kill 'em with courtesy.

Her glance let me know that she didn't approve of my presence. No doubt anything that upset Doctor's routine was viewed as an intrusion upon Paradise. But she finally left me alone in the office.

I took a look around the room. The desk was mahogany and battered. It was piled high with charts, medical journals, books, mail, drug samples, and a jar full of paper clips. The desk chairs and the easy chair in which I sat were once classy items—burnished leather—now both aged and cracked.

Two of the walls were covered with diplomas, many of which hung askew and at odds with one another. It looked like a room that had just been nudged by a minor earthquake—nothing broken, just shaken up a bit.

I casually examined the diplomas. Lionel W. Towle had amassed an impressive collection of paper over the years. Degrees, certificates of internship and residency, a walnut plaque with gavel commemorating his chairmanship of some medical task force, honorary membership in this and that, specialty board certification, commendations for public service on the Good Ship Hope, consultant to the California Senate subcommittee on child welfare. And on and on.

The other wall displayed photographs. Most were of Towle. Towle in fisherman's garb, knee-deep in some river holding aloft a clutch of steelhead. Towle with a marlin the size of a Buick. Towle with the mayor and some little squat guy with Peter Lorre eyes—everyone smiling, shaking hands.

There was one exception to this seeming self-obsession. In the centre of the wall hung a colour photograph of a young woman holding a small child. The colours were faded and from the style of clothing worn by the subjects, the picture looked three decades old. There was some of the tell-tale fuzziness of an enlarged snapshot. The hues were misty, almost pastel.

The woman was pretty, fresh-faced, with a sprinkle of freckles across her nose, dark eyes and medium-length brown hair with a natural wave. She wore a filmy-looking,

61

short-sleeved dress of dotted swiss cotton, and her arms were slender and graceful. They wrapped around the child—a boy—who looked around two or younger. He was beautiful. Rosy-cheeked, blond, with cupid's-bow lips and green eyes. He was dressed in a white sailor suit and sat beaming in his mother's embrace. The mountains and lake in the distance looked real.

'It's a lovely picture, isn't it?' said the voice I'd heard over the phone.

He was tall, at least six-three, and lean, with the kind of features bad novels label as chiselled. He was one of the most handsome middle-aged men I had ever seen. His face was noble—a strong chin bisected by a perfect cleft, the nose of a Roman senator, and twinkling eyes the colour of a clear sky. His thick, snow-white hair hung down over his forehead, Carl Sandburg style. His eyebrows were twin white clouds.

He wore a short white coat over a blue oxford shirt, burgundy print tie, and dark gray trousers of a subtle check. His shoes were black calfskin loafers. Very proper, very tasteful. But clothes didn't make the man. He would have looked patrician in doubleknits.

'Dr. Delaware? Will Towle.'

'Alex.'

I stood and we shook hands. His grip was firm and dry. The fingers that clasped mine were enormous and I was conscious of abundant strength behind them.

'Please, sit.'

He took his place behind the desk, swivelled back and threw his feet up on top, resting on a year's back issues of the *Journal of Pediatrics*.

I responded to his question.

'It is a beautiful shot. Somewhere in the Pacific Northwest?'

'Washington state. Olympic National Forest. We were vacationing there in fifty-one. I was a resident. That was my wife and son. I lost them a month later. In a car crash.'

62

'I'm sorry.'

'Yes.' A distant, sleepy look came on his face; it was a moment before he shook himself out of it and came back into focus.

'I know you by reputation, Alex, so it's a pleasure to get to meet you.'

'Same here.'

'I've followed your work, because I have a strong interest in behavioural paediatrics. I was particularly interested in your work with those children who'd been victimized by Stuart Hickle. Several of them were in the practice. The parents spoke highly of your work.'

'Thank you.' I felt as if I was expected to say more but that was one subject that was closed. 'I do remember sending consent forms to you.'

'Yes, yes. Delighted to cooperate.'

Neither of us spoke, then we both spoke at the same time.

'What I'd like to—' I said.

'What can I do for—' he said.

It came out a garbled mess. We laughed, good old boys at the University Club. I deferred to him. Despite the graciousness I sensed an enormous ego lurking behind that white forelock.

'You're here about the Quinn child. What can I do for you?'

I filled him in on as few details as possible, stressing the importance of Melody Quinn as a witness and the benign nature of the hypnotic intervention. I ended by requesting that he allow her to go off Ritalin for one week.

'You really think this child will be able to give you information of substance?'

'I don't know. I've asked the same question. But she's all the police have got.'

'And your role in all of this?'

I thought up a quicky title.

63

'I'm a special consultant. They call me in sometimes when there are children involved.'

'I see.'

He played with his hands, constructing ten-legged spiders and killing them.

'I don't know, Alex. When we start to remove a patient from what has been determined to be an optimal dosage we sometimes upset the entire pattern of biochemical response.'

'You think she needs to be on medication constantly.'

'Of course I do. Why else would I prescribe it for her?' He wasn't angry or defensive. He smiled calmly and with great forbearance. The message was clear: only an idiot would doubt him.

'There'd be no way to reduce the dosage?'

'Oh, that's certainly possible, but it creates the same type of problem. I don't like to tamper with a winning combination.'

'I see.' I hesitated, then continued. 'She must have posed quite a problem to merit sixty mgs.'

Towle placed a pair of reading glasses low on his nose, picked up the chart and flipped through it.

'Let me see. Ah, yes. Hmm. "Mother complains of severe behavioural problems." ' After thumbing through a few more pages: ' "Teachers report failure to complete school assignments. Difficulty in maintaining attention span for more than brief periods." Ah—here's a later notation—"Child struck mother during argument about keeping room clean." And here's a note of mine: "Poor peer relations, few friends." '

I was certain that the argument had something to do with giving away the giant walrus, Fatso. The gift from Daddy. And as for friends—it was easy to see that M and M Properties wouldn't truck with that kind of nonsense.

'That sounds pretty severe to me, don't you think?'

What I thought was that it was horseshit. There'd been nothing resembling a thorough psychological evaluation.

64

Nothing beyond taking the mother at her word. I looked at Towle and saw a quack. A nice-looking, white-haired quack with lots of connections and the right pieces of paper on his wall. I longed to tell him so, but that would do nobody—Melody, Milo—any good.

So I hedged.

'I can't say. You're her doc.' Faking the comradely grin was an exercise in moral self-control.

'That's right, Alex. I am.' He leaned back in his chair and placed his hands behind his head. 'I know what you're thinking. Will Towle is a pill pusher. Stimulants are just another form of child abuse.'

'I wouldn't say that.'

He waved away my objection.

'No, no, I know. And I don't hold it against you. Your training is behavioural and you see things behaviourally. We all do it, settle into professional tunnel vision. The surgeons want to cut everything out. We prescribe and you fellows like to analyse it to death.'

It was starting to sound like a lecture.

'Granted, drugs have risks. But it's a matter of cost-risk analysis. Let's consider a child like the little Quinn girl. What does she start out with? Inferior genes—both parents somewhat *limited* intellectually.' He made the word *limited* sound very cruel. 'Lousy genes and poverty, and a broken marriage. Absent father—although in some of these cases the children are better off without the kind of role models the fathers provide. Bad genes, bad environment. The child's got two strikes against her before she leaves the womb.

'Is it any wonder then that soon we're seeing all the telltale signs—antisocial behaviour, noncompliance, poor school performance, unsatisfactory impulse control?'

I felt a sudden urge to defend little Melody. Her genial doctor was describing her as some kind of total misfit. I kept silent.

'Now a child like this—' he took off his glasses and put

65

down the chart—'is going to have to do moderately well in school in order to achieve some semblance of a decent life for herself. Otherwise it's another generation of P.P.P.'

Piss-poor protoplasm. One of the quaint expressions dreamed up by the medical profession to describe especially unfortunate patients.

Playing straight man to Towle wasn't my idea of a fun afternoon. But I had a hunch it was some kind of ritual, that if I held out and let him smilingly browbeat me he might give me what I came for.

'But there is no way a child like this *can* achieve with her genes and her environment working against her. Not without help. And that's where stimulant medication comes in. Those pills allow her to sit still long enough and pay attention long enough to be able to learn something. They control her behaviour to the point where she no longer alienates everyone around her.'

'I got the impression that the mother was using the medication in a haphazard way—giving her an extra pill on days when there were lots of visitors at the apartment complex.'

'I'll have to check that.' He didn't sound concerned. 'You have to remember, Alex, that this child does not exist in a vacuum. There's a social context here. If there's nowhere for her mother and her to live, that isn't exactly therapeutic, is it?'

I listened, certain there was more. Sure enough: 'Now you may ask, what about psychotherapy? What about behaviour modification? My answer is: What about them? There is no chance of this particular mother developing the capacity for insight to successfully benefit from psychotherapy. And she lacks the ability to even comply with a stable system of rules and regulations necessary for behaviour mod. What she *can* deal with is administering three pills a day to her child. Pills that work. And I don't mind telling you, I don't feel a damn bit guilty about

66

prescribing them, because I think they're this child's only hope.'

It was a great ending. No doubt it made a big hit at the Western Pediatric Ladies Auxiliary Tea. But basically it was all crap. Pseudo-scientific gibberish mixed in with a lot of condescending fascism. Dope up the *Untermenschen* to make them good citizens.

He had worked himself up a bit. But now he was perfectly composed, as handsome and in control as ever.

'I haven't convinced you, have I?' He smiled.

'It's not a matter of that. You raise some interesting points. I'll have to think about it.'

'That's always a good idea, thinking things over.' He rubbed his hands together. 'Now, back to what you came for—and please forgive my little diatribe. You really think that taking this child off stimulants will make her more susceptible to hypnosis.'

'I do.'

'Despite the fact that her concentration will be poorer?'

'Despite that. I've got inductions that are especially suited for children with short attention spans.'

The snowy eyebrows rose.

'Oh, really? I'll have to find out about those. You know, I did some hypnosis, too. In the Army, for pain control. I know it works.'

'I can send you some recent publications.'

'Thank you, Alex.' He rose and it was clear that my time was up.

'Pleasure to meet you, Alex.' Another handshake.

'The pleasure is mine, Will.' This was getting sickening.

The unasked question hung in the air. Towle snagged it.

'I'll tell you what I'm going to do,' he said, smiling ever faintly.

'Yes?'

'I'm going to *think* about it.'

'I see.'

'Yes, I'll think it over. Call me in a couple of days.'

'I'll do that, Will.' And may your hair and teeth fall out overnight, you sanctimonious bastard.

On the way out Edna glared and Sandi smiled at me. I ignored them both and rescued Milo from the trio of munchkins that were climbing over him as if he were play-ground equipment. We made our way through the now-boiling mob of children and mothers and reached the car safely.

5

I TOLD Milo about the encounter with Towle as we drove back to my place.

'Power play.' His forehead creased and cherry-sized lumps appeared just above his jawline.

'That and something else that I can't quite figure. He's a strange guy. Comes across very courtly—almost obsequious—then you realize he's playing games.'

'Why'd he have you come all the way out there for something like that?'

'I don't know.' It was a puzzle, his taking time out from a frantic afternoon to deliver a leisurely lecture. Our entire conversation could have been handled in a five-minute phone call. 'Maybe it's his idea of recreation. One-upping another professional.'

'Hell of a hobby for a busy man.'

'Yeah, but the ego comes first. I've met guys like Towle before, obsessed with being in control, with being the boss. Lots of them end up as department heads, deans and chairmen of committees.'

'And captains and inspectors and police chiefs.'

'Right...'

'You going to call him like he said?' He sounded defeated.

'Sure, for what it's worth.'

'Yeah.'

Milo reclaimed his Fiat and after a few moments of prayer and pumping it started up. He leaned out of the window and looked at me wearily.

'Thanks, Alex. I'm going to go home and crash. This no-sleep routine is catching up with me...'

'You want to take a nap here and then head out?'

'No thanks. I'll make it if this pile of junk will.' He slapped the dented door. 'Thanks anyway.'

'I'll follow up with Melody.'

'Great. I'll call you tomorrow.' He drove away until I stopped him with my shout. He backed up.

'What?'

'It's probably not important, but I thought I'd mention it. The nurse in Towle's office told me Melody's dad's in prison.'

He nodded somnambulantly.

'So's half the country. It's that way when the economy goes bad. Thanks.'

Then he was off.

It was six-fifteen and already dark. I lay down on my bed for a few minutes and when I awoke it was after nine. I got up, washed my face, and called Robin. No one answered.

I took a quick shave, threw on a windbreaker and drove down to Hakata in Santa Monica. I drank sake and ate sushi for an hour, and bantered with the chef, who, as it turned out, had a master's degree in psychology from the University of Tokyo.

I got home, stripped naked, and took a hot bath, trying to erase all thoughts of Morton Handler, Melody Quinn and L.W. Towle, M.D., from my mind. I used self-hypnosis, imagining Robin and myself making love on top of

70

a mountain in the middle of a rain forest. Flushed with passion I got out of the tub and called her again. After ten rings, she answered, mumbling and confused and half-asleep.

I apologized for waking her, told her I loved her and hung up.

Half a minute later she called back.

'Was that you, Alex?' She sounded as if she was dreaming.

'Yes, hon. I'm sorry to wake you.'

'No, that's okay—what time is it?'

'Eleven-thirty.'

'Oh, I must have conked out. How are you, sweetie?'

'Fine. I called you around nine.'

'I was out all day buying wood. There's an old violin-maker out in Simi Valley who's retiring. I spent six hours choosing tools and picking out maple and ebony. I'm sorry I missed you.'

She sounded exhausted.

'I'm sorry too, but go back to bed. Get some sleep and I'll call you tomorrow.'

'If you want to come over, you can.'

I thought about it. But I was too restless to be good company.

'No, doll. You rest. How about dinner tomorrow? You pick the place.'

'Okay, darling.' She yawned—a soft, sweet sound. 'I love you.'

'Love you too.'

It took me a while to fall asleep and when I finally did, it was restless slumber, punctuated by black-and-white dreams with lots of frantic movement in them. I don't remember what they were about, but the dialogue was

71

sluggish and laboured, as if everyone were talking with paralysed lips and mouths filled with wet sand.

In the middle of the night I got up to check that the doors and windows were locked.

6

I WOKE UP at six the next morning, filled with random energy. I hadn't felt that way for over five months. The tension wasn't all bad, for with it came a sense of purpose, but by seven it had built up some, so that I paced around the house like a jaguar on the prowl.

At seven-thirty I decided it was late enough. I dialled Bonita Quinn's number. She was wide-awake and she sounded as if she'd been expecting my call.

'Morning, Doctor.'

'Good morning. I thought I'd drop by and spend a few hours with Melody.'

'Why not? She's not doin' anything. You know—' she lowered her voice—'I think she liked you. She talked about how you played with her.'

'That's good. We'll do some more today. I'll be there in half an hour.'

When I arrived she was all dressed and ready to go. Her mother had put her in a pale yellow sundress that exposed bony white shoulders and pipe-stem arms. Her hair was tied back in a ponytail, fastened by a yellow ribbon. She clutched a tiny patent-leather purse. I had thought we'd spend some time in her room and then per-

73

haps go out for lunch, but it was clear she was primed for an outing.

'Hi, Melody.'

She averted her gaze and sucked her thumb.

'You look very pretty this morning.'

She smiled shyly.

'I thought we'd take a drive, go to a park. How does that sound?'

'Okay.' The shaky voice.

'Great.' I peeked my head into the apartment. Bonita Quinn was pushing around a vacuum cleaner as if it were a wagonload of sins. She wore a blue bandanna on her head and a cigarette dangled from her lips. The television was tuned in to a gospel show, but snow obscured the picture and the choir was drowned out by the sound of the vacuum.

I touched her shoulder. She jumped.

'I'm taking her now, okay?' I yelled over the din.

'Sure.' When she spoke the cigarette bobbled like a trout lure in a rushing brook.

She resumed her chore, stooping over the roaring machine and ploughing it forward.

I rejoined Melody.

'Let's go.'

She walked alongside me. Midway to the parking lot a small hand slipped into mine.

Through a series of hilltop turns and lucky detours, I connected to Ocean Avenue. I drove south, toward Santa Monica, until we reached the park at the top of the cliff overlooking Pacific Coast Highway. It was eight-thirty in the morning. The sky was clear, pebbled only with a handful of clouds that might have been as distant as Hawaii. I found a parking space on the street, directly in front of the Camera Obscura and the Senior Citizens' Recreation Center.

Even that early in the morning the place was bustling.

74

Old people packed the benches and the shuffleboard court. Some of them jabbered nonstop to each other, or themselves. Others stared out at the boulevard in mute trance. Leggy girls in skimpy tops and satin shorts that covered a tenth of their gluteal regions skated by, transforming the walkways between the palms into fleshy freeways. Some of them wore stereo headsets—speeding spacewomen, with glazed, beatific expressions on their California-perfect faces.

Japanese tourists snapped pictures, nudged each other, pointed and laughed. Shabby bums loitered against the guardrail that separated the crumbling bluff from sheer space. They smoked behind cupped hands and regarded the world with distrust and fear. A surprising number of them were young men. They all looked as if they'd crawled out of some deep, dark, unproductive mine.

There were students reading, couples sprawled on the grass, small boys darting between the trees and a few furtive encounters that looked suspiciously like dope deals.

Melody and I walked along the outer rim of the park, hand in hand, talking little. I offered to buy her a hot pretzel from a street vendor, but she said she wasn't hungry. I remembered that loss of appetite was another side effect of Ritalin. Or maybe she'd just had a big breakfast.

We came to the walkway that led to the pier.

'Have you ever been on a merry-go-round?' I asked her.

'Once. We went on a school trip to Magic Mountain. The fast rides scared me but I liked the merry-go-round.'

'C'mon.' I pointed out toward the pier. 'There's one here. We'll take a ride.'

In contrast to the park, the pier was nearly deserted. There were a few men fishing here and there, mostly old blacks and Asians, but their expressions were pessi-

75

mistic, their buckets empty. Dried fish scales were embedded in the aged wooden planks of the walkway, giving it a sequined effect in the morning sun. There were cracks in several of the weathered boards, and as we walked I caught glimpses of the water below slapping against the pilings and retreating with a hissed warning. In the shadow of the pier's underbelly the water looked greenish black. There was a strong smell of creosote and salt in the air, a ripe, raw fragrance of loneliness and wasted hours.

The pool hall where I used to hide while playing hookey had been closed down. In its place was an arcade full of electric video games. A solitary Mexican boy intently pulled the joystick on one of the garishly painted robots. Computer noise emerged in blips and dreeps.

The merry-go-round was housed in a cavernous barn of a building that looked as if it would collapse with the next high tide. The operator was a tiny many with a pot-belly the size of a cantaloupe and flaky skin around his ears. He was sitting on a stool reading a racing form and trying to pretend we weren't there.

'We'd like to ride the merry-go-round.'

He looked up, gave us the once-over. Melody was staring at the ancient posters on the wall. Buffalo Bill. Victorian Love.

'Quarter a spin.'

I handed him a couple of bills.

'Keep it going for a while.'

'Sure.'

I lifted her up onto a large white-and-gilded horse with a pink plume for a tail. The brass rod upon which it was impaled had diagonal stripes running across it. A sure bet to go up and down. I stood next to her.

The tiny man was buried in his reading. He reached out a hand, pushed a button on a rusty console, pulled a lever and a rheumy rendition of the 'Blue Danube Waltz' piped

76

out of a dozen hidden speakers. The carousel started off slowly, and then it began to turn; horses, monkeys, chariots coming to life, moving in vertical counter-point to the revolution of the machine.

Melody's hands tightened around the neck of her steed; she stared straight ahead. Gradually, she relaxed her grip and allowed herself to look around. By the twentieth revolution, she was swaying with the music, eyes closed, mouth open in silent laughter.

When the music finally stopped I helped her down and she stepped dizzily onto the dirty concrete floor. She was giggling and swinging her purse in joyful rhythm, in time with the now dissipated waltz.

We left the barn and ventured to the end of the pier. She was fascinated by the enormous bait tanks teeming with squirming anchovies, amazed at the bin of fresh rockfish that was being brought up by a trio of muscled, bearded fishermen. The reddish fish lay dead in a heap. The quick ascent from the bottom of the ocean had caused the air bladders on several of them to explode and extrude from their open mouths. Crabs the size of bees crawled in and around the motionless bodies. Gulls swooped down to plunder and were waved off by the horned brown hands of the fishermen.

One of the fishermen, a boy of no more than eighteen, saw her staring.

'Pretty gross, huh?'

'Yeah.'

'Tell your daddy to take you to prettier places on his day off.' He laughed.

Melody smiled. She didn't try to correct him.

Someone was deep-frying shrimp. I saw her nose wrinkle.

'You hungry?'

'Kind of.' She looked uneasy.

'Anything wrong?'

'Mama told me not to be too grabby.'

77

'Don't you worry. I'm going to tell your mom what a good girl you've been. Have you had breakfast?'

'Kind of.'

'What'd you have?'

'Some juice. A piece of donut. The white powdery kind.'

'That's it?'

'Uh-huh.' She looked up at me as if expecting to be punished. I softened my tone.

'I guess you weren't hungry at breakfast time.'

'Uh-huh.' So much for the big-breakfast theory.

'Well, *I'm* pretty hungry.' It was true. All I'd had was coffee. 'What do you say we both get something?'

'Thank you, Doctor Del—' she stumbled over my name.

'Call me Alex.'

'Thank you, Alex.'

We located the source of the cooking smells at a shabby dinerette sandwiched between a souvenir shop and a bait and tackle stand. The woman behind the counter was pasty white and obese. Steam and smoke rose in billows around her moon face, creating a shimmering halo. Deep fryers crackled in the background.

I bought a large greasy bag full of goodies: foil-wrapped servings of shrimp and fried cod, a basket of french fries the size of billy clubs, plastic covered tubs of tartar sauce and ketchup, fluted paper tubes of salt, two cans of an off-brand of cola.

'Don't forget these, sir.'

The fat woman held out a handful of napkins.

'Thanks.'

'You know kids.' She looked down at Melody. 'You enjoy yourself now, hon.'

We carried the food off the pier and found a quiet spot on the beach, not far from the Pritikin Longevity Center. We ate our greasy fare watching middle-aged men

78

attempt to jog around the block, fuelled by whatever heartless menu the centre was serving nowadays.

She ate like a trucker. It was getting close to noon, which meant that normally she'd be ready for her second dose of amphetamine. Her mother hadn't offered the medication to me, and I hadn't thought—or wanted—to ask.

The change in her behaviour became evident halfway through lunch, and grew more obvious each minute.

She began to move more. She was more alert. Her face became more animated. She fidgeted, as if waking from a long, confusing sleep. She looked around, newly in touch with her environment.

'Look at them.' She pointed to a covey of wet-suited surfers riding waves in the distant.

'They look like seals, don't they?'

She giggled.

'Could I go in the water, Alex?'

'Take your shoes off and wade near the shoreline— where the water touches the sand. Try not to get your dress wet.'

I popped shrimp in my mouth, leaned back and watched her run along the tideline, skinny legs kicking up the water. Once she turned in my direction and waved.

I watched her play that way for twenty minutes or so, and then I rolled up my pants legs, took off my shoes and socks and joined her.

We ran together. Her legs worked better with every passing moment; soon she was a gazelle. She whooped and splashed and kept going until we were both out of breath. We walked back to our picnic site and collapsed on the sand. Her hair was a mess so I loosened the barettes and re-fastened them for her. Her small chest heaved. Her feet were crusted with grit from the ankle down. When she finally caught her breath she asked me:

'I—I've been a good girl, haven't I?'

'You've been great.'

She looked unsure.

'Don't you think so, Melody?'

'I don't know. Sometimes I think I am and Mama gets mad or Mrs. Brookhouse says I'm bad.'

'You're always a good girl. Even if someone thinks you've done something wrong. Do you understand that?'

'I guess so.'

'Not sure, huh?'

'I—I get mixed up.'

'Everyone gets mixed up. Kids and moms and dads. And doctors.'

'Dr. Towle, too?'

'Even Dr. Towle.'

She digested that for a while. The large, dark eyes darted around, moving from the water, to my face, to the sky, and back to me.

'Mama said you were going to hypnotize me.' She pronounced it hip-mo-tize.

'Only if you want me to. Do you understand why we think it might be helpful?'

'Sort of. To make me think better?'

'No. You think just fine. This—' I patted her head — 'works fine. We want to try hypnosis — hypnotizing — so that you can do us a favour. So that you can remember something.'

'About when the other doctor was hurt.'

I hesitated. My habit was to be honest with children, but if she hadn't been told about Handler and Gutierrez being dead I wasn't going to be the one to break the news. Not without the chance to be around to help pick up the pieces.

'Yes. About that.'

'I told the policeman I didn't remember anything. It was all dark and everything.'

80

'Sometimes people remember better after being hypnotized.'

She looked at me, frightened.

'Are you scared of being hypnotized?'

'Uh-huh.'

'That's okay. It's okay to be scared of new things. But there really isn't anything scary about hypnotizing. It's really kind of fun. Have you ever seen anyone hypnotized before?'

'Nope.'

'Never? Even in a cartoon?'

She lit up. 'Yeah, when the guy in the pointy hat hypnotized Popeye and the waves came out his hands and Popeye walked out of the window into the air and he didn't fall.'

'Right. I've seen that one too. The guy in the pointy hat made Popeye do all sorts of weird things.'

'Yeah.'

'Well that's great for cartoons, but real hypnotizing isn't anything like that.' I gave her a child's version of the lecture I'd delivered to her mother. She seemed to believe me, because fascination took the place of fear.

'Can we do it now?'

I hesitated. The beach was empty; there was plenty of privacy. And the moment was right. To hell with Towle...

'I don't see why not. First, let's get real comfortable.'

I had her fix her eyes upon a smooth shiny pebble as she held it in her hand. Within moments she was blinking in response to suggestion. Her breathing slowed and became regular. I told her to close her eyes and listen to the sound of the waves slapping against the shore. Then I instructed her to imagine herself descending a flight of stairs and passing through a beautiful door to a favourite place.

'I don't know where it is, or what's in it, but it's a special place for you. You can tell me or keep it secret, but being there makes you feel so comfortable, so happy, so in control...'

A bit more of that and she was in a deep hypnotic state.

'Now you can hear the sound of my voice without having to listen. Just continue to enjoy your favourite place, and have a real good time.'

I let her go for five more minutes. There was a peaceful, angelic expression on her thin little face. A soft wind rustled the loose strands of her hair. She looked tiny, sitting in the sand, hands resting in her lap.

I gave her a suggestion to go back in time, brought her back to the night of the murder. She tensed momentarily, then resumed the deep, regular breathing.

'You're still feeling totally relaxed, Melody. So comfortable and in control. But now you can watch yourself, just as if you were a star on TV. You see yourself getting out of bed...'

Her lips parted, she ran the tip of her tongue over them.

'And you go to the window and sit there, just looking out. What do you see?'

'Dark.' The word was barely audible.

'Yes, it's dark. And is there anything else.'

'No.'

'Okay. Let's sit there a while longer.'

A few minutes later:

'Can you see anything else in the dark, Melody?'

'Uh-uh. Dark.'

I tried a few more times, and then gave up. Either she had seen nothing, and the talk of two or three dark men had been confabulation, or she was blocking. In either event I wasn't going to get anything from her.

I let her enjoy her favourite place, gave her suggestions for mastery, control, and feeling refreshed and happy, and brought her gently out of hypnosis. She came out smiling.

'That was fun!'

'I'm glad you liked it. You seemed to have a real good favourite place.'

'You said I don't have to tell you!'

'That's true. You don't.'

'Well what if I want to?' she pouted.

'Then you can.'

'Hmm.' She savoured her power for a moment. 'I want to tell you. It was riding around on the merry-go-round. Going round and round, faster and faster.'

'That's a great choice.'

'Each time I went around I felt happier and happier. Can we go again some time?'

'Sure.' Now you've done it, Alex. Gotten yourself into something that won't be easy to pull out of. Instant daddy, just add guilt.

Back in the car she turned to me.

'Alex, you said hypnotizing makes you remember better?'

'It can.'

'Could I use it to remember my daddy?'

'When's the last time you saw him?'

'Never. He left when I was a little baby. He and Mama don't live together any more.'

'Does he visit?'

'No. He lives far away. Once he called me, before Christmas, but I was sleeping, so Mama didn't wake me up. That made me mad.'

'I can understand that.'

'I hit her.'

'You must have been really mad.'

'Yeah.' She bit her lip. 'Sometimes he sends me stuff.'

'Like Fatso?'

'Yeah, and other stuff.' She dug in her purse and pulled out what looked to be a large dried pit, or seed. It had been carved to resemble a face—a snarling face—with

83

rhinestone eyes, and strands of black acrylic hair glued to the top. A head, a shrunken head. The kind of hideous trash you can pick up at any Tijuana tourist stall. From the way she held it, it could have been the Crown Jewel of Kwarshiorkor.

'Very nice.' I handled the knobby thing and gave it back to her.

'I'd like to see him but Mama says she doesn't know where he is. Can hypnotizing help remember him?'

'It would be hard, Melody, because you haven't seen him in a long time. But we could try. Do you have anything to remember him by—any picture of him?'

'Yeah.' She searched in her purse again and came up with a spindled and mutilated snapshot. It had probably been fingered like a rosary. I thought of the photograph on Towle's wall. This was the week for celluloid memories. Mr. Eastman, if you only knew how your little black box can be used to preserve the past like a stillborn fetus in a jar of formalin.

It was a faded colour photograph of a man and woman. The woman was Bonita Quinn in younger, but not much prettier, days. Even in her twenties she had possessed a sad mask of a face that foreshadowed a merciless future. She wore a dress that exposed too much undernourished thigh. Her hair was long and straight and parted in the middle. She and her companion were in front of what looked like a rural bar, the kind of watering place you find peeking out around sudden highway curves. The walls of the building were rough-hewn logs. There was a Budweiser sign in the window.

Her arm was around the waist of the man, who had placed his arm around her shoulder. He wore a T-shirt, jeans and Wellington boots. The rump of a motorcycle was visible next to him.

He was a strange-looking bird. One side of him—the left—sagged and there was more than a hint of atrophy running all the way down from face to foot. He looked

84

crooked, like a piece of fruit that had been sliced and then put back together with less than full precision. When you got past the asymmetry he wasn't bad-looking—tall, slender, with shoulder-length shaggy blond hair and a thick moustache.

He had a wise-guy expression on his face that contrasted with Bonita's solemnity. It was the kind of look you see on the face of the local yokels when you walk into a small-town tavern in a strange place, just wanting a cold drink and some solitude. The kind of look you go out of your way to avoid, because it means trouble, and nothing else.

I wasn't surprised its owner had ended up behind bars.

'Here you go.' I handed the photo back to her and she carefully put it back in her purse.

'Want to take another run?'

'Naw. I'm kinda tired.'

'Want to go home?'

'Yeah.'

During the ride back to the apartment complex she was very quiet, as if she'd been doped up again. I had the uneasy feeling that I hadn't done right by this child, that I had overstimulated her, only to return her to a dreary routine.

Was I prepared to play the rescuing good guy on a regular basis?

I thought of the parting lecture one of the senior professors in graduate school had given our graduating class of aspiring pyschotherapists.

'When you choose to earn your living by helping people who are in emotional pain, you're also making a choice to carry them on your back for a while. To hell with all that talk of taking responsibility, assertiveness. That's crap. You're going to be coming up against helplessness every day of your lives. Your patients will imprint you, like goslings who latch on to the first creature they see

85

when they stick their heads out of the egg shell. If you can't handle it, become an accountant.'

Right now a ledger book full of numbers would have been a welcome sight.

7

I DROVE OUT to Robin's studio at half-past seven. It had been several days since I'd seen her and I missed her. When she opened the door she was wearing a gauzy white dress that accentuated the olive tint of her skin. Her hair hung loose and she wore gold hoops in her ears.

She held out her arms to me and we embraced for a long while. We walked inside, still clinging together.

Her place is an old store on Pacific Avenue in Venice. Like lots of other studios nearby, it's unmarked, the windows painted over in opaque white.

She led me past the front part, the work area full of power tools—table saw, band saw, drill press—piles of wood, instrument moulds, chisels, gauges and templates. As usual the room smelled of sawdust and glue. The floor was covered with shavings.

She pushed open swinging double doors and we were in her living quarters: sitting room, kitchen, sleeping loft with bath, small office. Unlike the shop, her personal space was uncluttered. She had made most of the furniture herself, and it was solid hardwood, simple and elegant.

She sat me down on a soft cotton couch. There was

coffee and pie set out on a ceramic tray, napkins, plates and forks.

She sidled next to me. I took her face in my hands and kissed her.

'Hello, darling.' She put her arms around me. I could feel the firmness of her back through the thin fabric, firmness couched in yielding, curving softness. She worked with her hands and it always amazed me to find in her that special combination of muscles and distinctly female lushness. When she moved, whether manipulating a hunk of rosewood around the rapacious jaws of a band saw or simply walking, it was with confidence and grace. Meeting her was the best thing that had ever happened to me. It alone had been worth dropping out for.

I'd been browsing at McCabe's, the guitar shop in Santa Monica, looking through the old sheet music, trying out the instruments that hung on the walls. I'd spied one particularly attractive guitar, like my Martin but even better made. I admired the craftsmanship—it was a hand-made instrument—and ran my fingers over the strings, which vibrated with perfect balance and sustain. Taking it off the wall I played it and it sounded as good as it looked, ringing like a bell.

'Like it?'

The voice was feminine and belonged to a gorgeous creature in her mid-twenties. She stood close to me—how long she'd been there I wasn't sure; I'd been lost in the music. She had a heart-shaped face topped by a luxuriant mop of auburn curls. Her eyes were almond-shaped, wide-set, the colour of antique mahogany. She was small, not more than five-two, with slender wrists leading to delicate hands and long tapering fingers. When she smiled, her upper two incisors, larger than the rest of her teeth, flashed ivory.

'Yes. I think it's terrific.'

'It's not that good.' She put her hands on her hips–very

88

definite hips. She had the kind of figure, small-waisted, busty and gently concave, that couldn't be camouflaged by the overalls she'd thrown on over her turtleneck.

'Oh, really?'

'Oh, really.' She took the guitar from me. 'There's a spot right here—' she tapped the soundboard '—where it's been sanded too thin. And the balance between head-stock and box could be better.' She strummed a few chords. 'All in all I'd give it an eight on a sale of one to ten.'

'You seem to be quite an expert on it.'

'I should be. I made it.'

She took me to her shop that afternoon and showed me the instrument she was working on. 'This one's going to be a ten. The other was one of my first. You learn as you go along.'

Some weeks later she admitted it had been her way of picking me up, her version of *come up and see my etchings*.

'I liked the way you played. Such sensitivity.'

We saw each other regularly after that. I learned that she had been an only child, the special daughter of a skilled cabinetmaker who had taught her everything he knew about how to transform raw wood into objects of beauty. She had tried college, majoring in design, but the regimentation had angered her, as had the fact that her dad had known more about form and function intuitively than all the teachers and books combined. After he died, she dropped out, took the money he left her and invested in a shop in San Luis Obispo. She got to know some local musicians, who brought her their instruments to fix. At first it was a sideline, for she was trying to make a living designing and manufacturing custom furniture. Then she began to take a greater interest in the guitars, banjos and mandolins that found their way to her workbench. She read a few books on instrument-making, found she had all the requisite skills and made her first guitar. It sounded

89

great and she sold it for five hundred dollars. She was hooked. Two weeks later she moved to L.A., where the musicians were, and set up shop.

When I met her she was making two instruments a month as well as handling repairs. She'd been written up in trade magazines and was back-ordered for four months. She was starting to make a living.

I probably loved her the first day I met her but it took me a couple of weeks to realize it.

After three months we started to talk about living together, but it didn't happen. There was no philosophical objection on either side, but her place was too small for two people and my house couldn't accommodate her shop. It sounds unromantic, letting mundane matters like space and comfort get in the way, but we were having such a good time with each other while maintaining our privacy, that the incentive to make a change wasn't there. Often she would spend the night with me, other times I'd collapse in her loft. Some evenings we'd go our separate ways.

It wasn't a bad arrangement.

I sipped coffee and eyed the pie.

'Have some, babe.'

'I don't want to pork out before dinner.'

'Maybe we won't go out for dinner.' She stroked the back of my neck. 'Ooh, such tension.' She began to knead the muscles of my upper back. 'You haven't felt this way in a long time.'

'There's good reason for it.' And I told her about Milo's morning visit, the murder, Melody, Towle.

When I was through she placed her hands on my shoulders.

'Alex, do you really want to get into something like this?'

'Do I have a choice? I see that kid's eyes in my sleep. I was a fool for getting sucked in, but now I'm stuck.'

She looked at me. The corners of her mouth lifted in a smile.

'You are such a pushover. And so sweet.'

She nuzzled me under my chin. I held her to me and buried my face in her hair. It smelled of lemon and honey and rosewood.

'I really love you.'

'I love you, too, Alex.'

We undressed each other and when we were totally naked, I lifted her in my arms and carried her up the stairs to the loft. Not wanting to be apart from her for one second I kept my mouth fastened upon hers while I manoeuvred myself on top of her. She clung to me, her arms and legs like tendrils. We connected, and I was home.

8

WE SLEPT until 10 P.M., then awoke famished. I went down to the kitchen and made sandwiches of Italian salami and Swiss cheese on rye, found a jug of burgundy and toted it all back upstairs for a late supper in bed. We shared garlicky kisses, got crumbs in the bed, hugged each other and fell back asleep.

We were jolted awake by the telephone.

Robin answered it.

'Yes, Milo, he's here. No, that's all right. Here he is.'

She handed me the receiver and buried herself under the covers.

'Hello, Milo. What time is it?'

'Three A.M.'

I sat up and rubbed my eyes. Through the skylight the heavens were black.

'What's going on.'

'It's the kid—Melody Quinn. She's freaked out—woke up screaming. Bonita called Towle who called me. Demanded you get over there. He sounds pissed.'

'Screw him. I'm not his errand boy.'

'You want me to tell him that? He's right here.'

'You're over there now? At her place?'

92

'Certainly. Neither rain nor hail nor darkness stays this trusted civil servant and all that shit. We're having a little party. The doctor, Bonita, me. The kid's sleeping. Towle gave her a shot of something.'

'Figures.'

'The kid spilled to her mom about the hypnosis. He wants you there if she wakes up again—to rehypnotize or something.'

'That asshole. The hypnosis didn't cause this. The kid's got sleep problems because of all the dope he's been shoving into her system.'

But I was far from certain of that. She *had* been troubled after the session on the beach.

'I'm sure you're right, Alex. I just wanted to give you the option to come down here, to know what was going on. If you want me to tell Towle to forget it, I will.'

'Hold on a minute.' I shook my head, trying to clear it. 'Did she say anything when she woke up—anything coherent?'

'I just caught the tail end of it. They said it was the fourth time tonight. She was screaming for her daddy: "Oh Daddy. Daddy, Daddy"—like that, but very loud. It looked and sounded pretty bad, Alex.'

'I'll be down there as soon as I can.'

I gave the sleeping mummy next to me a kiss on the fanny, got up, and threw on my clothes.

I sped along Pacific, heading north. The streets were empty and slick with marine mist. The guide lights at the end of the pier were distant pinpoints. A few trawlers sat on the horizon. At this hour the sharks and other nocturnal predators would be prowling the bottom of the ocean floor. I wondered how much carnage was hidden by the glossy black outer skin of the water; and how many of the night-hunters lurked on dry land, hiding in alleys, behind trash bins, concealed among the leaves and twigs of suburban shrubbery, wild-eyed, breathing hard.

As I drove I developed a new theory of evolution. Evil had its own metamorphic intelligence: the sharks and the razor-toothed serpents, the slimy, venomous things that hid in the silt, hadn't given way in an orderly progression to amphibian, reptile, bird and mammal. A single quantum leap had taken evil from water to land. From shark to rapist, eel to throat-slasher, poison slug to skullcrusher, with bloodlust at the core of the helix.

The darkness seemed to press against me, insistent, fetid. I pushed down harder on the accelerator and forced my way through it.

When I got to the apartment complex, Milo met me at the door.

'She's just started again.'

I could hear it before I got to the bedroom.

The light was dim. Melody sat upright in her bed, her body rigid, eyes wide open but unfocused. Bonita sat next to her. Towle, in sports clothes, stood on the other side.

The child was sobbing, a wounded animal sound. She wailed and moaned and rocked back and forth. Then the moan picked up volume, gradually, like a siren, until she was screaming, her thin voice a piercing, shrieking assault upon the silence.

'Daddy! Daddy! Daddy!'

Her hair was plastered against her face, slick with sweat. Bonita tried to hold her but she flailed and struck out. The mother was helpless.

The screaming continued for what seemed like forever, then it stopped and she began moaning again.

'Oh, Doctor,' Bonita pleaded, 'she's going at it again. Do something.'

Towle spotted me.

'Maybe Dr. Delaware can help.' His tone of voice was nasty.

'No, no, I don't want *him* near her! He caused all of this!'

94

Towle didn't argue with her. I could have sworn he looked smug.

'Mrs. Quinn—' I began.

'No. You stay away! Get out!'

Her screaming set Melody off, and she began calling for her father again.

'Stop it!'

Bonita went for her, putting her hand over the child's mouth. Shaking her.

Towle and I moved at the same time. We pulled her off. He took her aside and said something that quieted her down.

I moved next to Melody. She was breathing hard. Her pupils were dilated. I touched her. She stiffened.

'Melody,' I whispered. 'It's Alex. You're okay. You're safe.'

As I talked she calmed down. I blabbed on, knowing that what I said was less important than how I said it. I maintained a low, rhythmic pattern of speech, easy-going, reassuring. Hypnotic.

Soon she had slipped lower in the bed. I helped her lie down. Her hands unfolded. I kept talking to her soothingly. Her muscles began to relax and her breathing became slow and regular. I told her to close her eyes and she did. I stroked her shoulder, continued to talk to her, to tell her everything was all right, that she was safe.

She snuggled into a fetal position, drew the covers over her, and placed her thumb in her mouth.

'Turn off the light,' I said. The room became dark. 'Let's leave her alone.' The three of them left.

'Now you're going to continue sleeping, Melody, and you'll have a very peaceful, restful night, with good dreams. When you wake up in the morning you'll feel very good, very rested.'

I could hear her snoring ever so slightly.

'Goodnight, Melody.' I leaned over and gave her a light kiss on the cheek.

95

She mumbled one word.

'Da-da.'

I closed the door to her room. Bonita was in the kitchen, wringing her hands, She wore a frayed man's terry-cloth robe. Her hair had been pulled back in a bun and covered with a scarf. She looked paler than I remembered as she busied herself cleaning up.

Towle bent over his black bag. He clicked it shut, stood and ran his fingers through his hair. Seeing me he raised himself up to his full height and glared down, ready to give another lecture.

'I hope you're happy,' he said.

'Don't start,' I warned him. 'No I-told-you-so's.'

'You can see why I was reluctant to tamper with this child's mind.'

'Nobody tampered with anything.' I could feel tension rising in my gut. He was every hypocritical authority figure I'd detested.

He shook his head condescendingly.

'Obviously your memory needs some polishing.'

'Obviously you're a sanctimonious prick.'

The blue eyes flashed. He tightened his lips.

'What if I bring you up before the ethics committee of the State Medical Board?'

'You do that, Doctor.'

'I'm seriously considering it.' He looked like a Calvinist preacher, all stern and tight and self-righteous.

'You do it and we'll get into a little discussion on the proper use of stimulant medication with children.'

He smiled.

'It will take more than you to tarnish my reputation.'

'I'm sure it will.' My fists were clenched. 'You've got legions of loyal followers. Like that woman in there.' I pointed toward the kitchen. 'They bring their kids to you, human jalopies, and you tinker with them, give 'em a quick tune-up and a pill; you fix them to their specifi-

96

cations. Make them nice and quiet, compliant, and obedient. Drowsy little zombies. You're a goddamn hero.'

'I don't have to listen to this.' He moved forward.

'No you don't, hero. But why don't you go in there and tell her what you really think of her? Piss-poor protoplasm, and let's see—bad genes, no insight.'

He stopped in his tracks.

'Easy, Alex.' Milo spoke from the corner, cautiously.

Bonita came in from the kitchen.

'What's going on?' she wanted to know. Towle and I were facing each other like boxers after the bell.

He changed his manner and smiled at her charmingly. 'Nothing, my dear. Just a professional discussion. Doctor Delaware and I were trying to decide what was best for Melody.'

'What's best is no more hypnotizing. You told me that.'

'Yes.' Towle tapped his foot, tried not to look uncomfortable. 'That was my professional opinion.' He loved that word, professional. 'And it still is.'

'Well, you tell *him* that.' She pointed at me.

'That's what we were discussing, dear.'

He must have been just a little too smooth, because her face got tight and her voice lowered suspiciously.

'What's to discuss? I don't want him or him—' the second jab was at Milo '—around here no more.' She turned to us. 'You try and be a good Samaritan and help the cops and you get the shaft! Now my baby's got the seizures and she's screamin' and I'm gonna lose my place. I know I'm gonna lose it!'

Her face crumpled. She buried it in her hands and began to cry. Towle moved in like a Beverly Hills gigolo, putting his arms around her, consoling her, saying now, now.

He guided her to the couch and sat her down, standing over her, patting her shoulder.

'I'm gonna lose my place,' she said into her hands.

97

'They don't like noise here.' She uncovered her face and looked wet-eyed up at Towle.

'Now, now, it's going to be all right. I'll see to that.'

'But what about the the seizures!?'

'I'll see to that, too.' He gave me a sharp look, full of hostility and, I was sure, a bit of fear.

She sniffled and wiped her nose on her sleeve.

'I don't understand why she has to wake up screaming Daddy Daddy! That bastard's never been around to lift a finger or give me a cent of child support! He has no love for her! Why does she cry out for *him*, Doctor Towle?' She looked up at him, a novitiate beseeching the pope.

'Now, now.'

'He's a crazy man, that Ronnie Lee is. Look at this!' She tore the scarf from her head, shook her hair loose and lowered her head exposing the top of it. Giving a whimper she parted the strands at the centre of her crown. 'Look at this!'

It was ugly. A thick, raw red scar the size of a fat worm. A worm that had burrowed under her scalp and settled there. The skin around it was livid and lumpy, showing the results of bad surgery, devoid of hair.

'Now you know why I cover it!' she cried. '*He* did that to me! With a *chain!* Ronnie Lee Quinn.' She spat out the name. 'A crazy, evil bastard. That's the Daddy Daddy she's cryin' out for! That scum!'

'Now, now,' said Towle. He turned to us. 'Do you gentlemen have anything more to discuss with Mrs. Quinn?'

'No, Doctor,' said Milo and turned to leave. He took hold of my arm to guide me out. But I had something to say.

'Tell her, Doctor. Tell her those were not seizures. They were night terrors and they'll go away by themselves if you keep her calm. Tell her there'll be no need for phenobarbitol or Dilantin or Tofranil.'

Towle continued to pat her shoulder.

'Thank you for your professional opinion, Doctor. I'll manage this case as I see fit.'

I stood there rooted.

'Come on, Alex.' Milo eased me out of the door.

The parking lot of the apartment complex was crammed full of Mercedes, Porsches, Alfa Romeo's and Datsun Z's. Milo's Fiat, parked in front of a hydrant, looked sadly out of place, like a cripple at a track meet. We sat in it, glum.

'What a mess,' he said.

'The bastard.'

'For a minute I thought you were going to hit him.' He chuckled.

'It was tempting. The bastard.'

'It looked like he was baiting you. I thought you guys got along.'

'On his terms. On an intellectual level we were good old boys. When things fell apart he had to find a scapegoat. He's an egomaniac. *Doctor* is omnipotent. *Doctor* can fix anything. Did you see how she worshipped him, the goddamned Great White Father? Probably slit the kid's wrists if he told her to.'

'You're worried about the kid, aren't you?'

'You're damn right I am. You know exactly what he's going to do, don't you—more dope. She'll be a total space cadet in two days.'

Milo chewed on his lip. After a few minutes he said:

'Well, there's nothing we can do about it. I'm sorry I pulled you into it in the first place.'

'Forget it. It wasn't your fault.'

'Nah, it was. I've been lazy, trying for an instant miracle on this Handler mess. Been avoiding the old wear-down-the-shoe leather routine. Question Handler's associates, get the list of known bad guys with razor-happy fingers from the computer and plod through it. Go through

99

Handler's files. The whole thing was iffy in the first place, a seven year old kid.'

'She could have turned out to be a good witness.'

'Is it ever that easy?' He started up the engine, after three attempts. 'Sorry for ruining your night.'

'You didn't. He did.'

'Forget him, Alex. Assholes are like weeds—a bitch to get rid of and when you do, another one grows back in the same place. That's what I've been doing for eight years—pouring weed-killer and watching them grow back faster than I can clear them away."

He sounded weary and looked old.

I got out of the car and leaned in through the window.

'See you tomorrow.'

'What?'

'The files. We have to go through Handler's files. I'll be able to tell faster than you will which ones were dangerous.'

'You're kidding.'

'Nope. I'm carrying around a huge Zeigarnik.'

'A what?'

'Zeigarnik. She was a Russian psychologist who discovered that people develop tension for unfinished business. They named it after her. The Zeigarnik effect. Like most overachievers I've got a big one.'

He looked at me like I was talking nonsense.

'Uh-huh. Right, And this Zeigarnik is big enough for you to let it intrude upon the mellow life?'

'What the hell, life was getting boring.' I slapped him on the back.

'Suit yourself.' He shrugged. 'Regards to Robin.'

'You give regards to your doctor.'

'If he's still there when I get back. This middle-of-the-night stuff is testing that relationship.' He scratched at the corner of his eye and scowled.

I'm sure he'll put up with it, Milo.'

'Oh yeah? Why's that?'

100

'If he's crazy enough to go for you in the first place, he's crazy enough to stick with you.'

'That's very reassuring, pal.' He ground the Fiat into first and sped away.

9

AT THE TIME of his murder, Morton Handler had been in practice as a psychiatrist for a little under fifteen years. During that period he had consulted on or treated over two thousand patients. The records of these individuals were stored in manila folders and packed, one hundred and fifty to a box, in cardboard cartons that were taped shut and stamped with the L.A.P.D. seal.

Milo brought these boxes to my house, assisted by a slight, balding, black detective named Delano Hardy. Huffing and wheezing, they loaded the cartons in my dining room. Soon it looked as if I was either moving in or moving out.

'It's not as bad as it seems,' Milo assured me. 'You won't have to go through all of them. Right, Del?'

Hardy lit a cigarette and nodded assent.

'We've done some preliminary screening,' he said 'We eliminated anyone known to be deceased. We figured they'd be low probability suspects.'

The two of them laughed. Dark detective laughs.

'And the coroner's report,' he continued, 'says Handler and the girl were cut by someone with a lot of muscle.

102

The throat wound on him went clear back to the spine on the first try.'

'Which means,' I interrupted, 'a man.'

'Could be one hell of a tough lady,' laughed Hardy, 'but we're betting on a male.'

'There are six hundred male patients,' added Milo. 'Those four boxes over there.'

'Also,' said Hardy, 'we brought you a little present.'

He gave me a small package wrapped in green and red Christmas paper with a bugle and holly wreath pattern on it. It was tied with red ribbon.

'Couldn't find any other paper,' Hardy explained.

'We hope you like it,' added Milo. I began to feel as if I were the audience for a salt-and-pepper comedy team. A curious transformation had come over Milo. In the presence of another detective he had distanced himself from me and adopted the tough-wiseacre banter of the veteran cop.

I unwrapped the box and opened it. Inside, on a bed of cotton, was a plastic-coated L.A.P.D. identification badge. It bore a picture of me like the one on my driver's licence, with that strange, frozen look that all official photos seem to have. Under the picture was my signature, also from my licence, my name printed out, my degree and the title 'Special Consultant.' Life imitates art...

'I'm touched.'

'Put it on,' said Milo. 'Make it official.'

The badge wasn't unlike the one I had worn at Western Pediatric. It came with a clasp. I affixed it to my shirt collar.

'Very attractive,' said Hardy. 'That and ten cents might get you a local phone call.' He reached into his jacket and drew out a folded piece of paper. 'Now, if you'll just read and sign this.' He held out a pen.

I read it, all small print.

'This says you don't have to pay me.'

'Right,' said Hardy with mock sadness. 'And if you

get a paper cut looking over the files you can't sue the department.'

'It makes the brass happy, Alex,' said Milo.

I shrugged and signed.

'Now,' said Hardy, 'you're an o-fficial consultant to the Los Angeles Police Department.' He folded the paper and slipped it back in his pocket. 'Just like the rooster who was jumping the bones of all the hens in the henhouse. So they castrated him and turned him into a consultant.'

'That's very flattering, Del.'

'Any friend of Milo and all that.'

Milo, meanwhile, was opening the sealed cartons with a Swiss Army knife. He took out files in dozens and made neat little piles that covered the dining-room table.

'These are alphabetized, Alex. You can go through them and pull out the weird ones.'

He finished setting things up and he and Hardy got ready to go.

'Del and I will be talking to bad guys off the NCIC printout.'

'We've got our work cut out for us,' said Hardy. He cracked his knuckles and looked for a place to put out his cigarette, which was smoked down to the filter.

'Toss it in the sink.'

He left to do so.

When we were alone Milo said: 'I really appreciate this, Alex. Don't drive yourself—don't try to get it all done today.'

'I'll do as many as I can before the eyes start to blur.'

'Right. We'll call you a couple of times today. To see if you've got anything we can pick up while we're on the road.'

Hardy came back straightening his tie. He was dapper in a three-piece navy worsted suit, white shirt, blood-red tie, shiny black calfskin loafers. Next to him Milo looked more shopworn than ever in his sagging trousers and lifeless tweed sport coat.

'You ready, my man?' Hardy asked.

'Ready.'

'Onward.'

When they were gone I put a Linda Ronstadt record on the turntable. To the accompaniment of 'Poor, Poor Pitiful Me,' I started to consult.

Eighty per cent of the male patients in the files fell into two categories: affluent executive types referred by their internists due to a variety of stress-related symptoms— angina, impotence, abdominal pain, chronic headaches, insomnia, skin rashes of unknown origins—and depressed men of all ages. I reviewed these and put aside the remaining twenty per cent for more detailed perusal.

I knew nothing about what kind of psychiatrist Morton Handler had been when I started, but after several hours of reviewing his charts I began to build an image of him— one that was far from saintly.

His therapy session notes were sketchy, careless, and so ambiguous as to be meaningless. It was impossible to know from reading them what he had done during those countless forty-five-minute hours. There was scant mention of treatment plans, prognoses, stress histories—anything that could be considered medically or psychologically relevant. This shoddiness was most evident in notes taken during the last five or six years of his life.

His financial records, on the other hand, were meticulous and detailed. His fees were high, his form letters to debtors strongly worded.

Though during the last few years he had done less talking and more prescribing, the rate at which he ordered medication wasn't unusual. Unlike Towle, he didn't appear to be a pusher. But he wasn't much of a therapist, either.

What really bothered me was his tendency, again more common during later years, to inject snide comments into the notes. These, which he didn't even bother to couch in jargon, were nothing more than sarcastic put-downs of his patients. 'Likes to alternately whimper and simper' was the description of one older man with a mood disorder. 'Unlikely to be capable of anything constructive' was his pronouncement on another. 'Wants therapy as camouflage for a boring, meaningless life.' 'A real washout.' And so on.

By late afternoon my psychological autopsy of Handler was complete. He was a burnout, one of the legions of worker ants who had grown to hate his chosen profession. He might have cared at one time—the early files were decent, if not inspired—but he hadn't by the end. Nevertheless, he had kept it up, day after day, session after session, unwilling to give up the six-figure income and the perquisites of prosperity.

I wondered how he had occupied his time as his patients poured out their inner turmoil. Did he daydream? Engage in fantasies (sexual? financial? sadistic?)? Plan the evening's dinner menu? Do mental arithmetic? Count sheep? Compute how many manic depressives could dance on the head of a pin?

Whatever it had been, it hadn't included really listening to the human beings who sat before him believing he cared.

It made me think of the old joke, the one about the two shrinks who meet on the elevator at the end of the day. One of them is young, a novice, and he is clearly bedraggled—tie askew, hair messed, fraught with fatigue. He turns and notices that the other, a seasoned veteran, is totally composed—tan, fit, every hair in place, a fresh carnation stuck jauntily in his lapel.

'Doctor,' beseeches the young one, 'please tell me how you do it?'

'Do what, my son?'

'Sit, hour after hour, day after day, listening to people's problems without letting it get to you.'

106

'Who listens?' replies the guru.

Funny. Unless you were shelling out ninety bucks a session to Morton Handler and getting a covert assessment as a simpering whimperer for your money.

Had one of the subjects of his nasty prose somehow discovered the sham and murdered him? It was difficult to imagine someone engaging in the kind of butchery that had been visited upon Handler and his girlfriend in order to avenge a peeve of that kind. But you never knew. Rage was a tricky thing; sometimes it lay dormant for years, only to be triggered by a seemingly trivial stimulus. People had been ripped apart over a nudged car bumper.

Still I found it hard to believe that the depressives and psychosomaticizers whose files I had reviewed were the stuff of which midnight skulkers were fashioned. What I really didn't want to believe was that there were two thousand potential suspects to deal with.

It was close to five. I pulled a Coors out of the refrigerator, took it out to the balcony and lay down on a lounger, my feet propped up on the guardrail. I drank and watched the sun dip beneath the tops of the trees. Someone in the neighbourhood was playing punk rock. Strangely enough it didn't seem discordant.

At five-thirty Robin called.

'Hi, hon. You want to come over? *Key Largo*'s on tonight.'

'Sure,' I said. 'Should I pick up anything to eat?'

She thought a moment.

'How about chili dogs? And beer.'

'I've got a head start on the beer.' Three squashed Coors empties sat on the kitchen counter.

'Give me time to catch up, love. See you around seven.'

I hadn't heard from Milo since one-thirty. He'd called in from Bellflower, just about to interrogate a guy who'd assaulted seven women with a screwdriver. Very little similarity to the Handler case but you had to work with what you had.

107

I phoned West L.A. Division and left the message for him that I'd be out for the evening.

Then I called Bonita Quinn's number. I waited for five rings and when nobody answered, hung up.

Humphrey and Lauren were great, as usual. The chili dogs left us belching, but satisfied. We held each other and listened to Tal Farlow and Wes Montgomery for a while. Then I picked up one of the guitars she had lying around the studio and played for her. She listened, eyes closed, a faint smile on her lips, then gently removed my hands from the instrument and pulled me to her.

I had planned to stay the night but at eleven I grew restless.

'Is anything the matter, Alex?'

'No.' Just my Zeigarnik tugging at me.

'It's the case, isn't it?'

I said nothing.

'I'm starting to worry about you, sweetie.' She put her head on my chest, a welcome burden. 'You've been so edgy since Milo got you into all of this. I never knew you before, but from what you told me it sounds like the old days.'

'The old Alex wasn't such a bad guy,' I reacted defensively.

She was wisely silent.

'No,' I corrected myself. 'The old Alex was a bore. I promise not to bring him back, okay?'

'Okay.' She kissed the tip of my chin.

'Just give me a little time to get through this.'

'All right.'

But as I dressed she looked at me with a combination of worry, hurt, and confusion. When I started to say something, she turned away. I sat down on the edge of the bed and took her in my arms. I rocked her until her arms slid around my neck.

108

'I love you,' I said. 'Give me a little time.'

She made a warm sound and held me tighter.

When I left she was sleeping, her eyelids fluttering in the throes of the first dream of the night.

I tore into the one hundred and twenty files I had set aside, working until the early morning hours. Most of these turned out also to be rather mundane documents. Ninety-one of the patients were physically ill men whom Handler had seen as a consultant when he was still working at Cedars-Sinai as part of the liaison psychiatry team. Another twenty had been diagnosed schizophrenic, but they turned out to be senile (median age, seventy-six) patients at a convalescent hospital where he'd worked for a year.

The remaining nine men were of interest. Handler had diagnosed them all as psychopathic character disorders. Of course those diagnoses were suspect, as I had little faith in his judgment. Nevertheless the files were worth examining more closely.

They were all between the ages of sixteen and thirty-two. Most had been referred by agencies—the Probation Department, the California Youth Authority, local churches. A couple had experienced several scrapes with the law. At least three were judged violent. Of these, one had beaten up his father, another had stabbed a fellow high school student, and the third had used an automobile to run down someone with whom he'd exchanged angry words.

A bunch of real sweethearts.

None of them had been involved in therapy for very long, which was not surprising. Psychotherapy hasn't much to offer the person with no conscience, no morals, and, quite often, no desire to change. In fact, the psychopath by his very nature is an affront to modern psychology, with its egalitarian and optimistic philosophical underpinnings.

109

Therapists become therapists because down deep they feel that people are really good and have the capacity to change for the better. The notion that there exist individuals who are simply evil—bad people—and that such evil cannot be explained by any existing combination of nature or nurture is an assault upon a therapist's sensitivities. The psychopath is to the psychologist and the psychiatrist what the terminal cancer patient is to the physician: walking, breathing evidence of hopelessness and failure.

I knew such evil people existed. I had seen a mercifully small number of them, mostly adolescents, but some children. I remember one boy, in particular, not yet twelve years old, but possessed of a cynical, hardened, cruelly grinning face that would have done a San Quentin lifer proud. He'd handed me his business card—a bright rectangle of shocking pink paper with his name on it, followed by the single word *Enterprises*.

And an enterprising young man he had been. Buttressed by my assurances of confidentiality, he had told me proudly of the dozens of bicycles he had stolen, of the burglaries he had pulled off, of the teenage girls he had seduced. He was so pleased with himself.

He had lost his parents in a plane crash at the age of four and had been brought up by a baffled grandmother who tried to assure everyone—and herself—that down deep he was a good boy. But he wasn't. He was a *bad* boy. When I asked him if he remembered his mother, he leered and told me she looked like a real piece of ass in the pictures he had seen. It wasn't defensive posturing. It was really him.

The more time I spent with him, the more discouraged I grew. It was like peeling an onion and finding each layer more rotten than the last. He was a bad boy, irredeemably so. Most likely, he would get worse.

And there was nothing I could do. There was little doubt he would end up establishing an anti-social career.

If society was lucky, it would be limited to con games. If not, a lot of blood would be shed. Logic dictated that he should be locked up, kept out of harm's way, incarcerated for the protection of the rest of us. But democracy said otherwise, and, on balance, I had to admit it shouldn't be any other way.

Still, there were nights when I thought of that eleven-year-old and wondered if I'd be seeing his name in the papers one day.

I set the nine files aside.

Milo would have more of his work cut out for him.

10

THREE DAYS of the old wear-down-the-shoe-leather routine had worn Milo down.

'The computer was a total bust,' he lamented, flopping down on my leather sofa. 'All of those bastards are either back in the joint, dead, or alibied. The coroner's report has no forensic magic for us. Just six and a half pages of gory details telling us what we knew the first time we saw the bodies: Handler and Gutierrez were hacked up like sausage filler.'

I brought him a beer, which he drained in two long gulps. I brought him another.

'What about Handler? Anything on him?' I asked.

'Oh yeah, you were definitely right in your initial impression. The guy was no Mr. Ethical. But it doesn't lead anywhere.'

'What do you mean?'

'Six years ago, when he was doing hospital consultations, there was a bit of a stink—insurance fraud. Handler and some others were running a little scam. They'd peek their heads in for a second, say hello to a patient, and bill it as a full visit, which I take it is supposed to be forty-five or fifty minutes long. Then they'd make a note in the chart, bill for another visit, talk to the nurse, another visit, talk to the doctor, etc., etc. It was big bucks—one guy could put in for thirty, forty visits a day, at seventy, eighty bucks a visit. Figure it out.'

'No surprise. It's done all the time.'

'I'm sure. Anyway, it blew wide open because one of the patients had a son who was a doctor, and he started to get suspicious, reading the chart, seeing all these psychiatric visits. Especially 'cause the old man had been unconscious for three months. He griped to the medical director, who called Handler and the others in on the carpet. They kept it quiet, on the condition that the crooked shrinks leave.'

Six years ago. Just before Handler's notes had started to get slipshod and sarcastic. It must have been hard going from four hundred grand a year to a measly one hundred. And having to actually work for it. A man could get bitter...

'And you don't see an angle in that?'

'What? Revenge? From whom? It was insurance companies that were getting bilked. That's how they kept it going so long. They never billed the patients, just billed insurance.' He took a swig of beer. 'I've heard bad things about insurance companies, pal, but I can't see them sending around Jack the Ripper to avenge their honour.'

'I see what you mean.'

He got up and paced the room.

'This goddamn case sucks. It's been a week and I've got absolutely zilch. The captain sees it as a dead end. He's pulled Del off and left me with the whole stinking mess. Tough breaks for the faggot.'

'Another beer?' I held one out for him.

'Yeah, goddammit, why not? Drown it all in suds.' He wheeled around. 'I tell you, Alex, I should have been a schoolteacher. Viet Nam left me with this big psychic hole, you know? All that death for nothing. I thought

113

becoming a cop would help me fill that hole, catch bad guys, make some sense out of it all. Jesus, was I wrong!'

He grabbed the Coors out of my hand, tilted it over his mouth, and let some of the foam dribble down his chin.

'The things that I see—the monstrous things that we supposed humans do to each other. The shit I've become inured to. Sometimes it makes me want to puke.'

He drank silently for a few minutes.

'You're a goddamn good listener, Alex. All that training wasn't for naught.'

'One good turn, my friend.'

'Yeah, right. Now that you mention it, Hickle was another shitty case. I never convinced myself that was suicide. It stunk to high heaven.'

'You never told me.'

'What's to tell? I've no evidence. Just a gut feeling. I've got lots of gut feelings. Some of them gnaw at me and keep me up at night. To paraphrase Del, my gut feelings and ten cents.'

He crushed the empty can between his thumb and forefinger, with the ease of someone pulverizing a gnat.

'Hickle stunk to high heaven, but I had no evidence. So I wrote it off. Like a bad debt. No one argued, no one gave a shit, just like no one'll give a shit when we write off Handler and the Gutierrez girl. Keep the records tidy, wrap it up, seal it, and kiss it good-bye.'

Seven more beers, another half-hour of ranting and punishing himself, and he was stoned drunk. He crashed on the leather sofa, going down like a B-52 with a bellyful of shrapnel.

I slipped his shoes off and placed them on the floor beside him. I was about to leave him that way, when I realized it had turned dark.

I called his home number. A deep, rich male voice answered.

'Hello.'

'Hello, this is Alex Delaware, Milo's friend.'

114

'Yes?' Wariness.

'The psychologist.'

'Yes, Milo's spoken of you. I'm Rick Silverman.'

The doctor, the mother's dream, now had a name.

'I just called to let you know that Milo stopped by here after work to discuss a case and he got kind of—intoxicated.'

'I see.'

I felt an absurd urge to explain to the man at the other end that there was really nothing going on between Milo and me, that we were just good friends. I suppressed it.

'Actually, he got stoned. Had eleven beers. He's sleeping it off now. I just wanted you to know.'

'That's very considerate of you,' Silverman said, acidly.

'I'll wake him, if you'd like.'

'No. that's quite all right. Milo's a big boy. He's free to do as he pleases. No need to check in.'

I wanted to tell him, listen you insecure, spoiled brat, I just called to do you a favour, to set your mind at ease. Don't hand me any of your delicate indignation. Instead, I tried flattery.

'Okay, just thought I'd call you to let you know, Rick. I know how important you are to Milo, and I thought he'd want me to.'

'Uh, thanks. I really appreciate it.' Bingo. 'Please excuse me. I've just come off a twenty-four-hour shift myself.'

'No problem.' I'd probably woken the poor devil. 'Listen, how about if we get something together some time—you and Milo and my girlfriend and myself?'

'I'd like that, Alex. Sure. Send the big slob home when he sobers up and we'll work out the details.'

'Will do. Good talking to you.'

'Likewise.' He sighed. 'Goodnight.'

At nine thirty Milo awoke with a wretched look on his face. He started to moan, turning his head from side to side. I mixed tomato juice, a raw egg, black pepper, and Tabasco in a tall glass, propped him up and poured it down his throat. He gagged, sputtered, and opened his eyes suddenly, as if a bolt of lightning had zapped him in the tailbone.

Forty minutes later he looked every bit as wretched but he was painfully sober.

I got him to the door and stuck the files of the nine psychopaths under his arm.

'Bedtime reading, Milo.'

He tripped down the stairs, swearing, made his way to the Fiat, groped at its door handle and threw himself in with a single lurching movement. With the aid of a rolling start, he got it ignited.

Alone at last, I got into bed, read the *Times*, watched TV—but damned if I could tell you what I saw, other than that it had lots of flat punch lines and jiggling boobs and cops who looked like male models. I enjoyed the solitude for a couple of hours, only pausing to think of murder and greed and twisted evil minds a few times before drifting off to sleep.

11

'ALL RIGHT,' said Milo. We were sitting in an interrogation room at West L.A. Division. The walls were pea-green paint and one-way mirrors. A microphone hung from the ceiling. The furniture consisted of a gray metal table and three metal folding chairs. There was a stale odour of sweat and falsehood and fear in the air, the stink of diminished human dignity.

He had fanned out the folders on the table and picked up the first one with a flourish.

'Here's the way your nine bad guys shape up. Number one, Rex Allen Camblin, incarcerated at Soledad, assault and battery.' He let the folder drop.

'Number two, Peter Lewis Jefferson, working on a ranch in Wyoming. Presence verified.'

'Pity the poor cattle.'

'That's a fact—he looked like a likely one. Number three, Darwin Ward—you'll never believe this—attending law school, Pennsylvania State University.'

'A psychopathic attorney—not all that amazing, really.'

Milo chuckled and picked up the next folder.

'Número cuatro—uh—Leonard Jay Helsinger, work-

117

ing construction on the Alaska pipeline. Location like-wise confirmed by Juncau P.D. Five, Michael Penn, student at Cal State Northridge. Him we talk to.' He put Penn's file aside. 'Six, Lance Arthur Shattuck, short-order cook on the Cunard Line luxury cruiser *Helena*, verified by the Coast Guard to have been floating around in the middle of the Aegean Sea somewhere for the past six weeks. Seven, Maurice Bruno, sales representative for Presto Instant Print in Burbank—another interviewee.' Bruno's file went on top of Penn's.

'Eight, Roy Longstreth, pharmacist for Thrifty's Drug chain, Beverly Hills branch. Another one. And—last but not least—Gerard Paul Mendenhall, Corporal, United States Army, Tyler, Texas, presence verified.'

Beverly Hills was closer than either Northridge or Bur-bank, so we headed for Thrifty's. The Beverly Hills branch turned out to be a brick-and-glass cube on Canon Drive just north of Wilshire. It shared a block with trendy boutiques and a Häagen Dazs ice-cream parlor.

Milo showed his badge surreptitiously to the girl behind the liquor counter and got the manager, a light-skinned middle-aged black, in seconds flat. The manager got nervous and wanted to know if Longstreth had done anything wrong. In classic cop style, Milo hedged.

'We just want to ask him a few questions.'

I had trouble keeping a straight face through that one, but the cliché seemed to satisfy the manager.

'He's not here now. He comes on at two-thirty, works the night shift.'

'We'll be back. Please don't tell him we were here.'

Milo gave him his card. When we left he was studying it like a map to buried treasure.

The ride to Northridge was a half-hour cruise on the Venture Freeway West. When we got to the Cal State campus, we headed straight for the registrar's office. Milo obtained a copy of Michael Penn's class schedule. Armed with that and his mug shot, we located him in twenty minutes, walking across a wide, grassy triangle accompanied by a girl.

'Mr. Penn?'

'Yes?' He was a good-looking fellow, medium height, with broad shoulders and long legs. His light brown hair was cut preppy short. He wore a light blue Izod shirt and blue jeans, penny loafers with no socks. I knew from his file that he was twenty-six but he looked five years younger. He had a pleasant, unlined face, a real All-American type. He didn't look like the kind of guy who'd try to run someone down with a Pontiac Firebird.

'Police.' Again, the badge. 'We'd like to talk to you for a few moments.'

'What about?' The hazel eyes narrowed and the mouth got tight.

'We'd prefer to talk to you in private.'

Penn looked at the girl. She was young, no more than nineteen, short, dark, with a Dorothy Hamill wedge cut.

'Give me a minute, Julie.' He chucked her under the chin.

'Mike...?'

'Just a minute.'

We left her standing there and walked to a concrete area furnished with stone tables and benches. Students moved by as if on a treadmill. There was little standing around. This was a commuter campus. Many of the students worked part-time jobs and squeezed classes in during their spare time. It was a good place to get your B.A. in computer science or business, a teaching credential or a master's in accounting. If you wanted fun or leisurely intellectual debates in the shade of an ivy-encrusted oak, forget it.

Michael Penn looked furious but he was working hard at concealing it.

'What do you want?'

'When's the last time you saw Dr. Morton Handler?'

119

Penn threw back his head and laughed. It was a disturbingly hollow sound.

'That asshole? I read about his death. No loss.'

'When did you see him last?'

Penn was smirking now.

'Years ago, *officer*.' He made the title sound like an insult. 'When I was in *therapy*.'

'I take it you didn't think much of him.'

'Handler? He was a shrink.' As if that explained it.

'You don't think much of psychiatrists.'

Penn held out his hands, palms up.

'Hey listen. That whole thing was a big mistake. I lost control of my car and some paranoid idiot claimed I tried to kill him with it. They busted me, railroaded me and then they offered me probation if I saw a shrink. Gave me all those garbage tests.'

Those garbage tests included the Minnesota Multiphasic Personality Inventory and a handful of projectives. Though far from perfect, they were reliable enough when it came to someone like Penn. I had read his MMPI profile and psychopathy oozed from every index.

'You didn't like Dr. Handler?'

"Don't put words in my mouth.' Penn lowered his voice. He moved his eyes back and forth, restless, jumpy. Behind the handsome face was something dark and dangerous. Handler hadn't misdiagnosed this one.

'You did like him.' Milo played with him like a gaffed stingray.

'I didn't like him or dislike him. I had no use for him. I'm not crazy. And I didn't kill him.'

'You can account for your whereabouts the night he was murdered?'

'When was that?'

Milo gave him the date and time.

Penn cracked his knuckles and looked through us as if zeroing in on a distant target.

'Sure. That entire night I was with my girl.'

120

'Julie?'

Penn laughed.

'Her? No. I've got a mature woman, officer. A woman of means.' His brow creased and his expression changed from smug to sour. 'You're going to have to talk to her, aren't you?'

Milo nodded his head.

'That'll screw things up for me.'

'Gee, Mike, that's really too bad.'

Penn threw him a hateful look, then changed it to bland innocence. He could play his face like a deck of cards, shuffling, palming from the bottom, coming up with a new number every second.

'Listen, officer, that whole incident is behind me. I'm holding down a job, going to school—I'm getting my degree in six months. I don't want to get messed up because my name's in Handler's files.'

He sounded like Wally on 'Leave It to Beaver'—all earnest innocence. Gosh, Beave...

'We'll have to verify your alibi, Mike.'

'Okay, okay, do it. Just don't tell her too much, okay? Keep it general.'

Keep it general so I can fabricate something. You could see the gears spinning behind the high, tan forehead.

'Sure, Mike.' Milo took his pencil out and tapped it on his lips.

'Sonya Magary. She owns the Puff 'n' Stuff Children's Boutique in the Plaza de Oro in Encino.'

'Have you got the number handy?' Milo asked pleasantly.

Penn clenched his jaws and gave it to him.

'We'll call her, Mike. Don't you call her first, okay? We treasure spontaneity.' Milo put away his pencil and closed his notepad. 'Have a nice day, now.'

Penn looked from me to Milo, then back to me, as if seeking an ally. Then he got up and walked away in long, muscular strides.

121

'Oh, Mike!' Milo called.

Penn turned around.

'What are you getting your degree in?'

'Marketing.'

As we left the campus we could see him walking with Julie. Her head was on his shoulder, his arm around her waist. He was smiling down on her and talking very fast.

'What do you think?' Milo asked as he settled behind the wheel.

'I think he's innocent as far as this case goes, but I'll bet you he's got some kind of dirty deal going on. He was really relieved when he found out what we were there for.'

Milo nodded.

'I agree. But what the hell—that's someone else's headache.'

We got back on the freeway, heading east. We exited in Sherman Oaks, found a little French place on Ventura near Woodman and had lunch. Milo used the pay phone to call Sonya Magary. He came back to the table, shaking his head.

'She loves him. "That dear boy, that sweet boy, I hope he's not in trouble." ' He imitated a thick Hungarian accent. 'She verifies he was with her on the fateful night. Sounds proud of it. I expected her to tell me about their sex life—in Technicolor.'

He shook his head and buried his face in a plate of steamed mussels.

We caught up with Roy Longstreth as he got out of his Toyota in the Thrifty's parking lot. He was short and frail-looking, with watery blue eyes and an undernourished chin. Prematurely bald, what little hair he did have was on the sides; he had left it long, hanging down over his ears, so that the general effect was of a friar who'd been meditating too long and had neglected his personal

122

grooming. A mousy brown moustache snuck across his upper lip. He had none of Penn's bravado but there was that same jumpiness in the eyes.

'Yes, what do you want?' He piped up in a squeaky voice after Milo gave him the badge routine. He looked at his watch.

When Milo told him, he looked as if he were going to cry. Uncharacteristic anxiety for a supposed psychopath. Unless the whole thing was an act. You never knew the tricks those types could come up with when they had to.

'When I read about it I just knew you'd come after me.' The insignificant moustache trembled like a twig in a storm.

'Why's that, Roy?'

'Because of the things he said about me. He told my mother I was a psychopath. Told her not to trust me. I'm probably on some whacko list, right?'

'Can you account for your whereabouts the night he was killed?'

'Yes. That's the first thing I thought of when I read about it—they're going to come and ask me questions about it. I made sure I knew. I even wrote it down. Wrote a note to myself. Roy, you were at church that night. So when they come and ask you, you'll know where you were—'

He could have gone on that way for a couple of days but Milo cut him off.

'Church? You're a religious man, Roy?'

Longstreth gave a laugh that was choked with panic.

'No, no. Not praying. The Westside Singles group at Bel Air Presbyterian—it's the same place Ronald Reagan used to go to.'

'The singles group?'

'No, no, no. The church. He used to worship there before he was elected and—'

'Okay, Ron. You were at the Westside Singles group from when to when?'

The sight of Milo taking notes made him even more nervous. He began bouncing up and down, a marionette at the hands of a palsied puppeteer.

'From nine to one-thirty—I stayed to the end. I helped clean up. I can tell you what they served. It was guacamole and nachos and there was Gallo jug wine and shrimp dip and—'

'Of course there'll be lots of peole who saw you there.'

"Sure,' he said, then stopped. 'I—I didn't really mingle much. I helped out, tending bar. I saw lots of people but I don't know if any of them will—remember me.' His voice had quieted to a whisper.

'That could be a problem, Roy.'

'Unless—no—yes—Mrs. Heatherington. She's an older woman. She volunteers at church functions. She was cleaning up, too. And serving. I spent a lot of time talking to her—I can even tell you what we talked about, It was about collectables—she collects Norman Rockwells and I collect Icarts.'

'Icarts?'

'You know, the Art Deco prints.'

The works of Louis Icart went for high prices these days. I wondered how a pharmacist could afford them.

'Mother gave me one when I was sixteen and they—' he searched for the right word—'captivated me. She gives them to me on my birthday and I pick up a few myself. Dr. Handler collected them, too, you know. That—' he let his words trail off.

'Oh, really? Did he show you his collection?

Longstreth shook his head energetically.

'No. He had one in his office. I noticed it and we started talking. But he used it against me later on.'

'How's that?'

'After the evaluation—you know I was sent to him by the court after I was caught—' he looked nervously at the Thrifty's building—'shoplifting.' Tears filled his eyes. 'For God's sake, I took a tube of rubber cement at Sears

124

and they caught me! I thought Mother would die from the shame. And I worried the School of Pharmacy would find out—it was horrible!'

'How did he use the fact that you collected Icarts against you?' asked Milo patiently.

'He kind of implied, never came out and said it, but phrased it so you knew what he meant but he couldn't be pinned down.'

'Implied what, Roy?'

'That he could be bought off. That if I bribed him with an Icart or two—he even mentioned the ones he liked— he would write a favourable report.'

'Did you?'

'What? Bribe him? Not on your life. That would be dishonest!'

'And did he press the issue?'

Longstreth picked at his fingernails.

'Like I said, not so you could pin him down. He just said that I was a borderline case—psychopathic personality, or something less stigmatizing— anxiety reaction or something like that—that I could go either way. In the end he told Mother I was a psychopath.'

The wan face screwed up with rage.

'I'm glad he's dead! There, I've said it! It's what I thought the first time I read about it in the paper.'

'But you didn't do it.'

'Of course not. I couldn't. I run from evil, I don't embrace it!'

'We'll talk to Mrs. Heatherington, Roy.'

'Yes, ask her about the nachos and the wine—I believe it was Gallo Hearty Burgundy. And there was fruit punch with slices of orange floating in it, too. In a cut glass bowl. And one of the women got sick on the floor at the end. I helped mop it up—'

'Thanks, Roy. You can go now.'

'Yes. I will.'

125

He turned around like a robot, a thin figure in a short blue druggist's smock, and walked into Thrifty's.

'He's dispensing drugs?' I asked, incredulous.

'If he's not in some whacko file he should be.' Milo pocketed his notepad and we walked to the car. 'He look like a psychopath to you?'

'Not unless he's the best actor on the face of the earth. Schizoid, withdrawn. Pre-schizophrenic, if anything.'

'Dangerous?'

'Who knows? Put him up against enough stress and he might blow. But I'd judge him more likely to go the hermit route—curl up in bed, play with himself, wither, stay that way for a decade or two while Mommy propped his pillows.'

'If that story about the Icarts is true it sheds some light on our beloved victim.'

'Handler? A real Dr. Schweitzer.'

'Yeah.' said Milo. 'The kind of guy someone might want dead.'

We got on Coldwater Canyon before it clogged with the cars of commuters returning to their homes in the Valley, and made it to Burbank by half past four.

Presto Instant Print was one of scores of gray concrete edifices that filled the industrial park near the Burbank airport like so many oversized tombstones. The air smelled toxic and the flatulent roar of jets shattered the sky at regular intervals. I wondered about the life expectancy of those who spent their daylight hours here.

Maurice Bruno had come up in the world since his file had been compiled. He was now a vice-president, in charge of sales. He was also unavailable, we were told by his secretary, a lissome brunette with arched eyebrows and a mouth meant for saying no.

'Then give me his boss,' barked Milo. He shoved his badge under her nose. We were both hot and tired and discouraged. The last place we wanted to be stalled was Burbank.

'That would be Mr. Gershman,' she said as if discovering some new insight.

'Then that would be who I want to talk to.'

'Just one second.'

She wiggled off and came back with her clone in a blond wig.

'I'm Mr. Gershman's secretary,' the clone announced.

It must be the poison in the air, I decided. It caused brain damage, eroded the cerebral cortex to the point where simple facts took on an aura of profundity.

Milo took a deep breath.

'We'd like to talk with Mr. Gershman.'

'May I inquire what it's about?'

'No, you may not. Bring us to Gershman now.'

'Yes, sir.' The two secretaries looked at each other. Then the brunette pushed a buzzer and the blonde led us through double glass doors into an enormous production area filled with machines that chomped, stamped, bit, snarled, and smeared. A few people hung around the periphery of the rabid steel monsters, dull-eyed, lose-jawed, breathing in fumes that reeked of alcohol and acetone. The noise, alone, was enough to kill you.

She made a sudden left, probably hoping to lose us to the maws of one of the behemoths, but we hung on, following the movement of her swaying butt until we came to another set of double doors. These she pushed and let go, forcing Milo to fall forward to catch them. A short corridor, another set of doors, and we were confronted by silence so complete as to be overwhelming.

The executive suite at Presto Instant Print might have been on another planet. Plush, plum-coloured carpets that you had to bargain with in order to reclaim your ankles, walls panelled in real walnut. Large doors of walnut burl with names made of brass letters tastefully centred on the wood. And silence.

127

The blonde stopped at the end of the hall, in front of an especially large door with especially tasteful gold letters that said Arthur M. Gershman, President. She let us into a waiting room the size of an average house, motioned us to sit in chairs that looked and felt like unbaked bread dough. Settling behind her desk, a contraption of plexiglass and rosewood that afforded the world a perfect view of her legs, she pushed a button on a console that belonged at NASA Control Center, moved her lips a bit, nodded, and stood up again.

'Mr. Gershman will see you, now.'

The inner sanctum was as expected—the size of a cathedral, decorated like something conceived in the pages of *Architectural Digest*, softly lit and comfortable but hard-edged enough to keep you awake—but the man behind the desk was a complete surprise.

He wore khaki pants and a short sleeved white shirt that needed ironing. His feet were clad in Hush Puppies and since they were on the desk the holes in their soles were obvious. He was in his mid-seventies, bald, bespectacled, with one of the sidepieces of his glasses held together with masking tape, and potbellied.

He was talking on the phone when we came in.

'Hold the wire, Lenny.' He looked up. 'Thanks, Denise.' The blonde disappeared. To us: 'One second. Sit down, fix something.' He pointed to a fully stocked bar that covered half of one wall.

'Okay, Lenny, I got cops here, gotta go. Yeah, cops. I don't know, you wanna ask em? Ha ha. Yeah, I'll tell em that for sure, you *momzer*. I'll tell em what *you* did in Palm Springs the last time we were there. Yeah. Okay, the Sahara job in lots of three hundred thousand with coasters and matchbooks—not boxes, books. I got it. I give you delivery in two weeks. What? Forget it.' He winked at us. 'Go ahead, go to someone local, see if I care. I got maybe one, two more months before I drop dead from this business—you think I care if an order

128

drops dead? It's all gonna go to Uncle Sam and Shirley and my prince of a son who drives a German car. Nah, Nah. A BMW. With my money. Yeah. What can you do, it's out of control. Ten days?' He made a masturbating motion with his free hand and beamed at us. 'You're jerking off, Lenny. At least close the door, no one will see. Twelve days, tops. Okay? Twelve it is. Right. Gotta go, these cossacks are going to drag me away any minute. Good-bye.'

The phone slammed down, the man shot up like an uncoiled spring.

'Artie Gershman.'

He held out an ink-stained hand. Milo shook it, then I did. It was as hard as granite and horned with callus.

He sat down again, threw his feet back up on the desk.

'Sorry for the delay.' He had the joviality of someone who was surrounded by enough automatons like Denise to ensure his privacy. 'You deal with casinos they think they got a right to instant everything. That's the mob, you know—but what the hell am I telling you that, you're cops, you know that, right? Now, what can I do for you, officers? The parking situation I know is a problem. If it's that bastard at Chemco next door complaining, all I want to say is he can go straight to hell in a handbasket, because his Mexican ladies park in my lot all the time—you should also check how many of them are legal—if he wants to get really nasty, I can play that game too.'

He paused to catch his breath.

'It's not about parking.'

'No? What then?'

'We want to talk to Maurice Bruno.'

'Morry? Morry's in Vegas. We do a lot of our business there, with the casinos, the motels and hotels. Here.' He opened a drawer of the desk and tossed a handful of matchbooks at us. Most of the big names were represented.

Milo pocketed a few.

129

'When will he be back?'

'In a few days. He went on a selling trip two weeks ago, first to Tahoe, then Reno, end up in Vegas—probably playing around a bit on company time, not to mention the expense account—but who cares, he's a terrific salesman.'

'I thought he was a vice-president.'

'Vice-president in charge of sales. It's a salesman with a fancy title, a bigger salary, a nicer office—what do you think of this place—looks like some fag fixed it up, right?'

I searched Milo's face for a reaction, found none.

'My wife. She did this herself. This place used to be nice. There was papers all over the place, a couple of chairs, white walls—normal walls so you could hear the noise from the plant, know something was going on. This feels like death, you know. That's what I get for taking a second wife. A first wife leaves you alone, a second one wants to make you into a new person.'

'Are you sure Mr. Bruno's in Las Vegas?'

'Why shouldn't I be sure? Where else would he go?'

'How long has Mr. Bruno been working for you, Mr. Gershman.'

'Hey, what's this—this isn't child support or something like that?'

'No. We just want to talk to him about a homicide investigation we're conducting.'

'Homicide?' Gershman shot out of his chair. 'Murder? Morry Bruno? You got to be kidding. He's a gem of a guy!'

A gem who had been excellent at passing rubber checks.

'How long has he been working for you, sir?'

'Let me see—a year and a half, maybe two.'

'And you've had no problem with him?'

'Problem? I tell you he's a gem. Knew nothing about the business, but I hired him on hunch. Hell of a salesman. Outsold all the other guys—even the old-timers—by the fourth month. Reliable, friendly, never a problem.'

130

'You mentioned child support. Mr. Bruno's divorced?'

'Divorced,' said Gershman sadly. 'Like everyone. Including my son. They give up too easily nowadays.'

'Does he have family here in Los Angeles?'

'Nah. The wife, kids—three of em, I think—they moved back east. Pittsburg, or Cleveland, some place with no ocean. He missed 'em, talked about it. That's why he volunteered at the Casa.'

'Casa?'

'That kids' place, up in Malibu. Morry used to spend his weekends there, volunteering with the kids. He got a certificate. C'mon I'll show you.'

Bruno's office was a quarter the size of Gershman's, but decked out in the same eclectically elegant style. The place was neat as a pin, not surprising, since Bruno spent most of his time on the road. Gershman pointed to a framed plaque that shared wall space with a half-dozen Number One Salesman commendations.

'You see—"awarded to Maurice Bruno in recognition of voluntary service to the homeless children of La Casa de los Niños" blah blah blah. I told you he was a gem.'

The certificate was signed by the Mayor, as honorary witness, and by the director of the children's home, a Reverend Augustus J. McCaffrey. It was all calligraphy and floral intaglio. Very impressive.

'Very nice,' said Milo. 'Do you know what hotel Mr. Bruno was staying at?'

'He used to stay at the MGM, but after the fire, I don't know. Let's go back to the office and find out.'

Back in Office Beautiful, Gershman picked up the telephone, punched the intercom and barked into the receiver.

'Denise, where's Morry staying in Vegas? Do that.'

A half-minute later the intercom buzzed.

'Yeah? Good. Thanks, darling.' He turned to us. 'The Palace.'

'Caesar's Palace?'

131

'Yeah. You want me to call there, you can talk to him?'

'If you don't mind, sir. We'll charge it to the Police Department.'

'Nah!' Gershman waved his hand. 'On me. Denise, call Caesar's Palace, get Morry on the phone. He's not there, leave him a message to call—'

'Detective Sturgis. West L.A. Division.'

Gershman completed the instructions.

'You're not thinking about Morry as a suspect, are you?' he asked when he got off the phone. 'This is a witness thing, right?'

'We really can't say anything about it, Mr. Gershman.' Milo paid lip service to discretion.

'I can't believe it!' Gershman slapped his head with his hand. 'You think Morry's a murderer! A guy who works with kids on the weekend—a guy who never had a cross word with anybody here—go ask around, I give you permission. You find someone who has a bad word to say about Morry Bruno, I'll eat this desk!'

He was interrupted by the intercom buzzer.

'Yes, Denise. What's that? You're sure? Maybe it was a mistake. Check again. And then call the Aladdin, the Sands, maybe he changed his mind.'

The old man's face was solemn when he hung up.

'He's not at the Palace.' He said it with the sadness and fear of someone about to be torn from the comforting warmth of his preconceptions.

Maurice Bruno wasn't at the Aladdin or the Sands or any other major hotel in Las Vegas. Additional calls from Gershman's office revealed the fact that none of the airlines had a record of him flying from L.A. to Vegas.

'I'd like his home address and phone number, please.'

'Denise will give it to you,' said Gershman. We left him sitting alone in his big office, grizzled chin resting in his hands, frowning like a battered old bison who'd spent too many years at the zoo.

132

Bruno lived in Glendale, normally a ten-minute drive from the Presto plant, but it was 6 P.M., there had been an accident just west of the Hollywood–Golden State interchange, and the freeway was stagnant all the way from Burbank to Pasadena. By the time we exited on Brand, it was dark and both of us were in foul moods.

Milo turned north and headed toward the mountains. Bruno's house was on Armelita, a side street half a mile from where the boulevard ended. It was situated at the end of a cul-de-sac, a small, one-storey mock Tudor, fronted by a neat, square lawn, yew hedges and sprigs of juniper stuffed in the empty spaces. Two large arborvitae bushes guarded the entrance. It wasn't the kind of place I would have imagined for a Vegas-haunting bachelor. Then I remembered what Gershman had said about the divorce. No doubt this was the homestead left behind by the fleeing wife and children.

Milo rang the doorbell a couple of times, then he knocked hard. When no one answered he went to the car and called the Glendale police. Ten minutes later a squad car pulled up and two uniformed officers got out. Both were tall, beefy and sandy-haired and wore bushy, bristly, strawlike moustaches under their noses. They came over with that swagger unique to cops and drunks trying hard to look sober, and conferred with Milo. Then they got on their radio.

The street was quiet and devoid of visible human habitation. It stayed that way as the three additional squad cars and the unmarked Dodge drove up and parked. There was a brief conference that resembled a football huddle and then guns were drawn. Milo rang the bell again, waited a minute and then kicked the door in. The assault was on.

I stayed outside, watching, waiting. Soon the sound of gagging and retching could be heard. Then cops began running out of the house, spilling out on the lawn, their hands to their noses, an action sequence in reverse. One particularly stalwart patrolman busied himself puking into the junipers. When it appeared that they'd all retreated, Milo came to the door, a handkerchief held over his nose and mouth. His eyes were visible and they made contact with me. They gave me a choice.

Against my better judgment I pulled out my own handkerchief, masked the lower part of my face and went in.

The thin cotton was scant defense against the hot stench that rose up against me as I stepped across the threshold. It was as if raw sewage and swamp gas had blended into a bubbling, swirling soup, then vaporized and sprayed into the air.

My eyes watering, I fought the urge to vomit, and followed Milo's advancing silhouette into the kitchen.

He was sitting there at a Formica table. The bottom part of him, the part in clothing, still looked human. The sky-blue salesman's suit, the maize-coloured buttondown shirt with blue silk foulard. The dandy's touches—the breast pocket hankie, the shoes with tiny tassles, the gold bracelet that hung around a wrist teeming with maggots.

From the neck up he was something the pathologists threw out. It looked as if he'd been worked over with a crowbar—the entire front part of what used to be his face was caved in—but it was really impossible to know what the swollen bloody lump attached to his shoulders had been subjected to, so advanced was the state of decay.

Milo began throwing open windows and I realized that the house felt as hot as a blast furnace, fuelled by the hydrocarbons emitted by decomposing organic matter. A quick answer to the energy crisis: Save kilowatts, kill a friend. . .

I couldn't take any more. I ran for the door, gasping, and flung away the handkerchief when I reached the outdoors. I gulped hungrily at the cool night air. My hands shook.

There was lots of excitement on the block now. Neighbours—men, women and children—had come out of their castles, pausing in the middle of the evening news, interrupting their defrosted feasts to gawk at the blinking crimson lights and listen to the stuttering radio static of the squad car, staring at the coroner's van that had pulled up to the curb with the cold authority of a parading despot. A few kids rode their bikes up and down the street. Mumbling voices took on the sound of ravaging locusts. A dog barked. Welcome to suburbia.

I wondered where they'd all been when someone had gotten into Bruno's house, battered him into jelly, closed all the windows and left him to rot.

Milo finally came out, looking green. He sat on the front steps and hung his head between his knees. Then he got up and called the attendants from the coroner's office over. They had come prepared, with gas masks and rubber gloves. They went in with an empty stretcher and came out carrying something wrapped in a black plastic sheath.

'Ugh. Gross,' said a teenage girl to her friend.

It was as eloquent a way to put it as any.

12

THREE MORNINGS after we discovered the butchery of
Bruno, Milo wanted to come over to review the salesman's psychiatric file in detail. I postponed it until the
afternoon. Motivated by instincts that were unclear to
me, I called André Jaroslav at his studio in West Hollywood and asked him if he had time to help me refresh my
karate skills.

'Doctor,' he said, the accent as thick as goulash, 'such
a long time since I see you.'

'I know, André. Too long. I've let myself go. But I
hope you can help me.'

He laughed.

'Tsk, tsk. I have intermediate group at eleven and private lessons at twelve. Then I am going to Hawaii, Doctor. To choreograph fight scenes for new television pilot.
Girl policeperson who knows judo and catches rapists.
What do you think?'

'Very original.'

'Ya. I get to work with the redheaded chickie—this
Shandra Layne. To teach her how to throw around large
men. Like Wonder Woman, ya?'

'Ya. Do you have any time before eleven?'

136

'For you, Doctor—certainly. We get you in shape. Come at nine and I give you two hours.'

The Institute of Martial Arts was located on Santa Monica at Doheny, next to the Troubador nightclub. It was an L.A. institution, predating the Kung Fu craze by fifteen years. Jaroslav was a bandy-legged Czech Jew who'd escaped during the fifties. He had a high, squeaky voice that he attributed to having been shot in the throat by the Nazis. The truth was that he'd been born with the vocal register of a hysterical capon. It hadn't been easy, being a squeaky-voiced Jew in postwar Prague. Jaroslav had developed his own way of coping. Starting as a boy he taught himself physical culture, weight-lifting and the arts of self-defence. By the time he was in his twenties he had total command of every martial arts doctrine from sabre-fencing to hopkaido, and a lot of bullies received painful surprises.

He greeted me at the door, naked from the waist up, a spray of daffodils in his hand. The sidewalk was filled with anorectic individuals of ambiguous gender, hugging guitar cases as if they were life preservers, dragging deeply on cigarettes and regarding the passing traffic with spaced-out apprehension.

'Audition,' he squeaked, pointing a finger at the door to the Troubador and glancing at them scornfully. 'The artisans of a new age, Doctor.'

We went into the studio, which was empty. He placed the flowers in a vase. The practice room was an expanse of polished oak floor bordered by whitewashed walls. Autographed photographs of stars and near-stars hung in clusters. I went into a dressing room with the set of stiff white garments he gave me and emerged looking like an extra in a Bruce Lee movie.

Jaroslav was silent, letting his body and his hands talk. He positioned me in the centre of the studio and stood facing me. He smiled faintly, we bowed to each other and

137

he led me through a series of warm-up exercises that made my joints creak. It had been a long time.

When the introductory *katas* were through, we bowed again. He smiled, then proceeded to wipe the floor with me. At the end of one hour I felt as if I'd been stuffed down a garbage disposal. Every muscle fibre ached, every synapse quivered in exquisite agony.

He kept it up, smiling and bowing, sometimes letting out a perfectly controlled, high-pitched scream, tossing me around like a bean bag. By the end of the second hour, pain had ceased to be obtrusive—it had become a way of life, a state of consciousness. But when we stopped I was starting to feel in command of my body once again. I was breathing hard, stretching, blinking. My eyes burned as the perspiration dripped into them. Jaroslav looked as if he'd just finished reading the morning paper.

'You take a hot bath, Doctor, get some chickie to massage you, use a little witch hazel. And remember: practice, practice, practice.'

'I will, André.'

'You call me when I get back, in a week. I tell you about Shandra Layne and check if you've been practising.' He poked a finger in my gut, playfully.

'It's a deal.'

He held out his hand. I reached out to take it, then tensed, wondering if he was going to throw me again.

'Ya, good,' he said. Then he laughed and let me go.

The throbbing agony made me feel righteous and ascetic. I had lunch at a restaurant run by one of the dozens of quasi-Hindu cults that seem to prefer Los Angeles to Calcutta. A vacant-eyed, perpetually smiling girl swaddled in white robes and burnoose took my order. She had a rich kid's face coupled with the mannerisms of a nun and managed to smile while she talked, smile as she wrote, smile as she walked away. I wondered if it hurt.

I finished a plate heaped with chopped lettuce, sprouts,

refried soya beans and melted goat cheese on *chapati* bread—a sacred tostada—and washed it down with two glasses of pineapple-coconut-guava nectar imported from the holy desert of Mojave. The bill came to ten dollars and thirty-nine cents. That explained the smiles.

I made it back to the house just as Milo pulled up in an unmarked bronze Matador.

'The Fiat finally died,' he explained. 'I'm having it cremated and scattering the ashes over the offshore rigs in Long Beach.'

'My condolences.' I picked up Bruno's file.

'Contributions to the down payment on my next lemon will be accepted in lieu of flowers.'

'Get Dr. Silverman to buy you one.'

'I'm working on it.'

He let me read for a few minutes then asked, 'So what do you think?'

'No profound insights. Bruno was referred to Handler by the Probation Department after the bad-check bust. Handler saw him a dozen times over a four-month period. When the probationary period was over so was the treatment. One thing I did notice was that Handler's notes on him are relatively benign. Bruno was one of the more recently acquired patients. At the time he started therapy, Handler was at his nastiest, yet there are no vicious comments about him. Here, in the beginning Handler calls him a "slick con man".' I flipped some pages. 'A couple of weeks later he makes a crack about Bruno's "Cheshire grin". But after that, nothing.'

'As if they became buddies?'

'Why do you say that.'

Milo handed me a piece of paper. 'Here,' he said, 'Look at this.'

It was a printout from the phone company.

'This,' he pointed to a circled seven-digit code, 'is Handler's number—his home number, not the office. And this one is Bruno's.'

Lines had been drawn between the two, like lacing on a high-topped shoe. There's been lots of connections over the last six months.

'Interesting, huh?'

'Very.'

'Here's something else. Officially the coroner says it's impossible to fix a time of death for Bruno. The heat inside the house screwed up the decomposition tables— with the flack they've been getting they're not willing to go out on a limb and take the chance of being wrong. But I got one of the young guys to give me an off-the-record guess and he came up with ten to twelve days.'

'Right around the time Handler and Gutierrez were murdered.'

'Either right before or right after.'

'But what about the differing m.o.'s?'

'Who says people are consistent, Alex? Frankly there are other differences between the two cases besides m.o. In Bruno's case it looks like forced entry. We found broken bushes under a rear window and chisel marks on the pane—used to be a kid's room. Glendale P.D. also thinks they've got two sets of heelprints.'

'Two? Maybe Melody really saw something.' *Dark men. Two or three.*

'Maybe. But I've abandoned that line of attack. The kid will never be a reliable witness. In any event, despite the discrepancies, it looks like we might be on to something—what, I don't know. Patient and doctor, concrete proof that they maintained some kind of contact after treatment was over, both ripped off around the same time. It's too cute for coincidence.'

He studied his notes, looking scholarly. I thought about Handler and Bruno and then it hit me.

'Milo, we've been held back in our thinking by social roles.'

'What the hell are you talking about?'

'Roles. Social roles—prescribed sets of behaviours.

140

Like doctor and patient. Psychiatrist and psychopath. What are the characteristics of a psychopath?'

'Lack of conscience.'

'Right. And an inability to relate to other people except by exploiting them. The good ones have a glib, smooth façade, often they're good-looking. Usually above-average intelligence. Sexually manipulative. A predilection to engage in cons, blackmail, frauds.'

Milo's eyes opened wide.

'Handler.'

'Of course. We've been thinking of him as the doctor in the case and assuming psychological normalcy—he's been protected, in our eyes, by his role. But take a closer look. What do we know about him? He was involved in insurance fraud. He tried to blackmail Roy Longstreth, using his power as a psychiatrist. He seduced at least one patient—Elaine Gutierrez—and who knows how many more? And those putdowns in the margins of his notes— at first I thought they were evidence of burnout, but now I don't know. That was cold, pretending to listen to people, taking their money, insulting them. His notes were confidential—he never expected anyone else to read them. He could hang it all out, show his true colours. Milo, I tell you the guy comes across like your classic psychopath.'

'The evil doctor.'

'Not exactly a *rara avis*, is it? If there can be a Mengele, why not scores of Morton Handlers? What better façade for an intelligent psychopath than the title of Doctor—it yields instant prestige and credibility.'

'Psychopathic doctor and psychopathic patient.' He mulled it over.

'Not buddies, but partners in crime.'

'Sure. Psychopaths don't have buddies. Only victims and accomplices. Bruno must have been Handler's dream come true if he was plotting something and needed one of his own kind for help. I'll bet you those first sessions were incredible, the two of them hungry hyenas, checking

141

each other out, looking over their shoulders, sniffing the ground.'

'Why Bruno, in particular? Handler treated other psychopaths.'

'They were too crude. Short order cooks, cowboys, construction workers. Handler needed a smooth type. Besides, how do we know how many of those guys were deliberately misdiagnosed like Longstreth?'

'Just to play devil's advocate for one second—one of those jokers was in law school.'

I thought about it for a minute.

'Too young. In Handler's eyes a callow punk. In a few years, with degree in hand and a veneer of sophistication, maybe. Handler needed a businessman type for what he wanted to pull off. Someone really slick. And Bruno appears to have fit that bill. He fooled Gershman, who's no idiot.'

Milo got up and paced the room, running his fingers through his hair, creating a bird's nest.

'It's definitely appealing. Shrinker and shrinkee pulling off a scam.' He seemed amused.

'It's not the first time, Milo. There was a guy back East a few years ago—very good credentials. Married into a rich family and started a clinic for juvenile delinquents— back when they still called them that. He used his in-laws' social connections to organize fund-raising soirées for the clinic. While the champagne flowed, the j.d.'s were busy burglarizing the partygoers' townhouses. They finally caught him with a warehouse full of silver and crystal, furs and rugs. He didn't even need the stuff. He was doing it for the challenge. They sent him away to one of those discreet institutions in the rolling hills of southern Maryland—for all I know he's running the place by now. It never hit the papers. I found out about it through the professional grapevine. Convention gossip.'

Milo pulled out his pencil. He started writing, thinking out loud.

142

'To the marble corridors of high finance. Bank records, brokerage statements, businesses filed under fictitious names. See what's left in the safe-deposit boxes after the IRS has done its dirty work. County assessor for info on property ventures. Insurance claims out of Handler's office.' He stopped. 'I hope this gets me somewhere, Alex. This goddamn case hasn't helped my status in the department. The captain is aiming for promotion and he wants to show more arrests. Handler and Gutierrez weren't ghetto types he can afford to let fade away. And he's running scared that Glendale will solve Bruno first and make us look like shmucks. You remember Bianchi.'

I nodded. A small-town police chief in Bellingham, Washington, had caught the Hillside Strangler—something the L.A.P.D. war machine hadn't been able to do.

He got up, went into the kitchen and ate half of a cold chicken standing over the sink. He washed it down with a quart of orange juice and came back wiping his mouth.

'I don't know why I'm fighting not to laugh, up to my ass in dead bodies and no apparent progress, but it seems so funny, Handler and Bruno. You send a guy to a shrink to get his head straight and the doc is as fucked-up as the patient and *systematically* puts the warp on him.'

Put that way it didn't *sound* funny. He laughed anyway.

'What about the girl?' he asked.

'Gutierrez? What about her.'

'Well, I was thinking about those social roles. We've been looking at her as the innocent bystander. If Handler could connive with one patient, why not with two?'

'It's not impossible. But we know Bruno was psychopathic. Any of that kind of evidence about her.'

'No,' he admitted. 'We looked for Handler's file on her and couldn't find it. Maybe he shredded it when their relationship changed. Do you guys do that?'

'I wouldn't know. I never slept with my patients—or their mothers.'

'Don't be touchy. I tried to interview her family. The

143

old, plump *mamacita*, two brothers one of 'em with those angry, macho eyes. There's no father—he died ten years ago. The three of them live in a tiny place in Echo Park. When I got there they were in the middle of mourning. The place was full of the girl's pictures, in shrines. Lots of candles, baskets of food, weeping neighbours. The brothers were sullen. Mama barely spoke English. I made a serious attempt to be sensitive, culturally aware and all that. I borrowed Sanchez from Ramparts Division to translate. We brought food, kept a low profile. I got *nada*. Hear no evil, speak no evil. I honestly don't think they knew much about Elena's life. To them West L.A.'s as distant as Atlantis. But even if they did they sure as hell weren't going to tell me.'

'Even,' I asked, 'if it would help find her murderer.'

He looked at me wearily.

'Alex, people like that don't think the police can help them. To them *la policía* are the bastards who roust their *cholos* and insult their home girls and are never around when the low riders cruise the neighbourhood at night with their lights off and pop shotgun shells through bedroom windows. Which reminds me—I interviewed a friend of the girl. Her roommate, also a teacher. This one was outwardly hostile. Made it clear she wanted nothing to do with me. Her brother had been killed five years ago in a gang shootout and the police did nothing for her and her family then, so to hell with me now.'

He got up and padded around the room like a tired lion.

'In summation, Elaine Gutierrez is a cipher. But there's nothing to indicate she wasn't as pure as the freshly driven snow.'

He looked miserable, plagued with self-doubt.

'It's a tough case, Milo. Don't be so hard on yourself.'

'It's funny you should say that. That's what my mother used to tell me. Go easy, Milo Bernard. Don't be such a *profectionist*—that was the way she pronounced it. The

144

whole family had a tradition of low personal expectations. Drop out of school in tenth grade, go to work at the foundry, lay out a life for yourself of plastic dishes, TV, church picnics, and steel splinter that stuck in your skin. After thirty years enough pension and disability to give you a weekend in the Ozarks once in a while, if you're lucky. My Dad did it, his dad, and both of my brothers. The Sturgis game plan. But not the *profectionist*. For one, the game plan worked best if you got married and I'd been liking boys since I was nine. And second—this was more important—I figured I was too smart to do what the rest of those peasants were doing. So I broke the mould, shocked them all. And the hotshot who everyone thought was going to become a lawyer or a professor or at least some kind of accountant goes and ends up as a member of *la policía*. Ain't that something for a guy who wrote a goddamn thesis on transcendentalism in the poetry of Walt Whitman?'

He turned away from me and stared at the wall. He had worked himself into a funk. I had seen it before. The most therapeutic thing to say was nothing. I ignored him and did some calisthenics.

'Goddam Jack La Lanne,' he muttered.

It took him ten minutes to come out of it, ten minutes of clenching and unclenching his big fists. Then came the tentative raising of the eyes, the inevitable sheepish grin.

'How much for the therapy, Doctor?'

I thought a minute.

'Dinner. At a good place. No crap.'

He stood up and stretched, growled like a bear.

'How about sushi? I'm goddamn barbaric tonight. I'll eat those fish alive.'

We drove to Oomasa, in Little Tokyo. The restaurant was crowded, mostly with Japanese. This was no trendy hotspot decked out in shoji-screen elegance and waxed pine counters. The decor was red Naugahyde, stiff-backed chairs and plain white walls decorated only by a few Nikon calendars. The solitary concession to style was a large aquarium, in full view of the sushi bar, in which fancy goldfish struggled to propel themselves through bubbling, icy clear water. They gasped and bobbed, mutations ill-suited for survival in any but the most rarefied captivity, the products of hundreds of years of careful Oriental tinkering with nature—lionheads with faces obscured by glossy, raspberry growths, bug-eyed black moors, celestials with eyes forced perpetually heavenward, *ryukins* so overloaded with finnage that they could barely move. We stared at them and drank Chivas.

'That girl,' Milo said, 'the roommate. I felt she could help me. That she knew something about Elaine's lifestyle, maybe something about her and Handler. She was nailed tight, goddamn her.'

He finished his drink and motioned for another. It came and he gulped down half.

A waitress skittered over on geisha feet and handed us hot towels. We wiped our hands and face. I felt my pores open, hungry for air.

'You should be pretty good at talking to teachers, right? Probably did a lot of it back in the days when you were earning an honest living.'

'Sometimes teachers hate psychologists, Milo. They see us as dilettantes dropping theoretical pearls of wisdom on them while they do the dirty work.'

'Hmm.' The rest of the Scotch disappeared.

'But no matter. I'll talk to her for you. Where can I find her?'

'Same school Gutierrez taught at. In West L.A., not far from you.' He wrote the address on a napkin and gave it to me. 'Her name's Raquel Ochoa.' He spelled it, his voice thickening, slurring the words. 'Use your badge.' He slapped me on the back.

There was a grating sound above our heads. We looked up to find the sushi chef smiling and sharpening his knives.

We ordered. The fish was fresh, the rice just slightly

146

sweet. The *wasabe* horseradish cleared my sinuses. We ate in silence, against a backdrop of *samisen* music and foreign chatter.

13

I AWOKE as stiff as if I'd been spray-starched; a full-fledged charley horse had taken hold of my muscles, a souvenir of my dance with Jaroslav. I fought it by taking a two-mile run down the canyon and back. Then I practised karate moves out on the rear deck, to the amused comments of a pair of mockingbirds who interrupted their domestic quarrel long enough to look me over, then delivered what had to be the avian equivalent of a raspberry.

'Fly down here, you little bastards,' I grunted, 'and I'll show you who's tough.' They responded with hilarious screeching.

The day was shaping up as a lung-buster, grimy fingers of pollution reaching over the mountains to strangle the sky. The ocean was obscured by a sulfurous sheath of airborne garbage. My chest ached in harmony with the stiffness in my joints, and by ten I was ready to quit.

I planned to time my visit to the school where Raquel Ochoa taught for the noon break, hoping to find her free. That left enough time for a long, hot bath, a cold shower, and a carefully assembled breakfast of eggs with mushrooms, sourdough toast, grilled tomatoes and coffee.

I dressed casually in dark brown slacks, tan corduroy

148

sport coat, checked shirt and brown knit tie. Before I left I dialled a now-familiar number. Bonita Quinn answered.

'Yes?'

'Mrs. Quinn, Dr. Delaware. I just wanted to call to find out how Melody's been doing.'

'She's fine.' Her tone would have frosted a beer mug. 'Fine.'

Before I could say more she hung up.

The school was in a middle-class part of town, but it could have been anywhere. It was the old familiar layout of citadels of learning throughout the city: flesh-coloured buildings arranged in classic penitentiary style, surrounded by a desert of black asphalt and secured by ten-foot-high chain link fencing. Someone had tried to brighten it up by painting a mural of children playing along the side of one of the buildings but it was scant redemption. What helped a bit more were the sight and sound of real children playing—running, jumping, tumbling, chasing each other, screaming like banshees, throwing balls, crying out with the fervour of the truly persecuted ('Teacher, he *hit* me!'), sitting in circles, reaching for the sky. A small group of bored-looking teachers watched from the sidelines.

I climbed the front stairs and found the main office with little trouble. The internal floor plan of schools was as predictable as the drab exterior.

I used to wonder why all the schools I knew were so hopelessly ugly, so predictably oppressive, then I dated a nurse whose father was one of the chief architects for the firm that had been building schools for the state for the past fifty years. She had unresolved feelings about him, and talked a lot about him: a drunken, melancholic man who hated his wife and despised his children more, who saw the world in terms of minimally varying shades of disappointment. A real Frank Lloyd Wright.

The office reeked of mimeographing fluid. Its sole occupant was a stern, black woman in her forties, ensconced in

149

a fortress of scarred golden oak. I showed her my badge, which didn't interest her, and asked for Raquel Ochoa. The name didn't seem to interest her either.

'She's a teacher here. Fourth grade,' I added.

'It's lunchtime. Try the teachers' dining room.'

The dining room turned out to be an airless place, twenty feet by fifteen, into which folding tables and chairs had been crammed. A dozen men and women sat hunched over sack lunches and coffee, laughing, smoking, chewing. When I entered the room all activity ceased.

'I'm looking for Ms. Ochoa.'

'You won't find her here, honey,' said a stout woman with platinum hair.

Several of the teachers laughed. They let me stand there for a while and then a fellow with a young face and old eyes said:

'Room 304. Probably.'

'Thanks.'

I left. I was halfway down the hall before they started talking again.

The door to 304 was half-open. I went in. Rows of unoccupied school desks filled every square inch of space, with the exception of a few feet at the front that had been cleared for the teacher's desk, a boxy metal rectangle behind which sat a woman busy at work. If she had heard me enter she gave no indication, as she continued to read, make checkmarks, cross out errors. An unopened brown bag sat at her elbow. Light streamed in though dusty windows in beams that were suffused with dancing, suspended particles. The Vermeer softness was at odds with the utilitarian severity of the room: stark walls, a blackboard veneered with chalky residue, a soiled American flag.

'Ms. Ochoa?'

The face that looked up was out of a mural by Rivera. Reddish-brown skin stretched tightly over sharply defined but delicately constructed bones; liquid lips and melting

150

black eyes gabled by full, dark brows. Her hair was long and sleek, parted in the middle, hanging down her back. Part Aztec, part Spanish, part unknown.

'Yes?' Her voice was soft in volume but the timbre was defensively hard. Some of the hostility Milo had described was immediately apparent. I wondered if she was one of those people who had turned psychological vigilance into a fine art.

I walked over to her, introduced myself and showed her the badge. She inspected it.

'Ph.D, in what?'

'Psychology.'

She looked at me with disdain.

'The police don't get satisfaction, so they send in the shrinks?'

'It's not that simple.'

'Spare me the details.' She returned her eyes to her paperwork.

'I just want to talk to you for a few minutes. About your friend.'

'I told that big detective everything I know.'

'This is just a double-check.'

'How thorough.' She picked up her red pencil and began slashing at the paper. I felt sorry for the students whose work was coming under scrutiny at this particular moment.

'This isn't a psychological interview, if that's what you're worried about. It's—'

'I'm not worried about anything. I told him everything.'

'He doesn't think so.'

She slammed the pencil down. The point broke.

'Are you calling me a liar, Mr. Ph.D?' Her speech was crisp and articulate but it still bore a Latin tinge.

I shrugged.

'Labels aren't important. What is, is finding out as much as possible about Elaine Gutierrez.'

'*Elena*,' she snapped. 'There's nothing to tell. Let the

151

police do their job and stop sending their scientific snoop-
ers around harassing people who are busy.'

'Too busy to help find the murderer of your best friend?'

The head shot up. She brushed furiously at a loose strand
of hair.

'Please leave,' she said between clenched jaws. 'I have
work to do.'

'Yes, I know. You don't even eat lunch with the rest of
the teachers. You're very dedicated and serious—that's
what it took to get out of the *barrio*—and that puts you
above the laws of common courtesy.'

She stood up, all five feet of her. For a moment I thought
she was going to slap me, as she drew her hand back. But
she stopped herself, and stared.

I could feel the acid heat coming my way but I held my
gaze. Jaroslav would have been proud.

'I'm busy,' she finally said, but there was a pleading quality to the statement, as if she was trying to convince herself.

'I don't want to take you on a cruise. I just want to ask a
few questions about Elena.'

She sat down.

'What kind of psychologist are you? You don't talk like
one.'

I gave her a capsulized, deliberately vague history of my
involvement in the case. She listened and I thought I saw
her soften.

'A child psychologist. We could use you around here.'

I looked around the classroom, counted forty-six desks
in a space meant for twenty-eight.

'I don't know what I could do—help you tie them down?'

She laughed, then realized what she was doing and cut it
off, like a bad connection.

'It's no use talking about Elena,' she said. 'She only
got—into trouble because of being involved with that...'
She trailed off.

'I know Handler was a creep. Detective Sturgis—the big

152

guy—knows. And you're probably right. She was an innocent victim. But let's make sure, okay?'

'You do this a lot. Work for the police?' She evaded me.

'No. I'm retired.'

She looked at me with disbelief. 'At your age?'

'Post-burnout.'

That hit home. She dropped her mask a notch and a bit of humanity peeked through.

'I wish I could afford it. Retirement.'

'I know what you mean. It must be crazy working with this kind of bureaucracy.' I threw out the lure of empathy—administrators were the object of every teacher's ire. If she didn't go for it I wasn't sure what I'd do to gain rapport.

She looked at me suspiciously, searching for a sign that I was patronizing her.

'You don't work at all?' she asked.

'I do some free-lance investing. It keeps me busy enough.'

We chatted for a while about the vagaries of the school system. She carefully avoided mention of anything personal, keeping it all in the realm of pop sociology—how rotten things were when parents weren't willing to get emotionally and intellectually involved with their children, how difficult it was to teach when half the kids came from broken homes and were so upset they could barely concentrate, the frustration of dealing with administrators who'd given up on life and stuck around only for their pensions, anger at the fact that a teacher's starting salary was less than that of a trash collector. She was twenty-nine and she'd lost any shred of idealism that had survived the transition from East L.A. to the world of Anglo bourgeoisie.

She could really talk when she got going, the dark eyes flashing, the hands gesticulating—flying through the air like two brown sparrows.

I sat like the teacher's pet and listened, giving her what everyone wants when they're unloading—empathy, an understanding gesture. Part of it was calculated—I wanted

153

to break through to her in order to find out more about Elena Gutierrez—but some of it was my old therapeutic persona, thoroughly genuine.

I was starting to think I'd gotten through when the bell rang. She became a teacher again, the arbiter of right and wrong.

'You must go now. The children will be coming back.'

I stood up and leaned on her desk.

'Can we talk later? About Elena?'

She hesitated, biting her lip. The sound of a stampede began as a faint rumble and grew thunderous. High-pitched voices wailed their way closer.

'All right. I'm off at two-thirty.'

An offer to buy her a drink would have been a mistake. Keep it businesslike, Alex.

'Thank you. I'll meet you at the gate.'

'No. Meet me in the teachers' parking lot. At the south side of the building.' Away from prying eyes.

Her car was a dusty white Vega. She walked toward it carrying a stack of books and papers that reached up to her chin.

'Can I help you?'

She gave me the load, which must have weighed at least twenty pounds, and took a minute to find her keys. I noticed that she'd put on makeup—eye shadow that accentuated the depth of her orbs. She looked around eighteen.

'I haven't eaten yet,' she said. It was less an angling for an invitation than a complaint.

'No brown bag.'

'I threw it out. I make a lousy lunch. On a day like today it's too lousy to take. There's a chop house on Wilshire.'

'Can I drive you?'

She looked at the Vega.

'Sure, why not? I'm low on gas, anyway. Toss those on the front seat.' I put the books down and she locked the car. 'But I'll pay for my own lunch.'

154

We left the school grounds. I led her to the Seville. When she saw it her eyebrows rose.

'You must be a good investor.'

'I get lucky from time to time.'

She sank back in the soft leather and let out a breath. I got behind the wheel and started up the engine.

'I've changed my mind,' she said. 'You pay for the lunch.'

She ate meticulously, cutting her steak into tiny pieces, spearing each morsel individually and slipping it into her mouth, and wiping her mouth with her napkin every third bite. I was willing to bet she was a tough grader.

'She was my best friend,' she said, putting down her fork and picking up her water glass. 'We grew up together in East L.A. Rafael and Andy—her brothers—played with Miguel.' At the mention of her dead brother her eyes misted then grew hard as obsidian. She pushed her plate away. She'd eaten a quarter of her food. 'When we moved to Echo Park the Gutierrezes moved with us. The boys were always getting into trouble—minor mischief, pranks. Elena and I were good girls. Goody-goodies, actually. The nuns loved us.' She smiled.

'We were as close as sisters. And like sisters there was a lot of competition between us. She was always better-looking.'

She read the doubt in my face.

'Really. I was a scrawny kid. I developed late. Elena was—voluptuous, soft. The boys followed her around with their tongues hanging out. Even when she was eleven and twelve. Here.' She reached into her purse and took out a snapshot. More photographic memories.

'This is Elena and me. In high school.'

Two girls leaned against a graffiti-filled wall. They wore Catholic school uniforms—short-sleeved white blouses, gray skirts, white socks and saddle shoes. One was tiny, thin and dark. The other a head taller, had curves the uni-

155

form couldn't conceal and a complexion that was surprisingly fair.

'Was she a blonde?'

'Surprising, isn't it? Some German rapist way back, no doubt. Later she lightened it even more, to be really all-American. She got sophisticated, changed her name to Elaine, spent lots of money on clothes, her car.' She realized she was criticizing the dead girl and quickly changed her tune. 'But she was a person of substance underneath all of that. She was a truly gifted teacher—there aren't many like that. She taught EH, you know.'

Educationally Handicapped classes were for children who weren't retarded but still had difficulties learning. The category could include everything from bright kids with specific perceptual problems to youngsters whose emotional conflicts got in the way of their learning to read and write. Teaching EH was tough. It could be constant frustration or a stimulating challenge, depending on a teacher's motivation, energy and talent.

'Elena had a real gift for drawing them out—the kids no one else could work with. She had patience. You wouldn't have thought it to look at her. She was—flashy. She used lots of makeup, dressed to show herself off. Sometimes she looked like a party girl. But she wasn't afraid to get down on the floor with the children, didn't mind getting her hands dirty. She got into their heads—she dedicated herself to them. The children loved her. Look.'

Another photograph. Elena Gutierrez surrounded by a group of smiling children. She was kneeling and the kids were climbing on her, tugging at the hem of her skirt, putting their heads in her lap. A tall, well-built young woman, pretty rather than beautiful, with an earthy, open look, the yellow hair a styled, thick shag framing an oval face, and contrasting dramatically with the Hispanic features. Except for those features she was the classic California girl. The kind who should have been lying face down in the Malibu sand, bikini top undone, smooth brown back exposed to the sun. A girl for cola commercials and custom van shows and running down to the market in halter and shorts for a six-pack. She shouldn't have ended up as savaged, lifeless flesh in a refrigerated drawer downtown.

Raquel Ochoa took the picture out of my hands and I thought I saw jealousy in her face.

'She's dead,' she said, putting it back in her purse, frowning, as if I'd committed some kind of heresy.

'It looked like they adored her,' I said.

'They did. Now they've brought in some old bag who doesn't give a damn about teaching. Now that Elena's—gone.'

She started to cry, using her napkin to shield her face from my eyes. Her thin shoulders shook. She sank lower in the booth, trying to disappear, sobbing.

I got up, moved to her side and put my arms around her. She felt as frail as a cobweb.

'No, no. I'm all right.' But she moved closer to me, burying herself in the folds of my jacket, burrowing in for the long, cold winter.

As I held her I realized that she felt good. She smelled good. This was a surprisingly soft, feminine person in my arms. I fantasized swooping her up, featherweight and vulnerable, carrying her to bed where I'd still her painful cries with that ultimate panacea: orgasm. A stupid fantasy because it would take more than a fuck and a hug to solve her problems. Stupid because that wasn't what this encounter was all about. I felt an annoying heat and tension in my groin. Tumescence rearing its ugly head when least appropriate. Still, I held her until her sobbing slowed and her breathing became regular. Thinking of Robin, I finally let her go and moved back to my side.

She avoided my eyes, took out her compact and fixed her face.

'That was really dumb.'

'No it wasn't. That's what eulogies are for.'

She thought for a moment then managed a faint smile.

157

'Yes, I suppose you're right.' She reached across the table and placed a small hand on mine. 'Thank you. I miss her so much.'

'I understand.'

'Do you?' She drew her hand away, suddenly cross.

'No, I guess not. I've never lost anyone to whom I was that close. Will you accept a serious attempt at empathy?'

"I'm sorry. I've been rude—from the moment you walked in. It's been so hard. All of these feelings—sadness, and emptiness and anger at the monster who did it—it had to be a monster, didn't it?'

'Yes.'

'Will you catch him? Will that big detective catch him?'

'He's a very capable guy, Raquel. In his own way, quite gifted. But he's got little to go on.'

'Yes. I suppose I should help you, shouldn't I?'

'It would be nice.'

She found a cigarette in her purse and lit it with trembling hands. She took a deep drag and let it out.

'What do you want to know?'

'For starts, how about the old cliché—did she have any enemies?'

'The clichéd answer: No. She was popular, well-liked. And besides, whoever did this to her was no acquaintance—we didn't know anyone like that.' She shuddered, confronting her own vulnerability.

'Did she go out with a lot of men?'

'The same questions.' She sighed. 'She dated a few guys before she met *him*. Then it was the two of them all the way.'

'When did she begin seeing him?'

'She started as a patient almost a year ago. It's hard to know when she began sleeping with him. She didn't talk to me about that kind of thing.'

I could imagine sexuality being a taboo topic for the two best friends. With their upbringing there was bound to be lots of conflict. And given what I had seen of Raquel and

158

heard about Elena it was almost certain they had gone about resolving those conflicts in different ways: one, the party girl, a man's woman; the other, attractive but perceiving herself in pitched battle with the world. I looked across the table at the dark, serious face and knew her bed would be ringed with thorns.

'Did she tell you they were having an affair?'

'An affair? That sounds so light and breezy. He violated his professional ethics and she fell for it.' She puffed on her cigarette. 'She giggled about if for a week or so then came out and told me what a wonderful guy he was. I put two and two together. A month later he picked her up at our place. It was out in the open.'

'What was he like?'

'Like you said before—a creep. Too well-dressed—velvet jackets, tailored pants, sunlamp tan, shirt unbuttoned to show lots of chest hair—curly gray chest hair. He smiled a lot and got familiar with me. Shook my hand and held on too long. Lingered with a good-bye kiss—nothing you could pin him on.' The words were almost identical to Roy Longstreth's.

'Slick?'

'Exactly. Slippery. She's gone for that type before. I couldn't understand it—she was such a good person, so real. I figured it had something to do with losing her dad at a young age. She had no good male role model. Does that sound plausible?'

'Sure.' Life was never as simple as the psych texts but it made people feel good to find solutions.

'He was a bad influence on her. When she started going with him was when she dyed her hair and changed her name and bought all those clothes. She even went out and bought a new car—one of those Datsun-Z turbos.'

'How did she afford it?' The car cost more than most teachers made in a year.

'If you're thinking he paid for it, forget it. She bought it on payments. That was another thing about Elena. She had

159

no conception of money. Just let it pass through her fingers. She always joked how she was going to have to marry a rich guy to accommodate her tastes.'

'How often did they see each other?'

'At first once or twice a week. By the end she might as well have moved in with him. I rarely saw her. She'd drop in to pick up a few things, invite me to go out with them.'

'Did you?'

She was surprised at the question.

'Are you kidding? I couldn't stand to be around him. And I have a life of my own. I had no need to be the odd one out.'

A life, I suspected, of grading papers until ten and then retiring, nightgown buttoned high, with a gothic novel and a cup of hot cocoa.

'Did they have friends, other couples with whom they associated?'

'I have no idea. I'm trying to tell you—I kept out of it.' An edge crept into her voice and I retreated.

'She started out as his patient. Do you have any idea why she went to a psychiatrist in the first place?'

'She said she was depressed.'

'You don't think she was?'

'It's hard to tell with some people. When I get depressed everyone knows about it. I withdraw, don't want anything to do with anybody. It's like I shrink, crawl into myself. With Elena, who knows? It's not like she had trouble eating or sleeping. She would just get a little quiet.'

'But she said she was depressed?'

'Not until after she told me she was seeing Handler—after I asked her why. She said she was feeling down, the work was getting to her. I tried to help but she said she needed more. I was never a big fan of psychiatrists and psychologists.' She smiled apologetically. 'If you have friends and family you should be able to work it out.'

'If that's enough, great. Sometimes it's like she said, Raquel. You need more.'

She put out her cigarette.

'Well, I suppose it's fortunate for you that many people agree with that.'

'I suppose so.'

There was an awkward silence. I broke it.

'Did he prescribe any medication for her?'

'Not as far as I know. Just talked to her. She went to see him weekly, and then twice a week after one of her students died. Then she was obviously depressed—cried for days.'

'When was this?'

'Let me see, it was pretty soon after she started going to Handler, maybe after they were already dating—I don't know. About eight months ago.'

'How did it happen?'

'Accident. Hit-and-run. The kid was walking along a dark road at night and a car hit him. It destroyed her. She'd been working with him for months. He was one of her miracles. Everyone thought he was mute. Elena got him to talk.' She shook her head. 'A miracle. And then to have it all go down the drain like that. So meaningless.'

'The parents must have been shattered.'

'No. There were no parents. He was an orphan. He came from La Casa.'

'La Casa de los Niños? In Malibu Canyon?'

'Sure. Why the surprise? They contract with us to provide special education to some of their kids. They do it with several of the local schools. It's part of a state-funded project or something. To mainstream children without families into the community.'

'No surprise,' I lied. 'It just seems so sad for something like that to happen to an orphan.'

'Yes. Life is unfair.' The declaration seemed to give her satisfaction.

She looked at her watch.

'Anything more? I've got to get back.'

'Just one. Do you recall the name of the child who died?'

'Nemeth. Cary or Corey. Something like that.'

161

'Thanks for your time. You've been helpful.'

'Have I? I don't see how. But I'm glad if it brings you closer to that monster.'

She had a concrete vision of the murderer that Milo would have envied.

We drove back to the school and I walked her to her car.

'Okay,' she said.

'Thanks again.'

'You're welcome. If you have more questions you can come back.' It was as forward as she was going to get—for her the equivalent of asking me over to her place. It made me sad, knowing there was nothing I could do for her.

'I will.'

She smiled and held out her hand. I took it, careful not to hold on for too long.

14

I'VE NEVER BEEN a big believer in coincidence. I suppose it's because the notion of life being governed by the random collision of molecules in space cuts at the heart of my professional identity. After all, why spend all those years learning how to help people change when deliberate change is just an illusion? But even if I had been willing to give the fates their due, it would have been hard to see as coincidence the fact that Cary or Corey Nemeth (deceased), a student of Elena Gutierrez (deceased), had been a resident of the same institution where Maurice Bruno (deceased) had volunteered.

It was time to learn more about La Casa de los Niños.

I went home and searched through the cardboard boxes I had stored in the garage since dropping out, until I found my old office Rolodex. I located Olivia Brickerman's number at the Department of Social Services and dialled it. A social worker for thirty years, Olivia knew more about agencies than anyone in the city.

A recording answered the phone and told me D.P.S.S.'s number had been changed. I dialled the new number and another recording told me to wait. A tape of

Barry Manilow came on the line. I wondered if the city paid him royalties. Music to wait for your caseworker by.

'D.P.S.S.'

'Mrs. Brickerman, please.'

'One moment, sir.' Two more minutes of Manilow. Then: 'She's no longer with this office.'

'Can you please tell me where I can locate her?'

'One moment.' I was informed, once again, who wrote the music that made the whole world sing. 'Mrs. Brickerman is now at the Santa Monica Psychiatric Medical Group.'

So Olivia had finally left the public domain.

'Do you have that number?'

'One moment, sir.'

'Thanks anyway.' I hung up and consulted the Yellow Pages under Mental Health Services. The number belonged to an address on Broadway where Santa Monica approached Venice, not far from Robin's studio. I called it.

'S.M.P.M.G.'

'Mrs. Olivia Brickerman, please.'

'Who shall I say is calling?'

'Dr. Delaware.'

'One moment.' The line was silent. Apparently the utility of phonehold Muzak hadn't become apparent to S.M.P.M.G.

'Alex! How are you?'

'Fine, Olivia, and you?'

'Wonderful, wonderful. I thought you were somewhere in the Himalayas.'

'Why's that?'

'Isn't that where people go when they want to find themselves—somewhere cold with no oxygen and a little old man with a beard sitting on top of a mountain munching on twigs and reading *People* magazine?'

'That was the sixties, Olivia. In the eighties you stay home and soak in hot water.'

164

'Ha!'

'How's Al?'

'His usual extroverted self. He was hunched over the board when I left this morning, muttering something about the Pakistani defence or some such *naarishkeit*.'

Her husband, Albert D. Brickerman, was the chess editor for the *Times*. In the five years I'd known him I hadn't heard him utter a dozen words in a row. It was difficult to imagine what he and Olivia, Miss Sociability of 1930 through '80, had in common. But they'd been married thirty-seven years, had raised four children, and seemed content with each other.

'So you finally left D.P.S.S.'

'Yes, can you believe it? Even barnacles can be dislodged!'

'What led to such an impulsive move?'

'I tell you, Alex, I would have stayed. Sure the system stank—what system doesn't? But I was used to it, like a wart. I like to think I was still doing a good job—though I tell you, the stories got sadder and longer. Such misery. And with cuts in funding the people would get less and less—and madder and madder. They took it out on the caseworkers. We had a girl stabbed in the downtown office. Now there're armed guards in every office. But what the hell, I was brought up in New York. Then my nephew, my sister's boy, Steve, he finished medical school and decided to become a psychiatrist—can you believe that, another mental health person in the family? His father's a surgeon and that was the safest way for him to rebel. Anyway, he's always been very close to me and it's been a running joke that when he goes into practice he was going to rescue Aunt Livvy from D.P.S.S. and take her into his office. And would you believe he took me up on it? Writes me a letter, tells me he's coming out to California and joining a group, and they need a social worker for intakes and short-term counselling, would I like to do

165

it? So here I am, with a view of the beach, working for little Stevie—of course I don't call him that in front of other people.'

'That's great, Olivia. You sound happy.'

'I am. I go down to the beach for lunch, read a book, get a tan. After twenty-two years I finally feel like I'm living in California. Maybe I'll take up roller-skating, huh?'

The image of Olivia, who was built somewhat like Alfred Hitchcock, whizzing by on skates, made me laugh.

'Ah, you scoff now. Just wait!' She chuckled. 'Now, enough autobiography. Whan can I do for you?'

'I need some information on a place called La Casa de los Niños, in Malibu.'

'McCaffrey's place? You thinking of sending someone there?'

'No. It's a long story.'

'Listen, if it's that long why don't you give me a chance to dig in my files? Come over the house tonight and I'll give it to you in person. I'll be baking and Albert will be meditating over the board. We haven't seen you in a long time.'

'What are you baking?'

'Strudel, pirogis, fudge brownies.'

'I'll be over. What time?'

'Eightish. You remember the place?'

'It hasn't been that long, Olivia.'

'It's been twice as long. Listen, I don't want to be a yenta, but if you don't have a girlfriend there's a young lady—also a psychologist—who just came to work here. Very cute. The two of you would have brilliant children.'

'Thanks, but I've got someone.'

'Terrific. Bring her along.'

The Brickermans lived on Hayworth, not far from the

166

Fairfax district, in a small beige stucco house with Spanish tile roof. Olivia's mammoth Chrysler was parked in the driveway.

'What am I doing here, Alex?' Robin asked as we approached the front door.

'Do you like chess?'

'Don't know how to play.'

'Don't worry about it. This is one house where you don't have to be concerned about what to say. You'll be lucky if you get a chance to talk. Eat brownies. Enjoy yourself.'

I gave her a kiss and rang the doorbell.

Olivia answered it. She looked the same—maybe a few pounds heavier—her hair a hennaed frizz, her face rosy-cheeked and open. She was wearing a shift, a Hawaiian print, and ripples went through it as she laughed. She spread her hands and hugged me to a bosom the size and consistency of a small sofa.

'Alex!' She released me and held me at arm's length. 'No more beard—you used to resemble D.H. Lawrence. Now you look like a graduate student.' She turned and smiled at Robin. I introduced them.

'Pleased to meet you. You're very lucky, he's a darling boy.'

Robin blushed.

'Come in.'

The house was redolent with good, sweet baking smells. Al Brickerman, a prophet with white hair and beard, sat hunched over an ebony-and-maple chessboard in the living room. He was surrounded by clutter—books in shelves and on the floor, bric-a-brac, photographs of children and grandchildren, menorahs, souvenirs, over-stuffed furniture, an old robe and slippers.

'Al, Alex and his friend are here.'

'Hmm.' He grunted and raised his hand, never averting his eyes from the pieces on the board.

'Nice to see you again, Al.'

167

'Hmm.'

'He's a real schizoid,' Olivia confided to Robin, 'but he's dynamite in bed.'

She ushered us into the kitchen. The room was the same as it had been when the house had been built forty years ago: yellow tile with maroon borders, narrow porcelain sink, window sills filled with potted plants. The refrigerator and stove were vintage Kenmore. A ceramic sign hung over the doorway leading out to the service porch: *How Can You Soar Like An Eagle When You're Surrounded by Turkeys?*

Olivia saw me looking at it.

'My going-away present when I left D.P.S.S. To myself from myself.' She brought over a plate of brownies, still warm.

'Here, have some before I eat them. Look at this—I'm growing obese.' She patted her rear.

'More to love,' I told her and she pinched my cheek.

'Mmm. These are great,' Robin said.

'A woman with taste. Here, sit down.'

We pulled up chairs around the kitchen table, the plate set down before us. Olivia checked the oven and then she joined us. 'In about ten minutes you'll have strudel. Apples, raisins and figs. The latter an improvisation for Albert.' She crooked a thumb toward the living room. 'The system gets clogged, from time to time. Now then you want to know about Casa de los Niños. Not that it's any of my business but could you tell my why?'

'It has to do with some work I'm doing for the police department.'

'The police? You.'

I told her about the case, leaving out the gory details. She had met Milo before—they'd hit it off marvellously—but hadn't been aware of the extent of our friendship.

'He's a nice boy. You should find him a nice woman

168

like you found for yourself.' She smiled at Robin and handed her another brownie.

'I don't think that would work, Olivia. He's gay.'

It didn't stop her, only slowed her down. 'So? Find him a nice young man.'

'He's got one.'

'Good. Forgive me, Robin, I tend to run off at the mouth. It's all those hours I spend with clients listening and nodding and saying uh-huh. Then I get home and you can imagine the depth of conversational interplay I get with Prince Albert. Anyway, Alex, these questions about La Casa, Milo asked you to ask them?'

'Not exactly. I'm followng my own leads.'

She looked at Robin.

'Philip Marlowe here?'

Robin gave her a helpless look.

'Is this dangerous, Alex?'

'No. I just want to look into a few things.'

'You be careful, you understand?' She squeezed my bicep. She had a grip like a bouncer. 'Make sure he's careful, darling.'

'I try, Olivia. I can't control him.'

'I know. These psychologists, they get so used to being in a position of authority they can't take advice. Let me tell you about this handsome fellow. I first met him when he was an intern assigned for three weeks to D.P.S.S. to teach him what life was like for people without money. He started out as a wise guy but I could tell he was special. He was the smartest thing on two feet. And he had compassion. His big problem was he was too hard on himself, he drove himself. He was doing twice as much work as anyone else and he thought he was doing nothing. I wasn't surprised when he took off like a missile, the fancy title and the books and all that. But I was worried he was going to burn himself out.'

'You were right, Olivia,' I admitted.

'I thought he went to the Himalayas, or something,'

169

she laughed, continuing to address Robin. 'To get frozen so he could come back and appreciate California. Have more, both of you.'

'I'm stuffed.' Robin touched her flat tummy.

'You're probably right—keep the figure, if you have it. Me, I started out like a barrel, nothing to maintain. Tell me darling, do you love him?'

Robin looked at me. She put her arm around my neck. 'I do.'

'Fine, I pronounce you husband and wife. Who cares what he says?'

She got up and went to the oven, peering through the glass window.

'Still a few more minutes. I think the figs take longer to bake.'

'Olivia, about La Casa de los Niños?'

She sighed and her bosom sighed along with her. 'Okay. You're obviously serious about playing policeman.' She sat down. 'After you called I went into my old files and pulled out what I could find. You want coffee?'

'Please,' said Robin.

'I'll have some too.'

She came back with three steaming mugs, cream and sugar on a porcelain tray upon which had been silk-screened a panorama of Yellowstone Park.

'This is delicious, Olivia,' Robin said, sipping.

'Kona. From Hawaii. This dress is from there, too. My younger son, Gabriel, he's there. He's in import-export. Does very well.'

'Olivia—'

'Yes, yes, okay. La Casa de los Niños. The Children's Home. Started in 1974 by the Reverend Augustus McCaffrey, as a place of refuge for children with no home. That's right off the brochure.'

'Do you have the brochure with you?'

170

'No, it's at the office. You want me to mail you a copy?'

'Don't bother. What kind of kids stay there?'

'Abused and neglected children, orphans, some status offenders—you know runaways. They used to put them in jail or the CYA but those places got too crowded with fourteen-year-old murderers and rapists and robbers, so now they try to find foster placement for them or a place like La Casa. In general these institutions get the kids nobody wants, the ones they can't find foster placement or adoptive homes for. Lots of them have physical and psychological problems—spastic, blind, deaf, retarded. Or they're too old to be attractive adoptees. There are also the children of women in prison—mostly junkies and alcoholics. We tried to place them with individual families, but often nobody wanted them. To sum up, dear: chronic wards of the Dependency Court.'

'How's a place like that funded?'

'Alex, the way the state and federal systems are set up, an operator can pull in over a thousand dollars a month per child if he knows how to bill it right. Kids with disabilities bring in more—you get paid for all the special services. On top of that I hear McCaffrey's terrific at bringing in private donations. He's got connections—the land the place is on is an example. Twenty acres in Malibu, used to belong to the government. They interned the Japanese there during World War II. Then it was used as a labour camp for first offenders—embezzlers, politicians, that type. He got the county to give it to him on long-term lease. Ninety-nine years with token rent.'

'He must be a good talker.'

'He is. A good old boy. Used to be a missionary down in Mexico. I hear he ran a similar place there.'

'Why'd he move back up?'

'Who knows? Maybe he got tired of not drinking the

171

water? Maybe he longed for Kentucky Fried Chicken—although I hear they've got it down there now.'

'What about the place? Is it a good one?'

'None of those places is utopia, Alex. The ideal would be a little house in suburbia with a picket fence around it, gingham curtains and a green lawn, Mommy and Daddy and Rover the Dog. The reality is that there are over seventeen thousand kids on the Dependency Court docket in L.A. county alone. Seventeen thousand unwanted children! And they're piling into the system faster than they can be—here's a terrible word—processed.'

'That's unbelievable,' said Robin. She had a troubled look on her face.

'We've turned into a society of child-haters, darling. More and more abuse and neglect. People have kids and then change their minds. Parents don't want to take responsibility for them so they shunt them over to the government—how's that from an old Socialist, Alex? And abortion—I hope this doesn't offend you, because I'm for liberation as much if not more than the next woman. I was screaming for equal pay before Gloria Steinem went through puberty. But let's face it, this wholesale abortion we've got is just another form of birth control, another way out for people to avoid their responsibility. And it's killing kids, at least in some sense, isn't it? Maybe it's better than having them and then trying to get rid of them—I don't know.' She wiped the sweat from her forehead and dabbed at her upper lip with a paper napkin . 'Excuse me, that was a tedious polemic.'

She stood up and smoothed down her dress.

'Let me check the strudel.'

She came back with a steaming platter. 'Blow on it, it's hot.'

Robin and I looked at each other.

172

'You look so serious, I ruined your appetite with my polemic, didn't I?'

'No, Olivia.' I took a slab of strudel and ate a bite. 'It's delicious and I agree with you.'

Robin looked grave. We'd discussed the abortion issue many times, never resolving anything.

'In answer to your question, is it a good place, I can only say that we had no complaints when I was with D.P.S.S. They offer the basics, it looked clean, the area is certainly nice—most of those kids never saw a mountain except on TV. They bus the kids to the public schools when they have special needs. Otherwise they've got in-house teaching. I doubt if anyone helps them with their homework—it's certainly not "Father Knows Best" over there, but McCaffrey keeps the place up, pushes for lots of community involvement. That means public exposure. Why do you want to know so much about it, you think that kid's death was suspicious?'

'No. There's no reason to suspect anything.' I thought about her question. 'I guess I'm just fishing.'

'Well don't go fishing for minnows and come up with a shark, darling.'

We nibbled at the strudel. Olivia called into the living room:

'Al, you want some strudel—with the figs?'

There was no answer I could hear, but she put some pastry on a plate nonetheless and brought it into him.

'She's a nice lady,' said Robin.

'One in a million. And very tough.'

'And smart. You should listen to her when she says to be careful. Alex, please leave the detecting to Milo.'

'I'll take care of myself, don't worry.' I took her hand but she pulled away. I was about to say something but Olivia returned to the kitchen

'The dead man—the salesman, you said he volunteered at La Casa?'

'Yes. He had a certificate in his office.'

173

'He was probably a member of the Gentlemen's Brigade. It's something dreamed up by McCaffrey to get the business community involved with the place. He gets corporations to get their executives to volunteer weekend time with the kids. How much of it is voluntary on the part of the "Gentlemen" and how much is the result of pressure from the boss I don't know. McCaffrey give them blazers and lapel pins and certificates signed by the mayor. They also get brownie points with their bosses. Hopefully the kids get something out of it too.'

I thought of Bruno, the psychopath, working with homeless children.

'Is there any sort of screening?'

'The usual. Interviews, some paper-and-pencil tests. You know, dear boy, what that kind of thing is worth.'

I nodded.

'Still, like I said, we never got any complaints. I'd have to give the place a B-minus, Alex. The major problem is that it's too big of an operation for the kids to get any personalized attention. A good foster home would definitely be preferable to having four to five hundred kids in one place at the same time—that's how many he's got. Aside from that, La Casa is as good as any.'

'That's good to hear.' But in some perverse way I was disappointed. It would have been nice to find out that the place was a hellhole. Anything to connect it with the three murders. Of course that meant misery for four hundred children. Was I becoming just another member of the child-hating society Olivia had described? Suddenly the strudel tasted like sugar-coated paper and the kitchen seemed oppressively hot.

'So, is there anything else you want to know?'

'No. Thanks.'

'Now, darling.' She turned to Robin. 'Tell about yourself and how you met this impetuous fellow...'

174

We left an hour later. I put my arm around Robin. She let it lay there but was unresponsive. We walked to the car in silence as uncomfortable as a stranger's shoes.

Inside, I asked her:

'What's wrong?'

'Why did you bring me here tonight?'

'I just thought it would be nice...'

'Nice talking about murder and child abuse? Alex, that was no social call.'

I had nothing to say so I started the car and pulled away from the curb.

'I'm worried sick about you,' she said. 'The things you were describing in there were hideous. What she said about sharks is true. You're like a little boy adrift on a raft in the middle of the ocean. Oblivious to what's going on around you.'

'I know what I'm doing.'

'Right.' She looked out the window.

'What's wrong with my wanting to get involved in something other than hot tubs and jogging?'

'Nothing. But why can't it be something a little less hazardous than playing Sherlock Holmes? Something you know something about?'

'I'm a fast learner.'

She ignored me. We cruised through darkened empty streets. A light drizzle speckled the windshield.

'I don't enjoy hearing about people getting their faces bashed in. Or children run down by hit-run drivers, she said.

'That's part of what's out there.' I motioned toward the blackness of the night.

'Well, I don't want any part of it!'

'What you're saying is you'll go along for the ride as long as it's pretty.'

'Oh, Alex! Stop being so damned melodramatic— that's right out of a soap opera.'

'It's true, though, isn't it?'

175

'No, it's not—and don't try to put me on the defensive. I want the man I first met—someone who was satisfied with himself and not so full of insecurity that he had to run around trying to prove himself. That was what attracted me to you. Now you're like a—a man possessed. Since you've gotten involved in your little intrigues you haven't been there for me. I talk and your mind is somewhere else. It's like I told you before—you're going back to the bad old days.'

There was something to that. The last few mornings had found me waking up early with a taut sense of urgency in my gut, the old obsessive drive to take care of business. Funny thing was, I didn't want to let go of it.

'I promise you,' I told her, 'I'll be careful.'

She shook her head in frustration, leaned forward and switched on the radio. Loud.

When we got to her door she gave me a chaste peck on the cheek.

'Can I come in?'

She stared at me for a long moment and gave a resigned smile.

'Oh, hell, why not?'

Upstairs in the loft I watched her undress in the meagre share of moonbeam admitted by the skylight. She stood on one foot, undoing her sandal, and her breasts swung low. A diagonal stroke of illumination turned her white, then gray as she pivoted, then invisible as the slipped under the covers. I reached out for her, aroused, and pulled her hand down toward me. She touched me for a second, then removed her fingers, moved them upward, let them settle around my neck. I buried myself in the sanctuary between her shoulder and the arching sweetness under her chin.

We fell asleep that way.

In the morning her side of the bed was empty. I heard

176

rumbling and grinding and knew she was downstairs in the shop.

I got dressed, descended the narrow stairs and joined her. She was wearing bib overalls and a man's work shirt. Her mouth was covered with a bandanna, her eyes goggled.

The air was full of wood dust.

'I'll call you later,' I shouted over the din of the table saw.

She stopped for a moment, waved, then resumed working. I left her surrounded by her tools, her machines, her art.

15

I CALLED MILO at the station and gave him a full report of my interview with Raquel Ochoa and the Casa de los Niños connection, including the information given to me by Olivia.

'I'm impressed,' he said. 'You missed your calling.'

'So what do you think? Shouldn't this McCaffrey be looked into?'

'Wait a minute, friend. The man takes care of four hundred kids and one of them is killed in an accident. That's not evidence of major mayhem.'

'But that kid happended to be a student of Elena Gutierrez. Which means she probably discussed him with Handler. Not long after his death Bruno began volunteerring at the place. A coincidence?'

'Probably not. But you don't understand the way things work around here. I am in the toilet with this case. So far those bank records are showing nothing—everything in both the accounts looks kosher. I've got more work to do on it, but singlehanded it takes time. Every day the captain looks me up and down with that *no-progress, Sturgis?* stare. I feel like a kid who hasn't done his homework. I

178

expect him to pull me off the case any day and stick me on some garbage detail.'

'If things are so screwed up I'd expect you to jump for joy at the prospect of a new lead.'

'That's right. A lead. Not conjecture or a string of flimsy associations.'

'They don't look that damned flimsy to me.'

'Look at it this way—I start snooping around about McCaffrey, who's got connections from Downtown all the way to Malibu. He places a few strategic phone calls— no one can accuse him of obstructing justice because I've got no legitimate reason to be investigating him—and I'm yanked off the case faster than you can spit.'

'All right,' I conceded, 'but what about the Mexican thing? The guy was down there for years. Then all of a sudden he leaves, surfaces in L.A., and becomes a hotshot.'

'Upward mobility is no felony, and sometimes a cigar is a cigar, Dr. Freud.'

'Shit. I can't stand it when you get overly cute.'

'Alex, please. My life is far from rosy. I don't need crap from you on top of it all.'

I seemed to be developing a talent for alienating those close to me. I had yet to call Robin, to find out where last night's dreams had led her.

'I'm sorry. I guess I'm over-involved.'

He didn't argue.

'You've done good work. Been a big help. Sometimes things don't fall into place just because you do a good job.'

'So what are you going to do? Drop it?'

'No. I'll look into McCaffrey's background—quietly. Especially the Mexican bit. I'm going to continue sifting through Handler and Bruno's financial records and I'll add Gutierrez's to that. I'm even going to call the Malibu Sheriff Station and get copies of the accident report on that kid. What did you say his name was?'

179

'Nemeth.'

'Fine. That should be easy enough.'

'Is there anything else you want from me?'

'What? Oh. No, nothing. You've done a great job, Alex. I want you to know I really mean that. I'll take it from here. Why don't you take it easy for a while?'

'Okay,' I said without enthusiasm. 'But keep me posted.'

'I will,' he promised. 'Bye.'

The voice on the other end was female and very professional. It greeted me with the sing-song lilt of a detergent jingle, an isn't-life-wonderful buoyancy that bordered on the obscene.

'Good morning! La Casa!'

'Good morning. I'd like to speak to someone about becoming a member of the Gentlemen's Brigade.'

'Just one moment, sir!'

In twenty seconds a male voice came on the line.

'Tim Kruger. Can I help you?'

'I'd like to talk about joining the Gentlemen's Brigade.'

'Yes, sir. And what corporation do you represent?'

'None. I'm inquiring as an individual.'

'Oh. I see.' The voice lost a touch of its friendliness. Disruption of routine did that to some people—threw them off, made them wary.

'And your name, please.'

'Dr. Alexander Delaware.'

It must have been the title that did it because he shifted gears again, immediately.

'Good morning, Doctor, How are you today?'

'Just fine, thank you.'

'Terrific. And what kind of doctor are you, if I might ask.'

You might.

'Child psychologist. Retired.'

'Excellent. We don't get many mental health pro-

180

fessionals volunteering. I'm an M.F.C.C. myself, in charge of screening and counselling at La Casa.'

'I'd imagine most of them would consider it too much like work,' I said. 'Being away from the field for a while, the idea of working with children again appeals to me.'

'Wonderful. And what led you to La Casa?'

'Your reputation. I've heard you do good work. And you're well organized.'

'Well, thank you, Doctor. We *do* try to do well by our kids!'

'I'm sure you do.'

'We give group tours for prospective Gentlemen. The next one is scheduled a week from this Friday.'

'Let me check my calendar.' I left the phone, looked out the window, did a half-dozen knee bends, and came back. 'I'm sorry, Mr. Kruger. That's a bad day for me. When's the next one?'

'Three weeks later.'

'That's such a long way off. I was hoping to get going sooner.' I tried to sound wistful and just a little impatient.

'Hmm. Well, Doctor, if you don't mind something a bit more impromptu than the group orientation, I can give you a personalized tour. There'll be no way to assemble the video show in time, but as a psychologist you know a lot of that stuff, anyway.'

'That sounds just fine.'

'In fact, if you're free this afternoon, I could arrange it for then. Reverend Gus is here today—he likes to meet all potential Gentlemen—and that's not always the case, what with his travel schedule. He's taping Merv Griffin this week, then flying to New York for an "A.M. America".'

He imparted the news of McCaffrey's television activities with the solemnity of a crusader unveiling the Holy Grail.

'Today would be perfect.'

'Excellent. Around three?'

'Three it is.'

'Do you know where we are?'

'Not exactly. In Malibu?'

'In Malibu Canyon.' He gave me directions, then added: 'While you're there you can fill out our screening questionnaires. It would be a formality in a case such as yours, Doctor, but we do have to go through the motions. Though I don't imagine psychological tests would be very valid for screening a psychologist, would they?'

'I don't imagine so. We write 'em, we can subvert 'em.'

He laughed, straining to be collegial.

'Any other questions?'

'I don't think so.'

'Terrific. I'll see you at three.'

Malibu is as much an image as it is a place. The image is beamed into the living rooms of America on TV, splashed across the movie screen, etched into the grooves of LP's and emblazoned on the covers of trashy paperbacks. The image is one of endless stretches of sand; oiled, naked brown bodies; volleyball on the beach; sun-bleached hair; making love under a blanket with coital cadence timed to match the in-and-out of the tide; million-dollar shacks that teeter on pilings sunken into terra that isn't firma and, in fact, does the hula after a hard rain; Corvettes, seaweed and cocaine.

All of that is valid. But limited.

There's another Malibu, a Malibu that encompasses the canyons and dirt roads that struggle through the Santa Monica mountain range. This Malibu has no ocean. What little water it does possess comes in the form of streams that trickle through shaded gullies and disappear when the temperature rises. There are some houses in this Malibu, situated near the main canyon road, but there remain miles of wilderness. There are still mountain lions roaming the more remote regions of this Malibu, and packs of coyotes that prowl at night, making off with a chicken, a possum, a fat toad. There are shady groves

182

where the tree frogs breed so abundantly that you step into them thinking your foot is resting on soft, gray earth. Until it moves. There are lots of snakes—kings, garters and rattlers—in this Malibu. And secluded ranches where people live under the illusion that the latter half of the twentieth century never occurred. Bridle trails punctuated by steaming mounds of horse droppings. Goats. Tarantulas.

There are also lots of rumours surrounding the second, beachless Malibu. Of ritual murders carried out by Satanic cults. Of bodies that will never—can never be found. Of people lost while hiking and never heard from again. Horror stories, but perhaps just as valid as Beach Blanket Bingo.

I turned off Pacific Coast Highway, up Rambla Pacifica, and traversed the boundary from one Malibu to the other. The Seville climbed the steep grade with ease. I had Django Reinhardt on the tape deck and the music of the Gypsy was in synch with the emptiness that unfolded before my windshield—the serpentine ribbon of highway, assaulted by the relentless Pacific sun one moment and shaded by giant eucalyptus the next. A dehydrated ravine to one side, a sheer drop into space on the other. A road that urged the weary traveller to keep going, that offered promises it could never keep.

I had slept fitfully the night before, thinking of Robin and myself, seeing the faces of children—Melody Quinn, the countless patients I had treated over the last ten years, the remains of a boy named Nemeth, who had died just a few miles up this same road. What had been his last vision, I wondered, what impulse had crossed a crucial synapse at the last possible moment before a giant machine-monster roared down on him from nowhere...And what had led him to walk this lonesome stretch of road in the dead of night?

Now, fatigue, nursed by the monotony of the journey, was tracing a slow but inexorable passage along my spine, so that I had to fight to remain alert. I turned the music louder and opened all the windows in the car. The air smelled clean, but tinged with the odour of something burning—a distant bridge?

So occupied was I in the struggle for clarity of consciousness that I almost missed the sign the county had erected announcing the exit for La Casa de los Niños in two miles.

The turnoff itself was easy to miss, only a few hundred yards past a hairpin bend in the road. The road was narrow, barely wide enough for two vehicles to pass in opposite directions, and heavily shadowed by trees. It rose a half-mile at an unrelenting incline, steep enough to discourage any but the most purposeful foot traveller. Clearly the site had never been meant to attract the walk-in trade. Perfect for a labour camp, work farm, detention centre, or any nexus of activity not meant for the prying eyes of strangers.

The access road ended at a twelve-foot-high-barrier of chain link. Four-foot-high letters spelled out La Casa de los Niños in polished aluminium. A hand-painted sign of two huge hands holding four children—white, black, brown and yellow—rose to the right. A guardhouse was ten feet on the other side of the fence. The uniformed man inside took note of me, then spoke to me through a squawk box attached to the gate.

'Can I help you?' The voice came out steely and mechanical, like human utterance pureed into bytes, fed into a computer and regurgitated.

'Dr. Delaware. Here for a three o'clock appointment with Mr. Kruger.'

The gate slid open.

The Seville was allowed a brief roll until it was stopped by an orange and white striped mechanical arm.

'Good afternoon, Doctor.'

The guard was young, mustachioed, solemn. His uniform was dark gray, matching his stare. The sudden smile didn't fool me. He was looking me over.

'You'll be meeting Tim at the administration building. That's straight up this way and take the road to the left. You can park in the visitors' lot.'

'Thank you.'

'You're quite welcome, Doctor.'

He pushed a button and the striped arm rose in salute.

The administration building looked like it had once served a similar purpose during the days of Japanese internment. It had the low-slung, angry look of military architecture, but there was no doubt that the paint job— a mural of a baby blue sky filled with cotton candy clouds—was a contemporary creation.

The front office was panelled in cheap imitation oak and occupied by a grandmotherly type in a colourless cotton smock.

I announced myself and received a grandmotherly smile for my efforts.

'Tim will be right with you. Won't you please sit down and make yourself comfortable.'

There was little of interest to look at. The prints on the walls looked as if they'd been purloined from a motel. There was a window but it afforded a view of the parking lot. In the distance was a thick growth of forest—eucalyptus, cypress, and cedar—but from where I sat only the bottoms of the trees were visible, an uninterrupted stretch of gray-brown. I tried to busy myself with a two-year-old copy of *California Highways*.

It wasn't much of a wait.

A minute after I'd sat down the door opened and a young man came out.

'Dr. Delaware?'

I stood.

'Tim Kruger.' We shook hands.

He was short, mid-to-late twenties, and built like a

185

wrestler, all hard and knobby and endowed with just that extra bit of muscle in all the strategic places. He had a face that was well-formed, but overly stolid, like a Ken doll that hadn't been allowed to bake sufficiently. Strong chin, small ears, prominent straight nose of a shape that foreshadowed bulbousness in middle age, an out-doorsman's tan, yellowish-brown eyes under heavy brows, a low forehead almost totally hidden by a thick wave of sandy hair. He wore wheat-coloured slacks, a light blue short-sleeved shirt and a blue-and-brown tie. Clipped to the corner of his collar was a badge that said T. Kruger, M.A., M.F.C.C., Director, Counselling.

'I was expecting someone quite a bit older, Doctor. You told me you were retired.'

'I am. I believe in taking it early, when I can enjoy it.' He laughed heartily.

'There's something to be said for that. I trust you had no trouble finding us?'

'No. Your directions were excellent.'

'Great. We can begin the tour, if you'd like. Reverend Gus is on the grounds somewhere. He should be back to meet you by four.'

He held the door for me.

We crossed the parking lot and stepped onto a walkway of crushed gravel.

'La Casa,' he began, 'is situated on twenty-seven acres. If we stop right here, we can get a pretty good view of the entire layout.'

We were at the top of a rise, looking down on buildings, a playground, spiralling trails, a curtain of mountains in the background.

'Out of those twenty-seven, only five are actually fully developed. The rest is wide-open space, which we believe is great for the kids, many of whom come from the inner city.' I could make out the shapes of children, walking in groups, playing ball, sitting alone on the grass. 'To the north'—he pointed to an expanse of open fields—'is what

186

we call the Meadow. It's mostly alfalfa and weeds right now, but there are plans to begin a vegetable garden this summer. To the south is the Grove.' He indicated the forest I'd seen from the office. 'It's protected timberland, perfect for nature hikes. There's a surprising abundance of wildlife out there. I'm from the Northwest, myself, and before I got here I used to think the wildest life in L.A. was all on the Sunset Strip.'

I smiled.

'Those buildings over there are the dorms.'

He swivelled around and pointed to a group of ten large quonset huts. Like the administration building, they'd been gone at with the freewheeling paint brush, the corrugated iron sides festooned with rainbow-hued patterns, the effect bizarrely optimistic.

He turned again and I let my gaze follow his arm.

'That's our Olympic-sized pool. Donated by Majestic Oil.' The pool shimmered green, a hole in the earth filled with lime jello. A solitary swimmer sliced through the water, cutting a foamy pathway. 'And over there are the infirmary and the school.'

I noticed a grouping of cinder-block buildings at the far end of the campus where the perimeter of the central hub met the edge of the 'Grove.' He didn't say what they were.

'Let's take a look at the dorms.'

I followed him down the hill, taking in the idyllic panorama. The grounds were well-tended, the place bustling with activity but seemingly well-organized.

Kruger walked with long, muscular strides, chin to the wind, rattling off facts and figures, describing the philosophy of the institution as one that combined "structure and the reassurance of routine with a creative environment that encourages healthy development". He was resolutely positive—about La Casa, his job, the Reverend Gus, and the children. The sole exception was a grave lament about the difficulties of coordinating "optimal

187

care" with running the financial affairs of the institution on a day-to-day basis. Even this was followed, however, by a statement stressing his understanding of economic realities in the eighties and a few upbeat paeans to the free-enterprise system.

He was well-trained.

The interior of the bright pink quonset hut was cold, flat white over a dark plank floor. The dorm was empty and our footsteps echoed. There was a metallic smell in the air. The children's beds were iron double bunks arranged, barracks style, perpendicular to the walls, accompanied by foot lockers and bracket shelves bolted to the metal siding. There was an attempt at decoration— some of the children had hung up pictures of comic book superheroes, athletes, Sesame Street characters—but the absence of family pictures or other evidence of recent, intimate human connection was striking.

I counted sleeping space for fifty children.

'How do you keep that many kids organized?'

'It's a challenge,' he admitted, 'but we've been pretty successful. We use volunteer counsellors from UCLA, Northridge, and other colleges. They get intro psych credit, we get free help. We'd love a full time professional staff but it's fiscally impossible. We've got it staffed two counsellors to a dorm, and we train them to use behaviour mod—I hope you're not opposed to that.'

'Not if it's used properly.'

'Oh, very definitely. I couldn't agree with you more. We minimize heavy aversives, use token economies, lots of positive reinforcements. It requires supervision—that's where I come in.'

'You seem to have a good handle on things.'

'I try.' He gave an aw, shucks grin. 'I wanted to go for a doctorate but I didn't have the bucks.'

'Where were you studying?'

'U. of Oregon. I got an M.A. there—in counselling ed. Before that, a B.A. in psych from Jedson College.'

188

'I thought everyone at Jedson was rich.' The small college outside of Seattle had a reputation as a haven for the offspring of the wealthy.

'That's almost true,' he grinned. 'The place was a country club. I got in on an athletic scholarship. Track and baseball. In my junior year I tore a ligament and suddenly I was *persona non grata*.' His eyes darkened momentarily, smouldering with the memory of almost-buried injustice. 'Anyway, I like what I'm doing—plenty of responsibility and decision-making.'

There was a rustling sound at the far end of the room. We both turned toward it and saw movement beneath the blankets of one of the lower bunks.

'Is that you, Rodney?'

Kruger walked to the bunk and tapped a wriggling lump. A boy sat up, holding the covers up to his chin. He was chubby, black and looked around twelve, but his exact age was impossible to gauge, for his face bore the telltale stigmata of Down's syndrome: elongated cranium, flattened features, deep-set eyes spaced close together, sloping brow, low-set ears, protruding tongue. And an expression of bafflement so typical of the retarded.

'Hello, Rodney.' Kruger spoke softly. 'What's the matter?'

I had followed him and the boy looked at me questioningly.

'It's all right, Rodney. He's a friend. Now tell me what's the matter.'

'Rodney sick.' The words were slurred.

'What kind of sickness?'

'Tummy hurt.'

'Hmm. We'll have to have the doctor look at you when he makes his visit.'

'No!' the boy screamed. 'No docka!'

'Now, Rodney!' Kruger was patient. 'If you're sick you're going to have to get a checkup.'

'No docka!'

'All right, Rodney, all right.' Kruger spoke soothingly. He reached out and touched the boy softly on the top of the head. Rodney went hysterical. His eyes popped out and his chin trembled. He cried out and lurched backward so quickly that he hit the rear of his head on the metal bedpost. He yanked the covers over his face, uttering an unintelligible wail of protest.

Kruger turned to me and sighed. He waited until the boy calmed down and then spoke to him again.

'We'll discuss the doctor later, Rodney. Now where are you supposed to be? Where's your group right now?'

'Snack.'

'Aren't you hungry?'

The boy shook his head.,

'Tummy hurts.'

'Well you can't just lie here by yourself. Either come to the infirmary and we'll call someone to have a look at you or get up and join your group for snack.'

'No docka.'

'Okay. No doctor. Now get up.'

The boy crawled out of bed, away from us. I could see now that he was older than I'd thought. Sixteen at least, with the beginning of beard growth dotting his chin. He stared at me, eyes wide in fright.

'This is a friend, Rodney. Mr. Delaware.'

'Hello, Rodney.' I held out my hand. He looked at it and shook his head.

'Be friendly, Rodney. That's how we earn our goodie points, remember?'

A shake of the head.

'Come on, Rodney, shake hands.'

But the retarded boy was resolute. When Kruger took a step forward he retreated, holding his hands in front of his face.

It went on that way for several moments, a flat-out contest of wills. Finally Kruger gave in.

190

'Okay, Rodney,' he said softly, 'we'll forget social skills for today because you're ill. Now run along and join your group.'

The boy backed away from us, circling the bed in a wide arc. Still shaking his head and holding his arms in front of him like a punchy fighter, he moved away. When he was close to the door he turned, bolted and half-ran, half-waddled out, disappearing into the sun's glare.

Kruger turned to me and smiled weakly.

'He's one of our more difficult ones. Seventeen and functioning like a three-year-old.'

'He seems to be really afraid of doctors.'

'He's afraid of lots of things. Like most Down's kids he's had plenty of medical problems—cardiac, infections, dental complications. Add that to the distorted thinking going on in that little head and it builds up. Have you had much experience with m.r.'s?'

'Some.'

'I've worked with hundreds of them and I can't remember one who didn't have serious emotional problems. You know, the public thinks they're just like any other kids, but slower. It ain't so.'

A trace of irritation had crept into his voice. I put it down to the humiliation of losing at psychic poker to the retarded boy.

'Rodney's come a long way,' he said. 'When he first got here he wasn't even toilet-trained. After thirteen foster homes.' He shook his head. 'It's really pathetic. Some of the people the county gives kids to aren't fit to raise dogs, let alone children.'

He looked ready to launch into a speech, but stopped and slipped his smile back on quickly. 'Many of the kids we get are low-probability adoption cases—m.r., defective, mixed race, in and out of foster homes, or thrown on the trash heap by their families. When they come here they have no conception of socially appropriate behaviour, hygiene, or basic day-to-day living skills. Quite often

191

we're starting from ground zero. But we're pleased at our progress. One of the students is publishing a study on our results.'

'That's a great way to collect data.'

'Yes. And quite frankly, it helps us raise money, which is often the bottom line, Doctor, when you want to keep a great place like La Casa going. Come on.' He took my arm. 'Let's see the rest of the grounds.'

We headed toward the pool.

'From what I hear,' I said, 'Reverend McCaffrey is an excellent fund-raiser.'

Kruger gave me a sidelong glance, evaluating the intent of my words.

'He is. He's a marvellous person and it comes across. And it takes most of his time. But it's still difficult. You know, he ran another children's home in Mexico, but he had to close it down. There was no government support and the attitude of the private sector there was let the peasants starve.'

We were poolside now. The water reflected the forest, green-black dappled with streaks of emerald. There was a strong odour of chlorine mixed with sweat. The lone swimmer was still in the water doing laps—using a butter-fly stroke with a lot of muscle behind it.

'Hey, Jimbo!' Kruger called.

The swimmer reached the far end, raised his head out of the water and saw the counsellor's wave. He glided effortlessly toward us and pulled himself waist-high out of the water. He was in his early forties, bearded and sinewy. His sun-baked body was covered with wet, matted hair.

'Hey, Tim.'

'Dr. Delaware, this is Jim Halstead, our head coach. Jim, Dr. Alexander Delaware.'

'Actually your only coach.' Halstead spoke in a deep voice that emerged from his abdomen. 'I'd shake your hand, but mine's kinda clammy.'

192

'That's fine.' I smiled.

'Dr. Delaware's a child psychologist, Jim, He's touring La Casa as a prospective Gentleman.'

'Great to meet you, Doc, and I hope you join us. It's beautiful out here, isn't it?' He extended a long, brown arm to the Malibu sky.

'Gorgeous.'

'Jim used to work in the inner city,' said Kruger. 'At Manual Arts High. Then he got smart.'

Halstead laughed.

'It took me too long. I'm an easy-going guy but when an ape with a knife threatened me after I asked him to do pushups, that was it.'

'I'm sure you don't get that here,' I said.

'No way,' he rumbled. 'The little guys are great.'

'Which reminds me, Jim,' interrupted Kruger, 'I've got to talk to you about working out a programme for Rodney Broussard. Something to build up his confidence.'

'You bet.'

'Check you later, Jim.'

'Right on. Come back again, Doc.'

The hirsute body entered the water, a sleek torpedo, and swam otterlike along the bottom of the pool.

We took a quarter-mile walk around the periphery of the institution. Kruger showed me the infirmary, a spotlessly white, smallish room with an examining table and a cot, sparkling of chrome and reeking of antiseptic. It was empty.

'We have a half-time R.N. who works mornings. For obvious reasons we can't afford a doctor.'

I wondered why Majestic Oil or some other benefactor couldn't donate a part-time physician's salary.

'But we're lucky to have a roster of volunteer docs, some of the finest in the community, who rotate through.'

As we walked, groups of youngsters and counsellors passed us. Kruger waved, the councellors returned the greeting. More often than not the children were unre-

193

sponsive. As Olivia had predicted and Kruger had confirmed, most had obvious physical or mental handicaps. Boys seemed to outnumber girls by about three to one and the majority of the kids were black or Hispanic.

Kruger ushered me into the cafeteria, which was high-ceilinged, stucco walled and meticulously clean. Unspeaking Mexican women waited impassively behind a glass partition, serving tongs in hand. The food was typical institutional fare—stew, creative use of ground meat, jello, overcooked vegetables in thick sauce.

We sat down at a picnic-type table and Kruger went behind the food counter to a back room. He emerged with a tray of Danish pastries and coffee. The baked goods looked high-quality. I hadn't seen anything like them behind the glass.

Across the room a group of children sat at a table eating and drinking under the watchful eyes of two student counsellors. Actually, attempting to eat was more accurate. Even from a distance I could see that they suffered from cerebral palsy, some of them spastically rigid, others jerking in involuntary movements of head and limb, and had to struggle to get the food from table to mouth. The counsellors watched and sometimes offered verbal encouragement. But they didn't help physically and lots of custard and jello was ending up on the floor.

Kruger bit with gusto into a chocolate Danish. I took a cinammon roll and played with it. He poured us coffee and asked me if I had any questions.

'No. Everything looks very impressive.'

'Great. Then let met tell you about the Gentlemen's Brigade.'

He gave me a canned history of the volunteer group, stressing the wisdom of the Reverend Gus in enlisting the participation of local corporations.

'The Gentlemen are mature, successful individuals. They represent the only chance most of these kids have of being exposed to a stable male role model. They're

194

accomplished, the cream of our society and as such give the children a rare glimpse of success. It teaches them that it's indeed possible to be successful. They spend time with the kids here, at La Casa, and take them off-campus—to sporting events, movies, plays, Disneyland. And to their homes for family dinners. It gives the children access to a lifestyle they've never known. And it's fulfilling for the men, as well. We ask for a six-month commitment and sixty per cent sign up for second and third hitches.'

'Can't it be frustrating, for the kids,' I asked, 'to get a taste of the good life that's so far out of their grasp?'

He was ready for that one.

'Good question, Doctor. But we don't emphasize *anything* being out of our kids' reach. We want them to feel that the only thing limiting them is their own lack of motivation. That they must take responsibility for themselves. That they can reach the sky—that's the name of a book written for children by Reverend Gus. *Touch the Sky*. It's got cartoons, games, colouring pages. It teaches them a positive message.'

It was Norman Vincent Peale spiced up with humanistic psychological jargon. I looked over and saw the palsied children battling with their food. No amount of exposure to the members of the privileged class was going to bring them membership in the Yacht Club, an invitation to the Blue Ribbon Upper Crust Debutante Ball of San Marino, or a Mercedes in the garage.

There were limits to the power of positive thinking.

But Kruger had his script and he stuck to it. He was damned good, I had to admit, had read all the right journals and could quote statistics like a Rand Corporation whiz kid. It was the kind of spiel designed to get you reaching for your wallet.

'Can I get you anything else?' he asked after finishing a second pastry. I hadn't touched my first.

'No thanks.'

195

'Let's head back, then. It's almost four.'

We passed through the rest of the place quickly. There was a chicken coop where two dozen hens pecked at the bars like Skinnerian pigeons, a goat at the end of a long leash eating trash, hamsters treading endlessly on plastic wheels and a basset hound who bayed half-heartedly at the darkening sky. The schoolroom had once been a barracks, the gym a World War II storage depot, I was informed. Both had been remodelled artfully and creatively on a budget, by someone with a good feel for camouflage. I complimented the designer.

'That's the work of Reverend Gus. His mark is on every square inch of this place. A remarkable man.'

As we headed toward McCaffrey's office I saw, once again, the cinder-block buildings at the edge of the forest. From up close I could see there were four structures, roofed in concrete, windowless, and half-submerged in earth, like bunkers, with tunnel-like ramps sloping down to iron doors. Kruger showed no indication of explaining what they were, so I asked him.

He looked over his shoulder.

'Storage,' he said casually. 'Come on. Let's get back.'

We'd come full circle, back to the cumulus-covered administration building. Kruger escorted me in, shook my hand, told me he hoped to hear from me again and that he'd be dropping off the screening materials while I talked to the Reverend. Then he handed me over to the good graces of Grandma, the receptionist, who tore herself away from her Olivetti and bade me sweetly to wait just a few moments for The Great Man.

I picked up a copy of *Fortune* and worked hard at building an interest in a feature on the future of microprocessors in the tool-and-die industry, but the words blurred and turned into gelatinous gray blobs. Futurespeak did that to me.

I'd barely had a chance to uncross my legs when the door opened. They were big on punctuality here. I'd

196

started to feel like a hunk of raw material—what kind didn't really matter—being whisked along on an assembly line trough, melted, moulded, tinkered with, tightened, and inspected.

'Reverend Gus will see you now.' said Grandma.

The time had come, I supposed, for the final polishing.

16

IF WE'D been standing outdoors he would have blocked the sun.

He was six-and-a-half feet tall and weighed well over three hundred pounds, a pear-shaped mountain of pale flesh in a fawn-coloured suit, white shirt, and black silk tie the breadth of a hotel hand towel. His tan oxfords were the size of small sailboats, his hands, twin sandbags. He filled the doorway. Black horn-rimmed glasses perched atop a meaty nose that bisected a face as lumpy as tapioca pudding. Wens, moles and enlarged pores trekked their way across the sagging cheeks. There was a hint of Africa in the flatness of his nose, the full lips as dark and moist as raw liver, and the tightly kinked hair the colour of rusty pipes. His eyes were pale, almost without colour. I'd seen eyes like that before. On mullet, packed in ice.

'Dr. Delaware, I'm Augustus McCaffrey.'

His hand devoured mine then released it. His voice was strangely gentle. From the size of him I'd expected something along the lines of a tug horn. What came out was surprisingly lyrical, barely baritone, softened by the lazy cadence of the Deep South—Louisiana, I guessed.

198

'Come in, won't you?'

I followed him, a Hindu trailing an elephant, into his office. It was large and well-windowed but no more elegantly turned out than the waiting room. The walls were sheathed with the same false oak and were devoid of decoration save for a large wooden crucifix above the desk, a Formica-and-steel rectangle that looked like government surplus. The ceiling was low, perforated white squares suspended in a grid of aluminium. There was a door behind the desk.

I sat in one of a trio of vinyl upholstered chairs. He settled himself in a swivel chair that groaned in protest, laced his fingers together and leaned forward across the desk, which now looked like a child's miniature.

'I trust Tim has given you a comprehensive tour and has answered all of your questions.'

'He was very helpful.'

'Good,' he drawled, giving the word three syllables. 'He's a very capable young man. I handpick our staff.' He squinted. 'Just as I handpick all volunteers. We want only the best for our children.'

He sat back and rested his hands on his belly.

'I'm extremely pleased that a man of your stature would consider joining us, Doctor. We've never had a child psychologist in the Gentlemen's Brigade. Tim tells me you're retired.'

He gazed at me jovially. It was clear I was expected to explain myself.

'Yes. That's true.'

'Hmm.' He scratched behind one ear, still smiling. Waiting. I smiled back.

'You know,' he finally said, 'when Tim mentioned your visit I thought your name was familiar. But I couldn't place it. Then it came to me, just a few moments ago. You ran that programme for those children who were the victims of that day-care scandal, didn't you?'

'Yes.'

199

'Wonderful work. How are they doing, the children?'

'Quite well.'

'You—retired soon after the programme was over, did you?'

'Yes.'

The enormous head shook sadly.

'Tragic affair. The man killed himself, if I recall.'

'He did.'

'Doubly tragic. The little ones abused like that and a man's life wasted with no chance of salvation. Or,' he smiled, 'to use a more secular term, with no chance of rehabilitation. They're one and the same, salvation and rehabilitation, don't you think, Doctor?'

'I can see similiarity in the two concepts.'

'Certainly. It depends upon one's perspective. I confess,' he sighed, 'that I find it difficult, at times, to divorce myself from my religious training when dealing with issues of human relations. I must struggle to do so, of course, in view of our society's abhorrence of even a minimal liaison between church and state.'

He wasn't protesting. The broad face was suffused with calm, nourished by the sweet fruit of martyrdom. He looked at peace with himself, as content as a hippo sunning in a mudhole.

'Do you think the man—the one who killed himself—could have been rehabilitated?' he asked me.

'It's hard to say. I didn't know him. The statistics on treatment of lifelong pedophiles aren't encouraging.'

'Statistics.' He played with the word, letting it roll slowly off his tongue. He enjoyed the sound of his own voice. 'Statistics are cold numbers, aren't they? With no consideration for the individual. And, Tim informs me, on a mathematical level, statistics have no relevance for an individual. Is that correct?'

'That's true.'

'When folks quote statistics, it reminds me of the joke about the Okie—Okie jokes were fashionable before

200

your time—woman who had borne ten children with relative equanimity but who became very agitated upon learning she was pregnant with the eleventh. Her doctor asked her why, after having gone through the travails of pregnancy, labour and delivery ten times, she was suddenly so distraught. And she told him she had read that every eleventh child borne in Oklahoma was an Indian, and durned if she was going to raise a redskin!'

He laughed, the belly heaving, the eyes black slits. His glasses slid down his nose and he righted them.

'That, Doctor, sums up my view of statistics. You know, most of the children at La Casa were statistics prior to their coming here—doctor numbers in the Dependency Court files, codes for the D.P.S.S. caseworkers to catalogue, scores on IQ tests. And those numbers said they were beyond hope. But we take them and we work strenuously to transform those numbers into little *individuals*. I don't care about a child's IQ score, I want to help him claim his birthright as a human being—opportunity, basic health and welfare, and, if you'll permit a clerical lapse, a *soul*. For there is a soul in every single one of those children, even the ones functioning at a vegetative level.'

'I agree that it's good not to be limited by numbers.' His man, Kruger, had been pretty handy with statistics when they served his purpose and I was willing to bet La Casa made use of a computer or two to churn out the right numbers when the occasion called for it.

'Our work is effecting change. It's an alchemy of sorts. Which is why suicide—any suicide—saddens me deeply. For all men are capable of salvation. That man was a quitter, in the ultimate sense. But of course,' he lowered his voice, 'the quitter has become the archetype of modern man, hasn't he, Doctor? It has become fashionable to throw up one's hands after the merest travesty of effort. Everyone wants quick and easy solutions.'

Including, no doubt, those who retired at thirty-two.

'There are miracles happening every day, right on these

201

grounds. Children who've been given up on gain a new sense of themselves. A youngster who is incontinent learns to control his bowels.' He paused, like a politician after an applause line. 'So-called retarded children learn to read and write. Small miracles, perhaps, when measured against a man walking on the moon, or perhaps not.' His eyebrows arched, the thick lips parted to reveal widely spaced, horsey teeth. 'Of course, Doctor, if you find the word miracle unduly sectarian, we can substitute *success*. That is a word the average American can relate to. Success.'

Coming from someone else it could have been a cheap throwaway oration worthy of a Sunday morning Jesus-huckster. But McCaffrey was good and his words carried the conviction of one ordained to carry out a sacred mission.

'May I ask,' he inquired pleasantly, 'why you retired?'

'I wanted a change of pace, Reverend. Time to sort out my values.'

'I understand. Reflection can be profoundly valuable. However I trust you won't absent yourself from your profession for too long. We need good people in your field.'

He was still preaching, but now mixing it with an ego massage. I understood why the corporate honchos loved him.

'In fact I have begun to miss working with children, which is why I called you.'

'Excellent, excellent. Psychology's loss will be our gain. You worked at Western Pediatric, didn't you? I seem to remember that from the paper.'

'There and in private practice.'

'A first-rate hospital. We send many of our children there when the need for medical attention arises. I'm acquainted with several of the physicians on staff and many of them have been quite generous—giving of themselves.'

202

'Those are busy men, Reverend; you must be quite persuasive.'

'Not really. However, I do recognize the existence of a basic human need to *give*, an altruistic drive, if you will. I know this flies in the face of the modern psychologies which limit the notion of drive to self-gratification, but I'm convinced I'm right. Altruism is as basic as hunger and thirst. You, for example, satisfied your own altruistic need within the scope of your chosen profession. But when you stopped working, the hunger returned. And here,' he spread his arms,'you are.'

He opened a drawer of the desk, took out a brochure, and handed it to me. It was glossy and well-done, as polished as the quarterly report of an industrial conglomerate.

'On page six you'll see a partial list of our board.'

I found it. For a partial list it was long, running the height of the page in small print. And impressive. It included two county supervisors, a member of the city council, the Mayor, judges, philanthropists, entertainment biggies, attorneys, businessmen, and plenty of M.D.'s, some of whose names I recognized. Like L. Willard Towle.

'Those are all busy men, Doctor. And yet they find the time for our children. Because we know how to tap that inner resource, that well-spring of altruism.'

I flipped through the pages. There was a letter of endorsement from the governor, lots of photographs of children having fun, and even more pictures of McCaffrey. His looming bulk appeared pinstriped on the Donahue show, in tuxedo at a Music Center benefit, in a jogging suit with a group of his young charges at the victory line of the Special Olympics. McCaffrey with TV personalities, civil rights leaders, country singers and bank presidents.

Midway through the brochure I found a shot of McCaffrey in a room I recognized as the lecture hall at Western

203

Pediatric. Next to him, white hair gleaming, was Towle. On the other side was a small man, froggy, squat, grim even as he smiled. The guy with Peter Lorre eyes whose photograph I'd seen in Towle's office. The caption beneath the photo identified him as the Honorable Edwin G. Hayden, supervising judge of the Dependency Court. The occasion was McCaffrey's address to the medical staff on 'Child Welfare: Past, Present and Future'.

'Is Dr. Towle very involved in La Casa?' I asked.

'He serves on our board and is one of our rotating physicians. Do you know him?'

'We've met. Casually. I know him by reputation.'

'Yes, an authority on behavioural paediatrics. We find his services invaluable.'

'I'm sure you do.'

He spent the next quarter-hour showing me his book, a soft-covered locally printed volume of saccharine clichés and first-rate graphics. I bought a copy, for fifteen bucks, after he gave me a more sophisticated version of the pitch for cash Kruger had thrown my way. The bargain basement ambience of the office lent credibility to the spiel. Besides, I was O.D'ed on positive thinking and it seemed a small price to pay for respite.

He took the three five-dollar bills, folded them and placed them conspicuously in a collection box atop the desk. The receptacle was papered with a drawing of a solemn-looking child with eyes that rivalled Melody Quinn's in size, luminosity and the ability to project a sense of inner hurt.

He stood, thanked me for coming, and took my hand in both of his. 'I hope we see more of you, Doctor. Soon.'

It was my turn to smile.

'Plan on it, Reverend.'

Grandma was ready for me as I stepped into the waiting room, with a sheaf of stapled booklets and two sharpened number two pencils.

204

'You can fill these out right here, Doctor Delaware,' she said sweetly.

I looked at my watch.

'Gee, it's much later than I thought. I'll have to take a raincheck.'

'But—' She became flustered.

'How about you give them to me to take home? I'll fill them out and mail them back to you.'

'Oh no, I couldn't do that! These are psychological tests!' She clutched the papers to her breast. 'The rules are that you must fill them out here.'

'Well, then, I'll just have to come back.' I started to leave.

'Wait. Let me ask someone. I'll ask Reverend Gus if it's—'

'He told me he was going to retire for a period of meditation. I don't think he wants to be disturbed.'

'Oh.' She was disoriented. 'I must ask someone. You wait right here, Doctor, and I'll find Tim.'

'Sure.'

When she was gone I slipped out the door, unnoticed.

The sun had almost set. It was that transitional time of day when the diurnal palette is slowly scraped dry, colours falling aside to reveal a wash of gray, that ambiguous segment of twilight when everything looks just a little bit fuzzy around the edges.

I walked toward my car unsettled. I'd spent three hours at La Casa and had learned little other than that the Reverend Augustus McCaffrey was a shrewd old boy with overactive charisma glands. He'd taken the time to check me out and wanted me to know it. But only a paranoiac could rightfully see anything ominous in that. He was showing off, displaying how well-informed and prepared he was. The same went for his advertising the abundance of friends in high places. It was psychological muscle-flexing. Power respected power, strength gravitated to

205

strength. The more connections McCaffrey could show, the more he was going to get. And that was the way to big bucks. That, and collection boxes illustrated with sad-eyed waifs.

I had the key in the door of the Seville, facing the campus of the institution. It looked empty and still, like a well-run farm after the work's all done. Probably dinner time, with the kids in the cafeteria, the counsellors watching, and the Reverend Gus delivering an eloquent benediction.

I felt foolish.

I was about to open the door when I caught a glimpse of a flurry of movement near the forestlike Grove, several hundred feet in the distance. It was hard to be certain, but I though I saw a struggle, heard the sound of muffled cries.

I put the car keys back in my pocket and let the copy of McCaffrey's book drop to the gravel. There was no one else in sight, except for the guard in the booth at the entrance and his attention was focused in the opposite direction. I needed to get closer without being seen. Carefully I made my way down the hill upon which the parking lot sat, staying in the shadow of buildings whenever I could. The shapes in the distance were moving, but slowly.

I pressed myself against the flamingo-pink wall of the southernmost dormitory, as far as I could go without abandoning cover. The ground was moist and mushy, the air rotten with fumes given off by a nearby trash dumpster. Someone had tried to write FUCK in the pink paint, but the corrugated metal was a hostile surface and it came out chicken scratches.

The sounds were clearer and louder now, and they were definitely cries of distress—animal cries, bleating and plaintive.

I made out three silhouettes, two large, one much smaller. The small one seemed to be walking on air.

I inched closer, peering around the corner. The three figures passed before me, perhaps thirty feet away moving along the southern border of the institution. They walked across the concrete of the pool deck and came under the illumination of a yellow anti-bug light affixed to the eave of the poolhouse.

It was then that I saw them clearly, flash frozen in the lemon light.

The small figure was Rodney and he'd appeared suspended because he was being carried in the firm grip of Halstead, the coach, and Tim Kruger. They grasped him under the arms so that his feet dangled inches from the ground.

They were strong men but the boy was giving them a struggle. He squirmed and kicked like a ferret in a trap, opened his mouth and let out a wordless moan. Halstead clamped a hairy hand over the mouth but the child managed to wrench free and scream again. Halstead stifled him once more and it went on that way as they retreated out of the light and my line of vision, the alternating sounds of cries and muted grunts a crazy trumpet solo that grew faint then faded away.

Then it was silent and I was alone, back to the wall, bathed in sweat, clothes clammy and sticking to me. I wanted to perform some heroic act, to break out of the deadening inertia that had settled around my ankles like quick-drying cement.

But I couldn't save anybody. I was a man out of his element. If I followed them there'd be rational explanations for everything and a herd of guards to quickly turn me out, taking careful note of my face so that the gates of La Casa would never again open before it.

I couldn't afford that, just yet.

So I stood, up against the wall, rooted in the ghost-town stillness, feeling sick and helpless. I clenched my fists until they hurt and listened to the dry urgent sound of my own breathing like the scraping of boots against alley stones.

I forced the image of the struggling boy out of my mind. When I was sure it was safe I sneaked back to my car.

17

THE FIRST TIME I called, at 8 A.M., nobody answered. A half-hour later the University of Oregon was open for business.

'Good morning, Education.'

'Good morning. This is Dr. Gene Adler calling from Los Angeles. I'm with the Department of Psychiatry at Western Pediatric Medical Center in Los Angeles. We're currently recruiting for a counselling position. One of our applicants has listed on his resumé the fact that he received a master's degree in counselling education from your department. As part of our routine credentials check I was wondering if you could verify that for me.'

'I'll switch you to Marianne, in transcripts.'

Marianne had a warm, friendly voice but when I repeated my story for her she told me, firmly, that a written request would be necessary.

'That's fine with me,' I said, 'but that will take time. The job for which this individual has applied is being competitively sought by many people. We were planning to make a decision within twenty-four hours. It's just a formality—verification of records—but our liability insurance stipulates that we have to do it. If you'd like I

209

can have the applicant call you to release the information. It's in his best interests.'

'Well...I suppose it'll be all right. All you want to know is if this person received a degree, right? Nothing more personal than that?'

'That's correct.'

'Who's the applicant?'

'A gentleman named Timothy Kruger. His records list an M.A. four years ago.'

'One moment.'

She was gone for ten minutes, and when she returned to the phone she sounded upset.

'Well, Doctor, your formality has turned out to be of some value. There is no record of a degree being granted to a person of that name in the last ten years. We do have a record of a Timothy Jay Kruger attending one semester of graduate school four years ago, but his major wasn't in counselling, it was in secondary teaching, and he left after that single semester.'

'I see. That's quite disturbing. Any indication of why he left?'

'None. Does that really matter now?'

'No, I suppose not—you're absolutely certain about this? I wouldn't want to jeopardize Mr. Kruger's career—'

'There's no doubt whatsoever.' She sounded offended. 'I checked and double-checked, Doctor, and then I asked the head of the department, Dr. Gowdy, and he was positive no Timothy Kruger graduated from here.'

'Well, that settles it, doesn't it? And it certainly casts a new light on Mr. Kruger. Could you check one more thing?'

'What's that?'

'Mr. Kruger also listed a B.A. in psychology from Jedson College in Washington State. Would your records contain that kind of information as well?'

'It would be on his application to graduate school. We should have transcripts, but I don't see why you need to—'

'Marianne, I'm going to have to report this to the State Board of Behavioural Science examiners, because state licensure is involved. I want to know all the facts.'

'I see. Let me check.'

This time she was back in a moment.

'I've got his transcript from Jedson here, Doctor. He did receive a B.A. but it wasn't in psychology.'

'What was it in?'

She laughed.

'Dramatic arts. Acting.'

I called the school where Raquel Ochoa taught and had her pulled out of class. Despite that, she seemed pleased to hear from me.

'Hi. How's the investigation going?'

'We're getting closer,' I lied. 'That's what I called you about. Did Elena keep a diary or any kind of records around the apartment?'

'No. Neither of us were diary writers. Never had been.'

'No notebooks, tapes, anything?'

'The only tapes I saw were music—she had a tape deck in her new car—and some cassettes Handler gave her to help her relax. For sleep. Why?'

I ignored the question.

'Where are her personal effects?'

'You should know that. The police had them. I suppose they gave them back to her mother. What's going on? Have you found out something?'

'Nothing definite. Nothing I can talk about. We're trying to fit things together.'

'I don't care how you do it, just catch him and punish him. The monster.'

I dredged up a rancid lump of false confidence and smeared it all over my voice. 'We will.'

'I know you will.'

Her faith made me uneasy.

211

'Raquel, I'm away from the files. Do you have her mother's home address handy?'

'Sure.' She gave it to me.

'Thanks.'

'Are you planning on visiting Elena's family?'

'I thought it would be helpful to talk to them in person.'

There was silence on the other end. Then she spoke.

'They're good people. But they may shut you out.'

'It's happened before.'

She laughed.

'I think you'd do better if I went with you. I'm like a member of the family.'

'It's no hassle for you?'

'No. I want to help. When do you want to go?'

'This afternoon.'

'Fine. I'll get off early. Tell them I'm not feeling well. Pick me up at two-thirty. Here's my address.'

She lived in a modest West L.A. neighbourhood not far from where the Santa Monica and San Diego Freeways merged in blissful union, an area of crackerbox apartment buildings populated by singles who couldn't afford the Marina.

She was visible a block away, waiting by the curb, dressed in a pigeon-blood crepe blouse, blue denim skirt and tooled western boots.

She got in the car, crossed a pair of unstockinged brown legs and smiled.

'Hi.'

'Hi. Thanks for doing this.'

'I told you, this is something I want to do. I want to feel useful.'

I drove north, toward Sunset. There was jazz on the radio, something free form and atonal, with saxophone solos that sounded like police sirens and drums like a heart in arrest.

'Change it, if you'd like.'

She pushed some buttons, fiddled with the dial, and

212

found a mellow rock station. Someone was singing about lost love and old movies and tying it all together.

'What do you want to know from them?' she asked, settling back.

'If Elena told them anything about her work—specifically the child who died. Anything about Handler.'

There were lots of questions in her eyes but she kept them there.

'Talking about Handler will be especially touchy. The family didn't like the idea of her going out with a man who was so much older. And,' she hesitated, 'an Anglo, to boot. In situations like that the tendency is to deny the whole thing, not even to acknowledge it. It's cultural.'

'To some extent it's human.'

'To some extent, maybe. We Hispanics do it more. Part of it is Catholicism. The rest is our Indian blood. How can you survive in some of the desolate regions we've lived in without denying reality? You smile, and pretend it's lush and fertile and there's plenty of water and food, and the desert doesn't seem so bad.'

'Any suggestions how I might get around the denial?'

'I don't know.' She sat with her hands folded in her lap, a proper schoolgirl. 'I think I'd better start the talking. Cruz—Elena's mom—always liked me. Maybe I can get through. But don't expect miracles.'

She had little to worry about on that account.

Echo Park is a chunk of Latin America transported to the dusty, hilly streets that, buttressed by crumbling concrete embankments on either side of Sunset Boulevard, rise between Hollywood and downtown. The streets have names like Macbeth and Macduff, Bonnybrae and Laguna, but are anything but poetic. They climb to the south and dip down into the Union District ghetto. To the north they climb, feeding into the tiny lake-centred park that gives the area its name, continue through arid trails, get lost in an incongruous wilderness that looks

213

down upon Dodger Stadium, and Elysian Park, home of the Los Angeles Police Academy.

Sunset changes when it leaves Hollywood and enters Echo Park. The porno theatres and by-the-hour motels yield to *botánicas* and *bodegas*, outlets for Discos Latinos, an infinite array of food stands—taco joints, Peruvian seafood parlours, fast-food franchises—and first-rate Latino restaurants, beauty shops with windows guarded by styrofoam skulls wearing blond Dynel wigs, Cuban bakeries, storefront medical and legal clinics, bars and social clubs. Like many poor areas, the Echo Park part of Sunset is continually clogged with foot traffic.

The Seville cut a slow swath through the afternoon mob. There was a mood on the boulevard as urgent and sizzling as the molten lard spitting forth from the fryers of the food stands. There were homeboys sporting homemade tattoos, fifteen-year-old mothers wheeling fat babies in rickety strollers that threatened to fall apart at every curb, rummies, pushers, starched-collared immigration lawyers, cleaning women on shore leave, grandmothers, flower vendors, a never-ending stream of brown-eyed children.

'It's very weird,' said Raquel, 'coming back here. In a fancy car.'

'How long have you been gone?'

'A thousand years.'

She didn't seem to want to say more so I dropped it. At Fairbanks Place she told me to turn left. The Gutierrez home was at the end of an alley-sized twister that peaked, then turned into a dirt road just above the foothills. A quarter mile further and we'd have been the only humans in the world.

I'd noticed that she had a habit of biting herself—lips, fingers, knuckles—when she was nervous. And she was gnawing at her thumb right now. I wondered what kind of hunger it satisfied.

I drove cautiously—there was scarcely room for a single

214

vehicle— passing young men in T-shirts working on old cars with the dedication of priests before a shrine, children sucking candy-coated fingers. Long ago, the street had been planted with elms that had grown huge. Their roots buckled the sidewalk and weeds grew in the cracks. Branches scraped the roof of the car. An old woman with inflamed legs wrapped in rags pushed a shopping cart full of memories up an incline worthy of San Francisco. Graffiti scarred every free inch of space, proclaiming the immortality of Little Willie Chacon, the Echo Parque Skulls, Los Conquistadores, the Lemoyne Boys and the tongue of Maria Paula Bonilla.

'There.' She pointed to a cottagelike frame house painted light green and roofed with brown tarpaper. The front yard was dry and brown but rimmed with hopeful beds of red geraniums and clusters of orange and yellow poppies that looked like all-day suckers. There was rock trim at the base of the house and a portico over the entry that shadowed a sagging wooden porch upon which a man sat.

'That's Rafael, the older brother. On the porch.'

I found a parking space next to a Chevy on blocks. I turned the wheels to the curb and locked them in place. We got out of the car, dust spiralling at our heels.

'Rafael!' she called and waved. The man on the porch took a moment to lift his gaze, then he raised his hand— feebly, it seemed.

'I used to live right around the corner,' she said, making it sound like a confession. She led me up a dozen steps and through an open iron gate.

The man on the porch hadn't risen. He stared at us with apprehension and curiosity and something else that I couldn't identify. He was pale and thin to the point of being gaunt, with the same curious mixture of Hispanic features and fair colouring as his dead sister. His lips were bloodless, his eyes heavily lidded. He looked like the victim of some systemic disease. He wore a long-sleeved

215

white shirt with the sleeves rolled up just below the elbows. It bloused out around his waist, several sizes too large. His trousers were black and looked as if they'd once belonged to a fat man's suit. His shoes were bubble-toed oxfords, cracked at the tips, worn unlaced with the tongues protruding and revealing thick white socks. His hair was short and combed straight back.

He was in his mid-twenties but he had an old man's face, a weary, wary mask.

Raquel went to him and kissed him lightly on the top of his head. He looked up at her but was unmoved.

'H'lo, Rocky.'

'Rafael, how are you?'

'O.K.' He nodded his head and it looked for a moment as if it would roll off his neck. He let his eyes settle on me; he was having trouble focusing.

Raquel bit her lip.

'We came by to see you and Andy and your mom. This is Alex Delaware. He works with the police. He's involved in investigating Elena's—case.'

His face registered alarm, his hand tightened around the arm of the chair. Then, as if responding to a stage direction to relax, he grinned at me, slumped lower, winked.

'Yeah,' he said.

I held out my hand. He looked at it, puzzled, recognized it as a long lost friend, and extended his own thin claw.

His arm was pitifully undernourished, a bundle of sticks held together by a sallow paper wrapper. As our fingers touched his sleeve rode up and I saw the track marks. There were lots of them. Most looked old—lumpy charcoal smudges—but a few were freshly pink. One, in particular, was no antique, sporting a pinpoint of blood at its centre.

His handshake was moist and tenuous. I let go and the arm fell limply to his side.

216

'Hey, man,' he said, barely audible. 'Good to meetja.' He turned away, lost in his own timeless dream-hell. For the first time I heard the oldies music coming from a cheap transistor radio on the floor beside his chair. The puny plastic box crackled with static. The sound reproduction was atrocious, the music had the chalky quality of notes filtered through a mile of mud. Rafael had his head thrown back, enraptured. To him it was the Celestial Choir transmitting directly to his temporal lobes.

'Rafael,' she smiled.

He looked at her, smiled, nodded off and was gone.

She stared at him, tears in her eyes. I moved toward her and she turned away in shame and rage.

'Goddammit.'

'How long has he been shooting up?'

'Years. But I thought he'd quit. The last I'd heard he'd quit.' She raised her hand to her mouth, swayed, as if ready to fall. I got in position to catch her but she righted herself. 'He got hooked in Viet Nam. Came home with a heavy habit. Elena spent lots of time and money trying to help him get off. A dozen times he tried, and each time he slipped back. But he'd been off it for over a year. Elena was so happy about it. He got a job as a boxboy at the Lucky's on Alvarado.'

She faced me, nostrils flaring, eyes floating like black lilies in a salty pond, lips quivering like harp-strings.

'Everything is falling apart.'

She grasped the newel post on the porch rail for support. I came behind her.

'I'm sorry.'

'He was always the sensitive one. Quiet, never dating, no friends. He got beat up a lot. When their dad died he tried to take over, to be the man of the house. Tradition says the oldest son should do that. But it didn't work. Nobody took him seriously. They laughed. We all did. So he gave up, as if he'd failed some final test. He dropped out of school, stayed home and read comic books and

217

watched TV all day—just stared at the screen. When the army said they wanted him he seemed glad. Cruz cried to see him go, but he was happy...'

I looked at him, sitting so low he was almost parallel with the ground. Swallowed up by junkie-slumber. His mouth was open and he snored loudly. The radio played 'Daddy's Home'.

Raquel hazarded another look at him, then whipped her head away, disgusted. She wore an expression of noble suffering, an Aztec virgin steeling herself for the ultimate sacrifice.

I put my hands on her shoulders and she leaned back in my arms. She stayed there, tense and unyielding, allowing herself a miser's ration of tears.

'This is a hell of a start,' she said. Inhaling deeply, she let out her breath in a breeze of wintergreen. She wiped her eyes and turned around. 'You must think all I do is weep. Come on, let's go inside.'

She pulled the screen door open and it slapped sharply against the wood siding of the house.

We stepped into a small front room furnished with old but cared-for relics. It was warm and dark, the windows shut tight and masked by yellowing parchment shades— a room unaccustomed to visitors. Faded lace curtains were tied back from the window frames and matching lace coverlets shielded the arms of the chairs—a sofa and loveseat set upholstered in dark green crushed velvet, the worn spots shiny and the colour of jungle parrots, two wicker rockers. A painting of the two dead Kennedy brothers in black velvet hung over the mantel. Carvings in wood and Mexican onyx sat atop lace-covered end tables. There were two floor lamps with beaded shades, a plaster Jesus in agony hanging on the whitewashed wall next to a still life of a straw basket of oranges. Family portraits in ornate frames covered another wall and there was a large graduation picture of Elena suspended high above

218

those. A spider crawled in the space where wall met ceiling.

A door to the right revealed a sliver of white tile. Raquel walked to the sliver and peeked in.

'Señora Cruz?'

The doorway widened and a small, heavy woman appeared, dish-towel in hand. She wore a blue print dress, unbelted, and her gray-black hair was tied back in a bun, held in place by a mock tortoiseshell comb. Silver earrings dangled from her ears and salmon spots of rouge punctuated her cheekbones. Her skin had the delicate, baby-soft look common in old women who had once been beautiful.

'Raquelita!'

She put her towel down, came out, and the two women embraced for a long moment.

When she saw me over Raquel's shoulder, she smiled. But her face closed up as tight as a pawnbroker's safe. She pulled away and gave a small bow.

'Señor,' she said, with too much deference, and looked at Raquel, arching one eyebrow.

'Señora Gutierrez.'

Raquel spoke to her in rapid Spanish. I caught the words 'Elena', 'policía', and 'doctor'. She ended it with a question.

The older woman listened politely, then shook her head.

'No.' Some things are the same in any language.

Raquel turned to me. 'She says she knows nothing more than what she told the police the first time.'

'Can you ask her about the Nemeth boy? They didn't ask her about that.'

She turned to speak, then stopped.

'Why don't we take it slowly? It would help if we ate. Let her be a hostess, let her give to us.'

I was genuinely hungry and told her so. She relayed the message to Mrs. Gutierrez, who nodded and returned to her kitchen.

219

'Let's sit down,' Raquel said.

I took the loveseat. She tucked herself into a corner of the sofa.

The señora came back with cookies and fruit and hot coffee. She asked Raquel something.

'She'd like to know if this is substantial enough or would you like some homemade *chorizo*?'

'Please tell her this is wonderful. However if you think my accepting *chorizo* would help things along, I'll oblige.'

Raquel spoke again. A few moments later I was facing a platter of the spicy sausage, rice, refried beans and salad with lemon-oil dressing.

'*Muchas gracias, señora.*' I dug in.

I couldn't understand much of what they were saying, but it sounded and looked like small talk. The two women touched each other a lot, patting hands, stroking cheeks. They smiled, and seemed to forget my presence.

Then suddenly the wind shifted and the laughter turned to tears. Mrs. Gutierrez ran out of the room, seeking the refuge of her kitchen.

Raquel shook her head.

'We were talking about the old times, when Elena and I were little girls. How we used to play secretary in the bushes, pretend we had typewriters and desks out there. It became difficult for her.'

I pushed my plate aside.

'Do you think we should go?' I asked.

'Let's wait a while.' She poured me more coffee and filled a cup for herself. 'It would be more respectful.'

Through the screen door I could see the top of Rafael's fair head above the rim of the chair. His arm had fallen, so that the fingernails scraped the ground. He was beyond pleasure or pain.

'Did she talk about him?' I asked.

'No. As I told you, it's easier to deny.'

'But how can he sit there, shooting up, right in front of her, with no pretence?'

'She used to cry a lot about it. After a while you accept the fact that things aren't going to turn out the way you want them to. She's had plenty of training in it, believe me. If you asked her about him she'd say he was sick. Just as if he had a cold, or the measles. It's just a matter of finding the right cure. Have you heard of the *curanderos*?'

'The folk doctors? Yes. Lots of the Hispanic patients at the hospital used them along with conventional medicine.'

'Do you know how they operate? By caring. In our culture the cold, distant professional is regarded as someone who simply doesn't care, who is just as likely to deliver the *mal ojo*—the evil eye—as he is to cure. The *curandero*, on the other hand, has little training or technology at his disposal—a few snake powders, maybe. But he cares. He lives in the community, he is warm, and familiar, has tremendous rapport. In a way, he's a folk psychologist more than a folk doctor. That's why I suggested you eat—to establish a personal link. I told her you were a caring person. Otherwise she'd say nothing. She'd be polite, lady-like—Cruz is from the old school—but she'd shut you out just the same.' She sipped at her coffee.

'That's why the police learned nothing when they came here, why they seldom do in Echo Park, or East L.A., or San Fernando. They're too professional. No matter how well-meaning they may be, we see them as Anglo robots. You do care, Alex, don't you?'

'I do.'

She touched my knee.

'Cruz took Rafael to a *curandero* years ago, when he first started dropping out. The man looked into his eyes and said they were empty. He told her it was an illness of the soul, not of the body. That the boy should be given to the church, as a priest or monk, so that he could find a useful role for himself.'

'Not bad advice.'

221

She sipped her coffee. 'No. Some of them are very sophisticated. They live by their wits. Maybe it would have prevented the addiction if she'd followed through. Who knows? But she couldn't give him up. I wouldn't be surprised if she blames herself for what he's become. For everything.'

The door to the kitchen opened. Mrs. Gutierrez came out wearing a black band around her arm and a new face that was more than just fresh makeup. A face hardened to withstand the acid bath of interrogation.

She sat down next to Raquel and whispered to her in Spanish.

'She says you may ask any questions you'd like.'

I nodded with what I hoped was obvious gratitude.

'Please tell the señora that I express my sorrow at her tragic loss and also let her know that I greatly appreciate her taking the time during her period of grief to talk to me.'

The older woman listened to the translation and acknowledged me with a quick movement of her head.

'Ask her, Raquel, if Elena ever talked about her work. Especially during the last year.'

As Raquel spoke a nostalgic smile spread across the older woman's face.

'She says only to complain that teachers did not get paid enough. That the hours were long and the children could get difficult.'

'Any particular children?'

A whispered conference.

'No child in particular. The señora reminds you that Elena was a special kind of teacher who helped children with problems in learning. All the children had difficulties.'

I wondered to myself if there'd been a connection between growing up with a brother like Rafael and the dead girl's choice of speciality.

222

'Did she speak at all about the child who was killed. The Nemeth boy?'

Upon hearing the question Mrs. Gutierrez nodded, sadly, then spoke.

'She mentioned it once or twice. She said she was very sad about it. That it was a tragedy,' Raquel translated.

'Nothing else?'

'It would be rude to pursue it, Alex.'

'Okay. Try this. Did Elena seem to have more money than usual recently? Did she buy expensive gifts for anyone in the family?'

'No. She says Elena always complained about not having enough money. She was a girl who liked to have good things. Pretty things. One minute.' She listened to the older woman, nodding affirmation. 'This wasn't always possible, as the family was never rich. Even when her husband was alive. But Elena worked very hard. She bought herself things. Sometimes on credit, but she always made her payments. Nothing was repossessed. She was a girl to make a mother proud.'

I prepared myself for more tears, but there were none. The grieving mother looked at me with a cold, dark expression of challenge. I dare you, she was saying, to besmirch the memory of my little girl.

I looked away.

'Do you think I can ask her about Handler now?'

Before Raquel could answer, Mrs. Gutierrez spit. She gesticulated with both hands, raised her voice and uttered what had to be a string of curses. She ended the diatribe by spitting again.

'Need I translate?' asked Raquel.

'Don't bother.' I made a mental search for a new line of questioning. Normally, my approach would have been to start off with small talk, casual banter, and subtly switch to direct questions. I was dissatisfied with the crude way I was handling this interview, but working with a translator was like doing surgery wearing garden gloves.

223

'Ask her if there is anything else she can tell me that might help us find the man who—you phrase it.'

The old woman listened and answered vehemently.

'She says there is nothing. That the world has become a crazy place, full of demons. That a demon must have done this to Elena.'

'*Muchas gracias, señora.* Ask her if I might have a look at Elena's personal effects.'

Raquel asked her and the mother deliberated. She looked me over from head to toe, sighed, and got up.

'*Venga,*' she said, and led me to the rear of the house.

The flotsam and jetsam of Elena Gutierrez's twenty-eight years had been stored in cardboard boxes and stuck in a corner of what passed, in the tiny house, as a service porch. There was a windowed door with a view of the backyard. An apricot tree grew there, gnarled and deformed, spreading its fruit-laden branches across the rotting roof of a single car garage.

Across the hall was a small bedroom with two beds, the domicile of the brothers. From where I knelt I could see a maple dresser and shelves constructed of unfinished planks resting on cinder blocks. The shelves held a cheap stereo and a modest record collection. A carton of Marlboros and a pile of paperbacks shared the top of the dresser. One of the beds was neatly made, the other a jumble of tangled sheets. Between them was a single pine end table holding a lamp with a plastic base, an ashtray, and a copy of a Spanish girlie magazine.

Feeling like a Peeping Tom, I pulled the first box close and began my excursion in pop archaeology.

By the time I'd gone through three boxes I'd succumbed to an indigo mood. My hands were filthy with dust, my mind filled with images of the dead girl. There'd been nothing of substance, just the broken shards that surface at any prolonged dig. Clothing smelling of girl, half-empty bottles of cosmetics—reminders that someone had once tried to make her eyelashes look thick and lush,

224

to give her hair that Clairol shine, to cover her blemishes and gloss her lips and smell good in all the right places. Scraps of paper with reminders to pick up eggs at Vons and wine at Vendôme and other cryptograms, laundry receipts, gasoline credit-card stubs, books—lots of them, mostly biographies and poetry, souvenirs—a miniature ukelele from Hawaii, an ashtray from a hotel in Palm Springs, ski boots, an almost-full disc of birth control pills, old lesson plans, memos from the principal, children's drawings—none by a boy named Nemeth.

It was too much like graverobbing for my taste. I understood, more than ever, why Milo drank too much.

There were two boxes to go. I went at them, working faster, and was almost done when the roar of a motorcycle filled the air, then died. The back door opened, footsteps sounded in the foyer.

'What the fuck—'

He was nineteen or twenty, short and powerfully built, wearing a sweat-soaked brown tank top that showed every muscle, grease-stained khaki pants and work boots coated with grime. His hair was thick and shaggy. It hung to his shoulders and was held in place by a thonged leather headband. He had fine, almost delicate features that he'd tried to camouflage by growing a moustache and beard. The moustache was black and luxuriant. It dropped over his lips and glistened like sable fur. The beard was a skimpy triangle of down on his chin. He looked like a kid playing Pancho Villa in the school play.

There was a ring of keys hanging from his belt and the keys jingled when he came toward me. His hands were balled up into grimy fists and he smelled of motor oil.

I showed him my L.A.P.D. badge. He swore, but stopped.

'Listen man, you guys were here last week. We told you we had nothin'—' He stopped and looked down at the contents of the cardboard box strewn on the floor.

'Shit, you went through all that stuff already. I just packed it up, man, gettin' it ready for the Goodwill.'

'Just a recheck,' I said amiably.

'Yeah, man, why don't you dudes learn to get it right in the first fuckin' place, okay?'

'I'll be through in a moment.'

'You're through now, man. Out.'

I stood.

'Give me a few minutes to wrap it up.'

'Out, man.' He crooked his thumb toward the back door.

'I'm trying to investigate the death of your sister, Andy. It wouldn't hurt you to cooperate.'

He took a step closer. There were grease smudges on his forehead, and under his eyes.

'Don't "Andy" me, dude. This is my place and it's *Mr.* Gutierrez. And don't give me that shit about investigating. You guys aren't never gonna catch the dude who did it to Elena 'cause you don't really give a fuck. Come bustin' into a home and going through personal stuff and treatin' us like peasants, man. You go out on the street and find the dude, man. This was Beverly Hills, he'd already 'a' been caught, he do this to some rich guy's daughter.'

His voice broke and he shut up to hide it.

'Mr. Gutierrez,' I said softly, 'cooperation from family can be very helpful in these—'

'Hey, man, I told you, this family don't know nothing about this. You think we know what kind of crazy asshole do something like that? You think people around here act like that, man?'

He squinted at my badge, reading it with effort, moving his lips. He mouthed the word 'consultant' a couple of times before getting it.

'Aw, man, I don't believe it. You're not even a real cop. Fucking consultant, they send around here. What's Ph.D., man?'

226

'Doctorate in psychology.'

'You a shrink, man—fuckin' headshrinker they send aroun' here, think someone's crazy here! You think someone in this family is crazy, man? Do you?'

He was breathing on me now. His eyes were soft and brown, long-lashed and dreamy as a girl's. Eyes like that could make you doubt yourself, could lead a guy to get into some heavy macho posturing.

I thought the family had plenty of problems but I didn't answer his question.

'What the fuck you doin' here, psychin' us out, man?'

He sprayed me with spittle as he spoke. A balloon of anger expanded in my gut. Automatically my body assumed a defensive karate stance.

'It's not like that, I can explain. Or are you determined to be pig-headed?'

I regretted the words even as they left my mouth.

'Pig—goddammit man, you're the pig!' His voice rose an octave and he grabbed the lapel of my jacket.

I was ready but I didn't move. He's in mourning, I kept telling myself. He's not responsible.

I met his gaze and he backed off. Both of us would have welcomed an excuse to duke it out. So much for civilization.

'Get out, man. Now!'

'Antonio!'

Mrs. Gutierrez had come into the hallway. Raquel was visible behind her. Seeing her I felt suddenly ashamed. I'd done a great job of screwing up a sensitive situation. The brilliant psychologist. . .

'Mom, did you let this dude in?'

Mrs. Gutierrez apologized to me with her eyes and spoke to her son in Spanish. He seemed to wilt under mama's wagging finger and dark looks.

'Mom, I told you before, they don't give a—' He stopped, continued in Spanish. It sounded like he was

227

defending himself, the machismo slowly rendered impotent.

They went back and forth for a while. Then he started in on Raquel. She gave it right back to him: 'The man is trying to help you, Andy. Why don't you help him instead of chasing him away?'

'I don't need nobody's help. We're gonna take care of ourselves the way we always did.'

She sighed.

'Shit!' He went into his room, came out with a pack of Marlboros and made a big deal out of lighting one and jamming it into his mouth. He disappeared, momentarily, behind a blue cloud, then the eyes flashed once again, moving from me to his mother, to Raquel, and back to me. He pulled his key ring from his belt and held the keys sandwiched between his fingers, impromptu brass knuckles.

'I'm leaving now, dude. But when I get back you fucking well better be gone.'

He kicked the door open and jogged out. We heard the thunder of the motorcycle starting and the diminishing scream of the machine as it sped away.

Mrs. Gutierrez hung her head and said something to Raquel.

'She asks your forgiveness for Andy's rudeness. He's been very upset since Elena's death. He's working two jobs and under a lot of pressure.'

I held a hand up to stop the apology.

'There's no need to explain. I only hope I haven't caused the señora needless troubles.'

Translation was superfluous. The look on the mother's face was eloquent.

I rummaged through the last two boxes with little enthusiasm and came up with no new insights. The sour taste of the confrontation with Andy lingered. I experienced the kind of shame you feel upon digging too deep, seeing

228

and hearing more than you need or want to. Like a child walking in on his parents lovemaking or a hiker kicking aside a rock only to catch a glimpse of something slimy on the underside.

I'd seen families like the Gutierrezes' before; I'd known scores of Rafaels and Andys. It was a pattern: the slob and the superkid, playing out their roles with depressing predictability. One unable to cope, the other trying to take charge of everything. The slob, getting others to take care of him, shirking his responsibilities, coasting through life but feeling like—a slob. The superkid, competent, compulsive, working two jobs, even three when the situation called for it, making up for the slob's lack of accomplishment, earning the admiration of the family, refusing to stoop under the weight of his burden, keeping his rage under wraps—but not always.

I wondered what role Elena had played when she was alive. Had she been the peacemaker, the go-between? Getting caught in the crossfire between slob and superkid could be hazardous to one's health.

I repacked her things as neatly as I could.

When we stepped onto the porch Rafael was still stuporous. The sound of the Seville starting up jolted him awake, and he blinked rapidly, as if coming out of a bad dream, stood with effort, and wiped his nose with his sleeve. He looked in our direction, puzzled. Raquel turned away from him, a tourist avoiding a leprous beggar. As I pulled away I saw a spark of recognition brighten his doped-up countenance, then more bewilderment.

The approaching darkness had dimmed the activity level on Sunset but there was still plenty of life on the streets. Car horns honked, raucous laughter rose above the exhaust fumes and mariachi music blared from the open doors of the bars. Traces of neon appeared and lights flickered in the foothills.

'I really blew it,' I said.

'No, you can't blame yourself.' In the mood she was in,

boosting me took effort. I appreciated that effort and told her so.

'I mean it, Alex. You were very sensitive with Cruz— I can see why you were a successful psychologist. She liked you.'

'It obviously doesn't run in the family.'

She was silent for a few blocks.

'Andy's a nice boy—he never joined the gangs, took lots of punishment because of it. He expects a lot out of himself. Everything's on his shoulders, now.'

'With all that weight why add a two-ton chip?'

'You're right. He makes more problems for himself— don't we all? He's only eighteen. Maybe he'll grow up.'

'I keep wondering if there was some way I could have handled it better.' I recounted the details of my exchange with the boy.

'The pigheaded crack didn't help things, but it didn't make a difference. He came in ready to fight. When Latin men get that way there's little you can do. Add alcohol to that and you can see why we pack the emergency rooms with knifing victims every Saturday night.'

I thought of Elena Gutierrez and Morton Handler. They'd never made it to the emergency room. I allowed myself a short ride on that train of thought then skidded to a stop and dumped the thoughts in a dark depot somewhere in the south of my subconscious.

I looked over at Raquel. She sat stiffly in the soft leather, refusing to give herself over to comfort. Her body was still but her hands played nervously with the fabric of her skirt.

'Are you hungry?' I asked. When in doubt, stick to basics.

'No. If you want you can stop for yourself.'

'I can still taste the *chorizo*.'

'You can take me home, then.'

When I got to her apartment it was dark and the streets were empty.

230

'Thanks for coming with me.'

'I hope it was helpful.'

'Without you it would have been disastrous.'

'Thank you.' She smiled and leaned over. It started out as a kiss on the cheek but one or both of us moved and it turned into a kiss on the lips. Then a tentative nibble, nurtured with heat and want, that matured quickly into a gasping, ravenous adult bite. We moved closer simultaneously, her arms easing around my neck, my hands in her hair, on her face, at the small of her back. Our mouths opened and our tongues danced a slow waltz. We breathed heavily, squirming, struggling to get closer.

We necked like two teenagers for endless minutes. I undid a button of her blouse. She made a throaty sound, caught my lower lip between her teeth, licked my ear. My hand slithered around to the hot silk of her back, working with a mind of its own, undoing the clasp of her brassiere, cupping around her breast. The nipple, pebble-hard and moist, nestled against my palm. She lowered one hand, slender fingers tugging at my fly.

I was the one who stopped it.

'What's the matter?'

There's nothing you can say in a situation like that that doesn't sound like a cliché or totally idiotic, or both. I opted for both.

'I'm sorry. Don't take it personally.'

She threw herself upright, busied herself with buttoning, fastening, smoothing her hair.

'How else should I take it?'

'You're very desirable.'

'Very.'

'I'm attracted to you, dammit. I'd love to make love to you.'

'What is it, then?'

'A commitment.'

'You're not married, are you? You don't act married.'

'There are other commitments besides marriage.'

231

'I see.' She gathered up her purse and put her hand on the door handle. 'The person you're committed to, it would matter to her?'

'Yes. More important, it would matter to me.'

She burst out laughing, verging on hysteria

'I'm sorry,' she said, catching her breath. 'It's so damned ironic. You think I do this often? This is the first time I've been interested in a guy in a long time. The nun cuts loose and comes face to face with a saint.'

She giggled. It sounded feverish, fragile, made me uneasy. I was weary of being on the receiving end of someone's—anyone's—frustration but I supposed she was entitled to her moment of cathartic stardom.

'I'm no saint, believe me.'

She touched my cheek with her fingers. It was like being raked with hot coals.

'No, you're just a nice guy, Delaware.'

'I don't feel like that, either.'

'I'm going to kiss you again,' she said, 'but it's going to stay chaste this time. The way it should have been in the first place.'

And she did.

18

THERE WERE two surprises waiting for me when I got home.

The first was Robin, in my ratty yellow bathrobe, stretched out on the leather sofa, drinking hot tea. A fire burned in the hearth and the stereo played the Eagles' 'Desperado'.

She was wearing a magazine photograph of Lassie around her neck like a miniature sandwich sign.

'Hello, darling,' she said.

I threw my jacket over a chair.

'Hi. What's with the dog?'

'Just my way of letting you know that I've been a bitch and I'm sorry.'

'You have nothing to be sorry for.' I removed the sign.

I sat beside her and took her hands in mine.

'I was rotten to you this morning, Alex, letting you leave like that. The moment the door closed I started missing you. You know how it is when you let your mind wander around—what if something happens to him, what if I never see him again—you go crazy. I couldn't work, couldn't be around machines in that state. The day was

233

blown. I called you but I couldn't get through. So here I am.'

'Virtue has its rewards,' I muttered under my breath.

'What's that, sweetie?'

'Nothing.' Any recounting of my minor-league indiscretion would suffer in the retelling, emerging as either a boorish bathroom scribble—'Yeah, I hopped a fast feel from another broad, honey'—or, worse, a confession.

I lay down beside her. We held each other, said nice things, talked baby talk, stroked each other. I was pumped up from the waist down, some of it a residue of the curbside session with Raquel, most of it belonging to the moment.

'There are two giant porterhouses in the refrigerator and a Caesar salad and burgundy and sourdough.' She whispered, tickling my nose with her pinkie.

'You're a very oral person,' I laughed.

'Is that neurotic, Doctor?'

'No. It's wonderful.'

'How about this? And this?'

The robe fell open. She kneeled above me, letting it slide down her shoulders. Backlit by the glow of the fire, she looked like a piece of glorious, golden statuary.

'Come on sweetie,' she coaxed, 'get out of those clothes.' And she took the matter into her own hands.

'I do love you,' she said later. 'Even if you are catatonic.'

I refused to budge, and lay spreadeagled on the floor.

'I'm cold.'

She covered me, stood and stretched, and laughed with pleasure.

'How can you jump around afterwards?' I groaned.

'Women are stronger than men,' she said gaily, and proceeded to dance around the room, humming, stretching more so that the muscles of her calves ascended in the slender columns of her legs like bubbles rising in a

234

carpenter's level. Her eyes reflected orange Halloween light. When she moved a shudder went through me.

'Keep jiggling like that and I'll show you who's stronger.'

'Later, big boy.' She teased me with her foot and leaped away from my grabbing paws with fluid agility.

By the time the steaks were ready Mrs. Gutierrez's cuisine was a vague memory and I ate with gusto. We sat side by side in the breakfast nook, looking out through leaded glass as lights went on in the hills like the beacons of a distant search party. She rested her head on my shoulder. My arm went around her, my fingertips blindly traced the contours of her face. We took turns drinking from a single glass of wine.

'I love you,' I said.

'I love you too.' She kissed the underside of my chin. After several more sips:

'You were investigating those murders today, weren't you?'

'Yes.'

She fortified herself with a large swallow and refilled the glass.

'Don't worry,' she said. 'I'm not going to hassle you about it. I can't pretend I like it, but I won't try to control you.'

I hugged her by way of thanks.

'I mean, I wouldn't want you treating me that way, so I won't do it to you.' She was giving liberation the old school try, but worry remained suspended in her voice like a fly in amber.

'I'm watching out for myself.'

'I know you are,' she said, too quickly. 'You're a bright man. You can take care of yourself.'

She handed me the wine.

'If you want to talk about it, Alex, I'll listen.'

I hesitated.

235

'Tell me. I want to know what's going on.'

I gave her a rehash of the last two days, ending it with the confrontation with Andy Gutierrez, leaving out the ten turbulent minutes with Raquel.

She listened, troubled and attentive, digested it, and told me, 'I can see why you can't drop it. So many suspicious things, no connecting thread.'

She was right. It was reverse Gestalt, the whole so much less than the sum of its parts. A random assortment of musicians, sawing, blowing, thumping, yearning for a conductor. But who the hell was I to play Ormandy?

'When are you going to tell Milo?'

'I'm not. I spoke to him this morning and he basically told me to mind my own business, stay out of it.'

'But it's his job, Alex. He'll know what to do.'

'Honey, Milo will get bent out of shape if I tell him I visited La Casa.'

'But that poor child, the retarded one, isn't there something he could do about it?'

I shook my head.

'It's not enough. There'd be an explanation for it. Milo's got his suspicions—I'll bet they're stronger than he let on to me—but he's hemmed in by rules and procedures.'

'And you're not,' she said softly.

'Don't worry.'

'Don't worry, yourself. I'm not going to try to stop you. I meant what I said.'

I drank more wine. My throat had constricted and the cool liquid was astringently soothing.

She got up and stood behind me, putting her arms over my shoulders. It was a gesture of support not dissimilar from the one I'd offered Raquel just a few hours earlier. She reached down and played with the ridge of hair that vertically bisected my abdomen.

'I'm here for you, Alex, if you need me.'

236

'I always need you. But not to get involved in crap like this.'

'Whatever you need me for, I'm here.'

I rose out of the chair and drew her to me, kissing her neck, her ears, her eyes. She threw back her head and put my lips on the warm pulse at the base of her throat.

'Let's get into bed and snuggle,' she said.

I turned on the radio and tuned it to KKGO. Sonny Rollins was extracting a liquid sonata from his horn. I switched on a dim light and drew back the covers.

The second surprise of the evening lay there, a plain white envelope, business-size, unmarked and partially covered by the pillow.

'Was this here when you arrived?'

She'd taken off her robe. Now she held it to her breasts, seeking cover, as if the envelope were a living, breathing intruder.

'Could have been. I didn't go in the bedroom.'

I slit it open with my thumbnail and took out the single sheet of white paper folded inside. The page was devoid of date, address or any distinguishing logo. Just a white rectangle filled with lines of handwriting that slanted pessimistically downward. The penmanship, cramped and spidery, was familiar. I sat down on the edge of the bed and read.

Dear Doctor:

Here's hoping you sleep in your own bed in the near future so you have the opportunity to read this. I took the liberty of jimmying your rear door to get in and deliver this—you should get a better lock, by the way.

This afternoon I was relieved of my duties in the H-G case. El Capitán feels the case would benefit by the infusion of fresh blood—the tasteless choice of words was his, not mine. I have my doubts about his moti-

237

vation, but I haven't exactly set any new detection records so I was in no position to debate it with him.

I must have looked pretty shattered by it, cause he got suddenly empathetic and suggested I take some R and R. In fact, he was very well-versed in the details of my personnel file, knew that I'd accrued lots of vacation time and strongly urged me to use some of it.

At first I wasn't overjoyed at the idea, but I've since come to view it as an excellent one. I've found my place in the sun. A quaint little watering hole named Ahuacatlan, just north of Guadalajara. Some preliminary checking via long distance reveals that said burg is extremely well-suited for someone of my recreational interests. Hunting and fishing, in particular.

I expect to be gone for two or three days. Phone contact is tenuous and undesirable—the natives cherish privacy. Will call when I get back. Regards to Stradivarius (Stradivariette?) and stay out of trouble.

All the best,
Milo

I gave it to Robin to read. She finished it and handed it back.

'What's he saying—that he was kicked off the case?'

'Yes. Probably because of outside pressure. But he's going to Mexico to look into McCaffrey's background. Apparently when he called down there he got enough over the phone to make him want to pursue it.'

'He's going behind his captain's back.'

'He must feel it's worth it.' Milo was a brave man but no martyr. He wanted his pension as much as the next guy.

'You were right then. About La Casa.' She got under the covers and drew them up to her chin. She shivered, not from the cold.

'Yes.' Never had being right seemed of such meagre solace.

238

The music from the radio peeked around corners and took an unexpected pirouette. A drummer had joined Rollins, and he slapped out a tropical tattoo on his tom-toms . . . I could think only of cannibals and snake-encrusted vines. Shrunken heads . . .

'Hold me.'

I got in beside her and kissed her and held her and tried to act calm. But all the while my mind was elsewhere, lost on some frozen piece of tundra, floating out to sea.

19

THE ENTRANCE LOBBY of Western Pediatric Medical Center was walled with marble slabs engraved with the names of long-dead benefactors. Inside, the lobby was filled with the injured, the ill and the doomed, all simmering in the endless wait that is as much a part of hospitals as are intravenous needles and bad food.

Mothers clutched bundles to their breasts, wails escaping from within the layers of blanket. Fathers chewed their nails, grappled with insurance forms and tried not to think about the loss of masculinity resulting from encounters with bureaucracy. Toddlers raced about, placing their hands on the marble, withdrawing them quickly at the cold and leaving behind grimy mementoes. A loudspeaker called out names and the chosen plodded to the admissions desk. A blue-haired lady in the green-and-white-striped uniform of a hospital volunteer sat behind the information counter, as baffled as those she was mandated to assist.

In a far corner of the lobby, children and grownups sat on plastic chairs and watched television. The TV was tuned to a serial that took place in a hospital. The doctors and nurses on the screen wore spotless white, had coiffed

240

hair, perfect faces, and teeth that radiated a mucoid sparkle as they conversed in slow, low, earnest tones about love, hate, anguish and death. The doctors and nurses who elbowed their way through the throng in the lobby were altogether more human—rumpled, harried, sleepy-eyed. Those entering rushed, responding to beepers and emergency phone calls. Those exiting did so with the alacrity of escaping prisoners, fearing last-minute calls back to the wards.

I wore my white coat and hospital badge and carried my briefcase as the automatic doors allowed me through and the sixtyish, red-nosed guard nodded as I passed:

'Morning, Doctor.'

I rode the elevator to the basement along with a despondent black couple in their thirties and their son, a withered, gray-skinned nine-year-old in a wheelchair. At the mezzanine we were joined by a lab tech, a fat girl carrying a basket of syringes, needles, rubber tubing and glass cylinders full of the ruby syrup of life. The parents of the boy in the wheelchair looked longingly at the blood; the child turned his head to the wall.

The ride ended with a bump. We were disgorged into a dingy yellow corridor. The other passengers turned right, toward the lab. I went the other way, came to a door marked 'Medical Records,' opened it and went in.

Nothing had changed since I'd left. I had to turn sideways to get through the narrow aisle carved into the floor-to-ceiling stacks of charts. No computer here, no high tech attempt at organizing the tens of thousands of dog-eared manila files into a coherent system. Hospitals are conservative institutions, and Western Pediatric was the most stodgy of hospitals, welcoming progress the way a dog welcomes the mange.

At the end of the aisle was an unadorned gray wall. Just in front of it sat a sleepy-looking Filipino girl, reading a glamour magazine.

'May I help you?'

241

'Yes. I'm Dr. Delaware. I need to get hold of a chart of a patient of mine.'

'You could have your secretary call us, Doctor, and we'd send it to you.'

Sure. In two weeks.

'I appreciate that, but I need to look at it right now and my secretary's not here yet.'

'What's the patient's name?'

'Adams. Brian Adams.' The room was divided alphabetically. I picked a name that would take her to the far end of the A–K section.

'If you'll just fill out this form, I'll get it right for you.'

I filled out the form, falsifying with ease. She didn't bother to look at it and dropped it into a metal filebox. When she was gone, hidden between the stacks, I went to the L–Z side of the room, searched among the N's and found what I was looking for. I slipped it into my briefcase and returned.

She came back minutes later.

'I've got three Brian Adamses, here, Doctor. Which one is it?'

I scanned the three and picked one at random.

'This is it.'

'If you sign this'—she held out a second form—'I can let you have it on twenty-four-hour loan.'

'There'll be no need for that. I'll just examine it here.'

I made a show of looking scholarly, leafed through the medical history of Brian Adams, age eleven, admitted for a routine tonsillectomy five years previously, clucked my tongue, shook my head, jotted down some meaningless notes, and gave it back to her.

'Thanks. You've been most helpful.'

She didn't answer, having already returned to the world of cosmetic camouflage and clothing designed for the sado-intellectual set.

I found an empty conference room down the hall next to

242

the morgue, locked the door from the inside and sat down to examine the final chronicles of Cary Nemeth.

The boy had spent the last twenty-two hours of his life in the Intensive Care Unit at Western Pediatric, not a second of it in a conscious state. From a medical point of view it was open and shut: hopeless. The admitting intern had kept his notes factual and objective, labelling it Auto versus Pedestrian, in the quaint lexicon of medicine that makes tragedy sound like a sporting event.

He'd been brought in by ambulance, battered, crushed, skull shredded, all but his most rudimentary bodily functions gone. Yet thousands of dollars had been spent delaying the inevitable, and enough pages had been filled to create a medical chart the size of a textbook. I leafed through them: nursing notes, with their compulsive accounting of intake and output, the child reduced to cubic centimetres of fluid and plumbing; ICU graphs, progress notes—that was a cruel joke—consultations from neurosurgeons, neurologists, nephrologists, radiologists, cardiologists; blood test, X-rays, scans, shunts, sutures, intravenous feedings, parenteral nutritional supplements, respiratory therapy, and, finally, the autopsy.

Stapled to the back inside cover was the sheriff's report, another example of jargonistic reductionism. In this equally precious dialect, Cary Nemeth was V, for Victim.

V had been hit from behind while walking down Malibu Canyon Road just before midnight. He'd been barefoot, wearing pyjamas—yellow, the report was careful to note. There were no skid marks, leading the reporting deputy to conclude that he'd been hit at full force. From the distance the body travelled, the estimated speed of the vehicle was between forty and fifty miles per hour.

The rest was paperwork, a cardboard snack from some downtown computer.

It was a depressing document. Nothing in it surprised me. Not even the fact that Cary Nemeth's private paedia-

243

trician of record, the physician who'd actually signed the death report, was Lionel Willard Towle, M.D.

I left the chart stuck under a stack of X-ray plates and walked toward the elevator. Two eleven-year-olds had escaped from the ward and were waging a wheelchair drag race. They whooped by, I.V. tubing looping like lariats, and I had to swerve to avoid them.

I reached for the elevator button and heard my name called.

'H'lo, Alex!'

It was the medical director, chatting with a pair of interns. He dismissed them and walked my way.

'Hello, Henry.'

He'd put on a few pounds since I'd last seen him, jowls fighting the confines of his shirt collar. His complexion was unhealthily florid. Three cigars stuck out of his breast pocket.

'What a coincidence,' he said, giving me a soft hand. 'I was just about to call you.'

'Really? What about?'

'Let's talk in the office.'

He closed the door and scurried behind his desk.

'How've you been, son?'

'Just fine.' Dad.

'Good, good.' He took a cigar out of his pocket and made masturbatory motions up and down the cellophane wrapper. 'I'm not going to beat around the bush, Alex. You know that's not my way—always come right out and say what's on your mind is my philosophy. Let people know where you stand.'

'Please do.'

'Yes. Hmm. I'll come out and say it.' He leaned forward, either about to retch or preparing to impart some grave confidence. 'I've—we've received a complaint about your professional conduct.'

He sat back, pleasurably expectant, a boy waiting for a firecracker to explode.

244

'Will Towle?'

His eyebrows shot skyward. There were no fireworks up there, so they came back down again.

'You know?'

'Call it a good guess.'

'Yes, well, you're correct. He's up in arms about some hypnotizing you've done or some such nonsense.'

'He's full of shit, Henry.'

His fingers fumbled with the cellophane. I wondered how long it had been since he'd done surgery. 'I understand your point; however Will Towle is an important man, not to be taken lightly. He's demanding an investigation, some kind of—'

'Witch hunt?'

'You're not making this any easier, young man.'

'I'm not beholden to Towle or anyone else. I'm retired, Henry, or have you forgotten that? Check the last time I received my salary.'

'That's not the point—'

'The point is, Henry, if Towle has a gripe against me, let him bring it up before the State Board. I'm prepared to swap accusations. I guarantee it will be an educational experience for all concerned.'

He smiled unctuously.

'I like you, Alex. I'm telling you this to warn you.'

'Warn me of what?'

'Will Towle's family has donated hundreds of thousands of dollars to this hospital. They may very well have paid for the chair you're sitting on.'

I stood up.

'Thanks for the warning.'

His little eyes hardened. The cigar snapped between his fingers, showering the desk with shreds of tobacco. He looked down at his lost pacifier and for a moment I thought he'd break into tears. He'd be great fun on the analyst's couch.

'You're not as independent as you think you are. There's the matter of your staff privileges.'

'Are you telling me that because Will Towle complained about me I'm in danger of losing my right to practice here?'

'I'm saying: don't make waves. Call Will, make amends. He's not a bad fellow. In fact the two of you should have a lot in common. He's an expert in—'

'Behavioural Paediatrics. I know. Henry, I've heard his tune and we don't play in the same band.'

'Remember this, Alex—the status of psychologists on the medical staff has always been tenuous.'

An old speech came to mind. Something about the importance of the human factor and how it interfaced with modern medicine. I considered throwing it back in his face. Then I looked at his face and decided nothing could help it.

'Is that it?'

He had nothing to say. His type seldom does, when the conversation gets beyond platitudes, entendres, or threats.

'Good day, Doctor Delaware,' he said.

I left quietly, closing the door behind me.

I was down in the lobby, which had cleared of patients and was now filled with a group of visitors from some ladies' volunteer group. The ladies had old money and good breeding written all over their handsome faces—sorority girls grown up. They listened raptly as an administration lackey gave them a prefabricated spiel about how the hospital was in the forefront of medical and humanitarian progress for children, nodding their heads, trying not to show their anxiety.

The lackey prattled on about children being the resources of the future. All that came to my mind was young bones ground up as grist for someone's mill.

I turned and walked back to the elevator.

246

The third floor of the hospital housed the bulk of the administrative offices, which were shaped in an inverted T, panelled in dark wood, and carpeted in something the colour and consistency of moss. The medical staff office was situated at the bottom of the stem of the T, in a glass-walled suite with a view of the Hollywood Hills. The elegant blonde behind the desk was someone I hadn't counted upon seeing, but I straightened my tie and went in.

She looked up, contemplated not recognizing me, then thought better of it and gave me a regal smile. She extended her hand with the imperious manner of someone who'd been at the same job long enough to harbour illusions of irreplaceability.

'Good morning, Alex.'

Her nails were long and thickly coated with mother-of-pearl polish, as if she'd plundered the depths of the ocean for the sake of vanity. I took the hand and handled it with the care it cried out for.

'Cora.'

'How nice to see you again. It's been a long time.'

'Yes it has.'

'Are you returning to us—I'd heard you resigned.'

'No, I'm not, and yes, I did.'

'Enjoying your freedom?' She favoured me with another smile. Her hair looked blonder, coarser, her figure fuller, but still first-rate, packed into a chartreuse knit that would have intimidated someone of less heroic proportions.

'I am. And you?'

'Doing the same old thing,' she sighed.

'And doing it well, I'm sure.'

For a moment I thought the flattery was a mistake. Her face hardened and grew a few new wrinkles.

'We know,' I went on, 'who really keeps things together around here.'

247

'Oh, go on.' She flexed her hand like an abalone-tipped fan.

'It sure ain't the doctors.' I resisted calling her Ol' Buddy.

'Ain't that the truth. Amazing what twenty years of education won't give you in the way of common sense. I'm just a wage slave but I know which end is up.'

'I'm sure you could never be anyone's slave, Cora.'

'Well, I don't know.' Lashes as thick and dark as raven feathers lowered coquettishly.

She was in her early forties and under the merciless fluorescent lighting of the office every year showed. But she was well put together, with good features, one of those women who retain the form of youth but not the texture. Once, centuries ago, she'd seemed girlish, hearty and athletic, as we'd thrashed around the floor of the medical records office. It had been a one-shot deal, followed by mutual boycott. Now she was flirting, her memory cleansed by the passage of time.

'Have they been treating you okay?' I asked.

'As well as can be expected. You know how doctors are.'

I grinned.

'I'm a fixture,' she said. 'If they ever move the office, they'll pick me up with the furniture.'

I looked up and down her body.

'I don't think anyone could mistake you for furniture.'

She laughed nervously and touched her hair self-consciously.

'Thanks.' Self-scrutiny became too unsettling and she put me in the spotlight.

'What brings you down here?'

'Tying up loose ends—a few unfinished charts, paperwork. I've been careless about answering my mail. I thought I received a notice about overdue staff dues.'

'I don't remember sending you one but it could have

248

been one of the other girls. I was out for a month. Had surgery.'

'I'm sorry to hear that, Cora. Is everything all right?'

'Female troubles.' She smiled. 'They say I'm fine.' Her expression said that she thought 'they' were abject liars.

'I'm glad.'

We locked gazes. For just a moment she looked twenty, innocent and hopeful. She turned her back to me, as if wanting to preserve that image in my mind.

'Let me check your file.'

She got up and slid open the drawer of a black-lacquered file cabinet, and came up with a blue folder.

'No,' she said, 'you're all paid up. You'll be getting a notice for next year in a couple of months.'

'Thanks.'

'Don't mention it.'

She returned the folder.

'How about a cup of coffee?' I asked casually.

She looked at me, then at her watch.

'I'm not due for a break until ten, but what the hell, live it up, huh?'

'Right.'

'Let me go to the little girls' room and freshen up.' She fluffed her hair, picked up her purse and left the office to go into the lavatory across the hall.

When I saw the door shut after her I walked to the file cabinet. The drawer she'd opened was labelled. 'Staff A—G.' Two drawers down I found what I wanted. Into the old briefcase it went.

I was waiting by the door when she came out, flushed, pink and pretty, and smelling of patchouli. I extended my arm and she took it.

Over hospital coffee I listened to her talk. About her divorce—a seven-year-old wound that wouldn't heal—the teenage daughter who was driving her crazy by doing exactly what she'd done as an adolescent, car troubles, the insensitivity of her superiors, the unfairness of life.

249

It was bizarre, getting to know for the first time a woman whose body I'd entered. In the scrambled word game of contemporary mating rituals, there was greater intimacy in her tales of woe than there had been in the opening of her thighs.

We parted friends.

'Come by again, Alex.'

'I will.'

I walked to the parking lot marvelling at the ease with which I was able to slip on the cloak of duplicity. I'd always flattered myself with a self-assessment of integrity. But in the last three days I'd grown proficient at sneak-thievery, concealment of the truth, bald-faced lying and emotional whoring.

It must be the company I'd been keeping.

I drove to a cosy Italian place in West Hollywood. The restaurant had just opened and I was alone in my rear corner booth. I ordered veal in wine sauce, a side order of linguini with oil and garlic, and a Coors.

A shuffling waiter brought the beer. While I waited for the food I opened the briefcase and examined my plunder.

Towle's medical staff file was over forty pages long. Most of it consisted of Xeroxes of his diplomas, certificates and awards. His curriculum vitae was twenty pages of puffery, markedly devoid of scholarly publications—he'd coauthored one brief report while an intern, and nothing since—and filled with television and radio interviews, speeches to lay groups, volunteer service to La Casa and similar organizations. Yet he was a full clinical professor at the medical school. So much for academic rigour.

The waiter brought a salad and a basket of rolls. I picked up my napkin with one hand, started to return the

250

file to the briefcase with the other, when something on the front page of the resumé caught my eye.

Under *college or university attended*, he'd listed Jedson College, Bellevue, Washington.

20

I GOT HOME, called the *L.A. Times*, and asked for Ned Biondi at the Metro desk. Biondi was a senior writer for the paper, a short, nervous character right out of *The Front Page*. I'd treated his teenage daughter for anorexia several years back. Biondi hadn't been able to come up with the money for treatment on a journalist's salary—compounded with a penchant for playing the wrong horse at Santa Anita—but the girl had been in trouble and I'd let it go. It had taken him a year and a half to clear his debt. His daughter had gotten straightened out after months of my chipping away at layers of self-hatred that were surprisingly ossified in someone seventeen years old. I remembered her clearly, a tall, dark youngster who wore jogging shorts and T-shirts that accentuated the skeletal conditions of her body; a girl ashen-faced and spindly legged who alternated between deep, dark spells of brooding silence and flights of hyperactivity during which she was ready to enter every category of Olympic competition on three hundred calories a day.

I'd gotten her admitted to Western Pediatric, where she'd stayed for three weeks. That, followed by months of psychotherapy, had finally gotten through to her, and

252

allowed her to deal with the mother who was too beautiful, the brother who was too athletic, and the father who was too witty . . .

'Biondi.'

'Ned, this is Alex Delaware.'

It took a second for my name, minus title to register.

'Doctor! How are you?'

'I'm fine. How's Anne-Marie?'

'Very well. She's finishing up her second year at Wheaton—in Boston. She got A's and a few B's, but the B's didn't panic her. She's still too rough on herself, but she seems to be adjusting well to the peaks and troughs of life, as you called them. Her weight is stable at a hundred and two.'

'Excellent. Give my regards when you speak to her.'

'I certainly will. It's nice of you to call.'

'Well actually there's more to this than professional follow-up.'

'Oh?' A foxy edge, the conditioned vigilance of one who pried open locked boxes for a living, came into his voice.

'I need a favour.'

'Name it.'

'I'm flying up north to Seattle tonight. I need to get into some transcripts at a small college near there. Jedson.'

'Hey, that's not what I expected. I thought you wanted a blurb about a book in the Sunday edition or something. This sounds serious.'

'It is.'

'Jedson. I know it. Anne-Marie was going to apply there—we figured a small place would be less pressure for her—but it was fifty per cent more expensive than Wheaton, Reed, and Oberlin—and they're no giveaways themselves. What do you want with their transcripts?'

'I can't say.'

'Doctor.' He laughed. 'Pardon the expression, but

253

you're prick-teasing. I'm a professional snoop. Dangle something weird in front of me I get a hard-on.'

'What makes you think anything's weird?'

'Doctors running around trying to get into files is weird. Usually it's the shrinks who get broken into, if my memory serves me correctly.'

'I can't go into it now, Ned.'

I'm good with a secret, Doc.'

'No. Not yet. Trust me. You did before.'

'Below the belt, Doc.'

'I know. And I wouldn't gut-punch you if it wasn't important. I need your help. I may be onto something, maybe not. If I am you'll be the first to hear about it.'

'Something big?'

I thought about it for a moment.

'Could be.'

'Okay,' he sighed, 'what do you want me to do?'

'I'm giving your name as a reference. If anyone calls you, back up my story.'

'What's the story?'

He listened.

'It seems harmless enough. Of course,' he added cheerfully, 'if you get found out I'll probably be out of a job.'

'I'll be careful.'

'Yeah. What the hell, I'm getting ready for the gold watch, anyway.' There was a pause as if he were fantasizing life after retirement. Apparently he didn't like what he saw, because when he came back on the line, there was verve in his voice and he offered a reporter's priapic lament.

'I'm gonna go nuts wondering about this. You sure you don't want to give me a hint about what you're up to?'

'I can't, Ned.'

'Okay, okay. Go spin your yarn and keep me in mind if you knit a sweater.'

'I will. Thanks.'

'Oh, hell, don't thank me, I still feel crummy about

254

taking all that time to pay you. I look at my baby now and I see a pink-cheeked, smiling young lady, a beauty. She's still a little too thin for my taste, but she's not a walking corpse like before. She's normal, at least as far as I can tell. She can smile now. I owe you, Doctor.'

'Stay well, Ned.'

'You too.'

I hung up. Biondi's words of gratitude made me entertain a moment's doubt about my own retirement. Then I thought of bloody bodies and doubt got up and took a seat in the rear of the hearse.

It took several false starts and stops to reach the right person at Jedson College.

'Public relations, Ms. Dopplemeier.'

'Ms. Dopplemeier, this is Alex Delaware. I'm a writer with the *Los Angeles Times*.'

'What can I do for you, Mr. Delaware?'

'I'm doing a feature on the small colleges of the West, concentrating on institutions that are not well-known but academically excellent nonetheless. Claremont, Occidental, Reed, etcetera. We'd like to include Jedson in the piece.'

'Oh, really?' She sounded surprised, as if it was the first time anyone had labelled Jedson academically excellent. 'That would be very nice, Mr. Delaware. I'd be happy to talk to you right now and answer any questions you might have.'

'That wasn't exactly what I had in mind. I'm aiming for a more personal approach. My editor is less interested in statistics than in colour. The tenor of the story is that small colleges offer a degree of personal contact and—intimacy—that is missing from the larger universities.'

'How true.'

'I'm actually visiting the campuses, chatting with staff and students—it's an impression piece.'

255

'I understand exactly what you mean. You want to come across with a voice that's human.'

'Exactly. That's a marvellous way of putting it.'

'I did two years at a trade paper in New Jersey before coming to Jedson.' Within the soul of every flack there lurks a journalistic homunculus, chafing to be released to proclaim 'Scoop!' to the ears of the world.

'Ah, a kindred soul.'

'Well, I've left it, but I do think of going back from time to time.'

'It's no way to get rich, but it does keep me hopping, Ms. Dopplemeier.'

'Margaret.'

'Margaret. I'm planning to fly up tonight and wondered if I might come by tomorrow and pay you a visit.'

'Let me check.' I heard paper rustling. 'How about at eleven?'

'Fine.'

'Is there anything you'd like me to do by way of preparation?'

'One thing we're looking at is what happens to graduates of small colleges. I'd be interested in hearing about some of your notable alumni. Doctors, lawyers, that sort of thing.'

'I haven't had a chance to thoroughly acquaint myself with the alumni roster—I've only been here for a few months. But I'll ask around and find out who can help you.'

'I'd appreciate that.'

'Where can I reach you if I need to?'

'I'll be in transit most of the time. You can leave any message with my colleague at the *Times*, Edward Biondi.' I gave her Ned's number.

'Very good. It's all set for tomorrow at eleven. The college is in Bellevue, just outside of Seattle. Do you know where that is?'

'On the east shore of Lake Washington?' Years back I'd been a guest lecturer at the University of Washington and

256

had visited my host's home in Bellevue. I remembered it as an upper-middle-class bedroom community of aggressively contemporary homes, straight-edge lawns and low-rise shopping centres occupied by gourmet shops, antique galleries and high-priced haberdasheries.

'That's correct. If you're coming from downtown take 1-5 to 520 which turns into the Evergreen Point Floating Bridge. Drive all the way across the bridge to the east shore, turn south at Fairweather and continue along the coastline. Jedson is on Meydenbauer Bay, right next to the yacht club. I'm on the first floor of Crespi Hall. Will you be staying for lunch?'

'I can't say for sure. It depends upon how my time is running.' And what I find.

'I'll have something prepared for you, just in case.'

'That's very kind of you, Margaret.'

'Anything for a fellow journalist, Alex.'

My next call was to Robin. It took her nine rings to answer.

'Hi.' She was out of breath. 'I had the big saw going, didn't hear you. What's up?'

'I'm going out of town for a couple of days.'

'Tahiti, without me?'

'Nothing quite so romantic. Seattle.'

'Oh. Detective work?'

'Call it biographical research.' I told her about Towle's having attended Jedson.

'You're really going after this guy.'

'He's going after me. When I was at W.P. this morning Henry Bork grabbed me in the hall, trundled me off to his office and delivered a not-so-subtle version of the old arm twist. Seems Towle's been questioning my ethics in public. He keeps cropping up, like toadstools after a flood. He and Kruger share an alma mater and it makes me want to know more about the ivy-covered halls of Jedson.'

'Let me come up with you.'

257

'No. It's going to be all business. I'll take you on a real vacation, after this is all over.'

'The thought of you going up there all alone depresses me. It's dreary this time of year.'

'I'll be fine. You just take care of yourself and get some work done. I'll call you when I get settled.'

'You're sure you don't want me to come along?'

'You know I love your company, but there'll be no time for sight-seeing. You'd be miserable.'

'All right,' she said reluctantly. 'I'll miss you.'

'I'll miss you too. I love you. Take care.'

'The same goes for you. Love you, sweetie. Bye bye.'

'Bye.'

I took a 9 p.m. flight out of LAX and landed at Sea-Tac Airport at 11:25. I picked up a rented Nova at a Hertz desk. It was no Seville but it did have an F.M. radio that someone had left on a classical station. A Bach organ fugue in a minor key unravelled out of the dash speaker and I didn't cut it off: the music matched my mood. I confirmed my reservation at the Westin, drove away from the airport, connected to the Interstate highway and headed north toward downtown Seattle.

The sky was as cold and hard as a handgun. Minutes after I hit the blacktop the gun proved to be loaded: it fired a blast of thunder and the water started coming down. Soon it was one of those angry Northwest torrents that transforms a highway into miles of drive-thru car wash.

'Welcome to the Pacific Northwest,' I said out loud.

Pine, spruce and fir grew in opaque stands on both sides of the road. Starlit billboards advertised rustic motels and diners offering logger's breakfasts. Except for semis groaning under loads of timber I was the road's sole traveller. I thought to myself how nice it would be to be heading for a mountain cabin, Robin at my side, with a trunkload of fishing gear and provisions. I felt a sudden pang of loneliness and longed for human contact.

258

I reached downtown shortly after midnight. The Westin rose like a giant steel-and-glass test tube amid the darkened laboratory of the city. My seventh-floor room was decent, with a view of Puget Sound and the harbour to the west, Lake Washington and the islands to the east. I kicked off my shoes and stretched out on the bed, tired, but too jumpy for sleep.

I caught the sign-off edition of the news on a local station. The anchor man was wooden-jawed and shifty-eyed, and reported the day's events impersonally. He lent identical emphasis to an account of mass murder in Ohio and the hockey scores. I cut him off in midsentence, turned off the lights, stripped down in darkness and stared at the harbour lights until I fell asleep.

21

A THOUSAND YARDS of rain forest shielded the Jedson campus from the coastal road. The forest yielded to twin stone columns engraved with Roman numerals that marked the origin of a cobbled drive running through the centre of the college. The drive terminated in a circular turn-around punctuated by a pockmarked sundial under a towering pine.

At first glance, Jedson resembled one of those small colleges back East that specialize in looking like dwarf Harvards. The buildings were fashioned of weathered brick and embellished with stone and marble cornices, slate and copper roofing—designed in an era when labour was cheap and intricate mouldings, expansive arches, gargoyles and goddesses the order of the day. Even the ivy looked authentic, tumbling from slate peaks, sucking the brick, trimmed topiary-fashion to bypass recessed, leaded windows.

The campus was small, perhaps half a square mile, and filled with tree-shaded knolls, imposing stands of oak, pine, willow, elm and paper birch, and clearings inlaid with marble and bordered by stone benches and bronze monuments. All very traditional until you looked to the west and saw manicured lawns dipping down to the dock and the private harbour beyond. The slips were occupied by streamlined, teak-decked cruisers, fifty-foot craft and larger, topped with sonar and radar screens and clutches of antennae: clearly twentieth-century, obviously West Coast.

The rain had lifted and a triangle of light peeked out from under the charcoal folds of the sky. A few knots out of the harbour an armada of sailboats sliced through water that looked like tin foil. The boats were rehearsing some type of ceremony, for they each rounded the same buoy marker and unfurled outrageously coloured spinnakers—oranges, purples, scarlets and greens, like the tail-feathers of a covey of tropical birds.

There was a lucite-encased map on a stand and I consulted it to locate Crespi Hall. The students passing by seemed a quiet lot. For the most part they were apple-cheeked and flaxen-haired, their eye colour traversing the spectrum from light blue to dark blue. Their hairstyles were expensively executed but seemed to date from the Eisenhower age. Trousers were cuffed, pennies shined prettily from the tops of loafers and there were enough alligators on shirts to choke the Everglades. A eugenicist would have been proud to observe the straight backs, robust physiques and stiff-lipped self-assurance of those to the manor born. I felt as if I'd died and gone to Aryan Heaven.

Crespi was a three-storey rhomboid fronted by Ionic columns of varicose-veined white marble. The public relations office was hidden behind a mahogany door labelled in gold stencil. When I opened it, the door creaked.

Margaret Dopplemeier was one of those tall, rawboned women predestined for spinsterhood. She'd tried to couch an ungainly body in a tentlike suit of brown tweed, but the angles and corners showed through. She had a big-jawed face, uncompromising lips, and reddish-brown

261

hair cut in an incongruously girlish bob. Her office was hardly larger than the interior of my car—public relations was obviously not a prime concern for the elders of Jedson—and she had to squeeze between the edge of her desk and the wall to get up to greet me. It was a manoeuvre that would have looked clumsy performed by Pavlova and Margaret Dopplemeier turned it into a lurching stumble. I felt sorry for her but made sure not to show it: She was in her midthirties and by that age women like her have learned to cherish self-reliance. It's as good a way as any of coping with solitude.

'Hello, you must be Alex.'

'I am. Pleased to meet you, Margaret.' Her hand was thick, hard and chafed—from too much wringing or too much washing, I couldn't be sure.

'Please sit down.'

I took a slat-backed chair and sat in it uncomfortably.

'Coffee?'

'Please. With cream.'

There was a table with a hot plate to the back of her desk. She poured coffee into a mug and gave it to me.

'Have you decided about lunch?'

The prospect of looking across the table at her for an extra hour didn't thrill me. It wasn't her plainness, nor her stern face. She looked ready to tell me her life story and I was in no mood to fill my head with extraneous material. I declined.

'How about a snack, then?'

She brought forth a tray of cheese and crackers, looking uncomfortable in the role of hostess. I wondered why she'd gravitated toward p.r. Library science would have seemed more fitting. Then the thought occurred to me that public relations at Jedson was probably akin to library work, a desk job involving lots of clipping and mailing and very little face-to-face contact.

'Thank you.' I was hungry and the cheese was good.

'Well.' She looked around her desk, found a pair of

eyeglasses, and put them on. Behind the glass her eyes grew larger and somehow softer. 'You want to get a feel for Jedson.'

'That's right—the flavour of the place.'

'It's quite a unique place. I'm from Wisconsin myself, went to school at Madison, with forty thousand students. There are only two thousand here. Everyone knows everyone else.'

'Kind of like one big family.' I took out a pen and notepad.

'Yes.' At the word family her mouth pursed. 'You might say that.' She shuffled some papers and began reciting:

'Jedson College was founded by Josiah T. Jedson, a Scottish immigrant who made his fortune in mining and railroads in 1858. That's three years before the University of Washington was founded, so we're really the old school in town. Jedson's intention was to endow an institution of higher learning where traditional values coexisted side by side with education in the basic arts and sciences. To this day, primary funding for the college comes from an annuity from the Jedson Foundation, although other sources of income are existent.'

'I've heard tuition is rather high.'

'Tuition,' she frowned, 'is twelve thousand dollars a year, plus housing, registration and miscellaneous fees.'

I whistled.

'Do you give scholarships?'

'A small number of scholarships for deserving students are given each year, but there is no extensive programme of financial aid.'

'Then there's no interest in attracting students from a wide socio-economic range.'

'Not particularly, no.'

She took off her glasses, put her prepared material aside and stared at me myopically.

263

'I would hope we don't get into that particular line of questioning.'

'Why is that, Margaret?'

She moved her lips, trying on several unspoken words for size, rejecting them all. Finally she said: 'I thought this was going to be an impression piece. Something positive.'

'It will be. I was simply curious.' I had touched a nerve—not that it did me any good, for upsetting my source of information was the last thing I needed. But something about the upper-class smugness of the place was irritating me and bringing out the bad boy.

'I see.' She put her glasses back on and picked up her papers, scanned them and pursed her lips. 'Alex,' she said, 'can I speak to you off the record—one writer to another?'

'Sure.' I closed the notepad and put the pen in my jacket pocket.

'I don't know how to put this.' She played with one tweed lapel, twisting the coarse cloth then smoothing it. 'This story, your visit—neither are particularly welcomed by the administration. As you may be able to tell from the grandeur of our surroundings, public relations is not avidly sought by Jedson College. After I spoke to you yesterday I told my superiors about your coming, thinking they'd be more than pleased. In fact, just the opposite was true. I wasn't exactly given a pat on the back.'

She pouted, as if recalling a particularly painful spanking.

'I didn't intend to get you in trouble, Margaret.'

'There was no way to know. As I told you, I'm new here. They do things differently. It's another way of life—quiet, conservative. There's a timeless quality to the place.'

'How,' I asked, 'does a college attract enrolment without attracting attention?'

She chewed her lip.

'I really don't want to get into it.'

264

'Margaret, it's off the record. Don't stonewall me.'

'It's not important,' she insisted, but her bosom heaved and conflict showed in the flat, magnified eyes. I played on that conflict.

'Then what's the fuss? We writers need to be open with one another. There are enough censors out there.'

She thought about that for a long time. The tug-of-war was evident on her face and I couldn't help but feel rotten.

'I don't want to leave here,' she finally said. 'I have a nice apartment with a view of the lake, my cats and my books. I don't want to lose—everything. I don't want to have to pack up and move back to the Midwest. To miles of flatland with no mountains, no way of establishing one's perspective. Do you understand?'

Her manner and tone were brittle—I knew that manner, for I'd seen it in countless therapy patients, just before the defences came tumbling down. She wanted to let go and I was going to help her, manipulative bastard that I was . . .

'Do you understand what I'm saying?' she was asking.

And I heard myself answer, so smooth, so sweet:

'Of course I do.'

'Anything I tell you has to be confidential. Not for print.'

'I promise. I'm a feature writer. I have no aspirations of becoming Woodward or Bernstein.'

A faint smile appeared on the large, bland features.

'You don't? I did, once upon a time. After four years on the Madison student paper I thought I was going to turn journalism on its ear. I went for one solid year with no writing job—I did waitressing. I hated it. Then I worked for a dog magazine, writing cutesy-poo press releases on poodles and schnauzers. They brought the little beasts into the office for photographs and they fouled the carpet. It stunk. When that folded I spent two years covering union meetings and polka parties in New

265

Jersey and that finally squeezed all the illusions out of me. Now all I want is peace.'

Again the glasses came off. She closed her eyes and massaged her temples.

'When you get down to it, that's what all of us want,' I said.

She opened her eyes and squinted in my direction. From the way she strained I must have been a blur. I tried to look like a trustworthy blur.

She popped two pieces of cheese into her mouth and ground them to dust with lantern jaws.

'I don't know that any of it is relevant to your story,' she said. 'Especially if it's a puff piece you're after.'

I forced a laugh.

'Now that you've got me interested, don't leave me dangling.'

She smiled. 'One writer to another?'

'One writer to another.'

'Oh,' she sighed, 'I suppose it's no biggie.'

'In the first place,' she told me, between mouthfuls of cheese, 'no, Jedson College is not interested in attracting outsiders, period. It's a college, but in name and formal status only. What Jedson College really is—functionally—is a *holding pen*. A place for the privileged class to stash their children for four years before the boys enter Daddy's business and the girls marry the boys and turn into Suzy Homemaker and join the Junior League. The boys major in business or economics, the girls in art history and home economics. The gentleman's C is the common goal. Being too smart is frowned upon. Some of the brighter ones do go on to law school or medical school. But when they finish their training they return to the fold.'

She sounded bitter, a wallflower describing last year's prom.

'The average household income of the families that send their kids here is over a hundred thousand dollars a

266

year. Think of that, Alex. Everyone is rich. Did you see the harbour?'

I nodded.

'Those floating toys belong to students.' She paused, as if she still couldn't believe it. 'The parking lot looks like the Monte Carlo Grand Prix. These kids wear cashmere and suede for horsing around.'

One of her raw, coarse hands found the other and caressed it. She looked from wall to wall of the tiny room as if searching for hidden listening devices. I wondered what she was so nervous about. So Jedson was a school for rich kids. Stanford had started out that way too and might have ended up similarly stagnant if someone hadn't figured out that not letting in smart Jews and Asians and other people with funny names and high IQ's would lead to eventual academic entropy.

'There's no crime in being rich,' I said.

'It's not just that. It's the utter mindlessness that goes along with it. I was at Madison during the sixties. There was a sense of social awareness. Activism. We were working to end the war. Now it's the anti-nukes movement. The university can be a greenhouse for the conscience. Here, nothing grows.'

I envisioned her fifteen years back, dressed in khakis and sweatshirt, marching and mouthing slogans. Radicalism had fought a losing battle with survival, eroded by too much of nothing. But she could still take an occasional hit of nostalgia . . .

'It's especially hard on the faculty,' she was saying. 'Not the Old Guard. The Young Turks—they actually call themselves that. They come here because of the job crunch, with their typical academic idealism and liberal views and last two, maybe three years. It's intellectually stultifying—not to mention the frustration of earning fifteen thousand dollars a year when the student's wardrobes cost more than that.'

'You sound as if you have first-hand knowledge.'

267

'I do. There was—a man. A good friend of mine. He came here to teach philosophy. He was brilliant, a Princeton graduate, a genuine scholar. It ate him up. He talked to me about it, told me what it was like to stand up in front of a class and lecture on Kierkegaard and Sartre and see thirty pairs of vacant blue eyes staring back, *Ubermensch U.* he called it. He left last year.'

She looked pained. I changed the subject.

'You mentioned the Old Guard. Who are they?'

'Jedson graduates who actually develop an interest in something other than making money. They go on to earn advanced degrees in humanities—something totally useless like history or sociology or literature—and then come crawling back here to teach. Jedson takes care of its own.'

'I'd imagine they find it easier to relate to the students, coming from the same background.'

'They must. They stay on. Most of them are older—there haven't been too many returning scholars lately. The Old Guard may be shrinking. Some are quite decent, really. I get the feeling they were always outcasts—the misfits. Even the privileged castes have those, I suppose.'

The look on her face bespoke firsthand experience with the pain of social rejection. She may have sensed she was in danger of crossing the boundary from social commentary to psychological striptease, for she drew back, put on her glasses and smiled sourly.

'How's that for public relations?'

'For someone new you've certainly got a handle on the place.'

'Some of it I've seen for myself. Some I learned.'

'From your friend the scholar?'

'Yes.' She stopped and picked up an oversized imitation leather handbag. It didn't take her long to find what she was looking for.

'This is Lee,' she said, and handed me a snapshot of herself and a man several inches shorter than she. The man was balding, with tufts of thick, dark, curling hair over each ear, a bushy dark moustache and rimless round spectacles. He wore a faded blue work shirt and jeans and high-laced hiking boots. Margaret Dopplemeier was dressed in a serape that accentuated her size, baggy cords and flat sandals. She had her arm around him, and looked maternal and childishly dependent at the same time. 'He's in New Mexico now, working on his book. In solitude, he says.'

I gave her back the photo.

'Writers often need that.'

'Yes. We've gone round and round about that.' She put her keepsake back, made a move toward the cheese and then retracted her hand, as if she'd suddenly lost her appetite.

I let a silent moment pass, then performed a lateral arabesque away from her personal life.

'What you're saying is fascinating, Margaret. Jedson is set up with all the enrolment it needs—it's a self-perpetuating system.'

The word 'system' can be a psychological catalyst for anyone who's flirted with the Left. It got her going again.

'Absolutely. The percentage of students whose parents are also Jedson graduates is unbelievably high. I'll bet that the two thousand students come from no more than five to seven hundred families. The same surnames keep cropping up when I compile lists. That's why when you called it a family before I was taken aback. I wondered how much you knew.'

'Nothing until I came here.'

'Yes. I've said too much, haven't I?'

'In a closed system,' I persisted, 'publicity is the last thing the establishment wants.'

'Of course. Jedson is an anachronism. It survives the twentieth century by staying small and keeping out of the headlines. My instructions were to wine you, dine you, see that you took a nice little stroll around the campus, then escort you off the grounds with little or nothing to write about. The Trustees of Jedson don't want exposure in the *Los Angeles Times*. They don't want issues like affirmative action or equal opportunity enrolment to rear their ugly heads.'

'I appreciate your honesty, Margaret.'

For a moment I thought she was going to cry.

'Don't make it sound as if I'm some kind of saint. I'm not and I know it. My talking to you was spineless. Deceitful. The people here aren't evil, I have no right to expose them. They've been good to me. But I get so weary of putting up a front, of attending quaint little teas with women who can talk all day about china patterns and place settings—they give a class here in place settings, do you believe that?'

She looked at her hands as if unable to envision them holding anything as delicate as china.

'My job is pretence, Alex. I'm a glorified mailing service. But I'll not leave,' she insisted, debating an unseen adversary. 'Not yet. Not at this point in my life. I wake up and see the lake. I have my books and a good stereo. I can pick fresh blackberries not far from here. I eat them in the morning with cream.'

I said nothing.

'Will you betray me?' she asked.

'Of course not, Margaret.'

'Then go. Forget about including Jedson in your story. There's nothing here for an outsider.'

'I can't.'

She sat straight in her chair.

'Why not?' There was terror and anger in her voice, something decidedly menacing in her eyes. I could understand her lover's flight to solitude. I was certain the mental deadness of Jedson's student body wasn't the only thing he'd been escaping.

I had nothing to offer her that would keep our lines of communication open, other than the truth and the chance

270

to be a coconspirator. I took a deep breath and told her the real reason for my visit.

When I was through she wore the same possessive-dependent look I'd seen in her photograph. I wanted to back away, but my chair was inches from the door.

'It's funny,' she said, 'I should feel exploited, used. But I don't. You have an honest face. Even your lies sound righteous.'

'I'm no more righteous than you are. I simply want to get some facts. Help me.'

'I was a member of SDS, you know. The police were pigs to me in those days.'

'These aren't those days, I'm not a policeman, and we're not talking about abstract theory and the polemics of revolution. This is triple murder, Margaret, child abuse, maybe more. Not political assassinations. Innocent people hacked into bloody gobbets, mashed into human garbage. Children run down on lonely canyon roads.'

She shuddered, turned away, ran an unpolished fingernail along the top of a tooth, then faced me again.

'And you think one of them—a Jedsonite—was responsible for all of that?' The very idea was delicious to her.

'I think two of them had some involvement in it.'

'Why are you doing this? You say you're a psychiatrist.'

'Psychologist.'

'Whatever. What's in it for you?'

'Nothing. Nothing you'd believe.'

'Try me.'

'I want to see justice done. It's been eating at me.'

'I believe you,' she said softly.

She was gone for twenty minutes and when she returned it was with an armful of oversized volumes bound in dark blue Morocco leather.

'These are the yearbooks, if your estimates of their ages are correct. I'm going to leave you with them and search

271

for the alumni files. Lock yourself in when I'm gone and don't answer the door. I'll knock three times, then twice. That will be our signal.'

'Roger.'

'Ha,' She laughed, and for the first time looked almost attractive.

Timothy Kruger had lied about being a poor boy at Jedson. His family had donated a couple of buildings and even a casual reading of the book made it obvious the Krugers were Very Important. The part about his athletic prowess, though, was true. He'd lettered in track, baseball and Greco-Roman wrestling. In his yearbook pictures he resembled the man I'd spoken to days before. There were shots of him jumping hurdles, throwing the javelin, and later on, in a section on drama, in the roles of Hamlet and Petruchio. The impression I got was that of a big man on campus. I wondered how he'd ended up at La Casa de los Niños operating under a phony credential.

L. Willard Towle's photo showed him to have been a Tab Hunter-type blond in his youth. Notations under his name mentioned presidency of the Pre-Med Club and the Biology Honor Society, as well as captain of the crew team. There was also an asterisk that led to a footnote advising the reader to turn to the last page of the book. I obeyed the instructions and came to a black-bordered photograph—the same picture I'd seen in Towle's office, of his wife and son against a backdrop of lake and mountains. There was an inscription beneath the photo:

In Memoriam
Lilah Hutchison Towle
1930–1951

Lionel Willard Towle, Jr.
1949–1951

Under the inscription were four lines of verse.

272

How swiftly doth the night move
To dash our hopes and dim our dreams;
But even in the darkest night
The ray of peace yet beams.

It was signed 'S'.

I was rereading the poem when Margaret Doppleme-ier's coded knock sounded on the door. I slid open the latch and she came in holding a manila envelope. She locked the door, went behind her desk, opened the packet and shook out two three-by-five index cards.

'These are straight out of the sacred alumni file.' She glanced at one and handed it to me. 'Here's your doctor.'

Towle's name was at the top, written out in elegant script. There were several entries under it, in different hands and different colours of ink. Most of them took the form of abbreviations and numeric codes.

'Can you explain it to me?'

She came around and sat down next to me, took the card and studied it.

'There's nothing mysterious about any of it. The abbreviations are meant to save space. The five digits after the name are the alumnus code, for mailing, filing, that kind of thing. After that you've got the number 3, which means he's the third member of his family to attend Jedson. the *med* is self-explanatory—it's an occupation code, and the *F:med* means medicine is also the family's primary business. If it were shipping, it would say *shp*, banking, *bnk*, and so on. *B:51* is the year he received his bachelor's degree. *M:J,148793* indicates that he married another Jedson student and her alumnus code is cross-referenced. Here's something interesting—there's a small *d* in parentheses after the wife's code, which means she's deceased, and the date of death is 6/17/51—she died when he was still a student here. Did you know that?'

'I did. Would there be any way of finding out more about that?' She thought for a moment.

'We could check the local papers for that week, for an obituary or funeral notice.'

'What about the student paper?'

'The *Spartan* is a rag,' she said scornfully, 'but I suppose it would cover something like that. Back issues are stored in the library, on the other side of campus. We can go there later. Do you think it's relevant?'

She was flushed, girlish, given over totally to our little intrigue.

'It just could be, Margaret. I want to know everything I can about these people.'

'Van der Graaf,' she said.

'What's that?'

'Professor Van der Graaf, from the history department. He's the oldest of the Old Guard, been around Jedson longer than anyone I know of. On top of that he's a great gossip. I sat next to him at a garden party and the sweet old thing told me all sorts of tidbits—who was sleeping with whom, faculty dirt and the like.'

'They let him get away with it?'

'He's close to ninety, rolling in family money, unmarried with no heirs. They're just waiting for him to croak and leave it all to their college. He's been emeritus from way back. Keeps an office on campus, sequesters himself there pretending to write books. I wouldn't be surprised if he sleeps there. He knows more about Jedson than anybody.'

'Do you think he'd talk to me?'

'If he was in the right mood. In fact I thought of him when you told me over the phone that you wanted to find out about illustrious alumni. But I figured it was too risky leaving him alone with a reporter. You never know what he's going to do or say.'

She giggled, enjoying the old man's ability to rebel from a position of power.

'Of course now that I know what you want,' she continued, 'he'd be perfect. You'd need some kind of story

274

about why you wanted to talk about Towle, but I don't imagine that would be very difficult for someone as artful as you.'

'How about this: I'm a reporter for *Medical World News*. Call me Bill Roberts. Dr. Towle's been elected President of the Academy of Pediatrics and I'm doing a background story on him.'

'Sounds good. I'll call him now.'

She reached for the phone and I took another look at Towle's alumnus card. The only information she hadn't covered was a column of dated entries under the heading $—donations to Jedson, I assumed. They averaged ten thousand dollars a year. Towle was a faithful son.

'Professor Van der Graaf,' she was saying, 'this is Margaret Dopplemeier from Public Relations. I've been fine, thank you, and yourself? Very good—oh, I'm sure we can work that out, Professor.' She covered the receiver with her hand and winked at me, mouthing the words 'good mood'. 'I didn't know you liked pizza, Professor. No. No, I don't like anchovies either. Yes, I do like Duesenbergs. I know you do . . . Yes, I know. The rain was coming down in sheets, Professor. Yes, I would. Yes, when the weather clears up. With the top down. I'll bring the pizza.'

She flirted with Van der Graaf for five more minutes and finally broached the subject of my visit. She listened, gave me the okay sign with thumb and forefinger and went back to flirting. I picked up Kruger's card.

He was the fifth member of his family to attend Jedson and his degree was listed as having been granted five years previously. There was no mention of current position—the family was recorded as being active in *stl*, and *rl-est*. No mention of matrimony was present, nor had he donated money to the school. There was however an interesting cross-reference. Under *REL-F*: it said Towle. Finally, the three letters DLT were written in large, block characters at the bottom of the card.

Margaret got off the phone.

275

'He'll see you. As long as I come along, and quote: give me a brisk massage, young lady. You'll be prolonging the years of a living fossil, unquote. The old lecher,' she added affectionately.

I asked her about Towle's name on Kruger's card

'REL-F—related family. Apparently your two subjects are cousins of some sort.'

'Why isn't that listed on Towle's card as well?'

'The heading was probably added after he graduated. Rather than go back and mark each card they simply used it on the new ones. DLT, though, is more interesting. He's been deleted from the file.'

'Why's that?'

'I don't know. It doesn't say. It never would. Some transgression. With his family background it had to be something big. Something that made the school want to wash its hands of him.' She looked up at me. 'This is getting interesting, isn't it?'

'Very.'

She put the cards back in the envelope and locked it in her desk.

'I'll take you to Van der Graaf now.'

22

A GILDED CAGE of an elevator took us to the fifth floor of a domed building on the west side of the campus. It relaxed its jaws and let us out into a silent rotunda, wainscoted in marble and veneered with dust. The ceiling was concave plaster upon which a now-faded mural of cherubs blowing bugles had been painted: we were inside the shell of the dome. The walls were stone and gave off an odour of rotting paper. A stationary diamond-paned window separated two oak doors. One was labelled MAP ROOM and looked as if it hadn't been opened in generations. The other was blank.

Margaret knocked on the unadorned door and, when no answer was forthcoming, pushed it open. The room it revealed was high-ceilinged and spacious, with cathedral windows that afforded a view of the harbour. Every free inch of wall space was taken up by bookshelves crammed haphazardly with ragged volumes. Those books that hadn't found a resting place in the shelves sat in precariously balanced stacks on the floor. In the centre of the room was a trestle table piled high with manuscripts and still more books. A globe on a wheeled stand and an ancient claw-footed desk were pushed into the corner. A

McDonald's take-out box and a couple of crumpled, greasy napkins sat atop the desk.

'Professor?' said Margaret. To me: 'I wonder where he's gone.'

'Peek-a-boo!' The sound came from somewhere behind the trestle table.

Margaret jumped and her purse flew out of her hands. The contents spilled on the floor.

A gnarled head peeked around the curled edges of a pile of yellowed paper.

'Sorry to startle you, dear.' The head came into view, thrown back in silent laughter.

'Professor,' said Margaret, 'shame on you.' She bent to retrieve the scattered debris.

He came out from behind the table looking sheepish. Until that point I'd thought he was sitting. But when the head didn't rise in my sight I realized he'd been standing all along.

He was four feet and a few inches tall. His body was of conventional size but it was bent at the waist, the spine twisted in an S, the deformed back burdened with a hump the size of a tightly packed knapsack. His head seemed too large for his frame, a wrinkled egg topped by a fringe of wispy white hair. When he moved he resembled a drowsy scorpion.

He wore an expression of mock contrition but the twinkle in the rheumy blue eyes said far more than did the downturned, lipless mouth.

'Can I help you, dear?' His voice was dry and cultured.

Margaret gathered the last personal effects from the floor and put them in her purse.

'No, thank you, Professor. I've got it all.' She caught her breath and tried to look composed.

'Will you still come with me on our pizza picnic?'

'Only if you behave yourself.'

He put his hands together, as if in prayer.

'I promise, dear,' he said.

278

'All right. Professor, this is Bill Roberts, the journalist I spoke to you about. Bill, Professor Garth Van der Graaf.'

'Hello, Professor.'

He looked up at me from under sleepy lids.

'You don't look like Clark Kent,' he said.

'I beg your pardon.'

'Aren't newspaper reporters supposed to look like Clark Kent?'

'I wasn't aware of that specific union regulation.'

'I was interviewed by a reporter after the War—the big one. Number two—pardon the scatological entendre. He wanted to know what place the war would have in history. *He* looked like Clark Kent.' He ran one hand over his liver-spotted scalp. 'Don't you have a pair or glasses or something, young man?'

'I'm sorry, but my eyes are quite healthy.'

He turned his back to me and walked to one of the bookshelves. There was a queer, reptilian grace to his movements, the stunted body seeming to travel sideways while actually moving forward. He climbed slowly up a footstool, reached up and grabbed a leatherbound volume, climbed down and returned.

'Look,' he said, opening the book which I now saw was a looseleaf binder containing a collection of comic books. 'This is who I mean.' A shaky finger pointed to a picture of the *Daily Planet*'s star reporter entering a phone booth. 'Clark Kent. *That's* a reporter.'

'I'm sure Mr. Roberts knows who Clark Kent is, Professor.'

'Then let him come back when he looks more like him and I'll talk to him,' the old man snapped.

Margaret and I exchanged helpless looks. She started to say something and Van der Graaf threw back his head and let out an arid cackle.

'April Fool!' He laughed lustily at his own wit, the merriment dissolving into a phlegmy fit of coughing.

'Oh, Professor!' Margaret scolded.

They went at each other again, verbally jousting. I began to suspect that their relationship was well-established. I stood on the sidelines feeling like an unwilling spectator at a freak show.

'Admit it, dear,' he was saying, 'I had you fooled!' He stamped his foot with glee. 'You thought I'd gone totally senile!'

'You're no more senile than I,' she replied. 'You're simply a naughty boy!'

My hopes of getting reliable information from the shrunken hunchback were diminishing by the moment. I cleared my throat.

They stopped and stared at me. A bubble of saliva had collected in the corner of Van der Graaf's puckered mouth. His hands vibrated with a faint palsy. Margaret towered over him, legs akimbo.

'Now I want you to cooperate with Mr. Roberts,' she said sternly.

Van der Graaf gave me a dirty look.

'Oh, all right,' he whined. 'But only if you drive me around the lake in my Doosie.'

'I said I would.'

'I have a thirty-seven Duesenberg,' he explained to me. 'Magnificent chariot. Four hundred snorting stallions under a gleaming ruby bonnet. Chromium pipes. Consumes petroleum with ravenous abandon. I can no longer drive it. Maggie, here, is a large wench. Under my tutelage she could handle it. But she refuses.'

'Professor Van der Graaf, there was a good reason why I turned you down. It was raining and I didn't want to get behind the wheel of a car worth two hundred thousand dollars in hazardous weather.'

'Pshaw. I took that baby from here to Sonoma in forty-four. It thrives on meteorological adversity.'

'All right. I'll drive you. Tomorrow, if I get a good report on your behaviour from Mr. Roberts.'

'I'm the professor. I do the grading.'

280

She ignored him.

'I have to go to the library, Mr. Roberts. Can you find your way back to my office?'

'Certainly.'

'I'll see you when you're through, then. Good-bye, Professor.'

'Tomorrow at one. Rain or shine,' he called after her. When the door had closed he invited me to sit.

'I'll stand, myself. Can't find a chair that fits me. When I was a boy Father called in carpenters and woodcarvers, trying to come up with some way to seat me comfortably. To no avail. They did produce some fascinating abstract sculpture, however.' He laughed, and held on to the trestle table for support. 'I've stood most of my life. In the end it probably was beneficial. I've got legs like pig iron. My circulation's as good as that of a man half my age.'

I sat in a leather armchair. We were at eye level.

'That Maggie,' he said. 'Such a sad girl. I flirt with her, try to cheer her up. She seems so lonely most of the time.' He rummaged among the papers and pulled out a flask.

'Irish whiskey. You'll find two glasses in the top right drawer of the desk. Kindly retrieve them and give them to me.'

I found the glasses, which looked none too clean. Van der Graaf filled them each with an inch of whiskey, without spilling a drop.

'Here.'

I watched him sip his drink and followed suit.

'Do you think she could be a virgin? Is such a thing possible in this day and age?' He approached the question as if it were an epistemological puzzle.

'I really couldn't say, Professor. I only just met her an hour ago.'

'I can't conceive of it, virginity in a woman her age. Yet the notion of those milkmaid's thighs wrapped around a pair of rutting buttocks is equally preposterous.' He drank

281

more whiskey, contemplated Margaret Dopplemeier's sex life in silence, and stared off into space.

Finally he said: 'You're a patient young man. A rare quality.'

I nodded.

'I figure you'll come around when you're ready, Professor.'

'Yes, I do confess to a fair amount of childish behaviour. It's a perquisite of my age and station. Do you know how long it's been since I taught a class or wrote a scholarly paper?'

'Quite a while, I imagine.'

'Over two decades. Since then I've been up here engaged in long solitary stretches of allegedly deep thought—actually I loaf. And yet, I'm an honoured Professor Emeritus. Don't you think it's an absurd system that tolerates such nonsense?'

'Perhaps there's a feeling that you've earned the right to retirement with honour.'

'Bah!' He waved his hand. 'That sounds too much like death. Retirement with honour and maggots gnawing at one's toes. I'll confess to you, young man, that I never earned anything. I wrote sixty-seven papers in learned journals, all but five utter garbage. I coedited three books that no one ever read, and, in general, pursued a life of a spoiled wastrel. It's been wonderful.'

He finished his whiskey and put the glass down on the table with a thump.

'They keep me around her because I've got millions of dollars in a tax-free trust fund set up for me by Father and they hope I'll bequeath it all to them.' He smiled crookedly. 'I may or may not. Perhaps I should will it all to some Negro organization, or something equally outrageous. A group fighting for the rights of lesbians, perhaps. Is there such a cabal?'

'I'm sure there must be.'

'Yes. In California, no doubt. Speaking of which, you

282

want to know about Willie Towle from Los Angeles, do you?'

I repeated the story about *Medical World News*.

'All right,' he sighed, 'if you insist, I'll try to help you. God knows why anyone would be interested in Willie Towle, for a duller boy never set foot on this campus. When I found out he became a physician, I was amazed. I never thought him intellectually capable of anything quite that advanced. Of course the family is firmly rooted in medicine—one of the Towles was Grant's personal surgeon during the Civil War—there's a morsel for your article—and I imagine getting Willie admitted to medical school was no particular challenge.'

'He's turned out to be quite a successful doctor.'

'That *doesn't* surprise me. There are different types of success. One requires a combination of personality traits that Willie did indeed possess: perseverance, lack of imagination, innate conservatism. Of course, a good, straight body and a conventionally attractive face don't hurt, either. I'll wager he hasn't climbed the ranks by virtue of being a profound scientific thinker or innovative researcher. His strengths are of a more mundane nature, are they not?'

'He has a reputation as a fine doctor,' I insisted. 'His patients have only good things to say about him.'

'Tells them exactly what they want to hear, no doubt. Willie was always good at that. Very popular, president of this and that. He was my student in a course on European civilization, and he was a charmer. Yes, Professor, no, Professor. Always there to hold out my chair for me— Lord, how I detested that. Not to mention the fact that I rarely sat.' He grimaced at the recollection. 'Yes, there was a certain banal charm there. People like that in their doctors. I believe it's called bedside manner. Of course his essay exams were most telling, revealing his true substance. Predictable, accurate but not illuminating, gram-

283

matical without being literate.' He paused. 'This isn't the kind of information you were expecting, is it?'

I smiled. 'Not exactly.'

'You can't print this, can you?' He seemed disappointed.

'No. I'm afraid the article is meant to be laudatory.'

'Hale and hearty blah-blah stuff—in the vernacular, bullshit, eh? How boring. Doesn't it bore you to have to write such drivel?'

'At times. It pays the bills.'

'Yes. How arrogant of me not to take that into consideration. I've never had to pay bills. My bankers do that for me. I've always had far more money than I know what to do with. It leads one to incredible ignorance. It's a common fault of the indolent rich. We're unbelievably ignorant. And inbred. It brings about psychological as well as physical aberrations.' He smiled, reached around with one arm, and tapped his hunch. 'This entire campus is a haven for the offspring of the indolent, ignorant, inbred rich. Including your Doctor Willie Towle. He descends from one of the most rarefied environments you will ever find. Did you know that?'

'Being a doctor's son?'

'No, no.' He dismissed me as if I were an especially stupid pupil. 'He's one of the Two Hundred—you haven't heard of them?'

'No.'

'Go into the bottom drawer of my desk and pull out the old map of Seattle.'

I did what I was told. The map was folded under several back issues of *Playboy*.

'Give it to me,' he said impatiently. He opened it and spread it on the table. 'Look here.'

I stood over him. His finger pointed to a spot at the north end of the Sound. To a tiny island shaped like a diamond.

Brindamoor Island. Three square miles of innately

284

unappealing terrain upon which are situated two hundred mansions and estates to rival any found in the United States. Josiah Jedson built his first home there—a Gothic monstrosity, it was—and others of his ilk mimicked him. I have cousins who reside there—most of us are related in one way or the other—though Father built *our* home on the mainland, in Windermere.'

'It's barely noticeable.'

The island was a speck in the Pacific.

'And meant to be that way, my boy. In many of the older maps the island isn't even labelled. Of course there's no land access. The ferry makes one round-trip from the harbour when the weather and tides permit. It's not unusual for a week or two to elapse without the trip being completed. Some of the residents own private airplanes and have landing strips on their properties. Most are content to remain in splendid isolation.'

'And Dr. Towle grew up there?'

'He most certainly did. I believe the ancestral digs have been sold. He was an only son and when he moved to California there seemed no reason to hold on to it—most of the homes are far larger than homes have a right to be. Architectural dinosaurs. Frightfully expensive to maintain—even the Two Hundred have to budget nowadays. Not all had ancestors as clever as Father.'

He patted his midriff in self-congratulation.

'Do you feel growing up in that kind of isolation had any effect on Dr. Towle?'

'Now you sound like a psychologist, young man.'

I smiled.

'In answer to your question: most certainly. The children of the Two Hundred were an insufferably snobbish lot—and to merit that designation at Jedson College requires extraordinary chauvinism. They were clannish, self-centred, spoiled, and not overly bright. Many had deformed siblings with chronic physical or mental problems—my remark about inbreeding was meant in all

285

seriousness—and seemed to have been left callous and indifferent by the experience, rather than the opposite.'

'You're using the past tense. Don't they exist today?'

'There are amazingly few young ones left. They get a taste of the outside world and are reluctant to return to Brindamoor—it really is quite bleak, despite the indoor tennis courts and one pathetic excuse for a country club.'

To stay in character I had to defend Towle.

'Professor, I don't know Doctor Towle well, but he's very well spoken of. I've met him and he seems to be a forceful man, of strong character. Isn't it possible that growing up in the type of environment you describe Brindamoor to be could increase one's individuality?'

The old man looked at me with contempt.

'Rubbish! I understand you have to pretty up his image, but you'll get nothing but the truth from me. There wasn't an individual in the bunch from Brindamoor. Young man, solitude is the nectar of individuality. Our Willie Towle had no taste for it.'

'Why do you say that?'

'I cannot recall ever seeing him alone. He palled around with two other dullards from the island. The three of them pranced around like little dictators. The Three Heads of State they were called behind their backs—pretentious, puffed-up boys. Willie, Stu and Eddy.'

'Stu and Eddy?'

'Yes, yes, that's what I said. Stuart Hickle and Edwin Hayden.'

At the mention of those names I gave an involuntary start. I struggled to neutralize my expression, hoping the old man hadn't noticed the reaction. Happily, he appeared oblivious, as he lectured in that parched voice:

'. . . and Hickle was a sickly, pimple-faced rotter with a spooky disposition, not a word out of him that wasn't censored by the other two. Hayden was a mean-spirited little sneak. I caught him cheating on an exam and he attempted to bribe me out of failing him by offering to

286

procure for me an Indian prostitute of supposedly exotic talents—can you imagine such gall, as if I were unable to fend for myself in affairs of lust! Of course I failed him and wrote a sharp letter to his parents. Got no reply—no doubt they never read it, off on some European jaunt. Do you know what became of him?' he ended rhetorically.

'No,' I lied.

'He's now a judge—in Los Angeles. In fact I believe all three of them, the glorious Heads, moved to Los Angeles. Hickle's some kind of chemist—wanted to be a doctor, just like Willie, and I believe he actually did begin medical school. But he was too stupid to pull through.'

'A judge,' he repeated. 'What does that say about our judicial system?'

The information was pouring in fast and, like a pauper suddenly discovering a sizeable inheritance, I wasn't sure how to deal with it. I wanted to shed my cover and wring every last bit of information out of the old man, but there was the case—and my promises to Margaret—to think about.

'I'm a nasty old bugger, am I not?' cackled Van der Graaf.

'You seem very perceptive, Professor.'

'Oh, do I?' He smiled craftily. 'Any other tidbits I can toss your way?'

'I know Dr. Towle lost his wife and child several years back. What can you tell me about that?'

He stared at me, then refilled his glass and sipped. 'All part of your story?'

'All part of fleshing out the portrait,' I said. It sounded feeble.

'Ah, yes, fleshing it out. Of course. Well, it was a tragedy, no two ways about it, and your doctor was rather young to be dealing with it. He was married during his sophomore year to a lovely girl from a good Portland family. Lovely, but outside his circle—the Two Hundred tended to marry each other. The engagement came as a bit of surprise. Six months later the girl gave birth to a son and that mystery was cleared up.

'For a while the trio seemed to be breaking up—Hickle and Hayden slinked off by themselves as Willie attended to the duties of a married man. Then the wife and child were killed and the Heads were reunited. I suppose it's natural that a man will seek the comfort of friends in the wake of such a loss.'

'How did it happen?'

He peered into his glass and downed the last few drops.

'The girl—the mother—was taking the child to the hospital. He'd woken up with the croup or some such ailment. The nearest emergency facility was at the Children's Orthopedic Hospital, at the University. It was in the early morning hours, still dark. Her car went over the Evergreen Bridge and plunged into the lake. It was daybreak before it was found.'

'Where was Dr. Towle?'

'Studying. Burning the midnight oil. Of course this caused him to be guilt-stricken, absolutely wretched. No doubt he blamed himself for not having been there and been drowned himself. You know the type of self-flagellation embraced by the bereaved.'

'A tragic affair.'

'Oh yes. She was a lovely girl.'

'Dr. Towle keeps her picture in his office.'

'A sentimentalist, is he?'

'I suppose.' I drank some whiskey. 'After the tragedy he began seeing more of his friends?'

'Yes. Though as I hear you use the term I realize something. In my concept of friendship there is implied a bond of affection, some degree of mutual admiration. Those three always looked so grim when they were together— they didn't seem to enjoy each other's company. I never knew what the link between them was, but it did exist. Willie went away to medical school and Stuart tagged along. Edwin Hayden attended law school at the same

288

university. They settled in the same city. No doubt you'll be contacting the other two in order to obtain *laudatory* quotes for your article. If there is an article.'

I struggled to remain calm.

'What do you mean?'

'Oh, I think you know what I mean, my boy. I'm not going to ask you to present identification confirming you're who you say you are—it wouldn't prove a thing anyway—because you seem like a pleasant, intelligent young man and how many visitors to whom I can blab do you think I receive? Enough said.'

'I appreciate that, Professor.'

'And well you should. I trust you have your reasons for wanting to ask me about Willie. Undoubtedly they're boring and I've no wish to know them. Have I been helpful?'

'You've been more than helpful.' I filled our glasses and we shared another drink, no conversation passing between us.

'Would you be willing to be a bit more helpful?' I asked.

'That depends.'

'Dr. Towle has a nephew. Timothy Kruger. I wonder if there's anything you could tell me about him.'

Van der Graaf raised his drink to his lips with trembling hands. His face clouded.

'Kruger.' He said the name as if it were an epithet.

'Yes.'

'Cousin. Distant cousin, not nephew.'

'Cousin, then.'

'Kruger. An old family. Prussians, every one of them. Power brokers. A powerful family.' His mellifluousness was gone and he spat out the words with mechanical intonation. 'Prussians.'

He took a few steps. The arachnid stagger ceased abruptly and he let his hands drop to his sides.

'This must be a police matter,' he said.

'Why do you say that?'

His face blackened with anger and he raised one fist in the air, a prophet of doom.

'Don't trifle with me, young man! If it has something to do with Timothy Kruger there's little else it could be!'

'It is part of a criminal investigation. I can't go into details.'

'Oh, can't you? I've wagged my tongue at you without demanding to know your true intentions. A moment ago I judged them to be boring. Now I've changed my mind.'

'What is it about the Kruger name that scares you so much, Professor?'

'Evil,' he said. 'Evil frightens me. You say your questions are part of a criminal investigation. How do I know what side you're on?'

'I'm working with the police. But I'm not a policeman.'

'I won't tolerate riddles! Either be truthful or be gone!'

I considered the choice.

'Margaret Dopplemeier,' I said. 'I don't want her to lose her job because of anything I tell you.'

'Maggie?' he snorted. 'Don't worry about her, I've no intention of letting on the fact that she led you to me. She's a sad girl, needs intrigue to spice up her life. I've spoken enough to her to know that she clings longingly to the Conspiracy Theory of Life. Dangle one before her—she'll go for it like a trout for a lure. Kennedy assassinations, Unidentified Flying Objects, cancer, tooth decay—all the result of a grand collusion of anonymous demons. No doubt you recognized that and exploited it.'

He made it sound Machiavellian. I didn't dispute it.

'No,' he said. 'I've no interest in crushing Maggie. She's been a friend. Apart from that, my loyalties to this institution are far from blind. I detest certain aspects of this place—my true home, if you will.'

'Such as the Krugers?'

'Such as the environment that allows Krugers and their ilk to flourish.'

290

He tottered, the too-large head lolling on its misshapen base.

'The choice is yours, young man. Put up or shut up.'

I put up.

'Nothing in your story surprises me,' he said. 'I didn't know of Stuart Hickle's death nor of his sexual proclivities, but neither are shocking. He was a bad poet, Dr. Delaware, very bad—and nothing is beyond a bad poet.'

I recalled the verse at the bottom of Lilah Towle's yearbook obituary. It was clear who 'S' was.

'When you mentioned Timothy I became alarmed, because I didn't know if you were in the employ of the Krugers. The badge you showed me is well and fine, but such trinkets are easily counterfeited.'

'Call Detective Delano Hardy at West Los Angeles Police Division. He'll tell you what side I'm on.' I hoped he wouldn't take me up on it—who knew how Hardy would react?

He looked at me thoughtfully. 'No, that won't be necessary. You're a dreadful liar. I believe I can intuitively tell when you're telling the truth.'

'Thank you.'

'You're welcome. A compliment was intended.'

'Tell me about Timothy Kruger,' I said.

He stood blinking, gnomelike, a concoction of a Hollywood special-effects lab.

'The first thing I'd like to emphasize is that the evil of the Krugers has nothing to do with wealth. They would be evil paupers—I imagine they were, at one time. If that sounds defensive, it is.'

'I understand.'

'The very wealthy are not evil, Bolshevist propaganda to the contrary. They are a harmless lot—overly sheltered, reticent, destined for extinction.' He took a step backward as if retreating from his own prediction.

I waited.

291

'Timothy Kruger,' he finally said, 'is a murderer, plain and simple, The fact that he was never arrested, tried or convicted does nothing to diminish his guilt in my eyes. The story goes back seven—no, eight years. There was a student here, a farm boy from Idaho. Sharp as a tack, built like Adonis. His name was Saxon. Jeffrey Saxon. He came here to study, the first of his family to finish high school, dreaming of becoming a writer.

'He was accepted on an athletic scholarship—crew, baseball, football, wrestling—and managed to excel in all of those while maintaining an A average. He majored in history and I was his faculty advisor, though by that time I wasn't teaching any more. We had many chats, up here in this room. The boy was a pleasure to converse with. He had an enthusiasm for life, a thirst for knowledge.'

A tear collected in the corner of one drooping, blue eye.

'Excuse me.' The old man pulled out a linen handkerchief and dabbed his cheek. 'Dusty in here, must get the custodial staff to clean.' He sipped his whiskey and when he spoke his voice was enfeebled by memories.

'Jeffrey Saxon had the curious, searching nature of a true scholar, Dr. Delaware. I recall the first time he came up here and saw all the books. Like a child let loose in a toy store. I lent him my finest antiquarian volumes—everything from the London edition of Josephus' *Chronicles* to anthropologic treatises. He devoured them. "For God's sake, Professor," he'd say, "it would take several lifetimes to learn even a fraction of what there is to know."—that's the mark of an intellectual, in my view, becoming cognizant of one's own insignificance in relation to the accumulated mass of human knowledge.

'The others, of course, thought him a rube, a hick. They made fun of his clothes, his manner, his lack of sophistication. He spoke to me about it—I'd become a kind of surrogate grandfather I suppose—and I reassured him that he was meant for more noble company than what

292

Jedson had to offer. In fact I'd encouraged him to put in for a transfer to an Eastern school—Yale, Princeton—where he could achieve significant intellectual growth. With his grades and a letter from me, he might have made it. But he never got a chance.

'He became attached to a young lady, one of the Two Hundred, pretty enough, but vapid. This in itself, was no error, as the heart and the gonads must be satisfied. The mistake was in choosing a female already coveted by another.'

'By Tim Kruger?'

Van der Graaf nodded painfully.

'This is difficult for me, Doctor. It brings back so much.'

'If it's too difficult for you, Professor, I can leave now and come back some other time.'

'No, no. That would serve no purpose.' He took a deep breath. 'It comes down to a smarmy soap opera of a tale. Jeffrey and Kruger were interested in the same girl, they had words in public. Tempers flared, but it seemed to pass. Jeffrey visited me and vented his spleen. I played amateur psychologist—professors so often are required to provide emotional support to their students and I confess I did a fine job of it. I urged him to forget the girl, knowing her type, understanding full well that Jeffrey would be the loser in any battle of wills. The young of Jedson are homing pigeons, as predictable as their ancestors, reverting to type. The girl was meant to mate with one of her own. There were better things, finer things, awaiting Jeffrey, an entire lifetime of opportunity and adventure.

'He wouldn't listen. He was like a knight of old, imbued with the nobility of his mission. Conquer the Black Jouster, rescue the fair maiden. Total rubbish—but he was an innocent. *An innocent.*'

Van der Graaf paused, out of breath. His face had turned a sickly greenish shade of pale and I feared for his health.

293

'Perhaps we should stop for the moment,' I suggested. 'I can return tomorrow.'

'Absolutely not! I'll not be left here in solitary confinement with a poisonous lump lodged in my craw!' He cleared his throat. 'I'll be on with it—you sit there and pay close attention.'

'All right, Professor.'

'Now then, where was I—ah, Jeffrey as a White Knight. Foolish boy. The enmity between him and Timothy Kruger continued and festered. Jeffrey was ostracized by all the others—Kruger was a campus luminary, socially established. I became Jeffrey's sole source of support. Our conversations changed. No longer were they cerebral exchanges. Now I was conducting psychotherapy on a full-time basis—an activity with which I was most uncomfortable, but I felt I couldn't abandon the boy. I was all he had.

'It culminated in a wrestling match. Both the boys were Greco-Roman wrestlers. They agreed to meet, late at night, in the empty gymnasium, just the two of them for a grudge match. I'm no wrestler myself, for obvious reasons, but I do know that the sport is highly structured, replete with regulations, the criteria for victory clearly drawn. Jeffrey liked it for that reason—he was highly self-disciplined for one so young. He walked into that gym alive and left on a stretcher, neck and spine snapped, alive in only the most vegetative sense of the word. Three days later he died.'

'And his death was ruled an accident,' I said softly.

'That was the official story. Kruger said the two of them had gotten involved in a complicated series of holds and in the ensuing tangle of torsos, arms and legs, Jeffrey had been injured. And who could dispute it—accidents do occur in wrestling matches. At worst it seemed a case of two immature men behaving in an irresponsible manner. But to those of us who knew Timothy, who understood the depth of the rivalry between them, that was far from

294

a satisfactory explanation. The college was eager to hush it up, the police all too happy to oblige—why go up against the Kruger millions when there are hundreds of poor people committing crimes?

'I attended Jeffrey's funeral—flew to Idaho. Before I left I ran into Timothy on campus. Looking back I see he must have sought me out.' Van der Graaf's mouth tightened, the wrinkles deepening as if controlled by some internal drawstring. 'He approached me near the Founder's statue. "I hear you're travelling, Professor," he said. "Yes," I replied, "I'm flying to Boise tonight." "To attend the last rites for your young charge?" he asked. There was a look of utter innocence on his face, feigned innocence—he was an actor, for God's sake, he could manipulate his features at will.

' "What's it to you?" I replied. He bent to the ground, picked up a dry oak twig and sporting an arrogant smirk—the same smirk one can see in photographs of Nazi concentration camp guards tormenting their victims—snapped the twig between his fingers, and let it drop to the ground. Then he laughed.

'I've never in my life been so close to committing murder, Doctor Delaware. Had I been younger, stronger, properly armed, I would have done it. As it was, I simply stood there, for once in my life at a loss for words. "Have a nice trip," he said, and, still smirking, backed away. My heart pounded so, I was assaulted with a spell of dizziness, but fought to maintain my equilibrium. When he was out of eyesight I broke down and sobbed.'

A long moment passed between us.

When he appeared sufficiently composed I asked him: 'Does Margaret know about this? About Kruger?'

He nodded.

'I've spoken of it to her. She's my friend.'

So the awkward publicist was more spider than fly after all. The insight cheered me for some reason.

295

'One more thing—the girl. The one they were fighting over. What became of her?'

'What do you expect?' He sneered, some of the old vitriol returning to his voice. 'She shunned Kruger—most of the others did. They were afraid of him. She attended Jedson for three more undistinguished years, married an investment banker and moved to Spokane. No doubt she's a proper hausfrau, shuttling the kiddies to school, brunching at the club, boffing the delivery boy.'

'The spoils of battle,' I said.

He shook his head. 'Such a waste.'

I looked at my watch. I'd been up in the dome for a little over an hour, but it seemed longer. Van der Graaf had unloaded a truckful of sewage during that time, but he was a historian, and that's what they're trained to do. I felt tired and tense, and I longed for fresh air.

'Professor,' I said. 'I don't know how to thank you.'

'Putting the information to good use would be a step in the right direction.' The blue eyes shone like twin gaslights. 'Snap some twigs of your own.'

'I'll do my best.' I got up.

'I trust you can see yourself out.'

I did.

When I was halfway across the rotunda I heard him cry out: 'Remind Maggie of our pizza picnic!'

His words echoed against the smooth, cold stone.

296

23

AMONG CERTAIN PRIMITIVE TRIBES, there exists the belief that when one vanquishes an enemy it is not enough to destroy all evidence of corporeal life: the soul must be vanquished as well. That belief is at the root of the various forms of cannibalism that have been known to exist—and still exist—in many regions of the world. You are what you eat. Devour your victim's heart, and you encompass his very being. Grind his penis to dust and swallow the dust, and you've co-opted his manhood.

I thought of Timothy Kruger—of the boy he'd killed and how he'd assumed the identity of a struggling scholarship student when describing himself to me—and visions of lip-smacking, bone-crunching savagery intruded upon the idyllic verdancy of the Jedson campus. I was still struggling to erase those visions when I climbed the marble steps of Crespi Hall.

Margaret Dopplemeier responded to my coded knock with a 'Wait one second!' and an open door. She let me in and locked the door.

'Did you find Van der Graaf helpful?' she asked airily.

'He told me everything. About Jeffrey Saxon and Tim Kruger and the fact that you were his confidante.'

297

She blushed.

'You can't expect me to feel guilty for deceiving you when you did the same to me,' she said.

'I don't,' I assured her, 'I just wanted you to know that he trusted me and told me everything. I know you couldn't until he did.'

'I'm glad you understand,' she said primly.

'Thank you for leading me to him.'

'It was my pleasure, Alex. Just put the information to good use.'

It was the second time in ten minutes that I'd received that mandate. Add to that a similar order from Raquel Ochoa and it made for a heavy load.

'I will. Do you have the clipping?'

'Here.' She handed me the photocopy. The death of Lilah Towle and 'Little Willie' had made the front page, sharing space with a report on fraternity hijinks and a reprint of an Associated Press report on the dangers of 'mariwuana reefers'. I started to read but the copy was blurred and barely legible. Margaret saw me straining.

'The original was rubbed out.'

'It's okay.' I skimmed the article long enough to see that it was consistent with Van der Graaf's recollection.

'Here's another story, several days later—about the funeral. This one's better.'

I took it from her and examined it. By now the Towle affair was on page six, a social register item. The account of the ceremony was maudlin and full of dropped names. A photograph at the bottom caught my eye.

Towle led the mourners' procession, haggard and grim, hands folded in front of him. To one side was a younger, still toadlike Edwin Hayden. To the other, slightly to the rear, was a towering figure. There was no mistaking the identity of the mourner.

The kinky hair was black, the face bloated and shiny. The heavy framed eyeglasses I'd seen a few days before

298

were replaced by gold-rimmed, round spectacles resting low on the meaty nose.

It was the Reverend Augustus McCaffrey in younger days.

I folded both papers and slipped them in my jacket pocket.

'Call Van der Graaf,' I said.

'He's an old man. Don't you think you've questioned him enou—'

'Just call him,' I cut her off. 'If you don't I'll run back there myself.'

She winced at my abruptness, but dialled the phone.

When the connection was made she said, 'Sorry to bother you, Professor. It's *him* again.' She listened, shot me an unhappy look and handed me the receiver, holding it at arm's length.

'Thank you,' I said sweetly. Into the phone: 'Professor, I need to ask you about another student. It's important.'

'Go on. I've only Miss November of 1973 occupying my attention. Who is it?'

'Augustus McCaffrey—was he a friend of Towle, too?'

There was silence on the other end of the line and then the sound of laughter.

'Oh, dear me! That's a laugh! Gus McCaffrey, a Jedson student! And him touched by the tar brush!' He laughed some more and it was a while before he caught his breath. 'Mary Mother of God, no, man. He was no *student* here!'

'I've got a photograph in front of me showing him at the Towle funeral—'

'Be that as it may, he was no student. Gus McCaffrey was—I believe they call themselves maintenance engineers today—Gus was a janitor. He swept the dormitories, took out the trash, that kind of thing.'

What was he doing at the funeral? It looks like he's right behind Towle, ready to catch him if he falls.'

'No surprise. He was originally an employee of the Hickle family—they had one of the largest homes on Brinda-

299

moor. Family retainers can grow quite close to their masters—I believe Stuart brought him over to Jedson when he began college here. He did eventually attain some kind of rank within the custodial staff—supervising janitor or something similar. Leaving Brindamoor may very well have been an excellent opportunity for him. What's big Gus doing today?'

'He's a minister—the head of that children's home I told you about.'

'I see. Taking out the Lord's trash, so to speak.'

'So to speak. Can you tell me anything about him.'

'I honestly can't, I'm afraid. I had no contact with the nonacademic employees—there's a tendency to pretend they're invisible that's acquired over time. He was a big brute of a fellow, that I do recall. Slovenly, seemed quite strong, may very well have been bright—your information certainly points in that direction, and I'm no social Darwinist with a need to dispute it. But that is really all I can tell you. I'm sorry.'

'Don't be. One last thing—where can I get a map of Brindamoor Island?'

'There's none that I know of outside the County Hall of Records—wait, a student of mine did an undergraduate thesis on the history of the place, complete with residential map. I don't have a copy but I believe it would be stored in the library, in the thesis section. The student's name was—let me think—Church? No, it was something else of a clerical nature—Chaplain. Gretchen Chaplain. Look under C, you should find it.'

'Thanks again, Professor. Good-bye.'

'Good-bye.'

Margaret Dopplemeier sat at her desk, glaring at me.

'I'm sorry for being rude,' I said. 'It was important.'

'All right,' she said. 'I just thought you could have been a little more polite in view of what I've done for you.' The possessive look slithered into her eyes like a python into a lagoon.

300

'You're right. I should have. I won't trouble you further.' I stood up. 'Thanks so much for everything.' I held out my hand, and when she reluctantly extended hers, I took it. 'You've really made a big difference.'

'That's good to know. How long will you be staying?'

Gently I broke the handclasp.

'Not long.' I backed away, smiled at her, finally got my hand on the knob and pushed. 'All the best, Margaret. Enjoy your blackberries.'

She started to say something, then thought better of it. I left her standing behind her desk, a circle of pink tongue-tip visible in the corner of her unattractive mouth, searching for a taste of something.

The library was properly austere and very respectably stocked with books and journals for a college the size of Jedson. The main room was a marble cathedral draped in heavy red velvet and lit by oversized windows placed ten feet apart. It was filled with oak reading tables, green-shaded lamps, leather chairs. All that was missing were people to read the august volumes that papered the walls.

The librarian was an effete young man with close-cropped hair and a pencil moustache. His shirt was red plaid, his tie a yellow knit. He sat behind his reference table reading a recent copy of *Artforum*. When I asked him where the thesis section was, he looked up with the astonished expression of a hermit observing the penetration of his lair.

'There,' he said, languidly, and pointed to a spot at the south end of the room.

There was an oak card catalogue and I found Gretchen Chaplain's thesis listed in it. The title of her magnum opus had been *Brindamoor Island: Its History and Geography*.

Theses by Frederick Chalmers and O. Winston Chastain were present, but Gretchen's rightful place between them was unfilled. I checked and doublechecked the

301

Library of Congress number but that was a fruitless ritual: the Brindamoor study was gone.

I went back to Plaid Shirt and had to clear my throat twice before he tore himself away from a piece on Billy Al Bengston.

'Yes?'

'I'm looking for a specific thesis and can't seem to find it.'

'Have you checked the card file to make sure it's listed?'

'The card's there but the thesis isn't.'

'How unfortunate. I would guess it's been checked out.'

'Could you check for me, please?'

He sighed and took too long to raise himself out of his chair. 'What's the author's name?'

I gave him all the necessary information and he went behind the checkout counter with an injured look. I followed him.

'Brindamoor Island—dreary place. Why would you want to know about *that*?'

'I'm a visiting professor form UCLA and it's part of my research. I didn't know an explanation was necessary.'

'Oh, it's not,' he said, quickly, and buried his nose in a stack of cards. He lifted out a portion of the cards and shuffled them like a Vegas pro. 'Here,' he said, 'that thesis was checked out six months ago—my, it's overdue, isn't it?'

I took the card. Scant attention had been paid to Gretchen's masterpiece. Prior to its last withdrawal a half year ago, the last time it had been checked out was in 1954, by Gretchen herself. Probably wanted to show it to her kids—Mummy was once quite a scholar, little ones . . .

'Sometimes we get behind on checking on overdue notices. I'll get right on this, Professor. Who checked it out last?'

I looked at the signature and told him. As the name left

302

my mouth my brain processed the information. By the time the two words had dissolved I knew my mission wouldn't be complete without a trip to the island.

24

THE FERRY TO Brindamoor Island made its morning trip at seven-thirty.

When the wake-up call from the desk came in at six it found me showered, shaved and tensely bright-eyed. The rain had started again shortly after midnight, pounding the glass walls on the suite. It had roused me for a dream-like instant during which I was certain I'd heard the sound of cavalry hooves stampeding down the corridor, and had gone back to sleep anyway. Now it continued to come down, the city below awash and out of focus, as if viewed from inside a dirty aquarium.

I dressed in heavy slacks, leather jacket, wool turtleneck, and took along the only raincoat I had: an unlined poplin doublebreasted affair that was fine for Southern California but of uncertain utility in the present surroundings. I caught a quick breakfast of smoked salmon, bagels, juice and coffee and made it to the docks at ten after seven.

I was among the first to queue up at the entrance to the auto bay. The line moved and I drove down a ramp into the womb of the ferry behind a VW bus with Save the Whale stickers on the rear bumper. I obeyed the gesticulations of a crewman dressed in dayglo orange overalls and parked two inches from the slick, white wall of the bay. An ascent of two flights brought me on deck. I walked past a gift shop, tobacconist and snack bar, all closed, and a blackened room furnished wall to wall with video games. A waiter played Pac Man in solitude, devouring dots with brow-furrowing concentration.

I found a seat with a view at the stern, folded my raincoat across my lap and settled back for the one-hour ride.

The ship was virtually empty. My few fellow passengers were young and dressed for work: hired help from the mainland commuting to their assigned posts at the manors of Brindamoor. The return trip, no doubt, would be filled with commuters of another class: lawyers, bankers, other financial types, on their way to downtown offices and panelled boardrooms.

The ocean pitched and rolled, frothing in response to the surface winds that drag-raced along its surface. There were smaller craft at sea, mostly fishing boats, tugs and scows, and they danced in command, curtsying and dipping. For all the ferry moved it might have been a toy model on a shelf.

A group of six young men in their late teens came aboard and sat down ten feet away. Blond, bearded in varying degrees of shagginess, dressed in rumpled khakis and dirt-grayed jeans, they passed around a thermos full of something that wasn't coffee, joked, smoked, put their feet up on chairs and emitted a collective guffaw that sounded like a beery laugh track. One of them noticed me and held up the thermos.

'Swig, my man?' he offered.

I smiled and shook my head.

He shrugged, turned away and the party started up again.

The ferry's horn sounded, the rumble of its engines reverberating through the floorboards, and we started to move.

305

Halfway through the trip I walked over to where the six young drinkers sat, now slumped. Three of them slept, snooring open-mouthed, one was reading an obscene comic book, and two, including the one who'd offered me the drink, sat smoking, hypnotized by the glowing ends of their cigarettes.

'Excuse me.'

The two smokers looked up. The reader paid no attention.

'Yeah?' The generous one smiled. He was missing half of his front teeth: bad oral hygiene or a quick temper. 'Sorry, man, we got no more Campbell's soup.' He picked up the thermos and shook it. 'Ain't that right, Dougie?'

His companion, a fat boy with drooping moustaches and muttonchop sideburns, laughed and nodded his head.

'Yeah, no more soup. Chicken noodle. Ninety proof.'

From where I was standing the whole bunch of them smelled like a distillery.

'That's all right. I appreciate the offer. I was just wondering if you could give me some information about Brindamoor.'

Both boys looked puzzled, as if they'd never thought of themselves as having any information to give.

'What do you want to know? Place is a drag,' said Generous.

'Fuckin-A.' Fat Boy nodded assent.

'I'm trying to find a certain house on the island, can't seem to get hold of a map.'

'That's 'cause there ain't any. People there like to hide from the rest of the world. They got private cops ready to roust you for spittin' the wrong way. Me 'n' Doug and the rest of these jokers go over to do groundswork on the golf course, pickin' up crap and litter and stuff. Finish the day and head straight back for the boat, man. We want to keep our jobs, we stick to that—exactly.'

'Yeah,' said the fat one. 'No shootin' for the local beaver, no partyin'. Workin' people been doin' it for

306

years and years—my dad worked Brindamoor before he got in the union, and I'm just doin' it until he gets me in. Then, fuck those hermits. He told me they had a song for it, back in those days: Heft and tote, then float on the boat.' He laughed and slapped his buddy on the back.

'What you interested in findin'?' Generous lit another cigarette and placed it in the snaggled gap where his upper incisors should have been.

'The Hickle house.'

'You related to them?' Doug asked. His eyes were the colour of the sea, bloodshot and suddenly dull with worry, wondering if I was someone who could turn his words against him.

'No. I'm an architect. Just doing a little sightseeing. I was told the Hickle house would be of interest. Supposed to be the biggest one on the island.'

'Man,' he said, 'they're all big. You could fit my whole fuckin' neighbourhood in one of them.'

'Architect, huh?' Generous's face brightened with interest. 'How much school it take to do that?'

'Five years of college.'

'Forget it,' the fat one kidded him. 'You're an airhead, Harm. You got to learn how to read and write first.'

'Fuck you!' said his friend, good-naturedly. To me: 'I worked construction last summer. Architecture's probly pretty interestin'.'

'It is. I do mostly private houses. Always looking for new ideas.'

'Yeah, hey, right. Gotta keep it interestin'.'

'Aw, man,' chided Dougie. 'We don't do nothing interestin'. Clean up goddam garbage—hell, man, there's fun going on there at that club, 'cause last week Matt 'n' me found a couple of used rubbers out by hole number eleven—and we're missin' it, Harm.'

'I don't need those people for my fun,' said the generous one. 'You want to know about houses, mister, let's ask Ray.' He turned and leaned across one sleeping boy

307

to elbow the one with the comic book, who'd kept his nose buried in his reading and hadn't looked up once. When he did, his face had the glazed look of someone very stupid or very stoned.

'Huh?'

'Ray, you dumbshit, man wants to know about the Hickle house.'

The boy blinked, uncomprehending.

'Ray's been droppin' too much acid out in the woods. Just can't seem to shake himself out of it.' Harm grinned, his tonsils visible. 'C'mon, man, where's the Hickle place?'

'Hickle,' Ray said. 'My old man used to work there—spooky place he said. Weird. I think it's on Charlemagne. The old man used to—'

'All right, man.' Harm shoved Ray's head down and he returned to his comic book. 'They got strange names for streets on the island, Mister. Charlemagne, Alexander, Suleiman.'

Conquerors. The little joke of the very rich was evidently lost on those who were its intended butt.

'Charlemagne is an inland road. You go just past the main drag, past the market, a quarter mile—look hard because the street signs are usually covered by trees—and turn, lemme see, turn right, that's Charlemagne. After that you'd best ask around.'

'Much obliged.' I reached in and pulled out my wallet. 'Here's for your trouble,' I said, taking out a five.

Harm held out his hand—in protest, not collection. 'Forget it, mister. We didn't do nothin'.'

Doug, the fat boy, gave him an angry look and grunted.

'Up yours, Dougie,' said the boy with the missing teeth. 'We didn't do nothin' for the man's money.' Despite his unkempt hair and the war zone of a mouth, he had intelligence and a certain dignity. He was the kind of kid I wouldn't mind having at my side when the going got rough.

'Let me buy you a round, then.'

'Nah,' said Harm. 'We can't drink no more, Mister. Got to hit the course in half an hour. Be slick as snot on a day like this. Bubble Butt here, drink any more, he could fall and bounce down and crush the rest of us.'

'Fuck you, Harm,' said Doug, without heart.

I put the money back. 'Thanks much.'

'Think nothin' of it. You build some houses that don't need union help, you want reliable construction muscle, remember Harmon Lundquist. I'm in the book.'

'I will.'

Ten minutes before the boat reached shore the island emerged from behind a dressing screen of rain and fog, an oblong, squat, gray chunk of rock. Except for the coiffure of trees that covered most of its outer edges, it could have been Alcatraz.

I went down to the auto bay, got behind the wheel of the Nova and was ready when the man in orange waved us down the ramp. The scene outside might have been lifted off the streets of London. There were enough black topcoats, black umbrellas, and black hats to fill Piccadilly. Pink hands held briefcases and the morning's *Wall Street Journal*. Eyes stared straight ahead. Lips set grimly. When the gate at the foot of the gangway opened they moved in procession, each man in his place, every shiny black shoe rising and falling in response to an unseen drummer. A squadron of perfect gentlemen. A gentlemen's brigade . . .

Just beyond Brindamoor Harbor was a small town square built around an enormous towering elm and rimmed with shops: a bank with smoked glass windows, a brokerage house, three or four expensive looking clothiers with conservatively dressed, faceless mannequins in their windows, a grocer, a butcher, a dry cleaner's that also housed the local post office, a book store, two restaurants—one French, the other Italian—a gift shop, and

309

a jewellers. All the stores were closed, the streets empty and, except for a flock of pigeons convening under the elm, devoid of life.

I followed Harm's directions and found Charlemagne Lane with no trouble. A thousand yards out of the square the road narrowed and darkened, shadowed by walls of fern, devil ivy and shrub maple. The green was broken by an occasional gate—wrought iron or redwood, the former usually backed by steel plating. There were no mailboxes on the road, no public display of names. The estates seemed to be spaced several acres apart. A few times I caught a glimpse of the properties behind the gates: lots of rolling lawns, sloping drives paved with brick and stone, the houses imposing and grand—Tudor, Regency, Colonial—the driveways stabling Rolls Royces, Mercedes and Cadillac limousines, as well as their more utilitarian four-wheeled cousins—stationwagons panelled with phony wood, Volvos, compacts. Once or twice I saw gardeners labouring in the rain, their power mowers sputtering and belching.

The road continued for another half-mile, the properties growing larger, the houses set back further from the gates. It came to an abrupt halt at a thicket of cypress. There was no gate, no visible means of entry, just the forestlike growth of thirty-foot trees, and for a moment I thought I'd been misled.

I put on my raincoat, pulled up the collar and got out. The ground was thick with pine needles and wet leaves. I walked to the thicket and peered through the branches. Twenty feet ahead, almost totally hidden by the overgrowth of tangled limbs and dripping vegetation, was a short stone pathway leading to a wooden gate. The trees had been planted to block the entry; from the size of them they were at least twenty years old. Discounting the possibility that someone had taken the trouble to transplant a score of full grown cypress to the site, I decided it

310

had been a long time since the normal human business of living had taken place here.

I pushed my way to the gate and tried it. Nailed shut. I took a good look at it—two slabs of tongued-and-grooved redwood hinged to brick posts. The posts connected to chain link fencing piled high with thorny spirals. No sign of electricity or barbed wire. I found a foothold on a wet rock, slipped a couple of times and finally managed to scale the gate.

I landed on another world. Acres of wasteland spread before me; what had once been a formal lawn was now a swamp of weeds, dead grass and broken rock. The ground had sunk in several places, creating pools of water that stagnated and provided oases for the mosquitoes and gnats that hovered overhead. Once-noble trees had been reduced to jagged stumps and felled, rotten hulls crawling with fungus. Rusted auto parts, old tyres and discarded cans and bottles were scattered throughout what was now a sodden trash dump. Rain fell on metal and made a hollow, clanging sound.

I walked up a pathway paved in herringbone brick, choked with weeds and covered by slimy moss. In the places where the roots had pushed through, the bricks stuck out of the ground like loose teeth in a broken jaw. I kicked aside a drowned field mouse and slogged toward the former residence of the Hickle clan.

The house was massive, a three-storey structure of hand-hewn stone that had blackened with age. I couldn't imagine it as ever being beautiful but doubtless it had once been grand: a brooding, slate-roofed mansion trimmed with gingerbread, festooned with eaves and gables and girdled by wide stone porches. There was rusted wrought-iron furniture on the front porch, a nine-foot-high cathedral door and a weather vane at the highest peak in the shape of a witch riding a broomstick. The old crone twirled in the wind, safely above the desolation.

I climbed the stairs to the front entry. Weeds had grown

311

clear up to the door, which was nailed shut. The windows were similarly boarded and bolted tight. In spite of its size—perhaps because of it—the house seemed pathetic, a forgotten dowager, abandoned to the point where she no longer cared how she looked and sentenced to a fate of decaying in silence.

I forced my way through a makeshift barrier of rotting boards that had been stacked in front of the porte-coch-ere. The house was at least a hundred and fifty feet long and it took me a while to check each window on the ground floor: all were sealed.

The rear property was another three acres of swamp. A four-car garage, designed as a miniature of the house, was inaccessible—nailed and fastened. A fifty-foot swim-ming pool was empty save for several inches of muddy water in which floated a host of organic debris. The remains of a grape arbour and trellised rose garden were evident only as a jumble of peeling wood and cracked stone supporting a bird's nest of lifeless twigs. Stone benches and statues slanted and pitched on broken bases, Pompeii in the wake of Vesuvius.

The rain began to come down harder and colder. I put my hands in the pocket of my raincoat, by now soaked through, and looked for shelter. It would take tools—hammer and crowbar—to get into the house or the gar-age, and there were no large trees that could be trusted not to topple at any moment. I was out in the open like a bum caught in a blitz.

I saw a flash of light and braced myself for an electric storm. None came and the light flashed again. The heavy downpour made it difficult to see but the third time the light appeared I was able to draw a bead on it and walk in its direction. Several squishy footsteps later I could see it had come from a glass greenhouse at the rear of the estate, just beyond the bombed-out arbour. The panes were opaque with dirt, some of which ran in brown trickles, but they appeared intact. I ran toward it, following the light that flickered, danced, disappeared, then flickered again.

The door to the greenhouse was closed but it opened silently to the prompting of my hand. Inside it was warm, steamy and sour with the aroma of decomposition. Waist-high wooden tables ran along both sides of the glass room; between them was a walkway floored with woodchips, peat, mulch and topsoil. A collection of tools—pitch-forks, rakes, spades, hoes—stood in one corner.

Upon the tables were pots of gorgeously flowering plants: orchids, bromeliads, blue hydrangea, begonias of every hue, scarlet and white impatiens—all in full bloom and spilling abundantly from their terracotta houses. A wooden beam into which metal hooks had been embed-ded was suspended above the tables. Hanging from the hooks were fuchsias dripping purple, ferns, spider plants, creeping charlies, more begonias. It was the Garden of Eden in the Great Void.

The room was dim, and it reverberated with the sound of the rain assaulting the glass roof. The light that had drawn me appeared again, brighter and closer. I made out a shape at the other end of the greenhouse, a figure in yellow slicker and hood holding a flashlight. The figure shone the flashlight on plants, picking up a leaf here, a flower there, examining the soil, pinching off a dry branch, setting aside a ripe blossom.

'Hello,' I said.

The figure whirled and the flashlight beam washed over my face. I squinted in the glare and brought my hand up to shield my eyes.

The figure came closer.

'Who are you?' demanded a voice, high and scared.

'Alex Delaware.'

The beam lowered. I started to take a step.

'Stay right there!'

I put my foot down.

The hood was pulled back. The face it revealed was

313

round, pale, flat, utterly Asian, female but not feminine. The eyes were two razor cuts in the parchment skin, the mouth an unsmiling hyphen.

'Hello, Mrs. Hickle.'

'How do you know me—what do you want?' There was toughness diluted by fear in the voice, the toughness of the successful fugitive who knows vigilance must never cease.

'I just thought I'd pay you a visit.'

'I don't want visitors. I don't know you.'

'Don't you? Alex Delaware—doesn't the name mean anything to you?'

She didn't bother to lie, just said nothing.

'It was my office darling Stuart chose for his last big scene—or maybe it was chosen for him.'

'I don't know what you're talking about. I don't want your company.' Her English was clipped and slightly accented.

'Why don't you call the butler and have me ejected?'

Her jaws worked; white fingers tightened around the flashlight.

'You refuse to leave?'

'It's wet and cold outside. I'd appreciate the chance to dry off.'

'Then you'll go?'

'Then I stay and we talk awhile. About your late husband and some of his good buddies.'

'Stuart's dead. There's nothing to talk about.'

'I think there's plenty. Lots of questions.'

She put down the flashlight and folded her arms in front of her. There was defiance in the gesture. Any trace of fear had faded and her demeanour was one of irritation at being disturbed. It puzzled me—she was a lone woman accosted by a stranger in a deserted place but there was no panic.

'Last chance,' she said.

314

'I'm not interested in blowing your cover. Just let me—'

She clicked her tongue against the roof of her mouth.

A large shadow materialized into something living and breathing.

I saw what it was and my bowels went weak.

'This is Otto. He doesn't like strangers.'

He was the largest dog I'd ever seen, a Great Dane the size of a healthy pony, coloured like a Dalmatian—white dappled with gray-black splotches. One ear was partially shredded. His maws were black and wet with saliva, hanging loose in that half-smile, half-snarl so characteristic of attack dogs, revealing pearly-white fangs and a tongue the size of a hot-water bag. His eyes were piggy and too small for his head. They reflected orange pinpoints of light as they scanned me.

I must have moved, because his ears perked. He panted and looked up at his mistress. She cooed at him. He panted faster and gave her hand a fast swipe with the pink slab of tongue.

'Hi there, big fella,' I said. The words came out strangled. His jaws opened wider in a growling yawn.

I backed away and the dog arched his neck forward. He was a muscular beast, from head to quivering haunch.

'Now maybe I don't want you to go,' said Kim Hickle.

I backed away further. Otto exhaled and made a sound that came from deep in his belly.

'I told you I won't give you away.'

'So you say.'

I took two more steps backward. Baby steps. Playing a deranged version of Simon Says. The dog moved closer.

'I just wanted to be alone,' she said. 'Nobody to bother me. Me and Otto.' She looked lovingly at the great brute. 'You found out. You bother me. How did you find me?'

'You left your name in a library file at Jedson College.'

'So you hunted me.'

315

'No. It was an accident, finding the card. It's not you I'm after.'

She clicked her tongue again and Otto came a few feet closer. His malevolent leer loomed larger. I could smell him, rank and eager.

'First you, now others will follow. Asking questions. Blaming me, saying I'm bad. I'm not bad. I'm a good woman, good for children. I was a good wife to a sick man, not a sick woman.'

'I know,' I soothed. 'It wasn't your fault.'

Another click. The dog moved within springing distance. She had him controlled, like a radio-operated toy. Start, Otto. Stop, Otto, Kill, Otto . . .

'No. Not my fault.'

I stepped back. Otto followed me, stalking, one paw scraping the ground, the shorthairs rising.

'I'll go,' I said. 'We don't have to talk. It's not that important. You deserve your privacy.' I was rambling, stalling for time, my eyes on the tools in the corner. Mentally, I measured the distance to the pitchfork, covertly rehearsing the move I might have to make.

'I gave you a chance. You didn't take it. Now it's too late.'

She clicked twice and the dog sprang, coming at me in a blur of snarling darkness. I saw the forepaws raised in the air, the wet, hungry, gnashing mouth, the orange eyes zeroed on their target, all in a fraction of a second. Still within that second, I feinted to the right, sank to my knees and lunged for the pitchfork. My fingers closed around wood and I snatched it and jabbed upward.

He came down on me, a ton of coiled monster, crushing the breath from my chest, the paws and teeth scraping and snapping. Something went through cloth, then leather, then skin. Pain took hold of my arm from elbow to shoulder, piercing and sickening. The handle of the pitchfork slipped from my grasp. I shielded my face with one sleeve, as Otto nuzzled at me with his wet nose, trying

316

to get those buzz-saw jaws around my neck. I twisted away, reached out blindly for the pitchfork, got hold of it, lost it and found it again. I landed a knuckle punch on the crown of his skull. It was like pummelling armour plate. He reared up on his hind legs, roaring with rage and bore down. I turned the pitchfork prong-upwards. He lunged, throwing his full weight down on me. My legs bent and my back hit the dirt. The air went out of me and I fought for consciousness, swallowed up in churning fur and struggling to keep the fork between us.

Then he whinnied shrilly; at the same time I felt the pitchfork hit bone, scrape and slide as I twisted the handle, full of hate. The prongs went into him like a warm knife into butter.

We embraced, the dog's tongue on my ear, his mouth slavering, open in agony, an inch from carving out a chunk of my face. I put all of my strength behind the pitchfork, pushing and twisting, vaguely aware of the sound of a woman screaming. He cried out like a puppy. The prongs went in a final inch and then could sink no deeper. His eyes opened wide with injured pride, blinked spasmodically, then closed. The huge body shuddered convulsively atop me. A tide of blood shot out of his mouth, splashing across my nose, lips and chin. I gagged on the warm, salty muck. Life passed out of him and I struggled to roll free.

The whole thing had taken less than half a minute.

Kim Hickle looked at the dead dog, then at me, and made a run for the door. I pulled myself to standing position, yanked the pitchfork out of the barrel chest and blocked her way.

'Get back,' I gasped. I moved the pitchfork and droplets of gore flew through the air. She froze.

The greenhouse was silent. The rain had stopped. The silence was broken by a low, rumbling noise: bubbles of gas escaping from the big dog's corpse. A mound of faeces

317

followed, running down the limp legs and mingling with the mulch.

She watched it and started to cry. Then she went limp and sat on the floor with the hopeless, stuporous look of a refugee.

I jammed the pitchfork into the ground and used it to lean on. It took me a full minute to catch my breath, another two or three to check for damages.

The raincoat was ruined, torn and blood-soaked. With some effort I got it off and let it fall to the ground. One arm of the leather jacket was shredded. I slipped out of it, too, and rolled up the sleeve of the turtleneck. I inspected my bicep. The layers of clothing had prevented it from being worse but it wasn't pretty: three puncture wounds that had already begun to swell, surrounded by a maze of abrasions. The arm felt stiff and sore. I bent it and nothing felt broken. The same went for my ribs and my other limbs, although my entire body floated just above agony. I stretched carefully, using a limbering routine I'd learned from Jaroslav. It made me feel a little better.

'Did Otto have his shots?' I asked.

She didn't answer. I repeated the question, punctuating it with a grasp of the pitchfork handle.

'Yes. I have the papers.'

'I want to see them.'

'It's true. You can believe me.'

'You just tried to get that monster to rip out my throat. Right now your credibility isn't high.'

She looked at the dead animal and went into a meditative sway. She seemed to be one who was used to waiting. I was in no mood for a battle of endurance.

'You've got two choices, Mrs. Hickle. One, cooperate and I'll leave you to your little Walden. Or, you can make it hard for me and I'll see that your story makes page one of the *L.A. Times* Metro section. Think of it: Molester's

318

widow finds refuge in abandoned homesite. Poetic, isn't it? Ten to one the wire services pick it up.'

'What do you want from me?'

'Answers to questions. I've no reason—or desire—to hurt you.'

'You're really the one whose office Stuart—died in?'

'Yes. Who else were you expecing?'

'No one,' she said too quickly.

'Towle? Hayden? McCaffrey?'

At the mention of each name her face registered pain sequentially, as if her bones were being broken in stages.

'I'm not with them. But I want to know more about them.'

She raised herself to a squat, stood, and picked up the bloodied raincoat. Carefully she placed it over the dog's still form.

'I'll talk to you,' she said.

25

THERE WAS an entrance to the four-car garage that had
eluded me: At ground level, hidden behind an untrimmed
blue spruce, was a window covered with chicken-coop
wire mesh. She kneeled, played with a couple of strategic
strands and the mesh came loose. A push, a wriggle and
she was inside. I followed. I was much larger and it wasn't
easy. My injured arm brushed against the pane and I had
to hold my breath to stop from crying out as I squeezed
through.

A half-jump brought me to a narrow room that had
originally been a root cellar. It was damp and dark, the
walls lined with shallow wooden shelving, the floor of
poured concrete painted red. There was a wooden shutter
above the window, held in place by an eye and hook. She
unfastened it and it slammed shut. There was a second
of darkness during which I braced myself for something
devious. Instead came the pleasing pungence of kerosene, reminiscent of teenage love by the light of the camp-
fire, and smoky illumination. She tilted the slats of the
shutter so that additional light came in but visibility from
the outside was obscured.

My eyes adjusted to the light and the details came into

focus: a thin pallet and bedroll lay on the floor. The kerosene lamp, a hot plate, a can of Sterno and a packet of plastic utensils shared space on a rickety wooden table that had been painted and repainted so many times it looked like soft sculpture. There was a utility sink in one corner and above it a rack holding an empty jam jar, a toothbrush, toothpowder, safety razor and a bar of laundry soap. Most of the remaining floor space was taken up by wooden milk cartons of a type I hadn't seen since childhood. The boxes had tube-shaped hand holes on two sides and bore the imprint of 'Farmer Del's Dairy, Tacoma, Wash—Our Butter Is Best, Put It to the Test'. Below the slogan was a picture of a bored-looking heifer and a phone number with a two-letter prefix. She'd stacked the cartons three-high in places. The contents of some of them were visible—packets of freeze-dried food, canned goods, paper towels, folded clothing. Three pairs of shoes, all rubber-soled and sturdy, were lined up neatly against the wall. There were metal hooks hammered into a raw wood support beam. She hung her slicker on one of them and sat down on a straight-backed chair of unfinished pine. I settled myself on an overturned milk carton.

We looked at each other.

In the absence of competing stimuli the pain in my arm took over. I winced, and she saw it.

She got up, soaked a paper towel in warm water, came over and swabbed the wound. She poked around in one of the boxes and found sterile gauze, adhesive tape and hydrogen peroxide. Tending to me like Florence Nightingale, she bandaged the arm. The craziness of the situation wasn't lost on me—minutes ago she'd tried to kill me, now she clucked maternally and smoothed down the tape. I stayed karate-wary, expecting her to revert at any moment to murderous rage, to dig her fingers into the inflamed flesh and take advantage of the blinding pain to jab me in the eye.

But when she was finished she returned to her seat.

321

'The papers,' I reminded her.

More poking around. But quick. She knew exactly where everything was. A sheaf of papers bound with a thick rubber band found its way into my hand. There were veterinarian's bills, rabies vaccination records, Kennel Club registration—the dog's full name had been Otto Klaus Von Schulderheis out of Stuttgart-Munsch and Sigourn-Daffodil. Quaint. There were also diplomas from two obedience schools in L.A. and a certificate stating that Otto had been trained as an attack dog for defensive purposes only. I handed the papers back to her.

'Thank you,' she said.

We sat across from one another, pleasant as school chums. I took a good look at her and tried to work up some genuine animosity. What I saw was a sad-looking Oriental woman in her forties, her hair chopped China-doll short, sallow, frail, homely in baggy work clothes and shabby as a churchmouse. She sat, hands in lap, docile. The hatred wouldn't come.

'How long have you been living here?'

'Six months. Since Stuart's death.'

'Why live like this—why not open up the house?'

'I thought this would be better for hiding. All I want is to be alone.'

She didn't make much of a Garbo.

'Hiding from whom?'

She looked at the floor.

'Come on. I won't hurt you.'

'The others. The other sick ones.'

'Names.'

'The ones you mentioned and others.' She spit out a half-dozen other names I didn't recognize.

'Let's be specific. By sick you mean child molesters—all those men are child molesters?'

'Yes, yes. I didn't know it. Stuart told me later, when he was in prison. They volunteered at a children's home, took the kids to their houses. Did sick things with them.'

322

'And at your school, too.'

'No! That was only Stuart. The others never came to the school. Only at the children's home.'

'La Casa de los Niños. Your husband was a member of the Gentlemen's Brigade.'

'Yes. He told me he was doing it to help children. His friends recruited him, he said. The judge, the doctor, the others. I thought it was so nice of him—we didn't have children of our own—I was proud of him. I never knew what he was really doing—just like I didn't know about what he did at the school.'

I said nothing.

'I know what you're thinking—what they all thought. That I knew all along. How could I not know what my own husband was doing in my own house? You blame me as much as you blame Stuart. I tell you, I didn't know!'

Her arms went out beseechingly, the hands saffron talons. I noticed that the nails had been gnawed to the quick. There was a desperate, feral look on her face.

'I did not know,' she repeated, turning it into a self-punishing mantra. 'I did not know. He was my husband but I did not know!'

She was in need of absolution but I didn't feel like a father confessor. I stayed tight-lipped and observed her with forced detachment.

'You must understand the kind of marriage Stuart and I had to see how he could have been doing all of those things without my knowledge.'

My silence said, convince me.

She bowed her head and began.

'We met in Seoul,' she said, 'shortly after the war. My father had been a professor of linguistics. Our family was prosperous, but we had ties to the socialists and the KCIA killed them all. They went on rampages after the war, murdering intellectuals, anyone who wasn't a blind slave to the regime. Everything we owed was confiscated or destroyed. I was hidden, given to friends the day before

323

KCIA thugs broke into the house and slit the throats of everyone—family, servants, even the animals. Things got worse, the government clamped down harder. The family that took me in grew frightened and I was turned out to the street. I was fifteen years old, but very small, very skinny, looking twelve. I begged, ate scraps. I—I sold myself. I had to. To survive.'

She stopped, looked past me, gathered her strength and continued.

When Stuart found me I was feverish, infested with lice and venereal disease, covered with sores. It was at night. I was huddled under newspapers in an alley at the back of a café where the GI's went to eat and drink and find bar girls. I knew it was good to wait in such places because Americans threw away enough food to feed entire families. I was so sick I could barely move, but I waited for hours, forcing myself to stay awake so the cats wouldn't get my dinner first. The restaurant closed shortly after midnight. The soldiers came out, loud, drunk, staggering through the alley. Then Stuart, by himself, sober. Later I found out he never drank alcohol. I tried to keep quiet but my pain made me cry out. He heard, came over, so big, a giant in uniform, bending over me saying 'Don't worry, little girl.' He picked me up in his arms and took me to his apartment. He had lots of money, enough to rent his own place off base. The GI's were on R and R, celebrating, making lots of unwanted babies. Stuart had nothing to do with those kinds of things. He used his place to write poetry. To fiddle with his cameras. To be alone.'

She seemed to lose track of time and space, and staring absently at the dark wooden walls.

'He took you to his place,' I prompted.

'For five weeks he nursed me. He brought doctors, bought medicine. Fed me, bathed me, sat at my bedside reading comic books—I loved American comic books because my father had always brought them home to me from his travels. Little Orphan Annie. Terry and the

324

Pirates. Dagwood. Blondie. He read them all to me, in a soft, gentle voice. He was different from any man I'd ever met. Thin, quiet, like a teacher, with those eyeglasses that made his eyes look so big, like a big bird.

'By the sixth week I was well. He came into bed and made love to me. I know now it was part of the sickness—he must have thought I was a child, that must have excited him. But I felt like a woman. Over the years as I became a woman, when I was clearly no longer a child, he lost interest in me. He used to like to dress me up in little girl's things—I'm small, I could fit into them. But when I grew up, saw the world outside, I would have nothing to do with that. I asserted myself and he withdrew. Maybe that was when he started to act out his sickness. Maybe,' she said in a wounded voice, 'it was my fault. For not satisfying him.'

'No. He was a troubled man. You don't have to bear that responsibility,' I said, not with total sincerity. I didn't want it all to deteriorate into a wet session of self-recrimination.

'I don't know. Even now it seems so unreal. The papers, the stories about him. About us. He was such a kind man, gentle, quiet.'

I'd heard similar pictures painted of other child molesters. Often they were exceptionally mild-mannered men, with a natural ability to gain rapport with their young victims. But of course it had to be that way: kids won't flock to an unshaven ogre in a soiled trenchcoat. They *will* be drawn to Uncle Wally who's so much nicer than mean old Mom and Dad and all the other grownups who don't *understand*. To Uncle Wally with his magic tricks and neat collection of baseball cards and really terrific toys at his house and mopeds and video recorders, and cameras and neat, weird books . . .

'You must understand how much I loved him,' she was saying. 'He saved my life. He was American. He was rich. He said he loved me too. "My little geisha" he called me.

325

I'd laugh and tell him "No, I'm Korean, you silly. The Japanese are pigs!" He'd smile and call me his little geisha again.

We lived together in Seoul for four months. I waited for him to get off base on leave, cooked for him, cleaned, brought him his slippers. Was his wife. When his discharge papers came, he told me he was taking me back to the States. I was in heaven. Of course his family—there was only a mother and some elderly aunts—would have nothing to do with me. Stuart didn't care. He had money of his own, trust funds from his father. We travelled together to Los Angeles. He said he'd gone to school there—he did go to medical school, but flunked out. He took a job as a medical technician. He didn't need to work, it was a job that didn't pay much, but he liked it, said it kept him busy. He liked the machines—the meters and the test tubes—he was always a tinkerer. Gave me his entire paycheck, as if it was petty cash, told me to spend it on myself.

'We lived together that way for three years. I wanted marriage, but couldn't ask. It took me a while to get used to American ways, to women not being just property, to having rights. I pushed it when I wanted children. Stuart was indifferent to the idea, but he went along with it. We married. I tried to get pregnant but couldn't. I saw doctors, at UCLA, Stanford, Mayo. They all said there was too much scarring. I'd been so sick in Korea, it shouldn't have surprised me, but I didn't want to believe it. Looking back now, I know it was a good thing we did not have any little ones. At the time, after I finally accepted it, I became depressed. Very withdrawn, not eating. Eventually Stuart couldn't ignore it any longer. He suggested I go to school. If I loved children I could work with them, become a teacher. He may have had his own motives, but he seemed concerned for me—whenever I was sick or low he was at his best.

'I enrolled in junior college, then college, and learned

so much. I was a good student,' she recalled, smiling. 'Very motivated. For the first time I was out in the world, with other people—until then I'd *been* Stuart's little geisha. Now I began to think for myself. At the same time he drifted away from me. There was no anger, no resentment that he put into words. He simply spent more time with his cameras and his bird books—he used to like to read books and magazines on nature, though he never hiked or walked. An armchair bird lover. An armchair man.

'We became two distant cousins living in the same house. Neither of us cared, we were busy. I studied every spare moment, by now I knew I wanted to go beyond the bachelor's and get a credential in early childhood. We went our own ways. There were weeks when we never saw each other. There was no communication, no marriage. But no divorce either—what would have been the point? There were no fights. It was live and let live. My new friends, my college friends, told me I was liberated, I should be happy to have a husband who didn't bother me. When I became lonely I went deeper into my studies.

'I finished the credential and they gave me field placements at local preschools. I liked working with the little ones but I thought I could run a better school than those I had seen. I told Stuart, he said sure, anything to keep me happy, out of his way. We bought a big house in Brentwood—there always seemed to be money for anything—and I started Kim's Korner. It was a wonderful place, a wonderful time. I finally stopped mourning not having children of my own. Then he—'

She stopped, covered her face with her hands and rocked back and forth.

I got up and put a hand on her shoulder.

'Please don't do that. It's not right. I tried to have Otto kill you.' She lifted her face, dry and unlined. 'Do you understand that? I wanted him to *kill* you. Now you are being kind and understanding. It makes me feel worse '

I removed the hand and sat back down.

'Why the need for Otto, why the fear?'

'I thought you were sent by the ones who killed Stuart.'

'The official verdict was that he killed himself.'

She shook her head.

'No. He didn't commit suicide. They said he was depressed. It was a lie. Of course when he was first arrested, he was very low. Humiliated and guilty. But he bounced out of it. That was Stuart's way. He could block out reality as easily as exposing a roll of film. Poof, and the image is gone. The day before he was arraigned we spoke on the phone. He was in high spirits. To hear him talk, the arrest was the best thing that ever happened to him—to us. He'd been ill, now he would get help. We'd start all over again, as soon as he got out of the hospital. I could even get another school, in another city. He suggested Seattle and talked of our reclaiming the family mansion—that was how I got the idea to come here.

'I knew it would never happen. By then I'd decided to leave him. But I went along with the fantasies, saying, yes dear, certainly, Stuart. Later we had other conversations and it was the same thing. Life was going to be better than ever. He was not talking like a man about to blow his brains out.'

'It's not that simple. People often kill themselves right after an upswing in mood. The suicide season is spring, you know.'

'Perhaps. But I know Stuart and I know he didn't kill himself. He was too shallow to let something like the arrest bother him for a long time. He could deny anything. He denied me for all those years, denied our marriage—that's why he could do those things without my knowing about them. We were strangers.'

'But you know him well enough to be sure he didn't commit suicide.'

'Yes,' she insisted. 'That story about the false phone call to you, the picked locks. That kind of scheming isn't—

328

wasn't Stuart. For all his sickness he was naïve, almost simple. He wasn't a planner.'

'It took planning to get those children down in the cellar.'

'You don't have to believe me. I don't care. He's done his damage. Now he's dead. And I'm in a cellar of my own.'

Her smile was pitiful.

The lamp sputtered. She got up to adjust the wick and add more kerosene. When she sat back down I asked her: 'Who killed him and why?'

'The others. His so-called friends. So he wouldn't expose them. And he would have. During our last visits he'd hint around. Say things like, "I'm not the only sick one, Kimmy" or "Things aren't what they seem with the Gentlemen." I knew he wanted me to ask him, to help him spill it out. But I didn't. I was still in shock over losing the school, wrapped in my own shame, I didn't want to hear about more perversions. I cut him off, changed the subject. But after he died it came back to me and I put it all together.'

'Did he mention anyone by name as being sick?'

'No. But what else could he have meant? They'd come to pick him up, parking their big soft cars in the driveway, dressed in those sport jackets with the Casa insignia. When he'd leave with them he'd be excited. His hands trembling. He'd come back in the early hours of the morning, exhausted. Or the next day. Isn't it obvious what they were doing?'

'You haven't told anyone of your suspicions?'

'Who would believe me? Those men are powerful—doctors, lawyers, executives, that horrid little Judge Hayden. I wouldn't stand a chance, the wife of a molester. To the public I'm as guilty as Stuart. And there's no evidence—look what they did to him to shut him up. I had to run.'

'Did Stuart ever mention knowing McCaffrey from Washington?'

'No. Did he?'

'Yes. What about a child named Cary Nemeth. Did his name come up?'

'No.'

'Elena Gutierrez? Morton Handler—Doctor Morton Handler?'

'No.'

'Maurice Bruno?'

She shook her head. 'No. Who are these people?'

'Victims.'

'Violated like the others?'

'The ultimate violation. Dead. Murdered.'

'Oh my God.' She put her hands to her face.

Telling her story had made her sweat. Strands of black hair stuck to her forehead. 'So it continues,' she said mournfully.

'That's why I'm here. To put an end to it. What else can you tell me that would help?'

'Nothing. I've told you everything. They killed him. They're evil men, hiding their ugly secret under a cloak of respectability. I ran to escape them.'

I looked around the dingy room.

'How long can you continue this way?'

'Forever, if no one gives me away. The island is secluded, this property is hidden. When I have to go to the mainland to shop I dress like a cleaning maid. No one notices me. I stockpile as much as possible to avoid making too many trips. The last one was over a month ago. I live simply. The flowers are my one extravagance. I planted them from seed packets and bulbs. They occupy my time, with watering, feeding, pruning, re-potting. The days go by quickly.'

'How safe can you be—Towle and Hayden have roots here.'

'I know. But their familities haven't lived here for a

330

generation. I checked. I even went by their old homes. There are new faces, new names. There's no reason for them to look for me here. Not unless you give them one.'

'I won't.'

'On my next trip I'll buy a gun. I'll be prepared for them if they come. I'll escape and go somewhere else. I'm used to it. The memory of Seoul returns in my dreams. It keeps me watchful. I'm sorry to hear about the other murders, but I don't want to know about them. There's nothing that I can do.'

I got up and she helped me on with my jacket.

'The funny thing is,' she said, 'this estate probably belongs to me. As does the Brentwood property and the rest of the Hickle fortune. I'm Stuart's sole heir—we wrote our wills several years ago. He never discussed finances with me so I don't know how much he left, but it has to be considerable. There were bearer bonds, other pieces of real estate all up and down the coast. In theory I'm a rich woman. Do I look it?'

'There's no way to get in touch with the executors of his will?'

'The executor is a partner in Edwin Hayden's law firm. For all I know he's one of *them*. I can do without wealth when all it means is a fancy funeral.'

She used her chair to climb out of the window. I followed her. We walked in the direction of the big, black house.

'You worked with the children from my school. How are they doing?'

'Very well. The prognosis is good. They're amazingly resilient.'

'That's good.'

A few steps later:

'And the parents—did they hate me?'

'Some. Others were surprisingly loyal and defended you. It created a schism in the group. They worked it out.'

'I'm glad. I think about them often.'

331

She accompanied me to the edge of the swamp that fronted the mansion.

'I'll let you go the rest of the way by yourself. How does the arm feel?'

'Stiff, but nothing serious. I'll survive.'

I held out my hand and she took it.

'Good luck,' she said.

'Same to you.'

I walked through weeds and mud, chilled and tired. When I turned around to look she was gone.

I stayed in the ferry's dining room drinking coffee for much of the return trip to the mainland, going over what I'd learned. When I got back to the hotel I called Milo at the station, was told he wasn't there and tried his home number. Rick Silverman answered.

'Hi, Alex. There's static. Is this long distance?'

'It is. Seattle. Is Milo back yet?'

'No. I expect him tomorrow. He went to Mexico on a supposed vacation but it sounds like work to me.'

'It is. He's looking into the background of a guy named McCaffrey.'

'I know. The minister with the children's home. He said you turned him on to it.'

'I may have sparked his interest but when I spoke to him about it he brushed me off. Did he mention what led him to make the trip?'

'Let me see—I recall his saying he phoned the police down there—it's some small town, I forget the name—and they jerked him around. They implied they had something juicy for him but that he'd have to come up with some bucks to get it. It surprised me—I thought cops cooperated with each other—but he said that's the way they always are.'

'That's it?'

'That's it. He invited me to come along but it didn't work out well with my schedule—I had a twenty-four-hour shift coming up and it would have required too much trading with the other guys.'

'Have you heard from him since he left?'

'Just a postcard from the airport at Guadalajara. An old peasant pulling a burro next to a Saguaro cactus that looked plastic. Very classy stuff. He wrote "Wish you were here" on it.'

I laughed.

'If he does call, tell him to give me a ring. I've got some more information for him.'

'Will do. Anything specific?'

'No. Just have him call.'

'Okay.'

'Thanks. Look forward to meeting you some day, Rick.' .

'Likewise. Maybe when he gets back and wraps things up.'

'Sounds good.'

I got out of my clothes and examined the arm. There was some oozing, but nothing bad. Kim Hickle had done a good patchup job. I did a half-hour of limbering exercises and a bit of karate, then soaked in a hot bath for forty-five minutes while reading the throwaway guide to Seattle the hotel had furnished.

I called Robin, got no answer, dressed and went for dinner. I remembered a place from my previous visit, a cedar-panelled room overlooking Lake Union, where they barbecued salmon over alder wood. I found it, using my memory and a map, arrived early enough to get a table with a view, and proceeded to put away a large salad with Roquefort, a beautiful coral-coloured chinook fillet, potatoes, beans, a basket of hot cornbread and two Coors. I topped it off with homemade blackberry ice cream and coffee and, with a full belly, watched the sun go down over the lake.

I browsed a couple of bookstores in the University District, found nothing exciting or uplifting, and drove back to the hotel. There was an Oriental imports shop in the lobby, still open. I went in, bought a green cloisonné necklace for Robin and rode the elevator back up to my room. At nine I called her again. This time she answered.

'Alex! I was hoping it was you.'

'How are you, doll? I called you a couple of hours ago.'

'I went out for dinner. By my lonesome. Ate an omelette in a corner of the Cafe Pelican all by myself. Isn't that a pathetic image?'

'I supped alone, too, my lady.'

'How sad. Come home soon, Alex. I miss you.'

'I miss you too.'

'Was the trip productive?'

'Very.' I filled her in on the details, careful to exclude my encounter with Otto.

'You're really on to something. Don't you feel strange, uncovering all those secrets?'

'Not really, but I'm not looking at it from the outside.'

'I am, and believe me, it's freaky, Alex. I'll just be glad when Milo gets back and he can take over.'

'Yes. How are things going with you?'

'Nothing nearly as exciting. One thing new. This morning I got a call from the head of a new feminist group— it's a kind of a women's chamber of commerce. I fixed this woman's banjo, she came down to pick it up and we got to talking. This was a couple of months ago. Anyway, she called and invited me to give a lecture to their group next week. The topic's something like The Female Artisan in Contemporary Society subtitle Creativity Meets the Business World.'

'That's fantastic. I'll be sure to be there listening if they let me in.'

'Don't you dare! I'm scared enough as it is. Alex, I've never given a speech before—I'm absolutely petrified.'

'Don't worry. You know what you're talking about, you're bright and articulate, they'll love you.'

'So you say.'

334

'So I say. Listen, if you're really nervous I'll do a little hypnosis with you. To help you relax. It'll be a piece of cake.'

'You think hypnosis will help?'

'Sure. With your imagination and creativity you'll be a terrific subject.'

'I've heard you talk about it, how you used to do it with patients, but I never thought of asking you to do it with me.'

'Usually, darling, we find other ways to occupy our time together.'

'Hypnosis,' she said. 'Now I've got something else to worry about.'

'Don't worry. It's harmless.'

'Totally?'

'Yes. Totally, in your case. The only time you run into a problem is when the subject has major emotional conflicts or deep-seated problems. In those cases hypnosis can dredge up primal memories. You get a stress reaction, some terror. But even that can be helpful. The trained psychotherapist uses the anxiety constructively, to help the patient work it through.'

'And that couldn't happen to me?'

'Certainly not. I guarantee it. You're the most normal person I've ever met.'

'Ha. You've been retired too long!'

'I challenge you to come up with one single symptom of psychopathology.'

'How about extreme horniness, hearing your voice and wanting to be able to touch you and grab you and put you in me?'

'Hmmm. Sounds serious.'

'Then come on back and do something about it, Doctor.'

'I'll be back tomorrow. Treatment will commence immediately.'

'What time?'

'The plane lands at ten—a half-hour after that.'

'Damn, I forgot—I have to go to Santa Barbara tomorrow morning. My aunt's sick, in the ICU at Cottage Hospital. It's a family thing, I have to be there. If you came in earlier we could have breakfast before I leave.'

'I'm taking the earliest flight, hon.'

'I suppose I could postpone it, show up later.'

'Visit your aunt. We'll have dinner.'

'It might be a late dinner.'

'Drive straight to my place and we'll take it from there.'

'All right. I'll try to make it by eight.'

'That's great. Speedy recovery to your aunt. I love you.'

'Love you too. Take care.'

26

SOMETHING BOTHERED ME the next morning. The troubled feeling persisted during the ride to Sea-Tac and up the ramp to the plane. I couldn't get a handle on what it was that lurked in a bottom drawer of my mind, that lingered through the serving of the plastic food, the forced smiles of the flight attendants, the copilot's bad jokes. The harder I tried to bring it to the forefront of my consciousness the further back it sank. I felt the impatience and frustration of a child encountering Chinese finger puzzle for the first time. So I decided to just ride with it, sit back and wait and see if it came to me on its own.

It wasn't until shortly before landing that it did. What had stuck in my head was last night's conversation with Robin. She'd asked me about the dangers of hypnosis and I'd given her a speech about it being harmless unless the experience stirred up latent conflicts. *Dredged up primal memories* had been my exact words. Dredge up primal memories and the reaction is often terror . . .

I was stuffed with tension as the landing wheels touched down. Once free, I jogged through and out of the airport, picked up the Seville in the overnight lot, paid a considerable ransom to get it out the gate and headed east on

Century Boulevard. Caltrans, in its infinite wisdom, had chosen to set up construction in the middle of the road during the morning rush in and out of LAX and, caught in a jam, I cooked in the Cadillac for the mile to the San Diego Freeway on-ramp. I took the freeway north, connected to Santa Monica West, and exited just before Pacific Coast Highway. A drive down Ocean and a few turns brought me to the Palisades and the place where Morton Handler and Elena Gutierrez had lost their lives.

The door to Bonita Quinn's apartment was open. I heard cursing from within and entered. A man was standing in the front room kicking the floral sofa and muttering under his breath. He was in his forties, curly-haired, flabby and putty-coloured with discouraged eyes and a steel-wool goatee separating his first chin from his second. He wore black slacks and a light blue nylon shirt that clung to every tuck and roll of his gelatinous torso. One hand held a cigarette and flicked ashes onto the carpet. The other groped for treasure behind a meaty ear. He kicked the couch again, looked up, saw me and waved the smoking hand around the tiny room.

'Okay, you can get to work.'

'Doing what?'

'Loading this shit outta here—aren't you the mover—' he looked at me again, this time with sharpened eyes. 'No, you don't look like a mover. Excuse me.' He threw back his shoulders. 'What can I do for you?'

'I'm looking for Bonita Quinn and her daughter.'

'You and me both.'

'She's gone?'

'Three friggin' days. With who knows how many rent checks. I've got tenants complaining their calls weren't answered, repairs that haven't been done. I call her, no answer. So I come down here myself and find she's been gone for three days, left all this junk, hightailed it. I never had a good feeling about her. You do someone a favour, you get shafted. Happens every time.'

338

He inhaled his cigarette, coughed and sucked again. There was yellow around the irises of his eyes; gray, unhealthy flesh pouched the wary orbs. He looked like a man recuperating from a coronary or just about to have one.

'What are you, collection agency?'

'I'm one of her daughter's doctors.'

'Oh yeah? Don't tell me about doctors. It's one of you that got me into this in the first place.'

'Towle?'

His eyebrows rose. 'Yeah? You from his office? Cause if you are, I got plenty—'

'No. I just know him.'

'Then you know he's a nag. Gets into stuff he has no business getting into. My wife hears me say this, she'll kill me. She loves the guy. Says he's terrific with the kids, so who am I to argue, right? What kind of doctor are you, anyway?'

'Psychologist.'

'The kid had problems, hugh? Wouldn't surprise me. She looked a little iffy, if you know what I mean.' He held out his hand, tilted it like the wing of a glider.

'You said Dr. Towle got you into the mess with Bonita Quinn?'

'That's right. I met the guy once or twice, maybe. I don't know him from Adam. One day he calls me out of the clear blue and asks me if I could give a job to a patient of his. He heard there was an opening for a manager in this place, and could I help this lady out. I say does this person have experience—we're talking multiple units here, not some duplex. He says no, but she can learn, she's got a kid, needs the money. I say, listen, Doc, this particular building is singles-oriented, the job's not right for someone with a kid. The manager's place is too small.' He looked at me scowling. 'Would you stick a kid in a hole like this?'

'No.'

339

'Me neither. You don't have to be a doctor to see it's not fit. I tell Towle this. I explain it to him. I say, Doc, this job is meant for a single person. Usually I get a student from UCLA to do it—they don't need a lot of space. I've got other buildings, I tell him. In Van Nuys, a couple in Canoga Park, more family-oriented. Let me call my man in the Valley, have him check it out, I'll see if I can help this person.

'Towle says, no, it has to be this building. The kid's already enrolled in school in this neighbourhood, to move her would be traumatic, he's a doctor, he knows this to be a fact. I say, but Doc, you can't have kids making noise in a place like this. The tenants are mostly singles, some like to sleep late. He says I guarantee you this kid is well-behaved, she makes no noise. I think to myself this kid makes no noise, there's gotta be something wrong with her—now *you* show up and it makes sense.

'I try to put him off, but he presses me. He's a nag. My wife loves him, she'll kill me if I get him pissed off, so I say okay. He makes an appointment for me to meet this lady, shows up with the Quinn broad and the kid. I was surprised. I gave it a little thought the night before, figured he was humping this broad, that's why the Albert Schweitzer routine. I expected something classy, with curves. One of those aspiring actress types, you know what I mean? He's older, but he's a classy-looking guy, right? So in he walks with her and the kid and they look like a pair outta the Dust Bowl, real hicks. The mother is scared outta her skull, she's smoking more than me, which is a feat—the kid's, like I told you, a little iffy, just stares into space, though I'll grant you she's quiet. Didn't make a sound. I had my doubts she could handle the job, but what could I do, I already committed myself. I hired her. She did okay. She was a hard worker, but she learned very slowly. No complaints about the kid, though. Anyway, she stays for a few months, then she flies the coop leaving me with this junk and she's probably got five

340

grand worth of rent checks. I have to go back and trace 'em and have the tenants put stops on 'em and write new ones. I gotta clean this place, hire someone new. Let me tell you, no more Mister Nice Guy for Marty. For doctors or anyone else.'

He folded his arms over his chest.

'You have no idea where she went?' I asked.

'I did, would I be standing here jawing with you?'

He went into the bedroom. It was as bleak as I remembered it.

'Look at this. How can people raise kids like this? I got three, each has his own room, they got TV's, bookshelves, Pac Mans, all that stuff. How can a kid's mind grow in a place like this?'

'If you hear from her or find out where she is, would you please call me?' I took out an old business card, crossed out the number and wrote my home phone number on it.

He glanced at it, and put it in his pocket. Running one finger along the top of the dresser he came up with a digit cloaked with dust kittys. He flung the dust away. 'Yecch. I hate dirt. I like things to be clean, know what I mean? My apartments are always clean—I pay extra for the best cleaning service. It's important tenants should feel healthy in a place.'

'You'll call me?'

'Sure, sure. You do the same for me, too, okay? I wouldn't mind finding Miss Bonita, get my checks back, give her a piece of my mind.' He fished in his pocket, pulled out an alligator billfold and from it produced a pearl-gray business card that said M and M Properties, Commercial and Residential, Marduk I. Minassian, President, followed by a Century City address.

'Thanks, Mr. Minassian.'

'Marty.'

He continued probing and inspecting, opening drawers and shaking his head, bending to look under the bed Bon-

341

ita Quinn had shared with her daughter. He found something under there, stood up, looked at it and tossed it in a metal wastebasket where it landed with a clang.

'What a mess.'

I looked in the basket, saw what he had discarded, and pulled it out.

It was the shrunken head Melody had shown me the day we'd spent together at the beach. I held it in my palm and the rhinestone eyes glared back, glossy and evil. Most of the synthetic hair had come loose but a few black strands stuck out of the top of the snarling face.

'That's junk,' said Minassian. 'It's dirty. Throw it away.'

I closed my hand over the child's keepsake, more sure than ever that the hypothesis I'd developed on the plane was right. And that I had to move fast. I put the shrunken head in my pocket, smiled at Minassian, and left.

'Hey!' he called after me. And then he muttered something that sounded like 'Crazy doctors!'

I retraced my route, got back on the freeway and headed East, driving like a demon and hoping the Highway Patrol wouldn't spot me. I had my L.A.P.D. consultant badge in my pocket but I doubted it would help. Even police consultants aren't supposed to weave in and out of traffic going eighty miles an hour.

I was lucky. Traffic was light, the guardians of the asphalt were nowhere to be seen, and I made it to the Silver Lake exit just before one. Five minutes later I was walking up the steps to the Gutierrez home. The orange and yellow poppies drooped, thirsty. The porch was empty. It creaked as I stepped onto it.

I knocked on the door. Cruz Gutierrez answered, knitting needles and bright pink yarn in her hands. She didn't seem surprised to see me.

'*Sí señor?*'

'I need your help, señora.'

342

'*No habio inglés.*'

'Please. I know you understand enough to help.'

The dark, round face was impassive.

'Señora, the life of a child is at stake.' That was optimism speaking. '*Una niña.* Seven years old—*siete años.* She's in danger. She could be killed. *Muerta*—like Elena.'

I let that sink in. Liver-spotted hands tightened around the blue needles. She looked away.

'Like the other child—the Nemeth boy. Elena's student. He didn't die in an accident, did he? Elena knew that. She died because of that knowledge.'

She put her hand on the door and started to close it. I blocked it with the heel of my palm.

'I feel for your loss, señora, but if Elena's death is to take on meaning, it can be through preventing more killing. Through stopping the deaths of others. Please.'

Her hands started shaking. The needles rattled like chopsticks in the grasp of a spastic. She dropped them and the ball of yarn. I bent and retrieved them.

'Here.'

She took them, held them to her bosom.

'Come in, please,' she said, in English that was barely accented.

I was too edgy to want to sit but when she motioned me to the green velvet sofa I settled in it. She sat across from me as if awaiting sentence.

'First,' I said, 'you must understand that darkening Elena's memory is the last thing I want to do. If other lives were not at stake I wouldn't be here at all.'

'I understand,' she said.

'The money—is it here?'

She nodded, got up, left the room and came back minutes later with a cigar box.

'Take.' She gave me the box as if it held something alive and dangerous.

The bills were in large denominations—twenties, fifties, hundreds—neatly rolled and held together by thick

343

rubber bands. I made a cursory count. There was at least fifty thousand dollars in the box, probably a good deal more.

'Take it,' I said.

'No, no. I don't want. Black money.'

'Just keep it here, until I come back for it. Does anyone else know about it—either of your sons?'

'No.' She shook her head adamantly. 'Rafael know he take it and buy the dope. No. Only me.'

'How long have you had it here?'

'Elena, she bring it over the day before she was killed.' The mother's eyes filled with tears. 'I say, what is this, where you get this. She say, can't tell you, Mama. Jus' keep it for me. I come back for it. She never come back.' She pulled a lace-trimmed handkerchief from up her sleeve and dabbed at her eyes.

'Please. Take it back. Hide it again.'

'Only a little while, señor, okay? Black money. Bad eye. *Mal ojo.*'

'I'll come back for it if that's what you want.'

She took the box, disappeared again, and returned shortly.

'You're sure Rafael didn't know?'

'I sure. He know, it would all be gone.'

That made sense. Junkies weren't known for being able to hold on to their nickels and dimes, let alone a small fortune.

'Another question, señora. Raquel told me that Elena had in her possession certain tapes—recorded tapes. Of music, and of relaxation exercises given to her by Dr. Handler. When I went through her things I found no such tapes. Do you know anything about that?'

'I don' know. This is the truth.'

'Has anyone been through those boxes before I got here?'

'No. Only Rafael an' Antonio, they look for books, things to read. The *policia* take boxes first. Nothin' else.'

'Where are your sons, now?'

She stood up, suddenly agitated.

'Don' hurt. They good boys. They don' know nothin'.'

'I won't. I just want to talk to them.'

She looked to one side, at the wall covered with family portraits. At her three children, young, innocent and smiling; the boys with short hair, slicked and parted, and open-necked white shirts; the girl in a frilly blouse between them. At the graduation picture: Elena in mortarboard and gown, wearing a look of eagerness and confidence, ready to take on the world with her brains and her charm and her looks. At the sombre-tinted photo of her long-dead husband, stiff and solemn in starched collar and gray serge suit, a workingman unaccustomed to the fuss and fiddling that went with having one's countenance recorded for posterity.

She looked at the pictures and her lips moved, almost imperceptively. Like a general surveying a smouldering battlefield, she conducted a silent body count.

'Andy working,' she said, and gave me the address of a garage on Figueroa.

'And Rafael?'

'Rafael I don' know. He say he go look for work.'

She and I both knew where he was. But I'd opened enough wounds for one day, so I kept my mouth shut, except to thank her.

I found him after a half-hour's cruising up and down Sunset and in and out of several side streets. He was walking south on Alvarado, if you could call the stumbling, self-absorbed lurch that propelled him headfirst, feet following, a walk. He stayed close to buildings, veering toward the street when people or objects got in his way, quickly returning to the shadow of awnings. It was close to eighty but he wore a long-sleeved flannel shirt hanging loose over khakis and buttoned to the neck. On his feet were

345

high-topped sneakers; the laces on one of them had come loose. He looked even thinner than I remembered.

I drove slowly, staying in the right lane, out of his field of vision, and keeping pace with him. Once he passed a group of middle-aged men, merchants. They pointed at him behind his back, shook their heads and frowned. He was oblivious to them, cut off from the external world. He pointed with his face, like a setter homing in on a scent. His nose ran continuously and he wiped it with his sleeve. His eyes shifted from side to side as his body kept moving. He ran his tongue over his lips, slapped his thin thighs in a steady tattoo, pursed his lips as if in song, bobbed his head up and down. He was making a concentrated effort at looking cool but he fooled no one. Like a drunk working hard at coming across sober his mannerisms were exaggerated, unnatural and lacking spontaneity. They produced the opposite effect: he appeared to be a hungry jackal on the prowl, desperate, gnawed upon from within and hurting all over. His skin was glossy with sweat, pale and ghostly. People got out of his way as he boogied toward them.

I sped up and drove two blocks before pulling to the curb and parking near an alley behind a three-storey building that housed a Latin grocery on the ground floor and apartments on the upper two.

A quick look shot backward confirmed that he was still coming.

I got out of the car and ducked into the alley, which stunk of rotting produce and urine. Empty and broken wine bottles littered the pavement. A hundred feet away was a loading dock, unattended, its steel doors closed and bolted. A dozen vehicles were illegally parked on both sides; exit from the alley was blocked by a half-ton pickup left perpendicular to the walls. Somewhere off in the distance a mariachi band played 'Cielito Lindo'. A cat screeched. Horns honked out on the boulevard. A baby cried.

346

I peeked my head out and retracted it. He was half a block away. I got ready for him. When he began crossing the alley I said in a stage whisper: 'Hey, man. I got what you need.'

That stopped him. He looked at me with great love, thinking he'd found salvation. It threw him off when I grabbed him by his scrawny arm and pulled him into the alley. I dragged him several feet until we'd found cover behind an old Chevy with peeling paint and two flat tyres. I slammed him against the wall. His hands went up protectively. I pushed them down and pinioned both of them with one of my own. He struggled but he had no strength. It was like tussling with a toddler.

'Whadyou want, man?'

'Answers, Rafael. Remember me? I visited you a few days ago. With Raquel.'

'Hey, yeah, sure,' he said, but there was only confusion in the watery hazel eyes. Snot ran down one nostril and into his mouth. He let it sit there a while before reaching up with his tongue and trying to flick it away. 'Yeah, I remember, man. With Raquel, sure, man.' He looked up and down the alley.

'You remember, then, that I'm investigating your sister's murder.'

'Oh, yeah, sure. Elena. Bad stuff, man.' He said it without feeling. His sister had been sliced up and all he could think of was that he needed a packet of white powder that could be transformed into his own special type of milk. I'd read dozens of tomes on addiction, but it was there, in that alley, that the true power of the needle became clear to me.

'She had tapes, Rafael. Where are they?'

'Hey, man, I don't know shit about tapes.' He struggled to break loose. I slammed him against the wall again. 'Oh, man, I'm hurting, just let me go fix myself up and then I talk to you about tapes. Okay, man?'

'No. I want to know now, Rafael. Where are the tapes?'

347

'I don't know, man, I told you that!' He was whining like a three-year-old, snotfaced and growing more frantic with each passing second.

'I think you do and I want to know.'

He bounced in my grasp, clattering like a sack of loose bones.

'Lemme go, motherfucker!' he gasped.

'Your sister was murdered, Rafael. Turned into hamburger. I saw pictures of what she looked like. Whoever did it to her took their time. It hurt her. And you're willing to deal with them.'

'I don't know what you're talkin' about, man.'

More struggling, another slam against the wall. He sagged this time, closed his eyes and for a moment I thought I'd knocked him out. But he opened them, licked his lips and gave a dry, hacking cough.

'You were off the stuff, Rafael. Then you started shooting up again. Right after Elena's death. Where'd you get the dough? How much did you sell her out for?'

'I don't know nothin'.' He shook spastically. 'Lemme go. I don't know nothin'.'

'Your own sister,' I said. 'And you sold out to her murderers for the price of a fix.'

'Pu*leeze*, mister. Lemme go.'

'Not until you talk. I don't have time to waste time with you. I want to know where those tapes are. You don't tell me soon I'll take you home with me, tie you up and let you go cold turkey in the corner. Imagine that—think how bad you hurt now, Rafael. Think how much worse it's going to get.'

He crumpled.

'I gave them to some dude,' he stuttered.

'For how much?'

'Not money, man. Stuff. He gave me stuff. Enough for a week's fixing. Good stuff. Now lemme go. I gotta appointment.'

'Who was the guy?'

348

'Just some dude. Anglo. Like you.'

'What did he look like?'

'I don't know, man, I can't think straight.'

'The corner, Rafael. Tied up.'

'Twenty-five, six. Short. Built good, solid. Real straight-lookin'. Light hair, over the forehead, okay?'

He'd described Tim Kruger.

'Why did he say he wanted the tapes?'

'He dint say, man, I dint ask. He had good stuff, you unnerstand?'

'Didn't you wonder? Your sister was dead and you didn't wonder why some stranger would give you smack for her tapes?'

'Hey, man, I dint wonder, I don' wonder. I don' think. I just go flyin'. I gotta go flyin' now. I'm hurtin', man. Lemme go.'

'Did your brother know about this?'

'No! He kill me, man. You hurt me, but he *kill* me, you unnerstand? Don' tell him!'

'What was on the tapes, Rafael?'

'I dunno. I don' listen, man!'

On principle I refused to believe him.

'The corner. Tied up. Bone dry.'

'Jus' some kid talkin', man, I swear that's it. I dint hear the whole thing, but when he offered me the stuff for them I took a listen before I gave them to the dude. Some kid talkin' to my sister. She's listenin' and sayin' tell me more and he's talkin'.'

'About what?'

'I don' know man. It started to get heavy, the kid's cryin', Elena's cryin', I switched it off. I don' wanna know.'

'What were they crying about, Rafael?'

'I don' know, man, something about how somebody hurt the kid, Elena's askin' him if they hurt him, he's sayin' yes, she's cryin', then the kid's cryin', too.'

'What else?'

'That's it.'

I throttled him just hard enough to rattle his teeth.

'You wan' me to make somethin' up, I can do it, man, but that's all I know!'

He cried out, snuffling and sucking for air.

I held him at arm's length, then let go. He looked at me unbelievingly, slithered against the wall, found a space between the Chevy and a rusted Dodge van. Staring at me, he wiped his nose, passed between the two cars and made a run for freedom.

I drove to a gas station at Virgil and Sunset, filled up, and used the pay phone to call La Casa de los Niños. The receptionist with the upbeat voice answered. Slipping into a drawl I asked her for Kruger.

'Mr. Kruger isn't in, today, sir. He'll be in tomorrow.'

'Oh yeah, that's right! He told me he'd be off the day I got in.'

'Would you care to leave a message, sir?'

'Heck no. I'm an old friend from school. Tim and I go way back. I just blew in on a business trip—I'm selling tool and die, Becker Machine Works, San Antonio, Texas—and I was supposed to look old Tim up. He gave me his number at home but I must have lost it. Do you have it?'

'I'm sorry, sir, we're not supposed to give out personal information.'

'I can dig that. But like I say, Tim and me are tight. Why don't you call him at home, tell him old Jeff Saxon's on the line, ready to drop in but stuck without the address.'

A clatter of ringing phones sounded in the background.

'One moment, sir.'

When she returned I asked her:

'You call him yet, ma'am?'

'No—I—it's rather busy right now, Mr . . .'

'Saxon. Jeff Saxon. You call old Tim and tell him old

350

Jeff Saxon's in town to see him, I guarantee you he'll
be—'

'Why don't I just give you the number?' She recited
seven digits, the first two of which signified a beach cities
location.

'Thank you much, I believe Tim told me he lived near
the beach—that far from the airport?'

'Mr. Kruger lives in Santa Monica. It's about a twenty-
minute ride.'

'Hey, that's not bad—maybe I'll just drop in on him,
kind of a surprise, what do you think?'

'Sir, I have to—'

'You wouldn't happen to have the address? I tell you,
it's been one hell of a day, what with the airline losing my
sample case and I've got two meetings tomorrow. I think
I packed the address book in the suitcase, but now I can't
be sure and—'

'Here's the address, sir.'

'Thank you much, ma'am. You've been very helpful.
And you have a nice voice.'

'Thank you, sir.'

'You free tonight?'

'I'm sorry, sir, no.'

'Fellow's gotta try, right?'

'Yes, sir. Good-bye, sir.'

I'd been driving north for a good five minutes before I
heard the buzzing. I realized, then, that the sound had
been with me since I'd pulled out of the gas station. The
rearview mirror revealed a motorcycle several lengths
back, bouncing in the distance like a fly on a hot windshield. The driver twisted the handle accelerator and the
fly grew like a monster in a Japanese horror flick.

He was two lengths behind, and gaining. As he
approached I got a look at him, jeans, boots, black leather
jacket, black hemlet with full-face tinted sun visor that
completely masked his features.

351

He rode my tail for several blocks. I changed lanes. Instead of passing, he hung back, allowing a Ford full of nuns to come between us. A half mile past Lexington the nuns turned off. I steered sharply toward the curb and came to a sudden stop in front of a Pup 'n Taco. The motorcycle sped by. I waited until he'd disappeared, told myself I was being paranoid, and got out of the Seville. I looked for him, didn't see him, bought a Coke, got behind the wheel and reentered the boulevard.

I'd turned east on Temple headed for the Hollywood Freeway when I heard him again. Verifying his presence in the mirror caused me to miss the on ramp, and I stayed on Temple, dipping under the bridge created by the overpass. The motorcycle stayed with me. I gave the Seville gas and ran a red light. He maintained his position, buzzing and spitting. The next intersection was filled with pedestrians and I had to stop.

I kept a watch on him through the side mirror. He rolled toward me, three feet away, now two, approaching on the driver's side. One hand went inside the leather jacket. A young mother wheeled a small child in a stroller, passing directly in front of my bumper. The child wailed, the mother chewed gum, heavy-legged, moving oh so slowly. Something metallic came into the hand in the mirror. The motorcycle was just behind me, almost flush with the driver's window. I saw the gun now, an ugly little snub-nosed affair, easy to conceal in a large palm. I raced my engine. The gum-chewing young matron wasn't impressed. She seemed to move in slow motion, indolently working her jaws, the child now screaming at the top of his lungs. The light remained red but its catercornered cousin had turned amber. The longest light in the history of traffic engineering . . . how long could an amber light last?

The snout of the revolver pressed against the glass, directly in line with my left temple. A black hole miles long wrapped in a concentric halo of silver. The mother

352

still dragged her heavy body lazily across the intersection, her heel in line with my right front tyre, unaware that the man in the green Cadillac was going to be blown away any second. The finger on the trigger blanched. The mother stepped clear by an inch. I twisted the steering wheel to the left, pressed down hard on the accelerator and shot diagonally across the intersection into the path of the ongoing traffic. I gunned the engine, laid a long patch of rubber, heard a Delphic chorus of curses, shouts, honking horns and squealing brakes, and shot up the first side street, narrowly missing a head-on collision with a Water and Power van coming from the opposite direction.

The street was narrow and winding, and pocked with potholes. The Seville was no sports car and I had to fight its slack steering system to maintain speed and control around the turns. I climbed, bounced down hard, and swooped steeply down a hill. A boulevard stop at the bottom was clear. I sped through. Three blocks of level turf at seventy miles an hour and the buzz was back, growing louder. The motorcycle, so much easier to manoeuvre, was catching up fast.

The road came to an end at a cracked masonry wall. Left or right? Decisions, decisions, with the adrenaline shooting through every corpuscle, the buzz now a roar, my hands sweaty, slipping off the wheel. I looked in the mirror, saw one hand come off the bars and aim the gun at my tyres. I chose left and floored the Seville, putting my body into it. The road rose, scaling empty streets, higher, spiralling into the smog, a roller coaster of a street planned by a berserk engineer. The motorcyclist kept riding up on my rear, raking his gun hand off the bars whenever he could, striving for steady aim . . .

I swerved continuously, dancing out of his sights, but the narrowness of the street gave me little leeway. I knew I had to avoid slipping unconsciously into a regular rhythm—back and forth, back and forth, a gasoline-fuelled metronome—for to do so would be to offer an

353

easy target. I drove erratically, crazily, jerking the wheel, slowing down, speeding up, careening against the curb, losing a hubcap that spun off like a chromium Frisbee. It was a direct assault on my axle and I didn't know how long it could last.

We continued to climb. A view of Sunset below appeared around a corner. We were back in Echo Park, on the south side of the boulevard. The road hit its peak. A shot whizzed by so close that the Seville's windows vibrated. I swerved and a second shot went far afield.

The terrain changed as the altitude rose, thinning from residential blocks of frame houses to progressively empt-ier stretches of dusty lots, with here and there a decrepit shack. No more telephone poles, no cars, no signs of human habitation . . . perfect for an afternoon killing.

We began to race downhill and I saw with horror that I was heading full-speed into a dead end, mere yards from slamming into a pile of dirt at the mouth of an empty construction site. There was no escape—the roar termin-ated at the site and was additionally blocked by piles of cinder block, stacks of drywall, lumber and more mounds of excavated dirt. A goddam *box canyon*. If the impact of smashing nose-first into the dirt didn't kill me, I'd be imbedded, tyres spinning hopelessly, as immobile as parsley in aspic, a perfect, passive target . . .

The man on the motorcycle must have harboured simi-lar thoughts in that same instant, for he engaged in a quick series of confident actions. He removed his gun hand from the bars, slowed, and came around to the left, ready to be at my side when my escape came to an end.

I made the only move left for me: I jammed on the brakes. The Seville convulsed, skidded violently, spun and rocked on its bearings, threatening to capsize. I needed the skid to continue, so I steered away from it. The car spun like a rotor blade.

Then a sudden impact threw me across the seat.

My front end had gone out of control and collided with

354

the cycle as it came out of a spin with full torque behind it. The lighter vehicle bounced off the car, caromed and sailed through the air in a wide arc over the hill of earth. I watched as man and machine parted ways, the cycle climbing, stuntlike, falling, its rider thrown loose, flying higher, a scarecrow cut free from its stake, then falling too, landing unseen.

The Seville stopped spinning and its engine died. I pulled myself up. My sore arm had been knocked against the passenger door panel and it hummed with pain. No sign of movement came from the site. I got out quietly, crouched behind the car and waited there as my head cleared and my breathing slowed. Still nothing. I spied a two-by-four several feet away, snatched it, hefted it like a stave and circled the mound of dirt, staying low to the ground. Creeping onto the site I saw that a partial foundation had been laid—a right angle of concrete from which corrugated steel rods protruded like flowerless stalks. The remains of the motorcycle were visible immediately, a rubbish heap of seared metal and shattered windshield.

It took several more minutes of poking amid the rubble to find the body. It had landed in a ditch at the junction of the two cement arms, a spot where the earth was etched with caterpillar tread marks, next to a broken fibreglass shower stall and half-concealed by moulding sheets of insulation.

The opaque helmet was still in place but it had offered no protection from the steel rod that stuck out through a large, jagged hole in the rider's throat. The shaft extended just below the Adam's apple; it had created a good-sized exit wound coming through. Blood seeped from the hole, turning muddy in the dirt. The trachea was visible, still pink, but deflated, leaking fluid. A fleck of gore tipped the rod.

I knelt and undid the helmet strap, and tried to pull off the headpiece. The neck had bent unnaturally upon being

355

pierced and it proved a difficult task. As I struggled I felt steel scrape against vertebrae, cartilage and gristle. My belly quaked with nausea. I heaved and turned away to vomit in the dirt.

With a bitter taste in my mouth and eyes brimming with tears, breathing hard and loud, I returned to the grisly chore. The helmet finally came loose and the bare skull flopped to the ground. I stared down into the lifeless, bearded face of Jim Halstead, the coach at La Casa de Los Niños. His lips were drawn back in death, cast in a permanent sneer. The force of landing after his final free fall had snapped his jaws down upon his tongue, and the severed tip rested on the hairy chin like some fleshy, parasitic grub. His eyes were open and rolled backward, the whites flooded with blood. He cried crimson tears.

I looked away from him and saw the sun hit something shiny several feet to the right. I walked to it, found the gun and examined it—a chrome-plated .38. I took it and tucked it in the waistband of my trousers.

The ground at my feet radiated heat and the stench of something burning. Congealed tar. Toxic waste. Bio-undegradable garbage. Polyvinyl vegetation. A bluejay had landed on Halstead's face. It pecked at his eyes.

I found a dusty drop cloth peppered with specks of dried cement. The bird fled at my approach. I covered the body with the cloth, weighted down the corners with large stones and left him that way.

27

THE ADDRESS the receptionist had given me for Tim Kruger matched the oversized steel numbers on the face of a bone-white highrise on Ocean, just a mile or so from where the Handler-Gutierrez murders had taken place.

The entry hall was a crypt of marble floors and mirrors, furnished with a single white cotton sofa and two rubber plants in wicker canisters. The upper half of one wall was given over to rows of alphabetically arranged brass mailboxes. It didn't take long to locate Kruger's apartment on the twelfth floor. I took a short silent ride on an elevator padded with gray batting and exited into a corridor floored in royal-blue plush and paper with grasscloth.

Kruger's place was located in the northwest corner of the building. I knocked on the royal-blue door.

He opened it, dressed in jogging shorts and a Casa de los Niños T-shirt, shiny with perspiration and smelling as if he'd been exercising. He saw me, stifled his surprise and said 'Hello, Doctor' in a stagey voice. Then he noticed the gun in my hand and the stolid face turned ugly.

'What the—'

'Just get in,' I said.

357

He backed into the apartment and I followed. It was a small place, low ceilings sprayed with plaster cottage cheese and starred with glitter. The walls and carpet were beige. There was little furniture and what was there looked rented. A wall of glass offering a panoramic view of Santa Monica Bay saved it from being a cell. There was no artwork on the walls, except for a single, framed wrestling poster from Hungary. A tiny convenience kitchen was off on one side, a foyer to the other.

Athletic equipment filled a good portion of the living room—snow skis and boots, a pair of waxed wooden oars, several sets of tennis rackets, running shoes, a mountaineer's backpack, a football, a basketball, a bow and quiver of arrows. A beige-painted brick mantel was topped by a dozen trophies.

'You're an active boy, Tim.'

'What the hell do you want?' The yellow-brown eyes moved around like pachinko balls.

'Where's the little girl—Melody Quinn?'

'I don't know what you're talking about. Put that thing away.'

'You know damn well where she is. You and your fellow murderers abducted her three days ago because she's a witness to your dirty work. Have you killed her too?'

'I'm no killer. I don't know any kid named Quinn. You're crazy.'

'No killer? Jeffrey Saxon might not agree.'

His mouth dropped open, then shut abruptly.

'You left a trail, Tim. Pretty arrogant to think no one would find it.'

'Who the hell are you, anyway?'

'I'm who I said I was. A better question is who are *you*? A rich boy who can't seem to stay out of trouble? A guy who enjoys snapping twigs at hunchbacks and waiting for the tears? Or just an amateur actor whose best bit is an impression of Jack the Ripper?'

358

'Don't try to pin that on me!' He rolled his hands into fists.

'Hands up.' I waved the gun.

He obeyed very slowly, straightening his thick, brown arms and lifting them above his head. It drew my attention upward, and away from his feet. That enabled him to make his move.

The kick came at me like a boomerang, catching the underside of my wrist and numbing the fingers. The gun flew from my grasp and landed on the carpet with a thud. We both leaped for it and ended in a tangle on the floor, punching, kicking, gouging. I was oblivious to pain and seething with fury. I wanted to destroy him.

He was an iron man. It was like fighting an outboard motor. I clawed at his abdomen, but couldn't find an inch of extra flesh. I elbowed him in the ribs. It knocked him backward, but he rebounded as if on springs and landed a punch to the jaw that threw me off-balance long enough for him to get me in a headlock, then hold me skilfully at bay so that my arms were ineffective.

He grunted and increased the pressure. My head felt ready to burst. My vision blurred. I struck at him helplessly. With a strange kind of delicacy he danced out of reach, squeezing me tighter. Then he started pulling my head back. A little more and I knew my neck would snap. I experienced a sudden kinship with Jeffrey Saxon, drew upon a reserve of strength and brought my heel down hard on his instep. He cried out and reflexively let go, then tried to renew the lock, but it was too late. I landed a kick that snapped his head to the side and followed it with a series of rapid straightarm punches to the lower belly. When he doubled over I chopped down on the place where his head joined his neck. He sank to his knees, but I didn't take any chances—he was strong and skilled. Another kick to the face. Now he was down. I placed one foot under bridge of his nose. One quick forward motion and splinters of bone would lobotomize him. It turned out to be an unnecessary precaution. He was out.

I found a coil of thick nylon rope in the mountaineer's pack and trussed him as he lay on his abdomen, feet drawn up behind him, bound and secured to another piece of rope that similarly raised his arms. I checked the knots, drew them tight and dragged him clear of any weapon. I retrieved the .38, kept it in one hand, went into his kitchen and soaked a towel in cold water.

When several minutes of slapping him with the towel elicited no more than a half-conscious groan, I made another trip to the kitchen, pulled a Dutch oven out of a dish drainer, filled it with water and dumped the contents on his head. That brought him around.

'Oh, Jesus,' he moaned. He tried those first struggles that all prisoners attempt, gnashed his teeth, finally realized his predicament and sank back down, gasping.

I prodded the back of one leg with the muzzle of the .38.

'You like sports, Tim. That's fortunate because they'll let you exercise in prison. Without exercise the time can go very slowly. But I'm going to ask you questions and if you don't give me satisfactory answers I'm going to maim you, bit by bit. First I'll shoot you right here.' I pressed cold steel into warm flesh. 'After that your leg might be good for getting you on the john. Then I'll do the same to the other leg. From there to fingers, wrists, elbows. You'll do your time as a vegetable, Tim.'

I listened to myself talk, hearing a stranger. To this day I don't know if I would have followed through on the threat. I never had to find out.

'What do you want?' His speech came out in spurts, constricted with fear and hampered by the uncomfortable position.

'Where's Melody Quinn?'

'At La Casa.'

'Where at La Casa?'

360

'The storage rooms. Near the forest.'

'Those cinder block buildings—the ones you avoided discussing when you gave me the tour?'

'Uh-huh. Yes.'

'Which one? There were four.'

'The last one—furthest from the front.'

A spreading stain darkened the carpet at my feet. He'd wet himself.

'Jesus,' he said.

'Let's keep going, Tim. You're doing fine.'

He nodded, seemingly eager for praise.

'Is she still alive?'

'Yes. As far as I know. Cousin Will—Doctor Towle wanted to keep her alive. Gus and the judge agreed. I don't know for how long.'

'What about her mother?'

He closed his eyes and said nothing.

'Talk, Tim, or your leg goes.'

'She's dead. The guy they sent to get the kid and her did it. They buried her in the Meadow.'

I remembered the stretch of field at the north side of La Casa. *We're planning to plant a vegetable garden this summer* he'd told me . . .

'Who is he?'

'Some crazy guy. A gimp—kind of paralyzed on one side. Gus called him Earl.'

It wasn't the name I expected but the description was right.

'Why'd he do it?'

'Leave as few loose ends as possible.'

'On McCaffrey's orders?'

He was silent. I exerted pressure on the gun. High thigh quivered.

'Yeah. On his orders. Earl doesn't operate on his own.'

'Where is this Earl character now?'

More hesitation. Without thinking I flicked the tip of

361

the .38 over his kneecap. His eyes widened with surprise and hurt. Tears ran out of them.

'Oh, God!'

'Don't get religious. Just talk.'

'He's gone—dead. Gus had Halstead rip him off. After they buried the woman. He was filling the grave and Halstead hit him with the shovel, pushed him in with her and covered them both with dirt. He and Gus were laughing about it later. Halstead said when he hit Earl on the head it gave off a hollow sound. They used to talk like that, behind the guy's back—call him the gimp, damaged goods . . .'

'Mean guy, that Halstead.'

'Yeah. He is.' Kruger's visage brightened, eager to please. 'He's after you too. You were snooping around. Gus didn't know how much the kid told you. I'm tipping you off, man, watch your—'

'Thanks, pal, but Halstead's no threat anymore. To anyone.'

He looked up at me. I answered the unspoken question with a quick nod.

'Jesus,' he said, broken.

I didn't give him time to reflect.

'Why'd you kill Handler and Gutierrez?'

'I told you, I *didn't*. That was Halstead and Earl. Gus told 'em to make it look like a sex thing. Halstead told me later Earl was a natural for the job—carved 'em up like he enjoyed it. Really went to town on the teacher. Halstead held her and Earl used the knife.'

Two men, maybe three, Melody had said.

'You were there, too, Tim.'

'No. Yeah. I—I drove them there. With the headlights out. It was a dark night, no moon, no stars. I circled the parking lot, then figured I might get noticed, so I drove around in the Palisades and came back. They still weren't through—I remember wondering what was taking them so long. I left again, drove around some more, came back

362

and they were just coming out. They wore black, like demons. I could see the blood, even against the black. They smelled of blood. It was all over them, dark, like the clothing, but a different texture—you know, shiny. Wet.'

Dark men. Two, maybe three.

He stopped.

'That's not the end of the story, Tim.'

'That's it. They undressed in the car, stuffed the knife in a duffel bag. We burned it in one of the canyons—the clothes, bag, everything. Dumped whatever was left off the Malibu pier.' He paused again, out of breath. 'I didn't kill anybody.'

'Did they say anything in the car?'

'Halstead was stone silent. It bothered me, how freaked-out he looked, because he's a mean one—that story about getting a knife pulled on him by a kid is bullshit. He was kicked out of Manual Arts for beating up a couple of students pretty badly. Before that he was booted out of the marines. He loved violence. But whatever happened in that apartment got to him—he was silent, man.'

'How about Earl?'

'Earl was—different—like he *dug* it, you know? He was licking his lips and rocking back and forth like an autistic kid. Jabbering, saying "Sonofabitch" over and over. Weird. Crazy. Finally Halstead told him to shut the fuck up and he yelled something back—in Spanish. The guy spoke a lot in Spanish. Halstead yelled back and I thought the two of them were going to tear each other up right there. It was like driving around with two caged beasts. I calmed them down, used Gus's name—that always worked for Earl. I couldn't wait to get away from them that night. Prototypical psychopaths, both of them.'

'Save the scholarly stuff and tell me how you killed Bruno.'

He looked at me with renewed fear.

363

'You know everything, don't you.'

'What I don't you're going to fill in.' I waved the gun in the air. '*Bruno.*'

'We—they did that the night after doing the doctor and the teacher. Halstead didn't want Earl along but Gus insisted. Said two men on the job was better. I had the feeling he played them off against each other. I wasn't there at all. Halstead drove and did the killing. He used a baseball bat from the athletic supplies bin. I was there when he came back and told Gus about it. They found the salesman eating dinner, beat him to death right there at the table. Earl ate the rest of the meal.'

Two murders pinned on two dead men. Very neat. It stunk and I told him so.

'That's the way it was. I'm not saying I'm totally innocent. I knew what they were going to do when I drove them to the shrink's place. I gave them the key. But I didn't do any of the killing.'

'How'd you get the key?'

'Cousin Will gave it to me. I don't know where he got it.'

'All right. We've talked about who. Now tell me why all the butchery.'

'I assumed you knew—'

'Don't assume a goddam thing.'

'Okay, okay. It's the Brigade. It's a cover for child molesters. The shrink and the girl found out and they were blackmailing him. Stupid of them to think they could get away with it.'

I remembered the pictures Milo'd shown me that first day. They'd paid far too high a price for their stupidity.

I chased the bloody images from my mind and returned to Kruger.

'Are all the Gentlemen perverts?'

'No. Only about a quarter. The rest are straight-arrows. It makes it easier to conceal, sneaking the perverts in among them.'

364

'And the kids never talk?'

'Not until—we pick the ones that the pervs take home with care, mostly those who can't talk back. Retarded, or they don't know English, severely c.p. Gus likes orphans because they don't have family ties, no one looks out for them.'

'Was Rodney one of the chosen ones?'

'Uh-huh.'

'Did his fear of the doctor have something to do with that?'

'Yeah. One of the weirdos got a little rough with him. A surgeon. Gus warns them to go easy. He doesn't want the kids actually *hurt*—spoiled merchandise isn't worth as much. But it doesn't always work out. Those guys aren't normal, you know.'

'I know.' Anger and disgust made it hard to see straight. Kicking his head in would have been primally satisfying, but it was a pleasure I was going to have to deny myself . . .

'I'm not one of them,' he was insisting, sounding almost as if he'd convinced himself. 'I think it's disgusting, actually.'

I bent down and grabbed him by the throat.

'You went along with it, asshole!'

His face purpled, the butterscotch eyes bulging. I let go of his head. It dropped to the floor. He landed on his nose and it started to bleed. He writhed in confinement.

'Don't say it. You were just following orders.'

'You don't understand!' he sobbed. Real tears mixed with the moustache of blood on his upper lip creating a momentary illusion of harelip. But for his degree in drama I might have been impressed. 'Gus took me in when the rest of them—my so-called friends and family, everyone—blackballed me for the Saxon thing. You can think what you want but that wasn't murder. It was—an accident. Saxon was no innocent victim. He wanted to kill *me*—that's the truth.'

365

'He's in no position to state his case.'

'Shit! No one believed me. Except Gus. He knew what it could be like at that place. They all thought I was a washout—shame of the family and all that crap. He gave me responsibility. And I lived up to his expectations—I showed my stuff, showed you don't need a degree. Everything was perfect, I ran La Casa as smooth as—'

'You're a terrific stormtrooper, Tim. Right now I want answers.'

'Ask,' he said weakly.

'How long has the Brigade been a cover for child molesters?'

'From the beginning.'

'Just like in Mexico?'

'Just like. Down there, to hear him tell it—the police knew all about it. All he had to do was grease a few palms. They let him bring in rich businessmen from Acapulco—Japanese, lots of Arabs—to play with the kids. The place was called Father Augustino's Christian Home—whatever that is in Spanish. It went good for a long time until a new police commissioner, some religious nut, took over and didn't like it. Gus claims the guy ripped him off for thousands in payoff then double-crossed him and shut the place down anyway. He moved up here and set up camp. Brought Crazy Earl with him.'

'Earl was his boy in Mexico?'

'Yup. I figure he did the shitwork. Followed Gus like a lap dog. The guy spoke Spanish like a beaner—I mean the accent was fine but what he said was gibberish—we're talking brain damage, man. A robot with the screws loose.'

'McCaffrey had him killed anyway.'

Kruger gave the closest approximation to a shrug the ropes would allow.

'You have to know Gus. He's cold. Loves power. Get in his way and you're done. Those suckers didn't have a chance.'

366

'How did he get set up so fast in L.A.?'

'Connections.'

'Cousin Willie?'

He hesitated. I prodded him with the .38.

'Him. Judge Hayden. Some others. One seemed to lead to another. Each one knew at least one other closet sicko. Amazing how many of those guys there are. Cousin Will was a surprise to me, 'cause I knew him really well. Always seemed such a priss, holier than thou. My folks held him up as an example to follow—fine, upstanding Cousin Doctor.' He laughed hoarsely. 'And the guy's a kiddy boffer.' More laughter. 'Though I can't say I actually saw him take a kid home—I set up the schedules and I never set him up with anything. All I *know* he did was patch injured kids up whenever we called. Still, he must be as sick as the rest, why else would he be kissing up to Gus?'

I ignored the question and asked one of my own.

'How long was the blackmail going on?'

'A few months. Like I told you we screened the kids, to make sure they wouldn't talk. One time we blew it. There was this one boy, an orphan, just perfect. Everyone thought he was mute. Jesus, he never talked to *us*. We had speech and hearing tests—the government pays for all of that—and everything came back no speech. We were sure, and we were wrong. The kid talked all right. He told the teacher plenty. She freaked out and reported it to Cousin Will—he was the kid's paediatrician. She didn't know he was involved in it himself. He told Gus.'

And Gus had him killed. Cary Nemeth.

'Then what?'

'I—do we have to talk about it?'

'We goddamn as hell do! How did it happen?'

'They ran him down with a truck. They took him out of bed in the middle of the night, must have been close to midnight. Nothing's out there at that hour. Put him on the road, walking. In his pyjamas. I remember the pyjamas.

367

Yellow, with baseballs and mitts all over. I—I could have tried to stop it but it wouldn't have made a difference. The kid knew, he had to go. Simple as that. They would have done it later and probably me, too. It was wrong to do that to a little kid. Cold-blooded. I started to say something. Gus squeezed my arm. Told me to shut up. I wanted to scream. The kid was walking on the road, all alone, half-asleep, like he was dreaming. I kept quiet. Halstead got into the truck, drove it a ways down the road. I could hear him revving it up, from around the bend. He came back speeding, headlights on high beam. Hit the kid from behind—he never knew what happened, he was half-asleep.'

He stopped talking, panting, and closed his eyes.

'Gus talked about doing the teacher right then and there but he decided to wait, see if she'd told anyone else. He had Halstead follow her. He staked out her place. She wasn't there. Just her roommate. Halstead wanted to kidnap *her*, beat it out of *her*, see if she knew anything. Then he saw the teacher come back with some guy—it was Handler—to pick up her stuff. Like she was moving in with him. Halstead reported it back to Gus. Now it was getting complicated. They kept watching the two of them and finally saw them meet with Bruno. We knew Bruno—he'd volunteered at La Casa, seemed like a great guy. Very outgoing. The kids loved him. It was clear, at that point, that he'd been a spy. Now it was three mouths that had to be closed.

'The calls came a few days later. It was Bruno, disguising his voice, but we knew it was him. Saying he had tapes of the Nemeth kid telling all. He even played a few seconds over the phone. They were amateurs, they didn't know Gus had them from day one, right in the crosshairs. It was pathetic.'

Pathetic *was* the word for the scenario. Take one nice girl. Elena Gutierrez, up from the barrio, attractive, vibrant. A little materialistic, but warm-hearted. A gifted

368

teacher. Depressed about her job, burned out, she seeks help, enters therapy with Morton Handler, M.D., psychopath cum psychiatrist. Ends up going to bed with Handler but continues to tell him her problems—one major one being the kid who never talked before who's suddenly opening up and telling her terrible things about strange men doing bad things to him. He opens up to Miss Gutierrez because she's warm and understanding. A real talent for drawing them out, Raquel Ochoa had said. A talent for working with the ones who didn't respond to anyone else. A talent that cost Elena her life. Because what was human tragedy to her smelled profitable to Morton Handler. Nasty things in high places—what could be juicier?

Of course Handler thinks these things but he keeps them to himself. After all, maybe the kid is making it all up. Maybe Elena is overreacting—you know women, especially Latin women—so he tells her to keep listening, emphasizes what a good job she's doing, what a source of support she is for the child. Bides his time.

Shouldn't I report this to someone? she asks him. Wait, dear, be cautious, until you know more. But the child is crying out for help, the bad men are still coming for him . . . Elena takes it upon herself to call Cary's doctor. And thus signs his death warrant.

When Elena hears of the child's death, she suspects the awful truth; she falls apart. Handler shoves tranquillizers down her throat, calms her down. All the while his psychopathic mind is going click click click, because now he *knows* there's money to be made.

Enter Maurice Bruno: fellow psychopath, former patient, new buddy. A real smoothie. Handler recruits him and offers him a cut of the yield if he infiltrates the Gentlemen's Brigade and finds out as much as he can. Names, places, dates. Elena wants to call the police. Handler quiets her down with more pills and more talk. The police are ineffectual, my darling. They won't do

369

anything about it. I know from experience. Slowly, gradually, he gets her to go along with the blackmail scheme. This is the real way to punish them, he assures her. Hit them where it hurts. She listens, so unsure, so confused. Something seems so wrong about profiting from the death of a helpless little boy, but then again, nothing will bring him back, and Morton seems to know what he's talking about. He's very persuasive and besides, there's that Datsun 280ZX she's always wanted, and those outfits she saw last week at Neiman-Marcus. She could never afford them on what the damned school pays her. And who the hell ever did anything for her, anyway? *Look out for number one* Morton always says, and maybe he's got a point there . . .

'Earl and Halstead looked for the tapes,' Kruger was saying, 'after they tied them up. They tortured them to get them to tell where they kept them but neither of them talked. Halstead complained to Gus that he could have gotten it out of them but Earl went to work too fast with the knife. Handler passed out when he cut his throat, the girl freaked out totally, screaming, they had to jam something in her mouth. She choked, then Earl finished her, played with her.'

'But you finally found the tapes, didn't you, Timmy?'

'Yes. She'd kept them at her mother's. I got them from her junkie brother. Used smack as a bribe.'

'Tell me more.'

'That's it. They tried to put the squeeze on Gus. He paid them once or twice—big amounts 'cause I saw large rolls of bills—but it was just to give them false confidence. They never had a chance from the start. We never got the money back, but I don't think it mattered. It was a drop in the bucket. Besides, money doesn't seem to turn Gus on. He lives simply, eats cheap. There's big bucks rolling in every day. From the government—state and federal. Private donations. Not to mention the thousands the pervs pay him for their jollies. He stashes some away but

I've never seen him do anything extravagant. It's power he's after, not bread.'

'Where are the tapes?'

'I gave them to Gus.'

'Come on.'

'I gave them to him. He sent me on an errand and I delivered.'

'That's a strong-looking knee. Pity to pulverize it to bone meal.' I stepped on the back of his leg and bore down. It forced his head up, had to hurt.

'Stop! Okay. I made a copy. I had to. For leverage. What if Gus wanted me out of the way one day? I mean I was his golden boy now but you could never know, right?'

'Where are they?'

'In my bedroom. Taped to the bottom of the mattress.'

'Don't go away.' I released my foot.

He gnashed his teeth like a netted shark.

I found three unmarked cassettes where he said they'd be, pocketed them and returned.

'Tell me some names. Of the molesters in the Brigade.'

He recited like a kid delivering his confirmation speech. Automatic. Nervous. Overly rehearsed.

'Any more?'

'Isn't that enough?'

He had a point. He'd mentioned a well-known film director, a deputy D.A., a political biggie—a behind-the-scenes man who managed to stay in front—corporate attorneys. Doctors. Bankers. Real estate honchos. Men whose names usually got in print when they donated something or won an award for humanitarian service. Men whose names on a campaign endorsement roster brought in votes. Ned Biondi would have enough to turn L.A. society on its ear for quite some time.

'You're not going to forget all of this when the police ask you about it, are you, Tim?'

371

'No! Why should I? Maybe cooperating can buy me out?'

'You're not getting out. Accept it. But at least,' I added, 'you won't end up fertilizing McCaffrey's vegetable patch.'

He considered that. It must have been hard to count his blessings with the ropes biting into his wrists and ankles.

'Listen,' he said, 'I've helped you. Help me make a deal. I'll cooperate—I didn't kill anyone.'

The power he attributed to me was fictitious. I used it anyway.

'I'll do what I can,' I said magnanimously, 'but a lot of it's up to you. If the Quinn kid gets out of this healthy, I'll go to bat for you. If not, you're down the toilet.'

'Then get going, for God's sake! Get her out of there! I don't give her more than a day. Will put Gus off but it won't be for long. She'll have an accident. They'll never find the body. It's just a matter of time. Gus is sure she saw too much.'

'Tell me what I need to get her out of there safely.'

He looked away.

'I lied about where she is. It's not the furthest building, it's the one just before it. With the blue door. Metal door. There's a key in the pocket of my tan pants. Hanging in the closet in my room.'

I left him, fished it out and came back dangling the key.

'You're batting a thousand, Tim.'

'I'm being straight with you. Just help *me*.'

'Is anyone with her?'

'No. There's no need. Will has her on sedatives. Mostly she's out of it or sleeping. They send in someone to feed her, clean her up. She's strapped to the bed. The room's solid, concrete block. Only one way in—through the door. There's a single skylight window they keep open. Close it, anyone inside suffocates in forty-eight hours.'

'Could Will Towle get into La Casa without arousing suspicion?'

372

'Sure. Like I told you, he's on twenty-four-call for when the Gentlemen get too rough on the kids. Most of the time it's nothing serious—scrapes, lacerations. Sometimes the kids freak out, he gives them Valium or Mellaril, or a quick dose of Thorazine. Yeah, he could show up any time.'

'Good. You're going to call him. Tim. You're going to tell him he needs to make just such an emergency call. I want him entering La Casa a half-hour after dark—let's say seven-thirty. Make sure he's on time. And alone. Make it sound convincing.'

'I could be more convincing if I could move around a little bit.'

'Work with what you've got. I have faith in you. Use your dramatic training. You were pretty good as Bill Roberts.'

'How'd you kn—'

'I didn't. Now I do. It was an educated guess. You're a trained actor, you were a natural for the part. Did your role include killing Hickle, too?'

'Ancient history,' he said. 'Yeah, I made the call. Setting it up in your office was Hayden's idea of a joke. He's a mean little mother. Sick sense of humour. But like I told you before, I didn't *kill* anybody. For the Hickle thing I wasn't even there. That was all Hayden and Cousin Will. They—and Gus—decided to shut him up—same old story, I guess. Hickle was a member of the Brigade, one of the originals. But he free-lanced with the kids at his wife's school.

'I remember after he got busted, the three of them were talking about it. Gus was ranting. "Damned stupid shithead!" he was yelling, "I furnish that fool with enough hairless pussy to keep him smiling for the rest of his life and he goes and does a dumbshit thing like this!" The way I figured it Hickle'd always been regarded as weak and stupid, easily influenced. They bet that once he

373

started confessing the school stuff he'd open his yap and bring it all down around them. They had to put him away.

'The way they did it was for Hayden to call him and tell him he had good news. Hickle'd asked Hayden to pull strings downtown with the D.A., which just goes to show you how stupid he was. I mean at that time Hickle was page one. Just knowing him was the kiss of death. But he called Hayden, asked him anyway. Hayden faked it like he was going to try to help. Couple days later he called him, said yeah, there was good news, he could help. They met at Hayden's house, very hush-hush, no one around. From what I gather Will slipped something in his tea— the guy didn't drink booze. Something you could time precisely and that wore off, so traces were hard to find unless you were looking for something specifically. Will fixed the dosage—he's good at that. When Hickle was out they moved him to your place. Hayden picked the lock— he's good with his hands, does magic shows for the kids at La Casa. Dresses up like a clown—Blimbo the Clown— and does magic tricks.'

'Forget magic. Go on about Hickle.'

'That's it. They got him up there, faked the suicide. I don't know who pulled the trigger. I wasn't there. The only reason I know anything about it is I did the Bill Roberts bit and a few days later Gus told me what it was all about. He was in one of those dark moods when he talks like a megalomaniac. "Don't think your cousin the doctor is all that noble, my boy," he was saying. "I can fry his ass and the asses of lots of noble men with one phone call." He gets that way—anti-rich, after he thinks back to how he was poor and all us rich folk mistreated him. That night, after they killed Hickle, we were sitting in his office. He was drinking gin and he started to reminisce about how he used to work for Mr. Hickle—Hickle's father—from the time he was a little kid. He was an orphan and some agency basically sold him to the Hickles, like a slave. He said old Hickle had been a monster.

374

Vicious temper, liked to kick the help around. He told me how he took it, kept his eyes open, learned all the nasty family secrets—like Stuart's kinks, other stuff—saved it all up and used it to get off Brindamoor, to get the job at Jedson. I remember him smiling at me, half-drunk, looking crazy. "I learned early," he said, "that knowledge is power." Then he talked about Earl, how the guy was damaged goods, but would do anything for him. "He'd eat my shit and call it caviar," he said. "That's power." '

Kruger had arched his back, picking his head up, stiff-necked, as he talked. Now exhausted, he sank back down.

'I guess,' he said, 'he's getting back at all of us.'

He lay in the ochre stain of dried urine, pitiful.

'Anything else you want to tell me, Tim?'

'I can't think of anything. You ask, I'll tell.'

I saw the tension travel up and down his bound limbs like a handcar on a twisted track and kept my distance.

There was a phone on the floor several feet away. I brought it near, stayed away from his arms and laid the speaker near his mouth. Holding the gun to his brow I punched in Towle's office number and stepped back.

'Make it good.'

He did. I would have been convinced. I hoped Towle was. He signalled me the conversation was through by moving his eyes back and forth. I hung up and had him make a second call, to the security desk at La Casa to set up the doctor's visit.

'How was that?' he asked when he was through.

'Rave review.'

Oddly enough that seemed to please him.

'Tell me, Tim, how are your sinuses?'

The question didn't throw him. 'Great,' he blurted out, 'i'm never sick.' He said it with the bravado of the habitual athlete who believes exercise and firm muscles are guarantees of immortality.

'Good. Then this shouldn't bother you.' I crammed a

towel into his mouth while he made enraged, muffled noises through the terry-cloth.

Carefully I dragged him to the bedroom, emptied the closet of anything that resembled a tool or weapon and shoved him inside, moulding him to the confines of the tiny space.

'*If* I get out of La Casa with the kid and myself in good shape I'll tell the police where to find you. If I don't, you'll probably suffocate. Anything else you want to tell me?'

A shake of the head. Beseeching eyes. I closed the door and moved a heavy dresser in front of it. I replaced the gun in my waistband, closed all the windows in the apartment, drew the bedroom curtains and shut the bedroom door, blocking it with two chairs stood on end. I cut his phone line with a kitchen knife, drew the drapes so that the view of the ocean was erased and gave the place a final once-over. Satisfied, I walked out the door, slamming it tight.

28

THE SEVILLE was running, but shakily, as a result of the grand prix with Halstead. It was also too conspicuous for my purposes. I left it in a lot in Westwood Village, walked two blocks to a Budget Rent-A-Car and picked up a dark brown Japanese compact—one of those square little boxes of moulded plastic papered with an allegedly metal shell. It took fifteen minutes to putt-putt through the traffic from one end of the village to the other. I pulled into the Bullocks garage, locked the gun in the glove compartment, locked the car and went shopping.

I bought a pair of jeans, thick socks, crepe-soled shoes, navy blue turtleneck and a windbreaker of the same dark hue. Everything in the store was tagged with plastic alarm clips and it took the salesgirl several minutes to liberate the garments after she'd taken my money.

'Wonderful world,' I muttered.

'You think this is bad, we have the expensive stuff—leather, furs—under lock and key. Otherwise they just waltz right out with it.'

We shared righteous sighs and, after being informed I was likely to be under surveillance, I decided not to change in the store's dressing room.

It was just past six and dark by the time I was back on the street. Time enough to grab a steak sandwich, Greek salad, vanilla ice cream and lots of black coffee and watch the starless sky from the vantage point of a front table in a mom-and-pop eatery on West Pico. At six-thirty I paid the tab and went into the restaurant's men's room to change. While slipping into my new duds I noticed a piece of folded paper on the floor. I picked it up. It was the copy of the Lilah Towle accident story given to me by Margaret Dopplemeier. I tried to read it again, with not much great success. I was able to make out something about the Coast Guard and high tides, but that was it. I put it back in the jacket pocket, straightened up and got ready to head for Malibu.

There was a pay phone at the back of the café, and I used it to call the West L.A. station. I thought of leaving a convoluted message for Milo, then thought better of it and asked for Delano Hardy. After being kept waiting for five minutes I was finally told he was out on a call. I left the convoluted message for him, paid the check, and headed for Malibu.

It was slow going but I'd constructed my schedule with that in mind. I reached Rambla Pacifica just before seven, and the county sign announcing La Casa de los Niños at ten after. The sky was empty and dark, like a drop down an endless well. A coyote howled from a distant gully. Nightbirds and bats flittered and squeaked. I switched off my headlights and navigated the next mile and a half by sense of touch. It wasn't all that difficult, but the little car resonated at every crack and bump in the road, and transmitted the shock waves directly though my skeletal system.

I came to a stop a half-mile before the La Casa turnoff. It was seven-fifteen. There were no other vehicles on the road. Praying it stayed that way, I swung the car perpendicular to the road and blocked both lanes: rear wheels facing the ravine that bordered the highway, front tyres nosing the thick brush to the west. I sat in the darkened compartment, gun in hand, waiting.

At twenty-three after seven I heard the sound of an approaching engine. A minute later the Lincoln's square headlights came into view a quarter-mile up the road. I jumped out of the car, ran for cover in the brush and crouched, holding my breath.

He saw the empty car late and had to screech to a stop. He left his motor running, the lights on, and walked into the beam, cursing. The white hair gleamed silver. He wore a charcoal double-breasted blazer over a white open-necked shirt, along with black flannel pants and black-and-white golf shoes with tassles. Not a crease, not·a wrinkle.

He ran a hand alongside the flank of the little car, touched the hood, grunted, and leaned through the open driver's door.

It was then that I sprang silently on crepe and put the gun in the small of his back.

As a matter of taste and principle I hate firearms. My father loved them, collected them. First there were the Lugers he brought home as World War II mementos. Then the deer rifles, the shotguns, automatic pistols picked up in pawn shops, an old rusted Colt .45, nasty-looking Italian pistols with long snouts and engraved butts, blue steel .22's. Lovingly polished and displayed in the den, behind the glass of a cherrywood case. Most of them loaded, the old man toying with them while watching TV. Calling me over to show off the details of construction, the niceties of ornamentation; talk of chamber velocity, core, bore, muzzle, grip. The smell of machine oil. The odour of burnt matches that permeated his hands. As a small child I'd have nightmares of the guns leaving their perches, like pets slipping out of their cages, taking on instincts of their own, barking and snarling . . .

One time he had a fight with my mother, a loud and nasty one. In anger he went to the case and snatched at

379

the first thing he put his hands on—a Luger: Teutonically efficient. He pointed it at her. I could see it now: she screaming 'Harry!'; he realizing what he was doing; horrified, dropping the gun as if it were a venomous sea creature; reaching out to her, stuttering apologies. He never did it again, but the memory changed him, them—and me, five years old, standing, blanket in hand, half-hidden by the door, watching. Since then I've hated guns. But at that moment I loved the feel of the .38 as it dented Towle's blazer.

'Get in the car,' I whispered. 'Sit behind the wheel and don't move or I'll blow your guts out.'

He obeyed. Quickly I ran to the passenger side and in beside him.

'You,' he said.

'Start the engine.' I put the gun in his side, rougher than I had to be.

The little car coughed to life.

'Pull it to the side of the road, so that the driver's door is right up against that rock. Then turn off the engine and throw the key out the window.' He did as he was told, the noble profile steady.

I got out and ordered him to do likewise. The way I'd had him park, the exit from the driver's side was blocked by forty feet of granite. He slid out the passenger's side and stood motionless and stoic at the edge of the empty road.

'Hands up.'

He gave me a superior look and complied.

'This is outrageous,' he said.

'Use one hand to remove your car keys. Toss them *gently* on the ground over there.' I pointed to a spot fifteen feet away. Keeping the gun trained on him, I scooped them up.

'Walk to your car, get in on the driver's side. Put both hands on the wheel where I can see them.'

I followed him to the Lincoln. I got in the back, right

380

behind him, and placed the tip of the gun in the hollow at the base of his skull.

'You know your anatomy,' I said softly. 'One bullet to the medulla oblongata and the lights go out forever.'

He said nothing.

'You've done a fine job of mucking up your life and the lives of plenty of others. Now it's coming down on you. What I'm offering you is a chance for partial redemption. Save a life for once, instead of destroying it.'

'I've saved many lives in my day. I'm a physician.'

'I know, you're a saintly healer. Where were you when it came to saving Cary Nemeth?'

A dry, croaking sound came from deep inside of him. But he maintained his composure.

'You know everything, I suppose.'

'Just about. Cousin Tim can be talkative when the circumstances are right.' I gave him a few examples of what I knew. He was unmoved, stoic, hands melded to the wheel, a white-haired mannikin set up for display.

'You knew my name before we met,' I said, 'from the Hickle thing. When I called you invited me to the office. To see how much Melody had told me. It didn't make sense to me then, a busy paediatrician taking the time to sit and chat face-to-face. Anything we spoke about could have been discussed over the phone. You wanted to sound me out. Then you tried to block me.'

'You had a reputation as a persistent young man,' he said. 'Things were piling up.'

'Things? Don't you mean bodies?'

'There's no need to be melodramatic.' He talked like a Disneyland android: flat, without inflection, devoid of self-doubt.

'I'm not trying to be. It's just that multiple murder still gets to me. The Nemeth boy. Handler. Elena Gutierrez. Morry Bruno. Now, Bonita Quinn and good old Ronnie Lee.'

At the mention of the last name he gave a small, but noticeable start.

'Ronnie Lee's death bother you, in particular?'

'I'm not familiar with that name. That's all.'

'Ronnie Lee Quinn. Bonita's ex. Melody's father. *R.L.* A blond fellow, tall, crazy-looking, with a bad left side. Hemiparesis. With McCaffrey's southern accent it may have sounded like he was calling him Earl.'

'Ah,' he said, pleased that things made sense once again, 'Earl. Disgusting fellow. Unwashed. I remember meeting him once or twice.'

'Piss-poor protoplasm, right?'

'If you will.'

'He was one of McCaffrey's bad guys from Mexico, brought back to do a dirty job or two. Probably wanted to see his kid, so McCaffrey found her and Bonita for him. Then it dawned on him how she could fit in. She was a bright one, Bonita, wasn't she? Probably thought you were Santa Claus when you got her the job managing Minassian's building.'

'She was appreciative,' said Towle.

'You were doing her a big favour. You set her up so you could have access to Handler's apartment. She's the manager, she gets a master key. Then the next time she's in the office for Melody's checkup, she "loses" her purse. It's easy to do, the lady's a scatterbrain. She didn't *have it together*. That's what your office girl told me. Always losing things. Meanwhile you lift the key and McCaffrey's monsters can get in whenever they want—look for tapes, do a little slashing and hacking. No sweat off poor Bonita's back, except when she becomes expendable and ends up as food for next season's zucchini crop. A dull woman. More piss-poor protoplasm.'

'It wasn't supposed to happen that way. That wasn't in the plan.'

'You know how it is, the best-laid plans and all that.'

382

'You're a sarcastic young man. I hope you aren't that way with your patients.'

'Ronnie Lee finishes off Bonita—he may have done it because McCaffrey told him to, or perhaps it was just settling an old score. But now McCaffrey has to get rid of Ronnie Lee, too, because fiend that he is, even he may baulk at watching his own daughter die.'

'You're very bright, Alex,' he said. 'But the sarcasm really is an unattractive trait.'

'Thanks for the advice. I know you're an expert on bedside manner.'

'As a matter of fact, I am. I pride myself on it. Obtain early rapport with the child and family no matter how disparate your background may be from theirs. That's the first step in delivering good care. It's what I instruct the first-year students when I proctor the pediatric section of Introduction to Clinical Medicine.'

'Fascinating.'

'The students give me excellent ratings on my teaching. I'm an excellent teacher.'

I exerted forward pressure with the .38. His silver hair parted but he didn't flinch. I smelled his hair tonic, cloves and lime.

'Start the car and pull it to the side of the road. Just behind that giant eucalyptus.'

The Lincoln rumbled and rolled, then stopped.

'Turn off the engine.'

'Don't be rude,' he said. 'There's no need to try to intimidate me.'

'Turn it off, Will.'

'*Doctor* Towle.'

'Doctor Towle.'

The engine quieted.

'Is it necessary to keep that thing at the back of my head?'

'I'll ask the questions.'

383

'It seems needless—superfluous. This isn't some cheap Western movie.'

'It's worse. The blood is real and nobody gets up and walks away when the smoke clears.'

'More melodrama. Mellow drama. Strange phrase.'

'Stop playing around,' I said angrily.

'Playing? Are we playing? I thought only children played. Jump rope, Hopscotch.' His voice rose in pitch.

'Grownups play too,' I said. 'Nasty games.'

'Games. Games help the child maintain ego integrity. I read that somewhere—Erikson? Piaget?'

Either Kruger wasn't the only actor in the family or something was happening that I hadn't been prepared for . . .

'Anna Freud,' I whispered.

'Yes. Anna. Fine woman. Would have loved to meet her, but both of us so busy . . . Pity . . . The ego must maintain integrity. At all costs.' He was silent for a minute, then: 'These seats need cleaning. I see spots on the leather. They make a good leather cleaner now . . . I saw it at the car wash.'

'Melody Quinn,' I said, trying to reel him back in. 'We need to save her.'

'Melody. Pretty girl. A pretty girl is like a melody. Pretty little child. Almost familiar . . .'

I talked to him but he kept fading away. Minute by minute he regressed, the rambling growing progressively more incoherent and out of context, so that at his worse, he was emitting word salad. He seemed to be suffering, the aristocratic face crowded with pain. Every few minutes he repeated the phrase, 'The ego must maintain integrity,' as if it was a catechism.

I needed him to get into La Casa but in his present state he was useless. I started to panic. His hands remained on the steering wheel but they trembled.

'Pills,' he said.

'Where?'

'Pocket . . .'

'Go ahead.' I said, not without suspicion, 'reach in and get them. The pills and nothing else. Don't take too many.'

'No . . . two pills . . . recommended dosage . . . never more . . . nevermore . . . quoth the raven . . . nevermore . . .'

'Get them.'

I kept the gun trained on him. He lowered one hand and drew out a vial not unlike the one that had held Melody's Ritalin. Carefully he shook out two white tablets, closed the vial and put it down.

'Water?' he asked, childlike.

'Take them dry.'

'I shall . . . nuisance.'

He swallowed the pills.

Kruger had been right. He *was* good at adjusting dosages. Within twelve minutes on my watch he was looking and sounding much better. I thought of the strain he underwent each day maintaining himself in the public eye. No doubt talking about the murders had hastened the deterioration.

'Silly of me to miss . . . the afternoon dose. Never forget.'

I observed him with morbid fascination, watching the changes in his speech and behaviour as the psychoactive chemicals took hold of his central nervous system, making note of the gradually increasing attention span, the diminishing non sequiturs, the restoration of adult conversational patterns. It was like peering into a microscope and watching a primitive organism mitose into something far more complex.

When the drug was still in its initial stage he said:

'I've done many . . . bad things. Gus had me do bad things. Very wrong for a . . . man of my stature. For someone of my breeding.'

385

I let it pass.

Eventually he was lucid. Alert, seemingly undamaged.

'What is it, Thorazine?' I asked him.

'A variant. I've managed my own pharmacologic care for some time now. Tried a number of the phenothiazines . . . Thorazine was good but it made me too drowsy. Couldn't have that while conducting physicals . . . Wouldn't want to drop a baby. No, nothing like that. Dreadful, drop an infant. This is a new agent, far superior to the others. Experimental. Sent to me by the manufacturer. Just write away for samples, use M.D. after the name, no need to justify or explain. They're more than happy to oblige . . . I have a healthy supply. Must take the afternoon dose, though, or everything gets confused—that's what happened, isn't it?'

'Yes. How long does it take for kick in?'

'In a man my size twenty to twenty-five minutes—remarkable, isn't it? Pop, down the hatch, wait, and the picture tube regains clarity. Life is so much more bearable. Things hurt so much less. Even now I feel it working, like muddy waters turning crystalline. Where were we?'

'We were talking about the nasty games McCaffrey's perverts play with little children.'

'I'm not one of those,' he said quickly.

'I know. But you helped those perverts molest hundreds of children, gave time and money to McCaffrey, set up Handler and Gutierrez and Hickle. You overdosed Melody Quinn to keep her mouth shut. Why?'

'It's all over, isn't it?' he asked, sounding relieved.

'Yes.'

'They'll take away my licence to practise medicine.'

'Definitely. Don't you think that's best?'

'I suppose so,' he said reluctantly. 'I still feel there's plenty left in me, plenty of good work to be done.'

'You'll have your chance,' I reassured him, realizing that the pills were less than perfect. 'They'll send you

386

some place for the rest of your life where you'll experience little in the way of stress. No paperwork, no billing, none of the hassles of medical practice. No Gus McCaffrey telling you what to do, how to run your life. Just you—and you'll look and feel fine because they'll let you continue to take your pills—and help other people. People in need of help. You're a healer, you'll be able to help them.'

'I'll be able to help,' he repeated.

'Absolutely.'

'One human being to another. Unencumbered.'

'Yes.'

'I have a good bedside manner. When I'm well. When I'm not well things get confused and things hurt—even ideas hurt, thoughts can be painful. I'm not at my best, when that happens. But when I'm functioning well I can't be beat for helping people.'

'I know that, Doctor. I know your reputation.'

McCaffrey had spoken to me of an innate drive toward altruism. I knew whose buttons he'd been pushing with that one.

'I'm beholden to Gus,' he said, 'not due to any unusual sexual proclivity. That's his link with the others—with Stuart and Eddy. Since we'd been boys I'd known of their—strange ways. We all grew up in an isolated place, a strange place. We were cultivated, like orchids. Private lessons for this and that, having to look appropriate, act appropriately. Sometimes I wonder if that refined atmosphere didn't do us more harm than good. Look how we turned out, I, with my spells—I know there are labels for it these days, but I prefer to avoid them—Stuart and Eddy with their strange sexual habits.

'They started fooling with each other one summer, when we were nine or ten. Then with other children. Smaller children, much smaller. I didn't think much of it except to know that I wasn't interested in it. The way we were raised, right or wrong didn't seem as relevant as—appropriate and inappropriate. "That's not appropriate,

387

Willie," Father would say. I imagine had Stuart or Eddy's fathers caught them with the little ones, that would have been their description of the entire affair: *inappropriate*. Like using the wrong fork at dinner.'

His description of coming of age on Drindamoor was strikingly like the one Van der Graaf had given me. At that moment he seemed akin to the fancy goldfish in the tank at Oomasa: beautiful, showy, cultivated by mutation and centuries of inbreeding, raised in a protected environment. But ultimately stunted and unadaptable to the realities of life.

'In that sense, the sexual one,' he said, 'I was quite normal. I married, fathered a child, a son. I performed quite adequately. Stuart and Eddy continued as my chums, going about their perverted ways. It was live and let live. They never mentioned my—spells. I let them be. Stuart was really a fine fellow, not overly bright, but well-meaning. It was a pity he had to . . . Except for that one kink, he was a good boy. Eddy was, is different. A sense of humour but a mean one. A nasty streak runs through him. He is habitually caustic and sarcastic—that's why I'm sensitive to that type of thing. Perhaps it's because of his size . . .'

'Your tie to McCaffrey,' I prompted.

'Small men often get that way. You're—I can't see you now, but I recall you as being medium-sized. Is that correct?'

'I'm five-eleven,' I said wearily.

'That's medium-sized. I've always been large. Father was large. It's just as Mendel predicted—long peas, short peas—fascinating field, genetics, isn't it?'

'Doctor—'

'I've wondered about the genetic impact on many traits. Intellect, for example. The liberal dogma would have us believe that environment makes the largest contribution to intelligence. It's an egalitarian premise, but reality doesn't bear it out. Long peas, short peas. Smart parents,

388

smart children. Stupid parents, stupid children. I, myself, am a heterozygote. Father was brilliant. Mother was an Irish beauty, but very simple. She lived in a world where that combination served to create the perfect hostess. Father's showpiece.'

'Your tie to McCaffrey,' I said sharply.

'My tie? Oh nothing more serious than life and death.'

He laughed. It was the first time I'd heard his laugh and I hoped it would be the last. It was a vacant discordant note, a blatant musical error screaming out in the middle of a symphony.

'I lived with Lilah and Willie Junior on the third floor of the Jedson dormitory. Stuart and Eddy shared a room on the first. As a married student I was given larger quarters—really a nice little apartment, when you got down to it. Two bedrooms, bath, living room, small kitchen. But no library, no study, so I did my reading at the kitchen table. Lilah had made it a cheerful place—bunting, trim, curtains, womanly types of things. Willie Junior was a little over two at the time, I remember. It was my senior year. I'd been having trouble with some of the premedical courses—physics, organic chemistry. I've never been a brilliant person. However, if I apply myself and keep my attention span steady I can do quite well. I desperately wanted to get into medical school on my own merits. My father and his father before him were doctors, all had been brilliant students. The joke, behind my back, was that I'd inherited my mother's brains as well as her looks—they didn't think I heard but I did. I wanted so much to show them that I could succeed on my own merits, not because I was Adolf Towle's son.

'The night it happened Willie Junior had been feeling poorly, unable to sleep. He'd been screaming and crying out, Lilah was frazzled. I ignored her requests for help, plunging myself into my studies, trying to shut out everything else. I had to bring my science grades up. It was imperative. The more anxious I got, the less able I was to

389

pay attention. I tried to deal with it by embracing a kind of tunnel vision.

'Lilah had always been patient with me, but that night she became furious, started to come unglued. I looked up, saw her coming at me, her hands—she had tiny hands, a delicate woman—rolled up into fists, mouth open—I suppose she was screaming—eyes full of hatred. She seemed to me a bird of prey, about to swoop down and pick at my bones. I pushed her away with my arm. She fell, tumbling back, hit her head on the corner of a bureau—a hideous piece, an antique her mother had given her—and lay there, simply lay there.

'I can see the whole thing clearly now, as if it had just happened yesterday. Lilah lies there, motionless. I rise out of my chair, dreamlike, everything is swaying, everything is confusing. A small shape coming at me from the right, like a mouse, a rat. I swat it away. But it's not a rat, no, no. It's Willie Junior, coming back at me, crying for his mother, hitting me. Only dimly aware of his presence I strike out at him again, catch him on the side of his head. Too hard. He falls, lands, lies still. Unmoving. A large bruise masks the side of his face . . . My wife, my child, dead at my hands. I prepare to find my razor, cut my wrists, be done with it.

'Then Gus's voice is at my back. He stands in the doorway, huge, obese, sweaty, in work clothes, broom in hand. The janitor, cleaning the dormitories at night. I smell him—ammonia, body odour, cleaning fluids. He's heard the noise and has come to check. He looks at me, a long hard look, then at the bodies. He kneels over them, feels for a pulse. "They're dead," he tells me in a flat voice. For a second I think he's smiling and I'm ready to pounce on him, to attempt a third murder. Then the smile becomes a frown. He's thinking. "Sit down," he commands me. I'm not used to being ordered around by one of his class but I'm weak and sick with grief, my knees are buckling, everything's unravelling . . . I turn away from

390

Lilah and Willie Junior, sit, put my face in my hands. Start to cry. I begin to grow more confused . . . A spell is coming on. Everything is starting to hurt. I have no pills, not like I'll have years later, when I'm a doctor. Now I'm merely a premedical student, powerless, hurting.

'Gus makes a telephone call. Minutes later my friends Stuart and Eddy appear in the room, like characters walking onstage in the midst of a dreadful play . . . The three of them talk among themselves, sometimes looking at me, muttering. Stuart comes to me first. He places a hand on my shoulder. "We know it was an accident, Will," he says. "We know it wasn't your fault." I start to argue with him but the words stick in my throat . . . The spells make it so hard to talk, so painful . . . I shake my head. Stuart comforts me, tells me everything will be all right. They will take care of everything. He rejoins Gus and Eddy.

'They wrap the bodies in a blanket, tell me not to leave the room. At the last moment they decide Stuart should stay with me. Gus and Eddy leave with the bodies. Stuart gives me coffee. I cry. I cry myself to sleep. Later that evening they return and tell me the story I'm to report to the police. They rehearse me, such good friends. I do a fine job. They tell me so. I feel some sense of relief at that. At least there is something I'm good at. Play-acting. That's what a bedside manner is, after all. Give the audience what it clamours for . . . My first audience is made up of the police. Then an officer of the Coast Guard— a family friend. They've found Lilah's car. Her body is macerated and bloated, I needn't identify it if it's too much of an ordeal. Scraps of Willie Junior's clothing have been found clinging to her hands. His body has drifted away. The tides, explains the officer. They'll continue to search . . . I break down and ready myself for the next show, the well-wishers, the press . . .'

The tides, I thought, the Coast Guard. Something there . . .

'Several months later I'm accepted at the medical

school,' Towle was saying. 'I move to Los Angeles. Stuart comes with me, though we both know he'll never be able to finish. Eddy goes to law school in Los Angeles. The Heads are reunited—that's what they called us. The Three Heads of State.

'We go about our new lives, there is never a mention of the favour they've done for me. Of that night. However they are far more open than ever before about their sexual perversions, leaving nasty photographs where I can see them, not bothering to hide or conceal anything. They know I'm powerless to say a thing, even should I find a ten-year-old in my bed. A rotten mutual interdependence now binds us.

'Gus has disappeared. Years later, when I'm a doctor, on my way to prominence, the bedside manner fully developed, he appears at my office after the patients have all gone home. Further fattened, well-dressed, no longer a janitor. Now, he jokes, he's a man of God. He shows me the mail-order divinity degree. And he's come to ask a few favours from me. To *cash in some old IOU's* is the way he puts it. I paid him that evening and I've been paying him, in one way or another, ever since.'

'It's time to stop paying,' I said. 'Let's not sacrifice Melody Quinn to him.'

'The child is doomed, as things stand. I urged Gus to put it off. Her accident. Told him it was by no means evident that she'd seen or heard anything. But he won't be delayed much longer. What's one more life to a man like that?' He paused. 'Does she really pose a danger to him?'

'Not really. She sat at the window and saw shadows of men.' One of whom she'd recognized as her father—she didn't know him but she had a picture. On the day I hypnotized her, right after the session, she went into a spontaneous discussion of him. She showed me the picture and a trinket he'd given her. When she had the night terrors I should have figured it out. I thought the hypnosis hadn't

392

evoked anything in her. It had. It had brought back memories of her father, of seeing him lurking outside her window, entering Handler's place. She knew something bad had happened in the apartment. She knew her daddy had done something terrible. She suppressed it. And it came back in her sleep.

It had started coming together for me when I'd seen the clue she'd left behind when Ronnie Lee had come by and abducted her and her mother. A shrunken head, precious until now, a symbol of Daddy. For her to have abandoned it meant she'd kissed him off, had come to grips with the fact that Daddy was a bad man, come back, not to visit, but to hurt. Perhaps she'd watched him manhandle Bonita, or maybe it was the rough, uncaring way he'd spoken to her. Whatever it had been, the child had known.

Looking back it seemed so logical, but at the time the associations had been remote.

'It's ironic,' Towle was saying. 'I prescribed Ritalin to control her behaviour and it was that same prescription that caused her insomnia, that led her to be awake at the wrong time.'

'Ironic,' I said. 'Now let's go in there and get her out. You're going to help me. When it's over I'll see to it that you're cared for properly.'

He didn't say anything. Simply sat straight in the seat, working hard at looking noble.

'Are you requesting my help?'

'I am, Doctor.'

'Request granted.'

29

I LAY on the floor of the Lincoln, covered by a blanket.

'My gun is pointed at your spine,' I told him. 'I don't expect any trouble but we haven't known each other long enough for trust to be worth much.'

'I understand,' he said. 'I'm not offended.'

He drove to the La Casa access road, turned left and steered smoothly and slowly to the chain link barrier. He identified himself to the voice on the squawk box and was let in. A brief stop at the guardhouse, an exchange of pleasantries, plenty of 'Doctor, Sirs' from the guard and we were in.

He drove to the far end of the parking lot.

'Park away from the light,' I whispered.

The car came to a halt.

'It's clear now,' he said.

I crawled from under the blanket, got out of the car and motioned him to follow. We walked up the path, side by side. Counsellors passed us in pairs, greeted him with deference and moved on. I tried to look like his associate.

La Casa was peaceful at night. Camp songs filtered through the trees. 'A Hundred Bottles of Beer.' 'Oh Susanna.' Children's voices. An off-key guitar. Microphoned adult commands. Mosquitoes and moths vied for space around mushroom lights imbedded in the foliage at our feet. The sweet smell of jasmine and oleander in the air. An occasional whiff of brine from the ocean, so close but unseen. To the right the open gray-green expanse of the Meadow. A pleasant enough graveyard . . . The Grove, dark as fudge, a piney refuge . . .

We passed the pool, taking care not to slip on the wet cement. Towle moved like an old warrior heading into his last battle, chin up, arms at his side, marching. I kept the .38 within easy reach.

We made it to the bunkers unnoticed.

'That one,' I said. 'With the blue door.'

Down the ramp. A hard twist of the key and we were in.

The building was divided into two rooms. The one in the front was empty except for a single folding chair pushed under an aluminum bridge table. The walls were of unpainted block and smelled of mildew. The floors were cold slab concrete, as was the ceiling. A square black wound of skylight marked the ceiling's centre. The only light came from a single, unadorned bulb.

She was in the back, on an army cot, covered with a coarse olive drab blanket and restrained with leather straps across her ankles and chest. Her arms were pinioned under the blanket. She breathed slowly, mouth open, sleeping, head to one side, her pale, tear-streaked skin translucent in the semidarkness. Wisps of hair hung loosely around her face. Tiny, vulnerable, lost.

At the foot of the cot was a plastic tray holding an uneaten, congealed fried egg, limp french fries, shrivelled brown-tipped lettuce and an open wax container of milk.

'Untie her.' I pointed the gun.

Towle bent over her, working in the dimness to unfasten the straps.

'What do you have her on?'

395

'Valium, high dose. Thorazine on top of that.'

Dr. Towle's magic elixir.

He got the restraints loose and peeled back the blanket. She was wearing dirty jeans and a red-and-white striped T-shirt with Snoopy on the front. He lifted the shirt and palpated her abdomen, took her pulse, felt her forehead: played doctor.

'She looks thin, but otherwise healthy,' he pronounced.

'Wrap her back up. Can you carry her?'

'Certainly,' he replied, miffed that I could doubt his strength.

'All right then, let's go.'

He gathered her up in his arms, looking for all the world like the Great White Father. The child let out a sigh, a shudder, and clung to him.

'Keep her totally covered once we get outside.'

I began a half-turn. A soft, musical voice at my back drawled:

'Don't move, Doctor Delaware, or you'll lose your fucking head.'

I stood still.

'Put the young one down, Will. Take his gun.'

Towle looked at me blankly. I shrugged. He placed Melody on the the cot gently and covered her. I handed him the .38.

'Against the wall with your hands up, Doctor. Search him, Will.'

Towle patted me down.

'Turn around.'

McCaffrey stood there grinning, filling the opening between the two rooms, a .357 magnum in one hand, a Polaroid camera in the other. He wore an iridescent lime-green jumpsuit decorated with a score of snap-pockets and buckles, and matching lime patent leather shoes. In the dim light his complexion reflected greenly as well.

'Task, tsk, Willie. What mischief are we up to tonight?'

396

The great physician hung his head and shuffled nervously.

'Not feeling loquacious tonight, Willie? That's all right. We'll talk later.' The colourless eyes narrowed. 'Right now there's business to attend to.'

'Is this your idea of altruism?' I looked at Melody's limp form.

'Shut up!' he snapped. To Towle: 'Remove the child's clothing.'

'Gus—I—why?'

'Just do as I say, Willie.'

'No more, Gus,' Towle pleaded. 'We've done enough.'

'No, you idiot. We haven't done enough at all. This smartass here has the potential to cause us—you *and* me—lots of trouble. I made plans to eliminate him, but apparently I'll have to do the job myself.'

'Plans,' I sneered. 'Halstead's rotting in a vacant lot with a spike in his throat. He was a bumbler, like all of your slaves.'

McCaffrey pursed his thick lips.

'I'm warning you,' he said.

'That's your speciality, isn't it?' I continued, playing for time. I saw his massive silhouette shift as he tried to keep me in his sights. But the darkness made it difficult as did Towle's body, which had gotten between us as he fidgeted under his master's glare. 'You have a knack for finding bumblers and losers, emotional cripples, misfits. The same knack flies have for locating shit. You zero in on their open wounds, sink your fangs into them, suck them dry.'

'How literary,' he replied in a lilting voice, obviously fighting to maintain control. We were in close quarters and impulsiveness could prove hazardous.

'Her clothes, Will,' he said. 'Take them all off.'

'Gus—'

'Do it, you snivelling piece of turd!'

Towle raised his arm in front of his face like a child

397

warding off a blow. When none was forthcoming he moved toward the child.

'You're a doctor,' I said. 'A respected physician. Don't listen to him—'

Fast, faster than I thought possible, McCaffrey stepped forward in the clearing Towle had created. He slashed with one elephantine sleeve and raked the side of my head with his gun. I fell to the floor, my face exploding with pain, hands protecting myself from further assault, blood running between my fingers.

'Now you stay there, sir, and keep your fucking mouth shut.'

Towle removed Melody's T-shirt. Her chest was concave and white, the ribs twin grilles of gray-blue shadow.

'Now the pants. The panties. Everything.'

'Why are we doing this, Gus?' Towle wanted to know. To my ears, which were far from perfect, one being ripped and bloody, the other filled with watery echoes, his speech sounded slurred. I wondered if stress could break through the biochemical barrier he'd erected around his damaged mind.

'Why?' McCaffrey laughed. 'You're not used to seeing this type of thing firsthand, are you, Willie? You've had a sanitized role up until now, enjoying the luxury of distance. Well, no matter, I'll explain it to you.'

He raised an eyebrow at Towle contemptuously, looked down at me and laughed again. The sound reverberated painfully in my injured skull. The blood continued to run down my face. My head felt mushy, loose on its stalk. I began to grow nauseated and dizzy, and the floor rose up at me. Terror gripped me as I wondered if he'd hit me hard enough to cause brain damage. I knew what a subdural hematoma could do to the fragile gray jelly that made life worth living . . . Crazily, fighting for strength and clarity, I pictured my brain in an anatomist's tray, pinioned and splayed, and tried to localize the site of the injury. The gun had smashed against my left side—

the dominant hemisphere, for I am right-handed . . . that was bad. The dominant side controlled logical processes: reasoning, analysis, deduction—the stuff to which I'd grown addicted over thirty-three years. I thought about losing all of that, of fading into dimness and confusion, then remembered two-year-old Willie Junior, struck down in much the same way. He'd lost it all . . . which might have been merciful. For had he survived, the damage would have been great. Left side/right side . . . the tides . . .

'We're going to put on a little stage play, Willie,' McCaffrey lectured. 'I'll be the producer and director. You'll be my assistant, helping me with the props.' He swung the camera in an arc. 'The stars of the show will be little Melody and our friend Doctor Alex Delaware. The name of the play will be—"Death of a Shrink", subtitled "Caught in the Act". A morality play.'

'Gus—'

'The plot is as follows: Doctor Delaware, our erstwhile villain, is well-known as a caring, sensitive child psychologist. However, unbeknownst to his colleagues and his patients, his choice of profession did not arise out of any great sense of—altruism. No, Doctor Delaware has chosen to become a kiddy shrink to be closer to the kiddies. To be able to fondle and abuse their genitals. In short, a deviate, an opportunist, the lowest of the low. An evil and gravely sick man.' He paused to look down on me, chuckling, breathing hard. Despite the chill, he was sweating, his glasses sliding low on his nose. The top of his kinky head was a halo of moisture. I looked at the .38 in Towle's hand, and measured the distance between it and the spot where I lay. McCaffrey saw me, shook his head, and mouthed the word *no*, showing me his teeth.

'With these same depraved motivations in mind, Doctor Delaware applies for membership in the Gentlemen's Brigade. He visits La Casa. We show him around. We screen him and our tests reveal him to be unsuitable for

399

inclusion into our honourable fraternity. We reject him. Furious and frustrated at being denied a lifetime supply of hairless pussy and tiny little pricks, he simmers.'

He stopped the narration and made loud slurping noises. Melody stirred in her sleep.

'He simmers,' he repeated. 'Stews in his own juices. Finally, at the height of his sick rage, he breaks into La Casa one night and roams the grounds until he finds a victim. A poor orhan girl, defenseless, alone in her dormitory because she is sick in bed with the flu. The madman loses control. Rapes her, virtually tears her apart—the autopsy will show uncommon savagery. Will. Takes pictures of the ghastly deed. A hideous crime. As the child cries out, screaming for her life, we—you and me, Will—happen to be passing by. We rush to her aid, but it is too late. The child has succumbed.

'We take in the carnage before us with horror and disgust. Delaware, discovered, rises up against us, gun in hand. Heroically we wrestle him to the ground, struggle for the weapon and in the process the murderer is fatally wounded. The good guys win, and there is peace in the valley.'

'Amen,' I said.

He ignored me.

'Not bad, eh, Will?'

'Gus, it won't work.' Towle stepped between us again. 'He knows everything—the teacher and the Nemeth boy—'

'Quiet. It will work. The past is the best predictor of the future. We have succeeded before, we will continue to triumph.'

'Gus—'

'Silence! I'm not asking you, I'm telling you. Strip her!'

I propped myself on my elbows and spoke through aching, swollen jaws, struggling to make sense out of what I was saying even as I told it.

'How about another script? This one's called The Big

400

Lie. It's about a man who thinks he's murdered his wife and child and sells out his entire life to a blackmailer.'

'Shut up.' McCaffrey advanced on me. Towle blocked his way, aiming the .38 at the half-acre of green-clad fat. It was a Mexican standoff.

'I want to hear what he has to say, Gus. Things are confusing me. Things hurt. I want him to explain . . .'

'Think,' I said, talking as fast as the pain allowed. 'Did you ever check Willie Junior's body for signs of life? No. *He* did. *He* told you your boy was dead. That you'd killed him. But was the body ever found? Did you ever actually see the body?'

Towle's face tightened with concentration. He was slipping, losing his grip on reality, digging his nails in, fighting to hold on.

'I—I don't know. Willie was dead. They told me. The tides . . .'

'Maybe. But think: it was a golden opportunity. Lilah's death wouldn't have brought a charge greater than involuntary manslaughter. Domestic violence wasn't even taken seriously in those days. With the lawyers your family would have hired, you might have gotten off with probation. But two deaths—especially with one a child—would have been impossible to brush off. He needed you to believe Junior was dead to be able to hook you.'

'Will,' said McCaffrey, threateningly.

'I don't know—such a long time . . .'

'Think! Did you hit him hard enough to kill him? Maybe not. Use your brain. It's a good one. You remembered before.'

'I used to have a good brain,' he muttered.

'You still do! Remember. You hit little Willie on the side of the head. What side?'

'Don't know—'

'Will, it's all lies. He's trying to poison your mind.' McCaffrey looked for a way to silence me. But Towle's gun rose and nudged the spot where a normal person would have had a heart.

'What side, Doctor?' I demanded.

'I'm right-handed,' he answered, as if discovering the fact for the first time. 'I use my right hand. I hit him with my right hand . . . I see it . . . He's coming at me from his bedroom. Crying for Mommy. Coming from the right, throwing herself at me. I—hit him—on his right side. The right side.'

The pain in my head turned the act of talking into torture, but I bore down.

'Yes. Exactly. Think! What if McCaffrey hoaxed you— you didn't *kill* Willie. You injured him, but he survived. What kind of damage, what kind of symptoms, could be caused by trauma to the right hemisphere in a developing child?'

'Right hemisphere cerebral damage—the right brain controls the left side,' he recited. 'Right brain damage causes left-side dysfunction.'

'Perfect,' I urged him on. 'A severe blow to the right brain could bring about left-side hemiparesis. *A bad left side.*'

'Earl . . .'

'Yes. The body was never found because the child never died. McCaffrey felt his pulse, found one, saw you in shock over what you'd done and exploited your guilt. He wrapped up both bodies, with a little help from your buddies. Lilah was put behind the wheel of the car and dumped off the Evergreen Bridge. McCaffrey took the child. Probably got him some kind of medical help, but not the best, because a reputable doctor would have had to report the incident to the police. After the funeral he disappeared. Those were *your* words. He disappeared because he had to. He had the child with him. He took him to Mexico, who knows where, renamed him, changed him from your son into the kind of person someone raised

402

by a monster would turn out to be. He made him his *robot*.'

'Earl . . . Willie Junior.' Towle's brows knitted.

'Ridiculous! Out of the way, Will! I order it!'

'It's the truth,' I said through the pounding in my head. 'Tonight, before you took your pills, you said Melody looked vaguely familiar. Turn carefully—don't let *him* out of your sight—and take a look at her. Tell me why.'

Towle backed away, kept the gun on McCaffrey, took a short look at Melody, and then a longer one.

'She looks,' he said, softly, 'like Lilah.'

'Her grandmother.'

'I couldn't know—'

Of course he couldn't. The Quinns were poor, illiterate, the dregs of society. Piss-poor protoplasm. His views on the genetic superiority of the upper class would have prevented him from even fantasizing a connection between them and his bloodline. Now his defences were down and the insights were hitting his consciousness like drops of acid—each point of contact raising psychic wounds. His son a murderer, a man conditioned to be a night-hunting beast. Dead. His daughter-in-law, intellectually limited, a helpless, pathetic creature. Dead. His granddaughter, the child on whom he'd plied his trade and medicated into stupour. Alive. But not for long.

'He wants to murder her. To tear her apart. You heard him. The autopsy will show *uncommon savagery*.'

Towle turned on the man in green.

'Gus—' he sobbed.

'Now, now, Will,' said McCaffrey soothingly. Then he blew Towle away with the .357. The bullet entered his abdomen and exited through his back in a fine spray of blood, skin and cashmere. He slammed backward, landing at the side of the cot. The report of the big gun echoed through the concrete room. A thunderstorm. The child awoke and began screaming.

McCaffrey pointed the gun at her, reflexively. I threw

403

myself at him and kicked his wrist, knocking the gun loose. It sailed backward, into the front room. He howled, rabid. I kicked him again, in the shin. His leg felt like a side of beef. He backed into the front room, wanting the gun. I went after him. He lunged, his bulk rolling. I used both hands to hit him in the lower back. My fists sank into his softness. He barely budged. His hand was inches from the magnum. I kicked it away, then used my foot to smash his ribs with little effect. He was too damned big and too damned tall to be able to get a facial punch in. I went for his legs and thighs, and tripped him.

He came crashing down, a felled redwood, taking me with him. Snarling, cursing, drooling, he rolled on top of me and got his hands around my throat. He panted his sour breath on me, the lumpy face crimson, the fish eyes swallowed by fleshy folds, squeezing. I fought to get out from under him but couldn't move. I experienced the panic of the sudden paralytic. He squeezed tighter. I pushed up helplessly.

His face darkened. With effort, I thought. Crimson to maroon to red-black, then a splash of colour. The kinky hair exploding. The blood bright and fresh, pouring out of his nose, his ears, his mouth. The eyes opening wide, blinking furiously. A look of great insult on the grotesque face. Gargling noises from the jowl-wrapped gullet. Needles and triangles of broken glass raining down upon us. His inert carcass a shield from the rain.

The skylight was an open wound now. A face peered down. Black, serious. Delano Hardy. Something else black: the nose of a rifle.

'Hold on, Consultant,' he said. 'We're coming to get you.'

'Your face looks uglier than mine,' Milo said when he'd pulled McCaffrey off me.

'Yeah,' I said, struggling to articulate through a mouth

404

that felt as if I'd sucked on razor blades, 'but mine will look better in a couple of days.'

He grinned.

'The kid seems okay,' said Hardy from the back room. He came out with Melody in his arms. She was shivering. 'Scared but unharmed, as the papers say.'

Milo helped me to my feet. I walked to her and stroked her hair.

'It's going to be all right, sweetheart.' Funny how clichés seem to find their niche during rough times.

'Alex,' she said. She smiled. 'You look funny.'

I squeezed her hand and she closed her eyes. Sweet dreams.

In the ambulance Milo kicked his shoes off and sat, yoga style, by the side of my stretcher.

'My hero,' I said. It came out *Mmmm mirrow.*

'This one's going to be good for a *long* time, pal. Free use of the Caddy on demand, cash loans with no interest, gratis therapy.'

'In other words,' I fought to enunciate through swollen jaws, 'business as usual.'

He laughed, patted my arm and told me to shut up. The ambulance attendant agreed.

'The man may need wires,' he said. 'He shouldn't talk.'

I started to protest.

'Shh!' said the attendant.

A half-mile later Milo looked at me and shook his head.

'You are one lucky turkey, friend. I got into town an hour and a half ago and got Rick's note to call you. I call your place. Robin was there, sans you, worried. You had a dinner date at seven, but no you. She says it's not like compulsive old you to be late, please could I do something. She also filled me in on your jaunts—you've been a busy little bee in my absence, haven't you? I call in to the station—on a vacation day, I might add—and get this schitzy message about Kruger written in Del Hardy's fine cursive scrawl; also something about he's going to La

405

Casa. I went to Kruger's, got through your barricade, found him trussed, scared shitless. He was a wreck, spilled his guts without being asked—amazing what a little sensory deprivation will do, huh? I beep Del, catch him in his car on Pacific Coast Highway which is still full of traffic at this hour, what with producers and starlets going home—make believe it's code three and siren it all the way along the side of the road. The pros take over and the rest is goddamn history.'

'I didn't want a full-scale raid.' I forced out the words, in agony. 'Didn't want anything to happen to the kid—'

'Please shut up, sir,' said the attendant.

'Shush,' said Milo, gently. 'You did a great job. Thanks. Okay? Don't do it again. Turkey.'

The ambulance came to a halt at Santa Monica Hospital's Emergency Room. I knew the place because I'd given a series of lectures to the staff on the psychological aspects of trauma in children. There'd be no lecture tonight.

'You okay?' Milo asked.

'Um-hmm.'

'Okay. I'll let the white coats take over. Gotta go and arrest a judge.'

30

ROBIN TOOK one look at me, jaws wired shut, eyes blackened, and burst into tears. She hugged me, fussed over me and sat by my side feeding me soup and soda. That lasted for a day. Then she got in touch with her anger and let me have it for being so crazy to put my life on the line. I was in no position to defend myself. She tried not speaking to me for six hours, then relented and things started to get back to normal.

When I could talk I called Raquel Ochoa.

'Hi,' she said. 'You sound funny.'

I told her the story, keeping it brief because of the pain.

She said nothing for a moment, then softly:

'There *were* monsters.'

'Yes.'

The silence between us was uncomfortable.

'You're a man of principle,' she said, finally.

'Thank you.'

'Alex—that evening—us. I don't regret it. It got me thinking. Made me realize I have to go out and find something—someone—for myself.'

'Don't settle for less than the best.'

'I—thanks. Take care of yourself. Mend fast.'

407

'I'll work on it. Good-bye.'

'Good-byc.'

My next call was to Ned Biondi, who rushed over that afternoon and interviewed me until the nurses kicked him out. I read his stories for days. He had it all down McCaffrey's Mexico days, the Hickle murder, the Gentlemen's Brigade, the suicide of Edwin Hayden the night he was arrested. The judge had shot himself in the mouth while dressing to go to the station with Milo. It seemed fitting in light of what he'd done to Hickle, and Biondi didn't miss the chance to wax philosophical.

I phoned Olivia Brickerman and asked her to take care of Melody. Two days later she found an older, childless couple up in Bakersfield, people she knew and trusted, with lots of patience and five acres for running. Nearby was a gifted child psychologist, a woman I'd known from graduate school, with experience in stress and bereavement. To them would be entrusted the task of helping the little girl piece her life together.

Six weeks after the fall of La Casa de los Niños, Robin and I met Milo and Rick Silverman for dinner at a quiet, elegant seafood place in Bel Air.

My friend's amour turned out to be a guy who could have walked out of a cigarette ad—six feet tall, broad-shouldered, narrow-hipped, masculine, handsome face overlaid with just a touch of crag, head of tight bronze curls, matching bristle mustache. He wore a tailored black silk suit, black-and-white striped shirt and a black knit tie.

'Lucky Milo,' Robin whispered as they joined our table.

Next to him, Milo looked baggier than ever, though he'd tried to spruce himself up, his hair slicked down like that of a kid in church.

Milo made the introductions. We ordered drinks and got acquainted. Rick was quiet and reserved, with nervous, surgical hands that had to be holding something—

a glass, a fork, a stirrer. He and Milo exchanged loving glances. Once I saw them touch hands, for just a second. As the evening progressed he opened up and talked about his work, about what he liked and didn't like about being a doctor. The food came. The others had lobster and steak. I had to content myself with soufflé. We chatted, the evening went well.

After the dishes had been cleared away, before the pastry cart and the brandy, Rick's beeper went off. He excused himself and went to the phone.

'If you gentlemen don't mind, I'll make a stop in the ladies' room.' Robin patted her mouth with her napkin and rose. I followed her sway until she disappeared.

Milo and I looked at each other. He picked a piece of fish off his tie.

'Hello, friend,' I said.

'Hello.'

'He's a nice guy, Rick. I like him.'

'I want this one to last. It's hard, the way we live.'

'You look happy.'

'We are. Different in lots of ways, but we also have a lot in common. He's getting a Porsche 928,' he said with a laugh.

'Congratulations. You're a good-lifer now.'

'All comes to he who waits.'

I motioned the waiter over and we ordered fresh drinks. When they came I said: 'Milo, there's something I've been wanting to talk to you about. About the case.'

He took a long swallow of scotch.

'What about?'

'Hayden.'

His face grew grave.

'You're my shrink—so that this conversation is confidential?'

'Better than that. I'm your friend.'

'Okay,' he sighed. 'Ask what I know you're going to ask.'

409

'The suicide. It doesn't make sense on two grounds. First, the kind of guy he was. I got the same picture from everyone. An arrogant, nasty, sarcastic little bastard. Loved himself. Not a trace of self-doubt. That kind don't kill themselves. They search for ways to shift the blame to others, they weasel out of things. Second, you're a pro. How could you get so sloppy as to let him do it?'

'The story I told Internal Affairs was that he was a judge. I treated him with deference. I let him get dressed. In his study. They bought it.'

'Tell me about it. Please.'

He looked around the restaurant. The tables nearby were empty. Rick and Robin were still gone. He gulped down the rest of his drink.

'I went for him right after I left you. Must have been after ten by then. He lived in one of those huge English Tudor palaces in Hancock Park. Old money. Big lawn. Bentley in the driveway. Topiary. A doorbell out of a Karloff Flick.

'He answered the door, a little wimp of a guy, maybe five-four. Strange eyes. Spooky. He was wearing a silk dressing gown, holding a brandy in one hand. I told him what I'd come for. It didn't faze him.

'He was very proper, distant, as if what I was there for had nothing to do with him. I followed him inside the house. Lots of family portraits. Mouldings around the ceilings, chandeliers—I want you to get the flavour of this. Lord of the Manor. Led me to his study in the back. The requisite oak panels, wall-to-wall leather-covered books, the kind people collect but never read. A fireplace with two porcelain greyhounds, carved desk, blah blah blah.

'I pat him down, find a .22, take it. "It's for protection at night, officer," he tells me. "You never know who'll come knocking at your door." He's laughing, Alex, I swear I couldn't believe it. The guy's life is crashing down around him, he's going to hit the front page as a kiddy-diddler and he's laughing.

410

'I read him his rights, go into the spiel, he looks bored. Sits down at his desk, like I'm there for a favour. Then he starts talking to me. Laughing in my face. "How amusing," he says, "that they send you, the *faggot cop*, after me in a case like this. You of all people should understand." He goes on like that for a while, smirking, implying, then coming right out and saying it. That we're birds of a feather. Partners in crime. Perverts. I'm standing there listening to this and getting hotter and hotter. He laughs some more and I see that's what he wants, to stay in control of the situation. So I cool down, smile back. Whistle. He starts telling me the things they did to the kids, like it's supposed to arouse me. Like we're buddies at a stag party. My stomach is turning and he's putting us in the same boat.

'As he talks, he comes into focus, psychological focus. It's like I can see behind the spooky eyes, into his brain. And all I see is dark and bad. Nothing good in there. Nothing good can come from this guy. He's a washout. I'm judging the judge. I'm prophesying. Meanwhile he's going on about the parties they used to have with the kids, how much he's going to miss them.'

He stopped and cleared his throat. Took my drink and finished it.

'I'm still looking through him, into his future. And I know what's going to happen. I look around that big room. I know the kind of money behind this guy. He'll get a Not Guilty by Reason, they'll cart him off to some country club. Eventually he'll buy his way out and start all over again. So I make a decision. Right there on the spot.

'I walk around behind him, grab his scrawny little head and tilt it back. I take out the .22 and jam it in his mouth. He's struggling, but he's an old wimp. It's like holding down an insect, a goddamn bug. I position him—I've seen enough forensic reports to know what it should look like.

411

I say "Nighty-night, Your Honour," and pull the trigger. The rest you know. Okay?'

'Okay.'

'Now how about another drink? I'm thirsty as hell.'

BLOOD TEST

1

I SAT in the courtroom and watched Richard Moody get the bad news from the judge.

Moody'd come dressed for the occasion in a chocolate polyester suit, canary yellow shirt, string tie, and lizard skin boots. He grimaced and bit his lip and tried to lock eyes with the judge, but she out-stared him and he ended up looking at his hands. The bailiff at the rear of the room held his gaze on Moody. As a result of my warning he'd been careful to keep the Moodys apart all afternoon and had gone so far as to frisk Richard.

The judge was Diane Severe, girlish for fifty, with ash blonde hair and a strong, kind face; soft-spoken, and all business. I'd never been in her court but knew her reputation. She'd been a social worker before going to law school and after a decade in juvenile

7

court and six years on the family bench was one of the few judges who really understood children.

'Mr. Moody,' she said, 'I want you to listen very carefully to what I'm going to say.'

Moody started to assume an aggressive body posture, hunching his shoulders and narrowing his eyes like a bar fighter, but his attorney nudged him and he loosened up and forced a smile.

'I've heard testimony from Dr. Daschoff and Dr. Delaware, both eminently qualified as experts in this court. I've spoken to your children in my chambers. I've watched your behaviour this afternoon and I've heard your allegations against Mrs. Moody. I've learned of your instructions to your children to run away from their mother so that you could rescue them.'

She paused and leaned forward.

'You've got serious emotional problems, sir.'

The smirk on Moody's face vanished as quickly as it appeared, but she caught it.

'I'm sorry you think this is funny, Mr. Moody, because it's tragic.'

'Your Honor,' Moody's lawyer interjected.

She cut him off with the flick of a gold pen.

'Not now, Mr. Durkin. I've heard quite enough wordplay today. This is the bottom line and I want your client to pay attention.'

Turning back to Moody:

'Your problems may be treatable. I sincerely hope they are. There's no doubt in my mind that psycho-therapy is essential – a good deal of it. Medication may be called for as well. For your sake and the sake of your children I hope you get whatever treatment you need. My order is that you have no further contact with your children until I see psychiatric evidence that you are no longer a threat to yourself or to others – when the death threats and talk of suicide

8

cease, and you have accepted the reality of this divorce and are able to support Mrs. Moody in the raising of the children.

'Should you get to that point – and your word won't be sufficient to convince me, Mr. Moody – the court will call upon Dr. Delaware to set up a schedule of limited and monitored visitation.'

Moody took it in, then made a sudden move forward. The bailiff was out of his chair and at his side in a flash. Moody saw him, gave a sick grin, and let his body go slack. The tears flowed down his cheeks. Durkin pulled out a handkerchief, gave it to him, and raised an objection concerning the judge's encroachment upon his client's privacy.

'You're free to appeal, Mr. Durkin,' she said evenly.

'Judge.'

It was Moody now, the bass voice dry and strained.

'What is it, Mr. Moody?'

'You don't unnerstand.' He wrung his hands. 'Those kids, they're my life.'

For a moment I thought she was going to tongue-lash him. Instead she regarded him with compassion.

'I do understand, sir. I understand that you love your children. That your life is in shambles. But what *you* need to understand – the whole point of the psychiatric testimony – is that children can't be responsible for anyone's life. That's too big a burden for any child to bear. They can't raise *you*, Mr. Moody. You need to be able to raise them. And right now you can't. You need help.'

Moody started to say something but choked it back. He shook his head in defeat, gave the handkerchief back to Durkin, and tried to salvage a few shards of dignity.

The next quarter hour was spent on property settlement. I had no need to listen to the distribution of the

9

meagre estate of Darlene and Richard Moody and would have left, but Mal Worthy had said he wanted to talk to me afterward.

When the legal mumbling was over, Judge Severe took off her glasses and ended the hearing. She looked my way and smiled.

'I'd like to see you in chambers for a moment if you've got the time, Dr. Delaware.'

I smiled back and nodded. She swept out of the courtroom.

Durkin ushered Moody out under the watchful eye of the bailiff.

At the next table Mal was pep-talking Darlene, patting her plump shoulder as he scooped up handfuls of documents and stashed them in one of the two suitcases he'd brought. Mal was compulsive and while other lawyers made do with an attaché case, he carted around boxes of documents on a chromium luggage rack.

The former Mrs. Richard Moody looked up at him, bewildered, cheeks feverishly rosy, bobbing her head in assent. She'd stuffed her milkmaid's body into a light blue summer dress as frothy as high tide. The dress was ten years too young for her and I wondered if she'd confused new-found freedom with innocence.

Mal was decked out in classic Beverly Hills attorney mufti: Italian suit, silk shirt and tie, calfskin loafers with tassles. His hair was styled fashionably long and curly, his beard cut close to the skin. He had glossy nails and perfect teeth and a Malibu tan. When he saw me he winked and waved and gave Darlene one last pat. Then he held her hand in both of his and saw her to the door.

'Thanks for your help, Alex,' he said when he came back. Piles of papers remained on the table and he busied himself with packing them.

10

'It wasn't fun,' I said.

'No. The ugly ones aren't.' He meant it but there was a lilt in his voice.

'But you won.'

He stopped shuffling papers for a moment. 'Yeah. Well, you know, that's the business I'm in. Jousting.' He flipped his wrist and looked at a wafer-thin disc of gold. 'I won't say it pains me to dispose of a turkey like Mr. M.'

'You think he'll take it? Just like that?'

He shrugged.

'Who knows? If he doesn't we'll just keep bringing in the heavy artillery.'

At two hundred dollars an hour.

He lashed the suitcases to the rack.

'Hey listen, Alex, this wasn't a stinker. For those I don't call you – I've got hired guns up the wazoo. This was righteous, no?'

'We were on the right side.'

'Precissimoso. And I thank you again. Regards to the lady judge.'

'What do you think she wants?' I asked.

He grinned and slapped me on the back.

'Maybe she likes your style. Not a bad looking gal, heh? She's single, you know?'

'Spinster?'

'Hell, no. Divorced. I handled her case.'

Her chambers were done in mahogany and rose, and permeated with the scent of flowers. She sat behind a glass-topped, carved wood desk upon which stood a cut-crystal vase filled with stalks of gladiolus. On the wall behind the desk were several photographs of two hulking blond teenage boys – in football jerseys, wetsuits, and evening wear.

'My gruesome twosome,' she said, following my eyes. 'One's at Stanford, the other's selling firewood up at Arrowhead. No telling, eh, Doctor?'

11

'No telling.'

'Please have a seat.' She motioned me to a velvet sofa. When I'd settled she said, 'Sorry if I was a little rough on you in there.'

'No problem.'

'I wanted to know if the fact that Mr. Moody wears women's underwear was relevant to his mental status, and you refused to be pinned down.'

'I didn't think his choice of lingerie had much to do with custody.'

She laughed. 'I get two types of psych experts. The puffed-up, self-proclaimed authorities, so taken with themselves they think their opinions on any topic are sacrosanct, and the cautious ones, like you, who won't give an opinion unless it's backed up by a double-blind, controlled study.'

I shrugged. 'At least you won't get a Twinkie Defense out of me.'

'Touché. How about some wine?' She unlatched the doors of a credenza carved to match the desk and took out a bottle and two long-stemmed glasses.

'My pleasure, Your Honor.'

'In here, Diane. Is it Alexander?'

'Alex is fine.'

She poured red wine into the glasses. 'This is a very fine cabernet that I saved for the termination of particularly obnoxious cases. Positive reinforcement, if you will.'

I took the glass she offered.

'To justice,' she said, and we sipped. It was good wine and I told her so. It seemed to please her.

We drank in silence. She finished before I did and set down her glass.

'I want to talk to you about the Moodys. They're off my docket but I can't help thinking about the kids. I read your report and you have good insights on the family.'

12

'It took a while but they opened up.'

'Alex, are those children going to be all right?'

'I've asked myself the same thing. I wish I could tell you yes. It depends on whether or not the parents get their act together.'

She clicked her nails against the rim of the wineglass.

'Do you think he'll kill her?'

The question startled me.

'Don't tell me it didn't cross your mind – the warning to the bailiff and all that.'

'That was meant to prevent an ugly scene,' I said, 'but yes, I do think he could do it. The man's unstable and profoundly depressed. When he gets low, he gets nasty and he's never been lower than right now.'

'And he wears ladies' panties.'

I laughed. 'That too.'

'Refill?'

'Sure.'

She put the bottle aside and laced her fingers around the stem of her wineglass, an angular, attractive older woman, not afraid to let a few wrinkles show.

'A real loser, our Mr. Richard Moody. And maybe a killer.'

'If he gets in a killing mood, she'd be the obvious target. And the boyfriend – Conley.'

'Well,' she said, running the tip of her tongue over her lips, 'one must be philosophical about such things. If he kills her it's because she fucked the wrong guy. Just as long as he doesn't kill someone innocent, like you or me.'

It was hard to tell if she were serious or not.

'It's something I think about,' she said, 'some warped loser coming back and taking out his troubles on me. The losers never want to take responsibility

13

for their crappy little lives. You ever worry about it?'

'Not really. When I was clinically active most of my patients were nice kids from nice families – not much potential for mayhem there. I've been pretty much retired for the last couple of years.'

'I know. I saw the gap in your resumé. All that academic stuff, then blank space. Was that before the Casa de Los Ninos thing or after?'

I wasn't surprised she knew about it. Though it had been over a year, the headlines had been bold and people remembered. I had my own personal reminder – a reconstructed jaw that ached when the weather got clammy.

'A half year before. Afterwards I didn't exactly feel like jumping back in.'

'No fun being a hero?'

'I don't even know what the word means.'

'I'll bet.' She gazed levelly at me and adjusted the hem of her robe. 'And now you're doing forensic work.'

'On a limited basis. I accept consultations from attorneys I trust which narrows the field substantially and I get some directly from judges.'

'Which ones?'

'George Landre, Ralph Siegel.'

'Both good guys. I went to school with George. You want more work?'

'I'm not hustling. If the referrals come, okay. If not, I can always find things to do.'

'Rich kid, huh?'

'Far from it, but I made a few good investments that are still paying off. If I don't get sucked into a Rodeo Drive mentality I'm okay.'

She smiled.

'If you want more cases, I'll spread the word. The members of the psych panel are booked up for four months and we're always looking for guys who can

14

think straight and put it into language simple enough
for a judge to understand. Your report *was* really
good.'

'Thanks. If you send me cases I won't turn you
down.'

She finished the second glass. 'Very mellow, isn't
it? Comes from a tiny little vineyard up in Napa.
Three years old and still operating at a loss, but the
place is turning out limited bottlings of very fine
reds.'

She got up and walked around the room. From the
pocket of her robe she removed a pack of Virginia
Slims and a lighter. For the next few moments she
stared at a wall decorated with diplomas and
certificates and dragged deeply on the cigarette.

'People really manage to fuck up their lives, don't
they? Like Miss Bright Eyes Moody. Nice country
girl, moves to L.A. for a taste of excitement, gets a job
as a checker at Safeway and falls in love with the
macho man in lace undies – I forget, what is he, a
construction worker?'

'Carpenter. For Aurora Studios.'

'Right. I remember. Builds set. The guy's an
obvious loser but it takes her twelve years to figure it
out. Now she's extricating herself and who does she
hook up with? The loser's clone.'

'Conley's a lot more mentally intact.'

'Maybe so. But take a look at them side by side.
Twins. She's being pulled to the same type. Who
knows, maybe Moody was a charmer too in the
beginning. Give this Conley a few years, he'll turn.
Bunch of losers.'

She turned and faced me. Her nostrils flared and
the hand holding the cigarette trembled almost imper-
ceptibly: alcohol, emotion, or both.

'I hooked up with an asshole and it took me a while
to get out of it, Alex, but I didn't turn around and do

15

the same damn thing first chance I got. Makes you wonder if women will ever get smart.'

'I wouldn't bet on Mal Worthy having to give up his Bentley,' I said.

'Nor I. Mal's a smart boy. Did *my* divorce, did you know?'

I feigned ignorance.

'Probably conflict of interest, my hearing this case, but who cares, it was open and shut. Moody's crazy, he's screwing up his kids, and my order was the best shot at getting him straightened out. Any chance he'll follow through on therapy?'

'I doubt it. He doesn't think anything's wrong with him.'

'Of course not. The craziest ones never do. Baloney afraid of the slicer. Assuming he doesn't kill her, you know what's going to happen, don't you?'

'More days in court.'

'Absolutely. That idiot Durkin'll be here every other week with some ploy to reverse the order. In the meantime Moody will harass Bright Eyes and if it keeps up long enough the kids will be permanently screwed up.' She walked back to her desk with a long graceful stride, took a compact out of her purse and powdered her nose.

'On and on. He'll drag her through the system, she'll bleat and weep, but she'll have no choice.' Her expression hardened. 'But I don't give a damn. In two weeks I'm out of it. Retirement with pension. I've got some investments of my own. And one big money-loser. A tiny little vineyard up in Napa.' She grinned. 'This time next year I'll be in my cellar sampling the vintage until I reel. If you travel that way, be sure to drop in.'

'I'll make it a point to do that.'

She looked away from me, talked to her diplomas.

'Do you have a lady friend, Alex?'

16

'Yes. She's in Japan now.'

'Miss her?'

'Very much.'

'Figures,' she said good-naturedly. 'The good ones get snapped up.' She rose to indicate the audience was concluded. 'Good to meet you, Alex.'

'My pleasure, Diane. Good luck with the vines. What I tasted was great.'

'It's gonna get better and better. I can feel it.'

Her handshake was firm and dry.

My Seville had cooked in the open parking lot and I pulled my hand away from the heat of the door handle. Midway through the motion I sensed his presence and turned to face him.

'S'cuse me, Doc.' He was looking into the sun and squinting. His forehead was sweat-glossed and the canary-coloured shirt had darkened to mustard under the arms.

'I can't talk now, Mr. Moody.'

'Just a sec, Doc. Just lemme connect with ya. Lemme zero in. on some main points. *Communicate*, you know?' His words came out in a rush. As he spoke, the half-closed eyes darted back and forth, and he rocked on his boot heels. In rapid succession he smiled, grimaced, bobbed his head, scratched his Adam's apple, and tweaked his nose. A discordant symphony of tics and twitches. I'd never seen him this way but I'd read Larry Daschoff's report and had a good idea what was happening.

'I'm sorry. Not now.' I looked around the lot but we were alone. The rear of the court building faced a quiet side street in a run-down neighbourhood. The sole sign of life was a scrawny mutt nuzzling a patch of overgrown grass on the other side of the road.

'Aw, c'mon, Doc. Just lemme make a few main points, lemme break on through, lemme zero in on

17

the main facts, like the shysters say,' His speech picked up velocity.

I turned away from him and his hard brown hand closed on my wrist.

'Please let go, Mr. Moody,' I said with forced patience.

He smiled.

'Hey, Doc, I jus' wanna talk. State my case.'

'There's no case. I can't do anything for you. Let go of my arm.'

He tightened his grip but no tension registered on his face. It was a long face, sun-cured and leathery, with a broken pug nose at centre, a thin-lipped mouth, and an oversized jaw – the kind of mandibular development you get from chewing tobacco or gritting your teeth.

I put my car keys in my pocket and reached around to pry his fingers loose but his strength was phenomenal. That, too, made sense, if what I suspected was true. It felt like his hand had become heat-welded to my arm and it was starting to hurt.

I found myself assessing my chances in a fight: we were the same height and probably just about the same weight. Years of hauling lumber had given him an edge in the physical strength department, but I'd been sufficiently diligent about karate practice to have a few good moves. I could stomp down hard on his instep, hit him when he was off-balance, and drive away as he writhed on the cement . . . I interrupted that train of thought, ashamed, telling myself that fighting him would be absurd. The guy was disturbed and if anyone should be able to defuse him, I should.

I dropped my free arm and let it fall idly to my side.

'Okay. I'll listen to you. But first let go so I can concentrate on what you have to say.'

He thought about it for a second, then grinned broadly His teeth were bad and I wondered why I hadn't noticed it during the evaluation, but he'd been different then – morose and defeated, barely able to open his mouth to speak.

He released my wrist. The piece of sleeve where he'd held me was grimy and warm.

'I'm listening.'

'Okay, okay, okay.' His head continued to bob. 'Just gotta connect with you, Doc, show you I got plans, tell you how she twisted you roun' her little finger jus' like she did me. There's bad stuff in that house, my boys tell me how he's makin' the kids do things his way, and she lets it happen, she says okay, okay. Fine and dandy with her, they be cleanin' up after a scumbag like that, who knows what kind of dirt he's leavin' around, the guy's not normal, you know? Him wantin' to be man of the house and all that, all I gotta say is har, har, you know.

'Know why I'm laughin', doc, huh? To keep from cryin', that's why, keep from cryin'. For my babies. The boy and the girl. My boy tol' me the two of them be sleeping together, him wantin' to be the daddy, to be the big shot in the house that I built with these two hands here.'

He held out ten large-knuckled, bruised fingers. There was an oversized turquoise and Indian silver ring on each ring finger, one in the shape of a scorpion, the other a coiled snake.

'You unnerstan', Doc, you grab what I'm tossin' at you? Those kids are my life, I carry the burden, not nobody else, that's what I tol' the lady judge, the bitch in black. I carry it. From me, from here.' He grabbed his crotch. 'My body into hers when she was still decent – she could be decent again, you unnerstan', I get hold of her, speak some sense, straighten her out, right? But not with that Conley there, no way, no fuckin' way. My kids, my life.'

He paused for breath and I took advantage of it.

19

'You'll always be their father,' I said, trying to be reassuring without patronizing him. 'No one can take that away from you.'

'Right. Hunnerd procent right. Now you go in there and tell that to the bitch in black, straighten her out. Tell her I got to have those kids.'

'I can't do that.'

He pouted like a child denied dessert.

'You *do* it. Right *now*.'

'I can't. You're under a lot of stress. You're not ready to take care of them.' You're going through a full-fledged manic episode, Mr. Moody. You're a manic-depressive and you need help badly . . .

'I can handle it, I got plans. Get a trailer, get a boat, take 'em outta the dirty city, outta the smog-clouds, take 'em to the country, – fish for trout, hunt for meat, teach 'em the way to survive. Like Hank Junior says, country boy will *survive*. Teach 'em to shovel shit and eat good breakfasts, get away from scumbags like him and her until she gets straightened out, who knows when it'll come she keep up with him, humpin' him in front of them, a disgrace.'

'Try to calm down.'

'Here, watch me calm down.' He inhaled deeply and let the air out in a noisy whoosh. I smelled the stench of his breath. He cracked his knuckles and the silver rings sparkled in the sun. 'I'm relaxed, I'm clean, I'm ready for action, I'm the father, go in and tell her.'

'It doesn't work that way.'

'Why not?' he growled and grabbed the front of my jacket.

'Let go. We can't talk if you keep doing that, Mr. Moody.'

Slowly his fingers parted. I tried to edge away from him but my back touched the car. We were close enough to slow-dance.

20

'Tell her! You fucked me up, you fix it, Head-shrinker!'

His voice had taken a decidedly menacing tone. Manics could do damage when they got worked up. As bad as paranoid schizes. It was obvious that the power of persuasion wasn't going to do the trick.

'Mr. Moody – Richard – you need help. I won't do anything for you until you get it.'

He sputtered, sprayed me with saliva, and jacked upward viciously with his knee, a classic street brawler's move. It was one of the gambits I'd figured him for and I swiveled so that all he made contact with was gabardine.

The miss threw him off-balance and he stumbled. Consciously sad, I caught his elbow and threw him off my hip. He landed on his back, stayed down for a quarter second, and was at me again, arms chopping like a thresher gone mad. I waited until he was almost on me, ducked low, and hit him in the belly just hard enough to knock some wind out. Moving out of the way I let him double over in privacy.

'Please, Richard, calm down and pull it all together.'

His response was a growl and a snivel and a grab for my legs. He managed to get hold of one cuff and I felt myself going down. It would have been a good time to jump in the car and tool out of there, but he was between me and the driver's boot.

I contemplated a move for the passenger door, but that would mean turning my back to him and he was strong and crazy-fast.

As I contemplated, he bounded up and charged toward me shouting gibberish. My pity for him had made me too careless and he was able to connect with a punch to the shoulder that made my body rattle. Still stunned, I cleared my eyes soon enough to see the follow-through: a left hook aimed squarely at my

21

man-made jaw. Self-preservation won out over pity and I slid away, took hold of his arm, and threw him full-force against the car. Before he could have second thoughts I jerked him up, yanked the arm behind him, and pulled up to the point where it was just short of snapping. It had to be agonizing, but he evinced no sign of suffering. Manics could get like that, on a perpetual speed trip, impervious to minor details like pain.

I kicked him in the butt as hard as I could and he went flying. Grabbing for my keys, I jumped in the Seville and spun out.

I caught a glimpse of him in the rear-view mirror just before turning onto the street. He was sitting on the asphalt, head in hands, rocking back and forth and, I was pretty sure, weeping.

2

THE BIG black and gold koi was the first to surface, but the other fish soon followed his lead and within seconds all fourteen of them were sticking whiskered snouts out of the water and gobbling down food pellets as fast as I tossed them in. I knelt by a large smooth rock fringed with creeping juniper and lavender azaleas and held three pellets in my fingers just beneath the surface of the water. The big one caught the scent and hesitated, but gluttony got the better of him and his glistening muscular body snaked its way over. He stopped inches from my hand and looked up at me. I tried to appear trustworthy.

The sun was on its way down but enough light lingered over the foothills to catch the metallic glint of the gold scales, dramatizing the contrast with the velvety black patches on his back. A truly magnificent kin-ki-utsuri.

Suddenly the big carp darted and the pellets were gone from my hand. I replaced them. A red and white kohaku joined in, then a platinum ohgon in a moon-light-coloured blur. Soon all the fish were nibbling at my fingers, their mouths soft as baby kisses.

The pond and surrounding garden refuge had been a gift from Robin during the painful months of recuperation from the shattered jaw and all the unwanted publicity. She'd suggested it, sensing the value of something to calm me down during the period of enforced inactivity, and knowing of my fondness for things oriental.

At first I'd thought it unfeasible. My home is one of those creations peculiar to southern California, tucked into a hillside at an improbable angle. It's an architectural gem with spectacular views from three sides but there's very little usable flat land and I couldn't envision room for a pond.

But Robin had done some research, sounding out the idea with several of her craftsmen friends, and had been put in touch with an inarticulate lad from Oxnard – a young man so outwardly stuporous his nickname was Hazy Clifton. He had arrived with cement mixers, wooden forms, and a ton or two of crushed rock, and had created an elegant, meander-ing, naturalistic pond, complete with waterfall and rock border, that weaved its way in and around the sloping terrain.

An elderly Asian gnome materialized after Hazy Clifton's departure and proceeded to embroider the young man's artistry with bonsai, zen grass, juniper, Japanese maple, long-necked lilies, azalea, and bamboo. Strategically placed boulders established meditative spots and patches of snowy gravel suggested serenity. Within a week the garden looked centuries old.

I could stand on the deck that bisected the two

24

levels of the house and look down on the pond, letting my eyes trace patterns etched in the gravel by the wind, watching the koi, jewel-like and languid in their movement. Or I could descend to the floor of the garden and sit by the water's edge feeding the fish, the surface breaking gently in concentric waves.

It became a ritual: each day before sunset I tossed pellets to the koi and reflected on how good life could be. I learned how to banish unwanted images – of death and falsehood and betrayal – from my mind with Pavlovian efficiency.

Now I listened to the gurgling of the waterfall and put aside the memory of Richard Moody's debasement.

The sky darkened and the peacock-coloured fish greyed and finally melted into the blackness of the water. I sat in the dark, content, tension a vanquished enemy.

The first time the phone rang I was in the middle of dinner and I ignored it. Twenty minutes later it rang again and I picked it up.

'Dr. Delaware? This is Kathy from your service. I had an emergency call for you a few minutes ago but nobody answered.'

'What's the message, Kathy?'

'It's from a Mr. Moody. He said it was urgent.'

'Shit.'

'Dr. D?'

'Nothing, Kathy. Please give me the number.'

She did and I asked her if Moody had sounded strange.

'He *was* kind of upset. Talking real fast – I had to ask him to slow down to get the message.'

'Okay. Thanks for calling.'

'I've got another one, came in this afternoon. Do you want to take it?'

25

'Just one? Sure.'

'This one's from a doctor – let me get the pronun-
ciation right – Melendrez – no Melen*dez*-Lynch. With
a hyphen.'

Now that was a blast from the past . . .

'He gave me this number.' She recited an exchange
I recognized as Melendez-Lynch's office at Western
Peds. 'Said he'd be there until eleven tonight.'

That figured. Raoul was a notable workaholic in a
profession famous for them. I recalled seeing his
Volvo in the doctors' lot no matter how early I arrived
at the hospital or how late I left.

'That's it?'

'That's it, Dr. D. Have a nice one and thanks for
the cookies. Me and the other girls finished 'em off in
one hour.'

'Glad you enjoyed them.' That was a five-pound
box she was talking about. 'Munchies?'

'What can I say?' she giggled.

A switchboard staffed by potheads and they never
fouled up a message. Someone should be researching
it.

I drank a Coors before addressing the question of
whether or not to return Moody's call. The last thing
I wanted was to be on the receiving end of a manic
tirade. On the other hand, he might be calmer and
more receptive to suggestions for treatment. Unlikely,
but there's enough of the therapist left in me to be
optimistic past the point of realism. Recalling that
afternoon's scuffle on the parking lot made me feel
like a jerk, though I was damned if I knew how it
could have been avoided.

I thought it over and then called, because I owed it
to the Moody kids to give it my best shot.

The number he'd left had a Sun Valley exchange –
a rough neighbourhood – and the voice on the other
end belonged to the night clerk at the Bedabye Motel.

26

Moody'd found the perfect living quarters if he wanted to feed his depression.

'Mr. Moody, please.'

'Second.'

A series of buzzes and clicks and Moody said, 'Yeah.'

'Mr. Moody, it's Dr. Delaware.'

''lo, Doc. Don't know what got into me, jus' wanted to say sorry, hope I dint shake you up too badly.'

'I'm fine. How are you?'

'Oh fine, jus' fine. Got plans, gotta get myself together. I can see that. What everyone's saying, gotta have some sense to it.'

'Good. I'm glad you understand.'

'Oh, yeah, oh yeah. I'm catchin' on, jus' takes me a while. Like the firs' time I used a circular saw, supervisor tol' me Richard – this was back when I was a kid, jus' learning the trade – gotta take your time, take it slow, concentrate, 'thwise this thing chew you up. And he'd hold up his left hand with a stump where the thumb shoulda been, said, Richard, don' learn the hard way.'

He laughed hoarsely and cleared his throat.

'Guess sometimes I learn the hard way, huh? Like with Darlene. Mighta listened to her before she got involved with that scumbag.'

The pitch of his voice rose when he talked about Conley so I tried to ease him away from the subject.

'The important thing is that you're learning now. You're a young man, Richard. You've got a lot ahead of you.'

'Yeah. Well . . . old as you feel, y'know, and I'm feeling ninety.'

'This is the roughest time, before the final decree. It can get better.'

27

'They say that – the lawyer tol' me too – but I don' feel it. I feel shit on, y'know, shit on first class.'

He paused and I didn't fill it in.

'Anyway, thanks for listenin', and now you can talk to the judge and tell her I can see the kids, take 'em with me fishin' for a week.'

So much for optimism.

'Richard, I'm glad you're getting in touch with the situation but you're not ready to care for your children.'

'*Whythefucknot?*'

'You need help to stabilize your moods. There are medications that are effective. And get someone to talk to, like you're talking to me.'

'Yeah?' he sneered, 'if they're assholes like you, goddamn money-chasing fuckers, talkin' to them ain't gonna do me no good. I'm telling you I'm gonna take care of the problems now don't give me any shit, who the fuckareyou to tell me when I can see my kids.'

'This conversation isn't going anywhere – '

'Hunnerd procent right, Headshrinker. You listen and you listen good, they'll be hell to pay'f I'm not set up in my rightful place as daddy . . . '

He emptied a bucket of verbal swill and after listening for several minutes I hung up to avoid being sullied.

In the silence of the kitchen I became aware of the pounding of my heart and the sick feeling at the pit of my stomach. Maybe I'd lost the touch – the therapist's ability to put distance between himself and the ones who suffered so as to avoid being battered by a psychological hailstorm.

I looked down at the message pad. Raoul Melendez-Lynch. He probably wanted me to give a seminar to the residents on the psychological aspects of chronic disease or behavioural approaches to pain control.

28

Something nice and academic that would let me hide behind slides and videotape and play professor again.

At that moment it seemed an especially attractive prospect and I dialled his number.

A young woman answered the phone, breathless.

'Carcinogenesis lab.'

'Dr. Melendez-Lynch, please.'

'He's not here.'

'This is Dr. Delaware returning his call.'

'I think he's over at the hospital,' she said, sounding preoccupied.

'Could you connect me to the page operator, please.'

'I'm not sure how to do that – I'm not his secretary, Dr. Delray. I'm in the middle of an experiment and I really have to run. Okay?'

'Okay.'

I broke the connection, dialled the message desk at Western Peds, and had him paged. Five minutes later the operator came and told me he hadn't answered. I left my name and number and hung up, thinking how little had changed over the years. Working with Raoul had been stimulating and challenging, but fraught with frustration. Trying to pin him down could be like sculpting with shaving cream.

I went into the library and settled in my soft leather chair with a paperback thriller. Just when I'd decided the plot was forced and the dialogue too cute, the phone rang.

'Hello.'

'Hello, Alex!' His accent turned it into *Ahleex*. 'So good of you to return my call.' As usual, he talked at a breakneck pace.

'I tried to reach you at the lab but the girl who answered wasn't too helpful.'

'Girl? Ah yes, that would be Helen. My new post-doc. Brilliant young lady from Yale. She and I are

29

collaborating on an N.I.H. study aimed at clarifying the metastatic process. She worked with Brewer at New Haven – construction of synthetic cell walls – and we've been examining the relative invasiveness of varying tumour forms on specific models.'

'Sounds fascinating.'

'It is.' He paused. 'Anyway, how have you been, my friend?'

'Fine. And you?'

He chuckled.

'It's – nine forty-three and I haven't yet finished charting. That tells you how I've been.'

'Oh come on, Raoul, you love it.'

'Ha! Yes I do. What did you call me years ago – the quintessential type. A personality?'

'A *plus*.'

'I will die of a myocardial infarct but my paper-work will be completed.'

It was only a partial jest. His father, dean of a medical school in pre-Castro Havana, had keeled over on the tennis court and died at forty-eight. Raoul was five years from that age and he'd inherited his sire's lifestyle as well as some bad genes. I'd once thought him changeable but had long ago given up trying to slow him down. If four failed marriages hadn't done the trick, nothing would.

'You'll win the Nobel Prize,' I said.

'And it will all go for alimony!' He thought that tremendously funny. When his laughter died down he said:

'I need a favour, Alex. There's a family that's giving us some trouble – noncompliance problems – and I wondered if you could talk to them.'

'I'm flattered but what about the regular staff?'

'The regular staff made a mess of it,' he said, peeved. 'Alex, you know the high regard I have for you – why you abandoned a brilliant career I'll never

30

know, but that's another issue. The people Social Services are sending me are *amateurs*, my friend. Rank amateurs. Starry-eyed caseworkers who see themselves as patient advocates – provocateurs. The psych people will have nothing to do with us because Boorstin has a death phobia and is terrified of the word cancer.'

'Progress, huh?'

'Alex, nothing's changed in the last five years. If anything it's gotten worse. I've even started opening my ears to other offers. Last week I was given the chance to run an entire hospital in Miami. Chief of Staff. More money and a full professorship.'

'Considering it?'

'No. The research facilities were Mickey Mouse and I suspect they want me more for my Spanish than my medical brilliance. Anyway, what do you say about lending the department a hand – you're still officially listed as our consultant, you know.'

'To be honest, Raoul, I'm not taking on any therapy cases.'

'Yes, yes, I'm aware of that,' he said impatiently, 'but this is not therapy. Short term liaison consultation. I don't want to sound melodramatic, but the life of a very sick little boy is at stake.'

'Exactly what kind of noncompliance are you talking about?'

'It's too complicated to explain over the phone, Alex. I hate to be rude, but I must get over to the lab and see how Helen is doing. We're pacing an in vitro hepatoblastoma as it approaches pulmonary tissue. It's painstaking work and it requires constant vigilance. Let's talk about it tomorrow – nine, my office? I'll have breakfast sent up, and voucher forms. We're prepared to pay for your time.'

'All right, Raoul. I'll be there.'

'Excellent.' He hung up.

Being released from a conversation with Melendez-Lynch was a jarring experience, a sudden shift into low gear. I put down the receiver, regained my bearings, and reflected on the complexity of the manic syndrome.

3

WESTERN PAEDIATRIC Medical Center occupies a square block of mid-Hollywood real estate in a neighbourhood that was once grand but is now the turf of junkies, hookers, drag queens, and fancy dancers of every stripe. The working girls were up early this morning, halter-topped and hot-panted, and as I cruised eastward on Sunset they stepped out from alleys and shadowed doorways sashaying and hooting. The whores were as much a fixture of Hollywood as the brass stars inlaid in the sidewalks, and I could swear I recognized some of the same painted faces I'd seen there three years ago. The streetwalkers seemed to fall into two categories: doughy-faced runaways from Bakersfield, Fresno, and the surrounding farmlands, and lean, leggy, shopworn black girls from South Central L.A. All of them raring to go at eight forty-five in the morning. If the whole country ever got that industrious the Japanese wouldn't stand a chance.

The hospital loomed large, a compound of aged dark stone buildings and one newer column of concrete and glass. I pulled the Seville into the doctors' lot and walked to Prinzley Pavilion, the contemporary structure.

The Department of Oncology was situated on the fifth floor. The doctors' offices were cubicles arranged in a U around the secretarial pool. As head of the department, Raoul got four times as much space as any of the other oncologists, as well as privacy. His office was at the far end of the corridor and cordoned off by double glass doors. I went through them and walked into the reception area. Seeing no receptionist, I kept going and entered his office through a door marked PRIVATE.

He could have had an executive suite but had chosen to use almost all the space for his lab, ending up with an office only ten by twelve. The room was as I remembered it, the desk piled high with correspondence, journals, and unanswered messages, all ordered and precisely stacked. There were too many books for the floor-to-ceiling bookcase and the overflow was similarly heaped on the floor. One shelf was filled with bottles of Maalox. Perpendicular to the desk, faded beige curtains concealed the office's sole window as well as a view of the hills beyond.

I knew that view well, having spent a significant proportion of my time at Western Peds staring out at the crumbling letters of the HOLLYWOOD sign while waiting for Raoul to show up for meetings he had scheduled but inevitably forgot about, or cooling my heels during his interminable long-distance phone chats.

I searched for signs of habitation and found a Styrofoam cup half-filled with cold coffee and a

34

cream-coloured silk jacket draped neatly over the desk chair. Knocking on the door leading to the lab brought no response, and the door was locked. I opened the curtains, waited a while, paged him and got no callback. My watch said ten after nine. Old feelings of impatience and resentment began to surface.

Fifteen minutes more, I told myself, and then I'll leave. Enough is enough.

Ninety seconds before the deadline he blew in.

'Alex, Alex!' He shook my hand vigorously. 'Thank you for coming!'

He'd aged. The paunch had grown sizeably ovoid and it strained his shirt buttons. The last few strands of hair on his crown had vanished and the dark curls around the sides bordered a skull that was high, knobby, and shiny. The thick moustache, once ebony, was a variegated thatch of grey, black and white. Only the coffee bean eyes, ever moving, ever alert, seemed agelessly charged and hinted at the fire within. He was a short man given to pudginess and though he dressed expensively, his wardrobe wasn't selected with an eye toward camouflage. This morning he wore a pale pink shirt, a black tie with pink clocks, and cream-coloured slacks that matched the jacket over the chair. His shoes were mirror-polished, sharp-toed tan loafers of perforated leather. His long white coat was starched and immaculate but a size too large. A stethoscope was draped around his neck, and pens and documents stuffed the pockets of the coat, causing them to sag.

'Good morning, Raoul.'

'Have you had breakfast, yet?' He turned his back to me and moved his thick fingers rapidly over the piles on the desk like a blind man speedreading Braille.

'No, you said you'd – '

35

'How about we go to the doctor's dining room and the department will buy you some?'

'That would be fine,' I sighed.

'Great, great.' He patted his pockets, searched in them, and muttered a profanity in Spanish. 'Just let me make a couple of calls and we'll be off – '

'Raoul, I'm under some time pressure. I'd appreciate it if we could get going now.'

He turned and looked at me with great surprise.

'What? Oh, of course. Right now. Certainly.'

A last glance at the desk, a grab for the current copy of *Blood,* and we were off.

Though his legs were shorter than mine by a good four inches, I had to trot to keep up with him as we hurried across the glassed-in bridge that connected Prinzley with the main building. And since he talked as he walked, keeping up was essential.

'The family's name is Swope.' He spelled it. 'The boy is Heywood – Woody for short. Five years old. Non-Hodgkin's lymphoma, localized. The initial site was in the G.I. tract with one regional node. The metastatic scan was beautiful – very clean. The histology is nonlymphoblastic, which is excellent, because the treatment protocol for nonlympho-blastics is well-established.'

We reached the elevator. He seemed out of breath, tugging at his shirt collar and loosening his tie. The doors slid open and we rode down in silence to the ground floor. Silence – but not serenity, because he couldn't stand still: he tapped his fingers on the elevator wall, played with strands of his moustache, and clicked a ball-point pen open and shut repeatedly.

The ground floor corridor was a tunnel of noise, glutted with doctors, nurses, techs, and patients. He continued talking until I tapped his shoulder and shouted that I couldn't hear him. His head gave a curt little nod and he picked up his pace. We zipped

36

through the cafeteria and passed into the dimly lit elegance of the doctors' dining room.

A group of surgeons and surgical residents sat eating and smoking around a circular table, dressed in greens, their caps hanging across their chests like bibs; otherwise the room was unoccupied.

Raoul ushered me to a corner table, motioned for service, and spread a linen napkin over his lap. He picked up a packet of artificial sweetener and turned it on its side, causing the powder within to shift with a dry whisper, like sand through an hourglass. He repeated the gesture half a dozen times and started talking again, stopping only when the waitress came and took our order.

'Do you remember the COMP protocol, Alex?'

'Vaguely. Cyclophosphamide, um – methotrexate and prednisone, right? I forget what the O stands for?'

'Very good. Oncovin. We've refined it for non-Hodgkin's. It's working wonders when we combine it with intrathecal methotrexate and radiation. Eighty-one percent of patients are achieving three-year, relapse-free survival. That's a national statistic – the figures on my patients are even better – over ninety percent. I'm following a growing number of kids who are five, seven years and looking great. Think of that, Alex. A disease that killed virtually every child it got hold of a decade ago is potentially curable.'

The light behind his eyes picked up extra wattage.

'Fantastic,' I said.

'Perfect word – fantastic. The key is *multimodal chemotherapy*. More and better drugs in the right combinations.'

The food came. He put two rolls on his plate, cut them into tiny chunks, and systematically popped each piece in his mouth, finishing all of it before I'd downed half my bagel. The waitress poured coffee,

37

which was inspected, creamed, stirred, and quickly swallowed. He dabbed his lips and picked imaginary crumbs out of his moustache.

'Notice that I used the word curable. No timid talk of extended remission. We've beaten Wilm's Tumour, we've beaten Hodgkin's disease. Non-Hodgkin's lymphoma is next. Mark my words, it will be cured in the near future.'

A third roll was dissected and dispatched. He waved the waitress over for more coffee.

When she'd gone he said, 'This isn't really coffee, my friend. It is a hot drink. My mother knew how to make coffee. Back in Cuba we had the pick of the coffee crop. One of the servants, an old black man named José, would grind the beans by hand with great finesse – the grind is essential – and we would have *coffee!*' He drank some more and pushed his cup away, taking a glass of water as a replacement and emptying it. 'Come to my home and I'll make you real coffee.'

It occurred to me that though I'd worked with the man for three years and had known him twice that long, I'd never seen his living quarters.

'I may take you up on that one day. Where do you live?'

'Not far from here. Condo on Los Feliz. One bedroom – small but sufficient for my needs. When one lives alone it is best to keep things simple, don't you agree?'

'I suppose so.'

'You do live alone, don't you?'

'I used to. I'm living with a wonderful woman.'

'Good, good.' The dark eyes seemed to cloud. 'Women. They have enriched my life. And torn it apart. My last wife, Paula, has the big house in Flintridge. Another's in Miami, and two others, God knows where. Jorgé – my second oldest, Nina's boy –

38

tells me his mother is in Paris, but she never stayed in one place very long.'

His face drooped and he drummed on the table with his spoon. Then he thought of something that made him suddenly brighten.

'Jorgé's going to medical school next year at Hopkins.'

'Congratulations.'

'Thank you. Brilliant boy, always was. Summers he would visit me and work in the lab. I'm proud to have inspired him. The others are not so on the ball, who knows what they will do, but their mothers were not like Nina – she was a concert cellist.'

'I didn't know that.'

He picked up another roll and hefted it.

'Drinking your water?' he asked.

'It's all yours.'

He drank it.

'Tell me about the Swopes. What kind of noncompliance problems are you having?'

'The worst kind, Alex. They're refusing treatment. They want to take the boy home and subject him to God knows what.'

'Do you think they're holistic types?'

He shrugged. 'It's possible. They're rural people, come from La Vista, some little town near the Mexican border.'

'I know the area. Agricultural.'

'Yes, I believe so. But more important, close to Laetrile country. The father is some kind of farmer or grower. Crass man, always trying to impress. I gather he'd had some scientific training at one time or another – likes to throw around biological terms. Big heavyset fellow, in his early fifties.'

'Old to have a five year old.'

'Yes. The mother's in her late forties – makes you wonder if the boy was an accident. Maybe it's guilt

39

that's making them crazy. You know – blaming them selves for the cancer and all that.'

'That wouldn't be unusual,' I said. Few night-mares compare to finding out one's child has cancer. And part of the nightmare is the guilt parents inflict upon themselves, searching for an answer to the unanswerable question: *why me?* It's not a rational process. It occurs in doctors and biochemists and other people who should know better – the mental flogging, the I should haves and I could haves. Most parents get over it. The ones who don't can be crippled . . .

'Of course in this case,' Raoul was hypothesizing, 'there would be more of a basis for it, wouldn't there? Aged ovaries, etc. Well, enough conjecture, let me go on. Where was I – ah, Mrs. Swope. Emma. A mouse. Obsequious even. The father's the boss. One sibling, a sister, around nineteen or so.'

'How long's the boy been diagnosed?'

'Officially just a couple of days. A local G.P. picked up the distended abdomen on exam. There'd been pain for a couple of weeks and fevers for the last five days. The G.P. had sneaking suspicions – not bad for a country doc – didn't like the local facilities and sent them up here. We had to do an extensive eval – repeat physical, bloodwork, BUN, uric acid, bone marrows from two sites, immunodiagnostic markers – the non-Hodgkin's protocol demands it. It wasn't until a couple of days ago that we had it staged. Localized disease, no disseminated mets.

'I had a diagnostic conference with the parents, told them the prognosis was good because the tumours hadn't spread, they filled out informed consents, and we were ready to go. The boy has a recent history of multiple infections and there was pneumocystis swimming around in his blood so we put him in Laminar Flow, planned to keep him there

40

for the first course of chemo, and then check how the immune system was working. It looked open and shut and then I got a call from Augie Valcroix, my clinical Fellow – I'll get to him in a minute – and he told me the parents were having cold feet.'

'No indication of problems when you first spoke to them?'

'Not really, Alex. The father does all the talking in this family. She sat there and wept, I did my best to comfort her. He asked lots of picky questions – like I said, he was trying to impress – but it was all very friendly. They seemed like intelligent people, not flaky.'

He shook his head in frustration.

'After Valcroix's call I went right over, talked to them, thinking it was momentary anxiety – you know sometimes parents hear about treatment and get the idea we're out to torture their child. They start looking for something simple, like apricot pits. If the doctor takes the time to explain the value of chemo, they usually return to the fold. But not the Swopes. They had their minds made up.

'I used a chalkboard. Drew out the survival graphs – that eighty-one percent stat I gave you was for localized disease. Once the tumours spread the figure drops to forty-six. It didn't impress them. I told them speed was of the essence. I laid on the charm, cajoled, pleaded, shouted. They didn't argue. Simply refused. They want to take him home.'

He tore a roll to shreds and arranged the fragments in a semicircle on his plate.

'I'm going to have eggs,' he announced.

He beckoned the waitress back. She took the order and gave me a look behind his back that said *I'm used to this*.

'Any theory as to what caused the turnaround?' I asked.

41

'I have two. One, Augie Valcroix mucked it up. Two, those damned Touchers poisoned the parents' minds.'

'Who?'

'*Touchers*. That's what I call them. Members of some damned sect that has its headquarters near where the family lives. They worship this guru named Noble Matthias – that's what the social worker told me – and call themselves the Touch.' Raoul's voice filled with contempt. '*Madre de Dios*, Alex, California has become a sanctuary for the psychic refuse of the world!'

'Are *they* holistic types?'

'The social worker says yes – big surprise, no? *Ass*-holistic is more like it. Cure disease with carrots and bran and foul-smelling herbs thrown over the shoulder at midnight. The culmination of centuries of scientific progress – *voluntary* cultural regression!'

'What did these Touch people do, exactly?'

'Nothing I can prove. But all I know is things were going smoothly, the consents were signed, then two of them – a man and a woman – visited the parents and *disaster!*'

A plate heaped with scrambled eggs arrived along with a dish of yellow sauce. I remembered his affection for hollandaise. He poured the sauce on the eggs and used his fork to divide the mound into three sections. The middle segment was consumed first, followed by the one on his right, and finally the left third disappeared. More dabbing, more imaginary crumb disposal.

'What does your Fellow have to do with it?'

'Valcroix? Probably plenty. Let me tell you about this character. On paper he looked great – M.D. from McGill – he's a French-Canadian – internship and residency at Mayo, a year of research at Michigan. He's close to forty, older than most applicants, so I

42

thought he'd be mature. When I interviewed him I talked to a well-groomed, intelligent man. What showed up six months later was an ageing flower child.

'The man is bright but he's unprofessional. He talks and dresses like an adolescent, tries to get down to the patients' level. The parents can't relate to him and eventually the kids see through it, too. There are other problems, as well. He's slept with at least one mother of a patient that I know about and I suspect there've been several others. I chewed him out and he looked at me as if I were crazy to be worried about it.'

'A little loose in the ethics department?'

'He has no ethics. Sometimes I'm convinced he's drunk or on something, but I can't trip him up on rounds. He's prepared, always has the right answer. But he's still no doctor, just a hippie with a lot of education.'

'How'd he get along with the Swopes?' I asked.

'Maybe too well. He was very chummy with the mother and seemed to relate to the father as well as anyone could.' He looked into his empty coffee cup. 'I wouldn't be surprised if he wanted to sleep with the sister – she's a looker. But that's not what's bothering me right now.'

He narrowed his eyes.

'I think Dr. August Valcroix has a soft spot in his heart for quacks. He's spoken up at staff meetings about how we should be more tolerant of what he calls *alternative health care approaches*. He spent some time on an Indian reservation and was impressed with the medicine men. The rest of us are discussing the *New England Journal* and he's going on about shamans and snake powders. Unbelievable.'

He grimaced in disgust.

'When he told me they were pulling the boy out of treatment I couldn't help but feel he was gloating.'

43

'Do you think he actually sabotaged you?'

'The enemy from within?' He considered it. 'No, not overtly. I just don't think he supported the treatment plan the way he should have. Dammit, Alex, this isn't some abstract philosophy seminar. There's a sick boy with a nasty disease that I can treat and cure and they want to prevent that treatment. It's – *murder*!'

'You could,' I suggested, 'go to court on it.'

He nodded sadly.

'I've already broached the subject with the hospital attorney and he thinks we'd win. But it would be a Pyrrhic victory. You remember the Chad Green case – the child had leukaemia, the parents pulled him out of Boston Children's and ran away to Mexico for Laetrile. It turned into a media circus. The parents became heroes, the doctor and the hospital, big bad wolves. In the end, with all the court orders, the boy never got treated and died.'

He placed an index finger against each temple and pressed. A pulse quivered under each fingertip. He winced.

'Migraine?'

'Just started. I can handle it.' He sucked in his breath. The paunch rippled.

'I may have to take them to court. But I want to avoid it. Which is why I called you, my friend.'

He leaned forward and placed his hand over mine. His skin was unusually warm and just a bit moist.

'Talk to them, Alex. Use any tricks you've got up your sleeve. Empathy, sympathy, whatever. Try to get them to see the consequences of what they're doing.'

'It's a tall order.'

He withdrew his hand and smiled.

'The only kind we have around here.'

44

4

THE WALLS of the ward were covered with sunny yellow paper patterned with dancing teddy bears and grinning rag dolls. But the hospital smells that I'd grown used to when I worked there - disinfectant, body odour, wilting flowers - assaulted my nostrils and reminded me I was a stranger. Though I'd walked this same corridor a thousand times, I was gripped with the chilling uneasiness that hospitals inevitably evoke.

The Laminar Airflow Unit was at the east end of the ward behind a windowless grey door. As we approached, the door swung open and a young woman stepped into the hallway. She lit up a cigarette and began to walk away, but Raoul hailed her and she stopped, turned, bent a knee and froze the pose, one hand on the cigarette, the other on her hip.

'The sister,' he whispered.

He'd called her a looker but it was an understatement.

The girl was stunning.

She was tall, five eight or nine, with a body that managed to be both womanly and boyish. Her legs were long, coltish, and firm, her breasts high and small. She had a swan's neck and delicate, slender hands ending in crimson lacquered nails. She wore a white dress made of T-shirt material and had cinched it with a silver cord that showed off a tiny waist and flat belly. The soft fabric moulded to every angle and curve and ended midthigh.

Her face was oval with a strong cleft chin. She had prominent cheekbones and a clean jawline leading to lobeless ears. Each ear was pierced with two thread-like hoops of hammered gold. Her lips were straight and full, her mouth a generous red slash.

But it was her colouring that was most striking.

Her hair was long, lustrous, combed straight back from her high smooth forehead, and coppery red. But unlike most redheads she had no freckles and lacked the buttermilk complexion. Her skin was blemishless and burnished a deep California tan. Her eyes were wide-set, thick-lashed, and inky black. She'd used a bit too much makeup but had left her eyebrows alone. They were full and dark, with a natural arch that gave her a sceptical look. She was a girl anyone would notice, with a strange combination of simplicity and flash, almost overwhelmingly physical without trying to be.

'Hello,' said Raoul.

She shifted her weight and looked both of us over.

'Hi.' She spoke sullenly and regarded us with boredom. As if to underscore her apathy, she gazed past us and sucked on her cigarette.

'Nona, this is Dr. Delaware.'

She nodded, unimpressed.

46

'He's a psychologist, an expert in the care of children with cancer. He used to work here, in Laminar Flow.'

'Hello,' she said, dutifully. Her voice was soft, almost whispery, the inflection flat. 'If you want him to talk to my parents, they're not here.'

'Uh, yes, that is what I wanted. When will they be back?'

The girl shrugged and flicked ashes onto the floor.

'They didn't tell me. They slept here so they probably went back to the motel to clean up. Maybe tonight, maybe tomorrow.'

'I see. And how have you been doing?'

'Fine.' She looked up at the ceiling and tapped her foot.

Raoul raised his hand to offer the classic physician's pat on the back, but the look in her eyes stopped him and he immediately lowered it.

Tough kid, I thought, but then, this was no day at the beach for her.

'How's Woody?' he asked.

The question infuriated her. Her lean body tensed, she dropped the cigarette and ground it under her heel. Tears collected in the inner corners of the midnight eyes.

'You're the damned doctor! Why don't you tell *me!*' She tightened her face, turned, and ran away.

Raoul avoided eye contact. He picked up the crushed butt and deposited it in an ashtray. Covering his forehead with one hand he took a deep breath and gave a migraine grimace. The pain must have been excruciating.

'Come on,' he said. 'Let's go in.'

A hand-scrawled sign in the nurses' office said 'Welcome to Space Age Medasin.'

The bulletin board was tacked with layers of paper - shift schedules, cartoons cut out of magazines, chemotherapy dosage charts, and an autographed picture of a famous Dodger with a young bald boy in a wheelchair. The child held a bat with both hands and gazed up at the baseball player, who looked slightly ill at ease among the I.V. lines.

Raoul picked a medical chart out of a bin and flipped through it. He grunted and pushed a button on a panel above the desk. Seconds later a heavyset woman dressed in white stuck her head in.

'Yes – oh, hi, Doctor Melendez.' She saw me and gave a nod with a question mark stuck to the end of it.

Raoul introduced me to the nurse, whose name was Ellen Beckwith.

'Good,' she said, 'we could use you around here.'

'Dr. Delaware used to coordinate psychological care on this unit. He's an international expert on the psychological effects of reverse isolation.'

'Oh. Great. Pleased to meet you.'

I took the proferred fleshy hand.

'Ellen,' said Raoul, 'when are Mr. and Mrs. Swope due back on the unit?'

'Gee, I dunno, Doctor. They were here all last night and then they left. They usually come in every day, so they should be around sometime.'

He clenched his teeth.

'That's very helpful, Ellen,' he said sharply.

The nurse grew flustered and her meaty face took on the look of an animal corralled in an unfamiliar pen. 'I'm sorry, Doctor, it's just that they're not required to tell us – '

'Never mind. Is there anything new with the boy that hasn't been charted?'

'No sir, we're just waiting for – ' she saw the look on his face and stopped herself. 'Uh, I was just going to change the linens in unit three, Doctor, so if you have nothing more – '

48

'Go. But first get Beverly Lucas over here.'

She glanced at a chalkboard across the room.

'She's signed out to page, sir.'

Raoul looked up and stroked his moustache. The only evidence of his agony was the slight tremble beneath the bristly hairs.

'Then *page* her, for God's sake.'

She hurried off.

'And they want to be professionals,' he said. 'Working hand in hand with the doctor as equal partners. Ludicrous.'

'Do you use anything for the pain?' I asked.

The question threw him.

'What – oh, it's not so bad,' he lied, and forced a smile. 'Once in a while I take something.'

'Ever tried biofeedback or hypnosis?'

He shook his head.

'You should. It works. You can learn to vaso-dilate and constrict at will.'

'No time to learn.'

'It doesn't take long if the patient's motivated.'

'Yes, well – ' he was interrupted by the phone. He answered it, barked orders into the receiver, and hung up.

'That was Beverly Lucas, the social worker. She'll be here shortly to fill you in.'

'I know Bev. She was a student here when I was an intern.'

He held out his hand palm down and moved it side to side. 'So-so, eh?'

'I always thought she was pretty sharp.'

'If you say so.' He looked doubtful. 'She wasn't much use with this family.'

'That may be true of me as well, Raoul.'

'You're different, Alex. You think like a scientist but can relate to patients like a humanist. It's a rare combination. That's why I chose you, my friend.'

49

He'd never chosen me but I didn't argue. Maybe he'd forgotten the way it really started.

Several years back, he was awarded a government grant to study the medical value of isolating children with cancer in germ-free environments. The 'environments' came from NASA – plastic modules used to prevent returned astronauts from infecting the rest of us with cosmic pathogens. The modules were filtered continuously and flooded with air blown out rapidly and smoothly in laminar flow. Such smooth flow was important because it prevented pockets of turbulence where germs collected and bred.

The value of an effective way to protect cancer patients from microbes was obvious if you understood a little about chemotherapy. Many of the drugs used to kill tumours also knock out the body's immune system. It was as common for patients to die of infection brought about by treatment as to perish from the disease itself.

Raoul's reputation as a researcher was impeccable and the government sent him four modules and lots of money to play with. He constructed a randomized study, dividing the children into experimental and control groups, the latter treated in regular hospital rooms using conventional isolation procedures such as masks and gowns. He hired microbiologists to monitor the germ count. He gained access to a computer at Cal Tech to analyze the data. He was ready to go.

Then someone raised the issue of psychological damage.

Raoul pooh-poohed the risk, but others weren't convinced. After all, they reasoned, the plans were to subject children as young as two to what could only be termed sensory deprivation – months in a plastic room, no skin to skin contact with other human beings, segregation from normal life activities. A

50

protective environment, to be sure, but one that could be harmful. It needed to be looked into.

At the time I was a junior level psychologist and was offered the job because none of the other therapists wanted anything to do with cancer. And none of them wanted to work with Raoul Melendez-Lynch.

I saw it as an opportunity to do some fascinating research and prevent emotional catastrophe. The first time I met Raoul and tried to tell him about my ideas, he gave me a cursory glance, returned his attention to the *New England Journal*, and nodded absently.

When I finished my pitch he looked up and said, 'I suppose you'll be needing an office.'

It wasn't an auspicious beginning, but gradually his eyes were opened to the value of psychological consultation. I badgered him into building the unit so that each module had access to a window and a clock. I nagged him until he obtained funds for a full-time play therapist and a social worker for the families. I cadged a healthy chunk of computer time for psychological data. In the end it paid off. Other hospitals were having to release patients from isolation because of psychological problems but our children adjusted well. I collected mountains of data and published several articles and a monograph with Raoul as co-author. The psychological findings received more scientific attention than the medical articles, and by the end of three years he was an enthusiastic supporter of psychosocial care and somewhat humanized.

We grew friendly, though on a relatively superficial level. Sometimes he talked about his childhood. His family, originally Argentine, had escaped from Havana in a fishing boat after Castro nationalized their plantation and most of their wealth. He was proud of a family tradition of physician-businessmen.

51

All of his uncles and most of his cousins, he explained, were doctors, many of them professors of medicine. (All were fine gentlemen except Cousin Ernesto, who was a scum-sucking Communist pig. Ernesto had been a doctor, too, but he'd abandoned his family and his profession for the life of a radical murderer. No matter that thousands of fools worshipped him as Ché Guevara. To Raoul he'd always be despicable Cousin Ernesto, the black sheep of the family.)

As successful as he was in medicine, his personal life was a disaster. Women were fascinated by him but ultimately repelled by his obsessive character. Four of them endured marriage with him and he sired eleven children, most of whom he never saw.

A complex and difficult man.

Now he sat in a plastic chair in a drab little office and tried to be macho about the buzz saw ripping through his skull.

'I'd like to meet the boy,' I said.

'Of course. I can introduce you now, if you like.'

Beverly Lucas came in just as he was about to get up.

'Good morning, gentlemen,' she said. 'Alex – how nice to see you.'

'Hi, Bev.'

I rose and we embraced briefly.

She looked good, though considerably thinner than I remembered. Years ago, she'd been a cheerful, rather innocent trainee, full of enthusiasm. The kind voted Miss Bubbly in high school. She had to be thirty by now, and some of the pixie cuteness had turned to womanly determination. She was petite and fair, with rosy cheeks and straw-coloured hair worn in a long soft perm. Her round open face was dominated by hazel saucer eyes and untouched by makeup. She wore no jewellery and her clothes were simple – knee-

52

length navy skirt, short-sleeved blue-and-red plaid blouse, penny loafers. She carried an oversized purse, which she swung up on the desk.

'You look svelte,' I said.

'Running. I'm doing long distance, now.' She flexed a muscle and laughed.

'Very impressive.'

'It helps centre me.' She sat on the edge of the desk. 'What brings you around here after all this time?'

'Raoul wants me to help out with the Swopes.'

Her expression changed without warning, the features hardening and gaining a few years. With forced amiability she said, 'Good luck.'

Raoul stood up and started to lecture.

'Alex Delaware is an expert in the psychological care of children with malignant – '

'Raoul,' I interrupted, 'why don't you let Beverly fill me in on the case. There's no need for you to spend any more time at this point.'

He looked at his watch.

'Yes. Of course.' To Beverly: 'You'll give him a comprehensive rundown?'

'Of course, Dr. Melendez-Lynch,' she said sweetly.

'You want me to introduce you to Woody?'

'Don't bother. Bev will handle it.'

His eyes darted from me to her and then back to his watch.

'All right. I'm off. Call if you need me.'

He removed the stethoscope from around his neck and swung it at his side as he left.

'I'm sorry,' I said to her when we were alone.

'Forget it, it's not your fault. He's such an asshole.'

'You're the second person he's riled this morning.'

'There'll be plenty of others before the day's up. Who was the first?'

'Nona Swope.'

'Oh. Her. She's angry at the world.'

'It must be rough for her,' I said.

'I'm sure,' she agreed, 'but I think she was an angry young lady long before her brother got cancer. I tried to develop a rapport with her — with all of them — but they shut me out. Of course,' she added, bitterly, '*you* may do much better.'

'Bev, I've got no stake in being a miracle worker. Raoul called me in a panic, gave me no background, and I tried to do a friend a favour, okay?'

'You should pick your friends with greater care.'

I said nothing, just let her listen to the echoes of her own words.

It worked.

'Okay, Alex, I'm sorry for being such a bitch. It's just that he's impossible to work for, gives no credit when you do a good job, and throws these incredible tantrums when things so wrong. I've put in for a transfer, but until they find a sucker to replace me, I'm stuck.'

'No one can do this type of work for very long,' I said.

'Don't I know it! Life's too short. That's why I got into running — I come home all burnt out and after a couple of hours of pushing my body to the limit I'm renewed.''

'You look great.'

'Do I? I was starting to worry about getting too thin. Lately I've been losing my appetite — oh, hell, I must sound like a real egomaniac, griping like this when I'm surrounded by people in real crises.'

'Griping is a God-given right.'

'I'll try to look at it that way.' She smiled and pulled out a notebook. 'I suppose you want a psycho-social rundown on the Swopes.'

'It would help.'

'The name of the game is *weird* — these are strange

54

people, Alex. The mother never talks, the father talks all the time, and the sister can't stand either of them.'

'Why do you say that?'

'The way she looks at them. And the fact that she's never around when they are. It's like she feels out of place. She doesn't pay much attention to Woody when she's here, keeps strange hours – shows up late at night, or really early in the morning. The night staff says she mostly sits and stares at him – usually he's asleep, anyway. Once in a while she'll go in the unit and read him a book, but that's about it. The father doesn't do much in the way of stimulation, either. He likes to flirt with the nurses, acts like he knows it all.'

'Raoul told me the same thing.'

'Raoul's not totally incapable of insight.' She laughed maliciously. 'Seriously, Mr. Swope is a different kind of guy. Big fellow, grey-haired with a beer gut and a little goatee. Kind of like Buffalo Bill without the long hair. He's really cut off from his feelings – I know it's denial and I know it's not unheard of, but he goes beyond what we normally see. His son's diagnosed with cancer and he's laughing and joking with the nurses, trying to be one of the gang, talking about his orchard and his precious plants, throwing around horticultural jargon. You know what can happen to guys like that.'

'Sudden breakdown.'

'Exactly. All at once it hits them and pow! Pathological grief reaction.'

'Doesn't sound like the boy has much support.'

'The mother. She's got to be the most unliberated thing I've ever seen – Garland Swope is the *king* of his castle – but she does seem to be a good mother – nurturant, gives lots of hugs and kisses, goes into the unit a lot, and without any hesitation. You know how scary the spacesuit can be for lots of parents. *She*

55

jumped right in. The nurses see her go off into the corner and cry when she thinks no one's looking, but when Garland comes around she puts on a great big smile, lots of "Yes, Dears" and "No, Dears." It's really sad.'

'Why do you think they want to pull the kid out?' I asked.

'I know Raoul believes it was those people from the Touch – he's so paranoid about anything holistic – but how can he be so sure? Could be he's to blame for the whole thing. Maybe he screwed up communication with them – he's very aggressive when he describes the treatment protocols and lots of people are put off.'

'He seemed to think the Fellow was at fault.'

'Augie Valcroix? Augie marches to his own drummer but he's a good guy. One of the few docs who actually takes time to sit down with the families and act like a human being. He and Raoul hate each other's guts, which makes sense if you know them. Augie thinks Raoul's a fascist and Raoul sees him as a subversive influence. It's been great fun working in this department, Alex.'

'What about those cultists?'

She shrugged.

'What can I say? Another group of lost souls. I don't know much about them – there are so many fringe groups it would take a specialist to understand all of them. Two of them showed up a couple of days ago. The guy looked like a teacher – glasses, scuzzy beard, wimpy manner, brown oxfords. The lady was older, in her forties or fifties, the kind who was probably a hot number when she was younger but lost it. Both of them had that glazed look in their eyes – the I-know-the-secret-of-the-universe-but-I-won't-tell-you trance. Moonies, Krishnas, esties, Touchers, they're all the same.'

'You don't think they turned the Swopes around?'

'They may have been the straw that broke it,' she conceded, 'but I don't see how they could be entirely responsible. Raoul's looking for a scapegoat, for easy answers. That's his style. Most of the docs are like that. Instant fix-its for complex issues.'

She looked away and folded her arms across her chest.

'I'm really tired of all of it,' she said softly.

I steered her back to the Swopes.

'Raoul wondered if the parents' being older had anything to do with it. You pick up any hints the boy was an unwanted accident?'

'I didn't get close enough to even touch on stuff like that. I was lucky to get enough for a bare-bones intake. The father smiled and called me "dear" and made sure I never got enough time alone with his wife to develop a relationship. This family's *armoured*. Maybe they've got lots of secrets they don't want coming out.'

Maybe. Or maybe they're terrified at being in a strange environment so far from home with a gravely ill child and don't want to strip themselves bare in front of strangers. Maybe they don't like social workers. Maybe they're simply private people. Lots of maybes . . .

'What about Woody?'

'A cutie pie. He's been sick since he got here, so it's hard to judge what kind of kid he really is. Seems like a little sweetie – isn't it always the sweet ones who suffer?' She took out a tissue and blew her nose. 'Can't stand the air in here. Woody's a nice little boy who's agreeable and kind of passive. A people pleaser. He cries during procedures – the spinal tap really hurt him – but he holds still and gives no serious problems.' She stopped for a moment and fought tears.

57

'It's a goddamn crime, their pulling him out of treatment. I don't like Melendez-Lynch, but goddamn it, he's right this time! They're going to kill that little boy because somehow we screwed up, and it's driving me nuts.'

She pounded a small fist on the desk, snapped herself to a standing position, and paced the cramped office. Her lower lip quivered.

I stood up and put my arms around her and she buried her head in the warmth of my jacket.

'I feel like such a fool!'

'You're not.' I held her tightly. 'None of it is your fault.'

She pulled away and dabbed at her eyes. When she seemed composed I said, 'I'd like to meet Woody.'

She nodded and led me to the Laminar Airflow Unit.

There were four modules, placed in series, like rooms in a railroad flat, and shielded from one another by a wall of curtain that could be opened or drawn by pushing buttons inside each room. The walls of the units were transparent plastic and each room resembled an oversized ice cube, eight feet square.

Three of the cubes were occupied. The fourth was filled with supplies – toys, cots, bags of clothing. The interior side of the curtained wall in each room was a perforated grey panel – the filter through which air blew audibly. The doors of the modules were segmented, the bottom half metal and closed, the top plastic, and left ajar. Microbes were kept out of the opening by the high speed at which the air was expelled. Running parallel to all four units were corridors on both sides, the rear passage for visitors, the front for the medical staff.

Two feet in front of the doorway to each module was a no-entry area marked off by red tape on the vinyl floor. I stood just outside the tape at the entrance of Module Two and looked at Woody Swope.

He lay on the bed, under the covers, facing away from us. There were plastic gloves attached to the front wall of the module, which permitted manual entry into the germ-free environment. Beverly put her hands inside them and patted him on the head gently.

'Good morning, sweetie.'

Slowly and with seeming effort, he rolled over and stared at us.

'Hi.'

A week before Robin left for Japan, she and I went to an exhibition of photographs by Roman Vishniac. The pictures had been a chronicle of the Jewish ghettos of Eastern Europe just before the Holocaust. Many of the portraits were of children, and the photographer's lens had caught their small faces unaware, flash-freezing the confusion and terror it found there. The images were haunting, and afterward we cried.

Now, looking into the large dark eyes of the boy in the plastic room, these same feelings came back in a rush.

His face was small and thin, the skin stretched across delicate bone structure, translucently pale in the artificial light of the module. His eyes, like those of his sister, were black, and glassy with fever. The hair on his head was a thick mop of henna-coloured curls. Chemotherapy, if it ever happened, would take care of those curls in a brutal, though temporary, reminder of the disease.

Beverly stopped stroking his hair and held out her glove. The boy took it and managed a smile.

'How we doing this morning, doll?'

'Okay.' His voice was soft and barely audible through the plastic.

'This is Dr. Delaware, Woody.'

At the mention of the title he flinched and moved back on the bed.

'He's not the kind of doctor who gives shots. He just talks to kids, like I do.'

That relaxed him somewhat, but he continued to look at me with apprehension.

'Hi, Woody,' I said. 'Can we shake hands?'

'Okay.'

I put my hand into the glove Beverly relinquished. It felt hot and dry – coated with talc, I recalled. Reaching into the module I searched for his hand and found it, a small treasure. I held it for a moment and let go.

'I see you've got some games in there. Which is your favourite?'

'Checkers.'

'I like checkers, too. Do you play a lot?'

'Kind of.'

'You must be very smart to know how to play checkers.'

'Kind of.' The hint of a smile.

'I bet you win a lot.'

The smile widened. His teeth were straight and white but the gums surrounding them were swollen and inflamed.

'And you like to win.'

'Uh huh. I always win my mom.'

'How 'bout your dad?'

He gave a perplexed frown.

'He doesn't play checkers.'

'I see. But if he did, you'd probably win.'

He digested that for a moment.

'Yeah, I pro'ly would. He doesn't know much about playing games.'

'Anyone else you play with besides Mom?'

'Jared – but he moved away.'

60

'Anybody besides Jared?'

'Michael and Kevin.'

'Are they guys at school?'

'Yeah. I finished K. Next year I go into one.'

He was alert and responsive but obviously weak. Talking to me was taxing, and his chest heaved with the effort.

'How about you and I play a game of checkers?'

'Okay.'

'I could play from out here with these gloves, or I could put on one of those spacesuits and come in the room with you. Which would you like better?'

'I dunno.'

'Well, *I'd* like to come in the room.' I turned to Bev. 'Could somebody help me suit up? It's been a long time.'

'Sure.'

'I'll be there in a minute, Woody.' I smiled at him and stepped away from the plastic wall. Rhythm-and-blues music blared from the module next door. I glanced over and caught a glimpse of a pair of long brown legs dangling over the foot of a bed. A black boy around seventeen was sprawled atop the covers, staring at the ceiling and moving to the sounds that screamed from the ghetto blaster on his nightstand, seemingly impervious to the I.V. needles imbedded in the crooks of both arms.

'See,' said Bev, speaking up to be heard, 'I told you. A sweetie.'

'Nice kid,' I agreed. 'He seems bright.'

'The parents describe him as having been very sharp. The fevers have pretty much knocked him out but he still manages to communicate very well. The nurses love him – this whole pullout thing is making everyone very uptight.'

'I'll do what I can. Let's start by getting me in there.'

61

She called for help and a tiny Filipino nurse appeared bearing a package wrapped in heavy brown paper and marked STERILE.

'Take off your shoes and stand there,' ordered the nurse, pint sized but authoritative. She pointed to a spot just outside the red taped no-entry zone. After washing her hands with Betadyne, she unwrapped a pair of sterile gloves and slipped them on her hands. Having inspected the gloves and found them free from flaws, she removed a folded spacesuit from the brown paper and placed it inside the red border. It took a bit of playing with the suit - which, in a collapsed state, looked like a heavy paper accordion - but she found the footholes and had me step inside them. Gingerly, she took hold of the edges and pulled it up over me, tying the top seam around my neck. Being so short, she had to stretch to do the job so I bent my knees to make it easier.

'Thanks,' she giggled. 'Now your gloves - don't touch anything until they're on.'

She worked quickly and soon my hands were sheathed in surgical plastic, my mouth concealed behind a paper mask. The headpiece - a hood fashioned of the same heavy paper as the suit attached to a plastic, see-through visor - was slipped over my face and fastened to the suit with Velcro strips.

'How does that feel?'

'Very stylish.' The suit was oppressively hot and I knew that within minutes, despite the cool rapid airflow in the unit, I'd be drenched with sweat.

'It's our continental model,' she smiled. 'You can go in now. Half hour maximum time. The clock's over there. We may be too busy to remind you, so keep an eye on it and come out when the time's up.'

'Will do.' I turned to Bev. 'Thanks for your help. Any idea when the parents will be in?'

62

'Vangie, did the Swopes say when they'd be in?'

The Filipino nurse shook her head. 'Usually they're here in the morning – right around now. If they don't come soon, I don't know when. I can leave a message for them to call you, Doctor – '

'Delaware. Why don't you tell them I'll be here tomorrow at eight thirty and if they arrive earlier, please have them wait.'

'Eight thirty you should catch them.'

'I'll tell you what,' said Bev, 'I've got the number of the place they're staying – some motel on the west side. I'll call and leave a message. If they show up today do you want to come back?'

I considered it. Nothing on the agenda that couldn't wait. 'Sure. Call my exchange. They'll know where to reach me.' I gave her the number.

'All right, Alex, you'd better get in there before you truck a few million pathogens over the border. See ya.'

She hoisted the large purse over her shoulder and walked out the door.

I stepped into the Laminar Airflow Room.

He'd sat up and his dark eyes followed my entry.

'I look like a spaceman, huh?'

'I can tell who you are,' he said gravely, 'everyone looks different.'

'That's good. I always had trouble recognizing people when they wore these things.'

'Ya gotta look close, with strong eyes.'

'I see. Thanks for the advice.'

I got the box of checkers and unfolded the board on the armlike table that swung across the bed.

'What colour do you want to be?'

'Dunno.'

'Black goes first, I think. You wanna go first?'

'Uh huh.'

He was precociously good at the game, able to plot,

63

set up moves, and think sequentially. A bright little boy.

A couple of times I tried to engage him in conversation but he ignored me. It wasn't shyness or lack of good manners. His attention was focused on the checkerboard and he didn't even hear the sound of my voice. When he completed a move he'd lean back against the pillows with a satisfied look on his grave little face and say, 'There! Your turn,' in a voice made soft by fatigue.

We were halfway through the game and he was giving me a run for my money when he clutched his abdomen and cried out in pain.

I eased him down and felt his brow. Low-grade fever.

'Your tummy hurts, doesn't it?'

He nodded and wiped his eyes with the back of his hand.

I pressed the call button. Vangie, the Filipino nurse, appeared on the other side of the plastic.

'Abdominal pain. Febrile,' I told her.

She frowned and disappeared, returning with a cup of liquid acetominophen held in a gloved hand.

'Swing that counter over this way, would you.'

She set the medicine on the slab of Formica.

'You can take it now and give it to him. The resident's due by within the hour to check him over.'

I returned to the boy's bedside, propped him up with one hand behind his head, and held the liquid to his lips with the other.

'Open up, Woody. This will make it hurt less.'

'Okay, Doctor Delaware.'

'I think you'd better rest now. You played a good game.'

He nodded and the curls bounced. 'Tie?'

'I'd say so. Although you were getting me pretty

good at the end. Can I come back and play with you again?'

'Uh huh.' He closed his eyes.

'Rest up, now.'

By the time I was out of the unit and had shed the paper suit, he was asleep, lips parted, sucking gently at the softness of the pillow.

5

THE NEXT morning I drove east on Sunset under a sky streaked with tin-strip clouds and thought about last night's dreams – the same kind of spooky, murky images that had plagued my sleep when I first started working in oncology. It had taken a good year to chase those demons away and now I wondered if they'd ever been gone or had just been lurking in my subconscious, ever ready for mischief.

Raoul's world was madness and I found myself resenting him for drawing me back into it.

Children weren't supposed to get cancer.

Nobody was supposed to get cancer.

The diseases that fell under the domain of the marauding crab were ultimate acts of histologic treason, the body assaulting, battering, raping, murdering itself in a feeding frenzy of rogue cells gone berserk.

I slipped a Lenny Breau cassette into the tape deck and hoped that the guitarist's fluid genius would take my mind far away from plastic rooms and bald children and one little boy with henna-coloured curls and a Why Me? look in his eyes. But I could see his face and the faces of so many other sick children I'd known, weaving in and out of the arpeggios, ephemeral, persistent, begging for rescue . . .

Given that state of mind, even the sleaze that heralded the entry into Hollywood seemed benign, the half-naked whores nothing more than big-hearted welcome wagoners.

I drove through the last mile of boulevard in a blue funk, parked the Seville in the doctors' lot, and walked through the front door of the hospital with my head down, warding off social overtures.

I climbed the four flights to the oncology ward and was halfway down the hall before hearing the ruckus. Opening the door to the Laminar Airflow Unit turned up the volume.

Raoul stood, bug-eyed, his back to the modules, alternately cursing in rapid Spanish and screaming in English at a group of three people:

Beverly Lucas held her purse across her chest like a shield, but it wouldn't stay in one place because the hands that clutched it were shaking. She stared at a distant point beyond Melendez-Lynch's white-coated shoulder and bit her lip, straining not to choke on anger and humiliation.

The broad face of Ellen Beckwith bore the startled, terrified look of someone caught in the midst of a smarmy, private ritual. She was primed for confession, but unsure of her crime.

The third member of the audience was a shaggy-haired man with a hound dog face and squinty, heavy-lidded eyes. His white coat was unbuttoned and worn carelessly over faded jeans and a cheap-

67

looking shirt of the sort that used to be called psychedelic but now looked merely garish. A belt with an oversized buckle in the shape of an Indian chief bit into a soft-looking middle. His feet were large and the toes were long, almost prehensile. I could tell because he'd encased them, sockless, in Mexican huaraches. His face was clean-shaven and his skin was pale. The shaggy hair was medium brown, streaked with grey, and it hung to his shoulders. A puka shell necklace ringed a neck that had begun to turn to wattle.

He stood impassively, as if in a trance, a serene look in the hooded eyes.

Raoul saw me and stopped his harangue.

'He's gone, Alex.' He pointed to the plastic room where I'd played checkers less than twenty-four hours ago. The bed was empty.

'Removed from under the noses of these so-called *professionals*.' He dismissed the trio with a contemptuous wave of his hand.

'Why don't we talk about it somewhere else,' I suggested. The black teenager in the unit next door was peering out through the transparent wall with a puzzled look on his face.

Raoul ignored me.

'*They* did it. Those quacks. Came in as radiation techs and kidnapped him. Of course, if anyone had possessed the good sense to *read the chart* to find out if radiologic studies had been ordered, they might have prevented this – felony!'

He was boring in on the fat nurse now, and she was on the verge of tears. The tall man came out of his trance and tried to rescue her.

'You can't expect a nurse to think like a cop.' His speech was just barely tinged with a Gallic lilt.

Raoul wheeled on him.

'You! Keep your damned comments to yourself! If

68

you had an iota of understanding of what medicine is all about we might not be in this mess. *Like a cop!* If that means exercising vigilance and care to insure a patient's safety and security, then she damn well does have to think like a cop! This isn't an Indian reservation, Valcroix! It's life-threatening disease and invasive procedures and using the brain that God gave us to make inferences and deductions and *decisions*, for God's sake! It's *not* managing a reverse isolation unit like a bus terminal, where people come in and out and tell you they're someone they're not and whisk your patient away from under your lazy, sloppy, careless nose!'

The other doctor's response was a cosmic smile as he zoned back out into never-never land.

Raoul glared at him, ready to pounce. The gangly black boy watched the confrontation, eyes wide and frightened, from behind his plastic screen. A mother visiting her child in the third module stared, then drew the curtains protectively.

I took Raoul by the elbow and escorted him to the nurses' office. The Filipino nurse was there, charting. After one look at us, she grabbed her paperwork and left.

He picked up a pencil from the desk and snapped it between his fingers. Tossing the broken pieces to the floor, he kicked them into a corner.

'That bastard! The arrogance, to debate me in front of ancillary staff – I'll terminate his fellowship and get rid of him once and for all.'

He ran a hand over his brow, chewed on his moustache, and tugged at his jowls until the swarthy flesh turned rosy.

'They took him,' he said. 'Just like that.'

'What do you want to do about it?'

'What I want is to find those Touchers and strangle them with my bare hands and – '

69

I picked up the phone. 'You want me to call Security?'

'Ha! A bunch of senile alcoholics who need help finding their own flashlights – '

'What about the police? It's an abduction now.'

'No,' he said quickly. 'They won't do a damned thing and it will be a freakshow for the media.'

He found Woody's chart and leafed through it, hissing.

'Radiology – why would I schedule x-rays for a child whose treatment is up in the air! It makes no sense. Nobody thinks anymore. Automatons, all of them!'

'What do you want to do about it?' I repeated.

'Damned if I know,' he admitted and slapped the chart on the desktop.

We sat in glum silence for a moment.

'They're probably halfway to Tijuana,' he said, 'on a pilgrimage to some damned Laetrile *clinica* – did you ever see those places? Murals of crabs on filthy adobe walls. That's their salvation! Fools!'

'It's possible they haven't gone anywhere. Why don't we check?'

'How?'

'Beverly has the number of the place they're staying. We can call and find out if they've checked out.'

'Play detective – yes, why not? Call her in.'

'Be civil to her, Raoul.'

'Fine, fine.'

I beckoned the social worker away from a powwow with Valcroix and Ellen Beckwith, who gave me the kind of look usually reserved for plague carriers.

I told her what I wanted and she nodded wearily.

Once in the office she avoided looking at Raoul and silently dialled the phone. There was a brief exchange with the motel clerk, after which she hung up and said:

70

'The guy was real uncooperative. He hasn't seen them today but they haven't checked out. The car's still there.'

'If you'd like,' I offered, 'I'll go there, try to make contact with them.'

Raoul consulted his appointment book.

'Meetings until three. I'll cancel out. Let's go.'

'I don't think you should be there, Raoul.'

'That's absurd, Alex! I'm the *physician!* This is a medical issue – '

'Only nominally. Let me handle it.'

His thick brows curled and fury rose in the coffee bean eyes. He started to say something but I cut him off.

'We have to at least consider the possibility,' I said softly, 'that this whole thing may be due to a conflict between the family and you.'

He stared at me, making sure he'd heard right, purpled, choked on his anger, and threw up his hands in despair.

'How could you even – '

'I'm not saying it's so. Just that we need to consider it. What we want is that boy back in treatment. Let's maximize the probability of success by covering all contingencies.'

He was mad as hell but I'd given him something to think about.

'Fine. There's no shortage of things for me to do anyway. Go yourself.'

'I want Beverly along. Of anyone she's got the best feel for the family.'

'Fine, fine. Take Beverly. Take whomever you want.'

He straightened his tie and smoothed nonexistent wrinkles in the long white coat.

'Now, if you'll excuse me, my friend,' he said, straining to be cordial, 'I'll be off to the lab.'

* * *

71

The Sea Breeze Motel was on west Pico, set amid cheap apartments, dusty storefronts, and auto garages on a dingy slice of the boulevard just before L.A. surrenders to Santa Monica. The place was two storeys of pitted chartreuse stucco and drooping pink wrought-iron railing. Thirty or so units looked down upon an asphalt motor court and a swimming pool half-filled with algae-clogged water. The only breeze evident was the steaming layer of exhaust fumes that rose from the oily pavement as we pulled in beside a camper with Utah plates.

'Not exactly five star,' I said, getting out of the Seville. 'And far from the hospital.'

Beverly frowned.

'I tried to tell them that when I saw the address but there was no convincing the father. Said he wanted to be near the beach where the air was good. Even launched into a speech about how the whole hospital should move to the beach, how the smog was harmful to patients. I told you, the man is weird.'

The front office was a glass booth on the other side of a warped plywood door. A thin, bespectacled Iranian with the numb demeanour of a habitual opium smoker sat behind a chipped, hinged plastic counter poring over the Motor Vehicle Code. A revolving rack of combs and cheap sunglasses took up one corner, a low table covered with ancient copies of throwaway travel magazines squatted in the other.

The Iranian pretended not to notice us. I cleared my throat with tubercular fervour and he looked up slowly.

'Yes?'

'What room is the Swope family in?'

He looked us over, decided we were safe, said, 'Fifteen,' and returned to the wondrous world of road signs.

There was a dusty brown Chevy station wagon

72

parked in front of Room 15. Except for a sweater on the front seat and an empty cardboard box in the rear deck, the car was empty.

'That's theirs,' said Beverly. 'They used to leave it parked illegally by the front entrance. One time when the security guard put a warning sticker on the windshield, Emma ran out crying about her sick child and he tore it up.'

I knocked on the door. No answer. Knocked again harder. Still no response. The room had a single grimy window, but the view within was blocked by oilcloth curtains. I knocked one more time, and when the silence was unbroken, we returned to the office.

'Excuse me,' I said, 'do you know if the Swopes are in their room?'

A lethargic shake of the head.

'Do you have a switchboard?' Beverly asked him.

The Iranian raised his eyes from his reading and blinked.

'Who are you? What do you want?' His English was heavily accented, his manner surly.

'We're from Western Paediatric Hospital. The Swopes' child is being treated there. It's important that we speak to them.'

'I don't know anything.' He shifted his glance back to the vehicle code.

'Do you have a switchboard?' she repeated.

A barely visible nod.

'Then please ring the room.'

With a theatrical sigh, he dragged himself up and walked through a door at the rear. A minute later he reappeared.

'Nobody there.'

'But their car's there.'

'Listen, lady, I don't know cars. You want a room, okay. Otherwise, leave alone.'

'Call the police, Bev,' I said.

73

Somehow he must have sneaked in a bit of amphetamine because his face came alive suddenly and he spoke and gesticulated with renewed vigour.

'What for police? What for you cause trouble?'

'No trouble,' I said. 'We just need to talk to the Swopes.'

He threw up his hands.

'They take walk – I see them. Walking that way.' He pointed east.

'Unlikely. They've got a sick child with them.' To Bev: 'I saw a phone at the gas station on the corner. Call it in as a suspicious disappearance.'

She moved toward the door.

The Iranian lifted the hinged counter and came around to our side.

'What do you want? Why you make trouble?'

'Listen,' I told him, 'I don't care what kind of nasty little games you've got going on in the other rooms. We need to talk to the family in fifteen.'

He pulled a ring of keys out of his pocket. 'Come, I show you, they not here. Then you leave me alone, okay?'

'It's a deal.'

His pants were baggy and they flapped as he strode across the asphalt, muttering and jingling the keys.

A quick turn of the wrist and the lock released. The door groaned as it opened. We stepped inside. The desk clerk blanched, Beverly whispered Ohmigod, and I fought down a rising feeling of dread.

The room was small and dark and it had been savaged.

The earthly belongings of the family Swope had been removed from three cardboard suitcases, which lay crushed on one of the twin beds. Clothing and personal articles were strewn about: lotion, shampoo, and detergent leaked from broken bottles in viscous trails across the threadbare carpeting. Female under-

74

garments hung limply over the chain of the plastic swag lamp. Paperback books and newspapers had been shredded and scattered like confetti. Open cans and boxes of food were everywhere, the contents oozing out in congealing mounds. The room reeked of rot and dead air.

Next to the bed was a patch of carpet that was clear of litter, but far from empty. It was filled with a dark brown amoebalike stain half a foot across.

'Oh no,' said Beverly. She staggered, lost her balance, and I caught her.

You don't have to spend much time in a hospital to know the sight of dried blood.

The Iranian's face was waxen. His jaws worked soundlessly.

'Come on,' I took hold of his bony shoulders and guided him out, 'we have to call the police now.'

It's nice to know someone on the force. Especially when that someone is your best friend and won't assume you're a suspect when you call in a crime. I bypassed 911 and called Milo's extension directly. He was in a meeting but I pushed a bit and they called him out.

'Detective Sturgis.'

'Milo, it's Alex.'

'Hello, pal. You pulled me out of a fascinating lecture. It seems the west side has become the latest hot spot for PCP labs - they rent glitzy houses and park Mercedes in the driveway. Why I need to know all about it is beyond me but tell that to the brass. Anyway, what's up?'

I told him and he turned businesslike immediately.

'All right. Stay there. Don't let anyone touch anything. I'll get everything moving. There's gonna be a lot of people converging so don't let the girl get spooked. I'll crap out of this meeting and be there as

75

soon as I can but I may not be the first, so if someone gives you a hard time, drop my name and hope they don't give you a harder time because you did. Bye.'

I hung up and went to Beverly. She had the drained, lost look of a stranded traveller. I put my arm around her and sat her down next to the clerk, who'd progressed to muttering to himself in Farsi, no doubt reminiscing about the good old days with the Ayatollah.

There was a coffee machine on the other side of the counter and I went through and poured three cups. The Iranian took his gratefully, held it with both hands, and gulped noisily. Beverly put hers down on the table, and I sipped as we waited.

Five minutes later we saw the flashing lights.

6

THE TWO uniformed policemen were muscular giants, one white and blond, the other coal-black, his partner's photographic negative. They questioned us briefly, spending most of their time with the Iranian desk clerk. They didn't like him instinctively, and showed it in the way L.A.P.D. cops do – by being overly polite.

Most of their interrogation had to do with when he'd last seen the Swopes, what cars had come in and out, how the family had been behaving, who had called them. If you believed him, the motel was an oasis of innocence and he was the original see-no-evil, hear-no-evil kid.

The patrolmen cordoned off the area around room fifteen. The sight of their squad car in the centre of the motor court must have ruffled some feathers – I saw fingers drawing back corners of curtains in several of the rooms. The policemen noticed, too, and joked about calling Vice.

Two additional black and whites pulled into the lot and parked haphazardly. Out of them stepped four more uniforms, who joined the first two for a smoke and a huddle. They were followed by a crime scene technical van and an unmarked bronze Matador.

The man who got out of the Matador was in his midthirties, big and heavily built, with a loose, ungainly walk. His face was broad and surprisingly unlined, but bore the stigmata of severe acne. Thick drooping brows shadowed tired eyes of a startling bright green hue. His black hair was cut short around the back and sides but worn full on top in defiance of any known style. A thick shock fell across his forehead like a frontal cowlick. Similarly unchic were the sideburns that reached to the bottom of his soft-lobed ears and his attire - a rumpled checked madras sportcoat with too much turquoise in it, a navy shirt, gray-and-blue striped tie, and light blue slacks that hung over the tops of suede desert boots.

'That one's got to be a cop,' said Beverly.

'That's Milo.'

'Your friend - oh.' She was embarrassed.

'It's okay, that's what he is.'

Milo conferred with the patrolmen then took out a pad and pencil, stepped over the tape strung across the doorway to room fifteen, and went inside. He stayed in there awhile and came out taking notes.

He loped over to the front office. I got up and met him at the entrance.

'H'lo, Alex.' His big padded hand gripped mine. 'Hell of a mess in there. Not really sure what to call it yet.'

He saw Beverly, walked over, and introduced himself.

'Stick with this guy,' he pointed to me, 'and

78

inevitably you're going to get into trouble.'

'I can see that.'

'Are you in a hurry?' he asked her.

'I'm not going back to the hospital,' she said. 'All I've got, otherwise, is a run at three thirty.'

'Run? Oh, like in cardiovascular stimulation? Yeah, I tried that but the chest began to hurt and visions of mortality danced before my eyes.'

She smiled uneasily, not knowing what to make of him. Milo's great to have around – in more ways than one – when your preconceptions get overly calcified.

'Don't worry, you'll be out of here long before then. Just wanted to know if you could wait while I interview Mr. – ' he consulted the pad, 'Fahrizbadeh. Shouldn't take long.'

'That would be fine.'

He escorted the desk clerk outside and over to fifteen. Beverly and I sat in silence.

'This is horrible,' she said, finally. 'That room. The blood.' She sat stiffly in her chair and pressed her knees together.

'He could be okay,' I said without much conviction.

'I hope so, Alex. I really do.'

After a while Milo returned with the desk clerk, who slunk behind the counter without a glance at us and disappeared into the back room.

'Very unobservant guy,' said Milo. 'But I think he's on the level, more or less. Apparently his brother-in-law owns the place. He's studying business administration at night and works here instead of sleeping.' He looked at Beverly. 'What can you tell me about these Swope people?'

She gave him a history similar to the one I'd received in the Laminar Airflow Unit.

'Interesting,' he reflected, chewing on his pencil.

'So this could be anything. The parents taking the kid out of town in a hurry, which might not be a crime at all unless the hospital wants to make a thing out of it. Except if that was the case, they wouldn't leave the car behind. Hypothesis B is the cultists did the job with the parents' permission, which is still no crime. Or, without, which would be good old-fashioned kidnapping.'

'What about the blood?' I asked.

'Yeah, the blood. The techs say O positive. That tell you anything?'

'I think I remember from the chart,' said Beverly, 'that Woody and both of the parents are O. I'm not sure about the Rh factor.'

'So much for that. It's not a hell of a lot anyway, not what you'd expect if someone got shot or cut – ' He saw the look on her face and stopped himself.

'Milo,' I said, 'the boy's got cancer. He's not terminally ill – or wasn't as of yesterday. But his disease is unpredictable. It could spread and invade a major blood vessel, or convert to leukaemia. And if either of those occur, he could suddenly haemorrhage.'

'Jesus,' said the big detective, looking pained. 'Poor little guy.'

'Isn't there something you can do?' demanded Beverly.

'We'll do our best to find them but to be honest it won't be easy. They could be just about anywhere by now.'

'Don't you put out A.P.B.s or something like that?' she insisted.

'That's already been done. As soon as Alex called I got in touch with the law in La Vista – it's a one-man show run by a sheriff named Houten. He hasn't seen them but he promised to keep a lookout. He also gave me a good physical description of the family and I put

80

it over the wire. Highway patrol's got it, as well as L.A. and San Diego P.D.s and all the decent-sized departments in between. But we've got no vehicle to look for, no plates. Anything you'd like to suggest in addition to all of that?'

It was a sincere request for ideas, devoid of sarcasm, and it threw her off guard.

'Uh, no,' she admitted, 'I can't think of anything. I just hope you find him.'

'I hope so, too – can I call you Beverly?'

'Oh, sure.'

'I don't have any brilliant theories about this, Beverly, but I promise to give it a lot of thought. And, if *you* think of anything, call *me*.' He gave her a card. 'Anything at all, okay? Now, can I have one of the men give you a life home?'

'Alex could – '

He flashed her a wide, loose-lipped smile. 'I'm going to be needing to talk to Alex for a while. I'll get you a ride.' He went out to the six patrolmen, selected the best-looking of the bunch, a trim six-footer with curly black hair and shiny teeth, and brought him back to the office.

'Ms. Lucas, this is Officer Fierro.'

'Where to, ma'am?' Fierro tipped his hat. She gave him an address in Westwood and he guided her to his squad car.

Just as she was getting in, Milo rummaged in his shirt pocket and called out, 'Hey, Brian, hold on.'

Fierro stopped and Milo bounded over to the car. I jogged along with him.

'This mean anything to you, Beverly?' He handed her a matchbook.

She examined it. 'Adam and Eve Messenger Service'? Yeah. One of the nurses told me Nona Swope had gotten a job as a messenger. I remember thinking it was strange – why would she get a job

81

when they were only in town temporarily?' She looked at the matchbook more closely. 'What is this, a hooker service or something like that?'

'Something like that.'

'I knew she was a wild one,' she said angrily, and gave him back the matchbook. 'Is that all?'

'Uh huh.'

'Then I'd like to go home.'

Milo gave the signal and Fierro got behind the wheel and started up the engine.

'Uptight lady,' said Milo after they drove away.

'She used to be a sweet young thing,' I said. 'Too much time on the cancer ward can do things to you.'

He frowned.

'Quite a mess in there,' he said.

'Looks bad, doesn't it?'

'You want me to speculate? Maybe, maybe not. The room was tossed by someone who was *angry*. But couldn't it have been one of the parents, furious at having a sick kid, all scared and confused about pulling him out? You worked with people in that situation. Ever see anyone freak like that?'

I reeled back a few years.

'There was always anger,' I told him. 'Most of the time people talked it out. But sometimes it got physical. I can recall at least one intern getting slugged by a father. Plenty of threats. One guy who'd lost his leg in a hunting accident three weeks before his daughter came down with kidney tumours carried a couple of pistols into the hospital the day after she died. It was usually the ones who denied it and held it in and didn't communicate with anyone who were the most explosive.' Which fitted the description Beverly had given me of Garland Swope. I told him so.

'So that could be it,' he said uneasily.

'But you don't think so.'

The heavy shoulders shrugged.

82

'I don't think anything at this point. Because this is a crazy city, pal. More homicides each year and folks are getting wasted for the weirdest reasons. Last week, some old character jammed a steak knife in his neighbour's chest because he was *sure* the guy was killing his tomato plants with evil rays from his navel. Deranged assholes walk into fast-food joints and mow down kids eating *burgers*, for chrissake. When I first went into Homicide things seemed relatively logical, pretty simple, really. Most of the stuff we used to catch was due to love or jealousy, or money, family feuds – your basic human conflicts. Not now, *compadre*. Too many holes in the Swiss cheese? Ice the deli man. Looney Tunes.'

'And this looks like the work of a crazy?'

'Who the hell knows, Alex? We're not talking hard science. Most probably we'll find it was what I said before. One of them – probably the father – got a good look at the shitty cards he'd been dealt and tossed the room. They left the car behind so it's probably temporary.'

'On the other hand, I can't guarantee they didn't happen to be in the wrong place at the wrong time, didn't collide with a nutcase who thought they were Pluto Vampires out to take over his liver.' He held the matchbook between thumb and forefinger and waved it like a miniature flag.

'Right now,' he said, 'All we've got is this. It's not in my ballpark but I'll pay the place a visit and follow it up for you, okay?'

'Thanks, Milo. Getting to the bottom of it would calm a few people down. Want company?'

'Sure, why not? Haven't seen you in a good while. If missing the lovely Ms. Castagna hasn't made you unbearably morose, you might even turn out to be *good* company.'

83

7

THERE WAS a phone number on the matchbook but no address, so Milo called Vice and got one, along with some background on the Adam and Eve Messenger Service.

'They know the operation,' he said, tooling onto Pico and heading east. 'Owned by a sweetheart named Jan Rambo, has her finger in a little bit of everything. Daddy's a mob biggie in Frisco. Little Jan's his pride and joy.'

'What is it, a cover for an outcall service?'

'That and a few other things. Vice thinks sometimes the messengers transport dope, but that's only a sideline - impromptu, when someone needs a favour. They do some relatively legit stuff - party gags, like when it's the boss's birthday and a nubile young thing shows up at the office party, strips and rubs herself all over him. Mostly it's sex for sale, one way or another.'

'Which sheds new light on Nona Swope,' I said.

'Maybe. You said she was good looking?'

'Gorgeous, Milo. Unusually so.'

'So she knows what she's got and decides to profit from it – it might be relevant, but what the hell, when you get right down to it, this town was built on the buying and selling of bodies, right? Small town girl hits glitter-city, gets her head turned. Happens every day.'

'That has got to be the most hackneyed soliloquy you've ever delivered.'

He broke out laughing and slapped the dashboard with glee, then realized he'd been squinting into the sun and put on a pair of mirrored shades.

'Oka-ay, time to play cop. What do you think?'

'Very intimidating.'

Jan Rambo's headquarters were on the tenth floor of a flesh-coloured high rise on Wilshire just west of Barrington. The directory in the lobby listed about a hundred businesses, most with names that told you nothing about what they did – a free hand had been used with words like *enterprise, system, communications,* and *network*. A good third of them ended with Ltd. Jan Rambo had outdone them all, christening her meat market, *Contemporary Communications Network, Ltd.* If that didn't convince you it was all very respectable, the brass letters on the teak door and the matching thunderbolt logo were sure to do the trick.

The door was locked but Milo pounded it hard enough for the walls to shake, and it opened. A tall well-built Jamaican in his midtwenties stuck his head out and started to say something hostile, but Milo shoved his badge in the mahogany face and he shut his mouth.

85

'Hi,' said Milo, grinning.

'What can I do for you, Officers?' asked the black, over-enunciating in a show of arrogance.

'First, you can let us in.' Without waiting for co-operation, Milo leaned on the door. Taken by surprise, the Jamaican stepped back and we walked in.

It wasn't much of a reception room, barely larger than a closet, but Contemporary Communications probably didn't do much receiving. The walls were flat ivory and the only furniture was a chrome and vinyl desk upon which sat an electric typewriter and a phone, and the steno chair behind it.

The wall backing the desk was adorned with a photographic poster of a California surfer couple posing as Adam and Eve, underscored by the legend 'Send that Special Message to that Special person.' Eve had her tongue in Adam's ear and though the expression on his face was one of stuporous boredom, his fig leaf bulged appreciatively.

To the left of the desk was a closed door. The Jamaican stood in front of it, arms folded, feet apart, a scowling sentry.

'We want to speak with Jan Rambo.'

'You got a warrant?'

'Jesus,' said Milo, disgustedly, 'everyone in this lousy city thinks he's in the movies. "You got a warrant?" ' he mimicked. 'Strictly grade B, dude. C'mon, knock on the door and tell her we're here.'

The Jamaican remained impassive.

'No warrant, no entry.'

'My, my, an assertive one.' Milo whistled. He put his hands in his pockets, slouched and walked forward until his nose was a millimetre short of Eskimo-kissing the Jamaican.

'There's no need to get unpleasant,' he said. 'I know Ms. Rambo is a busy lady and as pure as the

86

freshly driven snow. If she wasn't, we might be here to search the premises. *Then* we'd need a warrant. All we want to do is *talk* with her. Since you obviously haven't advanced far enough in your legal studies to know this, let me inform you that no warrant is necessary when one simply wants to make conversation.'

The Jamaican's nostrils widened.

'Now,' Milo continued, 'you can choose to facilitate that conversation or continue to be obstructive, in which case I will cause you grievous bodily injury, not to mention significant pain, and arrest you for interfering with a police officer in the performance of his duty. Upon arrest, I will fasten the cuffs tight enough to cause gangrene, see to it that you are body-searched by a sadist, and make sure you are tossed in a holding cell with half a dozen charter members of the Aryan Brotherhood.'

The Jamaican pondered his choices. He backed away from Milo, but the detective bird-dogged him, breathing into his face.

'I'll see if she's free,' he muttered, opening the door a crack and slithering through.

He reappeared momentarily, eyes smouldering with emasculation, and jerked his head toward the open door.

We followed him into an empty anteroom. He paused before double doors and punched a code into a pushbutton panel. There was a low-pitched buzz and he opened one of the doors.

A dark-haired woman sat behind a marble-topped tubular metal desk in an office as big as a ballroom. The floor was covered with springy industrial carpenting the colour of wet cement. To her back was a wall of smoked glass offering a muted view of the Santa Monica mountains and the Valley beyond. One side of the office had been given over to some

87

West Hollywood decorator's fantasies – mercilessly contemporary mauve leather chairs, a lucite coffee table sharp enough to slice bread, an art deco sideboard of rosewood and shagreen similar to one I'd seen recently in a Sotheby's catalogue; that piece had gone for more than Milo took home in a year. Across from this assemblage was the business area: rosewood conference table, bank of black file cabinets, two computers, and a corner filled with photographic equipment.

The Jamaican stood with his back to the door and resumed his sentry pose. He worked at fashioning his face into a war mask but a rosy flush incandesced beneath the dusky surface of his skin.

'You can go, Leon,' the woman said. She had a whiskey voice.

The Jamaican hesitated. She hardened her expression and he left hastily.

She remained behind the desk and didn't invite us to sit. Milo sat anyway, stretching out his long legs and yawning. I sat next to him.

'Leon told me you were very rude,' said the woman. She was about forty, chunky, with small muddy eyes and short pudgy hands that drummed the marble. Her hair was cut blunt and short. She wore a tailored black business suit. The ruffled bodice of her white crêpe de chine blouse seemed out of character.

'Gee,' said Milo, 'I'm really sorry, Ms. Rambo. I hope we didn't hurt his feelings.'

The woman laughed, an adenoidal growl. 'Leon's a prima donna. I keep him around for decoration.' She pulled out an extra-long black cigarette from a box of Shermans and lit it up. Blowing out a cloud of smoke, she watched it rise to the ceiling. When it had dissipated completely she spoke.

'The answers to your first three questions are: One:

88

They're messengers, not hookers. Two: What they do on their own time is their own business. Three: Yes, he is my father and we talk on the phone every month or so.'

'I'm not from Vice,' said Milo, 'and I don't give a damn if your messengers end up giving fuck shows for horny old men snarfing nose candy and playing pocket pool.'

'How tolerant of you,' she said coldly.

'I'm known for it. Live and let live.'

'What do you want then?'

He gave her his card.

'Homicide?' Her eyebrows rose but she remained impassive. 'Who bit it?'

'Maybe no one, maybe a whole bunch of people. Right now it's a suspicious disappearance. Family from down near the border. The sister worked for you. Nona Swope.'

She dragged deeply and the Sherman glowed.

'Ah, Nona. The red-haired beauty. She a suspect or a victim?'

'Tell me what you know about her,' said Milo, taking out his pad.

She removed a key from a desk drawer, stood, smoothed her skirt, and went to the files. She was surprisingly short – five one or two. 'I guess I'm supposed to play hard to get, right?' She inserted the key in the file lock and twisted. A drawer slid open. 'Refuse to give you the information, scream for my lawyer.'

'That's Leon's script.'

That amused her. 'Leon's a good guard dog. No,' she said, taking out a folder. 'I don't care much if you read about Nona. I've got nothing to hide. She's nothing to me.'

She settled back behind the desk and passed the folder across to Milo. He opened it and I looked over

89

his shoulder. The first page was an application form filled out in halting script.

The girl's full name was Annona Blossom Swope. She'd listed a birthdate that made her just twenty and physical measurements that matched my memory of her. Under residence she'd claimed a Sunset Boulevard address – Western Paediatric Medical Center – with no phone number to go along with it.

The eight-by-ten glossies had been taken in the office – I recognized the leather furniture – and they'd framed her in a variety of poses, all sultry. The photos were black-and-white and short-changed her by their inability to capture her dramatic colouring. Nevertheless, she had what professionals call *presence* and it came through in these pictures.

We thumbed through the photos – Nona in a string bikini rolled down over her pelvis, Brazilian style; Nona braless in a sheer tank top and jeans, nipples budding through the fabric; Nona making love to an all-day sucker; Nona, feline, in a filmy negligee with a fuck-you look in her dark eyes.

Milo whistled softly. I felt an involuntary tug below the waist.

'Quite a gal, eh?' asked Jan Rambo. 'A lot of skin passes through these portals, gentlemen. She stood out from the rest of them. I started calling her Daisy Mae because there was a naive quality to her. Limited life experience. Despite that, she was a little girl who knew her way around, know what I mean?'

'When were these taken?' asked Milo.

'First day she got here – what's it say, a week ago? I took one look at her and called the cameraman. We shot and developed 'em the same day. I saw her as a good investment, started her off on messenger service.'

'Doing what, exactly?' he pushed.

90

'Doing messenger work, *exactly*. We've got a few basic skits – doctor and nurse, professor and coed, Adam and Eve, dominatrix and slave or vice versa. The old clichés, but your average yahoo can't break out of clichés even when it's fantasy time. The client picks the skit, we send out couples, and they do it like a message – you know, Happy Birthday, Joe Smith, this is from the boys in the Tuesday night poker group, and presto, the show is on. It's all legal – they joke around, but nothing that challenges the penal code.'

'How much does that run the poker buddies?'

'Two hundred. Sixty goes to the messengers, split fifty-fifty. Plus tips.'

I did some quick mental arithmetic. Working half-time Nona could have pulled in a hundred dollars a day or more. Big bucks for a country girl barely out of her teens.

'What if the client is willing to pay more to see more?' I asked.

She looked sharply at me. 'I was wondering if you talked. Like I said before, the messengers are free to do what they want on their own time. Once the skit is over, it's their own time. You like jazz?'

'Good jazz?' I answered.

'Me, too. Like Miles and Coltrane and Bird. Know what makes them great? They know how to improvise. Far be it from me to discourage improvisation.'

She took out another Sherman and lit it from the one smouldering in her mouth.

'That's all she did, huh?' asked Milo. 'Skits.'

'She could've done more – I had plans for her. Movies, magazine layouts.' The meaty face creased into a smile. 'She was cooperative – took off her clothes without batting an eye. They must raise 'em wild in the country.' She rolled the cigarette between stubby fingers. 'Yeah, I had plans but she split on me.

91

Worked a week and – ' She snapped her fingers – 'poof.'

'Any word where she was going?'

'Not a hint. And I didn't ask. This is no surrogate family. It's a business. I don't play mommy and I don't want to be treated like one. Skin comes and skin goes – this city's full of perfect bodies who think their buns are gonna make 'em rich. Some learn faster than others. High volume, high turnover. Still,' she admitted, 'that redhead had something.'

'Anyone else who'd know anything about her?'

'Can't think of anyone. She kept to herself.'

'What about the guys she messengered with?'

'Guy. Singular. She was only here a week. I don't remember his name offhand, and I'm not gonna comb through the files to find it. You guys have just been handed a big freebie.' She pointed to the file. 'You can even keep it, okay?'

'Tax your memory,' pressed Milo. 'It's not like it's a big deal – how many studs do you have in your stable?'

'You'd be surprised,' she said, stroking the marble desktop. 'Meeting adjourned.'

'Listen,' he persisted, 'you've been minimally helpful but it doesn't make you Suzy Citizen. It's hot outside, you've got great air conditioning in here, a fantastic view. Why sweat it at the station, waiting who knows how long for your lawyer to show up?' He held out his hands, palms up, and gave her a boyish grin. 'Want to try again?'

The muddy eyes narrowed and her face turned nastily porcine. She pressed a button and Leon materialized.

'Who was the guy teamed up with that redhead, Swope?'

'Doug,' he said without hesitation.

'Last night,' she snapped.

92

'Carmichael. Douglas Carmichael.'

Turning to us: 'Okay?'

'The file.' Milo held out his hand.

'Get it.' She ordered and the Jamaican fetched. 'Let them look at it.'

Milo took the folder from him and we walked to the door.

'Hey, wait a minute!' she protested hoarsely. 'That's an active one. You can't take it!'

'I'll make a Xerox, mail you back the original.'

She started to argue then stopped midsentence. As we left I could hear her screaming at Leon.

8

ACCORDING TO his file, Doug Carmichael lived in the upscale part of Venice, near the Marina. Milo had me call him from a phone booth near Bundy while he used the radio to find out if anything had come in on the Swopes.

A phone machine answered at Carmichael's. Classical guitar music played in the background while a rich baritone said, 'Hi, this is Doug,' and strove to convince me that receipt of my message was *really* important for his emotional well-being. I waited for the beep, told him it was *really* important to call Detective Sturgis at West L.A. Division, and left Milo's number.

I got back in the car and found Milo with his eyes closed, head tilted back against the seat.

'Anything?' he asked.

'I got a machine.'

94

'Figures. Zilch from this end, too. No Swopes spotted from here to San Ysidro.' He yawned and growled and started up the Matador. 'Moving right along,' he mumbled, steering into the broth of westbound traffic, 'I haven't eaten since six. Early dinner or late lunch, take your pick.'

We were a couple of miles from the ocean but a mild easterly wind was blowing and it wafted a hint of brine our way. 'How about fish?'

'Righto.'

He drove to a tiny place on Ocean at the mouth of the pier that resembles a thirties diner. Some nights during the dinner hour it's hard to find a parking space in the back lot among all the Rolls, Mercedes, and Jags. They don't take reservations or plastic, but people who know seafood are willing to wait and don't mind paying with real money. At lunch it's significantly more relaxed and we were seated at a corner table immediately.

Milo drank two lemonades, which they squeeze fresh and serve unsweetened, and I nursed a Grolsch.

'Trying to cut down,' he explained, holding up his glass. 'Rick's been on my case. Preaching and showing me slides of what it does to the liver.'

'That's good. You were hitting it pretty hard for a while. Maybe we'll have you around a little longer.'

He grunted.

The waiter, a cheerful Hispanic, informed us that there'd been a huge albacore run and a prime load had come up from San Diego that morning. We both ordered some and shortly were feasting on huge grilled steaks of the white tuna, baked potatoes, steamed zucchini, and chunks of sourdough bread.

Milo devoured half his meal, took a long swallow of lemonade, and gazed out the window. A chrome sliver of ocean was visible above the rooftops of the

95

ramshackle buildings that hid in the shadow of the sagging pier.

'So how you been, pal?' he asked.

'Not bad.'

'What do you hear from Robin?'

'I got a card a few days ago. The Ginza at night. They're wining and dining her. Apparently it's the first time they've entertained a woman that way.'

'What is it they're after, exactly?' he asked.

'She designed a guitar for Rockin' Billy Orleans and he played it onstage in Madison Square Garden. The music trades interviewed him after the concert and he raved about the instrument and the fantastic female luthier who'd created it. The U.S. rep for a Japanese conglomerate picked up on it and sent it to his bosses. They decided it was worth mass-producing as a Billy Orleans model and invited her over there to talk about it.'

'Maybe she'll end up supporting you, huh?'

'Maybe,' I said glumly and signalled the waiter for another beer.

'I see you're real overjoyed about it.'

'I'm happy for her,' I said quickly. 'It's the big break she's been waiting for. It's just that I miss her like crazy, Milo. It's the longest we've been apart and I've lost my taste for solitude.'

'That all of it?' he asked, picking up his fork.

I looked up sharply. 'What else?'

'Well,' he said, between mouthfuls, 'I may be totally off base here, Doctor, but it seems to me that this Japanese thing puts a new perspective on your – pardon the expression – *relationship*.'

'How so?'

'Like for the past couple of years, you've been the one with the bread, right? She makes a living, but the life the two of you've been leading – Maui, theatre tickets, that incredible garden – who pays for it?'

96

'I don't get the point,' I said, annoyed.

'The point is that despite your pretending it ain't so, you guys have had a traditional setup. Now she's got the chance to become a big shot and it could all change.'

'I can handle it.'

'Sure you can. Forget I brought it up.'

'Consider it forgotten.' I looked down at my plate. All of a sudden my appetite was gone. I pushed the food away and fixed my gaze on a flock of gulls raiding the pier for bait scraps. 'You insightful bastard,' I said. 'Sometimes you're spooky.'

He reached across the table and patted my shoulder. 'Hey, you're not a very subtle guy. Everything registers on that lean and hungry face.'

I rested my chin in my hands. 'Things were going along so nice and simple. She kept the studio after she moved in, we prided ourselves on giving each other room to move. Lately we'd started talking marriage, babies. It was great, both of us moving at the same pace, mutual decisions. Now,' I shrugged, 'who knows?' I took a long swallow of the Dutch brew. 'I'll tell you, Milo, they don't cover it in the psych books, but there's such a thing as the paternal urge, and at thirty-five I'm feeling it.'

'I know,' he said. 'I've felt it, too.'

My stare was involuntary.

'Don't look so surprised. Just because it's never gonna happen doesn't mean I don't think about it.'

'You never can tell. They're getting pretty liberal.'

He loosened his belt a notch and buttered a piece of bread. 'Not *that* liberal.' He laughed. 'Besides, Rick and I are not equipped for motherhood or whatever you wanna call it. Can't you just see it – me shopping at Toys "Я" Us and Dr. Fastidious changing diapers?'

We shared a good laugh over that.

'Anyway,' he said, 'I didn't mean to bring up a sore point, but it's something you're gonna have to deal with. I did. For most of my life I made my own way. My parents didn't give me squat. I've been working at one dodge or another since eleven, Alex. Paper routes, tutoring, picking pears, construction, a little time out for the M.A., then Saigon and the force. You don't get rich in Homicide, but a single guy can get by nicely. I was lonely as hell but my needs were met. After I met Rick and we started living together, it all changed. You remember my old Fiat – piece of shit that it was. I never drove anything but garbage and unmarkeds. Now we tool around in that Porsche like a pair of coke dealers. And the house – no way I could ever have had a place like that on my salary. He goes shopping at Carrols or Giorgio, picks me up a shirt or tie. I'm not a – kept man, but my lifestyle has changed. For the better, but that hasn't made it easy to accept. Surgeons make more than cops, always have, always will, and I've finally accomodated myself to it. Makes you stop and think about what women go through, huh?'

'Yup.' I wondered if Robin had been faced with the type of adjustment he'd described. Had there been a struggle that I'd been too insensitive to notice?'

'In the long run,' he said, 'it's better if both parties feel like adults, don't you think?'

'What I think, Milo, is that you're an amazing guy.'

He hid his embarrassment behind the menu. 'If I remember correctly the ice cream is good, right?'

'Right.'

Over dessert he had me tell him more about Woody Swope and childhood cancer. He was shocked, like most people, that it was the second most common cause of death in children; only accidents kill more.

The mechanics of the Laminar Airflow rooms

particularly fascinated him and he asked me detailed analytical questions until my fund of answers was exhausted.

'Months in that plastic box,' he said, troubled. 'And they don't freak out?'

'Not if it's handled right. You've got to orient the child to time and space, encourage the family to spend as much time there as possible. You sterilize favourite toys and clothes and bring them in, provide lots of stimulation. The key is to minimize the difference between home and hospital – there's always going to be some, but you can buffer it.'

'Interesting. You know what I'm flashing on, don't you?'

'What's that?'

'AIDS. Same principle, right? Lowered resistance to infection.'

'Similar but not identical,' I said. 'The laminar airflow filters out bacteria and fungi in order to protect the kids during treatment. But the loss of immunity is temporary – after chemotherapy's over, their systems rebound. AIDS is permanent and AIDS victims have other problems – Kaposi's Sarcoma, viral infections. The modules might protect them for a while, but not indefinitely.'

'Yeah, but you gotta admit, it's a hell of an image: Santa Monica Boulevard lined with thousands of plastic cubes, each one with some poor guy wasting away inside. You could charge admission, raise enough money to find a cure.'

He let out a bitter laugh.

'The wages of sin,' he shook his head. 'Enough to make you a Puritan. I hear the horror stories and thank God I'm monogamous. Rick's been fielding a lot of shit from both sides. Last week a patient came to the E.R. with a mangled arm – bar fight – and glommed onto the fact that Rick was gay. Probably a

99

paranoid guess, because Rick doesn't exactly swish, but he didn't deny it when this turkey demanded to know if they were giving him a faggot doctor. The guy refused to let Rick touch him, screamed about AIDS – no matter that he's bleeding all over the place. So Rick walked away. But the rest of the docs were up to their elbows in shit – Saturday night and they were wheeling 'em in one after the other. It threw the whole system out of whack. Everyone ended up getting pissed at Rick. He was a goddamn leper for the rest of the shift.'

'Poor guy.'

'Poor guy is right. The man was top of his class, chief resident at Stanford, and he's taking this kind of crap? He came home in a *dark* mood. The hell of it is, the night before, *he* was telling *me* that working with gay patients – especially the ones who came in bleeding – was making him antsy. I did heavy-duty therapy that night, Alex.'

He spooned the last bit of ice cream into his mouth.

'Heavy-duty,' he repeated and brushed the hair out of his eyes. 'But hey, that's what love's all about, right?'

9

MILO BEGGED off the case during the drive back to the Sea Breeze Motel.

'I can't take it any further,' he said apologetically. 'All we've got at this point is a missing persons squeal, and that's stretching it.'

'I know. Thanks for coming down.'

'No big deal. It was a break from routine. Just so happens I've got a particularly cruddy routine right now. Gang shooting – two *cholos* blown away – liquor store clerk ripped with a broken bottle, and a real sweetheart – a rapist who shits on his victims' abdomens when he's through with them. We know he's attacked at least seven women. The last one ended up more than defiled.'

'Jesus.'

'Jesus won't forgive this creep.' He frowned and

101

turned on Sawtelle toward Pico. 'Each year I tell myself I've witnessed the depths of depravity and each year the scumbags out there prove me wrong. Maybe I should have taken the exam.'

Fifteen months ago he and I had exposed a prominent orphanage as a brothel catering to paedophiles, solving a handful of murders in the process. He'd been a hero and had been invited to take the lieutenant's exam. There was no doubt he'd have passed, because he's brilliant, and the brass had let him know the city was ready for a gay loot as long as he didn't flaunt it. He'd debated it internally for a long time before turning it down.

'No way, Milo. You would have been miserable. Think back to what you told me.'

'What's that?'

'I didn't give up Walt Whitman to push paper.'

He chuckled. 'Yeah, that's right.'

Prior to his hitch in Vietnam, Milo had been enrolled in the graduate programme in American Lit. at Indiana U., contemplating life as a teacher, hoping the academic world would be a setting where his sexual preferences would be tolerated. He'd gotten as far as an M.A. and then the war had turned him into a policeman.

'Just imagine,' I reminded him, 'endless meetings with desk jockeys, considering the political implications of taking a leak, no contact with the streets.'

He held up a hand and feigned suffering.

'Enough, I'm gonna puke.'

'Just a little aversive therapy.'

He pulled the Matador into the motel lot. The sky had darkened in anticipation of twilight and the Sea Breeze benefited from it aesthetically. Take away the sunlight and the place looked almost habitable.

The office was brightly lit and the Iranian clerk was visible behind the counter, reading. My Seville was

102

the lone occupant of the lot. The half-empty pool looked like a crater.

Milo stopped the car and let the engine idle.

'You understand about my stepping out of this?'

'Of course. No homicide, no homicide detective.'

'They'll probably be back for the car. I had it impounded so they'll have to check in to get it back. They do, I'll call you and give you a chance to talk to them. Even if they don't show, we'll probably find out they're back home, no harm done.'

He realized what he'd said and grimaced.

'Shit. Where's my head? The kid.'

'He could be all right. Maybe they've taken him to another hospital.' I wanted to sound hopeful but memories – the pain on Woody's face, the bloodstain on the motel carpet – eroded my faith in a happy ending.

'If they don't treat him that's it, right?'

I nodded.

He stared out the windshield. 'That's one kind of murder I've never dealt with.'

Raoul had said the same thing in different words. I told him so.

'And this Melendez-Lynch doesn't want to go the legal route?'

'He was trying to avoid it. It may end up in court yet.'

He gave his big head a shake and placed a hand on my shoulder. 'I'll keep my ears open. Anything comes up I'll let you know.'

'I'd appreciate it. And thanks for everything, Milo.'

'It was nothing. Literally.' We shook hands. 'Say hello to the entrepreneur when she gets back.'

'Will do. The best to Rick.'

I got out of the car. The Matador's headlights striped the gravel as Milo swung out of the lot. The

103

truncated patter of the radio dispatcher created a punk rock concerto that hung in the air after he was gone.

I drove north to Sunset, planning to turn off at Beverly Glen and head home. Then I remembered that the house would be empty. Talking to Milo about Robin had opened a few wounds and I didn't want to be alone with my thoughts. I realized that Raoul knew nothing about what we'd found at the Sea Breeze, and decided now was as good a time as any to tell him.

He was hunched over his desk scrawling notations on the draft of a research paper. I knocked lightly on the open door.

'Alex!' He rose to greet me. 'How did it go? Did you convince them?'

I recounted what we'd found.

'Oh my God!' He slumped in his chair. 'This is unbelievable. Unbelievable.' He exhaled, compressed his jowls with his hands, picked up a pencil and rolled it up and down the surface of the desk.

'Was there much blood?'

'One stain about six inches wide.'

'Not enough for a bleed-out,' he muttered to himself. 'No other fluids? No bile, no vomitus?'

'I didn't see any. It was hard to tell. The place was a shambles.'

'A barbaric rite, no doubt. I told you, Alex, they are madmen, those damned Touchers! To steal a child and then to run amok like that! Holism is nothing more than a cover for anarchy and nihilism!'

He was jumping to conclusions in quantum leaps but I had neither the desire nor the energy to argue with him.

'The police, what did they do?'

'The detective who ran the show is a friend of mine.

104

He came down as a favour. There's an All Points Bulletin out on the family, the sheriff in La Vista has been notified to watch for them. They did a crime scene analysis and filed a report. That's it. Unless you decide to push it.'

'Your friend – is he discreet?'

'Very.'

'Good. We can't afford a media side show. Have you ever talked to the press? They are idiots, Alex, and vultures! The blondes from the television stations are the worst. Vapid, with paste-on smiles, always trying to trick you into making outrageous statements. Barely a week goes by that one of them doesn't attempt to get me to say that the cure for cancer is just around the corner. They want instant information, immediate gratification. Can you imagine what they'll do with something like this?'

He'd gone quickly from defeatism to rage and the excess energy propelled him out of his chair. He traversed the length of the office with short nervous steps, pounding his fist into his hand, swerved to avoid the piles of books and manuscripts, walked back to the desk, and cursed in Spanish.

'Do you think I should go to court, Alex?'

'It's a tough question. You need to decide if going public will help the boy. Have you done it before?'

'Once. Last year we had a little girl who needed transfusions. The family were Jehovah's Witnesses and we had to get an injunction to give her blood. But that was different. The parents weren't fighting us. Their attitude was, our beliefs don't allow us to give you permission, but if we're forced to comply we will. They *wanted* to save their child, Alex, and were happy when we took the responsibility away from them. That child is alive today and *thriving*. The Swope boy should be thriving, too, not dying in the back room of some scabrous voodoo den.'

He thrust his hand into the pocket of his white coat, removed a packet of saltine crackers, tore open the plastic, and nibbled on the crackers until they were consumed. After brushing crumbs out of his moustache he continued.

'Even in the Witness case the media tried to make a cause célèbre of it, implying that we were coercing the family. One of the stations sent around a moron masquerading as a medical reporter to interview me – probably one of those fellows who wanted to be a doctor but flunked his science courses. He swaggered in with a little tape recorder and addressed me by my *first name*, Alex! As if we were buddies! I dismissed him and he made the "no comment" sound like concealment of guilt. Fortunately the parents took our advice and refused to talk to them, too. At that point the so-called *controversy* died a quick death – no carrion, the vultures go elsewhere.'

The door leading to the lab opened and a young woman clutching a clipboard entered the office. She had light brown hair cut in a page boy, round eyes that uncannily matched the hair, pinched features, and a petulant mouth. The hand holding the clipboard was pale, and her nails were gnawed to the quick. She wore a lab coat that reached below her knees and crêpe-soled flats on her feet.

She looked through me to Raoul and said, 'There's something you should see. Could be exciting.' The lack of inflection in her voice belied the content of her message.

Raoul got up. 'Is it the new membrane, Helen?'

'Yes.'

'Wonderful.' He looked as if he were going to hug her then stopped suddenly, remembering my presence. Clearing his throat, he introduced us: 'Alex, meet a fellow Ph.D., Dr. Helen Holroyd.'

We exchanged the most cursory of pleasantries.

106

She edged closer to Raoul, a proprietary gleam in the beige eyes. He fought, unsuccessfully, to erase the naughty boy look from his face.

The two of them were trying so hard to look platonic that for the first time all day I felt like smiling. They were sleeping together and it was supposed to be a secret. Without a doubt everyone in the department knew about it.

'I've got to get going,' I said.

'Yes, I understand. Thank you for everything. I may call you to discuss this further. In the meantime, send your bill to my secretary.'

As I walked out the door they were gazing into each other's eyes and discussing the wonders of osmotic equilibrium.

On the way out I stopped in the hospital cafeteria for a cup of coffee. It was after seven and the dining room was sparsely populated. A tall Mexican man wearing a hair net and blue scrubs ran a dry mop over the floor. A trio of nurses laughed and ate doughnuts. I lidded the coffee and was preparing to leave when movement fluttered in the corner of my eye.

It was Valcroix and he was waving me over. I walked to his table.

'Care to join me?'

'All right.' I put down my cup and took a chair facing him. The remains of a giant salad sat on his tray along with two glasses of water. He used his fork to move a tumbleweed of alfalfa sprouts around the bowl.

He'd traded his psychedelic sport shirt for a black Grateful Dead T-shirt and had tossed his white coat over the chair next to him. From up close I could see that the long hair was thinning on top. He needed a shave but his beard growth was sparse, spotting only the moustache and the chin areas. The drooping face

107

had been worked over by a bad cold; he sniffled, red-nosed and bleary-eyed.

'Any news on the Swopes?' he asked.

I was tired of telling the story but he'd been their doctor and deserved to know. I gave him a brief summary.

He listened with equanimity, no emotion registered in the hooded eyes. When I was finished he coughed and dabbed at his nose with a napkin.

'For some reason I feel an urge to proclaim my innocence to you,' he said.

'That's hardly necessary,' I assured him. I drank some coffee and put it down quickly, having forgotten how awful it was.

His eyes took on a faraway look and for a moment I thought he was meditating, retreating to an internal world as he'd done during Raoul's harangue. I found my attention wandering.

'I know Melendez-Lynch blames me for this. He's blamed me for everything that's gone wrong in the department since I began my fellowship. Was he that way when you worked with him?'

'Let's just say it took a while to develop a good working relationship.'

He nodded solemnly, picked some strands from the ball of sprouts and chewed on them.

'Why do you think they ran away?' I asked him.

He shrugged. 'I have no idea.'

'No insights at all?'

'None. Why should I have, any more than anyone else?'

'I was under the impression they related well to you.'

'Who told you that?'

'Raoul.'

'He wouldn't recognize relating if it bit him in the ass.'

108

'He felt you'd developed especially good rapport with the mother.'

His hands were scrubbed and pink. They tightened around the salad fork.

'I was a nurse before I became a doctor,' he said.

'Interesting.'

'Is it?'

'Nurses are always complaining about their lack of status and money and threatening to quit and go to med school. You're the first I've met who actually did it.'

'Nurses gripe because their lot in life is shit. But there are insights to be learned at the bottom of the ladder. Like the value of talking to patients and families. I did it as a nurse but now that I'm a doc it makes me a deviate. What's pathetic is that it's viewed as sufficiently deviant to be noticed. Rapport? Hell, no. I barely knew them. Sure I spoke to the mother. I was sticking her son every day with needles, puncturing his bone and sucking out marrow. How could I not speak to her?'

He gazed into his salad bowl.

'Melendez-Lynch can't understand that, my wanting to come across as a human being instead of some white-coated technocrat. He didn't bother to get to know the Swopes but it doesn't occur to him that his remoteness has anything to do with their – defection. I extended myself, so I'm the goat.' He sniffed, wiped his nose, and drained one of the water glasses. 'What's the use of dissecting it? They're gone.'

I remembered Milo's conjecture about the abandoned car.

'They may be back,' I said.

'Be serious, man. They see themselves as having escaped to freedom. No way.'

'Freedom's going to sour pretty quickly when the

109

disease gets out of control.'

'The fact is,' he said, 'they hated everything about this place. The noise, the lack of privacy, even the sterility. You worked in Laminar Flow, right?'

'Three years.'

'Then you know the kind of food the kids in there get – processed and overcooked and dead.'

It was true. To a patient without normal immunity a fresh fruit or vegetable is a potential medium for lethal microbes, a glass of milk a breeding pond for lactobacillus. Consequently, everything the kids in the plastic rooms ate was processed to begin with, then heated and sterilized, sometimes to the point where no nutrients remained.

'*We* understand the concept,' he said, 'but lots of parents have difficulty grasping why this horribly sick kid can have his fill of cola and potato chips and all kinds of junk while carrots are out. It goes against the grain.'

'I know,' I said, 'but most people accept it pretty quickly because their child's life is at stake. Why not the Swopes?'

'They're country folk. They come from a place where the air is clean and people grow their own food. They see the city as a poisonous place. The father used to rail on about how bad the air was. "You're breathing sewage" he'd tell me every time I saw him. He had a thing for clean air and natural foods. For how healthy it was back home.'

'Not healthy enough,' I said.

'No, not healthy enough. How's that for a frontal assault on a belief system?' He gave a mournful look. 'Isn't there a term in psych for when it all comes tumbling down like that?'

'Cognitive dissonance.'

'Whatever. Tell me,' he leaned forward, 'what do people do when they're in that state?'

110

'Sometimes change their beliefs, sometimes distort reality to fit those beliefs.'

He leaned back, ran his hands through his hair and smiled.

'Need I say more?'

I shook my head and tried the coffee again. It had gotten colder, but no better.

'I keep hearing about the father,' I said. 'The mother sounds like his shadow.'

'Far from it. If anything, she was the tougher of the two. It's just that she was quiet. She let him run off at the mouth while she stayed with Woody, doing what needed to be done.'

'Could she have been behind their leaving?'

'I don't know,' he said. 'All I'm saying is she was a strong woman, not some cardboard cutout.'

'What about the sister? Beverly said there was no love lost between her and her parents.'

'I wouldn't know about that. She wasn't around much, kept to herself when she was.'

He wiped his nose and stood.

'I don't like to gossip,' he said. 'I've indulged in too much of it already.'

He snatched up his white coat, flung it over his shoulder, turned his back and left me sitting there. I watched him walk away, lips moving, as if in silent prayer.

It was after eight by the time I reached Beverly Glen. My house sits atop an old bridle path forgotten by the city. There are no streetlights and the road is serpentine, but I know every twist by heart and drove home by sense of touch. In the mailbox was a love letter from Robin. I got high on it for a while but after the fourth reading, a hazy sense of sadness set in.

It was too late to feed the koi so I took a hot bath, towelled off, put on my ratty yellow robe, and carried

111

a brandy into the small library off the bedroom. I finished writing a couple of overdue forensic reports then settled in an old chair and went through the stack of books I'd promised myself to read

The first volume I grabbed was a collection of Diane Arbus photographs but the unforgiving portraits of dwarfs, derelicts, and other walking wounded made me more depressed. The next couple of choices were no better so I went out on the deck with my guitar, sat looking at the stars, and forced myself to play in a major key.

10

THE NEXT morning I went out on the terrace to get the paper and saw it lying there, sluglike and bloated.

It was a dead rat. A crude noose of hemp had been tied around its neck. Its lifeless eyes were open and clouded, its fur matted and greasy. A pair of disturbingly humanoid forepaws were frozen in supplication. The half-open mouth revealed frontal incisors the colour of canned corn.

Underneath the corpse was a piece of paper. I used the *Times* to push the rodent away – it resisted, sticking, then slid like a puck to the edge of the terrace.

It was straight out of an old gangster movie: letters had been cut out of a magazine and pasted up to read:

HERES TO YOU MONEYCHASER HEADSHRINK

I'd probably have figured it out anyway, but that made it a cinch.

Sacrificing the classified section to the task, I wrapped up the rat and carried it down to the garbage. Then I went inside and got on the phone.

Mal Worthy's secretary had a secretary and I had to be assertive with both of them to get through to him.

Before I could speak he said, 'I know, I got one, too. What colour was yours?'

'Brownish grey, with a noose around its scrawny little neck.'

'Count yourself lucky. Mine came decapitated, in a box. I almost lost a damn good mailgirl because of it. She's still washing her hands. Daschoff's was ratburger.'

He was trying to make light of it, but sounded shaken.

'I knew the guy was a sicko,' he said.

'How'd he find out where I live?'

'Your address on your resumé?'

'Oh shit. What did the wife get?'

'Nothing. Does that make sense?'

'Forget making sense. What can we do about it?'

'I've already begun drafting a restraining order keeping him a thousand yards from any of us. But to be honest, there's no way to prevent him from defying it. If he gets caught at it, that's another story, but we don't want it to get that far, do we?'

'Not too comforting, Malcolm.'

'That's democracy, my friend.' He paused. 'This taped?'

'Of course not.'

'Just checking. There is another option, but it would be too risky before the property settlement has been completed.'

'What's that?'

114

'For five hundred dollars I can have him sufficiently damaged so he'll never be able to piss without
crying.'

'Democracy, huh?'

He laughed.

'Free enterprise. Fee for service. Anyway, it's just
an option.'

'Don't exercise it, Mal.'

'Relax, Alex. Just theorizing.'

'What about the police?'

'Forget it. We have no evidence it was him. I mean
we both know it but there's no proof, right? And
they're not going to fingerprint a rat because sending
rodents to your loved ones is no felony. Maybe,' he
laughed, 'we could get Animal Regulation on it. A
stern lecture and a night at the pound?'

'Wouldn't they at least go out and talk to him?'

'Not with the workload they've got. If it had been
more explicit, something that constituted a threat,
maybe. ''Here's to You Motherfucking Shyster'' won't
do, I'm afraid – the cops feel the same way he does
about lawyers. I'm going to file a report just for the
record, but don't count on help from the blue guys.'

'I know someone on the force.'

'Metermaids don't carry much weight, fella.'

'How about detectives?'

'That's different. Give him a call. You want me to
talk to him, I will.'

'I'll handle it.'

'Great. Let me know how it goes. And Alex – sorry
for the hassle.' He sounded eager to get off the phone.
At three and a half bucks a minute it doesn't pay to
give it away free for any length of time.

'One more thing, Mal.'

'What's that?'

'Call the judge. If she hasn't gotten a care package
yet, warn her she may.'

'I've already called her bailiff. Scratch up a few more brownie points for our side.'

'Describe this asshole as precisely as you can,' said Milo.

'My size almost exactly. Say five eleven, one seventy-five. Raw-boned, muscles. Long face, a reddish tan like construction workers get, busted nose, big jaw. Wears Indian jewellery – two rings, one on each hand. A scorpion and a snake. A couple of tattoos on the left arm. Bad dresser.'

'Eye colour?'

'Brown. Bloodshot. A binge drinker. Brown hair combed back, greasy kid stuff.'

'Sounds like a shitkicker.'

'Exactly.'

'And this Bedabye Motel's where he lives?'

'As of a couple of days ago. He may be living in his truck for all I know.'

'I know a couple of guys in Foothill Division. If I can get one of them in particular to go down and talk to this Moody, your troubles'll be over. Guy name of Fordebrand. Has the worse breath you've ever smelled. Five minutes of face to face with him and the asshole will *repent*.'

I laughed but my heart wasn't in it.

'He got to you, huh?'

'I've had better mornings.'

'If you're spooked and wanna stay at my place, feel free.'

'Thanks, but I'll be okay.'

'If you change your mind, let me know. Meanwhile, be careful. He may be just an asshole and a wiseguy, but I don't have to tell you about crazies. Keep your eyes open, pal.'

I spent most of the day doing mundane things and

116

appearing outwardly relaxed. But I was in what I call my karate state - a heightened level of consciousness typified by perceptual vigilance. The senses are finely tuned to a point, just short of paranoia, where looking over one's shoulder at frequent intervals seems perfectly normal.

To get that way I avoid alcohol and heavy foods, do limbering exercises and practice katas - karate dances - until exhausted. Then I relax with a half hour of self-hypnosis and auto-suggest hyper-alertness.

I learned it from my martial arts instructor, a Czech Jew named Jaroslav, who had honed his self-preservation skills fleeing the Nazis. I sought his advice during the first weeks after the Casa de Los Ninos affair, when the wires in my jaw made me feel helpless and nightmares were frequent visitors. The regimen he taught me had helped me mend where it counted - in my head.

I was ready, I told myself, for anything Richard Moody had in store.

I was dressing to go out for dinner when the service called.

'Good evening, Dr. D., it's Kathy.'

'Hi, Kathy.'

'Sorry to bother you but I've got a Beverly Lucas on the line. She says it's an emergency.'

'No problem. Put her on, please.'

'Okay. Have a nice night, Doc.'

'You too.'

The phone hissed as the lines connected.

'Bev?'

'Alex? I've got to talk t'you.'

There was loud music in the background - synthesized drums, screaming guitars, and a heart-stopping bass. I could hardly hear her.

'What's up?'

'Can't talk about it here – using the bar phone. Are you busy right now?'

'No. Where are you calling from?'

'The Unicorn. In Westwood. Please I need to talk to you.'

She sounded on edge but it was hard to tell with all that noise. I knew the place, a combination bistro-discotheque (bisco?) that catered to the upscale singles crowd. Once Robin and I had stopped in for a bite after a movie but had left quickly, finding the ambience too nakedly predatory.

'I was just about to have dinner,' I said. 'Want to meet somewhere?'

'How 'bout right here? I'll put my name down for a table and it'll be ready when you get here.'

Dinner at the Unicorn wasn't an appealing prospect – the noise level seemed likely to curdle the gastric juices – but I told her I'd be there in fifteen minutes.

Traffic in the Village was heavy and I was late getting there. The Unicorn was a narcissist's paradise, mirrored on every surface except the floor. Hanging Boston ferns, half a dozen fake Tiffany lamps, and some brass and wood trim had been tossed in, but the mirrors were the essence of the place.

To the right was a smallish restaurant, twenty tables draped with parrot green damask, to the left a glassed-in disco where couples boogied to a live band, the glass shimmying with the backbeat. In between was the lounge. Even the bar was covered with reflective glass, its base a display of trendy footwear.

The lounge was dim and packed with bodies. I edged my way through the throng, surrounded by laughing faces in triplicate, quadruplicate, unsure what was real, what was illusion. The place was a damned funhouse.

She was sitting at the bar next to a chesty guy in a

118

body shirt. He alternated between trying to make time with her, guzzling light beer, and visually trawling the crowd for a more hopeful prospect. She nodded from time to time but was clearly preoccupied.

I elbowed my way next to her. She was staring at a tall glass half-filled with foamy pink liquid, lots of candied fruit, and a paper parasol. One hand twirled the parasol.

'Alex.' She wore a lemon-coloured Danskin top and matching satin jogging shorts. Her legs were sheathed from ankle to knee with yellow and white warmers that matched her running shoes. She had on lots of makeup and plenty of jewellery – at work she'd always been conservative with both. A glittery sweatband circled her forehead. 'Thanks for comin'.' She leaned over and kissed me on the mouth. Her lips were warm. Body Shirt got up and left.

'Bet that table's ready,' she said.

'Let's check.' I took her arm and we wedged through waves of flesh. Plenty of male eyes followed her exit but she didn't seem to notice.

There was a bit of confusion because she'd given the maitre d' the name 'Luke' and hadn't told me, but we got it straightened out and were seated in a corner table under a colossal Creeping Charlie.

'Damn,' she said, 'left my zinger at the bar.'

'How about some coffee?'

She pouted.

'You think I'm drunk or somethin'?'

She was talking clearly and moving normally. Only her eyes gave her away, as they focused and unfocused in rapid succession.

I smiled and shrugged.

'Playing it safe, huh?' She laughed.

I called for the waiter and ordered coffee for myself. She had a glass of white wine. It didn't seem to affect

119

her. She was maintaining as only a heavy drinker can.

A while later the waiter returned. She asked me to order first while she scanned the menu. I kept it simple, choosing a small spinach salad and broiled chicken, because trendy places usually have lousy food and I wanted something they couldn't ruin too easily.

She continued to study the menu as if it were a textbook, then looked up brightly.

'I'll have an artichoke,' she said.

'Hot or cold, ma'am?'

'Uh, cold.'

The waiter wrote it down and looked at her expectantly. When she didn't say anything he asked if that was all.

'Uh huh.'

He left, shaking his head.

'I eat artichokes a lot because when you run you lose sodium and artichokes have lots of sodium.'

'Uh huh.'

'For dessert I'll have something with bananas because bananas are high in potassium. When you up your sodium you have to up your potassium to put your body in balance.'

I'd always seen her as a level-headed young lady, if a bit too hard on herself and prone to self-punishment. The dizzy broad across the table was a stranger.

She talked about running marathons until the food came. When the artichoke was set down before her she stared at it and began picking delicately at the leaves.

My food was unpalatable – the salad gritty, the chicken arid. I played with it to avoid eating.

When she'd dismantled and polished off the artichoke and seemed settled, I asked her what she wanted to talk about.

120

'This is very difficult, Alex.'

'You don't have to tell me if you don't want to.'

'I feel like a – traitor.'

'Against whom?'

'Shit.' She looked everywhere but at me. 'It's probably not even important and I'm just shooting off my mouth for nothing but I keep thinking about Woody and wondering how long it'll be before the metastases start popping up – if they haven't already – and I want to *do* something, to stop feeling so damned helpless.'

I nodded and waited. She winced.

'Augie Valcroix knew the couple from the Touch who came to visit the Swopes,' she said.

'How do you know?'

'I saw him talking to them, calling them by name, and I asked him about it. He said he visited the place once, thought it was nice. Peaceful.'

'Did he say why?'

'Just that he was interested in alternative lifestyles. I know that's true because in the past he'd spoken of checking out other groups – Scientologists, Lifespring, a Buddhist place in Santa Barbara. He's Canadian, thinks the whole California thing is fascinating.'

'Did you ever detect any collusion between them?'

'None. Just that they knew each other.'

'You said he used their names. Do you remember them?'

'I think he called the guy Gary or Barry. I never heard the woman's name. You don't really think this was some sort of conspiracy, do you?'

'Who knows?'

She squirmed as if her clothes were too tight, caught the waiter's eye, and ordered a banana liqueur. She sipped it slowly trying to appear relaxed, but she was jumpy and ill-at-ease.

121

She put the glass down with a furtive look in her eyes.

'Is there anything else, Bev?'

She nodded, embarrassed. When she spoke it was barely a whisper.

'This is probably even less relevant but as long as I'm blabbing I might as well spill it all out. Augie and Nona Swope had a thing going. I'm not sure when it started. Not too long ago because the family was only in town a couple of weeks.' She fiddled with her napkin. 'God, I feel like such a shit. If it weren't for Woody I'd never have opened my mouth.'

'I know that.'

'I wanted to tell your cop friend about it right there, at the motel – he seemed nice enough – but I just couldn't. Then I got to thinking about it later and I couldn't let go of it. I mean, what if there was a way to help that little boy and I let it go by? But I still didn't want to go to the police. I figured if I told you, you'd know what to do with it.'

'You did the right thing.'

'I wish doing right didn't feel so wrong.' Her voice broke. 'I wish I could be sure that my telling you has any meaning.'

'All I can do is let Milo know. At this point he's not even convinced a crime's been committed. The only one who seems sure of that is Raoul.'

'*He's* always sure of everything,' she said angrily. 'Ready to assess blame at the drop of a hat. He dumps on everyone but Augie's been his favourite scapegoat since he got here.'

She dug the nails of one hand into the palm of the other. 'And now I've made things worse for him.'

'Not necessarily. Milo may brush it off completely or he may choose to talk to Valcroix. But he doesn't care what Raoul thinks. No one's going to get rail-roaded, Bev.'

That was meagre balm for her conscience.

'I still feel like a traitor. Augie's my friend.'

'Look at it this way, if Valcroix's sleeping with Nona had anything to do with this mess, you did a good deed. If not, he can endure a few questions. It's not like the guy's a total innocent.'

'What do you mean?'

'The way I hear it he makes a habit of sleeping with his patients' mothers. This time it was a sister, for variety. At the very least it's unethical.'

'That's so self-righteous,' she snapped, turning scarlet, 'so damned judgemental!'

I started to reply but before I knew what was happening she got up from the table, grabbed her purse, and ran out of the restaurant.

I pulled out my wallet threw down a twenty and went after her.

She was half-running, half-walking north on Westwood Boulevard, swinging her arms like a foot soldier, heading into the crush and commotion of the Village at night.

I ran, caught up, and took her arm. Her face was wet with tears.

'What the hell's going on, Bev?'

She didn't answer but let me walk with her. The Village seemed especially Felliniesque that evening, litter-strewn sidewalks clogged with street musicians, grim-faced college students, squealing packs of junior high kids wearing oversized clothes pocked with high-priced holes, empty-eyed bikers, gawking tourists from the exurbs, and assorted hangers-on.

We walked in silence all the way to the southern edge of the UCLA campus. Inside the grounds of the university the pandemonium and bright lights died and were replaced by tree-shadowed darkness and a silence so pure it was startling. Except for an occasional passing car, we were alone.

123

A hundred yards into the campus I got her to stop and sit on a bench at a shuttle stop. The buses had stopped running for the night and the lights near the stop had been turned off. She turned away and buried her face in her hands.

'Bev – '

'I must be going nuts,' she mumbled, 'running out like that.'

I tried to put my arm around her for comfort but she jerked away.

'No, I'm okay. Let me spit it out, once and for all.'

She sucked in her breath, bracing herself for an ordeal.

'Augie and I were – involved. It started pretty soon after he came to Western Peds. He seemed so different from the men I'd been meeting. Sensitive, adventurous. I thought it was serious. I allowed myself the luxury of romance and it turned to shit. When you talked about his sleeping around it brought back all that shit.

'I was a fool, Alex, because he never promised me anything, never lied to me or told me he was anything other than what he was. It was me. I chose to see him as some noble knight. Maybe he came along at a time when I was ready to believe anything, I don't know. We slept together for six months. Meanwhile he was making it with every woman he could find – nurses, lady docs, mothers.

'I know what you're thinking. He's an unethical creep. I doubt I can convince you of this, but he's not a bad man, just a weak one. He was always loving and gentle. And open. When I confronted him with the stories I was hearing he said sure, he was giving pleasure and receiving it in return. What could be wrong with that, especially with all the pain and suffering and death we had to deal with. He was so

124

convincing I didn't stop seeing him even then. It took me a long time to get my head straight.

'I thought I'd gotten over it until a week ago when I saw him with Nona. I was out on a date – a fix-up, a real disaster – at an intimate little Mexican place not far from the hospital. The two of them were across the room, tucked away in a dark little booth. I could barely see them. They were all over each other. Drinking margaritas and laughing. *Tongue-duelling*, for God's sake. Like a couple of reptiles.'

She stopped, caught her breath.

'It hurt bad, Alex. She was so confident, so beautiful. The jealousy went through me like a knife. I'd never felt that kind of jealousy before – I was *bleeding*. Their eyes were horribly orange from the candlelight. Two vampires. There I was, stuck with some dull creep, dying for the evening to be over, and they were just about fucking on the table. It was obscene.'

Her shoulders shook. She shivered and hugged herself.

'So you can see why I was so torn about telling anyone about it. I'd be seen as the woman scorned, doing it out of spite. That's a degrading role and I've been degraded enough for a lifetime.'

Her eyes implored me to understand.

'Everyone takes a bite out of me and I'm fucking disappearing, Alex. I want to forget him, her, everyone. But I can't. Because of that little boy.'

This time she accepted my comfort and put her head on my shoulder, her hand in mine.

'You've got to get some distance from it,' I said, 'so you can start to see straight again. He may have been gentle and "honest" in some perverse way but he's no hero. The guy's got problems and you're best off without him. He's a druggie, isn't he?'

'Yes. How'd you know that?'

I decided not to cite Raoul's suspicions. Mention of his name would set her off. Besides, I had suspicions of my own.

'I talked to him last night. He was sniffing the whole time. At first it looked like a cold but later I started wondering about coke.'

'He's into coke pretty heavily. Grass and downers, on the side. Sometimes speed when he's on call. He talked about dropping acid in med school but I don't think he does that anymore. He does booze, too. I started drinking heavily when I was with him and kept it up ever since. I know I have to stop.'

I gave her a squeeze.

'You deserve a lot better, hon.'

'It's nice to hear that,' she said in a small voice.

'I'm saying it because it's true. You're intelligent, you're attractive, and you have a good heart. That's why you're hurting so badly. Get the hell away from all the death and misery. It'll destroy you. I know.'

'Oh, Alex,' she sobbed into my shoulder, 'I'm so cold.'

I gave her my jacket. When the tears stopped I walked her back to her car.

11

NEITHER THE Swopes' disappearance nor Richard Moody's rat fell under Milo's jurisdiction. Out of friendship he'd helped me with both and I was reluctant to bother him so soon with the information on Valcroix.

But what Beverly had told me the night before was disturbing. As Raoul had claimed, the Canadian was unethical and a drunk, and his familiarity with the Touch visitors fleshed out the suspicion of a conspiracy to remove Woody Swope from treatment. I felt some obligation to let him know what was going on, but I didn't look forward to it because he was sure to flip out. Before the pyrotechnics began I wanted to consult a professional.

·Milo, bless his soul, sounded genuinely glad to hear from me.

'No sweat. I was gonna call you anyway. Fordebrand went out to the Bedabye to breathe on Moody but when he got there the asshole was gone. Left behind a room full of b.o. - it would have been a battle of the stinkers - and candy wrappers. Foothill will keep an eye out for him and I'll have the boys here do the same, but be careful. Also, I got a call back from that Carmichael character - the one who messengered with the Swope girl. Normally I might have just talked to him on the phone but this guy sounded *very* uptight. Like he's sitting on something. He's also got a record - busted for prostitution a couple of years ago. So I'm gonna head out and do a face to face. Now what's on your mind?'

'I'll go with you to Carmichaels and tell you in the car.'

He absorbed the information on Valcroix while speeding along the Santa Monica Freeway.

'What is he, some kind of stud?'

'Far from it. An old, ersatz hippie. Saggy face, flabby body, kind of a slob really.'

'No accounting for taste. Maybe he's hung like a horse.'

'I doubt the appeal's strictly physical. He's a scavenger, Milo. Moves in on women when they're under stress, plays Mr. Sensitive, gives them what passes for love and understanding.'

He put a finger to his nose and sniffed.

'And a little blow, too?'

'Could be.'

'I'll tell you what, after we're finished with Carmichael we'll head out to the hospital and interview him. I've got a little slack because the gang thing resolved nicely - confessions all around. The shooters were fourteen years old. They'll end up at the Youth Authority. The liquor store cutting's due to close any day - Del Hardy's interviewing a snitch who looks

128

promising. The main thing pending is the stomach-shitter. We're praying to the computer on that.'

He exited at Fourth Avenue, headed south to Pico, took Pico to Pacific, and continued southward into Venice. We passed Robin's studio, an unmarked storefront with the windows painted opaque white, but neither of us mentioned it. The neighbourhood changed from sleazy to slick as we approached the Marina.

Doug Carmichael's house was on a walk-street west of Pacific, half a block from the beach. It resembled a landlocked cabin cruiser, all peaks and portholes, narrow and high, and wedged into a lot no wider than thirty feet. The exterior was teal blue wood siding and white trim. Fish-scale shingles graced the gable-like peak above the door. A planter brimming with nail-polish pink geraniums hung from the sill of the front window. A white picket fence ringed the dwarf lawn. The door was inlaid with a stained-glass window. Everything looked clean and well tended.

This close to the beach the place had to cost a pretty piece of change.

'Fulfilling fantasies must be paying well,' I said.

'Hasn't it always?'

Milo rang the doorbell. It opened quickly and a tall muscular man in a red-and-black plaid shirt, faded jeans, and topsiders flashed us a smile saturated with fear, introduced himself ('Hi, I'm Doug'), and asked us in.

He was about my age. I'd been expecting someone younger and was surprised. He had thick blond hair, layered and blow-dried to look dashingly mussed, a full but neatly trimmed reddish-blond moustache, sky blue eyes, artist's model features, and poreless golden skin. An ageing beachboy who'd preserved well.

The interior walls of the house had been torn down to create a thousand square feet of skylit living space.

129

The furniture was bleached wood, the walls oyster white. The scent of lemon oil was in the air. There were marine lithographs, a salt-water aquarium, a small but well-stocked kitchen, a partially folded futon bed. Everything in its place, neat as a pin.

In the centre of the room was a sunken area half-filled by a bottle green velvet modular couch. We stepped down and sat. He offered us coffee from a pot that had already been set out on the table.

He poured three cups and sat across from us, still smiling, still scared.

'Detective Sturgis – ' he looked from me to Milo who had identified himself with a nod – 'over the phone you said this had to do with Nona Swope.'

'That's correct, Mr. Carmichael.'

'I have to tell you at the outset, I'm afraid I won't be of much help. I barely know her – '

'You messengered with her several times.' Milo pulled out his pencil and pad.

Carmichael laughed nervously. 'Three, maybe four times. She didn't stick around very long.'

'Uh huh.'

Carmichael drank coffee, put the cup down, and cracked his knuckles. He had iron-pumper's arms, each muscle defined in bas relief and roped with veins.

'I don't know where she is,' he said.

'No one said she was missing, Mr. Carmichael.'

'Jan Rambo called and told me what it was all about. She said you took my file.'

'Does that bother you, Mr. Carmichael?'

'Yes, it does. It's private and I don't see what it has to do with anything.' He was trying to assert himself but despite the muscles there was something preternaturally meek and childish about him.

'Mr. Carmichael, you were pretty keyed up over the phone and you're just as nervous in person. Want

130

to tell us why?' Milo sat back and crossed his legs.

It's always pathetic when someone physically impressive starts to fall apart, like watching a monument crumble. I saw the look on the blond man's face and wanted to be somewhere else.

'Tell us about it,' said Milo.

'It's my own damned fault. Now I'm going to pay.' He got up, went into the kitchen, and came back with a bottle of pills.

'B-twelve. I need it when I'm stressed out.' He unscrewed the lid, shook out three capsules, swallowed, and washed them down with coffee. 'I shouldn't be taking in so much caffeine but it calms me down. Paradoxical reaction.'

'What's on your mind, Doug?'

'My working at Adam and Eve has been a - a secret. Until now. I knew all along it was risky, that I might run into someone who knew me. I don't know, maybe that was part of the thrill.'

'We're not interested in your private life. Just in what you know about Nona Swope.'

'But if it leads somewhere and ends up in court I'm gonna be subpoenaed, right?'

'Could happen,' admitted Milo, 'but we're a long way from that. Right now we just want to find Nona and her parents so we can save a little boy's life.'

The detective went on in great detail about Woody's lymphoma. He'd retained everything I told him and was throwing it back in Carmichael's handsome face. The blond man tried hard not to listen but failed. He took all of it in, obviously pained. He seemed a sensitive one and I found myself liking him.

'Jesus. She told me she had a sick brother but she never said how sick.'

'What else did she tell you?'

'Not much. Really. She didn't say much about

131

anything. Talked about wanting to be an actress – the usual delusional stuff you hear from most of the girls. But she didn't seem depressed like you'd expect with a brother that sick.'

Milo changed the subject.

'What kind of gigs did you two do?'

Returning to the topic of his work made Carmichael anxious again. He tangled his fingers together and twisted. Knots rose on the heavy arms.

'Maybe I should get an attorney before we go any further.'

'Suit yourself,' said Milo, pointing to the phone.

Carmichael sighed and shook his head. 'No. That would only complicate things even more. Listen, I can give you some insights into Nona's personality if that's what you're after.'

'It would help.'

'But that's all I've got. Insights, no facts. How about you forget where you got them from?'

'Doug,' said Milo, 'we know who your father is and we know all about the bust, so stop dancing around, okay?'

Carmichael looked like a stallion in a burning stable, ready to bolt despite the consequences.

'Don't panic,' said Milo. 'We couldn't care less about that stuff.'

'I'm not some kind of pervert,' Carmichael insisted. 'If you traced me that far back you know how it happened.'

'Sure. You were a dancer at Lancelot's. After the show one of the ladies in the audience picked you up. Sex for money was discussed and she busted you.'

'She entrapped me. The cunt!'

Lancelot's was a male stripper joint in west L.A. catering to women who thought liberation meant aping the crudest aspects of male behaviour. The club had long been the object of neighbourhood complaints

132

and a couple of years back the police and the fire inspectors had paid it lots of attention. A harassment suit by the owner had ended that.

Milo shrugged. 'Anyway, daddy got you off, the file was closed, and you promised to behave yourself.'

'Yeah,' said Carmichael, bitterly. 'End of story, right? Only it wasn't that simple.' The blue eyes burned. 'Dad commandeered my trust fund – money left to me by my mom. It was illegal, I'm sure of it, but the lawyer in charge of the trust is one of Dad's California Club buddies and before I knew it the old man had all of it under his control. And me by the balls. It was like being a kid again, having to ask permission for everything. He forced me to go to school, said I had to make something of myself. Christ, I'm thirty-six and I'm in junior college! If I get good grades there'll be a place for me at Carmichael Oil. What a crock. Nothing's gonna change me into someone I'm not. What the hell does he want from me?'

He looked at us beseechingly, wanting support. My instinct was to give it to him but this wasn't therapy. Milo let him cool down before he spoke.

'And if he finds out about your current job, kaput, eh?'

'Shit.' Carmichael stroked his beard. 'I can't help it. I like doing that kind of thing. God gave me a great body and a great face and I get off on sharing it with other people. It's like acting but private, so it's better, more intimate. When I used to dance I could feel the women's eyes on me. I played to them, treated them good. I wanted them to cream right there. It felt so – loving.'

'I told this to your boss and I'll tell it to you,' said Milo, 'we don't give a damn who fucks who in this city. It only becomes a problem when people get cut or shot or strangled in the process.'

133

Carmichael didn't seem to have heard.

'I mean it's not like I'm hooking or anything,' he insisted. 'I don't need the money – in a good week I pull in six, maybe seven hundred bucks.' He dismissed that kind of money with a wave of his hand, operating from the distorted value system of one born into wealth.

'Doug,' said Milo with authority in his voice, 'stop defending yourself and listen: we don't care about what you do with your dick. Your file will stay sealed. Just tell us about Nona.'

The message finally got through. The look on Carmichael's face was that of a child who'd received an unexpected gift. I realized that I kept thinking of him as a big kid because, except for the manly outer husk, everything about him was childlike, immature. A classic case of arrested development.

'She was a barracuda,' he said. 'You had to hold her back or she got too aggressive. The last time we worked together was a stag party for an older guy who was getting married for the second time. A bunch of middle-aged men, salesman types, in this apartment in Canoga Park. They'd been drinking hard and watching fuck films before we got there. We were doing jock and cheerleader that night. I had on a football uniform and she was wearing a jersey top, a little pleated skirt, and sneakers. Pompons, her hair in pigtails, the works.

'Those guys were harmless old farts. Before we got there they'd probably been talking big, hooting at the movies like guys do when they're nervous. Then we walked in, they saw her, and I thought a few hearts were gonna give out. She wiggled at 'em, batted her lashes, showed a lot of tongue. We had the skit all planned out but she decided to ad lib. The script says we do a little minor league fondling while trading suggestive lines – you know stuff like I ask her how

134

she'd like to be my wide receiver and she says "Do it
again, we like it, we like it!" She was a lousy actress,
by the way, real flat, no emotion. But the audiences
seemed to dig her – her looks made up for it, I guess.
Anyway, these old guys were eating it up and she got
off on it. That's probably what gave her the idea of
getting really outrageous.

'All of a sudden she reached into my pants,
grabbed my cock, did a bump and grind, started
jerking me off, all the time gyrating at them. I wanted
to stop her – we're not supposed to go past the script
unless we're asked to.' He stopped, looked uncomfortable. 'And paid to. But I couldn't do it because it
would have ruined the skit and been a downer for all
those old guys.

'They were staring at her and she was groping me
and I was smiling through it all. Then she let go and
waltzed over to the guy who was getting hitched –
pudgy little fellow with big eyeglasses – and slipped
her hand down *his* pants. Everything got real quiet
then. He was red as a beet but he couldn't say
anything cause it woulda made him look like a wimp
in front of his friends. He got a sick look on his face,
forced himself to smile. She started tonguing his ear,
kept yanking his chain. The other guys started to
laugh. To relieve their tension. Soon they were yelling
out lewd comments. Nona was high, like she was really
getting off on groping the poor sucker.

'Finally I was able to ease her away without it
looking like a hassle. We got out of there and I yelled
at her in the car. She looked at me like I was nuts, said
what was the matter, we got a big tip, didn't we. I
could see it was no use talking to her so I gave up. We
got on the freeway. I was driving fast because I
couldn't wait to get away from her. Then all of a
sudden I felt her pulling at my zipper. Before I know
it, my cock is out and she's got it in her mouth. We're

135

going seventy and she's sucking me off and telling me to admit it, I love it. I was helpless, just praying the highway patrol wouldn't pull us over – that would be my balls, right? I asked her to stop but she had me and she wouldn't let go until she finished me off.'

'The next day I complained to Rambo, insisted I wouldn't work with her anymore. She just laughed, said Nona would be great in films. Later I found out she'd left, just walked out.'

Telling the story had made him sweat. He excused himself, went to the bathroom, came back freshly combed and sprayed and smelling of aftershave. Milo started questioning before he sat back down.

'And you have no idea where she went?'

Carmichael shook his head.

'She ever talk about anything personal?'

'Nope. There was nothing personal about her. She was all on the surface.'

'No hint where she might be headed?'

'She never even said where she came from. Like I told you, we did three or four gigs, then she split.'

'How'd she connect with Adam and Eve?'

'No idea. Everyone gets into it differently. Rambo called me after she caught my act at Lancelot's. Some find out by word of mouth. She runs ads in the underground papers and skin mags. Gets more applications than she wants.'

'All right, Doug,' said Milo, standing, 'I hope you've been straight with us.'

'I really have, Detective. Please don't pull me into this.'

'I'll do the best I can.'

We left. Back in the car Milo checked in with the dispatcher. There were no important messages.

'So what's the diagnosis on Surfer Boy?' he asked.

'Off the cuff? Personality problems, probably narcissistic.'

136

'Which means?'

'That he's got low self-esteem and it expresses itself in self-obsession – muscles, vitamins, constant attention paid to his body.'

'Sounds like half of L.A.,' he growled and turned on the ignition. As we pulled away, Carmichael came out of his house in swim trunks carrying a surfboard, a towel, and tanning lotion. He saw us, smiled, waved, and headed toward the beach.

Milo parked in a no parking zone near the entrance to Western Peds. 'I hate hospitals,' he said, as we boarded the elevator and rode up to the fifth floor. It took a while to locate Valcroix. He was examining a patient and we waited for him in a small conference room off the ward.

He came in fifteen minutes later, gave me a disgusted look, and told Milo to hurry, he was busy. When the detective began talking, he made a show of pulling out a medical chart, perusing it, and writing notes.

Milo's a skilled interrogator but he struck out with the Canadian. Valcroix continued to chart, unflustered, as the detective confronted him with knowing the Touch visitors and his affair with Nona Swope.

'Are you through, Officer?'

'For the time being, Doctor.'

'What am I supposed to do, defend myself?'

'You might start by explaining your role in the disappearance.'

'That will be quite simple. There is none.'

'No collaboration between you and the couple from the Touch?'

'Absolutely not. I visited them once. That's the extent of it.'

'What was the purpose of your visit?'

137

'Educational. I'm interested in communal societies.'

'Did you learn much, Doctor?'

Valcroix smiled.

'It was a peaceful place. They have no need for policemen.'

'What were the names of the people who visited the Swopes?'

'The man was called Baron, the woman, Delilah.'

'Surnames?'

'They don't use them.'

'And you've only visited the Touch once or twice.'

'Once.'

'All right. We'll be verifying that.'

'Feel free.'

Milo fixed him with a hard stare. The Fellow smiled contemptuously.

'Did Nona Swope tell you anything that would lead us to her family's whereabouts?'

'We didn't talk much. We just fucked.'

'Doctor, I suggest you rethink your attitude.'

'Oh really?' The squinty eyes became hyphens. 'You interrupt my work to ask me stupid questions about my personal life and expect me to have a good attitude?'

'In your case personal and professional seem pretty enmeshed.'

'How insightful of you to notice.'

'Is that all you have to say, Doctor?'

'What more would you like to hear? That I like to fuck women? All right. I do. I crave it. I'm going to fuck as many women as I can in this life and if there's a life thereafter I hope it will provide an endless chain of warm, willing women so I can keep fucking. Last I heard, fucking was no crime, or have they passed a new law in America?'

'Go back to work, Doctor.'

138

Valcroix gathered his charts and left, dreamy-eyed.

'What an asshole,' said Milo walking back to the car. 'I wouldn't let him near my hangnail.' There was an illegal parking warning from Hospital Security taped on the windshield. He ripped it off and put it in his pocket. 'I hope he's not typical of what they're passing off as doctors nowadays.'

'He's one of a kind. He won't last much longer here.'

We headed west on Sunset.

'You going to check out his story?' I asked.

'I could ask the Touch people how well they know him but if there is some kind of conspiracy they'd lie. Best thing is to call the sheriff down there and find out if the joker's been spotted more than once. Small town like that the law tends to notice things.'

'I know someone who might be familiar with the Touch. Want me to call him?'

'Why not? Couldn't hurt.'

He drove me home and stayed for a minute to look at the koi. He was transfixed by the colourful fish and smiled as they gobbled down the pellets he tossed them. When he tore himself away to leave, his big body seemed heavy and slow.

'Any longer, I'd stay here till my beard turned white.'

We shook hands, he gave a little salute, turned and ambled off for another afternoon of witnessing the human animal at its worst.

12

I PHONED Professor Seth Fiacre at UCLA. He's an
old classmate from grad school, a social psychologist
who'd been studying cults for several years.

'Hi, Alex,' he said, cheerful as always, 'just got
back from Sacramento. Senate hearings. Stultifying.'

We reminisced and played catch-up and then I told
him why I'd called.

'The Touch? I'm surprised you've even heard of
them. They're not well-known and they don't prose-
lytize. They've got a place called the Retreat, used to
be a monastery, down near the Mexican border.'

'What about the leader – Matthias?'

'Noble Matthias. He was a lawyer originally. Used
to call himself Norman Matthews.'

'What kind of law did he practice?'

'I don't know. But it was high powered. Beverly
Hills.'

Attorney to guru seemed an unlikely metamorphosis.

'Why the change of lifestyle?' I asked.

'I don't know, Alex. Most charismatic leaders claim some sort of cosmic vision, usually after a trauma. Your basic voice in the desert stuff. Maybe he ran out of gas in the Mojave and saw God.'

I laughed.

'I wish I could tell you more, Alex. The group hasn't attracted much attention because it's so small, maybe sixty members. And like I said, they're not out looking for converts, so it'll probably stay small. Whether or not that'll change if there's increased attrition remains to be seen. They've only been around for three or four years. Another thing that's unusual is that most of their members are middle-aged. Groups that recruit tend to go after young people. In practical terms that means you don't have parents screaming to the cops or calling in the deprogrammers.'

'Are they into holistic health?'

'Probably. Most of these groups are. It's part of rejecting the values of the greater society. But I haven't heard about them obsessing on it, if that's what you mean. I think their focus is more on self-sustenance. Growing their own food, making their own clothes. Like the original utopians – Oneida, Ephrata, New Harmony. Can I ask why you want to know all of this?'

I told him about the Swopes' decision not to treat Woody and the family's subsequent disappearance.

'Does that sound like something this group could be involved in, Seth?'

'It doesn't seem likely, because they're reclusive. Taking on the medical establishment would subject them to lots of scrutiny.'

'They did visit the family,' I reminded him.

141

'If they wanted to be subversive why do it so publicly? You said the family lived near the Retreat?'

'From what I understand.'

'So maybe they were just being neighbourly. In a small town like La Vista there's bound to be plenty of distrust of oddballs on the part of the natives. A small oddball makes a special effort to be friendly. It's good survival strategy.'

'Speaking of survival,' I asked, 'how do they support themselves?'

'My guess is member contributions. On the other hand, Matthews was a rich man. He could be bank-rolling the whole thing himself just for the power and prestige. If they're really into self-reliance the overhead wouldn't be that high.'

'One more thing, Seth. Why do they call them-selves the Touch?'

He laughed. 'Damned if I know. I think I'll sic a grad student on it.'

Mal Worthy called me later that day.

'It appears that Mrs. Moody didn't get a rat because she was destined for bigger and better things. This morning she found a dog eviscerated, hanging from the front doorknob by its entrails. He castrated it too, stuffed the balls in its mouth.'

Revulsion kept me silent.

'What a guy, huh? On top of that he snuck in a phone call, in defiance of the order, talked to the boy and told him to run away. The kid obeyed and it took seven hours to find him. They finally caught up with him late last night, wandering around the parking lot of some mall, five miles from home. Apparently he thought his father was going to pick him up and take him away. No one showed up and he was scared out of his mind, poor kid. Needless to say Darlene is going bananas, and I'm calling to ask you to see the

142

kids. More for their mental health than anything else.'

'Did they see the dog?'

'Thank God, no. She cleaned it up before they had a chance. How soon can you see them?'

'I won't have access to the office until Saturday.' I'd been renting space for forensic evaluations in the Brentwood suite of a colleague, but only had use of the office on weekends.

'You can do it here. Just name the time.'

'Can you get them down there in a couple of hours?'

'You got it.'

The offices of Trenton, Worthy & La Rosa were located on the penthouse floor of a high-prestige building at the intersection of Roxbury and Wilshire. Mal, resplendent in a navy silk and worsted from Bijan, was in the waiting room to greet me personally. He informed me I'd be using his office. I remembered it as a cavernous, dark-walled room with an oversized amorphous desk that looked like a piece of free-form sculpture, saw-toothed abstract prints hanging from the panelling, and shelves full of expensive – and breakable – mementos. Not an ideal place for child therapy but it would have to do.

I rearranged some chairs, moved an end table, and created a play area in the centre of the room. Removing paper, pencils, crayons, hand puppets, and a portable playhouse from my carrying case, I placed them on the table. Then I went to fetch the Moody children.

They were waiting in the law library: Darlene, Carlton Conley, and the children, who'd been dressed as if for church.

The three year old, April, wore a white taffeta dress and white patent leather sandals over lace-hemmed

143

socks. Her blonde hair had been ribboned and braided. She nestled sleepily in her mother's lap, worrying a knee scab and sucking her thumb.

Her brother'd been costumed in a white western shirt, brown corduroy pants with the cuffs turned up, a snap-on tie and black oxfords. His face had been scrubbed, his dark hair slicked down in an unsuccessful attempt to make it behave. He looked as miserable in the getup as any nine year old could. When he saw me he turned away.

'Now, Ricky, don't be rude to the doctor,' admonished his mother. 'Say hello, nice and polite. Hello, Doctor.'

'Hello, Mrs. Moody.'

The boy shoved his hands in his pockets and scowled.

Conley got up from his seat next to her and shook my hand, grinning awkwardly. The judge had been right. Except for being significantly taller, he looked strikingly like the man he'd replaced.

'Doctor,' he said weakly.

'Hello, Mr. Conley.'

April stirred, opened her eyes, and smiled at me. She'd been the easy one during the evaluation, an expressive, happy child. Because she was a girl her father had chosen to ignore her and she'd been spared his destructive love. Ricky was the favourite; he'd suffered for it.

'Hi, April.'

She batted her lashes, lowered her face, and giggled, a natural coquette.

'Remember the toys we played with last time?'

She nodded and giggled again.

'I have them here. Would you like to play with them again?'

She looked at her mother, requesting permission.

'Go 'head, honey.'

144

The little girl climbed down and took my hand.

'I'll see you in a while, Ricky,' I said to the sullen boy.

I spent twenty minutes with April, mostly observing as she manipulated the miniature inhabitants of the playhouse. Her play was organized and structured and relatively untroubled. Though she enacted several episodes of parental conflict, she was able to resolve them by having the father leave and the family live happily ever after. For the most part, hope and determination emanated from the scenarios she constructed.

I drew her out about the situation at home and found that she had an age-appropriate understanding of what was going on. Daddy was angry at mommy, mommy was angry at daddy, so they weren't going to live with each other anymore. She knew it wasn't her fault or Ricky's and she liked Carlton.

Everything was consistent with what I'd learned during the initial evaluation. At that time she'd expressed little anxiety over her father's absence and had seemed to be growing attached to Conley. When I questioned her about him now her face lit up.

'Carlton's so nice, Docka Alek. He take me to da zoo. We saw da diraffe. An da cockadile.' Her eyes widened with wonder, the memory alive.

She went on singing his praises and I prayed Judge Severe's cynical prophecy would be proved wrong. I'd treated countless girls who'd suffered tortured relationships with their fathers or no relationship at all, and had witnessed the psychic damage they'd incurred, grievously handicapped in the relationship game. This little sweetheart deserved better.

When I'd observed long enough to convince myself she was functioning reasonably well, I took her back. She stood on tippy toes and reached out toothpick arms. I bent and she kissed my cheek.

'Bye, Docka Alek.'

'Bye, honey. If you ever want to talk to me, tell your mommy. She'll help you call.'

She said okay and crawled back to the pillowy sanctuary of her mother's thighs.

Ricky'd moved to a far corner where he stood alone, staring out the window. I walked over to him, put my hand on his shoulder, and spoke softly so only he could hear: 'I know you're really mad about having to do this.'

He thrust out his lower lip, stiffened his neck, and crossed his arms across his chest. Darlene got up, still holding April, and started to say something but I motioned her down.

'It must be real hard not to see your dad,' I said.

He stood as straight as a Marine, trying hard to look tough and grim.

'I heard you ran away.'

No reply.

'That must have been a real adventure.'

The hint of a smile danced across his lips and escaped.

'I knew you had strong legs, Ricky, but to go five miles all by yourself. Whew!'

The smile returned, staying a little longer this time.

'See anything interesting?'

'Uh huh.'

'Can you tell me about it?'

He looked back at the others.

'Not here,' I assured him. 'Let's go to another room. We can draw and play like the last time. Okay?'

He frowned but followed me.

Mal's office amazed him and he circled the immense room several times before settling down.

'Ever seen a place like this?'

'Uh uh. In a movie.'

146

'Oh yeah? Which one?'

'It was about bad guys who were taking over the world. They had an office with lasers and stuff. It looked like this.'

'Bad guy headquarters, huh?'

'Yeah.'

'Do you think Mr. Worthy's a bad guy?'

'My dad said he was.'

'Did he tell you anyone else was a bad guy?'

He looked uneasy.

'Like me? And Dr. Daschoff?'

'Uh huh.'

'Do you understand why your father said that?'

'He's mad.'

'That's right. He's really mad. Not because of anything you or April did, but because he doesn't want your mom and him to get divorced.'

'Yeah,' the boy said with sudden ferocity, 'it's her damn fault!'

'The divorce?'

'Yeah! She kicked him out and he even paid for the house with his money!'

I sat him down, took a chair opposite him, and put my hands on his small shoulders as I spoke:

'Ricky, I'm sorry everything is so sad. I know you want your mom and dad to get back together. But that's not going to happen. Do you remember how they used to fight all the time?'

'Yeah, but then they'd stop fighting and be happy to us.'

'When that happened it was nice.'

'Yup.'

'But the fighting got worse and worse and there wasn't much happiness left.'

He shook his head.

'Divorce is terrible,' I said. 'Like everything's falling apart.'

147

He looked away.

'It's okay to be angry, Ricky. I'd be angry, too, if my parents were getting divorced. But it's not okay to run away because you could get hurt that way.'

'My dad'll take care of me.'

'Ricky, I know you love your dad very much. You should. A dad is someone special. And a dad should be able to be with his children, even after a divorce. I hope some day your dad can see you a lot, and take you places and do fun stuff with you. But right now – and this is really sad – it's not a good idea for him to spend a lot of time with you and April. Do you understand why?'

'Cause he's sick?'

'Right. Do you know what kind of sickness?'

He ruminated on the question.

'He gets mad?'

'That's part of it. He gets real mad or real sad or real happy all of a sudden. Sometimes without a good reason. When he's real mad he could do mad things that wouldn't be right, like fight with somebody. That could be dangerous.'

'Uh *uh*! He could beat 'em up!'

'That's true, but it would be dangerous for the person he beat up. And you or April could get hurt, accidentally. Do you understand?'

A grudging nod.

'I'm not saying he'll always be sick. There are medicines he can take that can help. And talking to doctors, like me, can help, too. But right now your dad doesn't want to admit that he needs help. So the judge said he couldn't see you until he got better. That made him really mad and now he thinks everyone is a bad guy trying to hurt him. But we're really trying to help him. And to protect you.'

He stared at me, stood, found the drawing paper, and proceeded to construct a fleet of paper airlines.

148

For the next quarter hour he waged a solitary battle of epic proportions, destroying entire cities, massacring thousands, stomping and shouting and shredding paper until Mal's antique Saruk was covered with confetti.

After that he drew for a while but wasn't happy with any of his creations and tossed them, crumpled, in the trash. I tried to get him to talk about the runaway episode but he refused. I reiterated the danger and he listened, looking bored. When I asked him if he'd do it again he shrugged.

I brought him back and took Darlene into the office. She wore a pink pantsuit with a faint diamond pattern and silver sandals. Her dark hair was piled high and sprayed in place. She'd spent a lot of time on her makeup but still looked tired and worn and scared. After seating herself she pulled a handkerchief out of her purse and passed it from hand to hand, kneading and squeezing.

'This must be really hard on you,' I said.

Tears oozed out of her eyes. Up went the handkerchief.

'He's a crazy man, Doctor. He's been getting crazier all along and now he won't let me go without doing something really crazy.'

'How have the kids been doing?'

'April's a little clingy - you saw her out there. She gets up a couple of times at night, wants to come into our bed. But she's a sweet thing. *He's* my problem, just angry all the time, refusing to mind. Yesterday he said the ef word to Carlton.'

'What did Carlton do?'

'Told him he'd whip him if he did it again.'

Great.

'It's not a good idea to get Carlton involved in discipline at this point. Having him there is a big adjustment for the kids in the first place. If you let

149

him take over, they'll feel abandoned.'

'But Doctor, he can't use language like that!'

'Then you need to handle it, Mrs. Moody. It's important for the children to know that you're there for them. That you're in charge.'

'Okay,' she said, without enthusiasm. 'I'll try it.'

I knew she wouldn't comply. The word *try* was the tipoff. In a couple of months she'd be wondering why both children were ornery and miserable and impossible to manage.

I did my job anyway, telling her that both of the children could benefit from professional help. April, I explained, showed no serious problems but was insecure. Therapy for her was likely to be short-term and could reduce the risk of more severe problems in the future.

Ricky, on the other hand, was a troubled little boy, full of anger and likely to run away again. She interrupted at that point to blame the running away on the boy's father and said that come to think of it he reminded her of his father.

'Mrs. Moody,' I said, 'Ricky needs the chance to blow off steam on a regular basis.'

'You know,' she said, 'Carlton and him are starting to get along better. Yesterday they were playing catch in the backyard and having a great time. I know Carlton's gonna be a good influence on him.'

'Great. But that won't take the place of professional help.'

'Doctor,' she said, 'I'm broke. Do you know how much lawyers cost? Just being here today is draining me dry.'

'There are clinics that operate on a sliding scale based on ability to pay. I'll give some numbers to Mr. Worthy.'

'Are they far? I don't drive freeways.'

'I'll try to find one close to you, Mrs. Moody.'

'Thank you, doctor.' She sighed, picked herself up, and let me hold the door for her.

Watching her trudge down the hall like an old woman it was easy to forget she was twenty-nine years old.

I dictated my findings to Mal's secretary as she typed silently on a court stenographer's machine. When she left he brought out a bottle of Johnny Walker Black and poured us each a couple of fingers.

'Thanks for coming by, Alex.'

'No problem, but I don't know that it did any good. She won't follow through.'

'I'll see to it that she does. Tell her it's important for the case.'

We sipped Scotch.

'Incidentally,' he said, 'the judge hasn't gotten any nasty surprises so far – apparently Moody's crazy but not stupid. But she's mega-pissed about the whole thing. She called the D.A. and ordered him to get someone on it. He dumped it on Foothill Division.'

'Who said they'd been looking for him already.'

'Right.' He looked surprised. I told him about Milo's call to Fordebrand.

'Very impressive, Alex. More?' He picked up the bottle. I declined a refill. Good Scotch is hard to resist but talking about Moody reminded me of the importance of staying clear-headed.

'Anyway, Foothill claims to be looking for him seriously but they think he's gone into Angeles Crest.'

'Wonderful.'

Angeles Crest National Forest is 600,000 acres of wilderness bordering the city to the north. The Moodys had lived in nearby Sunland, and the forest would be familiar territory to Richard, a natural place to escape. Much of the acreage was impenetrable except on foot and a man could stay lost there for as long as he pleased. It was a haven for hikers, campers, naturalists, and climbers, as well as for packs of outlaw bikers who partied all night and sacked out in caves. And its ravines and washes were favourite dumping spots for bodies.

Just before we'd scuffled in the court parking lot, Moody'd talked about surviving in the wilderness, clearly indicating his children in the fantasy. I let Mal know that.

He nodded grimly.

'I've instructed Darlene to take the kids and get out of town for a while. Her folks have a farm up near Davis. They're leaving today.'

'Won't he be able to figure that out?'

'If he comes out in the open. I'm hoping he decides to play mountain man for a while.'

He threw up his arms.

'It's the best I can do, Alex.'

The conversation was taking an unsettling turn. I got up to go and we shook hands. At the door I asked him if he'd ever heard of a lawyer named Norman Matthews.

'Stormin' Norman? That's a golden oldie. I went up against him at least a dozen times. Biggest ball-breaker in Beverly Hills.'

'He was a divorce lawyer?'

'The best. Super-aggressive, had a reputation for getting his clients what they wanted no matter who he offended in the process. Handled lots of Hollywood dissolutions with big bucks at stake and got to thinking of himself as a star. Very image conscious – an Excalibur *and* a Corniche, conspicuous clothes, blondes on each arm, blew Dunhill latakia through a thousand-dollar meerschaum.'

'He's a bit more spiritual nowadays.'

'Yeah, I heard. Got a weird group down on the

152

border. Calls himself Grand Noble Poobah or something like that.'

'Noble Matthias. Why'd he leave law?'

He laughed uneasily.

'You might say it left him. This was five or six
years ago. It was in the papers. I'm surprised you
don't remember. Matthews was representing the wife
of some playwright. The guy had just hit it big – a
smash on Broadway – after ten years of eating air
sandwiches. At that point the wife found another loser
to mother and filed. Matthews got her everything – a
huge chunk of royalties from the play and a healthy
percentage of everything the guy would bring in for
the next ten years. It was a publicized case and there
was a press conference scheduled on the courtroom
steps. Matthews and the wife were headed there when
hubby came out of nowhere with a twenty-two. He
shot them both in the head. She died but Matthews
squeaked by after half a year of touch and go. Then
he dropped out of sight, resurfaced a couple of years
later as a maharishi. Your basic California story.'

I thanked him for the information and turned to
leave.

'Hey,' he said, 'why the interest?'

'Nothing important. His name came up in conversation.'

'Stormin' Norman,' he smiled. 'Sanctification
through brain damage.'

13

THE NEXT morning, Milo knocked on my door and woke me at six forty-five. The sky was alley-cat grey. It had rained all night and the air smelled like damp flannel. The glen harboured a relentless chill that seeped into my bones the moment I opened the door.

He wore a thin shiny black raincoat over a wrinkled white shirt, a brown and blue tie, and brown slacks. His chin was blued with stubble, his eyelids weighted by fatigue. There was mud on his brogues, which he scraped off along the edge of the terrace before coming in.

'We found two of the Swopes, the mother and father, up in Benedict Canyon. Shot in the head and back.'

He talked rapidly without making eye contact and walked past me into the kitchen. I followed him and put up coffee. While it brewed I washed my face in

154

the kitchen sink and he chewed on a log of French bread. Neither of us spoke until we'd sat down at my old oak table and punished our gullets with large swallows of scalding liquid.

'Some old character with a metal detector found them a little after one a.m. He's a rich guy, a retired dentist, has a big house off Benedict but likes to roam around in the dark prospecting. His gizmo picked up the coins in the father's pockets – the two of them weren't buried very deep. The rain had washed away some of the dirt and he could see part of a head in the moonlight. Poor fellow was shaking.'

He looked downward, dispiritedly.

'Another detective picked up the squeal but when they identified the bodies he remembered my involvement and called me. He was scheduled for vacation anyway and more than happy to hand it over. I've been there since three.'

'No sign of Woody and Nona?'

Milo shook his head.

'*Nada*. We combed the immediate area. The place we found them is just before the road climbs toward the Valley. Most of Benedict's pretty well built up but there's a small gully on the west side that the developers haven't gotten to. It's concave, kind of like a saucer in the ground, covered with brush and layered with about a foot of dead leaves. Easy to miss if you drive by quickly 'cause it's blocked from the road by big eucalyptus. We used the grid approach, went over it foot by foot. Funny thing is, we did dig up another body, but this one was all bones. From the shape of the pelvis, the M.E. says a woman. Been there for at least a couple of years.'

He was concentrating on details to avoid dealing with the emotional impact of the murders. Taking a large gulp of coffee, he rubbed his eyes and shivered.

'I'm soaked. Lemme peel out of this.'

155

He pulled off the raincoat and draped it over a chair.

'Let's hear it for sunny goddamn California,' he snarled. 'I feel like I've been marinating in a rice paddy.'

'Want a warm shirt?'

'Nah.' He rubbed his hands together, drank more coffee, and got up for a refill.

'Not a sign of the kids,' he reiterated upon returning to the table. 'Several possibilities present themselves: one, they weren't with the parents and escaped what went down. When they got back to the motel, they saw the blood and ran scared.'

'Why wouldn't the family stick together if they were returning home?' I asked.

'Maybe she took him for an ice cream. While the parents packed.'

'No way, Milo. He was too sick for that.'

'Yeah, I keep forgetting that. Must be unconscious repression, huh?'

'Must be.'

'Okay, hypothesis two, then. They weren't together because the sister snatched the kid. You told me Bev said she didn't like the parents. Could be it came to a head.'

'Anything Bev has to say about her needs to be taken with a shaker of salt, Milo. Nona made it with a man she once loved. Down deep, she hates the girl's guts.'

'You told me yourself the kid was pissed the time you met her, how she lit into Melendez-Lynch. And the picture we get of her after talking to Rambo and Carmichael is one strange little girl.'

'That's true. She sounds like she's got plenty of problems. But why would she abduct her brother? All indications are that she was self-centred, cut off from family feelings. She and Woody didn't have a close

156

relationship. She rarely visited and when she did it was at night when he was asleep. Her not being there with the others makes sense. But not the rest of it.'

'Gee, you're fun to be with,' said Milo. 'I'll call you next time I need a yes man.'

His face opened in a giant yawn. When he'd taken in enough air he continued. 'Everything you say is logical, pal, but I've gotta touch all bases. I called Houten in La Vista just before I came here. Woke the poor devil up and told him to scour the town for her and the kid. He was pretty broken up hearing about the parents, said he'd already searched carefully the first time I asked, but agreed to do it again.'

'Including the Touch's place?'

'Especially there. Melendez-Lynch may have been right from the beginning. Even if Houten comes up empty they're sweet suspects. I'm heading down there today to check them out. Especially the two that visited the Swopes. A couple of my guys are going to the hospital to interview anyone who took care of the Swopes. With special emphasis on squeezing that asshole Valcroix.'

I told him about Seth Fiacre's assessment of the Touch as a reclusive group that shunned the limelight and tacked on Mal's account of the greening of Norman Matthews.

'They don't seek converts,' I pointed out. 'They seclude themselves. What motivation would there be for them to get involved with outsiders?'

Milo seemed to ignore the question and expressed surprise at Noble Matthias's identity.

'Matthews is the guru? I always wondered what happened to him. I remember the case. It went down in Beverly Hills so we weren't involved. They locked the husband up in Atascadero and six months later he mixed himself a Draino cocktail.' He smiled mirthlessly. 'We used to call Matthews the "Shyster to the Stars." What do you know?'

He yawned again and drank more coffee.

'Motivation?' he repeated. 'Maybe they thought they'd convinced the parents to treat the kid their way, there was a change of heart and things got out of control.'

'That's pretty far out of control,' I said.

'Don't forget what I told you in the motel room. About the world getting crazier and crazier. Besides, maybe the cultists were camera-shy when your professor friend studied them but not anymore. Weirdos change, like anyone else. Jim Jones was everyone's hero until he turned into Idi Amin.'

'It's a good point.'

'Of course it is. I'm a pro-fesh-you-nole.' He laughed, a good warm sound soon replaced by silence made cold by unspoken words.

'There's another possibility,' I said, finally.

'Now that you've mentioned it, yes.' His green eyes darkened with melancholia. 'The kids are buried somewhere else. Whoever did it got scared before he could finish dumping them at Benedict and took off. There are coyotes and all sorts of creepy crawlies out there. You could see a pair of eyes and easily get spooked.'

I'd been heartsick and numb since learning of the killings, my attention vacillating between Milo's words and the images they evoked. But now the full impact of what he was saying slammed straight into me and I mustered up a wall of denial to block it out.

'You're still going to look for him, aren't you?'

He looked up at the urgency in my voice.

'We're canvassing Benedict from Sunset up into the Valley, Alex, doing door-to-doors on the chance someone saw something. But it was dark so an eyewitness is unlikely. We're also going to cruise the

158

other canyons – Malibu, Topanga, Coldwater, Laurel, right here in the Glen. About a thousand man hours and unlikely to be productive.'

I got back on the subject of the parents' murders because grim as it was, it was preferable to fantasizing about Woody's fate.

'Were they shot right there, in Benedict?' I asked.

'Not likely. There was no blood on the ground and we couldn't find any spent shells. The rain introduces a little uncertainty, but each of them had half a dozen bullet holes. That much shooting would make a lot of noise and there'd have to be some shells left behind. They were killed somewhere else, Alex, and then dumped. No footprints or tyretracks, but that you can definitely put down to the rain.'

He ripped viciously at the French bread with small, sharp teeth, and chewed noisily.

'More coffee?' I offered.

'No thanks. My nerves are scraped raw as it is.' He leaned forward, thick, spatulate fingers splayed on the table. 'Alex, I'm sorry. I know you cared about the kid.'

'It's like a bad dream,' I admitted. 'I'm trying not to think of him.' Perversely, the small pale face floated into consciousness. A game of checkers in a plastic room . . .

'When I saw the motel room I really thought they'd gone home, that it was a family thing,' he was saying morosely. 'From the looks of the bodies, the M.E. guessed they were murdered a couple of days ago. Probably not too long after the kid was pulled out of the hospital.'

'Hindsight is twenty-twenty, Milo,' I said, trying to sound supportive. 'There was no way anyone could have known.'

'Right. Let me use your john.'

159

After he left I set about pulling myself together – with meagre success. My hands were unsteady and my head buzzed. The last thing I needed was to be left alone with my helplessness and my anguish. I searched for absolution through activity. I'd have gone to the hospital to tell Raoul about the murders but Milo had asked me not to. I paced the room, filled a cup with coffee, tossed it down the sink, snatched up the paper and turned to the movie section. A revival house in Santa Monica was featuring an early matinee, a documentary on William Burroughs, which sounded sufficiently bizarre to crowd out reality. Just as I was stepping out the door Robin called from Japan.

'Hello, lover,' she said.

'Hello, babe. I miss you.'

'Miss you too, sweetie.'

I took the phone to the bed and sat down facing a framed picture of the two of us. I remember the day it had been taken. We'd gone to the arboretum on a Sunday in April and had asked a passing octogenarian to do us the favour. Despite his trembling hands and protestation of ignorance about modern cameras it had come out beautifully.

We held each other against a backdrop of royal purple rhododrendrons and snowy camellias. Robin stood in front, her back to my chest, my arms around her waist. She wore tight jeans and a white turtleneck that showed off her curves. The sun had picked up the auburn highlights in her hair, which hung long and curly, like coppery grapes. Her smile was wide and open, the perfect teeth a crescent of white. Her face was a valentine, her dark eyes liquid and dancing.

She was a beautiful woman, inside and out. Hearing the sound of her voice was sweetly painful.

'I bought you a silk kimono, Alex. Grey-blue, to match your eyes.'

'Can't wait to see it. When are you coming home?'

'About another week, honey. They're tooling up to actually manufacture a gross of instruments and they want me here to inspect them.'

'Sounds like things are going well.'

'They are. But you sound distant. Is something wrong?'

'No. Must be the connection.'

'You sure, baby?'

'Yes. Everything's fine. I miss you, that's all.'

'You're mad at me, aren't you? For staying so long.'

'No. Really. It's important. You have to do it.'

'It's not like I'm having fun, you know. The first couple of days they entertained me, but after the amenities were over it was strictly business. Design studies and factories all day. And no male geishas to help me unwind at night!'

'Poor baby.'

'You bet.' She laughed. 'I have to admit, though, it's a fascinating country. Very tense, very structured. Next time I go you have to come with me.'

'Next time?'

'Alex, they love my designs. If the Billy Orleans does well they're sure to want another. We could go during cherry blossom time. You'd love it. They've got beautiful gardens – larger versions of ours – in the public parks. And I saw a koi almost five feet long. Square watermelons, sushi bars you wouldn't believe. It's incredible, hon.'

'Sounds like it.'

'Alex, what's wrong? And stop saying nothing.'

'Nothing.'

'Come on. I was so lonely, sitting by myself in this sterile hotel room, drinking tea and watching "Kojak" with Japanese subtitles. I thought talking to

161

you would help me feel alive again. But it's only made me sadder.'

'I'm sorry, babe. I love you and I'm really proud of you. I'm trying really hard to be noble, to put my needs aside. But as it turns out, I'm just another selfish, sexist bastard, threatened by your success and worried that it won't be the same.'

'Alex, it'll always be the same. The most precious thing in my life is us. Didn't you once tell me that all the busy little things we do – career, achievement – are just trim around the edges? That what's important is the intimacy we establish in our lifetime? I bought it. I really believe that.'

Her voice broke. I wanted to hold her near.

'What's this about square watermelons?' I said.

We laughed together and the next five minutes were long-distance heaven.

She'd been travelling around the country but was now settled in Tokyo and would be there until returning to the States. I took down the address of her hotel and her room number. Her travel plan included an overnight stopover in Hawaii before the final flight back to L.A. The idea of my flying to meet her in Honolulu and our spending a week together on Kauai came up as a lark but ended up as a serious possibility. She promised to call when her departure date had been determined.

'Do you know what's been keeping me going?' she giggled. 'Remembering that wedding we went to last summer in Santa Barbara.'

'The Biltmore, room three fifty-one?'

'I'm getting wet right now just thinking about it.'

'Stop or I'll be limping all day.'

'That's good. You'll appreciate me.'

'Believe me, I already do.'

We prolonged the good-byes and then she was gone.

162

I hadn't told her about my involvement with the Swopes. We'd always had an open relationship and I couldn't help feeling that holding back had been an unfaithful act of sorts. Still, I rationalized, it had been the right thing to do, because hearing about such horror from so great a distance would only have burdened her with intractable anxiety.

In an attempt to quell my guilt I spent a long time on the phone with a histrionic florist, arranging for a dozen coral roses to be sent halfway around the world.

14

THE PERSON on the phone was female, agitated, and vaguely familiar.

'Dr. Delaware, I need your help!'

I tried to place her. A patient from years back reaching out in the throes of crisis? If so, not being remembered would only compound her anxiety. I'd fake it until I figured out who it was.

'What can I do for you?' I said soothingly.

'It's Raoul. He's gotten himself into terrible trouble.'

Bingo. Helen Holroyd. Her voice sounded different when heated by emotion.

'What kind of trouble, Helen?'

'He's in prison, down in La Vista!'

'What!'

'I just spoke to him – they allowed him one call. He

164

sounds terrible! Heaven knows what they're doing to him! A genius locked up like a common criminal! Oh, God, please help!'

She was falling apart, which didn't surprise me. Icy people often freeze themselves in order to hold in check a volcanic stew of disturbing and conflictual feelings. Emotional hibernation, if you will. Crack the ice and the stuff inside comes pouring out with all the discipline of molten lava.

She was sobbing and began to hyperventilate.

'Calm down,' I said. 'We'll clear it up. But first tell me how it happened.'

It took a couple of minutes for her to regain control.

'The police came to the lab late yesterday afternoon. They told him about those people being killed. I was there, working on the other side of the room. Hearing about it didn't seem to affect him. He was at the computer, typing in data, and he didn't stop the entire time they were there. Just kept on working. I knew something was wrong. It's not like him to be that impassive. He had to be really upset. When they were gone I tried to talk to him but he shut me out. Then he left, just walked out of the building without telling anyone where he was going.'

'And drove to La Vista.'

'Yes! He must have thought about it all night and left early in the morning because he got there by ten and had some kind of altercation with someone. I'm not sure who, they wouldn't let us talk long and he was so agitated he wasn't making much sense. I called back and talked to the sheriff but he said they were holding Raoul for the Los Angeles police to question. He wouldn't tell me more, said I was free to get a lawyer, and hung up. He was rude and insensitive, talking about Raoul as if he were a criminal and my knowing him made me a criminal, too.'

She sniffled, remembering the indignity.

165

'It's all so – Kafkaesque! I'm so confused, don't know how to help him. I thought of you because Raoul said you had connections with the police. Please tell me, what should I do?'

'Nothing for the time being. Let me make a few calls and get back to you. Where are you calling from?'

'The lab.'

'Don't go anywhere.'

'I rarely do.'

Milo wasn't available and the desk man at the station wouldn't tell me where he was so I asked for Delano Hardy, my friend's occasional partner, and was connected to him after being put on hold for ten minutes. Hardy is a dapper, balding black man with an easy wit and a ready smile. His skill with a rifle had once saved my life.

'Hey, Doc.'

'Hi, Del. I need to talk to Milo. The guy at the desk was all hush-hush. Isn't he back from La Vista?'

'He's not back because he never went. Change of plans. We've been working on a very hot case and a big break came through yesterday.'

'The stomach-shitter?'

'Yeah. We've got him cold and Milo and another guy have been locked up with the prick all morning, playing good-cop, bad-cop.'

'Congratulations on the bust. Could you give him a message to call me when he's free?'

'What's the trouble?'

I told him.

'Hold on. Lemme see if he's gonna break soon.'

He returned to the phone moments later.

'He said give him another half hour. He'll call you.'

'Thanks a lot, Del.'

'No sweat. By the way, I'm still digging that Strat.'

Hardy was a fellow guitarist, a first-rate musician who gigged with an R & B group after hours. I'd bought him a vintage Fender Stratocaster in gratitude for his marksmanship.

'Glad you're enjoying it. Let's jam again.'

'Absolutely. Come by the club and bring your axe. Gotta go now.'

I called Helen and told her it would take time. She sounded shaky so I talked her through it by getting her to tell me about her work. When the chill came back into her voice I knew she'd be okay. At least for a while.

Milo called an hour later.

'Can't talk long, Alex. We've got the asshole nailed. A Saudi Arabian student, related to the royal family. It's gonna get hairy but I'll be damned if this one is gonna slither away on diplomatic immunity.'

'How'd you get him?'

'I wish I could say it was brilliant police work. He attacked another woman and she had mace in her purse. Sprayed the fucker until he shrieked, knee-dropped him, and called us. Little wisp of a thing, too,' he added, with admiration. 'We found articles belonging to the other victims in his apartment. The guy shits his pants when he gets excited. It's been a giggle interrogating him. Only cheerful note is that his asshole lawyer has to sit there and smell it, too.'

'Sounds like fun. Listen, if you can't talk now – '

'It's okay. I took a break. Gotta come up for air. Del told me about the Cuban. I called Houten and he told me what happened. Seems your friend is a hothead. Drove into town this morning like Gary Cooper before the big showdown. Barged in on Houten, demanded he arrest the Touch people for the murder of the Swopes, and claimed the boy and Nona were being held captive at their place. Houten told him they'd already been questioned by him, that I was planning to come down and do it again, and that the premises had been thoroughly searched. Melendez-Lynch wouldn't listen, got really abusive and eventually Houten had to basically kick him out. He got in his car and drove straight to the Retreat.'

I groaned.

'Wait, it gets better. Apparently they have big iron gates at the front entrance that they keep locked. Melendez-Lynch drove up and started screaming for them to let him in. A couple of them came out to calm him down and it got physical. He absorbed most of the damage. They went back in, he started up his car and rammed the gate. At that point they called Houten and he busted Melendez-Lynch for disturbing the peace, malicious mischief, and who knows what else. Houten said the guy seemed like a lunatic and he got to wondering if we'd be interested in interviewing him. So he locked him up, offered him an attorney, which he refused, and gave him the proverbial one phone call.'

'Unbelievable.'

Milo laughed.

'Isn't it? Between him and Valcroix and the stories Rick tells me, I'm losing what little faith I had in modern medicine. I mean, these guys are *not* confidence inspiring.'

'Maybe the Swopes didn't think so either.'

'That's right. If they saw the kind of flakiness we've been uncovering I can understand them wanting out.'

'Not as far out as they got.'

'Yeah. Once we're sure the Saudi's off the streets their case will be my number one problem. But it's going to have to wait awhile because if we don't play close attention to Shitpants, he'll weasel out and be back in Riyadh before we know it.'

His words chilled me. Human life meant a lot to

168

Milo, and if he thought Woody and Nona were alive he'd find a way, Saudi or not, to pursue their case aggressively.

I fought back my anger.

'When did you decide they were dead?'

'What? – Jesus, Alex, stop analyzing! I haven't decided a goddamn thing. I've got *platoons* going through the canyons, I check the A.P.B.s at least two, three times a day. So, it's not like I'm sitting on my ass. But the fact is I've got a suspect in custody in one case and zilch on the other. Where would *you* put your priorities?'

'Sorry. I was way out of line. It's just that it's hard to think of that little boy as beyond hope.'

'I know, pal.' His tone softened. 'I'm on the rag, too. Too much time spent with blood and crud. Just be careful you're not getting overinvolved. Again.'

Unconsciously, I fingered my jaw.

'Okay. Now what's the story with Raoul? I need to tell his girlfriend something.'

'No story. I told Houten we didn't care if he let him go. The guy may be whacko but right now he's not a suspect. Houten says he wants him escorted out of there. Melendez-Lynch hasn't stopped ranting since they locked him up, and they don't want him causing trouble the minute they let him out. If you think you can keep him calm, I'll tell Houten to release him to your custody. Your being a shrink would make it look better, too.'

'I don't know,' I said. 'I've seen Raoul pull tantrums but never like this.'

'Up to you. Unless the guy calms down and agrees to talk to a lawyer or someone comes to get him, he could be there for a while.'

If word got out about Melendez-Lynch's incarceration, his professional reputation would be compromised. I knew of no one close to him except Helen

169

Holroyd and she was definitely not up to the task of dragging him away from La Vista.

'They're calling me back, Alex,' Milo was saying, 'gotta hold my nose and jump into it.'

'All right. Call the sheriff. Tell him I'll get down there as soon as I can.'

'What a nice guy. Bye.'

I called Helen again and told her I'd secured the release of the esteemed Dr. Melendez-Lynch. She thanked me effusively and was starting to lapse into tears before I cut her off. For her own good.

15

THE SEVILLE glided onto the interstate shortly past noon. The first half of the two-hour journey to La Vista was a southward slice through the industrial underbelly of California. I sped past stockyards and freight docks, mammoth auto dealerships, grimy warehouses, and factories belching effluvia into a sky obscured by billboards. I kept the windows closed, the air conditioning on, and Flora Purim on the tape deck.

At Irvine the terrain shifted suddenly to endless expanses of green – fields of rich, dark soil stitched precisely with emerald rows of tomatoes, peppers, strawberries, and corn, spasmodically bathed by whirligig sprinklers. I opened the window and let in the good stench of manure. A while later the highway edged closer to the ocean and the fields gave way to the affluent suburbs of Orange County, then thinned

171

to miles of empty scrub enclosed by barbed chain-link fence – government land, rumoured to harbour secret nuclear testing plants.

Just past Oceanside, traffic going the other way slowed to a crawl: the Border patrol had set up a spot check for illegal aliens. Grey-uniformed officers in Smoky the Bear hats peered into each vehicle, waving on the majority, pulling a few over for closer scrutiny. The process had a ceremonial look to it, which was appropriate, for stemming the tide of those yearning for the good life was as feasible as capturing the rain in a thimble.

I exited a few miles later, heading east on a state highway that slogged through blocks of fast-food joints and self-serve gas stations before turning into two-lane blacktop.

The road rose, climbing toward mountains veiled by lavender mist. Twenty minutes out of the junction and there wasn't another vehicle in sight. I passed a granite quarry where mantislike machines dipped into the earth and brought up piles of rocks and dirt, a horse ranch, a field of grazing Holsteins, then nothing. Dusty signs heralded the construction of 'luxury planned communities' and 'townhomes,' but apart from one abandoned project – the roofless remains of a warren of small houses crammed into a sun-baked gully – it was empty, silent land.

As the altitude increased the scenery grew lush. Acres of eucalyptus-shaded citrus groves and a mile of avocado preceded the appearance of La Vista. The town sat in a valley at the foot of the mountains, surrounded by forest, vaguely alpine. A wayward glance and I would have missed it.

The main drag was Orange Avenue and a good part of it was given over to a sprawling gravel yard filled with somnolent threshers, tillers, bulldozers, and tractors. A long, low, glass-fronted structure occupied one end of the yard and a worn wooden sign above the entrance announced sales, rental, and repair of farm equipment and power tools.

The street was quiet and ribbed with diagonal parking lines. Few of the spaces were occupied, those that were housed half-ton pickups and old sedans. The posted speed limit was 15 m.p.h. I decelerated and coasted past a dry-goods story, a market, an eight-dollar-a-visit chiropractor ('no appointment necessary'), a barbershop complete with spinning pole, and a windowless tavern named Erna's.

City Hall was a two-story square of pink cinder block midway through the town. A concrete walkway ran down the centre of a well-tended lawn, flanked by towering date palms, and leading to brass double doors, propped open. Weathered brass rods bearing Old Glory and the flag of California jutted out above the entrance.

I parked in front of the building, stepped out into the dry heat, and walked to the door. A plaque commemorating La Vista's World War II dead and dated 1947 was inlaid in the block at eye level, just left of the doorpost. I stepped into an entry hall containing a pair of slat-backed oak benches and nothing else. I looked for a directory, saw none, heard the sound of typing and walked toward it, footsteps echoing in the empty corridor.

There was a woman pecking at a Royal manual in a stuffy room full of oak file cabinets. Both she and her machine were of antique vintage. An electric fan perched atop one of the files spun and blew, causing the ends of the woman's hair to dance.

I cleared my throat. She looked up with alarm, then smiled, and I asked her where the sheriff's office could be found. She directed me to a rear stairwell leading to the second floor.

At the top of the stairs was a tiny courtroom that

173

looked as if it hadn't been used in a long time. The word SHERIFF had been painted in glossy black on lime green plaster. Underneath it, was an arrow pointing to the right.

La Vista law enforcement was headquartered in a small dark room containing two wooden desks, an unmanned switchboard, and a silent teletype machine. A map of the county covered one wall. Wanted posters and a well-stocked gun rack rounded out the decor. At the centre of the rear wall was a metal door with a four inch wire-glass window.

The beige-uniformed man at one of the desks looked too young to be a peace officer – pink chipmunk cheeks and guileless hazel eyes under brown bangs. But he was the only one there and the nametag over his breast pocket said Deputy W. Bragdon. He was reading a farm journal and when I entered, looked up and gave me a cop's stare: wary, analytic, and inherently distrustful.

'I'm Dr. Delaware, come to pick up Dr. Melendez-Lynch.'

W. Bragdon stood, hitched up his holster, and disappeared through the metal door. He returned with a man in his fifties who could have stepped off a Remington canvas.

He was short and bow-legged, but broad shouldered and rock-solid, and he walked with a hint of a bantam swagger. His razor-creased trousers were of the same tan material as the deputy's uniform, his shirt green plaid and pearl buttoned. A crisp, wide-brimmed Stetson rested squarely atop his long head. The suggestion of vanity was confirmed by his tailoring: the shirt and slacks had been tapered to hug a trim physique.

The hair under the hat was dun and cropped close to narrow temples. His facial features were prominent and somewhat avian. A thick grey handlebar mous-

174

tache flared under a strong beakish nose.

I was drawn to his hands, which were unusually thick and large. One rested on the butt of a long-barrelled Colt .45 nestling in a hand-tooled holster, the other extended in a handshake.

'Doctor,' said a deep mellow voice, 'Sheriff Raymond Houten.' His grip was solid but he didn't exert pressure – a man well aware of his own strength.

He turned to Bragdon. 'Wait.' The baby-faced deputy looked me over once more and returned to his desk.

'Come on in, Doctor.'

On the other side of the tiny mesh window were ten feet of corridor. To the left was a bolted metal door, to the right his office, high-ceilinged, sunlit, and redolent of tobacco.

He sat behind an old desk and motioned me to a scarred leather armchair. Removing his hat, he tossed it on a rack fashioned from elk antlers.

Pulling out a pack of Chesterfields, he offered me one and when I declined, lit up, leaned back, and looked out the window. A large bay window afforded a view of Orange Avenue and his eyes followed the path of a semi hauling a load of produce. He waited until the big truck had rumbled out of sight before speaking.

'You're a psychiatrist?'

'Psychologist.'

He held the cigarette between thumb and forefinger and inhaled.

'And you're here as Dr. Lynch's friend, not in a professional capacity.'

His tone implied the latter would have been more than appropriate.

'That's correct.'

'I'll take you to see him in just a minute. But I want

175

to prepare you. He looks like he fell into a combine. We didn't do it.'

'I understand. Detective Sturgis said he started a fight with members of the Touch and came out the worse for it.'

Houten's mouth twisted under his moustache.

'That about sums it up. From what I understand Dr. Lynch is a prominent man,' he said sceptically.

'He's an internationally renowned expert on children's cancer.'

Another look out the window. I noticed a diploma hanging on the wall behind the desk. He'd earned a bachelor's degree in criminology from one of the state colleges.

'Cancer.' He mouthed the word softly. 'My wife had it. Ten years ago. It ate her up like some wild animal before it killed her. The doctors wouldn't tell us anything. Hid behind their jargon till the end.'

His smile was frightful.

'Still,' he said, 'I don't recall any of them quite like Dr. Lynch.'

'He's one of a kind, Sheriff.'

'Seems to have a temper problem. What is he, Guatemalan?'

'Cuban.'

'Same thing. The *latino* temperament.'

'What he did here wasn't typical. To my knowledge he's never been in trouble with the law.'

'I know that, Doctor. We ran him through the computer. That's one reason I'm willing to be lenient and let him go with just a fine. I've got enough to hold him over for quite a while – trespassing, assault, malicious mischief, interfering with an officer. Not to mention the damage he did to their gate with his car. But the circuit judge doesn't get up this way until winter and we'd have to ship him to San Diego. It would be complicated.'

'I appreciate your leniency and I'll write a cheque for any damages.'

He nodded, put out his cigarette, and got on the phone.

'Walt, write up Dr. Lynch's fines and include the estimate on the gate . . . No need, Dr. Delaware will come by and pay for it.' A glance in my direction. 'Take his cheque, he looks like an honest man.'

When he hung up he said, 'It's going to be a sizeable sum. The man created lots of problems.'

'He must have been traumatized hearing about the Swope murders.'

'We were all *traumatized*, Doctor. Nineteen hundred and seven people live in this town, not counting migrants. Everyone knows everyone. Yesterday we flew the flag at half mast. When little Woody got sick it was a kick in the gut for all of us. Now this . . .'

The sun had changed position and it flooded the office. Houten squinted. His eyes disappeared in a thatch of crow's feet.

'Dr. Lynch seems to have gotten it into his head that the children are here, over in the Retreat,' he said expectantly. I got the feeling I was being tested, and turned it back on him.

'And you feel that's out of the question.'

'You bet. Those Touch people are – unusual – but they're not criminals. When folks found out who bought the old monastery, there was one hell of an uproar. I was supposed to play Wyatt Earp and run 'em out of town.' He smiled sleepily. 'Farmers don't always grasp the finer points of due process, so I had to do a bit of educating. The day they drove into town and actually moved in, it was a circus, everyone gawking and pointing.

'That very day I went over and had a chat with Mr. Matthias, gave him a sociology lesson. Told him they'd do best to keep a low profile, patronize local

177

businesses, make timely contributions to the church auxiliary.'

It was precisely the strategy Seth Fiacre had described.

'They've been here three years, without a traffic ticket. Folks have grown used to them. I drop in on them when I please, so that everyone knows there's no witchcraft brewing behind those gates. They're just as strange as the day they moved in. But that's all. Strange, not criminal. If felonies were being committed, I'd know about it.'

'Any chance Woody and Nona could be somewhere else around here?'

He lit up again and regarded me coldly.

'Those children were raised here. They played in the fields and explored the dirt roads and never fell into harm's way. One trip to your big city and all that's changed. A small town is like a family, doctor. We don't murder each other, or kidnap each other's young.'

His experience and training should have taught him that families are the cauldrons in which violence is brewed. But I said nothing.

'There's one more thing I want you to hear so that you can pass it along to Dr. Lynch.' He got up and stood in front of the window. 'This is one giant TV screen. The show is called La Vista. Some days it's a soap opera, other times a comedy. Once in a while there's action and adventure. No matter what's on, I watch it every day.'

'I understand.'

'I thought you would, Doctor.'

He retrieved his hat and put it on.

'Let's see how the renowned expert is doing.'

The bolt on the metal door responded noisily to Houten's key. On the other side were three cells in a

178

row. I thought of the Laminar Airflow rooms. The jail was hot and humid, and it stank of body odour and solitude.

'He's in the last one,' said Houten.

I followed his bootsteps down the windowless passageway.

Raoul was sitting on a metal bench bolted to the wall, staring at the floor. His cell was seven feet square and contained a bed, also bolted down and covered by a thin stained mattress, a lidless toilet, and a zinc washbasin. From the smell of things the toilet wasn't in peak condition.

Houten unlocked the door and we walked in.

Raoul looked up with one eye. The other was blackened and swollen shut. A crust of dried blood had formed under his left ear. His lip was split and the colour of raw steak. Several buttons were missing from his white silk shirt, which hung open, exposing his soft hairy chest. There was a blue-black bruise along his ribcage. A shirtsleeve had been ripped at the seam and it dangled vestigially. His belt, tie, and shoelaces had been taken from him and I found the sight of his alligator shoes, caked with dirt, the tongue protruding, especially pathetic.

Houten saw my expression and said, 'We wanted to clean him up but he started fussing so we let it be.'

Raoul muttered something in Spanish. Houten looked at me, his expression that of a parent faced with a tantruming child.

'You can go now, Dr. Lynch,' he said. 'Dr. Delaware will drive you home. You can have your car towed back to Los Angeles at your expense, or leave it here to be fixed. Zack Piersall knows foreign ca - '

'I'm not going anywhere,' snapped Raoul.

'Dr. Lynch - '

'It's *Melendez*-Lynch, and your deliberate failure to

179

remember that doesn't intimidate me. I'm not leaving until the truth comes out.'

'Doctor, you're in a lot of trouble, potentially. I'm letting you go with fines in order to simplify things for all of us. I'm sure you've been under a lot of strain – '

'Don't patronize me, Sheriff. And stop covering for those murderous quacks!'

'Raoul – ' I said.

'No, Alex, you don't understand. These people are close-minded imbeciles. The tree of knowledge could sprout on their doorstep and they wouldn't pick the fruit.'

Houten moved his jaws as if trying to bring up a cud of patience.

'I want you out of my town,' he said softly.

'I won't go,' Raoul insisted, gripping the bench with both hands to demonstrate his intransigence.

'Sheriff,' I said, 'let me speak to him alone.'

Houten shrugged, left the cell, and locked me in. He walked away, and after the metal door closed behind him I turned to Raoul.

'What the hell's the matter with you!'

'Don't lecture me, Alex.' He stood and shook a fist in my face.

I stepped back instinctively. He stared at his upraised hand, dropped it to his side and mumbled an apology. Collapsing as if he'd been filleted, he sat back down.

'What in the world possessed you to conduct a one-man invasion of this place?' I asked him.

'I know they're in there,' he panted. 'Behind those gates. I can feel it!'

'You turned the Volvo into an assault tank because of feelings? Remember when you called intuition ''just another form of soft-headed hocus-pocus''?'

'This is different. They wouldn't let me in. If that's not proof they're hiding something I don't know what

180

it is!' He punched his palm with his fist. 'I'll get in there somehow and tear that place apart until I find him.'

'That's crazy. What is it about the Swopes that's turned you into a damned cowboy?'

He covered his face with his hands.

I sat down next to him and put my arm around his shoulder. He was soaked with sweat.

'Come on, let's get out of here,' I urged.

'Alex,' he said hoarsely, his breath sour and strong, 'oncology is a specialty for those who are willing to learn how to lose graciously. Not to love failure or accept it, but to suffer with dignity, as a patient must. Did you know that I was first in my medical school class?'

'I'm not surprised.'

'I had my pick of residencies. Many oncologists are the cream of medicine. And yet we confront failure each day of our lives.'

He pushed himself up and walked to the bars, running his hands up and down the ragged and rusty cylinders.

'Failure,' he repeated. 'But the victories are uncommonly sweet. The salvage and reconstruction of a life. What could create greater illusions of omnipotence, eh, Alex?'

'There'll be many more victories,' I assured him. 'You know that better than anyone. Remember the speech you used to give at fund raisers – the slide show with all those pictures of cured kids? Let this one go.'

He swivelled around and faced me, eyes blazing.

'As far as I'm concerned that boy is alive. Until I see his corpse I won't believe otherwise.'

I tried to speak but he cut me off.

'I didn't go into this field because of mawkish sentimentality – no favourite cousin died of leukaemia, no

181

grandpapa wasted away of carcinoma. I became an oncologist because medicine is the science – and the art – of *fighting* death. And cancer is death. From the first time, as a medical student, when I viewed those monstrous, primitive, *evil* cells under the microscope, I was seized with that truism. And I knew what my life's work would be.'

Beads of perspiration had collected on his high dark forehead. The coffee bean eyes glistened and roamed the cell.

'I won't give up,' he said, radiating defiance. 'Only the conquest of death, my friend, allows a glimpse of immortality.'

He was unreachable, caught up in his own frantic vision of the world. Obsessive and quixotic and denying what was most probable: Woody and Nona were dead, buried somewhere in the shifting mulch beneath the city.

'Let the police handle it, Raoul. My friend's due to come down here soon. He'll check everything out.'

'The police,' he spat. 'A lot of good they've been. Bureaucratic pencil pushers. Mediocre minds of limited vision. Like that stupid cowboy out there. Why aren't they here right now – every day is crucial for that little boy. They don't care, Alex. To them he's just another statistic. But not to me!'

He folded his arms in front of him, as if warding off the indignity of confinement, unaware of his derelict appearance.

I'd long thought that a surfeit of sensitivity could be a killing thing, too much insight malignant in its own right. The best survivors – there are studies that show it – are those blessed with an inordinate ability to deny. And keep on marching.

Raoul would march till he dropped.

I'd always considered him a touch manic. Perhaps as manic at the core as Richard Moody, but more generously endowed intellectually so that the excess energy was channelled honourably. For the good of society.

Now, too many failures had converged upon him: the Swopes' rejection of treatment, which, because he lived his work, was seen as a rejection of *him*, an atheism of the worst sort. The abduction of his patient – humiliation and loss of control. And now, death, the ultimate insult.

Failure had made him irrational.

I couldn't leave him there but didn't know how to get him out.

Before either of us could speak, the sound of approaching footsteps punctuated the silence. Houten peered into the cell, keys in hand.

'Ready, gentlemen?'

'I've had no luck, Sheriff.'

The news deepened the worry lines around his eyes.

'You're choosing to stay with us, Dr. *Melendez-Lynch*?'

'Until I've found my patient.'

'Your patient isn't here.'

'I don't believe that.'

Houten's mouth tightened and his eyebrows lowered. 'I'd like you out of there, Dr. Delaware.'

He turned a key, held the door barely open and kept a watchful eye on Raoul as I slipped through.

'Good-bye, Alex,' said the oncologist with a martyr's solemnity.

Houten spoke to him in clipped cadence.

'If you think prison is fun, sir, you're going to learn different. I promise you that. In the meantime, I'm getting you a lawyer.'

'I refuse legal services.'

'I'm getting you one anyway, Doctor. Whatever happens to you is going to be by the book.'

183

He turned on his heel and stomped away.

As we left the jail I caught a last glimpse of Raoul behind the bars. There wasn't any good reason for me to feel unfaithful, but I did.

16

HOUTEN MADE a phone call out of earshot. Ten minutes later a man in shirtsleeves showed up and the sheriff came forward to greet him.

'Thanks for coming on such short notice, Ezra.'

'Pleased to help, Sheriff.' The man's voice was soft, modulated, and even.

He looked to be in his late forties, medium-sized but sparely built, with a scholar's stoop. Everything about him was compact and neat. The smallish head was covered with thin salt-and-pepper hair combed straight back. The ears were elfin and close set. His facial features were regular but too delicate to be handsome. His short-sleeved white shirt was spotless and, despite the heat, free of wrinkles. His khaki trousers seemed freshly laundered. He wore rimless octagonal eyeglasses and carried a clip-on case for them in his breast pocket.

He looked like a man who never perspired.

I stood up and he appraised me mildly.

'Ezra,' said Houten, 'this is Dr. Delaware, a psychologist from Los Angeles. Came all the way down to take back the one I told you about. Doctor, meet Mr. Ezra Maimon, the best lawyer in town.'

The neat man laughed gently.

'The Sheriff's engaging in a bit of hyperbole,' he said and held out a thin calloused hand. 'I'm the *only* attorney in La Vista, and the cases I usually work with are made of wood.'

'Ezra owns a rare fruit nursery just out of town,' explained Houten. 'Claims he's retired but we still get him to do a bit of lawyering from time to time.'

'Wills and small estates are comparatively simple matters,' said Maimon. 'If this turns into criminal defence you'll have to bring in a specialist.'

'That's all right,' Houten twirled one of his moustaches. 'This is no criminal case. Yet. Just a little problem, like I told you over the phone.'

Maimon nodded.

'Tell me the details,' he said.

He listened quietly and impassively, turning once or twice to smile at me. When Houten was through, the attorney placed a finger to his lips and gazed up at the ceiling, as if doing mental arithmetic. After a minute of silent contemplation he said, 'Let me see my client.'

He spent half an hour in the cell. I tried to kill the time by reading a magazine for highway patrolmen until I found that it specialized in graphic photo-essays of fatal road wrecks accompanied by detailed descriptions of the vehicular horrors. I couldn't imagine why those who witnessed such carnage as part of their daily routine would be attracted to a photographic reprise. Perhaps it provided distance –

186

the true solace of the voyeur. I put the magazine aside and contented myself with watching. W. Bragdon read about alfalfa culture while he picked at his cuticles.

Finally a buzzer rang.

'Go in and get him, Walt,' ordered Houten.

Bragdon said yessir, left, and came back with Maimon.

'I think,' said the attorney, 'we may be able to reach a compromise.'

'Run it by me, Ezra.'

The three of us sat around one of the desks.

'Dr. Melendez-Lynch is a very intelligent man,' said Maimon. 'Perhaps overly insistent. But not, in my opinion, at all malicious.'

'He's a pain in the butt, Ezra.'

'He's been a little overzealous in his attempts at fulfilling his medical obligations. But, as we all know, Woody's deathly ill. Dr. Melendez-Lynch feels he has the means to cure him and he sees himself as trying to save a life.'

Maimon spoke with quiet authority. He could have acted as Houten's mouthpiece but instead seemed to be functioning as a true advocate. I didn't think it was for my benefit and I was impressed.

Houten's face darkened with anger.

'The boy's not here. You know that as well as I do.'

'My client is an empiricist. He wants to see that for himself.'

'No way is he going near that place, Ezra.'

'I agree with you. That would be inviting trouble. However he did agree to Dr. Delaware's conducting a search of the Retreat. Promised to pay his fines and leave without a fuss if the good doctor finds nothing suspicious.'

It was a simple solution. But neither Houten nor I had come up with it. He, because his appetite for

187

concession wasn't hearty in the first place, and he'd already had his fill. And I'd been too overwhelmed by Raoul's fanaticism to think straight.

The sheriff digested it.

'I can't force Matthias to open the place up.'

'Of course not. He has every right to refuse. If he does we'll reapproach the problem.'

An eminently logical man.

Houten turned his attention to me.

'What about it? You up for it?'

'Sure. Whatever works.'

Houten went into his office and returned saying Matthias had okayed the visit. Maimon had another talk with Raoul, buzzed, was retrieved by Bragdon and left, telling the sheriff to call him if he was needed. Houten put on his hat and absently touched the butt of his Colt. He and I climbed down the stairs and out of the building. We got into a white El Camino decaled on the door with the sheriff's star. He gunned the engine, which sounded super-charged, and turned right in front of city hall.

The road forked a half mile out of town. Houten headed right, driving quickly and smoothly, accelerating around turns that would have given a stranger pause. The road narrowed and grew dim in the shadows of bordering conifers. The El Camino's tyres churned up dust as it sped past. A jackrabbit in our path froze, quivered, and bounded into the shelter of the tall trees.

Houten managed to pull out a Chesterfield and light it without reducing speed. He drove another two miles, sucking in smoke and surveying the countryside with a cop's scanning eyes. At the top of a rise he turned abruptly, drove a hundred feet, and braked to a stop in front of a pair of black-painted arched iron gates.

The entrance to the Retreat was unlabelled as such. Prickly mounds of cactus squatted at the outer edges of both gates. A tide of electric pink bougainvillaea flowed over one of the abode gateposts. A single climbing rosebush awash with scarlet blooms and studded with thorns embraced the other. He turned off the engine and we were greeted by silence. And all around, the deep, secretive green of the forest.

Houten stubbed out his cigarette, dismounted the truck, and strode up to the entrance. There was a long columnar lockbox affixed to one gate, but when he pushed the iron door, it swung open.

'They like it quiet,' he said. 'We'll walk from here.'

An unpaved path lined with smooth brown stones and meticulously barbered beds of succulents had been excised from the forest. It climbed and we moved briskly, the pace set by Houten. He hiked rather than walked, muscles swelling through the tautness of his slacks, arms swinging by his sides, military fashion. California jays squawked and fussed. Large fussy bees nuzzled up to the labia of wildflowers. The air smelled meadow-fresh.

The sun bore down relentlessly on the unshaded path. My throat was dry and I felt the sweat trickle down my back. Houten seemed as crisp as ever. Ten minutes of walking brought us to the top of the road.

'That's it,' said Houten. He stopped to pull out another cigarette and light it in the shelter of cupped hands. I mopped my brow and gazed down at the valley below.

I saw perfection and it unnerved me.

The Retreat still looked like a monastery, with its towering cathedral and high walls. An assortment of smaller buildings sat behind the walls and created a maze of courtyards. A large wooden crucifix topped the belfry of the churchtower, a brand burned into the azure flanks of the sky. The front windows were

189

leaded and supported by wooden balconies. The roofs and the tops of the walls were layered with red clay tile. The walls were fresh vanilla stucco splashed dove white where the sun hit. A great deal of care had been taken to preserve the intricate mouldings and borders scored into the stucco.

A running brook circled the compound like a moat. Above it floated an arched viaduct that bled into a brick pathway at the point where solid ground reasserted itself. The path was hooded by a stone arbour caressed by tendrils of grape vine, ruby clusters of fruit ponderous amid the green leaves.

To the front of the compound was a small patch of lawn shaded by ancient gnarled oaks. The big twisted trees danced like witches around a fountain that spat into an enormous stone urn. Beyond the buildings were acres of farmland. I made out corn, cucumbers, groves of citrus and olive, a sheep pasture and vineyards, but there was plenty more. A handful of white-garbed figures worked the land. Heavy machinery buzzed wasplike in the distance.

'Pretty, isn't it?' asked Houten resuming the hike.

'Beautiful. Like out of another time.'

He nodded. 'When I was a kid I used to climb around the hills, try to get a peek at the monks – they wore heavy brown robes no matter how hot it got. Never talked to anyone or had anything to do with folks in town. The gates were always locked.'

'Must have been nice growing up here.'

'Why's that?'

I shrugged.

'The open air, the freedom.'

'Freedom, huh?' His smile was abrupt and bitter. 'Farming is just another word for bondage.'

His jaw set and he kicked at a rock with sudden savagery. I'd hit some kind of nerve and quickly changed the subject.

190

'When did the monks leave?'

He sucked on his cigarette before answering.

'Seven years ago. The land went fallow. Scrub and brambles. Couple of corporations thought of buying it – executive resort and all that – but all of 'em backed out. The buildings weren't suited to it – rooms like cells, no heat, looked like a church any way you cut it. The cost of renovation would have been too high.'

'But perfect for the Touch.'

He shrugged.

'Something for everyone in this world.'

The front door was rounded at the top, a slab of stout boards braced by wide iron bands. Inside was a three-storey white-walled entrance floored with Mexican pavers and skylit from above. A smear of colour reflected from the stained-glass windows rainbowed the tiles. The spicy aroma of incense suggested itself. The air was cool, almost to the point of refrigeration.

A woman in her sixties sat at a wooden table in front of a pair of oversized doors that were rounded and banded like the one out front. Above them was a wooden sign that said SANCTUARY. The woman's hair had been tied back in a ponytail and fastened with a leather thong. She wore a sack dress of raw white cotton and sandals on her feet. Her face was weathered, bland and pleasant, and free of makeup or other pretence. Her hands were in her lap and she smiled, reminding me of a well-behaved schoolchild. The teacher's pet.

'Good afternoon, Sheriff.'

'Hello, Maria. Like to see Matthias.'

She rose gracefully. The skirt reached below her knees.

'He's waiting for you.'

She led us to the left of the sanctuary down a long hallway unadorned except for potted palms placed at

191

ten-foot intervals. There was a single door at the end, which she held open for us.

The room was dim and lined with books on three walls. The floor was pine plank. The incense smell was stronger. There was no desk, only three plain wooden chairs arranged in an isosceles triangle. At the peak of the triangle sat a man.

He was long, lean and angular and wore a tunic and drawstring trousers of the same raw cotton as Maria's dress. His feet were bare, but a pair of sandals lay on the floor by his chair. His hair was the waxy, amber-tinted white that is the heritage of some blonds grown to maturity, and was cropped short. His beard was a shade darker – more amber and less snow – and hung across his chest. It curled luxuriantly and he stroked it as if it were a pet. His brow was high and domed and I saw the crease just below the hairline, an indentation you could rest your thumb in. The eyes, cradled in deep sockets, were grey-blue in colour, not dissimilar from mine. But I hoped mine gave off more warmth.

'Please sit.' His voice was powerful and somewhat metallic.

'This is Dr. Delaware, Matthias. Doctor, Noble Matthias.'

The imperial title sounded silly. I searched for mirth on Houten's face but he looked dead serious.

Matthias kept stroking his beard. He sat meditatively still, a man not uncomfortable with silence.

'Thanks for cooperating,' said Houten stiffly. 'Hopefully we can clear this thing up and move along.'

The white head nodded. 'Whatever will help.'

'Dr. Delaware would like to ask you a few questions and then we'll take a stroll around.'

Matthias remained in repose.

Houten turned to me.

192

'It's your show.'

'Mr. Matthias,' I began.

'Just Matthias, please. We eschew titles.'

'Matthias, I'm not here to intrude upon you or your – '

He interrupted me with a wave of his hand.

'I'm well aware of the nature of your visit. Ask what you need to ask.'

'Thank you. Dr. Melendez-Lynch feels you had something to do with the removal of Woody Swope from the hospital and the family's subsequent disappearance.'

'Urban madness,' said the guru. 'Madness.' He repeated the word as if testing it for suitability as a mantra.

'I'd appreciate hearing any theories you might have about it.'

He inhaled deeply, closed his eyes, opened them, and spoke.

'I can't help you. They were private people. As are we. We barely knew them. There were brief encounters – passing each other on the road, perfunctory smiles. Once or twice we purchased seeds from them. In the summer of our first season the girl worked for us as a scullery maid.'

'Temporary job?'

'Correct. In the beginning we were not yet self-sufficient and we hired several of the local youngsters to help. Her duties were in the kitchen, as I recall. Scrubbing, scouring, readying the ovens for use.'

'How was she as a worker?'

A smile vented the cotton-candy beard.

'We are rather aescetic by contemporary standards. Most young people would not be attracted to that.'

Houten broke in. 'Nona was – is a live one. Not a bad kid, just a little on the wild side.'

The message was clear: she'd been a problem. I remembered Carmichael's story about the stag party. That kind of spontaneity could wreak havoc in a place that prized discipline. She'd probably come on to the men. But if that had anything to do with the issue at hand I couldn't see it.

'Anything else you could tell me that might help?'

He stared at me. His gaze was intense, almost tangible. It was hard not to look away.

'I'm afraid not.'

Houten shifted restlessly in his chair. Nicotine fidgets. His hand went up to his cigarette pocket then stopped.

'I'm gonna take some air,' he said and walked out. Matthias didn't seem to notice his exit.

'You didn't know the family well,' I went on. 'Yet two of your people visited them at the hospital. I'm not doubting your word but it's a question you're bound to be asked again.'

He sighed.

'We had business in Los Angeles. Baron and Delilah were assigned to handle it. We felt it would be gracious for them to visit the Swopes. They brought the family fresh fruit from our orchards.'

'Not,' I smiled, 'for medicinal purposes.'

'No,' he said, amused. 'For nourishment. And pleasure.'

'So this was a social call.'

'In a sense.'

'What do you mean?'

'We're not sociable. We don't make small talk. Visiting them was an act of good will, not part of some nefarious scheme. No attempt was made to interfere with the child's medical care. I've notified Baron and Delilah to join us momentarily so you'll have a chance to obtain additional details.'

'I appreciate that.'

194

A vein throbbed in the centre of the crater in his brow. He held out his hands as if to ask, What next? The remote look on his face reminded me of someone else. The association triggered my next question.

'There's a doctor who treated Woody by the name of August Valcroix. He told me he visited here. Do you remember him?'

He twirled the ends of his beard around one long finger.

'Once or twice a year we offer seminars on organic gardening and meditation. Not to proselytise, but to enlighten. He may have attended one of those. I don't remember him specifically.'

I gave him a physical description of Valcroix but it didn't evoke recognition.

'That's it, then. I appreciate your help.'

He sat there, unblinking and unmoving. In the stingy light of the room his pupils had expanded so that only a thin rim of pale iris was visible. He had hypnotic eyes. A prerequisite for charisma.

'If you have any more questions you may ask them.'

'No questions, but I would like to hear more about your philosophy.'

He nodded.

'We are refugees from a former life. We've chosen a new life that emphasizes purity and industry. We avoid environmental poisons and seek self-sufficiency. We believe that by changing ourselves we increase the positive energy in the world.'

Standard stuff. He rattled it off like some New Age pledge of allegiance.

'We're not killers,' he added.

Before I could reply, two of them came into the room.

Matthias stood up and left without acknowledging their presence. The man and woman took the two

195

empty seats. The transaction was oddly mechanical, as if the people were interchangeable parts in some smoothly functioning apparatus.

They sat, hands in laps – more good schoolkids – and smiled with the maddening serenity of the born-again and the lobotomized.

I was far from serene. Because I recognized both of them, though in quite different ways.

The man who called himself Baron was medium-sized and thin. Like Matthias, his hair was cut short and his beard left untrimmed. But in his case the effect was less dramatic than untidy. His hair was medium brown and wispy. Patches of skin showed through the sparse frizzy chin whiskers and his cheeks were covered with soft fuzz. It was as if he'd forgotten to wash his face.

In graduate school I'd known him as Barry Graffius. He was older than I, in his early forties, but had been a class behind, a late starter who'd decided to become a psychologist after trying just about everything else.

Graffius's family was wealthy, big in the movie business, and he'd been one of those rich kids who couldn't seem to settle down – inadequate drive level because he'd never been deprived of anything. The consensus was that family money had gotten him in, but that may have been a jaundiced view. Because Barry Graffius had been the most unpopular person in the department.

'I've always tended to be charitable in my evaluations of others but I'd despised Graffius. He was loudmouthed and contentious, dominating seminars with irrelevant quotes and statistics aimed at impressing the professors. He insulted his peers, bullied the meek, played devil's advocate with malicious glee.

And he loved to flaunt his money.

196

Most of us were struggling to get by, working extra jobs in addition to our teaching assistantships. Graffius delighted in coming to class in hand-tailored leather and suede, complaining about the repair bill on his XKE, lamenting the tax bite. He was an outrageous name dropper, recounting lavish Hollywood parties, offering a teasing glimpse into a glamorous world beyond the grasp of the rest of us.

I'd heard that after graduating he'd gone into practice on Bedford Drive – Beverly Hills Couch Row – planning to capitalize on his connections and become Therapist to the Stars.

I could see where he'd run into Norman Matthews.

He recognized me too. I could tell by the flurry of activity behind his watery brown eyes. As we looked at each other that activity crystallized: fear. The fear of being discovered.

His former identity was no secret in the strict sense. But he didn't want to be confronted by it: for those who imagine themselves reborn, bringing up the past has all the appeal of exhuming one's own mouldering corpse.

I said nothing, but wondered if he'd told Matthias about knowing me.

The woman was older, but uncommonly pretty despite the ponytail no-makeup look that seemed to be *de rigueur* for Touch women. Madonna-faced with ivory skin, raven hair now streaked with silver, and brooding gypsy eyes. Beverly Lucas had called her a hot number who'd lost it but that seemed unfairly bitchy. Perhaps knowing the woman's true age would have softened the critique.

She looked a well-preserved fifty but I knew she was at least sixty-five.

She hadn't made a film since 1951, the year I was born.

Desiree Layne, Queen of budget film noirs.

There'd been a revival of her movies when I was in college, with free screenings during finals week. I'd seen them all: *Phantom Bride, Darken My Doorstep, The Savage Place, Secret Admirer.*

An eon ago, before my early retirement, I'd been a frantic, lonely man, with little free time. But one of the few pleasures I'd allowed myself was a Sunday afternoon in bed with a tall glass of Chivas and a Desiree Layne flick.

It hadn't mattered who the leading man was as long as there were lots of closeups of those beautiful evil eyes, the dresses that looked like lingerie. The voice husky with passion . . .

She emitted no passion now, sitting statue-still, white-garbed, smiling vacantly. So goddamned *harmless.*

The place was really starting to spook me. It was like walking through a wax museum . . .

'Noble Matthias told us you have questions,' said Baron.

'Yes. I just wanted to hear more about your visit to the Swopes. It could help explain what's happened, aid in locating the children.'

They nodded in unison.

I waited. They looked at each other. She spoke.

'We wanted to cheer them up. Noble Matthias had us pick fruit - oranges, grapefruit, peaches, plums - the best we could find. We put it all in a basket, wrapped it with gay paper.'

She stopped talking and smiled, as if her narrative had explained everything.

'Was your graciousness well received?'

Her eyes widened.

'Oh yes. Mrs. Swope said she was hungry. She ate a plum - a Santa Rosa plum - right there. Said it was delicious.'

Baron's face hardened as she prattled on. When

198

she paused he said, 'You want to know if we tried to talk them out of treating the boy.' He sat impassively but there was an aggressive edge to his voice.

'Matthias told me you didn't. Did the subject of medical treatment come up?'

'It did,' he said. 'She complained about the plastic room, said she felt cut off from the boy, that the family was being divided.'

'Did she explain what she meant?'

'No. I assumed she was talking about the physical separation – not being allowed to touch him without gloves, only one person in the room at a time.'

Delilah nodded in assent.

'Such a cold place,' she said. 'Physically and spiritually.' To illustrate she gave a little shudder. Once an actress . . .

'They didn't feel the doctors treated them like human beings,' added Baron. 'Especially the Cuban.'

'Poor man,' said Delilah. 'When he tried to force his way in this morning I couldn't help feeling sorry for him. Overweight and flushed red as a tomato – he must have high blood pressure.'

'What were their complaints about him?'

Baron pursed his lips.

'Just that he was impersonal,' he said.

'Did they mention a doctor named Valcroix?'

Delilah shook her head.

Baron spoke again.

'We didn't talk about much of anything. It was just a brief visit.'

'I couldn't wait to get out of there,' recalled Delilah. 'Everything was so mechanical.'

'We dropped off the fruit, left, and drove back home,' Baron said with finality.

'A sad situation,' she sighed.

17

A GROUP of Touch people were sitting yoga-style on the grass when I came out, eyes closed, palms pressed together, faces glowing in the sun. Houten leaned against the fountain, smoking, eyes drifting idly in their direction. He saw me coming, dropped the butt, stomped on it, and tossed it in an earthenware trash-basket.

'Learn anything?'

I shook my head.

'Like I told you,' he cocked his head toward the meditators who had now started to hum, 'strange but harmless.'

I looked at them. Despite the white costumes, the sandals, and the untrimmed beards, they resembled participants in a corporate seminar, one of those glossy pop-psych affairs promoted by management to increase productivity. The faces gazing heavenward were middle-aged and well-fed, suffused with an executive look that bespoke prior lives of comfort and authority.

Norman Matthews had been described to me as an aggressive and ambitious man. A hustler. As Matthias he'd tried to come across a holy man but there was enough cynicism in me to wonder if he hadn't simply traded one hustle for another.

The Touch was a gold mine: offer the prosperous simplicity amid lush surroundings, remove the burden of personal responsibility, substitute an ethos that equated health and vitality with righteousness, and pass the collection plate. How could it miss?

But even if the whole thing was a scam it didn't spell kidnapping and murder. As Seth had pointed out, loss of privacy was the last thing Matthias wanted, be he prophet or con man.

'Let's take a look around,' said Houten, 'and be done with it.'

I was allowed free access to the grounds, permitted to open any door. The sanctuary was domed and majestic, with clerestory windows and biblical murals on the ceiling. The pews had been removed and the floor covered with padded mats. There was a rough pine table in the centre of the room and little else. A woman in white dusted and swept, stopping only to smile at us maternally.

The sleeping rooms were indeed cells – no larger than the one in which Raoul was confined – low-ceilinged, thick-walled, and cool, with a single window the size of a hardbound book and grilled with wood. Each room was furnished with a cot and a chest of drawers. Matthias's differed only in that it had a small bookcase. His literary taste was eclectic – the Bible, the Koran, Perls, Jung, Cousin's *Anatomy of An Illness*, Toffler's *Future Shock*, the Bhagavad-Gita,

201

several texts on organic gardening and ecology.

I took a tour of the kitchen, where cauldrons of broth simmered on industrial stoves and bread baked sweetly in brick ovens. There was a member's library, its stock leaning toward health and agriculture, and a conference room with textured adobe walls. And everywhere people in white working, smiling, bright-eyed and friendly.

Houten and I traipsed through the fields, watching Touch members tend the grapes. A black-bearded giant put down his shears and offered us a freshly picked cluster. The fruit was moist to the touch and it burst electrically upon my tongue. I complimented the man on the flavour. He nodded and returned to his work.

It was well into the afternoon but the sun continued to rage. My unprotected head began to ache and after cursorily inspecting the sheepyard and the vegetable plots I told Houten I'd had enough.

We turned and walked back toward the viaduct. I wondered what I'd accomplished, for the search had been symbolic, at best. There wasn't any reason to believe the Swope children were there. And if they were, there'd be no way to find them. The Retreat was surrounded by hundreds of acres, much of it forest. Nothing short of a bloodhound pack could cover it all. Besides, monasteries are secret places, designed for refuge, and the compound might very well harbour a maze of underground caverns, secret compartments, and hidden passages that only an archaeologist could unravel.

It had been a futile day, I thought, but if it helped Raoul confront reality it was worth it. Then I realized what *reality* meant and craved the balm of denial.

Houten had Bragdon bring Raoul's personal effects in a large manila envelope. In the end he'd agreed to

202

accept the oncologist's cheque for six hundred eighty-seven dollars' worth of fines and while he recorded the amount in triplicate, I walked around the room restlessly, eager to get going.

The county map caught my eye. I located La Vista and noticed a back road to the east that seemed to skirt the town, allowing entry to the region from the outlying woodlands without actually passing through a commercial district. If that was the case, avoiding Houten's scrutiny was easier than he'd let on.

After some hesitation I asked him about it. He fiddled with a piece of carbon paper and continued writing.

'Oil company bought up the land, got the county to seal off the road. There was big talk of deep deposits, prosperity just around the corner.'

'Did they strike it rich?'

'Nope. Bone dry.'

The deputy brought Raoul out. I told him about my visit to the Retreat and the negative findings. He took it in, looking downcast and beaten, and offered no protest.

The sheriff, pleased with his passivity, treated him with exquisite courtesy while he signed him out. He asked Raoul what he wanted to do about his Volvo, and the oncologist shrugged and said to have it fixed, he'd pay for it.

I led him out of the room and down the stairs.

He was silent throughout the ride home, not even losing his cool when a chubby female border guard pulled us over and asked for his identification. He accepted the indignity with a mute acquiescence that I found pitiful. Two hours ago he'd been aggressive and poised for battle. I wondered if he'd been laid low by the accumulated stress or if cyclical mood swings were a part of his makeup I'd never noticed.

I was famished but he looked too grungy to take to a restaurant so I bought a couple of burgers and Cokes at a stand in Santa Ana and pulled to the side of the road near a small municipal park. I gave Raoul his food and ate mine while watching a group of teenagers play softball, racing to finish before nightfall. When I turned to look at him, he was asleep, the food still wrapped and lying in his lap. I took it, stowed it in a trashcan and started up the Seville. He stirred but didn't awaken and by the time I got back on the freeway he was snoring peacefully.

We reached L.A. by seven, just as traffic on the downtown interchange was untangling. When I turned off at the Los Feliz exit he opened his eyes.

'What's your address?'

'No, take me back to the hospital.'

'You're in no shape to go back there.'

'I must. Helen will be waiting.'

'You'll only scare her looking like that. At least go home and freshen up first.'

'I have a change of clothes in my office. Please, Alex.'

I threw up my hands and drove to Western Peds. After parking in the doctors' lot I walked him to the front door of Prinzley.

'Thank you,' he said, looking at his feet.

'Take care of yourself.'

On the way back to the car I met Beverly Lucas leaving the wards. She looked tired and worn, the oversized purse seeming to weigh her down.

'Alex, I'm so glad to see you.'

'What's the matter?'

She looked around to make sure no one was listening.

'It's Augie. He's been making my life miserable ever since your friend interrogated him, calling me unfaithful, a quisling. He even tried to embarrass me on rounds but the attending doc stopped it.'

'Bastard.'

She shook her head.

'What makes it hard is that I see his point. We were – close, once. What he did in bed was nobody's business.'

I took her by the shoulders.

'What you did was right. If you got enough distance to see straight that would be obvious. Don't let him get to you.'

She flinched at the harshness in my voice.

'I know you're right. Intellectually. But he's falling apart and it hurts me. I can't help my feelings.'

She started to cry. A trio of nurses walked our way. I steered her off the walkway and into the stairwell to the doctors' level.

'What do you mean falling apart?'

'Acting strange. Doping and drinking more heavily than usual. He's bound to get caught. This morning he pulled me off the ward and into a conference room, locked the door, and came on to me.'

She lowered her eyes in embarrassment.

'He told me I was the best he'd ever had, actually tried to get physical. When I stopped him he looked crushed. Then he started to rant about Melendez-Lynch – how he'd scapegoated him and was going to try to use the Swope case to terminate the fellowship. He started to laugh – it was a freaky laugh, Alex, full of anger. He said he had an ace up his sleeve. That Melendez-Lynch would never get rid of him.'

'Did he say what that was?'

'I asked him. He just laughed again and walked out. Alex, I'm worried. I was just on my way to the residents' dorm. To make sure he was okay.'

I tried to talk her out of it but she was resolute. She had an infinite capacity for guilt. Someday she'd make someone a wonderful doormat.

It was clear she wanted me to accompany her to his apartment, and tired as I was, I agreed to go with her, in case things got hairy. And on the off-chance Valcroix really had an ace and might show it.

The residents' dorm across the boulevard from the hospital was a utilitarian affair, three storeys of unfinished concrete over a subterranean parking lot. Some of the windows had been brightened up with plants and flower arrangements resting on sills or hanging from macrame harnesses. But that didn't stop it from looking like what it was: low-cost housing.

An elderly black guard was stationed at the door – there had been rapes in the neighbourhood and the residents had screamed for security. He looked at our hospital badges and let us pass.

Valcroix's apartment was on the second floor.

'It's the one with the red door,' said Beverly, pointing.

The corridor and all the other doors were beige. Valcroix's was scarlet and stood out like a wound.

'Amateur paint job?' I ran my hand over the wood, which was rough and bubbled. A segment from a doper comic had been pasted to the door – furry people popping pills and hallucinating in technicolour, their fantasies sexually explicit and excessive.

'Uh huh.'

She knocked several times. When there was no answer she bit her lip.

'Maybe he went out,' I suggested.

'No. He always stays home when he's not on call. That was one thing that bothered me about our relationship. We never went out.'

I didn't remind her that she'd spotted him in a restaurant with Nona Swope. No doubt he was one of those men as stingy about giving as he was greedy about taking. He'd do the least amount possible to

206

enter a woman's body. With her lowered expectations, Beverly would have been his dream. Until he got bored with her.

'I'm worried, Alex. I know he's in there. He could be OD'ed on something.'

Nothing I said alleviated her anxiety. Finally, we went downstairs and convinced the guard to use his master key on the red door.

'I don't know 'bout this, Doctor,' he said, but he unlocked the apartment.

The place was a sty. Dirty laundry was piled on the grubby carpet. The bed was unmade. On the nightstand was an ashtray brimming with marijuana roaches. Nearby was an engraved roach clip in the shape of a pair of female legs. Medical books and more doper comics coexisted in the paper blizzard that covered half the living room floow. The kitchen sink was a swamp of dirty dishes and cloudy water. A fly circled overhead.

No one was home.

Beverly walked through and unconsciously began straightening up. The guard looked at her quizzically.

'Come on,' I said with surprising vehemence. 'He's not here. Let's get out.'

The guard cleared his throat.

She covered the bed, took a last look around, and left.

Outside the dorm she asked if we should call the police.

'What for?' I demanded sharply. 'A grown man leaves his apartment? They'd never take it seriously. And for good reason.'

She looked wounded and wanted to discuss it further but I begged off. I was weary, my head hurt, my joints were sore; it felt like I was coming down with something. Besides, my altruism account was already badly overdrawn.

We crossed the street in silence and parted ways.

By the time I got home I felt really lousy – feverish, logy, and aching all over. There was a bright spot – an express letter from Robin confirming her departure from Tokyo in a week. One of the Japanese executives owned a condo on Kauai and he'd offered her the use of it. She was hoping I could meet her flight in Honolulu and set aside two weeks for fun and sun. I called Western Union and wired a Yes on all accounts.

A hot bath didn't make me feel any better. Neither did a cool drink or self-hypnosis. I dragged myself downstairs to feed the koi but didn't linger to watch them eat. Back in the house I fell into bed with the paper, the rest of the mail, and Leo Kottke on the stereo. But I found myself too drained to concentrate, and surrendered to sleep without a struggle.

18

BY MORNING my malaise had matured to influenza. I took aspirin, drank lemon tea, and wished Robin were there to take care of me.

I kept the TV on for background noise and slept, on and off, all day. By evening I was feeling well enough to hobble out of bed and eat Jell-O. But even that tired me and soon I was back asleep.

In my dream I was adrift on an Arctic ice floe, seeking shelter from a violent hailstorm in a meagre cardboard leanto. Each new fusillade shredded the cardboard, leaving me increasingly terrified and exposed.

I awoke naked and shivering. The hailstorm continued. Digital numbers glowed in the dark: 11:26. Through the window I saw clear black skies.

The hail turned into bullets. Shotgun fire stinging the side of the house.

I dived to the floor, lay flat, belly-down, breathing hard.

More gunfire. A percussive pop, then the tinkle of broken glass. A cry of pain. A sickening dull sound, like a melon bursting under a sledgehammer. An engine starting. Automotive escape.

Then silence.

I crawled to the phone. Called the police. Asked for Milo. He was off-shift. Del Hardy, then. *Please.*

The black detective came to the phone. Between gasps I told him about the nightmare that had turned real.

He said he'd call Milo, both of them would be there code three.

Minutes later the wail of sirens stretched up the glen, trombones gone mad.

I put on a robe and stepped outside.

The redwood siding on the front of the house was peppered with holes and splintered in a dozen places. One window had been blown out.

I smelled hydrocarbons.

On the terrace were three open cans of gasoline. Wadded rags had been fashioned into oversized wicks and stuffed into the spouts. Oily footprints led to the edge of the landing and ended in a single smear of a skidmark. I looked over the railing.

A man sprawled face down and motionless in the Japanese garden.

I climbed down just as the black and white pulled up. Walked barefoot to the garden, the stone cool under feet burning with fever. I called out. The man didn't respond.

It was Richard Moody.

Half his face had been blown away. What remained was dog food. Or more precisely, fish food,

210

for his head was submerged in my pond and the koi nibbled at it, sucking up the bloody water, relishing the novelty of a new snack.

Sickened, I tried to wave them away but the sight of me was a conditioned stimulus for feeding and they grew more enthusiastic, feasting and slurping, scaly gourmands. The big black and gold carp came half out of the water to get a mouthful. I could swear he grinned at me with whiskered lips.

Someone was at my side. I jumped.

'Easy, Alex.'.

'Milo!'

He looked as if he'd crawled out of bed. He wore a lifeless windbreaker over a yellow Hang-Ten polo shirt and baggy jeans. His hair was a fright wig and his green eyes gleamed in the moonlight.

'Come on,' he took my elbow. 'Let's go upstairs, get something liquid in you and then you can tell me what happened.'

As the crime scene crew busied themselves with the technical minutiae of murder I sat in my old leather sofa and drank Chivas. The shock was beginning to slough off; I realized I was still sick – chilled and weak. The Scotch went down warm and smooth. Across from me sat Milo and Del Hardy. The black detective was dapper, as always, in a shaped dark suit, peach-coloured shirt, black tie, and spit-polished demiboots. He put on a pair of reading glasses and took notes.

'On the surface,' said Milo, 'it looks like Moody had plans to torch your place and somebody followed him, caught him in the act, and took him out.' He thought for a moment. 'There was a triangle, right? How do you like the boyfriend for the shooter role?'

'He didn't seem the type to stalk a man like that.'

211

'Full name,' said Hardy, pen poised.

'Carlton Conley. He's a carpenter from Aurora Studios. He and Moody were friends before it tri-angulated.'

Hardy scribbled. 'Did he move in with the wife?'

'Yes. They're all supposed to be up near Davis. On the advice of her lawyer.'

'The lawyer's name?'

'Malcolm J. Worthy. Beverly Hills.'

'Better call him,' said Milo. 'If Moody had a list he'd be on it. Find out the number up in Davis and check out if anything went down there – she's still next of kin, has to be notified anyway. Have the local law go over there and read her face – see if she's surprised by the news. Call the judge, too. Anyone else you can think of, Alex?'

'There was another psychologist involved in the case. Dr. Lawrence Daschoff. Lives in Brentwood. Office in Santa Monica.' I knew Larry's office number by heart and gave it to them.

'What about Moody's own lawyer?' asked Del. 'If the joker thought his case had been botched he might lash out, right?'

'True. The guy's name is Durkin. Emil or Elton or something like that.'

A grimace of recognition crossed the black detective's face.

'Elridge,' he growled. 'Fucker represented my ex-wife. Cleaned me out.'

'Well, then,' laughed Milo, 'you can have the pleasure of interviewing him. Or consoling his widow.'

Hardy grumbled, closed his pad, and went into the kitchen and left to make the calls.

A crime scene tech beckoned from the door and Milo patted my shoulder and went out to talk to him. He returned in a few minutes.

212

'They found tyre tracks,' he said. 'Fat ones, like on a hot rod. Ring any bells?'

'Moody drove a truck.'

'They already looked at his wheels. No match.'

'Nothing else comes to mind.'

'There were six more gas cans in the truck, which supports the hit list theory. But it also doesn't make sense. He was going to use three cans here. Let's assume that he planned this out as some kind of structured revenge ritual, three cans per victim. Given a minimum of five victims – you, the other shrink, both lawyers, and the judge, that adds up to fifteen cans. Six left means nine used. Not counting you, that makes two prior attempts. If he planned on torching the family home, make it twelve and three possible priors. Even if the numbers are wrong it's unlikely you were singled out for more gas than anyone else. Which means you probably weren't his first stop. Why would the shooter follow him around town, watch him set two or three fires, risk being seen, and wait until the third to do the job?'

I puzzled over that.

'Only thing I can think of,' I said, 'is this is a pretty secluded area. Lots of big trees, easy for a sniper to hide.'

'Maybe,' he said sceptically. 'We'll pursue the tyre angle. The Hot Rod Killer. Catchy.'

He chewed on a hangnail, looked at me gravely.

'Got any enemies I don't know about, pal?'

My stomach lurched. He'd put into words what had been fulminating in my mind. That I was the intended victim . . .

'Just the Casa de Los Ninos guys and they're behind bars. No one on the streets that I know of.'

'Way the system runs you never know whether they're on the streets or not. We'll run parole checks on all of them. Which'll be in my best interests, too.'

He sipped coffee and leaned forward.

'I don't want to raise your anxiety level, Alex, but there's something we should deal with. Remember when you called me about the rat and I asked you to describe Moody? You told me you and he were almost exactly the same size and colouring.'

I nodded numbly.

'You've been in the house all day, sick in bed. Someone arriving after dark wouldn't have known that. From a distance, the mistake would be easy to make.'

He waited a moment before continuing.

'It's not pretty to think about, but we've got to consider it,' he said, almost apologetically. 'In my gut I don't think the Casa thing'll pan out. What about the jokers you've run into on the Swope case?'

I thought of the people I'd encountered during the last couple of days. Valcroix. Matthias and the Touchers. Houten – did the sheriff's El Camino have fat tyres? Maimon. Bragdon. Carmichael. Rambo. Even Beverly and Raoul. None seemed remotely likely as suspects and I told Milo so.

'Of all of them, I like that asshole Canadian the best,' he said. 'Guy's a Class A bad actor.'

'I don't see it, Milo. He resented being interrogated and could have held that against me. But resentment isn't hatred and whoever fired those shots did it out of blood lust.'

'You told me he was a heavy doper, Alex. They've been known to get paranoid.'

I thought of what Beverly had said about Valcroix's increasingly strange behaviour and repeated it to Milo.

'There you go,' he said. 'Cokehead madness.'

'I guess it's possible, but it still doesn't feel right. I wasn't that important to him. Anyway, he seems more of an escapist, someone who'd retreat rather

214

than act out. The peace-love-Woodstock type.'

'So were the Manson family. What kind of car does he drove?'

'No idea.'

'We'll run it through D.M.V., then pick the guy up for questioning. Talk to the others, too. Hopefully the whole thing will boil down to Moody. When you get down to it he sounds like an easy one to hate.'

He stood and stretched.

'Thanks for everything, Milo.

He waved it off. 'Haven't done a damn thing so don't thank me yet. And I probably won't be able to handle it myself. Gotta travel.'

'Where to?'

'Washington, D.C. On the rape-murder. The Saudis have one of those slick public relations firms on retainer. Been putting millions into commercials showing they're just plain folks. Prince Stinky's exploits could make them look like the enemy again. So there's been pressure from the top to let him slink out of town to avoid a trial and all the publicity. The department won't let go of this one cause the crimes were too damned ugly. But the Arabs keep pushing and the politicos have to do a bit of symbolic brown-nosing.'

He shook his head in disgust.

'Other day a couple of grey suits from the State Department came down and took Del and me out to lunch. Three martinis and haute cuisine at the tax-payer's expense, followed by congenial chit-chat about the energy crisis. I let them talk, then I shoved a bunch of pictures of the girl Stinky killed right in front of them. Foreign Service types must have delicate constitutions. They almost heaved right into the coq au vin. That afternoon I got volunteered to fly to D.C. and discuss it further.'

215

'That'll be something to see,' I said. 'You and a room full of bureaucrats. When are you leaving?'

'Don't know. I'm on call. Could be tomorrow or the day after. Going first class for the first time in my deprived life.'

He looked at me with concern.

'At least Moody's out of the way.'

'Yeah,' I sighed. 'I wish it could have happened another way.' I thought of April and Ricky, what this would do to them. If Conley turned out to have been the one who blew away their father, the tragedy would be compounded. The entire case had a raw, primal stink that foreshadowed tragic endings for generations to come.

Hardy came back from the kitchen and gave his report.

'Coulda been worse than it was. Half of Durkin's house is up in smoke. He and his wife suffered second-degree burns and some smoke inhalation but they're gonna live. Worthy had smoke alarms and caught it in time. He lives in the Palisades, big property with lots of trees. Couple of 'em burned down.'

Which meant plenty of hiding places. Milo glanced at me meaningfully. Hardy kept on talking.

'The judge's and Daschoff's places haven't been touched so the cans in the car were probably meant for them. I sent uniforms to check out all of their offices.'

Richard Moody had ended his tormented life in a blaze of twisted passion.

Milo whistled and told Hardy the Delaware-as-victim scenario. Hardy found merit to it, which did nothing to improve my state of mind.

They thanked me for the coffee and stood. Hardy left the house and Milo lingered behind.

'You can stay here if you want,' he said, 'because

216

most of the forensic work will go on outside. But if you want to go somewhere else, that's okay, too.' It was intended more as advice than the granting of permission.

The glen was filled with blinking lights, footsteps, and muted human conversation. Safe, for now. But the police wouldn't be there forever.

'I'll move out for a couple of days.'

'If you wanna stay at my place, the offer's still open. Rick'll be on call next couple days, it'll be quiet.'

I thought for a moment.

'Thanks, but I really want to be alone.'

He said he understood, drained his coffee mug, and came closer.

'I see that gleam in your eyes and it worries me, pal.'

'I'm fine.'

'So far. I'd like to see it stay that way.'

'There's nothing to worry about, Milo. Really.'

'It's the kid, isn't it? You haven't let go of it.'

I was silent.

'Look, Alex, if what happened tonight has anything to do with the Swopes, that's all the more reason for you to stay out of it. I'm not saying cut off your feelings, just cover your ass.'

He touched my bad jaw gently. 'Last time you were lucky. Don't push it.'

I packed an overnight bag and drove around awhile before deciding on the Bel-Air Hotel as a good place to recuperate. And hide. It was just minutes away, quiet and secluded behind high stucco walls and towering subtropical shrubbery. The ambience – pink exterior, forest green interiors, swaying coconut palms, and a pond in which flamingos floated – had always reminded me of the old mythical Hollywood –

217

romance, sweet fantasy, and happy endings. All of which seemed in short supply.

I headed west on Sunset, turned north at Stone Canyon Road, and drove past immense gated estates until coming to the hotel's entrance. No one was parking cars at one forty in the morning; I slipped the Seville between a Lamborghini and a Maserati and left it looking like a dowager escorted by two gigolos.

The night clerk was a brooding Swede who didn't look up when I paid in advance with cash and registered as Carl Jung. Then I noticed he'd recorded it as Karl Young.

A tired-looking bellman took me to a bungalow overlooking a pool, which was lit up like an aquamarine. The room was under-stated and comfortable, with a big soft bed and heavy dark forties furniture.

I slid my body between cool sheets and remembered the last time I'd been there: the previous July, on Robin's twenty-eighth birthday. We'd heard the philharmonic do Mozart at the Music Center and followed the concert with a late supper at the Bel Air.

The dining room had been dark and quiet, our booth private and next to a picture window. Between the oysters and the veal a stately older woman in a formal gown had glided regally across the palm court.

'Alex,' Robin had whispered, 'look - no it couldn't be . . .'

But it was. Bette Davis. We couldn't have custom-ordered it.

Thinking of that perfect night helped keep the ghastliness of this quite imperfect one at bay.

I slept until eleven, dialled room service and ordered fresh raspberries, a herb omelette, bran muffins, and

218

coffee. The food came on china and silver and was superb. I chased images of death from my mind and ate heartily. Soon, I started to feel like a human being again.

I slept some more, woke, and called West L.A. Division at two. Milo had flown to Washington so I checked in with Del Hardy. He informed me that Conley was out as a suspect. While Moody was being blown apart, he'd been on location in Saugus for a night shoot on a new TV series. I took the news with equanimity, never having seen him as a calculating killer. Besides, I'd already convinced myself I was the sniper's intended victim. Accepting the role didn't make for tranquillity but at least I'd be vigilant.

I went for a swim at four, more for exercise than pleasure, returned to my room, and called for the evening paper and a Grolsch. The flu seemed to have surrendered. I sank into an armchair to read and drink.

The news of Valcroix's death was a two-inch filler piece on page twenty-eight entitled DOCTOR LOSES LIFE IN AUTO CRASH. From it I learned the genre, if not the make, of the car the Canadian had driven ('foreign compact') before crashing it into an abutment near the Wilmington harbour. He'd been pronounced dead at the scene and relatives in Montreal had been notified.

Wilmington is midway between L.A. and San Diego if you take the coastal route, a drab section of warehouses and shipyards. I wondered what he'd been doing there and which direction he'd been headed before the collision. He'd visited La Vista before. Was he returning from there when he crashed?

I thought of his boasts to Beverly about having an ace up his sleeve with regard to the Swopes. More questions reverberated relentlessly: was the crash an accident, the result of drug-numbed reflexes, or had he tried to play that ace and lost his life in the process? And what was the secret he'd considered his salvation? Could it solve the murder of the Swopes? Or help locate their children?

I turned it over, again and again, until my head hurt, sitting tensely on the edge of the chair, groping haphazardly like a blind man in a maze.

It wasn't until I realized what was missing that I was able to focus on what had to be done. Had I looked at it *clinically*, as a psychologist, clarity of purpose might have come sooner.

I'd been trained in the art of psychotherapy, the excavation of the past as a means of untangling the present and rendering it liveable. It's detective work of sorts, crouching stealthily in the blind alleys of the unconscious. And it begins with the taking of a careful and detailed history.

Four people had perished unnaturally. If their deaths seemed a jumble of unrelated horrors, I knew it was because such a history was missing. Because insufficient respect had been paid to the past.

That had to be remedied. It was more than an academic exercise. There were lives at stake.

I refused to compute the odds on the Swope children being alive. For the time being, it was sufficient that they were greater than zero. I thought, for the hundredth time, of the boy in the plastic room, helpless, dependent, potentially curable but harbouring an internal time bomb . . . He had to be found or he'd die in pain.

Seized with anger at my helplessness, I shifted from altruism to self-preservation. Milo had urged me to be careful but sitting still could be the most dangerous act of all.

Someone had hunted me. The news of my survival would eventually emerge. The hunter would return to claim his prey, taking his time so as to do it right. I wouldn't, couldn't play that waiting game, living like a man on death row.

There was work to be done. Exploration. Exhumation.

The compass pointed south.

19

TO TRUST someone is to take the greatest risk of all. Without trust nothing ever happens.

The issue, at this juncture, wasn't whether or not to take the risk. It was who could be trusted.

There was Del Hardy of course, but I didn't see him, or the police in general, as being much help. They were professionals who dealt with facts. All I had to offer were vague suspicions and intuitive dread. Hardy would hear me out politely, thank me for my input, tell me not to worry, and that would be it.

The answers I needed had to come from an insider; only someone who had known the Swopes in life could shed light on their deaths.

Sheriff Houten had seemed straight. But like many a large frog in a small pond, he'd overidentified with his role. He *was* the law in La Vista and crime was a

222

personal affront. I recalled his anger at my suggestion that Woody and Nona might be somewhere in town. Such things simply didn't happen on *his* turf.

That kind of paternalism bred a make-nice approach exemplified by the formal coexistence between the town and the Touch. On the positive side it could lead to tolerance, on the negative, tunnel vision.

I couldn't turn to Houten for help. He wouldn't welcome inquiries by outsiders under any circumstances and the hassles with Raoul were certain to have firmed his defences. Neither could I waltz into town and strike up conversations with strangers. For a moment it seemed hopeless, La Vista a locked box.

Then I thought of Ezra Maimon.

There'd been a simple dignity and independence of spirit about the man that had impressed me. He'd walked into a mess and cleaned it up within minutes. Representing an outside trouble-maker's interests against those of the sheriff could have proved intimidating to a less resolute man. Maimon had taken the job seriously and had done it damn well. He had spine and smarts.

Equally important, he was all I had.

I got his number from information and dialled it.

He answered the phone 'Rare Fruit and Seed Company' in the same quiet voice I remembered.

'Mr. Maimon, Alex Delaware. We met at the sheriff's station.'

'Good afternoon, Dr. Delaware. How is Dr. Melendez-Lynch?'

'I haven't seen him since that day. He was pretty depressed.'

'Yes. Such a tragic state of affairs.'

'That's why I called you.'

'Oh?'

I told him of Valcroix's death, the attempt on my

223

life, and my conviction that the situation would never be resolved without delving into the history of the Swopes, finishing with a straight-out plea for help.

There was silence on the other end and I knew he was deliberating, just as he had after Houten presented his case. I could almost hear the wheels turning.

'You've got a personal stake in this,' he said finally.

'That's a big part of it. But there's more. Woody Swope's disease is curable. There's no reason for him to die. If he's alive I want him found and treated.'

More silent cerebration.

'I'm not sure I know anything that will help you.'

'Neither am I. But it's worth a try.'

'Very well.'

I thanked him profusely. We agreed that meeting in La Vista was out of the question. For both our sakes.

'There's a restaurant in Oceanside named Anita's where I dine regularly,' he said. 'I'm a vegetarian and they serve fine meatless cuisine. Can you meet me there at nine tonight?'

It was five forty. Given even the heaviest traffic, I'd make it with time to spare.

'I'll be there.'

'All right, then, let me tell you how to find the place.'

The directions he gave were as expected: simple, straightforward, precise.

I paid for another two nights at the Bel Air, returned to my room and called Mal Worthy. He was out of the office but his secretary volunteered his home number.

He picked up on the first ring, sounding weary and drained.

224

'Alex, I've tried to get you all day.'

'I'm in seclusion.'

'Hiding? Why? He's dead.'

'It's a long story. Listen, Mal, I called for a couple of reasons. First, how did the children take it?'

'That's what I wanted to talk to you about. To get your advice. What a goddamned mess. Darlene didn't want to tell them but I told her she had to. I spoke to her afterward, and she said April cried a lot, asked questions, wouldn't let go of her skirt. She couldn't get Ricky to talk. Kid clammed up, went into his room and wouldn't come out. She had lots of questions and I tried my best to answer them but it's not my area of expertise. Do those reactions sound normal?'

'Normal or abnormal isn't the issue. Those kids have had to deal with more trauma than most people encounter in a lifetime. When I examined them in your office I felt they needed help and said so. Now it's absolutely necessary. Make sure they get it. In the meantime keep an eye on Ricky, He identified strongly with his father. Imitative suicide isn't out of the question. Neither is arson. If there are guns in the house get rid of them. Tell Darlene to watch him closely – keep him away from matches, knives, ropes, pills. At least until she gets him into therapy. After that she should do what the therapist says. And if the kid starts expressing his anger she should make sure not to clamp down. Even if it gets abusive.'

'I'll pass it on. I'd like you to see them once they get back to L.A.'

'I can't, Mal. I'm too close to the whole thing.' I gave him the names of two other psychologists.

'All right,' he said, with some reluctance. 'I'll give her the referrals, make sure she calls one of them.' He paused. 'I'm staring out the window. Place looks like a barbecue pit. Firemen sprayed it with something that's supposed to make the smell go away but it still stinks. I keep wondering if it could have turned out differently.'

'I don't know. Moody was programmed for violence. He had a violent upbringing. You remember the history – his own father was explosive, died in a brawl.'

'History repeats itself.'

'Get that boy in therapy and maybe it won't.'

The whitewashed walls of Anita's Café were backlit by lavender-tinted bulbs and trimmed with used brick. The entrance was through a lattice-wood arch. Dwarf lemon trees had been espaliered to the lattice and the fruit glowed turquoise in the artificial light.

The restaurant was tucked away, incongruously, in an industrial park, flanked on three sides by black-glass office buildings, acres of parking lot on the fourth. The songs of nightbirds mingled with the distant roar of the highway.

Inside, it was cool and dim. Baroque harpsichord music issued forth at low volume. The aroma of herbs and spices – cumin, marjoram, saffron, basil – saturated the air. Three quarters of the tables were occupied. Most of the diners looked young, hip, affluent. They spoke earnestly in subdued tones.

A stout blonde woman in peasant blouse and embroidered skirt showed me to Maimon's table. He rose in a courtly gesture and sat when I did.

'Good evening, Doctor.' He was dressed as before: spotless white shirt, pressed khaki trousers. His eyeglasses had slid down his nose and he pushed them back into place.

'Good evening. Thank you very much for seeing me.'

He smiled.

'You stated your case eloquently.'

226

The waitress, a slender girl with long dark hair and a Modigliani face, came to our table.

'They make an excellent lentil wellington,' said Maimon.

'That sounds fine.' My mind wasn't on food.

He ordered for both of us. The waitress returned with ice water in cut-crystal goblets, pillowy slices of whole-wheat bread and two small tubs of vegetable pâté that tasted uncannily like the real thing. A paper-thin lemon slice floated in each glass.

He spread pâté on bread, took a bite, chewed slowly and deliberately. After he swallowed he asked, 'How can I help you, Doctor?'

'I'm trying to understand the Swopes. What were they like before Woody's illness.'

'I didn't know them well. They were secretive people.'

'I keep hearing that.'

'I'm not surprised.' He sipped his water. 'I moved to La Vista ten years ago. My wife and I were childless. After she died I retired from my law practice and opened up the nursery - horticulture had been my first love. One of the first things I did after settling in was to contact the other growers in the area. For the most part I was welcomed warmly. Traditionally, horticulturists and orchardists are cordial people. So much of our progress depends upon cooperation - one grower will obtain seeds from an unusual species and distribute it to the others. It's in the best interests of all - scientifically and economically. A fruit that no one tastes will eventually die out, as did so many of the old American apples and pears. One that achieves some degree of circulation will survive.

'I'd expected to be welcomed warmly by Garland Swope, because he was my neighbour. It was a naive expectation. I dropped in on him one day and he stood by his gate, not inviting me in, curt, almost to

227

the point of hostility. Needless to say, I was taken aback. Not only by the unfriendliness but also by his lack of desire to show off – most of us love to exhibit our prize hybrids and rare specimens.'

The food came. It was surprisingly good, the lentils intriguingly spiced and wrapped in filo dough. Maimon ate sparingly then put his fork down before speaking again.

'I left quickly and never went back, though our properties are less than a mile apart. There were other growers in the area interested in collaboration and I quickly forgot about Swope. About a year later I attended a convention in Florida on the cultivation of subtropical Malaysian fruits. I met several people who'd· known him and they explained his behaviour.

'It seems the man was a grower in name only. He'd been prominent at one time, but hadn't done anything for years. There's no nursery behind his gates, only an old house and acres of dust.'

'What did the family live on?'

'Inheritance. Garland's father was a state senator, owned a large ranch and miles of coastal land. He sold some to the government, the rest to developers. Much of the proceeds were immediately lost to bad investments, but apparently there was enough left to support Garland and his family.'

He looked at me with curiosity.

'Does any of this help you?'

'I don't know. Why did he give up horticulture?'

'Bad investments of his own. Have you heard of the cherimoya?'

'There's a street in Hollywood by that name. Sounds like a fruit.'

He wiped his lips.

'You're correct. It is a fruit. One that Mark Twain called "deliciousness of deliciousness." Those who've

228

tasted it are inclined to agree. It's subtropical in nature, native to the Chilean Andes. Looks somewhat like an artichoke or a large green strawberry. The skin is inedible. The pulp is white and textured like custard, laced with many large, hard seeds. Some joke that the seeds were put there by the gods so the fruit wouldn't be consumed with undue haste. One eats it with a spoon. The taste is fantastic, Doctor. Sweet and tangy, with perfumed overtones of peach, pear, pineapple, banana, and citrus, but a totality that is unique.

'It's a wonderful fruit, and according to the people in Florida, Garland Swope was obsessed with it. He considered it the fruit of the future and was convinced that once the public tasted it, there would be instant demand. He dreamed of doing for the cherimoya what Sanford Dole had done for the pineapple. Even went so far as to name his first child after it – *Annona cherimola* is the full botanical name.'

'Was it a realistic dream?'

'Theoretically. It's a finicky tree, requiring a temperate climate and constant moisture, but adaptable to the subtropical strip that runs along the coast of California from the Mexican border up through Ventura County. Wherever avocados grow so can the cherimoya. But there are complications that I'll come to.

'He bought up land on credit. Ironically, much of it had originally been owned by his father. Then he went on expeditions to South America and brought back young trees. Propagated seedlings and planted his orchard. It took several years for the trees to reach fruiting size, but finally he had the largest cherimoya grove in the state. During all this time he'd been travelling up and down the state, talking up the fruit with produce buyers, telling them of the wonders that would soon be blossoming in his groves.

'It must have been an uphill battle, for the palate of the American public is quite unadventurous. As a nation, we don't consume much fruit. The ones we do eat have gained familiarity over centuries. The tomato was once believed poisonous, the eggplant thought to cause madness. Those are just two examples. There are literally hundreds of tantalizing food plants that would thrive in this climate but are ignored.

'However, Garland was persistent and it paid off. He received advance orders for most of his crop. Had the cherimoya caught on he would have cornered the market on a gourmet delicacy and ended up a rich man. Of course, the corporate growers would have moved in eventually and coopted everything, but that would have taken years and even then, his expertise would have been highly marketable.

'Almost a decade after he conceived his plan the first year's crop set – that in itself was an achievement. In its native habitat the cherimoya is pollinated by an indigenous wasp. Duplicating the process requires painstaking hand pollination – pollen from the anthers of one flower is brushed on the pistils of another. Time of day is important as well, for the plant undergoes fertility cycles. Garland babied the trees almost as if they were human infants.'

Maimon took off his glasses and wiped them. His eyes were dark and unblinking.

'Two weeks before harvest a killing frost borne by frigid air currents crept up from Mexico. There'd been a rash of tropical storms that had battered the Caribbean and the frost was an aftershock. Most of the trees died overnight and the ones that survived dropped their fruit. There was a frantic attempt at rescue. Several of the people I met in Florida had been there to help. They described it to me: Garland and Emma running through the groves with smudge-

230

pots and blankets, trying to wrap the trees, warm the soil, do anything to save them. The little girl watching them and crying. They struggled for three days but it was hopeless. Garland was the last to accept it.'

He shook his head sadly.

'Years of work were lost in a span of seventy hours. After that he withdrew from horticulture and became a virtual hermit.'

It was a classic tragedy – dreams savaged by the Fates. The agony of helplessness. Terminal despair.

I began to catch a glimpse of what Woody's diagnosis must have meant to them:

Cancer in a child was never less than monstrous. For any parent it meant confronting a sickening sense of impotence. But for Garland and Emma Swope the trauma would be compounded, the inability to save their child evoking past failures. Perhaps unbearably . . .

'Is all of this well-known?' I asked.

'To anyone who's lived here for a while.'

'What about Matthias and the Touch?'

'That I couldn't tell you. They moved here a few years ago. May or may not have found out. It's not a topic of public conversation.'

He smiled the waitress over and ordered a pot of herb tea. She brought it, along with two cups, which she filled.

He sipped, put his cup down, and looked at me through the steam.

'You still harbour suspicions about the Touch,' he said.

'I don't know,' I admitted. 'There's no real reason to. But something about them is spooky.'

'Somewhat contrived?'

'Exactly. It all looks too programmed. Like a movie director's version of what a cult should be.'

'I agree with you, Doctor. When I heard Norman

231

Matthews had become a spiritual leader I was rather amused.'

'You knew him?'

'By reputation only. Anyone in the legal profession had heard of him. He was the quintessential Beverly Hills attorney – bright, flamboyant, aggressive, ruthless. None of which jibed with what he presently claims to be. Still, I suppose odder transformations have taken place.'

'Someone took a pot shot at me yesterday. Can you see them doing that kind of thing?'

He thought about it.

'Their public face has been anything but violent. If you told me Matthews was a swindler I'd believe it. But a murderer . . . ' He looked doubtful.

I took a different tack.

'What kind of relationship was there between the Touch and the Swopes?'

'None, I would imagine. Garland was a recluse. Never came to town. Occasionally I'd see Emma or the girl out shopping.'

'Matthias told me Nona worked for the Touch one summer.'

'That's true. I'd forgotten.' He turned away and fiddled with a container of unfiltered honey.

'Mr. Maimon, forgive me if this sounds rude, but I don't see you forgetting anything. When Matthias talked about Nona, the sheriff got uncomfortable, as you just did. Broke in with a comment about what a wild kid she was, as if to end the conversation. You've been very helpful until now. Please don't hold back.'

He put his glasses back on, stroked his chin, started to lift his teacup but thought better of it.

'Doctor,' he said evenly, 'you seem a sincere young man and I want to help you. But let me explain the position I'm in. I've lived here for a decade but still

232

consider myself an outsider. I'm a Sephardic Jew, descended from the great scholar Maimonides. My ancestors were expelled from Spain in 1492, along with all the Jews. They settled in Holland, were expelled from there, went to England, Palestine, Australia, America. Five hundred years of wandering gets into the blood, makes one reluctant to think in terms of permanence.

'Two years ago, a member of the Ku Klux Klan was nominated for state assembly from this district. Part of it was subterfuge – the man concealed his membership – but too many people knew who he was to make the nomination an accident. He lost the election but shortly afterward there were cross-burnings, anti-Semitic leafleting, an epidemic of racist graffiti and harassment of Mexican-Americans along the border.

'I'm not telling you this because I think La Vista is a hotbed of racism. On the contrary, I've found it an extremely tolerant town, as witnessed by the smooth integration of the Touch. But attitudes can change rather quickly – my forebears were court physicians to the Spanish royal family one week, refugees the next.' He warmed both hands on his cup. 'Being an outsider means exercising discretion.'

'I know how to keep a secret,' I said. 'Anything you tell me will be kept confidential unless lives are at stake.'

He engaged in another bout of silent contemplation, the delicate features solemn and still. We locked eyes for a moment.

'There was some kind of trouble,' he said. 'Exactly what kind was never publicized. Knowing the girl, it had to be of a sexual nature.'

'Why's that?'

'She had a reputation for promiscuity. I don't seek out gossip, but in a small town one overheard things.

233

There's always been something libidinous about the girl. Even at twelve or thirteen when she walked through town every male head would turn. She exuded - physicality. I'd always thought it strange that she sprang from such a withdrawn, isolated family - as if somehow she'd sucked the sexual energy from the others and ended up with more than she could handle.'

'Do you have any idea what happened at the Retreat?' I asked, though from Doug Carmichael's story, I had a strong hypothesis.

'Only that her job was terminated abruptly and snickers and whispers circulated around town for the next few days.'

'And the Touch never hired town kids again.'

'Correct.'

The waitress brought the cheque. I put down my credit card. Maimon thanked me and called for another pot of tea.

'What was she like as a little girl?' I asked.

'I have only vague memories - she was a pretty little thing - that red hair always stood out. Used to pass by my place and say hello, always very friendly. I don't think the problems started until she was twelve or so.'

'What kinds of problems?'

'What I told you. Promiscuity. Wild behaviour. She started running with a bunch of older kids - the ones with fast cars and motorcycles. I suppose things got out of hand because they sent her away to boarding school. That I remember vividly because on the morning she left Garland's car broke down on the way to the train station. Just gave out in the middle of the road, a few yards from my nursery. I offered to give them a lift but of course he refused. Left her sitting there with her suitcase until he came back with a truck. She looked like a sad little child, though I

234

suppose she must have been at least fourteen. As if all the mischief had been knocked out of her.'

'How long was she away?'

'A year. She was different when she returned – quieter, more subdued. But still sexually precocious, in an angry kind of way.'

'What do you mean?'

He flushed and drank tepid tea.

'Predatory. One day she walked into my nursery wearing shorts and a halter top. Out of the blue. Said she'd heard I had a new kind of banana and she wanted to see it. It was true – I'd brought in several fifteen-gallon Dwarf Cavendish plants from Florida and had taken a lovely bunch of fruit to the town market for display. I wondered why she'd be interested in something like that, but showed her the plants anyway. She looked them over in a cursory manner and smiled – lasciviously. Then she leaned over and gave me a frank view of her chest, picked a banana and began eating it in a rather crude manner – ' He stopped, stammered – 'You'll have to excuse me, Doctor, I'm sixty-three, from another generation, and it's hard for me to be as uninhibited about this kind of thing as is fashionable.'

I nodded, trying to seem empathetic. 'You look much younger.'

'Good genes.' He smiled. 'Anyway, that's the story. She made a production out of eating the banana, smiled at me again and told me it was delicious. Licked her fingers and ran off down the road. The encounter unnerved me because even as she vamped there'd been hatred in her eyes. A strange mixture of sex and hostility. It's hard to explain.'

He sipped his tea, then asked, 'Has any of this been relevant?'

Before I could answer the waitress returned with

the charge slip. Maimon insisted upon leaving the tip.
It was a generous one.

We walked out to the parking lot. The night was
cool and fragrant. He had the springy step of a man a
third his age.

His truck was a long-bed Chevy pickup. Conventional tyres. He took out his keys and asked, 'Would
you like to stop by and visit my nursery? I'd like to
show you some of my most fascinating specimens.'

He seemed eager for companionship. He'd
unloaded a lot of alienation, probably for the first
time. Self-expression can become habit forming.

'It would be my pleasure. Could being seen with
me cause problems for you?'

He smiled and shook his head.

'Last I heard, Doctor, this was still a free country.
I'm located several miles southeast of town. Up in the
foothills where most of the big groves are. You will follow
me, but in case we disconnect I'll give you directions.
We'll cut under the freeway, ride parallel with it, and
turn right on an unmarked road – I'll slow down so
you don't miss it. At the foot of the mountains there'll
be a left turn onto an old utility trail. Too narrow for
commercial vehicles and it floods when the rains
come. But this time of year it's a handy shortcut.'

He went on for a while before I realized he was
directing me to the back road I'd seen on the county
map in the sheriff's office. The one that bypassed the
town. When I'd asked Houten about it he'd said it
was sealed off by the oil company. Perhaps he
considered a utility trail too insignificant to be
thought of as a road. Or maybe he'd lied.

I wondered about it as I got into the Seville.

236

20

THE TURNOFF was sudden. The road, apart from
being unmarked, was hardly a road at all. Just a
narrow dirt ribbon, at first glance one furrow of many
that cut through the vast table of farmland. Anyone
unfamiliar with the area would have missed it. But
Maimon drove slowly and I followed his taillights
through moonlit fields of strawberries. Soon the
freeway sounds were behind us, the night hushed and
aglitter with moths spiralling up toward the stars,
pressing frantically and hopelessly for the heat of
distant galaxies.

The mountains hovered above us, grim hulking
masses of shadow. Maimon's truck was old and it
lurched as he shifted into low gear and began the
climb into the foothills. I stayed several car-lengths
behind and trailed him into darkness so dense it was
palpable.

We climbed for miles, finally reaching a plateau. The road veered sharply to the right. To the left was a broad mesa surrounded by chain-link fence. Pyramidal towers rose from the flatlands, skeletal and still. The abandoned oilfields. Maimon turned away from them and resumed the ascent.

The next few miles were groves, unbroken stretches of trees recognizable as such by the serrated silhouette of star-kissed leaves, shiny satin against the velvet of the sky. Citrus, from the perfume in the air. Then came a series of homesteads, farmhouses on one-acre plots shadowed by sycamore and oak. The few lights that were on blurred as we drove by.

Maimon's turn signal went on two hundred feet before he swung left through an open gate. An unobtrusive sign said RARE FRUIT AND SEED CO. He pulled up in front of a big two-storey frame house girdled by a wide porch. On the porch were two chairs and a dog. The dog rose on its haunches and nuzzled Maimon's hand as he climbed out of the truck. A Labrador, heavy and stolid, seemingly unimpressed by my presence. Its master petted it and it went back to sleep.

'Come around to the back,' said Maimon. We walked along the left side of the house. There was an electrical junction box hanging from the rear wall. He opened it, flicked a switch, and a series of lights came on in sequence, as if choreographed.

What unfolded before my eyes was as textured and verdant as a painting by Rousseau. A masterpiece entitled *Variations on the Theme of Green.*

There were plants and trees everywhere, many in bloom, all thick with foliage. The larger ones sat in five and fifteen gallon containers, a few were rooted in the rich dark soil. Smaller plants and seedlings in peat pots rested on tables shielded by canopies of mesh. Beyond the canopies were three glass greenhouses.

238

The air was a cocktail of mulch and nectar.

He gave me a guided tour. Initially I recognized most of the species but found the varieties novel. There were unusual strains of peach, nectarine, apricot, plum, low-chill apples, and pears. Several dozen fig trees in pots were lined up against a fence. Maimon picked two figs from one of them, handed one to me and popped the other in his mouth. I'd never cared for raw figs but ate the fruit to oblige him. I was glad I did.

'What do you think?'

'Wonderful. Tastes like a dried fig.'

He was pleased.

'Celeste. Best taster by my standards, though some prefer Pasquale.'

It continued like that, Maimon pointing out choice hybrids with unconcealed pride, sometimes stopping to pick one and offer me a taste. His fruit was unlike anything I'd found on the produce shelves, larger, juicier, more vividly coloured and intensely flavoured.

Finally we came to the exotic specimens. Many were aflame with orchidlike blossoms in shades of yellow, pink, scarlet, and mauve. Each group of plants was accompanied by a wooden sign staked into the ground. On the sign was a colour photograph of fruit, flower, and leaf. Under the illustration were botanical and common names in neatly lettered text, along with geographic, horticultural, and culinary details.

There were species with which I was vaguely familiar - litchies, unusual varieties of mango and papaya, loquats, guavas, and passion fruits - and many others I'd never known existed - sapotes, sapodillas, acerola cherries, jujubes, jaboticaba, tamarinds, tree tomatoes.

One section was devoted to vines - grapes, kiwis,

raspberries hued from black to gold. In another, stocked with rare citrus, I saw Chandler pommelos three times the size of grapefruit and sugary sweet, Moro, Sanguinelli, and Tarocco blood oranges with pulp and juice the colour of burgundy wine, tangors, limequats, sweet limes, and Buddha's Finger citrons resembling the eight-digited human hands.

The greenhouses protected seedlings of the most fragile plants in the collection, those Maimon had obtained from young adventurers who explored the remote tropical regions of the world for new species of flora. By manipulating light, heat, and moisture he'd constructed microclimates that assured high success in propagation. He became animated as he described his work, tossing out esoterica followed by patient explanations.

Half of the last greenhouse was given over to stacks of carefully labelled boxes. On the table were a postage meter, scissors, tape, and padded envelopes.

'Seeds,' he said. 'The mainstay of my business. I ship all over the world.'

He held open the door and took me to a cluster of small trees.

'Family *annonaceae*.' He poked among the leaves of the first tree and uncovered a large yellow-green fruit covered with fleshy spines. '*Annona muricata*, the soursop. And this red one is *Annona reticulata*, the custard apple. Lindstroms variety. There are no fruit on this one here, won't be until August – *Annona squamosa*, sweetsop or custard apple, seedless Brazilian variety. And these,' he indicated half a dozen trees with drooping, elliptical leaves, 'are the cherimoyas. Right now I've got several varieties – Booth, Bonita, Pierce, White, Deliciosa.'

I reached out and touched a leaf. The underside was fuzzy. An orangelike scent issued forth.

240

'Lovely fragrance, isn't it?' More probing among the branches. 'This is the fruit.'

It didn't look like the stuff of which dreams were made - a large, globose, heart-shaped mound, pale green and dotted with protrusions, resembling a leathery green pine cone. I touched it gingerly. Firm and gently abrasive.

'Come inside. I'll open a ripe one.'

His kitchen was big and old and spotless. The refrigerator, oven, and sink were white enamel, the floor, linoleum waxed to a gleam. A table and chairs fashioned from rock maple occupied the centre. I pulled up a chair and sat down. The big Lab had moved indoors and lay snoring at the base of the stove.

Maimon opened the refrigerator, pulled out a cherimoya, and brought it, two bowls, two spoons, and a knife, to the table. The ripe fruit was mottled with brown and soft to the touch. He sliced it in two, put each half in a bowl, skin down. The pulp was a creamy off-white, the colour and consistency of fresh custard.

'Dessert,' said Maimon and spooned out a shimmering mouthful. He held it aloft then ate.

I put my spoon to the fruit. It slid in and sank. I pulled it out filled with custard and put it to my lips.

The taste was incredible, bringing to mind the flavours of many other fruits yet different from each; sweet, then tart, then sweet again, shifting elusively on the tongue, as subtle and satisfying as the finest confection. The seeds were plentiful, beanlike and hard as wood. An annoyance, but tolerable.

We ate in silence. I savoured the cherimoya, knowing it had brought heartbreak to the Swopes, but not permitting that to adulterate my pleasure until all that was left was an empty green shell.

Maimon ate slowly and finished a few minutes later.

241

'Delicious,' I said when he put down his spoon. 'Where can you get them?'

'Generally two places. At Hispanic markets they're comparatively cheap but the fruit is small and irregular. If you go to a gourmet grocer you'll pay fifteen dollars for two good-sized ones wrapped in fancy tissue paper.'

'So they're being grown commercially?'

'In Latin America and Spain. On a more limited basis here in the U.S., mostly up near Carpenteria. The climate there's too cool for true tropicals but it's even more temperate than what we get down here.'

'No frosts?'

'Not yet.'

'Fifteen dollars,' I thought out loud.

'Yes. It never caught on as a popular fruit - too many seeds, too gelatinous, people didn't like to carry spoons with them. No one's found a way to machine-pollinate so it's highly labour-intensive. Nevertheless, it's a delicacy with a loyal following and demand exceeds supply. But for the Fates, Garland would have been wealthy.'

My hands were sticky from handling fruit. I washed them in the kitchen sink. When I returned to the table the dog was curled at Maimon's feet, eyes closed, crooning low-pitched canine satisfaction as the grower stroked its fur.

A peaceful scene but it made me restless. I'd lingered too long in Maimon's Eden when there were things that needed to be done.

'I want to take a look at the Swopes' place. Is it one of those farms we passed on the way up?'

'No. They live - lived further up the road. Those weren't really farms, just old home tracts too small to be commercially viable. Some of the people who work in town like to live up here. They get a little more space and the chance to earn spare change growing

242

seasonal cash crops – pumpkins for Halloween, winter melons for the Asian trade.'

I remembered Houten's sudden anger when he talked of farming and asked if the sheriff had ever worked the land.

'Not recently,' he said hesitatingly. 'Ray used to have a plot nearby. Grew conifers that he sold to Christmas tree brokers.'

'Used to?'

'He sold the place to a young couple after he lost his daughter. Moved into a rooming house a block from city hall.'

The possibility that the sheriff had lied to discourage me from snooping around hadn't left my mind. I found myself wanting to know more about the man who was the law in La Vista.

'He told me about his wife dying of cancer. What happened to the daughter?'

Maimon raised his eyebrows and stopped stroking the Lab. The dog stirred and growled until the stimulation resumed.

'Suicide. Four or five years ago. She hung herself from an old oak on the property.'

He recalled it matter of factly, as if the girl's death hadn't been surprising. I commented on it.

'It was a tragedy,' he said, 'but not one of those cases where one's initial reaction is stunned disbelief. Marla'd always seemed a troubled child to me. Plain, overweight, excessively timid, no friends. Always had her nose buried in a book. Fairy tales, the times I noticed. I never saw her smile.'

'How old was she when she died?'

'Around fifteen.'

Had she lived she'd be the same age as Nona Swope. The two girls had lived nearby. I asked Maimon if there'd been any contact between them.

'I doubt it. As little girls they sometimes played

together. But not after they got older. Marla kept to herself and Nona ran with the wild crowd. You couldn't find two girls more dissimilar.'

Maimon stopped stroking the dog. He rose, cleared the table, and began washing dishes.

'Losing Marla changed Ray,' he said, turning off the water and picking up a dish towel. 'And the town along with him. Before her death he'd been a hell-raiser. Liked to drink, arm-wrestle, tell off-colour jokes. When they cut her body down from that tree he turned inward. Wouldn't accept solace from anyone. At first people thought it was grief, that he'd come out of it. But he never did.' He wiped a bowl past the gleaming point. 'Seems to me La Vista's been a little more sombre since then. Almost as if everyone's waiting for Ray to give them permission to smile.'

He'd just described mass anhedonia – the rejection of pleasure. I wondered if therein lay the key to Houten's tolerance of the ostensibly self-denying Touch.

Maimon finished drying and wiped his hands.

I got up.

'Thank you,' I said, 'for your time, the tour, and the fruit. You've created great beauty here.' I held out my hand.

He took it and smiled.

'Someone else created it. I've simply displayed it. It's been a pleasure talking to you, Doctor. You're a good listener. Will you be going to Garland's place now?'

'Yes. Just to look around. Can you direct me?'

'Proceed along the road the way we came. You'll pass half a mile of avocado. Owned by a consortium of La Jolla doctors as a tax shelter. Then a covered bridge over a dry bed. Once off the bridge drive another quarter mile. The Swope place is to the left.'

I thanked him again. He walked me to the door.

244

'I passed by the place a couple of days ago,' he said. 'There was a padlock on the gate.'

'I'm a pretty good climber.'

'I don't doubt it. But remember what I told you about Garland's being antisocial. There are coils of barbed wire on top of the fence.'

'Any suggestions?'

He pretended to look at the dog, and said with forced nonchalance: 'There's a toolshed next to my back porch. Odds and ends. Rummage around, see if you find anything helpful.'

He walked away from me and I exited the house.

The 'odds and ends' were a collection of high quality hand tools, oiled and wrapped. I selected a heavy-duty bolt cutter and a crowbar and carried them to the Seville. I put them on the floor of the car along with a flashlight retrieved from the glove compartment, started up the engine, and rolled forward.

I looked back at the brightly lit nursery. The taste of cherimoya lingered on my tongue. As I drove off the property the lights went out.

21

I'D RECEIVED impressions of the Swopes from multiple sources but had yet to form a coherent image of the shattered family.

Everyone had thought Garland unusual – emotionally inappropriate, secretive, hostile to outsiders. But for a hermit he'd been surprisingly outgoing – Beverly and Raoul had both described him as opinionated and talkative to the point of boorishness, anything but socially reticent.

Emma had emerged as her husband's cringing subordinate, almost a nonentity, except in Augie Valcroix's view. The Canadian doctor had described her as a strong woman and hadn't rejected the possibility that she'd instigated the disappearance.

On the subject of Nona there seemed to be the most agreement. She was wild, hypersexual, and angry. And had been that way for a long time.

And then there was Woody, a sweet little boy. Any way you looked at it, an innocent victim. Was I deluding myself into believing he might still be alive? Engaging in the same kind of denial that had turned a brilliant physician into a public nuisance?

I had an intuitive distrust of Matthias and the Touch but no evidence to back it up. Valcroix had visited them and I wondered if it had been only a single visit as claimed. Several times I'd watched him space out in a manner reminiscent of the meditation practiced by the Touch. Now he was dead. What was the connection, if any?

Something else stuck in my mind. Matthias had said the cult purchased seeds from Garland Swope once or twice. But according to Ezra Maimon, Garland had nothing to sell. All there was behind his gates, was an old house and acres of dust. A minor point? Perhaps. But why the need to fabricate?

Lots of questions, none of them leading anywhere.

It was like a jigsaw puzzle whose pieces had been improperly tooled. No matter how hard I worked, the end product was maddening off-kilter.

I passed through the covered bridge and slowed down. The entrance to the Swope property was fronted by a sunken dirt driveway leading to rusty iron gates. The gates weren't high – seven feet at most – but they wore a coiffure of barbed wire that stretched another yard, and were bound, as Maimon had said, by padlock and chain.

I drove a hundred feet before finding space to pull over. Nosing the Seville as close as possible to a stand of eucalyptus, I parked, took the tools and flashlight, and backtracked on foot.

The lock was brand new. Probably affixed by Houten. The chain was plastic-coated steel. It resisted the bolt cutters for a moment then split like over-cooked sausage. I opened the gate, slipped through, closed it, and rearranged the severed links to conceal the surgery.

The driveway was gravel and responded to my footsteps with breakfast cereal sounds. The flashlight revealed a two-storey frame house, at first glance not unlike Maimon's. But this structure seemed to sag on its foundation, the wood splintered and peeling. The roof was tar paper and bald in several places, the windows framed by warped casements. I placed my foot on the first porch step and felt the wood give way under my weight. Dry rot.

An owl hooted. I heard the rasping friction of wings, raised my beam to catch the big bird in flight. Then a broad swoop, the scurrying panic of prey, a thin squeak, and silence once again.

The front door was locked. I considered various means of snapping the lock and stopped midthought, feeling furtive and vaguely criminal. Looking up at the ravaged mass of the decrepit house, I remembered the fate of its inhabitants. Inflicting further damage seemed a heedless act of vandalism. I decided to try the back door.

I stumbled on a loose board, caught my balance, and walked around the side of the house. I hadn't taken a dozen steps when I heard the sound. An incessant dripping, rhythmic and oddly melodic.

There was a junction box in the same place as the one at Maimon's. It was rusted shut and I had to use the crowbar to pry it open. I tried several switches and got no response. The fourth brought on the lights.

There was a single greenhouse. I entered it.

Long heavy wooden tables ran the length of the glass building. The bulbs I'd switched on were dim and bluish, casting a milky glaze over the creations that rested on the heavy planks. At the peak of the ceiling were winches and pulleys designed to open the roof.

248

The source of the dripping sound became evident: a reptilian system of overhead irrigation operated by old-fashioned dialled timers and suspended from the crossbeam.

Maimon had been wrong about there being nothing but dust behind the Swopes' gate. The greenhouse contained a plethora of growing things. Not flowers. Not trees. *Things.*

I'd thought of the Sephardic grower's nursery as an Eden. What I saw now was a vision from Hell.

Exquisite care had been taken to create a jungle of botanic monstrosities.

There were hundreds of roses that would never fill a bouquet. Their blossoms were shrivelled, stunted, coloured a deathly grey. Each flower was ragged-edged, irregular, and covered with a layer of what looked like moist fur. Others boasted three inch thorns that turned stem and stalk into deadly weapons. I didn't stoop to smell the flowers but the stench reached me anyway, pungently warm, aggressively rancid.

Next to the roses was a collection of carnivorous plants. Venus's-flytraps, pitcher plants, others I couldn't identify. All were larger and more robust than any I'd seen. Green maws hung open. Sap oozed from tendrils. On the table was a rusty kitchen knife and a slab of beef cut into tiny pieces. Each cube teemed with maggots, many of them dead. One of the flesh-craving plants had managed to lower its mouth to the table and snare some of the white worms with its deadly-sweet exudate. Nearby were more goodies for the carnivores – a coffee can heaped to the brim with dried beetles and flies. The heap shuddered. Out crawled a live insect, a wasp-like creature with a pincer mouth and swollen abdomen. It stared at me and buzzed off. I followed its trajectory. When it had flown out the door, I ran over and slammed it shut.

The glass panes vibrated.

And all the while the steady drip-drip from the pipes overhead, keeping everything nice and healthy.

Weak-kneed with nausea I walked on. There was a collection of bonsai oleanders, leaves ground to powder and stored in canisters. The granulate had apparently been tested on field mice for poison content. All that remained of the rodents were teeth and bones enshrouded in flesh tanned by rigor mortis. They'd been left to their terminal agonies, paws begging stiffly. The droppings had been used to fertilize trays of toadstools. Each tray was labelled: *Amanita muscaria. Boletus miniato-olivaceus. Helvella esculenta.*

The plants in the next section were fresh and pretty but equally deadly: hemlock. Foxglove. Black henbane. Deadly nightshade. An ivylike beauty identified quaintly as poisonwood.

There were fruit trees as well. Acrid smelling oranges and lemons, pruned and twisted to nothingness. An apple tree laden with grotesquely misshapen tumours masquerading as fruit. A pomegranate bush slimy with mucoid jelly. Flesh-coloured plums harbouring colonies of gyrating worms. Mounds of fruit rotted on the ground.

On and on it went, a stinking, repulsive nightmare factory. Then suddenly, something different:

Against the far wall of the greenhouse was a single tree in a hand-painted clay pot. Well-shaped, healthy, and obtrusively normal. A hill had been formed from the dirt that floored the greenhouse and the potted tree rested on it, elevated, as if an object of worship.

A lovely looking tree, with drooping elliptical leaves and fruit resembling leathery green pine cones.

Once outside I gulped fresh air greedily. Behind the

greenhouse was a stretch of barren land ending at a black wall of forest. A good place for hiding. Using the flashlight beam for guidance I made my way between the massive trunks of redwood and fir. The forest floor was a spongy mattress of humus. Small animals scampered in the wake of my intrusion. Twenty minutes of searching and prodding revealed no trace of human habitation.

I walked back to the house and switched off the greenhouse lights. The padlock on the back door was fastened to a cheap hasp that yielded to a single twist of the crowbar.

I entered the dark house through a service porch that connected to a large cold kitchen. Electricity and water had been shut off. The greenhouse must have run off a separate generator. I used the flashlight to guide me.

The rooms downstairs were musty and stingily furnished, the walls devoid of paintings or photographs. An oval hooked rug covered the living room floor. Bordering it were a thrift shop sofa and two aluminium folding chairs. The dining room was storage space for cardboard cartons full of old newspapers and bound cords of firewood. Bedsheets had been used for curtains.

Upstairs there were three bedrooms, each containing crude, rickety furniture and cast-iron beds. The one that had been Woody's bore a semblance of cheer - a toybox next to the bed, superhero posters on the walls, a Padres banner over the headboard.

Nona's dresser was blanketed with cut-glass perfume atomizers and bottles of lotion. The clothes in her closet were mostly jeans and skimpy tops. The exceptions were a short rabbit jacket of the type Hollywood streetwalkers used to favour and two frilly party dresses, one red, one white. Her drawers were crammed with nylons and lingerie and scented with a homemade sachet. But like the rooms below, her private space was emotionally blank, unmarked by personal touches. No yearbooks, diaries, love letters, no souvenirs. I found a crumpled scrap of lined notebook paper in the bottom drawer of the dresser. It was brown with age and covered, like some classroom punishment, with hundreds of repetitions of the same single sentence: FUCK MADRONAS.

Garland and Emma's bedroom had a view of the greenhouse. I wondered if they'd woken in the morning, peered down at the chamber of mutations and been warmed by a self-congratulatory glow. There were two single beds with a nightstand between them. All available floorspace was given over to cardboard boxes. Some were filled with shoes, others with towels and linens. Still others held nothing but other cardboard boxes. I opened the closet. The parents' wardrobes were meagre, shapeless, decades out of style and biased toward greys and browns.

There was a small hinged trapdoor cut into the ceiling of the closet. I found a stepstool hidden behind a mildewed winter coat, pulled it out, and stretched high enough to give the door a strong push. It opened with a slow pneumatic hiss, and a ship's ladder slid down automatically through the aperture. I tested it, found it steady, and ascended.

The attic covered the full area of the house, easily two thousand square feet. It had been transformed into a library, though not an elegant one.

Plywood bookcases were propped against all four walls. A desk had been constructed of the same cheap wood. A metal folding chair sat before it. The floor was speckled with sawdust. I looked for another entry to the room and found none. The windows were small and slatted. Only one mode of construction was possible: planks had been slipped through the trapdoor and nailed together up here.

I ran the flashlight over the volumes that lined the shelves. With the exception of thirty years' worth of *Reader's Digest* condensed books, and a case full of *National Geographics*, all were on biology, horticulture and related topics. There were hundreds of pamphlets from the U.C. Riverside Agricultural Station and the Federal Government Printing Office. Stacks of mail-order seed catalogues. A set of oversized leather-bound *Encyclopaedia of Fruit* printed in England, dated 1879, and illustrated with hand-tipped colour lithographs. Scores of college texts on plant pathology, soil biology, forestry management, genetic engineering. A hiker's guide to the trees of California. Complete collections of *Horticulture* and *Audubon*. Copies of patents awarded to inventors of farm equipment.

Four shelves of the case closest to the desk were crowded with blue-cloth looseleaf binders labelled with Roman numerals. I pulled out Volume I.

The cover was dated 1965. Inside were eighty-three pages of handwritten text. The writer's penmanship was hard to decipher – cramped, blackslanted, and of uneven darkness. I held the flashlight with one hand, turned pages with the other, and finally got a perceptual fix on it.

Chapter One was a summary of Garland Swope's plan to be the Cherimoya King. He actually used that term, even doodling miniature crowns in the margins of the book. There was an outline of the fruit's attributes and a reminder to check out its nutritional value. The section ended with a list of adjectives to be used when describing it to prospective buyers. Succulent. Juicy. Mouth-watering. Refreshing. Heavenly. Other-worldly.

The rest of the first volume and the nine that followed continued in this vein. Swope had authored eight hundred and twenty-seven pages of text lauding the cherimoya over a ten-year period, recording the progress of each tree in his young grove and plotting his control of the market. ('Riches? Fame? Which is paramount? No matter, there will be both.')

Stapled in one of the books was an invoice from a printer and a sample brochure brimming with gushing prose and illustrated with colour photographs. One picture showed Swope holding a bushel of the exotic fruit. As a young man he'd resembled Clark Gable, tall, husky, with dark wavy hair and a pencil moustache. The caption identified him as a world-renowned horticulturist and botanical researcher specializing in the propagation of rare food crops and dedicated to ending world hunger.

I read on. There were detailed descriptions of cross-breeding experiments between the cherimoya and other members of *annonaceae*. Swope was a compulsive reporter, painstakingly listing every possible climactic and biochemical variable. In the end that line of research had been abandoned with the notation that 'No hybrid approaches the perfection that is *a. cherimoya.*'

The optimism came to an abrupt halt in Volume X: I opened to newspaper clippings reporting the freak frost that had decimated the cherimoya grove. There were descriptions of the agricultural damage wrought by the cold winds and projections of rises in food prices clipped from the San Diego papers. A mournful feature on the Swopes specifically had been printed in the La Vista *Clarion*. The next twenty pages were filled with jagged, obscene scribbles, the paper deeply indented often to the point of tearing; the pen had been used to stab and slash.

Then new experimental data.

As I turned the pages, Garland Swope's fascination with the grotesque, the stillborn, and the deadly evolved before my eyes. It started as theoretical notations about mutations, and rambling hypotheses

254

about their ecological value. Midway through the eleventh volume was the chilling answer Swope found to those questions: 'The sublimely repugnant mutations of otherwise mundane species must be evidence of the Creator's essential hatefulness.'

The notes grew progressively less coherent even as they increased in complexity. At times Swope's handwriting was so cramped as to be illegible, but I was able to make out most of it – tests of poison content on mice, pigeons, and sparrows; careful selection of deformed fruit for genetic culture; culling of the normal, nurturance of the defective. All part of a patient, methodical search for the ultimate horticultural horror.

Then there was yet another turn in the convoluted journey through Swope's mind: in the first chapter on Volume XII it appeared he'd dropped his morbid obsessions and gone back to working with *annonaceae*, concentrating on a species Maimon hadn't mentioned: *a. zingiber.* He'd conducted a series of pollinization experiments, carefully listing the date and time of each. Soon, however, the new studies were interrupted by accounts of work with deadly toadstool, foxglove, and dieffenbachia. There was a gleeful emphasis upon the neurotoxic qualities of the last exemplified by a footnote attributing the plant's common name, dumb cane, to its ability to paralyze the vocal chords.

This pattern of shifting between his pet mutations and the new annona became established by the middle of the thirteenth volume and continued through the fifteenth.

In Volume XVI, the notes took on an optimistic tone as Swope exulted in the creation of 'a new cultivar.' Then, as suddenly as it had appeared, *a. zingiber* was discarded and dismissed as 'showing robust breeder potential but lacking any further utility.' I put my strained eyes through another hundred pages of madness and set the binders aside.

The library contained several books on rare fruit, many of them exquisite editions published in Asia. I looked through all of them but could find no reference to *annona zingiber*. Puzzled, I searched the shelves for suitable reference material and pulled out a thick dog-eared volume titled *Botanical Taxonomy*.

The answer was at the end of the book. It took a while to comprehend the full meaning of what I'd just read. An unspeakable conclusion but agonizingly logical.

As the insights hit I was seized with acute claustrophobia and grew rigid with tension. Sweat ran down my back. My heart pounded and my breathing quickened. The room was an evil place and I had to get out.

Frantically I gathered up several of the blue cloth binders and placed them in a cardboard box. I carried it and my tools down the ladder, bolted the bedroom, and rushed to the landing. Teetering with vertigo, I ran recklessly down the stairs and crossed the frigid living room with four long strides.

After fumbling with the latch I managed to throw open the front door. I stood on the rotting porch until I caught my breath.

Silence greeted me. I'd never felt so alone.

Without looking back I made my escape.

22

ALONG WITH everyone else, I'd dismissed Raoul's conviction that Woody Swope had been abducted by the Touch. Now I wasn't so sure.

I'd seen no aberrant crops growing in the gardens of the Retreat, which meant Matthias had lied about buying seeds from the Swopes. On the surface it seemed a petty falsehood, serving no purpose. But habitual liars often lace their stories with demitruths for the sake of realism. Had the guru fabricated a casual connection between his group and the Swopes in order to obscure a deeper relationship?

The lie stuck in my craw. Along with the memory of my first visit to the Retreat, which, in retrospect, seemed suspiciously well orchestrated. Matthias had been too gracious about my intrusion, too pliant and cooperative. For a group that had been described as reclusive, the Touch had been strangely willing to endure scrutiny by a total stranger.

Had the generous welcome meant they had nothing to hide? Or that they had hidden their secret so well that discovery was out of the question.

I thought of Woody and allowed myself the luxury of hope: the boy might still be alive. But for how long? His body was a biological minefield ready to explode at any moment.

If Matthias and his cultists had stashed the boy somewhere on their grounds, a more spontaneous inspection was in order.

Houten had gotten to the Retreat by driving through La Vista and turning right at a fork just outside the town limits. I wanted to avoid being seen and if my recollection of the county map was correct, the road I now travelled intersected the one from town, forming the right prong of the fork. I sped along, headlights off and soon found myself nearing the gates of the former monastery.

Once again I hid the Seville under tall trees and walked to the entrance on foot. The bolt cutter was in my waistband, the flashlight in my jacket pocket, and the crowbar up one sleeve. I wouldn't stand a chance in an electrical storm.

My hopes for surreptitious entry were dashed by the sight of a male cultist patrolling inside the gates. His white uniform stood out in the darkness, the loose-fitting garments billowing, as he walked back and forth. A leather stash bag swung from the sash around his waist.

I'd come too far to turn back. A plan presented itself. I moved forward cautiously. Closer inspection revealed the guard to be Brother Baron, né Barry Graffius. This cheered me greatly. I'm not a violent person by inclination and had begun to feel more than a little guilty about what I was about to do. But if anyone deserved it, Graffius did. The rationalization didn't remove the guilt, but it did serve to lower it to a tolerable level.

I timed my footsteps to coincide with his and drew closer. Unloading my tools, I waited, concealed behind high shrubbery, but able to see him through the branches. He continued his walk for a few minutes, then obliged me by stopping to scratch his rear. I gave a low hiss and he snapped to attention, straining to locate the source of the sound. Edging closer to the gate he peered out, sniffing like a rabbit.

I held my breath until he resumed pacing. Another pause, this one deliberate, inquisitive. *Hiss.* He reached under his blouse and drew out a little pistol. Stepped forward, pointing the gun in the direction of the sound.

I waited until he'd stopped and listened three more times before hissing again. This time he let out a curse and pressed his belly up against the iron bars of the gate, eyes wide with suspicion and anxiety. He raised the weapon, moved it in an arc like a turret gunner.

When the barrel was pointing away from me I rushed him, grabbed the gun arm and yanked it forward through the bars. A sharp perpendicular twist against the metal made him cry out in pain and drop the weapon. I put my fist in his solar plexus and as he gasped, employed a little trick I'd learned from Jaroslav. Grabbing his neck, I felt for the right places, found them, squeezed and shut down his carotid arteries.

The choke-hold worked quickly. He went limp and passed out. As consciousness departed, his body grew heavy in my grasp. I struggled to keep my hold on him and lowered him carefully to the ground ι was tricky working through the bars but I managed ιo ·oιl him over and loosen the drawstrings of the stash bag.

The yield: a roll of breath mints, a small sack of sun-flower seeds, and a ring of keys.

I left him the snacks, took the keys and unlocked the gates. After retrieving the tools and the pistol, I walked through, closed and relocked the gates.

Stripping Graffius was harder than it looked. I used his clothes to bind his arms and legs. By the time I'd finished I was breathing hard. After ensuring that his nasal passages were clear I gagged him with one of his socks.

He'd be coming around soon and I didn't want him discovered, so I lifted him over my shoulder and carried him off the path, stepping into the bed of succulents. The plants squished underfoot, moist and cold against my trouser legs. I took him through to where the wooded area began, continued several yards, and deposited him between two red-woods.

Gathering my tools I began the walk to the Retreat.

A pale amber light shone above the door of the cathedral. The crucifix seemed to float above the belfry. A pair of male cultists patrolled the entrance at ten minute intervals.

I took my time crossing the viaduct, crouching to avoid detection, concealing myself behind the columns of the arbour. An arched gate was set into the wall to the right of the main building. When the time was right I made a run for it, found it unlocked, and walked through.

I was in one of the many courtyards I'd noticed during my first visit, a grassy rectangle trimmed on three sides by a hedge of eugenia. The church wall formed the fourth. At the far end of the lawn was a brass-topped sundial.

Draperies had been drawn over the clerestory windows, but a crescent of light escaped from one and

260

whitened the grass. I bounded over to look but the windows were too high to see through, the stucco walls free of toeholds.

I searched for something to stand on, saw only the sundial. It was solid stone, far too heavy to carry. Roots had wrapped themselves around the base. By rocking it back and forth I was able to free it from its earthly mooring. Laboriously I rolled it to the window, hoisted myself up, and peeked in through folds of brocade.

The huge domed room was brightly lit, the biblical murals vivid to the point of vulgarity. Matthias sat in its centre, cross-legged and naked, on a padded mat. His long body was as thin as a fakir's, soft and pale. Other mats ringed the periphery of the cathedral. Cultists squatted on them, fully garbed, men to the left, women to the right.

The pine table that had been at the centre of the room during my first visit was pushed back behind the guru. One of the men – the black-bearded giant from the vineyard – stood by it. Several red porcelain bowls sat on the table. I wondered what was in them.

Matthias meditated.

The flock waited silently and patiently as their shepherd retreated into an internal world, eyes closed, palms pressed together. He swayed and hummed and his penis began to harden, tilting upward. The others gazed at the tumescing organ as if it were sacred. When he was fully erect he opened his eyes and stood.

Stroking himself, he regarded his followers with authoritarian smugness.

'Let the Touch begin!' he thundered in a deep metallic voice.

A woman rose, fortyish, pudgy, and fair. She walked daintily to the table. Blackbeard inserted a golden straw into one of the bowls. The woman

261

stooped and put her nose to it, sniffed hard and inhaled the powder up into her sinuses.

The cocaine must have been high-quality. It took effect quickly. She swooned and grinned, broke into a giggle and did a little dancelike shuffle.

'Magdalene,' called Matthias.

She walked to him, undid her clothes and stood naked before her master. Her body was pink and plump, the buttocks marbled and stippled. She knelt and took him in her mouth, licking, nibbling, breasts bobbling with each movement. Matthias rocked on his heels, gritting his teeth with pleasure. She serviced him as the others watched until he pushed her head away and gestured for her to go.

She rose, walked to the left side of the cathedral and stood in front of the men, arms at her sides, completely at ease.

Matthias spoke the name 'Luther.'

A short man, bald and stooped, with a full grey beard, stood and disrobed. Upon command he went to the table, received a giant snootful of coke from the giant. Another stage direction from Matthias led him and the chubby woman to the centre of the room. She dropped to her knees, teased him hard and lay down on her back. The bald man mounted her and they copulated frantically.

The next woman to dip into the snow and kneel before the guru was tall, bony, and Spanish-looking. She was paired with a heavily built, bespectacled, florid man who looked like he'd been an accountant in a former life. He had an unusually small penis and the angular woman seemed to swallow it whole as she worked energetically to arouse him. Soon the two of them joined the first couple in the horizontal dance on the cathedral floor.

The third woman was Delilah. Her body was freakishly youthful, lithe, and firm. Matthias kept her with him longer than the first two and had four other women join in. They ministered to him like drones servicing a queen bee. Finally he released them and assigned them partners.

In the course of twenty minutes a fortune in coke had been consumed, with no letup in sight. I saw people go back for seconds and thirds, all in response to commands from Matthias. When one bowl was depleted the giant simply shoved his straw into another.

The padded mats held a writhing mass of wriggling bodies. The scene was sexual without being sensual, depressingly lacking in spontaneity, a mindless ritual, codified, choreographed, and based on the whims of one megalomaniac. A nod from Matthias and the cultists tumbled and thrust. The crook of an eyebrow and they heaved and moaned. I couldn't help being reminded of the maggots blindly burrowing through the meat in Garland Swope's greenhouse.

A roar rose from the cultists. Matthias had spurted. Women scurried to lick him clean. He lay back, sated, but their attentions made him hard again and the action resumed.

I'd seen enough. Climbing down from the sundial, I walked quietly to the gate. The two sentries were approaching from the right, brown-bearded, grim-faced, and goose-stepping in rhythm. I stepped back into the shadows until they had passed. When they'd turned the corner I sprinted out of the courtyard and raced to the iron-banded front door. Pulling it open a crack I peeked through and found the entrance unguarded. From behind the doors of the sanctuary came sounds of muffled bleating and the rhythmic slap of flesh on flesh.

To the left was the dead end punctuated by Matthias's office. I ran to the right, nearly tripping over a potted palm in my haste. The corridor was empty and white. I felt as conspicious as a roach on a

263

refrigerator. If discovered, I was a dead man: I'd seen the coke cache. I had no idea how long the orgy down the hall would last, or if the sentries' circuit took them indoors. Speed was of the essence.

I searched the laundry room, the kitchen, the members' library, looked for hidden tunnels, false walls, secret stairways. Found nothing.

Using a master key I discovered on the ring I'd taken from Graffius, I conducted a fruitless search of each room. Halfway through there was one false alarm: sudden movement under the bedcovers of one of the beds. For one heart-stopping moment I thought my search was over. But the body under the blanket was adult, male, hirsute, and thick, the face above it red-nosed, open-mouthed, and mottled: a cultist sleeping off a cold. The man stirred under the beam of my flashlight, passed wind, and rolled over, dead to the world. I left quietly.

The next room was Delilah's. She'd kept some of her old reviews and press clippings in the bottom of a drawer filled with plain cotton underwear. Other than that her sleeping quarters were as barren as those of the others.

I went from room to room, checking another dozen cells before coming to the one I remembered was Matthias's. The door wouldn't respond to any of the keys on the ring.

I used the crowbar. The bolt was a long one and wouldn't surrender until the door was nearly shattered. Anyone passing by would notice the damage. I slipped inside, taut with pressure.

It was as before. Identical to the others except for the small bookcase. Low ceilinged. Cool. Walled and floored with stone. Dominated by a hard narrow bed covered with a coarse grey blanket.

The humble domicile of a man who'd forsaken the pleasures of the flesh for those of the spirit.

Ascetic. And false to the core.

For the man was anything but spiritual. Minutes ago I'd watched him defile a church, drunk with power, cold as Lucifer. Suddenly the books on his shelves seemed to stare out at me. *Mockingly.* Righteous tomes on religion, philosophy, ethics, morality.

Books had revealed secrets once already this evening. Perhaps they would again.

Furiously, I emptied the shelves, examining each volume, opening, shaking, searching for false spines, hollowed out pages, clues scrawled in margins.

Nothing. The books were pristine, bindings stiff, pages crisp and unfoxed.

Not a single one had been read.

The empty bookcase teetered, shifted on its base. I caught it before it fell. And noticed something.

The portion of the floor that had been under the bookcase was a clearly demarcated rectangle, a shade lighter than the rest. I knelt, pointed the flashlight, ran my fingers over the edges. Seams. Cut into the stone. I pushed. Faint movement.

It took some experimenting to find the proper fulcrum. Stepping on one corner of the rectangle lifted the block sufficiently to lodge the crowbar in the opening. I exerted pressure. The slab rose and I pushed it aside.

The hole was about eighteen inches by a foot, four feet deep and lined with concrete. Too small for a body. But more than ample for other booty:

I found double plastic bags tightly packed with powder in shades of chocolate and vanilla: snowy cocaine and a brownish substance that I recognized as Mexican heroin. A metal strongbox full of sticky dark resin – raw opium. Several pounds of hashish in foil-wrapped chunks the size of soap bars.

And at the bottom of the hole, a single manila folder.

I opened it, read it, and slipped it into my shirt. By now I was carrying more cargo than the Southern Pacific. I turned off the flashlight, looked both ways down the hall. Heard the sounds of human voices. At the end of the corridor was a door leading outside. I sprinted, as fast as I could and hurled myself through it, lungs aching.

Cultists were streaming out of the sanctuary, most of them still naked. I made it to the base of the fountain without being seen and hid under the oak trees. Matthias came out surrounded by women. One wiped his brow. Another – Maria, the bland-faced, grandmotherly woman who'd sat at the entrance the day of my first visit – gave him a neck rub and fondled his penis. Apparently oblivious to these ministrations, he led the group to the lawn and bade them sit. Five dozen people obeyed, the crowd collapsing like deflated bellows. They were no more than thirty feet away.

Matthias looked up at the stars. Mumbled something. Closed his eyes and began chanting wordlessly. The others joined in. The sound was raw and atonal, a primal wail, passionately pagan. When they reached a crescendo, I sprinted to the viaduct and ran straight for the front gates.

Graffius was lying a few feet from where I'd placed him, twisting like a worm on a griddle, struggling to get free. He seemed to be breathing well. I left him there.

23

I HADN'T found what I was looking for. But between Swope's journals and the file I'd taken from Matthias's room I had plenty for show and tell. No doubt my pilferage violated all the rules of evidence, but what I'd found would be enough to get things going.

It was just past two a.m. I got behind the wheel of the Seville, adrenalized and hyperalert. Starting up the engine, I organized my thoughts: I'd drive to Oceanside, find a phone and call Milo or, if he was still in Washington, Del Hardy. It shouldn't take long to notify the proper authorities, and with luck the investigation could commence before dawn.

It was more important than ever to avoid La Vista. I turned the car around in the direction of the utility road and rolled into the dark. I passed the Swope place, Maimon's nursery, the homesteads and the

citrus groves, and had reached the plateau of the foothills when the other car materialized from the west.

I heard it before seeing it – its headlights, like mine,
were off. There was just enough moonlight to identify
the make as it sped past. A late model Corvette, dark,
possibly black, its snout nosing the asphalt. The
rumble of an oversized engine. A rear spoiler. Shiny
mag wheels.

But it wasn't until I saw the big fat tyres that I
changed my plan.

The Corvette turned left. I shot the intersection,
turned right and followed, lagging far enough behind
to stay out of earshot and struggling to keep the low
dark chassis in view from that distance. Whoever was
behind the wheel knew the road well and drove like a
teenage joyrider, popping the clutch, downshifting
around curves without breaking, accelerating with a
roar that signalled impending redline.

The road turned to dirt. The Corvette chewed it up
like a four-wheeler. The Seville's suspension shim-
mied but I held on. The other car slowed at the
sealed entrance to the oilfields, turned sharply and
drove along the perimeter of the mesa. It accelerated
and sped on, hugging the fence, casting an incision-
thin shadow against the chain link.

The abandoned fields stretched for miles, as
desolate as a moonscape. Moist craters pocked the
terrain. The fossils of tractors and trucks rose from
the sump. Row after row of dormant wells encased in
grid-sided towers erupted from the tortured earth,
creating the illusion of a skyline.

The Corvette was there one moment, gone the
next. I braked quickly but quietly, and coasted
forward. There was a car-sized gap in the fence. The
chain link was ragged and curly-edged around the
opening, as if it had unravelled under the force of
giant shears. Tyre tracks etched the dirt.

I drove through, parked behind a rusted derrick, got out, and inspected the ground.

The Corvette's tyres had created dual caterpillars that wove a corridor through convex metal walls: oil drums were stacked three-high, forming a hundred yards of barricade. The night air stank with tar and burnt rubber.

The corridor terminated in a clearing. In the open space sat an old mobile home on blocks. A smudge of light filtered through a single curtained window. The door was unadorned plywood. A few feet away was the sleek black car.

The driver's door opened. I pressed back, flat against the oil drums. A man got out, arms full, keys dangling from his fingertips. He carried four shopping bags as if they were weightless. Walking to the door of the mobile home, he knocked once, three times, then once again, and let himself in.

He stayed in there for half an hour, emerged carrying an axe, laid it on the Corvette's passenger seat, and got behind the wheel.

I waited ten minutes after he'd driven away before walking to the door and imitating his knock. When there was no response, I repeated it. The door opened. I looked into wide-set eyes the colour of midnight.

'Back so soo – ' The straight wide mouth froze in surprise. She tried to slam the door shut. I put my foot in and pressed. She pushed back. I got in and she edged away from me.

'You!' The girl was wild-eyed and beautiful. Her flaming hair had been tied up and pinned. A few fine strands had come loose, haloing the long supple neck. Two thin hoops pierced each ear. She wore cut-offs and a white midriff blouse. Her belly was tan and flat, her legs smooth and miles-long, tapering to bare feet. She'd painted her fingernails and toenails hunter green.

269

The trailer was partitioned into rooms. We were in a cramped yellow kitchen that smelled of mildew. One of the shopping bags had already been emptied. The other three sat on the counter. She fumbled in the dish drainer, came up with a plastic-handled bread knife.

'Get out of here or I'll cut you. I swear it!'

'Put it down, Nona,' I said softly. 'I'm not here to hurt you.'

'Bull*shit!* Just like the others.' She held the knife with both hands. The serrated blade made a wobbly arc. 'Get out!'

'I know what was done to you. Hear me out.'

She went slack and looked puzzled. For a moment I thought I'd calmed her. I took a step closer. Her young face contorted with hurt and rage.

She took a deep breath and lunged at me, knife held high.

I stepped away from the thrust. She plunged the blade where my thorax had been, stabbed air, and pitched forward awkwardly. I caught her wrist, squeezed and shook.

The knife fell, clicking against grubby linoleum. She went for my eyes with long green nails, but I got hold of both of her arms. She was delicately built, the bones fragile under smooth soft skin, but strengthened by anger. She kicked and coiled and spat, managed to gouge my cheek. On my bad side, I felt a warm trail flow ticklishly down the side of my face, then a sharp sting. Burgundy splotches dotted the floor.

I pinioned her arms to her sides. She went stiff, staring at me with the terror of a wounded animal. Suddenly she darted her face forward. I jerked back to avoid being bitten. Her tongue snaked out and caught a droplet of blood on its tip. She ran it over her lips, rouging them wetly. Forced a smile.

'I'll drink you,' she said huskily. 'Do anything you want. If you leave afterwards.'

'That's not what I'm after.'

'It would be if you knew. I can make you feel things you've never imagined.' It was a line from a low-budget skinflick, but she took it seriously, grinding her pelvis against mine. She licked me once more and made a show of swallowing the blood.

'Stop it,' I said, arching away.

'Aw, c'mon.' She wriggled. 'You're a hunk. Those nice blue eyes and all of those thick dark curls. I bet your cock is just as pretty, huh?'

'Enough, Nona.'

She pouted, and kept rubbing against me. Her skin was saturated with musky dimestore cologne.

'Don't be angry, Blue Eyes. There's nothing wrong with being a big healthy guy with a big gnarly cock. I can feel it now. Right *there.* Oh yeah, it's *big.* I'd *love* to play with it. Put it in my mouth. *Swallow* you. *Drink* you.' She batted her lashes. 'I'll take off my clothes and let you play with me while I do you.'

She tried to lick me again. I freed one hand and slapped her hard across the face.

She reeled backward, stunned, and looked at me with little-girl surprise.

'You're a human being,' I said. 'Not a piece of meat.'

'*I'm a cunt!*' She screamed and tore at her hair, ripping loose the long ginger tendrils.

'Nona – '

She shuddered with self-loathing, sculpted her hands into quivering hooks. But this time they were aimed at her own flesh, inches from ripping open that exquisite face.

I grabbed her and held her tight. She fought me, cursing, then exploded into sobs. She seemed to curl up and diminish in size, crying on my shoulder.

271

When the tears wouldn't come anymore, she collapsed against my chest, mute and limp.

I carried her to a chair, sat her down, wiped her face with a tissue and pressed another against my cheek. Most of the bleeding had stopped. I retrieved the knife and tossed it in the sink.

She was staring at the table. I cupped her chin in my hand. The inky eyes were glazed and unfocused.

'Where's Woody?'

'Back there,' she said dully. 'Sleeping.'

'Show me.'

She rose unsteadily. A shredded plastic shower curtain divided the trailer. I guided her through it.

The back room was stuffy and dim and furnished with thrift shop remnants. The walls were panelled with fake birch, scarred white. A filling station calendar hung lopsided from a roofing nail. Digital time beamed forth from a plastic clock radio atop a plastic Parsons table. On the floor was a pile of teen magazines. A blue velveteen sleeper sofa had been opened to a queen-size bed.

Woody slept under faded paisley covers, coppery curls spreading on the pillow. On the adjacent nightstand were comic books, a toy truck, an uneaten apple, a bottle of pills. Vitamins.

His breathing was regular but laboured, his lips swollen and dry. I touched his cheek.

'He's very hot,' I told her.

'It'll break,' she said defensively. 'I've been giving him vitamin C for it.'

'Has it helped yet?'

She looked away and shook her head.

'He needs to be in a hospital, Nona.'

'No!' She bent down, took his small head in her arms. Pressed her cheek to his and kissed his eyelids. He smiled in his sleep.

272

'I'm going to call an ambulance.'

'There's no phone,' she proclaimed with childish triumph. 'Go leave to find one. We'll be gone when you get back.'

'He's very sick,' I said patiently. 'Every hour we delay puts him in greater danger. We'll go together, in my car. Get your things ready.'

'They'll *hurt* him!' she screamed. 'Just like before. Sticking needles in his bones! Putting him in that plastic jail!'

'Listen to me, Nona. He has *cancer*. He could die from it.'

She turned away.

'I don't believe it.'

I held her shoulders.

'You'd better. It's true.'

'Why? Cause that beaner doctor said so? He's just like all the others. Can't be trusted.' She cocked her hip the way she'd done in the hospital corridor. 'Why should it be cancer? He never smoked or polluted himself! He's just a little kid.'

'Kids get cancer, too. Thousands of them each year. No one knows why but they do. Almost all of them can be treated and some can be cured. Woody's one of them. Give him a chance.'

She frowned stubbornly.

'They were poisoning him in that place.'

'You need strong drugs to kill the disease. I'm not saying it'll be painless but medical treatment's the only thing that can save his life.'

'S'that what the beaner told you to tell me?'

'No. It's what I'm telling you myself. You don't have to go back to Dr. Melendez-Lynch. We'll find another specialist. In San Diego.'

The boy cried out in his sleep. She ran to him, sang a low, wordless lullaby, and stroked his hair. He quieted.

273

She rocked him in her arms. A child cradling a child. The flawless features trembled on the brink of collapse. The tears started again, in a torrent that streamed down her face.

'If we go to a hospital they'll take him away from me. I can take care of him best right here.'

'Nona,' I said, summoning all my compassion, 'there are things even a mother can't do.'

The rocking ceased for a moment, then resumed.

'I was at your parents' house tonight. I saw the greenhouse and read your father's notebooks.' She gave a start. It was the first she'd heard of the journals. But she suppressed the surprise and pretended to ignore me.

I continued to talk softly. 'I know what you've been through. It started after the death of the cherimoyas. He was probably unbalanced all along, but failure and helplessness drove him over the edge. He tried to get back in control by playing God. By creating his own world.'

She stiffened, withdrew from the boy, put his head down on the pillow tenderly, and walked out of the room. I followed her into the kitchen, keeping an eye on the knife in the sink. Stretching, she took a bottle of Southern Comfort from a high cupboard shelf, poured a coffee cup half full, and leaning rangily against the counter, swallowed. Unaccustomed to hard drinking, she grimaced and went into a paroxysm of coughing as it hit bottom.

I patted her back and eased her to a chair. She took the bottle with her. I sat opposite her, waited until she'd stopped hacking to continue.

'It started out as a series of experiments. Weird stuff using inbreeding and complex grafts. And that's all it was for a while – weird. Nothing criminal happened until he noticed you'd grown up.'

She filled the cup again, threw her head back, and

274

tossed the liquor down her throat, a caricature of toughness.

Once upon a time she'd been anything but tough. A pretty little red-haired girl, Maimon had recalled, smiling and friendly. The problems hadn't started until she was twelve years old or so. He hadn't known why.

But I did.

She'd completed puberty three months before her twelfth birthday. Swope had recorded the day he'd discovered it: ('Eureka! Annona has blossomed. She lacks intellectual depth, but what physical perfection! First rate stock . . . ').

He'd been fascinated with the transformation of her body, describing it in botanical terms. And as he observed her development, a hideous plan had taken shape in the wreckage of his mind.

One part of him was still organized, disciplined. As analytical as Mengele. The seduction was undertaken with the precision of a scientific experiment.

The first step was dehumanization of the victim. In order to justify the violation, he reclassified her: the girl was no longer his daughter, or even a person. Merely a specimen of a new exotic species. *Annona zingiber*. The ginger annona. A pistil to be pollinated.

Next came semantic distortion of the outrage itself: the daily excursions into the forest behind the greenhouse weren't incest, simply a new, intriguing project. The ultimate investigation of inbreeding.

He'd wait eagerly each day for her return from school to take her by the hand, and lead her into darkness. Then the spreading of the blanket on ground softened by pine needles, casual dismissal of her protests. There had been a full half year of rehearsal – an intensive seminar in fellatio – then finally, entry into the young body, the spilling of seed on the ground.

275

Evenings were devoted to the recording of data: climbing into the attic, he'd log each union in his notebook, sparing no details. Just like any other research.

According to the journals, he'd kept his wife informed about the progress of the experiments. Initially, she'd offered faint protest, then stood by, passively acquiescent. *Following orders.*

Impregnating the girl hadn't been an accident. On the contrary, it had been Swope's ultimate goal, calibrated and calculated. He'd been patient and methodical, waiting until she was a bit older - fourteen - to fertilize her so that the health of the foetus would be optimized. Charting her menstrual cycle to pinpoint ovulation. Refraining from intercourse for several days to increase the sperm count.

It had taken on the first try. He'd rejoiced at the cessation of her menses, the swelling of her belly. A *new cultivar* had been created.

I told her what I knew, wording it gently and hoping the empathy came through. She listened with a blank look on her face, drank Southern Comfort until her eyelids drooped.

'He victimized you, Nona. Used you and discarded you when it was over.'

Her head gave an almost imperceptible nod.

'You must have been so frightened, carrying a child at that age. And being sent away to have it in secret.'

'Bunch of dykes,' she muttered, slurring her words.

'At Madronas?'

She took another drink.

'Fuck yeah. Las Fucking Madronas Home for Bad Little Fucking Girls. In Mexi-fucking-O.' Her head lolled. She reached for the bottle. 'Big fat fucking

276

beaner dykes running the place. Screaming in beaner. Pinching and poking. Telling us we were trash. Sluts.'

Maimon had remembered vividly the morning she'd left town. Had described her waiting with her suitcase in the middle of the road. A scared little girl with all the mischief knocked out of her. About to be banished for the sins of another.

She'd come back different, he'd noted. Quieter, more subdued. Angry.

She was talking now, softly, drunkenly.

'It hurt so bad to push that baby boy out. I screamed and they covered my mouth. I thought I was coming apart. When it was over, they wouldn't let me hold him. Took him away from me. *My* baby, and they took him away! I forced myself to sit up to get a look at him. It near killed me. He had red hair, just like me.'

She shook her head, baffled.

'I thought I could keep him after I got home. But *he* said no way. Told me I was nothing. Just a vessel. Just a fucking vessel. Fancy word for cunt. Good for nothing but fucking. Told me I wasn't really the momma. *She'd* already started being his momma. I was the cunt. All used up and tossed in the trash. Time to let the grownups take over.'

She dropped her head on the table and whimpered.

I rubbed the back of her neck, said comforting things. Even in that state she reacted reflexively to the touch of a male, lifting her face and flashing me an intoxicated, come-hither smile, leaning forward to expose the tops of her breasts.

I shook my head and she turned away shame-faced.

I had so much sympathy for her it ached. There were therapeutic things I could have said. But now was the time to manipulate her. The boy in the back room needed help. I was prepared to take him out of

277

there against her will but preferred to avoid another abduction. For both their sakes.

'It wasn't you who took him out of the hospital, was it? You loved him too much to endanger him like that.'

'It's true,' she said, wet-eyed. 'They did it. To stop me from being his momma. All these years I'd let them treat me like garbage. Stayed out of the way while *they* raised him. Not saying anything to him about it cause I was afraid it would freak him out. Too much for a little kid to handle. Dying inside all the time.' She raised one slender hand to her heart, reached down with the other and drained her glass.

'But when he got sick something tugged on me. Like a hook in my guts with someone reeling in the line. I had to reclaim my rights. I stewed about it, sitting with him in that plastic room, watching him sleep. My baby. Finally I decided to do it. Sat them down in the motel one night, told them the lies had gone on too long. That my time had come. To take care of my baby.

'They – *he* laughed at me. Put me down, told me I was unfit, a piece of shit. A fucking *vessel*. I should get the hell out and make it better for everyone. But this time I didn't take it. The pain in my guts was too strong. I gave it all back to them, told them they were evil. Sinners. That the ca – the sickness was God's punishment for what they'd done. *They* were the ones who were unfit. And I was gonna tell everyone about it. The doctors, the nurses. They'd kick them out and hand my baby over to his rightful momma when they found out.'

Her hands trembled violently around her glass. I walked behind her and steadied them with mine.

'It was my right!' she cried out, whipping her head around and begging confirmation. I nodded and she slumped against my chest.

278

During Baron and Delilah's hospital visit, Emma Swope had complained the cancer treatment was dividing the family. The cultists had construed it as anxiety about the physical separation imposed by the Laminar Airflow room. But the woman had been worrying out loud about a far more serious rupture, one that threatened to rend the family as irreparably as a guillotine on neck-flesh.

Perhaps she'd known, then, that the wound was too deep to heal. But she and her husband had attempted to patch it anyway. To prevent the leakage of the ugly secret by taking the child and running . . .

'They snuck him out behind my back,' Nona was saying, squeezing my hand, digging in with the green nails. The anger was percolating within her once again. A thin film of sweat moustached the rich, wide mouth. 'Like fucking thieves. *She* dressed up as an x-ray technician. In a mask and gown they swiped from the laundry bin. Took him down to the basement on a service elevator and out a side exit. *Thieves.*

'I came back to the motel and all three of them were there. My baby was lying on the bed, so small and helpless. *They* were packing and joking about getting away with it so easy. How nobody had recognized her behind the mask because none of them had ever looked her in the eye. Putting down the hospital. Him going on about smog and shit. Trying to justify what they'd done.'

She'd given me an opening. It was time to renew my pitch. To convince her to come with me peaceably as I carried her son out of there.

But before I could say anything the door burst open.

24

DOUG CARMICHAEL crouched in the doorway like a commando in a martial arts movie. The arm that extended into the room held a rifle. The other hefted a double-edged axe as if it were balsa. He wore a black mesh tank top that exposed lots of hypertrophied muscle. His legs were thick and corded, carpeted with curly blond hair and encased in tight white swim trunks. His knees were misshapen and lumpy – surfer's knots. Rubber beach sandals cushioned large rough feet. The reddish-blond beard was neatly cropped, the thick layered hair precisely blow-dried.

Only the eyes had changed from the day I'd met him. That afternoon in Venice they'd been the colour of a cloudless sky. Now I looked into a pair of bottomless black holes: dilated pupils surrounded by thin rings of ice. Mad eyes that scanned the trailer, shifting from the Southern Comfort bottle to the drowsy girl to me.

'I ought to kill you right now for giving her that poison.'

'I didn't. She took it herself.'

'Shut up!'

Nona tried to straighten up. She swayed groggily. Carmichael pointed the rifle at me.

'Sit down on the floor. Up against the wall, with your hands under you. Good. Now stay put or I'll have to hurt you.'

To Nona: 'C'mere, Sis.'

She went to his side and leaned against his bulk. One massive arm went around her protectively. The one with the axe.

'Did he hurt you, babe?'

She looked at me, knew she was my jury, considered her answer, and shook her head woozily.

'Naw, he's been okay. Just talking. Wants to take Woody to the hospital.'

'I'll bet he does,' sneered Carmichael. 'That's the party line. Pour more poison in and rake in the bucks.'

She looked up at him.

'I dunno, Doug, the fever's no better.'

'Did you give him the C?'

'Yeah, just like you said.'

'What about the apple?'

'He wouldn't eat it. Been too sleepy.'

'Try again. If he doesn't like the apple there are pears and plums, too. And oranges.' He tilted his head at the shopping bags on the counter. 'That stuff is super fresh. Just picked, totally organic. Get some fruit and fluid down him along with more C and he'll cool off.'

'The boy's in danger,' I said. 'He needs more than vitamins.'

281

'I said shut up! You want me to finish you off right here?'

'I don't think he means any harm,' said the girl, meekly.

Carmichael smiled at her with genuine warmth and just a touch of condescension.

'You go back in there with the little guy. Work on nutrition.'

She started to say something but Carmichael silenced her with a flash of white teeth and a reassuring nod. Obediently she disappeared behind the shower curtain.

When we were alone he kicked the trailer door shut and moved opposite me, his back to the counter. I stared up into the twin barrels of the rifle – a deadly figure eight.

'I'm going to have to kill you,' he said calmly, then shrugged apologetically. 'Nothing personal, you know? But we're a family and you're a threat.'

The last thing I'd wanted to display was scepticism and I was sure I hadn't. But his psychic radar was hot-wired to go off unpredictably, the scrambled apparatus of the truly paranoiac. He squinted angrily and lowered the rifle, aiming at the tender concavity between my eyes. Hunching his massive shoulders he stared down menacingly.

'We *are* a family. And we don't need a blood test to prove it.'

'Of course not,' I agreed with a mouth full of cotton. 'It's the emotional bond that's important.'

He looked at me hard to make sure I wasn't patronizing him. I moulded my face into a mask of sincerity. Froze it that way.

The axe swung loosely, whetted blade abrading the floor.

'Exactly. It's feelings that count. Our feelings have been *forged in pain*. We're three against the world. Our family is what it should be – a sanctuary against all the craziness out there. A safe zone. It's beautiful and precious. And I've got to protect it.'

I had no plan for escape. For the time being there was no hope but to buy time by keeping him talking.

'I understand. You're the head of the family.'

The blue eyes heated like gas flames.

'The only one there ever was. The other two were evil, parents in name only. They abused their rights. Tried to destroy the family from within.'

'I know, Doug. I was over at the house this evening. Saw that greenhouse. Read some diaries that Swope kept.'

A terrible look oozed onto his face. He lifted his arm and swung the axe in a blinding parabola, letting it smash into the counter. The trailer shook as the plastic shattered. The movement had been effortless, not even budging his rifle arm. There was stirring behind the curtain but no sign of the girl.

'I was going to destroy that shithole tonight,' he whispered, jerking the blade free. 'With this. Shatter every fucking pane. Take the house apart board by board. Then burn it to the ground. But when I got there the lock had been tampered with so I came back. Lucky I did.'

He sucked in his breath, let it out with a hiss. Iron-pumper's breathing. He was sweating heavily, sizzling with agitation. I fought back the fear, forced myself to think clearly: I had to steer his attention to the crimes of the Swopes. And away from me.

'It's an evil place,' I said. 'Hard to believe people could be like that.'

'Not hard for me, man. I lived it. Just like Sis did. My old man diddled me and beat me and told me I was shit for years. And the bitch who called herself mom just stood by and watched. Different theatres

283

but the same movie. When I said forged in pain I meant it.'

As he talked about the abuse he'd suffered, lots of things fell into place: the arrested development, the exhibitionism, the hatred and panic when he'd talked about his father.

'It's destiny, Nona and me,' he said, with a satisfied smile. 'Neither of us could have made it alone. But some kind of miracle brought us together. Made us a family.'

'How long have you been a family?' I asked.

'Years. I used to come up summers, worked this field, rough-necking, sinking wells. The old bastard had big plans for this place. Carmichael Oil was gonna rape the land, carve it up, and squeeze every greasy drop out of it. Unfortunately, it was dry as a dead woman's tit.' He laughed, banged the axe head against the floor.

'I hated the work. It was dirty and demeaning and boring but he forced me to do it. Every summer, like a jail sentence, I sneaked away any chance I got, went hiking through the back roads, breathing clean air. Thinking of ways to get back at him.

'One day I met her while I was walking through the forest. She was sixteen and the most beautiful thing I'd ever seen, sitting on a stump and crying. She saw me and got scared but I told her it was okay. Instead of running, or talking, she started to - ' The handsome face darkened and distorted with anger. 'Put it out of your filthy mind, man. I never touched her. And that story I told you and the cop about the freeway blow job was bullshit. I was just trying to throw you off.'

I nodded. Another explanation for the fantasy suggested itself: wishful thinking. But for now his sexual impulses toward the girl he called his sister were safely repressed and I hoped they'd stay that way.

284

'It was because I treated her differently from the other men that something special grew between us. Instead of jumping her bones I listened to her. To her pain. Shared my own. All summer we met and talked. And the summer after that. I started looking forward to working the wells. We got to know each other bit by bit, discovered we'd been through the same thing, realized we were alike – two halves of one person. Male and female components. Brother and sister, but more. Know what I mean?'

I strained to look sympathetic, wanting him to keep on talking. 'You formed a common identity. Like some twins do.'

'Yeah. It was beautiful. But then the old bastard closed down the wells. Locked everything up. I drove up anyway. On weekends. During holidays for a week at a time. Crashed right here – used to be the night watchman's place. I cooked for her. Taught her how to cook. Helped her with her homework. Showed her how to drive. Took long walks at night. Always talking. About how we wanted to kill our parents, erase our roots. Start fresh, with a new family. We had picnics in the forest. I wanted the little guy to come along, so he could be part of the family, too. But they wouldn't let him out of their sight. She talked a lot about him, how she wanted to claim her rights. I told her she should, taught her about liberation. We made plans for next summer. The three of us were gonna run away to some island. Australia, maybe. I'd started collecting brochures to find the best place, then he got sick.

'She called me as soon as she got to L.A. Wanted me to help her get a job as a prize girl on one of the game shows, but I told her you needed heavy connections for that. Besides, I'd already lined up the gig with Adam and Eve. Got Rambo to let us work as partners. The skits went smooth as silk. We didn't

285

need any rehearsal because each of us knew what the other was thinking. It was like working with yourself. We got big tips and I gave them to her to keep.

'Then one night she phoned me in a panic, Said she'd confronted them and they'd snatched the little guy out. I'd never liked the idea of him being in that hospital in the first place but I was afraid they were gonna disappear south of the border, take him where she'd never see him again.

'I rushed over and got there just as they were leaving. Swope was coming out the door when I opened it. I'd never met him, but I knew damn well what kind of shit he was. He started mouthing off and I hit him in the face. Knocked him out. The woman came at me then, screaming, and I hit her, too, along the side of the head.

'Both of them were lying there, grokked. The little guy was kind of dazed, mumbling in his sleep. Nona got pissed all of a sudden and started to tear up the room. I calmed her down, told her to wait right there, and managed to load both of them in the 'Vette. Stuffed her in the back, put him in the front seat. Drove 'em to the beach at Playa Del Rey and when one of the planes passed overhead, finished 'em off. Then I hauled them to a place I knew in Benedict and dumped them. They deserved to die.'

He twirled the axe handle like a baton, chewed on a strawlike moustache hair.

'The police found the remains of another body up there,' I said. 'A woman.' I let the question hang in the air

He grinned.

'I know what you're thinking, but no. I would have liked to put mom there but she had the bad manners to have a stroke and die in bed a couple of years ago. It pissed me off, because I'd been planning it for years – there's a plot reserved for the old man that I'll fill

286

one day. But she escaped. Then I got lucky. I was doing a late gig at Lancelot's and this old broad in the front row was really coming on to me. Stuffing ten dollar bills down my jock, licking my ankles. Turns out she was a doctor. Radiologist. Divorced a couple of months and out for a wild night. She came to my dressing room, sloshed to the gills, started pawing me, sending out real strong signals. It turned me off and I was gonna kick her out. But when I turned on the lights I saw it: she could have been the old bitch's twin sister. Same dried-up face, upturned nose, rich bitch manner.

'I smiled, said *Come on in, honey*. Let her do me, right there in the dressing room. The door was unlocked, anyone could have come in. She didn't care, just hiked up her skirt and got on top. Later we went to her place, condo penthouse in the Marina. Made it again and then I strangled her in her sleep.' His eyes widened innocently. 'The burial plot had been chosen. Someone had to fill it.'

He leaned the axe against the oven, reached into one of the shopping bags with his free hand and brought out a large peach.

'Want one?'

'No thanks.'

'They're good. Good for you, too. Calcium, potassium. Lots of A and C. Make a great last meal.'

I shook my head.

'Suit yourself.' He took a large bite out of the fruit, licked the juice from the ends of his moustache.

'I'm no threat to you,' I said, choosing my words carefully, 'I just want to help your little brother.'

'How? By pumping him full of poisons? I read all about the stuff they wanted to use on him That shit *causes* cancer.'

'I'm not going to lie and tell you the drugs they use are harmless. They're strong – poisons just like you

287

said. But that's what it takes to kill the tumours.'

'Sounds like a load of shit to me.' His jaw tightened and the beard bristled. 'She told me all about the doctors there. Who's to say you're any different?'

He finished the peach and threw the pit in the sink. Took out a plum and dispatched it, too.

'Come on,' he said, picking up the axe. 'Stand up. Let's get it over with. I wish for your sake that I'd gotten you the first time, with the shotgun. You wouldn't even have known what hit you. Now you're gonna have to suffer a bit, waiting for it to happen.'

25

I WALKED to the door, the tip of the rifle nudging the small of my back.

'Open it slowly and carefully,' instructed Carmichael. 'Keep your hands on your head and look straight ahead.'

I obeyed him shakily and heard the rustling of the shower curtain, the sound of Nona's voice.

'You don't need to hurt him, Doug.'

'Go back in. Let me handle this.'

'But what if he's right? Woody's burning up - '

'I said I'll handle it!' the blond man snapped, with sudden loss of patience.

Her unseen response caused him to soften his voice.

'I'm sorry, Sis. It's been heavy and we're all stressed out. When I finish with him, we'll settle down, drop some B-twelve. I'll show you how to cool the little guy down. Couple weeks he'll be fine and we'll split. This time next month I'll be teaching him how to shoot the waves.'

'Doug, I – ' she began. I hoped she'd continue to plead my case, providing diversion for a sudden run. But she stopped midsentence. Padded footsteps were followed by the whisper of the curtain closing.

'Move,' said Carmichael, angered by the hint of rebellion and expressing it by jamming cold steel into my kidney.

I pushed the door open and stepped into darkness. The chemical stench in the air seemed stronger, the bleakness of the mesa more pronounced. The husks of the unused machines were giant, rusting carcasses, sprawled passive and silent across the ravaged terrain. It was far too ugly a place in which to die.

Carmichael prodded me through the corridor created by the stacked oil drums. My eyes darted from side to side, searching for escape, but the black cylinders formed high metal barricades, mercilessly seamless.

Several yards before the end of the passageway he started talking, offering me options.

'I can do it while you're standing, kneeling, or lying on the ground the way I did the Swopes. Or, if being still freaks you out, you can make a run for it, get a little exercise to take your mind off what's coming. I won't tell you how many steps I'll give you, so you can pretend it's like a regular run. Make believe you're in some kind of marathon. When I run I get high. Maybe you will, too. I'm using a heavy load so you won't feel a thing. Kinda like one big rush.'

My knees buckled.

'Come on, man,' he said, 'don't fall part. Go out with style.'

'Killing me won't do you any good. The police

know I'm here. If I don't return they'll be swarming over this place.'

'No sweat. As soon as you're out of the way, we're splitting.'

'The boy can't travel in his condition. You'll kill him.'

The rifle jabbed painfully.

'I don't need your advice. I can take care of my own.'

We walked in silence until we reached the mouth of the metal hallway.

'So how do you want it,' he demanded, 'standing still or running?'

A hundred yards of flat, empty land lay before me. The darkness would provide some cover for a run but I'd still be easy to pick off. Just beyond the void were hills of scrap metal – strips of sheet-iron, coils of wire, the derrick behind which I'd hidden the Seville. Meagre sanctuary, but finding cover among the detritus would gain me time to plan . . .

'Take your time,' Carmichael said magnanimously, savouring the starring role.

He'd played this scene before, was working hard at coming across cool and in control. But I knew he was as unstable as nitro and just might start blowing his lines if provoked. The trick was to get him sufficiently distracted to lower his guard, then flee. Or attack. It was a deadly gamble – a sudden burst of rage could just as easily yank his trigger finger. But there wasn't much to lose at this point and the idea of submitting passively to slaughter was damned distasteful.

'Make up your mind?'

'It's a bullshit choice, Doug, and you know it.'

'What?'

'I said you're full of shit.'

Growling, he spun me around, tossed the rifle away, and grabbed the front of my shirt, pulling it

291

tight. He raised the axe and held it poised in the air.

'Move and I'll slice you like cheese.' He panted with anger, face glistening with sweat. A feral smell emanated from the mass of his body.

I kneed him hard in the groin. He yelped in pain and relinquished his grip reflexively. I pulled away, landed on the ground, scurried backward like a crab, scraping my knees and palms. While fighting to push myself upright I pressed my foot against something round. A large metal spring. It rolled, I was upended, and fell flat on my back.

Carmichael charged forward, hyperventilating like a child coming out of a tantrum. The edge of the axe caught a glint of moonlight. Shadowed against the blackness of the sky he seemed immense, fictional.

I yanked myself up and crawled away from him.

'You've got a big mouth,' he gasped. 'No class, no style. I gave you the opportunity to end it peacefully. I tried to be fair but you didn't appreciate it. Now it's gonna hurt. I'm gonna use this on you.' He hefted the axe for emphasis. 'Slowly. Turn you into garbage piece by piece and make it last. In the end you'll beg for a bullet.'

A figure stepped out from behind the oil drums.

'Put it down, Doug.'

Sheriff Houten stepped into the clearing, trim and sure-footed. The Colt .45 extended like a nickel-plated handshake.

'Put it down,' he repeated, levelling the firearm at Carmichael's chest.

'Leave it alone, Ray,' said the blond man. 'Got to finish what we started.'

'Not this way.'

'It's the only way,' insisted Carmichael.

The lawman shook his head.

'I just got off the phone with a fellow named Sturgis at L.A. Homicide. He was making inquiries about the doctor here. Seems somebody took a shot at him last night and gunned down the wrong man. Next day the doctor disappeared. They're looking for him in earnest. I figured he might have ended up here.'

'He's trying to break up my family, Ray. You warned me about him yourself.'

'You're confused, boy. I told you he'd asked about the back road so you'd find yourself another hiding place. Not to put you up to killing the man. Now drop that axe and we'll talk about it calmly.'

He held his gun steady and looked down at me.

'Damn stupid of you to go snooping around, Doctor.'

'It seemed better than being a stationary target. And there's a little boy in that trailer who needs medical attention.'

He shook his head fiercely.

'Boy's gonna die.'

'Not true, Sheriff. He can be treated.'

'That's what they told me about my wife. I let them cut her up and fill her with poisons and the cancer ate her up just the same.' He returned his attention to Carmichael:

'I backed you up to a point, Doug, but it's gone too far. Lay down the axe.'

The two of them locked eyes. I seized the opportunity to roll out of hacking range.

Carmichael saw me and swung his weapon.

The .45 blazed. Carmichael jumped back, screaming in pain. He clamped one hand to his side, blood seeping out around his fingers. Incredibly, the other continued to grip the axe.

'You – you hurt me,' he muttered, incredulous.

'Just a flesh crease,' said Houten evenly. 'You'll survive. Now let go of the damned axe, boy.'

I stood and inched toward the discarded rifle, staying out of the blond man's swinging range.

The door to the trailer opened, spilling cold white light down the pathway. Nona ran out calling Carmichael's name.

'Get the rifle, Sis!' he yelled. The command emerged from between pain-clenched jaws. The hand holding the axe was shaking. The one at his side was glossy red from wrist to fingertips. Blood rolled viscously over his knuckles and dripped to the ground.

The girl came to a stop, watching wide-eyed as the dirt at Carmichael's feet sprouted a spreading crimson flower.

'You killed him!' she shrieked and ran toward Houten, striking out blindly. He straight-armed her while keeping a bead on the wounded man. She flailed away at him without doing any damage. Finally he shoved her aside and she staggered off-balance before falling.

I edged closer to the rifle.

Nona picked herself up.

'You filthy old fuck!' she screamed at the Sheriff. 'You were supposed to help us and now you've killed him!' Houten looked past her woodenly. Suddenly she flung herself at Carmichael's feet. 'Don't die, Doug. Please. I need you so bad.'

'Get the rifle!' he screamed.

She looked up at him blankly, nodded, and marched toward the weapon. She was closer to it than I and it was time to move. As she stooped to retrieve it I dived.

Carmichael saw me out of the corner of his eye, pivoted and slashed down at my arm with the axe. I jerked back. He grunted in agony, his wound leaking copiously, and slashing again, missing me by inches.

Houten crouched, two-handed the .45, and shot Carmichael in the back of the head. The exit trajectory tore open his throat. He clutched at his

294

neck, sucked in air, gurgled, and dropped.

The girl snatched up the rifle and cradled it knowingly. She stared at the body on the ground. Carmichael's limbs twitched automatically and she watched, transfixed, until they were stiff. Her hair was loose and blowing in the night breeze, her eyes frightened and moist.

Carmichael's bowels opened with a burst of flatulence. The beautiful face hardened. She looked up, pointed the weapon at me, shook her head and arced around, aiming at the sheriff.

'You're just like the rest,' she spat at him.

Before he could reply she shifted her attention back to the corpse, began talking to it in a singsong voice.

'He's just like the rest, Doug. He didn't help us because he was good, because he was on our side like you thought. He did it because he was a fucking coward. Afraid I'd tell his dirty secrets.'

'Quiet girl,' warned the sheriff.

She ignored him.

'He fucked me, Doug, just like all the other, filthy, evil old men with their filthy cocks and their sagging balls. When I was just a little girl. After the monster broke me in. The righteous arm of the law.' She sneered. 'I flashed him a sample and he lapped it up. Couldn't get enough. Had to have it every day. In his house. In his truck. Picked me up while I walked home from school and drove me up to the hills to do it. What do you think of our old friend, Ray, now, Doug?'

Houten shouted for her to shut up. But his voice lacked conviction and he seemed to sag, looking shrivelled and helpless despite the big gun in his hand.

She continued to address the body, sobbing.

'You were so good and trusting, Doug . . . You thought he was being our friend, helping us hide out

295

because he didn't like doctors any better than we did
. . . Because he understood. But that wasn't it at all.
He would have given us up in a minute but I threatened to expose him if he did . . . To tell everyone that
he fucked me. And *knocked me up*.'

Houten looked at the Colt. Harboured a terrible
thought and dismissed it. 'Nona, you don't wa – '

'He thinks he's Woody's daddy, cause that's what
I've told him all these years.' She stroked the rifle and
giggled. 'Course now, maybe I was telling the truth,
maybe I wasn't. Maybe I don't even know. We never
did do any blood tests to find out, did we, Ray?'

'You're crazy,' he said. 'You'll be locked up.' To
me: 'She's crazy. You can see that, can't you?'

'Is that so?' She put her finger around the trigger
and smiled. 'I guess you know all about crazy. All
about crazy little girls. Like little old fat crazy Marla,
always sitting by herself, rocking and writing dumb
crazy poems. Talking to herself, wetting her pants,
and carrying on like a baby. *She* was crazy, wasn't
she, Ray? Fat and ugly and a real head case.'

'Shut your mouth – '

'You shut yours, you old bastard!' she screamed.
'Who the hell are you telling me what to do? You
fucked me every day, taking sloppy seconds without
complaining. Shot your scum into me and knocked
me up.' She smiled eerily. 'Maybe. Least that's
what I told Crazy Marla. You shoulda seen the look in
those piggy little eyes. I gave her *all* the details. About
how you lapped it up and begged for more. *Sheriff*. I
must have upset the poor thing, cause the next day
she took a rope and – '

Houten bellowed and came at her.

She laughed and shot him in the face.

He collapsed like wet tissue paper. She stood over
him and pulled the trigger again. Braced herself
against the recoil and put yet another slug into him.

I peeled her fingers off the weapon and let it fall between the two corpses. She offered no resistance. Put her head on my shoulder and gave me a lovely smile.

I took her with me and went looking for the El Camino. It wasn't hard to find. Houten had parked it just outside the gap in the fence. Watching her closely, I used the radio to make my calls.

26

LATE ON a quiet Sunday afternoon, I stood on the lawn across from the entrance to the Retreat and waited for Matthias. Furnace-blast winds had strafed the southern half of the state without letup for thirty-six hours and though sunset was drawing near the heat refused to dissipate. Sticky, itchy, and over-dressed in jeans, chambray shirt, and a calfskin jacket, I sought the shade of the old oaks circling the fountain.

He emerged from the main building encircled by a cocoon of followers, glanced in my direction and bade them disperse. They moved to a hilly spot, sat and began to meditate. He approached slowly and deliberately, staring downward, as if searching for something in the grass.

We came face to face. Instead of greeting me, he dropped to the ground, folded himself into a lotus

298

position, and stroked his beard.

'I don't see pockets in the outfit you're wearing,' I said. 'No place to hold a substantial wad of cash. I hope that doesn't mean you didn't take me seriously.'

He ignored me and stared off into space. I tolerated it for a few minutes then made a show of losing my patience.

'Cut the holy-man, crap, Matthews. It's time to talk business.'

A fly settled on his forehead, walked nimbly along the edge of the crater-scar. It didn't seem to bother him.

'State your business,' he said softly.

'I thought I was pretty clear over the phone.'

He picked a stalk of clover and twirled it in his long fingers.

'About certain things, yes. You confessed to trespassing, assault on Brother Baron, and burglary. What remains unclear is why there should be any – business for you and me to conduct.'

'And yet you're here. Listening.'

He smiled.

'I pride myself on maintaining an open mind.'

'Listen,' I said, turning to go. 'I've had a rough couple of days and my tolerance for bullshit is at an all time low. What I've got will keep. You want to think about it, go ahead. Just add a thousand a day in late fees.'

'Sit down,' he said.

I settled opposite him, crossing my legs and tucking them under me. The ground was as hot as a waffle iron. The itch in my chest and belly had intensified. Off in ·ıe distance the cultists bowed and scraped.

His hand left his beard and stroked the grass idly.

'You mentioned a substantial sum of money over the phone,' he said.

'A hundred and fifty thousand dollars. Three

instalments of fifty thousand each. The first today, the following two at six-month intervals.'

He worked hard at looking amused.

'Why in the world would I pay you that kind of money?'

'For you it's petty cash. If the party I saw a couple of nights ago is typical, you and your zombies shovel that much up your noses in a week.'

'Are you implying that we use illicit drugs?' he asked, mockingly.

'Perish the thought. No doubt you've removed the stash, stowed it somewhere else, and would welcome a police search with open arms. Just like you did the first time I was here. But I've got Polaroids from the party that would make great porno for the geriatric set. All those worn-out bodies grinding away. Bowls of snow and straws up noses. Not to mention a couple of clear shots of the cache under your bookcase.'

'Photographs of consenting adults having sex,' he recited, sounding suddenly like an attorney, 'bowls on a table containing an unknown substance. Plastic bags. It doesn't add up to much. Certainly not a hundred and fifty thousand.'

'How much is avoiding a murder rap worth?'

His eyes narrowed and his face changed into something lupine and predatory. He tried to stare me down but it was no contest. The itch had grown nearly unbearable and gazing back at the brutal mask was a welcome distraction.

'Go on,' he said.

'I made three copies of the file, added a page of interpretation to each one, and put them in separate safe places. Along with the pictures and instructions to several attorneys in the event of my untimely demise. Before I copied I read through it several times. Fascinating.'

He looked composed but his right hand gave him

300

away. The bony white fingers had clawed the ground and ripped out a handful of grass.

'Generalities are worthless,' he whispered harshly. 'If you have something to say, say it.'

'All right,' I said, 'Let's flash back a little over twenty years ago. Long before you discovered the guru scam. You're sitting in your office on Camden Drive. A mousy little woman named Emma is on the other side of the desk. She's travelled all the way from a hick town called La Vista to Beverly Hills and has paid you a hundred dollars for a confidential legal consultation. A lot of money in those days.

'Emma's story is a sad one, though no doubt you think of it as third-rate melodrama. Finding herself trapped in a loveless marriage she'd sought comfort in the arms of another man. A man who made her feel things she'd never imagined possible. The affair had been heavenly, true refuge. Until she became pregnant by her lover. Panicked, she hid the fact for as long as possible and when she started showing, told her husband the child was his. The cuckold had been ecstatic, ready to celebrate, and when he uncorked the champagne she nearly died of guilt.

'She'd considered an abortion but had been too scared to go through with it. She prayed for a miscarriage but none came. You ask her if she's told her lover about the problem and she says no, horrified at the thought. He's a pillar of the community, a deputy sheriff charged with upholding the law. On top of that, he's married, with a pregnant wife of his own. Why destroy two families? Besides he hasn't called in a long time, confirming her suspicions that for him the relationship had been primarily carnal all along. Does she feel abandoned? No. She's sinned and now she's paying for it.

'As the foetus grows in her womb so does the burden of her secret. She lives the lie for eight and a

301

half months until she can't take it any longer. On a day when her husband is out of town she gets on the bus and heads north, to Beverly Hills.

'Now she sits in your big glossy office, so out of her element, just weeks from delivery, confused and terrified. She's considered her options for plenty of sleepless nights and has finally come to a decision. She wants out. A divorce, quick and easy, with no explanation. She'll leave town, have the baby in solitude, maybe in Mexico, put it up for adoption, and start a new life far away from the site of her transgression. She's read about you in the pages of a Hollywood fan magazine and is sure you're the man for the job.

'As you listen to her, it's clear that quick and easy is out of the question. The case would be a messy one. That by itself wouldn't have stopped you from taking it on, because the messy cases bring in the fattest fees. But Emma Swope wasn't your type of client. Drab and unglamorous and strictly small town. Most important, she didn't smell of money.

'You took her hundred, and discouraged her from engaging your services. Gave her a line about doing better with a local attorney. She left red-eyed and heavy-bellied and you filed it away and forgot about it.

'Years later you get shot in the head and decide to make a career switch. You've built up lots of connections with the big money people, which in L.A. includes the dope trade. I don't know who suggested it first, you or one of them, but you decide to go for megabucks as a coke and smack middleman. The fact that it's illegal adds to the appeal because you see yourself as a victim, as having been failed by the system you'd served faithfully. Dealing dope is your way of saying fuck the system. The money and power aren't too shabby, either.

302

'For the enterprise to be successful you'll need a place close to the Mexican border and a good cover. Your new partners suggest one of the small agricultural towns south of San Diego. La Vista. They know of an old monastery for sale just outside the town limits. Secluded and quiet. They've been considering it for a while but need a way of keeping the locals from prying. You look at a map and something flashes. The bullet didn't destroy the old memory. Back into the files. How am I doing so far?'

'Keep talking.' His palm was wet and green from compressing the torn grass into a ball.

'You do a little research and find out that Emma Swope never did get another lawyer. Her visit to you had been a single burst of initiative in an otherwise timid existence. She reverted to type, swallowed the secret and lived with it. Gave birth to a beautiful little red-headed daughter who's now grown up into a wild young teenager. Lover Boy's still around, too, busy enforcing the law. But he's no longer a deputy. He's the head honcho. The man everyone looks up to. So powerful he sets the emotional tone of the town. With him in your pocket you'll have a free ride.'

All traces of serenity had passed from the long bearded face. He touched his beard and stained it green, tasted grass and spat.

'Sleazy little people with their stinking little intrigues,' he snarled. 'Labouring under the delusion that there's some meaning to their lives.'

'You sent him a copy of the file, invited him to Beverly Hills for a chat, half-expecting him to ignore you or tell you to go to hell. What's the worst that would have happened? A minor scandal? Early pension? But he was there the next day, wasn't he?'

Matthias laughed out loud. It wasn't a pleasant sound.

303

'Bright and early,' he said, nodding, 'in that ridiculous cowboy costume. Trying to look macho but quaking in his boots – the fool.'

He revelled cruelly in the memory.

'You knew, right away,' I continued, 'that you'd touched on something vital. Of course, it wasn't until the following summer, when the girl worked for you, that you figured it out, but you didn't have to understand the fear to capitalize on it.'

'He was a yokel,' said Matthias. 'A sucker for a bluff.'

'That summer,' I said, 'must have been an interesting one. Your brand-new social structure threatened by a sixteen-year-old girl.'

'She was a little nympho,' he said contemptuously. 'Had a thing for older men. Went after them like a vacuum cleaner. I heard rumours from the time she got here. One day I discovered her blowing a sixty year old in the pantry. Pulled her off and called Houten. The way they looked at each other tipped me off as to why the file had turned him to jelly. He'd been screwing his own daughter without knowing it. I knew then that his balls were in my pocket. Forever. From that point on I pressed him into service.'

'Must have come in handy.'

'Exceedingly,' he grinned. 'Before elections, when the Border Patrol came down hard, he'd go into Mexico and pick up the cargo for us. Nothing like a personal police escort.'

'It's a hell of a nice setup,' I said. 'Well worth preserving. If I were you I'd view the hundred and fifty as a bargain.'

He shifted his weight. I took the opportunity to recross my legs. One foot had fallen asleep and I shook it gently to restore circulation.

'All I've heard up to this point is pure supposition,' he said coolly. 'Nothing worth trading for.'

304

'There's more. Let's talk about Dr. August Valcroix. A refugee from the sixties and a devotee of situational ethics. I'm not sure how the two of you got together but he'd probably been dealing up in Canada and knew some of your partners. He became one of your salesmen, handling the hospital trade. What better cover for it than a bona fide M.D.?

'The way I see it, he could have gotten hold of the stuff in two ways. Sometimes he came down here to collect, under the guise of attending a seminar. When that was inconvenient, you sent it up to him. Which is what Graffius and Delilah were doing in L.A. the day they visited the Swopes. A courtesy call after a dope transfer. They had nothing to do with the Swopes' reluctance to treat Woody or the abduction, despite Melendez-Lynch's suspicions.

'Valcroix wasn't much of a human being but he knew how to listen to patients and get them to open up. He used that talent to seduce and – sometimes – to heal. He developed a good rapport with Emma Swope – he's the only one who described her as other than a nonentity, as being strong. Because he knew something about her no one else did.

'The diagnosis of cancer in a child can throw a family off-kilter, disrupt old patterns of behaviour. I've seen it happen plenty of times. For the Swopes, the stress was crushing; it turned Garland into a pompous jester and caused Emma to sit and brood about the past. No doubt Valcroix caught her at a particularly vulnerable moment. She got in touch with her guilt and spilled out her confession because he seemed like such a compassionate fellow.

'Anyone else would have considered it just another sad story and kept it confidential. But for Valcroix the information had larger implications. He'd probably observed Houten and wondered why he was so willing to take orders from you. Now he knew. And he was unethical – confidentiality meant nothing to him. When his future as a doctor began to look shaky, he drove down here and confronted you with his knowledge, demanding a bigger piece of the pie. You feigned concession, doped him up until he fell asleep, had one of your faithful drive him halfway back to L.A., to the Wilmington docks. Another followed in a second car. They set up a fatal accident, watched it happen, and drove off. The technique is simple enough – wedge a board between the seat and the accelerator . . . '

'Close.' Matthias smiled. 'We used a tree branch. Apple tree. Organic. He hit the wall at fifty. Barry said he looked like a tomato omelette afterward.' Licking his moustache, he gave me a hard meaningful look. 'He was a grasping, greedy pig.'

'If that's supposed to scare me off, forget it. A hundred and fifty. Firm.'

The guru sighed.

'By itself the hundred and fifty is a nuisance,' he said. 'And a palatable one. But who's to say it'll stop there? I've looked you up, Delaware. You were a top man in your field but now work only irregularly. Despite your apparent indolence, you like to live well. That worries me. Nothing feeds greed more quickly than a sizeable gap between want and have. A new car, couple of fancy vacations, down payment on a condo in Mammoth, and it's all gone. Next thing I know, you're back with an outstretched palm.'

'I'm not greedy, Matthews, just resourceful. If your research was thorough you'd know I made a bunch of good investments that are still paying off. I'm thirty-five and stable, have lived comfortably without your money and could do so indefinitely. But I like the idea of ripping off a master rip-off artist. As a one-shot deal. When the one fifty's safely in my hands you'll never see or hear from me again.'

He grew thoughtful.

'Would you consider two hundred in coke?'

'Not a chance. Never touch the stuff. Hard cash.'

He pursed his lips and frowned.

'You're a tough bastard, Doctor. You've got the killer instinct – which I admire in the abstract. Barry was wrong about you. He said you were a straight arrow, sickeningly self-righteous. In actuality you're a jackal.'

'He was a lousy psychologist. Never did understand people.'

'Neither do you, apparently.' He stood suddenly and gestured to the cultists on the hill. They rose in unison and marched forward, a battalion in white.

I bounded up quickly.

'You're making a mistake, Matthews. I've taken precautions for exactly this contingency. If I'm not back in L.A. by eight the files get opened. One by one.'

'You're an ass,' he snapped. 'When I was an attorney I chewed up people like you and spat them out. Shrinks were the easiest to terrorize. I made one wet his pants up on the stand. A full professor, no less. Your bush-league attempt at arm twisting is pathetic. In a matter of minutes I'll know the location of every single one of those files. Barry wants to handle the interrogation personally. I think it's an excellent idea – his desire for revenge is quite robust. He's a nasty little slime, very well suited to the job. It will be excruciating, Delaware. And when the information is in my hands you'll be dispatched. Another unfortunate accident.'

The cultists marched closer, robotlike and grim.

'Call them off, Matthews. Don't dig yourself deeper.'

'Excruciating,' he repeated and beckoned them closer.

307

They formed a circle around us. Blank, middle-aged faces. Tight little mouths. Empty eyes. Empty minds . . .

Matthias turned his back on me.

'What if there are other copies? Ones I didn't tell you about?'

'Good-bye, Doctor,' he said scornfully, and began to exit the circle.

The others stepped aside to let him through and closed ranks immediately after he'd passed. I spotted Graffius. His puny frame quivered with anticipation. An ellipse of drool dotted his lower lip. When our eyes met the lip drew back hatefully.

'Take him,' he ordered.

The black-bearded giant stepped forward and grabbed one of my arms. Another large man, heavyset and gap-toothed, grasped the other. Graffius gave the signal and they dragged me toward the main building, followed by two dozen others chanting a wordless dirge.

Graffius ran alongside and slapped my face teasingly. Cackling with glee, he told me about the party he'd planned in my honour.

'We've got a new designer hallucinogen that makes acid seem like baby aspirin, Alex. I'll shoot it right into your veins with a Methedrine chaser. It'll be like being dipped in and out of hell.'

He had lots more to say but his oration was cut short by a sudden, brief stutter of gunfire, punctuating the silence like a symphony of giant bullfrogs. The second burst was longer, the unmistakable belch of heavy-duty firearms.

'What the fuck!' exclaimed Graffius, chin whiskers trembling like charged filaments.

The procession stopped.

From that point on everything seemed to happen in fast-forward.

308

The sky filled with thunder. Whirring blades and blinking lights assaulted the gathering dusk. A pair of helicopers circled overhead. From one of them boomed an amplified voice:

'This is Agent Siegel of the Federal Drug Enforcement Agency. The shots were a warning. You are surrounded. Release Dr. Delaware and lie face down on the ground.'

The message was repeated. Over and over.

Graffius started screaming unintelligibly. The rest of the cultists stood rooted in place, looking up to the heavens, as baffled as primitives discovering a new god.

The helicopters swooped low, rustling the trees.

Agent Siegel continued to reiterate his command. The cultists didn't comply – out of shock, not defiance.

One of the helicopters aimed a high-intensity beacon on the group. The light was blinding. As the cultists shielded their eyes, the invasion began.

Scores of men, flak-jacketed and wielding automatic weapons, converged on the grounds with the silent efficiency of soldier ants.

One group of raiders materialized from beneath the viaduct. Seconds later another emerged from behind the main building transporting a downcast herd of shackled cultists. A third swept in from the fields and stormed the cathedral.

I tried to break loose but Blackbeard and Snaggletooth held catatonically firm. Graffius pointed at me and jibbered like a monkey on speed. He ran over and raised his fist. I kicked out with my right foot and caught him hard in the centre of kneecap. He yelped and did a one-legged rain dance. The big men looked at each other idiotically, unsure of how to react. Within seconds the decision had been taken out of their hands.

309

We were surrounded. The raiders from the viaduct had formed a concentric ring around the circle of cultists. They were a mixed group – D.E.A. agents, state police, county sheriffs, and at least one L.A. detective whom I recognized – but functioned with the smoothness of a seasoned unit.

A Hispanic officer with a Zapata moustache barked the order to lie down. This time compliance was immediate. The big men released my arms as if they were electrified. I stepped away and observed the action.

The raiders made the cultists spread their legs and frisked them, two officers for every captive. Once searched, they were handcuffed, removed from the group one by one like beads pulled off a string, read their rights, and taken into custody at gunpoint.

With the exception of Graffius, who was dragged away kicking and screaming, the men and the women of the Touch offered no resistance. Numb with fear and disorientation, they submitted passively to police procedure and shambled off to captivity in a forlorn procession periodically spotlit by the circling helicopters.

The heavy door to the main building swung open and disgorged another parade of captors and captives. The last to exit was Matthias, guarded by a phalanx of agents. He walked woodenly and his mouth worked frantically. From a distance it looked like one hell of a closing statement but the din from the copters blotted out the sound. Not that anyone was listening.

I watched his departure and, when the grounds were still, became once more aware of the heat. I removed my jacket and tossed it to the side, and was unbuttoning my shirt when Milo came over in the company of a hatchet-faced man with a five o'clock shadow. The man wore a grey suit, white shirt, and

310

dark tie under his flak jacket and walked with a military stride. This morning, I'd found him humourless but reassuringly thorough. The boss D.E.A. agent, Severin Fleming.

'Great performance, Alex.' My friend patted my back.

'Let me help you with that, Doctor,' said Fleming, untaping the Nagra body recorder from my chest. 'I hope it wasn't too uncomfortable.'

'As a matter of fact it itched like crazy.'

'Sorry about that. You must have sensitive skin.'

'He's a very sensitive guy, Sev.'

Fleming conceded a smile and concentrated on checking the Nagra.

'Everything looks in order,' he announced, returning the machine to its case. 'Reception in the van was excellent – we got a first-rate copy. An attorney from Justice was sitting in and she's of the opinion there's plenty to work with. Once again, Doctor, thanks. Be seeing you, Milo.'

He shook our hands, gave a small salute, and walked away, cradling the Nagra like a newborn.

'Well,' said Milo, 'You keep revealing new talents. Hollywood's bound to be knocking on your door.'

'Right,' I said, rubbing my chest. 'Call my agent. We'll take a meeting at the Polo Lounge.'

He laughed and undid his flak jacket.

'Feel like the Michelin tyre man in this thing.'

'You should be so cute.'

We walked together toward the viaduct. The sky had darkened and quieted. Beyond the gates engines rumbled to a start. We stepped onto the bridge, treading on cool stone. Milo reached up, plucked a grape from the arbour, split it with his teeth, and swallowed.

'You made a big difference, Alex,' he said. 'Eventually they'd have gotten him on the drug thing. But

311

it's the murder rap that'll put him away. Combine that with lowering the boom on Stinky Pants and I'd say it's been a fine week for the good guys.'

'Great,' I said wearily.

Several yards later:

'You okay, pal?'

'I'll be all right.'

'Thinking about the kid?'

I stopped and looked at him.

'Do you need to head back to L.A. right away?' I asked.

He put a heavy arm around my shoulder, smiled and shook his head.

'Getting back means diving into a mess of paperwork. It can wait.'

27

I STOOD at a distance and looked through the wall of plastic.

The boy lay on the bed, still but awake. His mother sat by his side, rendered nearly anonymous by spacesuit, gloves, and mask. Her dark eyes wandered around the room, settling momentarily on his face, then upon the pages of the story book in her hands. He struggled upright, said something to her and she nodded and held a cup to his lips. Drinking exhausted him quickly; he fell back against the pillow.

'Cute kid,' said Milo. 'What did that doc say his chances are?'

'He's severely infected. But the I.V. is pumping in high-dose antibiotics and they feel it will eventually clear up. The original tumour has enlarged – it's begun to press against the diaphragm, which isn't good – but there's no evidence of any new lesions.

Chemotherapy will start tomorrow. Overall, the prognosis is still good.'

He nodded and went into the nurses' office.

The boy was asleep, now. His mother kissed his forehead, drew the blankets around him, and looked at the book again. She flipped a few pages, put it down and began straightening the room. That done, she returned to sitting bedside, folded her hands in her lap, and remaining motionless. Waiting.

The two marshalls emerged from the nurses' office. The man was thick-waisted and middle-aged, the woman petite and dyed-blonde. He looked at his watch and said 'It's time' to his partner. She walked over to the module and tapped on the plastic.

Nona looked up.

The woman said, 'It's time.'

The girl hesitated, bent over the sleeping child and kissed him with sudden intensity. He called out and rolled over. The movement caused the I.V. pole to vibrate, the bottle to sway. She steadied it, stroked his hair.

'Come on, honey,' said the female marshall.

The girl stiffened, stumbled out of the module. She took off the mask and gloves and let the sterile suit fall around her ankles, revealing a jumpsuit underneath. On the back was stencilled PROPERTY SAN DIEGO COUNTY JAIL and a serial number. Her copper hair was drawn back in a ponytail. The golden hoops had been removed from her ears. Her face looked thinner and older, the cheekbones more pronounced, the eyes buried deeper. Jailhouse pallor had begun to dull the lustre of her skin. She was beautiful, but damaged, like a day-old rose.

They handcuffed her − gently, it seemed − and led her to the door. She passed by me and our eyes locked. The ebony irises seemed to moisten and melt. Then she hardened them, held her head high, and was gone.

314

28

I FOUND Raoul in his lab, staring at a computer screen on which were displayed columns of polynomials atop a multicoloured bar graph. He'd mutter in Spanish, examine a page of printout, then turn to the keyboard and rapidly type a new set of numbers. With each additional bit of datum the height of the bars in the graph changed. The lab was airless and filled with acrid fumes. High-tech doodads clicked and buzzed in the background.

I pulled up a stool next to him, sat and said hello.

He acknowledged me with a downward twist of his moustache and continued to work with the computer. The bruises on his face had turned to purplish-green smudges.

'You know,' he said.

'Yes. She told me.'

315

He typed, hitting the keyboard hard. The graph convulsed.

'My ethics were no better than Valcroix's. She came wiggling in here in a skintight dress and proved that.'

I'd come to the lab with the intention of comforting him. There were things I could have said. That Nona had been turned into a weapon, an instrument of vengeance, abused and twisted until sex and rage were inexorably intertwined, then launched and aimed at a world of weak men like some kind of heat-seeking missile. That he'd made an error in judgement but it didn't negate all the good he'd done. That there was more good work to be done. That time would heal.

But the words would have rung hollow. He was a proud man who'd shed his pride before my eyes. I'd witnessed him ragged and half-crazed in a stinking cell, obsessively intent on finding his patient. His quest had been ignited by guilt, by the mistaken belief that his sin – ten lust-blinded minutes of Nona kneeling before him, ravenous – had caused the removal of the boy from treatment.

Coming to see him had been a mistake. Whatever friendship we'd had was gone, and with it, any power I might have had to reassure.

If salvation existed, he'd have to find it for himself.

I placed my hand on his shoulder and wished him well. He shrugged and stared at the screen.

I left him with his nose buried in a pile of data, cursing out loud at some arcane numerical discrepancy.

I drove east on Sunset slowly, and thought about families. Milo had once told me that family disputes were a cop's most dreaded calls, for they were the most likely to erupt in violence that was murderously sudden, stunningly intense. A good chunk of my life had been spent sorting out the scrambled communications, festering hostilities, and frozen affections that characterized families in turmoil.

It was easy to believe that nothing worked. That blood ties strangled the soul.

But I knew that a cop's reality was skewed by the daily struggle against evil, that of the psychotherapist distorted by too many encounters with madness.

There were families that worked, that nurtured and loved. Places in the heart where a soul could find refuge.

Soon a beautiful woman would meet me on a tropical island. We'd talk about it.